THE PORTABLE TOLSTOY

THE PORTABLE

Tolstoy

*Selected and with a
Critical Introduction, Biographical Summary,
and Bibliography by*

JOHN BAYLEY

*Thomas Warton Professor of English Literature
at Oxford University*

THE VIKING PRESS · NEW YORK

First published in 1978 by The Viking Press
625 Madison Avenue, New York, N.Y. 10022

LIBRARY OF CONGRESS CATALOGING IN PUBLICATION DATA
Tolstoy, Lev Nikolaevich, graf, 1828–1910.
The portable Tolstoy.
(The Viking portable library)
Bibliography: p. 887
I. Bayley, John, 1925— II. Title.
PG3365.A2 1978   891.7'3'3   78-6784
ISBN 0-670-71869-6

Printed in the United States of America
Set in Linotype Times Roman

ACKNOWLEDGMENTS

Columbia University Forum: For George L. Kline's translation of *A History of Yesterday*, Vol. 11, No. 3 (Spring 1959).
Copyright © 1959 by The Trustees of Columbia University
in the City of New York. Reprinted by permission.

Farrar, Straus & Giroux, Inc.: From *A Window on Russia* by
Edmund Wilson. Copyright © 1943, 1944, 1952, 1957, 1971,
1972 by Edmund Wilson, renewed copyright © 1971, 1972 by
Edmund Wilson. Reprinted by permission.

Oxford University Press: For Louise and Aylmer Maude's
translation, published by Oxford University Press in the
Worlds Classics series, and reprinted by permission.

CONTENTS

EDITOR'S INTRODUCTION

I

Tolstoy's greatest works are of course *War and Peace* and *Anna Karenina,* and I saw no point in trying to select sections of those two great novels for inclusion in this Portable. On grounds of space I have also had to omit the later novel *Resurrection* and the last long story, *Hadji Murád,* which fortunately is easily available in other collections. But one cannot arrive at any true understanding of Tolstoy (and for the matter of that, one cannot enjoy him as he ought to be enjoyed) without studying his shorter and lesser-known works, particularly the experimental fiction that led up to *War and Peace.* There are also the most personally revealing of his works, *A Confession,* the parables and essays in which he set out his teaching, *The Kreutzer Sonata,* and the remarkable "The Memoirs of a Madman." Many of these are not easily available, and they are certainly not available in one volume, so a wide selection of them should prove valuable alike to readers who know the two big novels and wish to extend their acquaintance and to students who feel the need for a useful compendium at their elbow.

So much has been written on Tolstoy, so much is readily discoverable to read about him and on his ideas, that a lengthy preface is hardly needed. I shall confine myself to discussing the significance of the works included here, with a few others not included, in relation to Tolstoy's life and in relation to one another, for Tolstoy is not, obviously, a novelist in the ordinary sense. He does not, that is, turn from one subject to another or see the world and society as offering different themes and aspects which he might treat in one way or another. No novelist is less professional than he, which does not mean that he did not take pains. The manuscripts of his great novels exist in innumerable variations, and he labored long over their design and form. He was proud of the fact that the "keystone," as he called it, in the design of *Anna Karenina* had been so cunningly concealed in the architecture of the work that it was invisible to the reader's eye, and in his old age, he was heard to mutter dreamily, after some friends had been discussing his last story, *Hadji Murád*—"the old man wrote it well." None the less, he despised any notion of *artistry*, holding art itself to be the simple and passionate utterance of a human being communicating his vision to others in the most straightforward way. In this, as in much else, Tolstoy's attitude was highly equivocal. When he remarked, after a good day's work, that he had "left a little of his flesh in the inkpot," was he claiming that his word—like God's—had been made flesh to dwell among his readers, or that he had compressed into his story the living sense and apprehension of life itself?

Perhaps both. The Russian critic and thinker Dmitri Merezhkovsky called him "the seer of the flesh," in contrast to Dostoevsky, the seer of the spirit. And it is certainly true that Tolstoy can, as it were, only know his characters through the medium of their flesh, their living being. It is thus that we know Anna and Natasha, Pierre, Andrew, and Stephan Oblonsky. So powerful is the impact of Tolstoy's primary creative power that it never occurs to us that these human beings have been juggled into existence—like any other literary character—through the abstract medium of words: we meet them in the flesh as if they had always existed in it. Though the scope of the work is much slighter, this applies to *Childhood, Boyhood,* and *Youth* as much as to the two great novels, but where the flesh and all that pertains to it is not the lord of the matter (even though its dominance may be unadmitted by Tolstoy) this great primary power deserts him.

In a sense this may be because all his great characters, even the female ones, constitute a part of his physical being and are undivided from it. But when he concocted a character, such as Nekhlyudov in *Resurrection* or Pozdnyshev in *The Kreutzer Sonata,* to illustrate a dogma or an assertive point of view, the feeling of a stuffed dummy is very strong, because the instinctual bond between creator and created seems not to exist. This contrast between realized and invented characters is far more striking than in any other author and tells us a great deal about the unique nature of genius. *The Death of Ivan Ilyich* is a story too well known to need reprinting here. And even Ivan Ilyich, in one of the most moving and terrible accounts of a death that has ever been written, is an "invented" character in this reductive sense. In the nature of things, he and his fate—the two, as in *War and Peace*, are synonymous but in the novel each individual's fate fits with an exact and appropriate harmony—are analyzed by Tolstoy as things he has not known himself: even Tolstoy could only *imagine* what it was like to die.

Tolstoy's amazing gifts amount to a kind of inspired solipsism; in his own flesh he identified that of all other humans. But the seer of the flesh was never content with the flesh—that is the obvious but none the less towering paradox. His childhood was happy, happier than that of any other great writer, and was singularly lacking in any kind of disabling emotional connection; he never seems to have felt that to be orphaned was a forlorn state; he was surrounded by love and affection, his aunt Tanya in particular filling the roles of mother, friend, and housekeeper without making any demand on him. He belonged to one of the first families of Russia, and, though he often gambled and wasted large sums, money was never a problem. This aspect of Tolstoy has been admirably summed up by Edmund Wilson[1] in relation to Turgenev, whose early years brought a permanent legacy of paralysis and nightmare.

Tolstoy had been an orphan, exhilaratingly self-dependent; he had inherited his estate at nineteen with no hateful family memories, and during the years of his rather wild freedom and his service in the Crimean War, it had been kept for him as a home by an affectionate aunt whom he loved. When he married he founded a family that was completely his own. His property of Yasnaya Polyana was a romance he was always inventing,

[1] In *The Triple Thinkers: 12 Essays on Literary Subjects* (New York: Farrar, Straus & Giroux), 1976.

as he had invented—out of old family papers and legends—the idyll of *War and Peace*. And even in his latest phase of pretending to abdicate his status of landowner, nobleman and popular writer he was reserving for himself *le beau role*.

Between Yasnaya Polyana and Turgenev's property of Spasskoye there is indeed a great divide—the two are geographically close but spiritually a long way apart. Tolstoy is equally distant from every other great Russian writer: the critic Prince Mirsky observed that when we read him we wonder where on earth the Russia of Gogol and Dostoevsky comes from. But the very splendor of Tolstoy's freedom, the spaciousness of his idyll, brought their own nemesis. Spasskoye may have crippled Turgenev, but it saved him from the state of mind which Tolstoy portrayed with such vivid horror in "The Memoirs of a Madman," and more soberly in *A Confession;* and Dostoevsky struggled all his life against the kind of difficulties which make it totally unnecessary and indeed irrelevant for a man to ask himself "What is the point of life?" But when Tolstoy had got everything he wanted and achieved everything that the most voracious and ambitious genius could set itself, then the question of "why?" struck with deadly force. Again, Edmund Wilson has put the matter with more sense and concision than any of Tolstoy's numerous biographers.

Tolstoy found himself in the unusual, for a great writer perhaps the unprecedented, situation of having everything he could possibly want in a material way, and having realized, in a literary way, all of his possible ambitions. He had a title and a distinguished ancestry and an extensive country estate, no adverse parental pressures, an attractive and intelligent wife, first-rate intellectual powers, and an imaginative genius that had enabled him to produce two masterpieces of fiction that were bringing in a good deal of money: when he heard of his former colleagues receiving important official appointments he would sometimes remark ironically that "though he had not got a Generalship in the artillery, he had at any rate won a Generalship in literature." But he had served in the Caucasus war and been nearly killed by a shell; he had fought in the Crimean warfare and had declined or disregarded three crosses for valor; he had had innumerable women; he had seen all he wanted to see of Western Europe. He had acted as an Arbiter of the Peace, after the liberation of the serfs, with such an impartial justice as to infuriate many of his fellow nobles; he had instituted and directed a school for the peasants' children on a system of his own creation. It is no wonder—though so rare a phenomenon—that, having experienced and accomplished so much at a relatively early age, he should ask himself, as he does in *A Confession*, what there was to hope for and aim at next. Life at last had confronted him with a great blank. How is this blank to be filled? There is no further way to excel save through some effort of spiritual self-ennoblement.[2]

This is indeed the crux of the matter. We do not need to depreciate Tolstoy's spiritual efforts and aspirations, as some critics have done, but neither can we feel the unbounded reverence and admiration for his latter-day personality which has been displayed by disciples—and cranks—at the time and since. The bearded sage of Yasnaya Polyana is essentially the same personality as the vain and touchy young artillery cadet, the dandy, gambler, freethinker, and rake, who embarked sixty years earlier on a fantastic career of achievement and self-realization. If it were not so, Tolstoy would not be the enduringly remarkable monument that he is; he would be an ossified figure, a sage no longer relevant to us. For the fact is that the confrontation of Tolstoy with the futility of complete and dazzling worldly success, with life's unmeaning, with the finality and indifference of death, is a gigantic but straightforward analogue of the experience which we all, more dimly, go through. Each of us gets a little of what he achieved in superabundance, and our response is scaled down but inevitably similar. Tolstoy is not Everyman but a superman to whom life remorselessly brings the fate which Everyman, in the mediaeval play, had to undergo.

Tolstoy's is the egotism of a man like any other, but immensely *more so,* and his embodiment of the universal physical existence would be nothing if it was not always confronting the question of what lay outside itself. A Tolstoy who continued to write a series of novels with

[2] Ibid.

endings like that of *War and Peace* would be an intolerable phenomenon, for *War and Peace* is the grandest apotheosis in literature of self-realization, of art giving life everything it wants. However different in degree, it is ultimately one in kind with the almost equally popular (but for how long?) novelette *Love Story*. For the hero and heroine of that work its author arranges that they should get what their natures seem to require—in the one case the abnegation and dignity of a "right" death, in the other the complex satisfactions of grief, achievement, and release for more life. And thus in *War and Peace* it is right for Andrew to die, right for Sonya to devote herself in selfless (that is to say, selfish, right for herself) service to the loved family, right for Natasha and Nikolai and Pierre to get the marriages and the lives that exactly suit them. *War and Peace* is right for a moment of life, for the triumph of life. But growing in it and through it is the spreading knowledge of extinction, of the outfacing of self by what is not self, of life by death. Prince Andrew "dies" like Jenny of *Love Story*: a purposeful act of life that is not extinguished but goes on as a part, a supreme part, of a book. The death of Anna Karenina is not like that, nor is that of Hadji Murád, the hero of Tolstoy's last story. Death is not Anna's natural fate: it is imposed upon her by a situation that she feels, at a poignantly random moment, to be intolerable; and death for Ivan Ilyich is a monstrous intrusion, an ugly and unexpected visitor whose eruption into their lives seems to his family and friends to be, above all, *in the worst of taste.*

If the idyllic decorum of *War and Peace* represents the fullness of Tolstoy's life, its richness upon every side, then the work of his later years expresses his sense of desolation. For the great seer of the flesh, the flesh became not only not enough—it became a mockery. But one must emphasize again that this transformation is not a sudden arbitrary affair, a willful volte-face on Tolstoy's part. His life presents, and his art reflects, a logical and inevitable pattern of life, but a pattern on the heroic scale. In the old age of Tolstoy, as in that of King Lear, youth and maturity can be clearly seen, not as things that have passed away for the old man, but present to him and in him at every moment. As Thomas Hardy wrote:

> But time, to make me grieve
> Part steals, lets part abide,
> And shakes this fragile form at eve
> With throbbings of noontide.

That is why the full span of Tolstoy's creation is so continuous and harmonious, the whole being implied in each part, at each moment. Mirsky wrote that Tolstoy's life up to *A Confession* was like an enchanted ballroom: after it, like Ivan Ilyich's black bag. Not so, surely. Ballroom and black bag are always present to him, and it is because of the presence of the one that we accept the other. Tolstoy himself may have come to reject the ballroom utterly and to emphasize with a certain relish of morbidity the frivolous emptiness of ordinary life, but the balance of his work is not really affected by this.

As the extremely subtle Russian critic Shestov has shown, all Tolstoy's great fictions are shot through and through with equivocation. At the end of *War and Peace* he celebrates the simple Russian country gentleman that Nikolai Rostov has become and dares us—as it were— to notice the fact that not only is he now the main hero, but that Pierre, the seeker and would-be reformer, led on throughout the story by idealism and lofty hopes, has been tamed and reduced to the same condition. Only Andrew's son is left to restart the cycle of quest and unrest, to assume the human bondage to divine discontent: his elders are—from a spiritual point of view—finished. And yet Tolstoy does not portray this state of affairs as a defeat; on the contrary, the ending that from one point of view is total anticlimax, and what Flaubert called *une affreuse dégringolade* into the complacent self-sufficiency of satisfied country gentlemen, is also a majestic epic conclusion, fitting the work's whole huge scope of man and nature. Tolstoy makes no attempt to explain this curious state of affairs; he simply turns upon us, as Shestov says, the impassive face of a man whose forebears had been diplomats and high state officials as well as gentry. He declines to explain; and so, as always with great art, we find ourselves trusting the tale, not its teller.

It was no doubt for this reason that, later in his un-remitting search for a rational and moral justification of life, Tolstoy came to regard his great novels with con-tempt. Having written them, he could of course find this easy to do, and it cost him nothing, and yet we cannot call him dishonest for so regarding them. He came to believe more and more that art must be simple and direct, that its analysis of a situation (and Tolstoy was one of the greatest analysts who ever wrote) must be completely stark and ruthlessly straightforward. That is what he came to *believe*, as he forced himself to believe that love is the simple answer to human ills, but what he *knew*, as a writer, was something very different. Like some immensely cunning and experienced animal he knew the ways of the world, but he refused to believe in them. An animal simile seems strangely appropriate for Tolstoy: Gorki said that the aged Tolstoy and God were "like two bears living in one den," and Isaiah Berlin, in a particularly brilliant summation, described him as a fox who was always trying to be a hedgehog. There is a proverb which says: "The Fox knows many things but the Hedgehog knows one big thing"; like all good pro-verbs it is cryptic, but Tolstoy certainly knew many things and discarded them, threw them aside in search of the "one big thing"—the meaning and purpose of life. Naturally enough he never found it: the discovery for us is what he made out of his search.

II

Tolstoy's first attempt at a story is a kind of extract or *reductio ad absurdum* of a diary, the kind of detailed diary which he kept in adolescence. "A History of Yesterday" is a remarkable piece, which has seldom been translated, and which holds more than one clue to Tolstoy's future development as an artist. It is analysis run mad, used by a young man who has just discovered the intoxication of his talent for this, and its accumulation of factual detail also looks forward to the later novels and stories (Turgenev was to object that one really shouldn't spend ten pages describing exactly how a character gesticulated with his hand). But more significantly it shows right at the outset of Tolstoy's writing career that he was fascinated by technique and formal experiment. He chose not to follow up this experiment, and it would be highly interesting to see what would have come of it if he had. He may have felt—and it would be a remarkably mature reaction from a young man if he did so—that the form of a work should not be the most obvious and important thing about it, that originality should be concealed behind the mask of convention.

Childhood and its successors, *Boyhood* and *Youth,* are certainly original; the details of the past, which in "A History of Yesterday" are intruded upon the reader as something the writer holds to be important and gives emphasis to deliberately, are wholly inconspicuous, naturally and apparently artlessly brought out. The reality of the past is not turned into poetry; it remains scrappy; and its scrappiness is shot through alike with beauty and with boredom. Tolstoy has contrived not to sentimentalize the past in any way, but to give weight to the feeling of sheer nonentity and "unfinishedness" which we experience before our life takes on the habitual patterns of age, a kind of nonentity which is truer to the bulk and texture of childhood than are any Wordsworthian intimations and apprehensions of joy. What, for instance, could be truer—and, it must be admitted, more *lowering!*— than the account of the visit to the mother of a friend, after the narrator's mother has died? Tolstoy makes us feel the vacant embarrassment of the child, the discomfort and gloom which are not situated in his own emotions, in any sentiment of pity for the lady or of yearning for his mother, but spill into a vague limbo, almost a Sartrean *huis clos,* in which all that matters is that time should continue to get on with it. That is surely childhood as it really is for most of the time. And coupled with this uncanny sense of actuality, of the low-keyed nature of things, is the indeterminate portrait—appearance rather —of the young man, who has no idea of a personality, or how to acquire one; who is simply a blur of responses and reactions moving inevitably forward. Compare him with J. D. Salinger's Holden Caulfield in *The Catcher in the Rye* and the difference between truth and sentiment is instantly obvious. Caulfield is cunningly and lovingly made, but he is a waxwork constructed by the author out of himself as he imagines himself to have been. Dickens's David Copperfield—and this novel influenced Tolstoy greatly and was much admired by him—is not much different. But in *Childhood, Boyhood,* and *Youth* veracity excludes any build-up of a "character."

This is an important critical point, for Tolstoy was never again to be so unconventional. We might say that he learned by disconcerting and truthful experiments how to use and become the master of more normal fictional conventions, for just as *Childhood* is far less overtly and boldly experimental than "A History of Yesterday," so *The Cossacks* and the Sevastopol stories are much more conventional than *Childhood*; and when we come to *War and Peace* we find Tolstoy operating over the great length of the work almost every hoary fictional device in existence—coincidence, melodrama, a disputed will, a Byronic villain, and conventional groupings of "good" and "bad" characters. His development is thus quite different from that of most novelists, who usually begin by imitation and go on to develop a mode and a world of their own; Tolstoy, typically, did the thing entirely in his own way at first and then went on to borrow what he saw that he needed for full communication with the reader and for the reader's prolonged entertainment.

Two other points require notice before we leave *Childhood*. The first is Tolstoy's marvelous sense, which can also be extremely comic, of the solipsistic nature of human experience. Things seem wonderful and strange to the narrator, he is filled with a sense of the importance of what he is seeing and feeling, and yet no one else specially marks him or pays any attention to his account of his sensations. An example is the visit to the monastery for confession, and the talk with the cabman afterward. The cabman, whom the narrator thinks so sympathetic, is quite indifferent to his confidences and finally interrupts by asking if he belongs to the gentry, a possibility which in his eyes would explain any kind of inane behavior. The same point is made by a direct description of the narrator's sensations. "I imagined that beside myself nobody and nothing existed in the universe, that objects were not objects at all, but images which appeared only when I paid attention to them." This is not of course an uncommon sensation, especially among the young, but the ways in which Tolstoy experienced it, and the total independence of mind which it brought him ("I loved my father, but a man's mind lives independently of his heart."), might fairly be called, in the deepest sense, aristocratic. Tolstoy had the aristocrat's confidence in himself, his conviction of his own rightness, and his assumption that the world revolves around himself. These he never lost; the solipsism of the young Tolstoy and the dogmatism of the old man who portrayed himself in his play *The Light Shines in Darkness* are really one and the same. "Solipsism dogged him," says Shestov, "and as he grew older he came to terms with it, as men learn to come to terms with impertinent ideas."

The other Tolstoyan theme that runs through the sequence of *Childhood, Boyhood,* and *Youth* is the importance of what the narrator calls "understanding." This is an instinctive mode of communicating with others who share the same faculty, and it is in fact the most important and the most authentic kind of communication possible between human beings. It is based, significantly, on the family, and the great family connections in the big novels depend very much on it. Indeed, it would be true to say that Tolstoy communicates with his readers through this kind of instinctual appeal of "understanding," and the characters who don't possess it—Vera Rostov in *War and Peace,* Nekhlyudov in the *Childhood* sequence—are described by him from the outside: they are not, as it were, up to the sort of inner intimacy and apparently unconscious revealing of self which we experience with the narrator's family, with Olenin in *The Cossacks,* and with Natasha, Nikolai, and Petya in *War and Peace.* Tolstoy later repudiates this intimacy of presentation through the medium of "understanding," no doubt thinking it frivolous, and this explains to a very large extent why the characters in the later works are more distant and formal and have no instant and authentic reality. They are "non-understanders." It is symbolic that in *Resurrection* Irtenyev, the narrator of the *Childhood* sequence, is dead, and the main character is that same Prince

Nekhlyudov who in the early work was deficient in the Tolstoyan quality of "understanding." The ready understander and observer of all life dies; the earnest seeker after the truths that really matter goes marching on.

The beginning of *The Cossacks* might almost be a continuation of *Youth,* but we soon discover that the hero Olenin is to be seen much more objectively and ironically. Irtenyev resembled Tolstoy and yet was a fictional character, and Olenin's situation bears an even more marked resemblance to his author's—Tolstoy's description of him at the beginning puts us very much in mind of Edmund Wilson's words:

At the age of eighteen he was free—as only rich young Russians in the 'forties who had lost their parents at an early age could be. Neither physical nor moral fetters of any kind existed for him; he could do as he liked, lacking nothing and being bound by nothing. Neither relatives, nor fatherland, nor religion, nor wants, existed for him. He believed in nothing and admitted nothing. But although he believed in nothing he was not a morose or *blasé* young man, nor self-opinionated, but on the contrary continually let himself be carried away. He had come to the conclusion that there is no such thing as love, yet his heart always overflowed in the presence of any young and attractive woman. He had long been aware that honors and position were nonsense, yet involuntarily he felt pleased when at a ball Prince Sergius came up and spoke to him affably. But he yielded to his impulses only in so far as they did not limit his freedom.[3]

It is that freedom which for Tolstoy will be the great nemesis; the horrible nothingness and futility which waits for him at the end of the boundless and exuberant possibilities that Olenin sees stretching before him when he travels to the Caucasus. This freedom is a traditional thing in Russian literature, for *The Cossacks* is very much influenced by Pushkin's wonderful poem *The Gypsies,* in which a similarly "free" young man puts himself into the domestic bonds of a gypsy encampment. That tale ends catastrophically when the hero kills his gypsy mistress in a paroxysm of jealousy and is exiled into

[3] *Ibid.*

the total solitude of the steppe. Nothing so dramatic—Tolstoy being opposed to the device of drama—is allowed to happen in *The Cossacks,* but Olenin is compelled to feel, in a not entirely dissimilar fashion, that Cossack life is both outside the bounds his egoism can compass and fundamentally indifferent and alien to him. *The Cossacks,* in any case, is full of wonderful descriptions—like that of the shooting of the *abrek* by the riverside—which have nothing to do with the hero and his consciousness; and it contains, too, the first really solid and objective characters that Tolstoy created—the old Cossack Eróshka and the young girl Maryánka. Their objectivity is in part, and ironically, established by their basic total indifference to the hero and his world, though they are for him figures of romantic fantasy and enchantment.

After his service in the Caucasus Tolstoy took part in the siege of Sevastopol, the main focus of the Crimean war, and this resulted in further sketches of the kind he had already made in "The Raid" and "The Woodfelling." Tolstoy never wrote anything more vividly compelling than these accounts of men's fear, dignity, vanity, and cowardice in the face of death; they satisfy his own mature requirement for a simple "infective" art that anyone can understand and be moved by, though it is significant that—despite the need for getting past the censorship—these sketches do not by any means infect us with the total abhorrence of war and military prowess which constitutes their overt purpose. Patriotism, love of life, and that peculiar enhancement of the quality of living which danger and war bring—these are at least as much in evidence here as the exhortation: Thou shalt not kill. And indeed it is worth remembering that when Port Arthur was surrendered by the Russians during the Japanese war, the aged Tolstoy was highly indignant and recalled how much more determinedly Sevastopol had been defended.

"The Woodfelling" is my own favorite among Tolstoy's stories, not for any good reason, but because it provides a peculiarly transparent glimpse into his workshop. The effect of the soldier's death on his comrades, at once trivial and profound—"like something that had happened goodness knows how long ago or had never happened at all"—is searchingly analyzed but at the same time touched on very lightly: there is none of the weight, organization, and meaningfulness which Tolstoy put into his later stories. It is instructive to compare the lightness of "The Woodfelling" with the similar scenes in *Hadji Murád*, written at the end of Tolstoy's life, and also with the deliberately simplistic story *A Prisoner in the Caucasus*, which he wrote as a kind of commentary, even parody, on Pushkin's romantic narrative poem with the same title. Tolstoy's unspoken point is that Pushkin falsifies—both in the episodes of his plot, involving a sloe-eyed Circassian beauty, and in the psychology of his hero—and that he is determined to avoid this and give such a situation just as it would have been. Immediacy is lost in too scrupulous a search for simplicity.

"Two Hussars" shows Tolstoy in an unexpectedly jovial and sardonic mood; and indeed this, with "Strider" and the other less well-known stories, not only gives the reader a better idea of the breadth and variety of his talents than do the more famous ones, but also shows how comparatively slowly he came to literary maturity and in what directions he cast about in the period before he settled down to his *chef d'oeuvre.* "Family Happiness," written when Tolstoy was in love with a girl called Arseneva, has an unexpected lack of assurance in its meticulousness, as if it reflected the author's own inner doubts and queries about the possibilities of marriage, and the anxious pendantry with which he tried to educate the girl in his own views.

It is a curiously laborious tale, one of my reasons for omitting it here. But we hear in it for the first time that note of hypothesis which is the trademark of Tolstoy's later *nouvelles,* of which the most important is *The Kreutzer Sonata.* By inventing a situation, he explores a problem, often in a manner that seems over-rigid, abstract, and arbitrary. Thus Tolstoy puts himself in the place of a young girl getting married and tempted to have an affair; into the position of a man tormented with sexual desire, or obsessed with jealousy, and though what follows is unforgettably powerful in the case of the later stories, and lyrically charming in the case of "Family Happiness," we might feel that Tolstoy has too much *taken over* the protagonists of his tales and is using them for his own ends as he never uses the great independent characters of the long novels. Pozdnyshev of *The Kreutzer Sonata*, in particular, may strike us as a man more sinned against by his creator than sinning in his own life. None the less, the moment when he bids farewell to the narrator in the railway carriage is unforgettably moving.

Something very similar is true of the plays which Tolstoy wrote in later life. They are invaluable for helping us to understand him and his work, and they have their moments of genuine drama and feeling, but we cannot enter them with that hallucination of pure reality with which we enter his narrations. *The Power of Darkness* is powerful indeed—Maeterlinck called it the greatest of all plays, and Tolstoy is supposed to have commented sardonically, "Then why doesn't he imitate it?"—though we have space for only his most famous one, another play on which Tolstoy worked on and off for many years, *The Light Shines in Darkness,* is fascinating in that it is a pitiless and accurate portrait of a Tolstoyan, almost a self-portrait of the prophet by the artist, the hedgehog by the fox. With unswerving truth Tolstoy shows the blindness of Saryntsev and the solipsism—ignoring all ordinary human and family claims—that dominates the prophet who believes himself a vessel of revelation.[4] Such characters contain a forceful image of himself which he is not willing overtly to recognize. They constitute a quite different kind of self-portrait from the straightforward blend of autobiography and fictional invention in the *Childhood* sequence, "Family Happiness," and *War and Peace*. But in the plays we have a third projection of Tolstoy's own personality which the form determines and embodies—the virtual satire by the uncompromising solitary of the final period on the human and social difficulties which his position had brought about. Perhaps it was the acerbic wit in this realization which led Bernard Shaw—somewhat perversely—to pronounce that *The Light Shines in Darkness*, which we

---

[4] Tolstoy never completed the play, but his synopsis for the ending involved the shooting of the "Tolstoyan" Saryntsev by the distraught mother of a young man who has been persuaded by the Tolstoyan doctrine not to do his army service and who has been sentenced to prison and flogging.

have reluctantly omitted, was Tolstoy's masterpiece! Shaw perceived that derision was the keynote of intelligent modern drama, above all derision at the dramatist's expense.

Such considerations do not enter into the simple and impressive parables such as "God Sees the Truth but Waits," "What Men Live By," and "How Much Land Does a Man Need?" The last is perhaps the most effective of all Tolstoy's "popular" tales in the telling force of its moral and in its power to reach a wide audience —the two criteria that he came to value as the things that really mattered in a work of art.

What is Art?, which Tolstoy was working on in 1897, is a pedantic and polemical essay, but it contains unforgettable insights, and more of Tolstoy's mordant wit than is usually recognized. As in the theories on education which he had put forward thirty years earlier in his magazine *Yasnaya Polyana*. Tolstoy takes the line that no one before himself has seen the obvious: when he is at his most doctrinaire he is most aristocratic, convinced that he alone realizes how absurd all the bourgeois received ideas on the subject are. Opera for example— and Wagner's opera in particular—is ludicrous in itself, because of the grotesque artificiality of the way it works and the effects it sets out to achieve. By describing the goings-on of opera literally and in a dead-pan manner, Tolstoy seeks to ridicule them, as he had ridiculed the ballet through the eyes of Natasha in *War and Peace*, by the device known to Russian critics as "making it strange": that is to say, by gravely describing the antics of the performers as a child without preconceptions might perceive them. The artificial, used as one of the conventions of high art and for its own sake, is always his deadly enemy. He hates equally the elevated language of Shakespeare's plays and the way actors say it. His notorious denunciation of *King Lear* is really caused by what he regards as an intensely painful, distasteful, and embarrassing incongruity between high poetic language and artifice and the stark horror of the action.

The attack on Lear is repetitive and hysterical: Tolstoy makes the point as effectively and much more pithily in his aside on *Hamlet* in one of the sections I have included from *What Is Art?* The best-acted *Hamlet* he maintains to be a frigid performance compared to an acted presentation of a deer hunt by Vogul tribesmen, from which the audience experiences "that simple feeling familiar to the plainest man and even to a child, that sense of infection with another's feeling—compelling us to rejoice in another's gladness, to sorrow at another's grief and to mingle souls with another—which is the very essence of art." Ultimately a person's understanding of art depends on its involvement in his attitude to life, on what he considers to be good or evil, on how he thinks men should live.

The chapters I have included from *What Is Art?* contain the crux of Tolstoy's doctrine, but in some ways his theories are better shown by the real examples discussed in other pieces included in this book—the Introduction to the Works of Maupassant, the preface to a novel by the German naturalistic novelist Wilhelm von Polenz, and above all the afterword to a story of Chekhov's called "The Darling." In the first of these Tolstoy stresses the necessity of looking from the work—however artistically dazzling it may seem—to the author in order to ask the question: "Well now, what sort of a person are you?" and in connection with von Polenz, he emphasizes the fact that this writer, unlike playwrights and others who are making a deliberate attempt to "excite" their audience, really "loves his protagonists" and persuades the reader not only to pity but also to love them. Even more interestingly, he asserts, for example, that Chekhov intended to make fun of his heroine—"The Darling"—but that "by directing the close attention of a poet upon her he has exalted her." This is the closest Tolstoy comes to recognizing that an author's intention may not correspond to the actual effect of the work of art and that some of the best books, and those most full of infectious feeling, may be those in which the author's intention is lost sight of, or even contradicted by the close attention or "love" he devotes to his characters. This may be why we feel as we do about characters such as Stiva Oblonsky in *Anna Karenina* and the many other persons whom Tolstoy drew with close attention in spite of his disapproving of them in the terms of his own rigid philosophy.

A Confession, begun in 1879, is the first of the works that were written with what the critic Mikhaylov called "the left hand of Tolstoy," the hand of the preacher and dogmatic exponent of his own form of religion. But just as anything he wrote shows the hand of the master-craftsman, even when it is the left hand, so his earlier writings reveal, not only the genius of great art, but what might be called the dogmatism of the right hand. Few things could be more ultimately instructive for our knowledge of Tolstoy, it seems to me, than to compare the tone of *A Confession* and *What I Believe* with that of the defiant passage from an early draft of *War and Peace* in which Tolstoy attacked the prevailing Russian liberal and intellectual climate of the time—personified by such leaders of the intelligentsia as Belinsky—in defense of what he sees as the old Russian values of simplicity, aristocracy, and a certain down-to-earth honesty and hatred of cant: "I am an aristocrat because I cannot believe in the high intellect, the refined taste, or the absolute honesty of a man who picks his nose and whose soul converses with God." Tolstoy never wrote anything more characteristic and self-revealing than that.

JOHN BAYLEY

A NOTE ON THE TRANSLATIONS

Tolstoy, who knew English well, said in his later years that the best English translations of his works had been made by Aylmer Maude (1858–1938)—an English Quaker, long a businessman in Czarist Russia. Maude knew Russian perfectly, knew Tolstoy personally, was sympathetic to his ideas, visited frequently at Yasnaya Polyana; and with his Russian-born wife Louise he translated over the years almost all of Tolstoy's manifold published works.

Earlier, many of them had merely been translated into English second-hand from French versions; later, in certain cases, a particular work by another gifted translator from the Russian has sometimes been favored. But the consistently careful, sympathetic, and well-documented translations by the Maudes, issued by the Oxford University Press, have become the accepted standard for Tolstoy in English. When it was time to attempt a Portable Tolstoy, *it seemed logical and served consistency to use the Maude translations throughout wherever they existed. This proved to be the case for all of John Bayley's selections except the first:* A History of Yesterday—*never picked up by the Maudes but translated by an American, Professor George L. Kline of Bryn Mawr.*

Grateful acknowledgement is made to the Oxford University Press for permission to use its Maude translations in this Portable.

All unsigned footnotes may be assumed to be the Maudes'.

THE PUBLISHERS

A
TOLSTOY
CHRONOLOGY

1828　August 28, old style (September 9). Leo Nikolaye-
　　　　vich Tolstoy born at Yasnaya Polyana, province
　　　　of Tula, fourth son of Count Nikolai Ilyich Tolstoy.

1830　Death of mother.

1837　Family moves to Moscow. Death of father.

1841　Moves from Moscow to Kazan under guardian-
　　　　ship of his aunt Tatyana (the main model for
　　　　Sonya in *War and Peace*).

1844　Enters Faculty of Oriental Languages, Kazan Uni-
　　　　versity. Fails examinations.

1845　Transfers to Law Faculty. Leads a wild life with
　　　　all the usual student excesses.

1847　Abandons his studies on grounds of "ill health
　　　　and domestic circumstances." Short period in hospi-
　　　　tal with venereal disease. Returns to Yasnaya
　　　　Polyana, now his personal estate.

1848　Goes into Moscow society, gambling and drinking
　　　　heavily.

1849　Decides to enter Law Faculty at St. Petersburg
　　　　University and manages to pass two examinations.
　　　　Now has heavy gambling debts. Decides to with-
　　　　draw from the capital and retrench in the country.
　　　　Opens a school for the serf children on his estate
　　　　and interests himself in pedagogy.

1850　Becomes seriously interested in music—devotes
　　　　much time to piano playing and has thoughts of
　　　　becoming a composer—but still spends much time
　　　　in club life in Moscow and Tula.

1851　First attempt at literary composition. Writes "A
　　　　History of Yesterday," which remained unpublished
　　　　throughout his lifetime. He begins "Childhood" and
　　　　makes a partial translation of Sterne's *Sentimental*

Journey, which, together with Dickens's *David Copperfield* and the writings of the German novelist Töpfer, had a great influence on him at this time. Gives up literature for the moment and departs for the Caucasus with his brother. Sees first action against the tribesmen.

1852   "Childhood" published and at once successful; Tolstoy sent it to the leading St. Petersburg journal, *The Contemporary*, founded by Pushkin and at that time edited by Mekrasov; is angry because Mekrasov publishes it under the title "A History of My Childhood" ("I was extremely displeased to recognize it as the novel *Childhood* that I sent to you. . . . Who is interested in the history of *my* childhood?"), nonetheless he is pleased by the acceptance of the story and writes in his diary: "It made me happy to the limit of stupidity." Dostoevsky, exiled in Siberia, is impressed when he sees a copy of *Childhood,* and writes to a friend asking, "Who is this mysterious L.N.T.?" (the book appeared in *The Contemporary* under Tolstoy's initials only), and Turgenev observes: "When this wine is mature it will be a drink fit for the Gods." But toward the end of his life, Tolstoy denounces the childhood scenes as "insincere and badly written." Meanwhile has joined the army as a cadet and has nearly been killed by an exploding grenade. Is in the Gunners and is reasonably conscientious in his duties, which leave him plenty of time for writing, and for gambling. Visits spas in the Caucasus for treatment of his venereal complaint.

1853   "The Raid" published by *The Contemporary*. Takes part in a raid against the Chéchens in which he is nearly captured.

1854   *Boyhood* published. Outbreak of Crimean war. Sent to serve on the Danube and subsequently in Sevastopol.

1855   Two Sevastopol sketches and "The Woodfelling" published. Returns to St. Petersburg at the end of the war and meets a number of well-known Russian writers connected with *The Contemporary*.

1856   Leaves army. Brother Dmitri dies. Continues to frequent literary circles in St. Petersburg. Falls in love with Arseneva (who becomes the model for the heroine of "Family Happiness"). Publishes several stories, including "Two Hussars."

1857   Visits Europe for six months, chiefly Paris and Switzerland. In Paris attends Sorbonne lectures and sees a public execution. Works on stories, including "Lucerne." *Youth* published.

1858   Family at home. Tolstoy nearly killed by a bear while out hunting.

1859   Publishes "Family Happiness," which is rapidly recognized. Temporarily gives up literature for teaching theory and practice.

1860   Studies educational theory and practice in Germany. Brother Nicholas dies of consumption when they are in France together (he is recalled in the character and death of Levin's brother in *War and Peace*).

1861   Traveling in England, France, Italy, and Germany. Hears Dickens lecture on education. On returning to Russia, quarrels with Turgenev and challenges him to a duel, which does not take place.

1862   Starts magazine *Yasnaya Polyana*, on educational matters. Works as Arbiter of the Peace following the liberation of the serfs and acquires reputation for just conduct, which alienates some of his fellow landowners. After short courtship marries Sonya Behrs.

1863   *The Cossacks* published. Begins work on *War and Peace*. First child born.

1869   Completes *War and Peace*, which was published over the years in six volumes. In August, on a journey to view a property near the town of Arzamas, has a terrifying experience, a kind of "vastation" which he afterward refers to as "the Arzamas horror," in part certainly caused by the reaction from the six-year strain of composing his great work. Ten years later he intended to write it down as a personal account, but—perhaps because it still unnerved him—gave it the form of a story, "Memoirs of a Madman," which he never finished.

1870   Suffers from acute depression, but studies ancient Greek and the drama.

1872   "A Prisoner in the Caucasus" published. Works halfheartedly on a historical novel about Peter the Great and his times but soon abandons it.

1873   Travels to his new estate in Bashkiria, taking his family. Starts *Anna Karenina*, which begins to appear in installments in 1875.

1878   Publication of *Anna Karenina* in book form. Begins to work again on a novel about the Decembrist movement. Only fragments of this survive, though he does not finally abandon the idea for another five years. Becoming increasingly preoccupied with religion.

1879   Visits the monasteries of Kiev and began to write *A Confession* and other articles on religion.

1882   Finishes *A Confession*, publication of which was banned in Russia. Begins "The Death of Ivan Ilyich" and "What Then Must Be?" which are finished in 1886.

1885   Writing popular stories, "What Men Live By" and "Where Love Is God Is" published. Becomes a vegetarian.

1886   Writes *The Power of Darkness*. The play is banned in Russia but acted in Paris two years later. Publication of "The Death of Ivan Ilyich" and "How Much Land Does a Man Need?"

1888   Birth of his last child (the thirteenth). Increasing friction in the family circle, caused by the enmity between the Countess Tolstoy and Tolstoy's chief disciple, Chertkov.

1889   Completes *The Kreutzer Sonata* and begins work on *Resurrection*. Much interested at this time in the theories of Henry George and the single tax land-holding system, which are mentioned in *Resurrection*. The plot of the work is based partly on an anecdote about a seduced orphan girl told him by a lawyer friend, and partly on an episode in his own life. "When I was young I led a very evil life and the incidents still particularly haunt me . . . a liaison with a peasant girl before I was married—there is an allusion to it in my story *The Devil*—and the crime I perpetrated on Gasha, the maid who lived in my aunt's house. I seduced her and she was expelled from the house and came to grief." (Tolstoy had particular trouble with the ending of *Resurrection*. In one Version, almost the final one, Nekhlyúdov insists on marrying Maslova and they lead a peasant life together in Siberia before escaping to London, where Nekhlyúdov campaigns on behalf of Henry George and against the evils of private landownership. Tolstoy planned a sequel along this or other lines but never wrote it.)

1891   Tolstoy renounces his copyrights. Helps organize famine relief.

1894   Writes religious essays and the introduction to Maupassant's works.

1898   Decides to publish *Resurrection* and *Father Sergius* in order to raise funds for famine relief. Working on *What Is Art?* and his last long story, *Hadji Murád,* which harks back to his experiences as a youth in the Caucasus.

1899   Aids emigration of the Dukhobors to Canada.

1901   Excommunicated by the Orthodox Church. Convalesces in the Crimea after a serious illness and sees Chekhov, Gorky, and other writers.

1904   Decides to publish no more creative work in order to avoid quarrels with his wife over copyrights. Finishes *Hadji Murád,* which is published posthumously.

1905   Writes several stories, including "Alyosha Gorshok," which are published posthumously. Writes introduction to Chekhov's "The Darling."

1906   Death of his favorite daughter and disciple.

1907   Writes to the Russian prime minister advocating the Henry George solution to the land problem.

1908   Writes "I Cannot be Silent" against capital punishment. The authorities intervene and a newspaper editor is arrested for printing it. Tolstoy's secretary is also arrested and deported.

1909   Wife threatens suicide; their relations extremely

difficult. Crises with his wife and Chertkov over his diaries and over his will and surrender of copyright.

1910   Leaves home; on November 7, old style (November 20), dies of pneumonia at Astapovo railway station, aged eighty-two.

THE PORTABLE TOLSTOY

PART ONE
The Past
Recaptured

∿∿∿∿∿∿∿∿∿∿∿∿∿∿∿

A HISTORY OF YESTERDAY
Part of an unfinished work

Translated by George L. Kline

TRANSLATOR'S NOTE
Tolstoy planned "A History of Yesterday" as a major literary effort—his first. He wrote the surviving fragment between March 26 and 28, 1851 (old style calendar), set the work aside while he completed Childhood, and never returned to it. The fragment was not published until after his death; it was not translated into English until 1949.

The "yesterday" in question was March 25, but the story begins with the evening of the "day before yesterday" and gets little beyond it. Tolstoy actually spent that evening (March 24) in the home of his second cousin, Prince A. A. Volkonski, whose charming and flirtatious twenty-six-year-old wife seems to have been almost hypnotically attractive to the twenty-two-year-old Tolstoy. (She later served as the model for the "Little Princess," wife of Prince Andrei Bolkonski, in War and Peace.*) Tolstoy recalled in 1852 that his "best memories" of the preceding year were of her.*

At this time Tolstoy was devouring Goethe's Werther *and Sterne's* Sentimental Journey through France and Italy. *He admired the latter so much that he actually completed a Russian translation (based largely on a French one) of about a third of it. "A History of Yesterday" shows the influence of Sterne in many ways: in its innocent and "sentimental" eroticism, in the close analysis of subtle and evanescent feelings and reactions to feelings, in the "inaudible conversation," the frequent digressions—and digressions within digressions—and in the intrusion of commonplace aphorisms and observations. There is even direct borrowing, as when Sterne writes: "I [was] left alone with the lady with her hand in mine, and with our faces both turned closer to the door . . . than what was absolutely necessary," and Tolstoy echoes: "She very carefully drew something which I could not see, lifted the chalk a little higher than was necessary, and placed it on the table."*

Certain literary devices appear in this early work which Tolstoy later abandoned. Others—particularly the interior monologue, the "silent dialogue," and the suggestion of emotional states and processes through facial expression or bodily movement—were systematically developed in later works.

This English version is based upon the authoritative text of the Jubilee Edition of Tolstoy's collected works ("Istoriya vcherashnevo dnya," Polnoye sobraniye sochinenii L. N. Tolstovo, I, Moscow, 1928), edited by Tolstoy's long-time associate V. G. Chertkov. What follows is a slightly abridged revision of my earlier translation, which appeared in the Russian Review, vol. VIII, no. 2 (1949).

I am writing a history of yesterday not because yesterday was extraordinary in any way, for it might rather be called ordinary, but because I have long wished to trace the intimate side of life through an entire day. Only God knows how many diverse and diverting impressions, together with the thoughts awakened by them, occur in a single day. Obscure and confused they may be, but they are nevertheless comprehensible to our minds. If they could be recorded in such a way that I myself—and others after me—could easily read the account, the result would be a most instructive and amusing book. But there would not be ink enough in the world to write it, or typesetters to put it into print. However, let us get on with the story.

I arose late yesterday—at a quarter to ten—because I had gone to bed after midnight. (It has long been my rule never to retire after midnight, yet this happens to me at least three times a week.) But there are some circumstances in which I consider this a fault rather than a crime. The circumstances vary; yesterday they were as follows:

Here I must apologize for going back to the day before yesterday. But then, novelists devote whole chapters to their heroes' forebears.

I was playing cards—not from any passion for the game, as it might seem; no more, indeed, from a passion for the game than one who dances the polka does so from a passion for promenading. Rousseau, among the many things which he proposed and no one has accepted, suggested the playing of cup-and-ball in society in order to keep the hands occupied. But that is scarcely enough; in society the head too should be occupied or at the very least should be so employed as to permit silence as well as conversation.[1] Such an employment has been invented: cards. People of the older generation complain that "nowadays there is no conversation." I don't know how people were in the old days (it seems to me that people have always been the same), but conversation there can never be. As an employment conversation is the stupidest of inventions. It is not from any deficiency of intelligence but from egotism that conversation fails. Everyone wishes to talk about himself or about that which interests him. But if one person speaks while another listens, you have not a conversation but a lecture. If two people come together who are interested in the same thing, then a third person is enough to spoil the whole business: he interferes, you must try to give him a share too—and your conversation has gone to the devil.

There are also conversations between people who are interested in the same thing, and where no one disturbs them, but such cases are even worse. Each speaks of the same thing from his own viewpoint, transposing everything to his own key, and measuring everything with his own yardstick. The longer the conversation continues, the further apart they draw, until at last each one sees that he is no longer conversing, but is preaching with a freedom which he permits only to himself; that he is making a spectacle of himself, and that the other is not listening to him, but is doing the same thing. Have you ever rolled eggs during Holy Week? You start off two identical eggs with the same stick, but with their little ends on opposite sides.

[1] In fact, Rousseau too was concerned with occupying the head as well as the hands. "If ever I went back into society," he wrote in Book V of the *Confessions*, "I should carry a cup-and-ball in my pocket, and play with it all day long to excuse myself from speaking when I had nothing to say. If everyone were to do the same men would become less malicious, and society would become . . . more agreeable."—G.L.K.

At first they roll in the same direction, but then each one begins to roll away in the direction of its little end. In conversation, as in egg-rolling, there are little sloops that roll along noisily and not very far; there are sharp-ended ones that wander off heaven knows where. But, with the exception of the little sloops, there are no two eggs that will roll in the same direction. Each has its little end.

I am not speaking now of those conversations which are carried on simply because it would be improper not to say something, just as it would be improper to appear without a necktie. One person thinks, "You know quite well that I have no real interest in what I am saying, but it is necessary"; and the other, "Talk away, talk away, poor soul—I know it is necessary." This is not conversation, but the same thing as a swallowtail coat, a calling card, and gloves—a matter of decorum.

And that is why I say that cards are an excellent invention. In the course of the game one may chat, gratify one's ego, and make witty remarks; furthermore, one is not obligated to keep to the same subject, as one is in that society where there is only conversation.

One must reserve the last intellectual cartridge for the final round, when one is taking his leave. Then is the time to explode your whole supply, like a race horse approaching the finish line. Otherwise one appears pale and insipid. And I have noticed that people who are not only clever but capable of sparkling in society have lost out in the end because they lacked this sense of timing. If you have spoken heatedly and then become too bored and listless to reply, the last impression lingers, and people say, "How dull he is . . ." But when people play cards this does not happen. One may remain silent without incurring censure.

Besides, women—young ones—play cards, and what could be better than to sit beside a young lady for two or three hours? And if it is *the* young lady, nothing more can be desired.

And so I played cards. We took seats on the right, on the left, opposite—and everything was cozy.

This diversion continued until a quarter to twelve. We finished three rubbers. Why does this woman love (how I should like to finish this sentence with "me"!) to embarrass me? For even if she didn't I would not be myself in her presence. It seems to me either that my hands are very dirty or that I am sitting awkwardly, or else I am tormented by a pimple on my cheek—the one facing her. Yet she is in no way to blame for this: I am always ill at ease with people whom I either do not like or like very much. Why is this? Because I wish to convey to the former that I do not like them, and to the latter that I do, and to convey what you wish is very difficult. With me it always works out in reverse. I wish to be cool, but then this coolness seems overdone and to make up for it I become too affable. With people whom you love honorably, the thought that they may think you love them dishonorably unnerves you and you become short and brusque.

She is the woman for me because she has all those endearing qualities which compel one to love them, or rather, to love her—for I do love her. But not in order to possess her. That thought never entered my head.

She has the bad habit of billing and cooing with her husband in front of others, but this does not bother me; it means no more to me than if she should kiss the stove or the table. She plays with her husband as a swallow plays with a blossom, because she is warmhearted and this makes her happy.

She is a coquette; no, not a coquette, but she loves to please, even to turn heads. I won't say coquette, because either the word or the idea associated with it is bad. To call showing the naked body and deceiving in love coquetry! That is not coquetry but brazen impudence and baseness. But to wish to please and turn heads is fine and does no one any harm, since there are no Werthers; and it provides innocent pleasure for oneself and others. Thus, for example, I am quite content that she should please me; I desire nothing more. Furthermore, there is clever coquetry and stupid coquetry; clever coquetry is inconspicuous and you do not catch the culprit in the act; stupid coquetry, on the contrary hides nothing. It speaks thus: "I am not so good-looking, but what legs I have! Look! Do you see? What do you say? Nice?" Perhaps your legs are nice, but I did not notice, because you showed them. Clever coquetry says: "It is all the same to me whether you look or not. I was hot, so I took off my hat." I saw everything. "And what does it matter to me?" *Her* coquetry is both innocent and clever.

I looked at my watch and got up. It is astonishing: except when I am speaking to her, I never see her looking at me, and yet she sees all my movements. "Oh, what a pink watch he has!" I am very much offended when people find my Bréguet watch pink; it would be equally offensive if they told me that my vest is pink. I suppose I was visibly embarrassed, because when I said that on the contrary it was an excellent watch, she became embarrassed in her turn. I dare say she was sorry that she had said something which put me in an awkward position. We both sensed the humor of the situation and smiled. Being embarrassed together and smiling together was very pleasant to me. A silly thing, to be sure, but together. I love these secret, inexplicable relationships, expressed by an imperceptible smile or by the eyes. It is not only that one person understands the other, but that each understands that the other understands that he understands him, etc.

Whether she wished to end this conversation which I found so sweet, or to see how I would refuse, or if I would refuse, or whether she simply wished to continue playing, she looked at the figures which were written on the table, drew the chalk over the table—making a figure that could be classified neither as mathematical nor pictorial—looked at her husband, then between him and me, and said: "Let's play three more rubbers." I was so absorbed in the contemplation not of her movements alone, but of everything that is called *charme*—which it is impossible to describe— that my imagination was very far away, and I did not have time to clothe my words in a felicitous form. I simply said, "No, I can't."

Before I had finished saying this I began to regret it— that is, not all of me, but one part of me. There is no action which is not condemned by some part of the mind. On the other hand, there is a part that speaks in behalf of any action: what is so bad about going to bed after twelve, and when do you suppose you will spend another such delightful evening? I dare say this part spoke very eloquently and persuasively (although I cannot convey what it said), for I became alarmed and began to cast about for arguments. In the first place, I said to myself, there is no great pleasure in it, you do not like her at all, and you're in an awkward position; besides, you've already said that you can't stay, and you would fall in her estimation . . .

"Comme il est aimable, ce jeune homme."

This sentence, which followed immediately after mine, interrupted my reflections. I began to make excuses, to say I couldn't stay, but since one does not have to think to make excuses, I continued reasoning with myself. How I love to have her speak of me in the third person. In German this is rude, but I would love it even in German. Why doesn't she find a decent name for me? It is clearly awkward for her to call me either by my given name or by my surname and title. Can this be because I . . .

"Stay and have supper," said her husband. As I was busy with my reflections on the formula of the third person, I did not notice that my body, while very properly making its excuses that it could not stay, was putting down its hat again and sitting down quite coolly in an easy chair. It was clear that my mind was taking no part in this absurdity. I became highly vexed and was about to begin roundly reproaching myself, when a pleasant circumstance diverted me. She very carefully drew something which I could not see, lifted the chalk a little higher than was necessary, and placed it on the table. Then she put her hands on the divan on which she was sitting, and wriggling from side to side, pushed herself to the back of it and raised her head—her little head, with the fine rounded contours of her face, the dark, half-closed, but energetic eyes, the narrow, sharp little nose and the mouth that was one with the eyes and always expressed something new. At this moment who could say what it expressed? There was pensiveness and mockery, and pain, and a desire to keep from laughing, dignity, and capriciousness, and intelligence, and stupidity, and passion, and apathy, and much more. After waiting for a moment, her husband went out—I suppose to order the supper.

To be left alone with her is always frightening and oppressive to me. As I follow with my eyes whoever is leaving, it is as painful to me as the fifth figure of the quadrille: I see my partner going over to the other side and I must remain alone. I am sure it was not so painful for Napoleon to see the Saxons crossing over to the enemy at

Waterloo as it was for me, a young man, to watch this cruel maneuver. The stratagem that I employ in the quadrille I employed also in this case: I acted as though I did not notice that I was alone. And now even the conversation which I had begun before his exit came to an end; I repeated the last words that I had said, adding only, "And that's how it is." She repeated hers, adding, "Yes." But at the same time another, inaudible, conversation began.

She: "I know why you repeat what you have already said. It is awkward for you to be alone with me and you see that it is awkward for me—so in order to seem occupied you begin to talk. I thank you very much for this attention, but perhaps one could say something a little bit more intelligent."

I: "That is true, your observation is correct, but I don't know why *you* feel awkward. Surely you don't think that when we are alone I will begin to say things that will be distasteful to you? To prove that I am ready to sacrifice my own pleasures for your sake, however agreeable our present conversation is to me, I am going to speak aloud. Or else you begin."

She: "Well, go on!"

I was just opening my mouth to say something that would allow me to think of one thing while saying something else, when she began a conversation aloud which apparently could continue for a long while. In such a situation the most interesting questions are neglected because *the* conversation continues. Having uttered one sentence apiece, we fell silent, tried once more to speak, and again fell silent.

The conversation—

I: "No, it is impossible to talk. Since I see that this is awkward for you, it would be better if your husband were to return."

She (aloud to a servant): "Well, where is Ivan Ivanovich? Ask him to come in here."

If anyone does not believe that there are such secret conversations, that should convince him.

"I am very glad that we are now alone," I continued, speaking silently. "I have already mentioned to you that you often offend me by your lack of confidence. If my foot accidentally touches yours, you immediately hasten to apologize and do not give me time to do so, while I, having realized that it was actually your foot, was just about to apologize myself. Because I am slower than you, you think me indelicate."

Her husband came in. We sat for a while, had supper, and chatted. At about twelve-thirty I went home.

It was spring, the twenty-fifth of March. The night was clear and still; a young moon was visible from behind the red roof of a large white house opposite; most of the snow was already gone.

My night sledge was the only vehicle at the entrance; even without the footman's shout of "Let's go, there!" Dmitri knew quite well that it was I who was leaving. A smacking sound was audible, as though he were kissing someone in the dark, which, I conjectured, was intended to urge the little mare and the sledge away from the pavement stones on which the runners grated and screeched unpleasantly. Finally the sledge drew up. The solicitous footman took me under the elbow and assisted me to my seat. If he had not held me I should simply have jumped into the sledge, but as it was, in order not to offend him, I walked slowly, and broke through the thin ice which covered the puddle, getting my feet wet. "Thank you, my friend." "Dmitri, is there a frost?" "Of course, sir; we still have a bit of frost at night."

How stupid! Why did I ask that? No, there is nothing stupid about it. You wanted to talk, to enter into communication with someone, because you are in high spirits. And why am I in high spirits? Half an hour ago if I had gotten into my sledge, I wouldn't have started to talk. Because you spoke elegantly when taking your leave, because her husband saw you to the door and said, "When will we see you again?" Because as soon as the footman caught sight of you he jumped up, and despite the fact that he reeked of parsley, he took pleasure in serving you. I gave him a fifty-kopek piece a few days ago. In all our recollections the middle falls away and the first and last impressions remain, especially the last. For this reason there exists the splendid custom of the master of the house accompanying his guest to the door, where, twining one leg about the other as a rule, the host must say something kind to his guest. Despite any intimacy of relations, this rule must not be disregarded. Thus, for example, "When will we see you again?" means nothing, but from vanity the guest involuntarily translates it as follows: *When* means "please make it soon"; *we* means "not only myself but my wife, who is also pleased to see you"; *see you* means "give us the pleasure another time"; *again* means "we have just spent the evening together, but with you it is impossible to be bored." And the guest carries away a pleasant impression.

It is also necessary to give money to the servants, especially in homes that are not well regulated and where not all the footmen are courteous—in particular the doorman (who is the most important personage because of the first and last impression). They will greet you and see you off as if you were a member of the family, and you translate their solicitousness—whose source is your fifty-kopek piece—as follows: "Everyone here loves and respects you, therefore we try, in pleasing the masters, to please you." Perhaps it is only the footman who loves and respects you, but all the same it is pleasant. What's the harm if you are mistaken? If there were no mistakes, there would be no . . .

"Are you crazy! . . . What the de-e-evil!"

Dmitri and I were very quietly and modestly driving down one of the boulevards, keeping to the ice on the right-hand side, when suddenly some "chowderhead" (Dmitri gave him this name afterwards) in a carriage and pair ran into us. We separated, and only after we had gone on about ten paces did Dmitri say, "Look at him, the chowderhead, he doesn't know his right hand from his left!"

Don't think that Dmitri was a timid man or slow to answer. No, on the contrary, although he was of small stature, clean shaven—but with a moustache—he was deeply conscious of his own dignity and strictly fulfilled his duties. His weakness in this case was attributable to two circumstances: (1) Dmitri was accustomed to driving vehicles which inspired respect, but now we were driving in a small sledge with very long shafts, pulled by a very small horse, which he could hardly reach even with a whip; what is more, the horse dragged its hind feet pitifully—and all this could easily evoke the derision of bystanders. Consequently this circumstance was all the more difficult for Dmitri and could quite destroy his feelings of [self-confidence][2] (2) Probably my question, "Is there a frost?" had reminded him of similar questions that I had asked him in the autumn on starting out to hunt. He is a hunter, and hunters have something to daydream about; they forget to hurl a well-timed curse at the driver who does not keep to the right-hand side. With coachmen, as with everyone else, whoever shouts first and with the greatest assurance is right. There are certain exceptions. For example, a droshki-driver cannot shout at a carriage; a singleton—even an elegant one—can hardly shout at a four-in-hand; but then, everything depends on the nature of the individual circumstances, and, most important, on the personality of the driver and the direction in which he is going. I once saw in Tula a striking example of the influence that one man can have on others through sheer audacity.

Everyone was driving to the carnival: sleighs with pairs, four-in-hands, carriages, trotters, silk cloaks—all drawn out in a line on Kiev Street—and there were swarms of pedestrians. Suddenly there was a shout from a side street: "Hold back your horses! Out of the way there!" in a self-assured voice. Involuntarily the pedestrians made way, the pairs and four-in-hands were reined in. And what do you think? A ragged cabby, brandishing the ends of the reins over his head, standing on a broken-down sledge drawn by a vile jade, tore through with a shout to the other side, before anyone realized what was happening. Even the policemen burst out laughing.

Although Dmitri is a reckless fellow and loves to swear, he has a kind heart and spares his poor horse. He uses the whip not as an incentive but as a corrective, that is, he doesn't spur his horse on with the whip: this is incompatible with the dignity of a city driver. But if the trotter doesn't stand still at the entrance, he will "give him one." I had occasion to observe this presently: crossing from one street to another our little horse was hardly able to drag us along, and I noticed from the desperate movements of Dmitri's back and hands and from his clucking that he was having difficulties. Would he use the whip? That was not his custom. But what if the horse stopped? That he would not tolerate, even though here he didn't need to fear the wag

[2] This word is illegible in Tolstoy's manuscript.—G.L.K.

who would say, "Feeding time, eh?" Here was proof that Dmitri acted more from a consciousness of his duty than from vanity.

I thought much more about the many and varied relations of drivers among themselves, of their intelligence, resourcefulness, and pride. I suppose that at large gatherings those who have been involved in collisions recognize one another and pass from hostility to peaceable relations. Everything in the world is interesting, especially the relationships which exist in classes other than our own.

If the vehicles are going in the same direction the disputes last longer. The one who was to blame attempts to drive the other away or to leave him behind, and the latter sometimes succeeds in proving to him the wrongness of his action, and gains the upper hand; incidentally, when both are going the same way, the one with faster horses has the advantage.

All of these relationships correspond very closely to the general relationships in life. The relationships of gentlemen among themselves and with their drivers in the case of such collisions, are also interesting. "Hey there, you scoundrel, where do you think you're going?" When this cry is addressed to the whole vehicle, the passenger involuntarily tries to assume a serious, or gay, or unconcerned expression —in a word, one that he did not have before. It is evident that he would be pleased if the situation were reversed. I have noticed that gentlemen with moustaches[3] are especially sensitive to the insults sustained by their vehicles.

"Who goes there?"

This shout came from a policeman who had in my presence been very much offended by a driver this same morning. At the entrance across from his sentry-box a carriage was standing; a splendid figure of a driver with a red beard, having tucked the reins under him, and resting his elbows on his knees, was warming his back in the sun— with evident pleasure, for his eyes were almost completely closed. Opposite him the policeman walked up and down on the platform in front of his sentry-box and, using the end of his halberd, adjusted the plank which was laid across the nearby puddles. Suddenly he seemed to resent the fact

[3] That is, cavalry officers.—G.L.K.

that the carriage was standing there, or else he began to envy the driver who was warming himself with such pleasure, or perhaps he merely wished to start a conversation. He walked the length of his little platform, peered into the side street, and then thumped with his halberd on the plank: "Hey you, where are you stopping? You're blocking the road." The driver unscrewed his left eye a little, glanced at the policeman, and closed it again.

"Get a move on! I'm talking to you!" No sign of life. "Are you deaf? Eh? Move along, I said!" The policeman, seeing that there was no response, walked the length of his little platform, peered into the side street once more, and evidently was getting ready to say something devastating. At this point the driver raised himself a little, adjusted the reins under him, and turning with sleepy eyes to the policeman, said, "What are you gawking at? They wouldn't even let you have a gun, you simpleton, and still you go around yelling at people!"

"Get out of here!"

The driver roused himself and got out of there.

I looked at the policeman. He muttered something and looked angrily at me; apparently he was embarrassed that I had overheard and was looking at him. I know of nothing that can offend a man more deeply than to give him to understand that you have noticed something but do not wish to mention it. As a result I became embarrassed myself; I felt sorry for the policeman and went away.

TRANSLATOR'S NOTE

In the concluding pages, here omitted, Tolstoy describes his meticulous posting of the day's "weaknesses" from diary to "Franklin journal" by "putting little crosses in the columns." He goes on to reflect upon the nature of good and evil, to recount his sensations while falling asleep, and to expatiate on the causes of dream experience. Finally, he tells of planning a trip down the Volga from Saratov to Astrakhan and of the initial steps in hiring a boat for the purpose.—G.L.K.

From CHILDHOOD

I

OUR TUTOR, KARL IVÁNYCH

On the 12th of August 18—, exactly three days after my tenth birthday, on which I had received such wonderful presents, Karl Iványch woke me up at seven in the morning by hitting a fly just above my head with a flap of blue sugar-bag paper fastened to a stick. He did this so awkwardly that he caught the little picture of my patron-saint, which hung from the top of my oak bedstead, and the dead fly fell right on my head. I pushed my nose from under the bed-clothes, put out my hand to steady the little picture which was still swinging, threw the dead fly on the floor, and looked at Karl Iványch with angry though sleepy eyes. He however, in his variegated, quilted dressing-gown, girdled with a belt of the same material, and with a red tasselled smoking-cap on his head, continued to walk round the room in his soft leather boots, aiming at and hitting the flies.

"Of course I am small," I thought, "but why should he disturb me? Why does he not kill the flies round Volódya's bed? See what a lot of them there are! No, Volódya is older than I. I am the youngest of all—that's why he torments me. He thinks of nothing all his life long but how to make things unpleasant for me," I whispered. "He sees perfectly well that he has waked me up and frightened me, but he pretends not to notice it. Disgusting fellow! His dressing-gown and cap and tassel are all disgusting!"

While in my own mind I was thus expressing my vexation with Karl Iványch, he went up to his bed, looked at his watch which hung above it in a small beaded slipper, hung the flap on a nail in the wall, and, evidently in the best of spirits, turned to us.

"*Auf, Kinder, auf !. . . 's ist Zeit. Die Mutter ist schon im Saal!*"[1] exclaimed he in his kind, German voice. Then

[1] "Up, children, up! . . . It's time! Mother is already in the dining-room."

he came up to me, sat down at the foot of my bed, and took his snuff-box from his pocket. I pretended to be asleep. Karl Iványch first took a pinch of snuff, wiped his nose, snapped his fingers, and only then turned on me. He began, laughingly, to tickle my heels.

"*Nun, nun, Faulenzer!*"[2] he said.

Much as I dreaded being tickled, I did not jump up or answer him, but only hid my head deeper under the pillow and kicked with all my strength to keep from laughing.

"How kind he is and how fond of us! How could I think so badly of him?"

I was vexed with myself and with Karl Iványch and wanted to laugh and to cry: my nerves were upset.

"*Ach, lassen Sie, Karl Iványch!*"[3] I shouted with tears in my eyes, thrusting my head out from under the pillow.

Karl Iványch was surprised, left the soles of my feet in peace, and anxiously began to inquire what was the matter, and whether I had had a bad dream. . . . His kindly German face, and the solicitude with which he tried to discover the cause of my tears, made them flow the faster. I was ashamed, and could not understand how, but a moment before, I had been able to dislike him, and consider his dressing-gown, cap, and tassel disgusting. Now, on the contrary, all these things appeared extremely pleasing, and even the tassel seemed clear evidence of his goodness. I said that I was crying because of a bad dream—that mamma had died and was being carried to her funeral. I invented all this, for I could not at all remember what I had dreamt that night; but when Karl Iványch, touched by my words, began to console and calm me, it seemed to me that I had really had that dreadful dream and I now shed tears for another reason.

[2] "Now then, lazybones!"
[3] "Oh, leave me alone."

When Karl Iványch left me, and having sat up in bed I began drawing the stockings on to my small feet, my tears flowed more gently, but the gloomy thoughts of my invented dream did not leave me. Nicholas, our attendant, a clean little man, always serious, neat, respectful, and great friends with Karl Iványch, came in. He brought our clothes; for Volódya a pair of boots and for me those detestable shoes with bows which I still wore. I was ashamed to let him see me cry, besides which the morning sun shone gaily into the room, and Volódya, standing at the wash-stand and mimicking Márya Ivánovna (our sister's governess), was laughing so merrily and so ringingly that even the serious Nicholas, with a towel over his shoulder, a piece of soap in one hand, and a jug of water in the other, said with a smile: "Have done, Vladímir Petróvich. Please wash now."

I grew quite cheerful.

"*Sind Sie bald fertig?*"[4] came Karl Iványch's voice from the schoolroom.

His voice sounded severe and no longer had that kindly tone which had moved me to tears. In the schoolroom Karl Iványch was quite a different man: he was the instructor. I dressed and washed quickly and, with the brush still in my hand smoothing down my wet hair, obeyed his call.

Karl Iványch, spectacles on nose and book in hand, sat in his usual place between the door and the window. To the left of the door were two shelves, one of them ours—the children's—the other Karl Iványch's *own*. On ours were all sorts of books—lesson-books and others: some standing, others lying down. Only two volumes of *Histoire des Voyages* in red bindings stood decorously against the wall, and then came long, thick, big and little books—bindings without books and books without bindings. We used to jam and shove everything there when told, before recreation, to tidy up the "library," as Karl Iványch pompously called that shelf. The collection of books on his own shelf, if not so large as ours, was yet more varied. I remember three of them: an unbound German pamphlet on the manuring of cabbage plots, one volume of a *History of the Seven Years' War*, bound in parchment and burnt at one corner, and a

4 "Will you soon be ready?"

full course of hydrostatics. Karl Iványch spent most of his time reading, and had even injured his eyes at it, yet he never read anything but these books and the *Northern Bee*.

Among the things that lay on his shelf, the one chiefly connected in my memory with Karl Iványch was a cardboard disk attached to a wooden stand on which it could be moved by means of pegs. A caricature of a lady and a hairdresser was pasted on the disk. Karl Iványch, who was very clever at that sort of thing, had made the disk to protect his weak eyes from too bright a light.

I can still see before me his long figure in the quilted dressing-gown and red skull-cap, from beneath which one saw his thin grey hair. He sits beside a small table on which stands the disk with the hairdresser, throwing a shadow on his face; a book is in one hand and the other rests on the arm of his chair; before him lies his watch with the figure of a hunter on its face, a chequered handkerchief, a round, black snuff-box, his green spectacle-case, and a pair of snuffers on their tray. All this lies so precisely, so tidily in its place, that by this orderliness alone one can feel sure that Karl Iványch's conscience is clear and his soul at peace.

When one had had enough running about in the dancing-room downstairs, one would creep upstairs on tiptoe to the classroom and see Karl Iványch sitting in his arm-chair all alone and reading one or other of his favourite books with a calmly dignified expression on his face. Sometimes I caught him when he was not reading: his spectacles hung low on his large aquiline nose, his half-closed blue eyes had a peculiar expression in them, and there was a sad smile on his lips. All was quiet in the room; the only sounds to be heard were his regular breathing and the ticking of the watch with the hunter on its face.

Sometimes he did not notice me and I stood by the door thinking: "Poor, poor old man! There are many of us; we play, we are merry, and he is all alone, and no one caresses him. He says truly that he is an orphan. The story of his life is such a dreadful one! I remember how he told it to Nicholas. It is dreadful to be in his position!" And I felt so sorry for him that I would go up and take his hand and say, "*Lieber Karl Iványch!*"[5] He liked me to speak so and would always pet me and was evidently touched.

On the other wall hung maps, nearly all of them torn but skilfully repaired by Karl Iványch. On the third wall, in the middle of which was a door leading to the stairs, hung, on one side, two rulers: one of them, ours, all cut about, and the other, a new one, his *own*, used by him more for incitement than for ruling lines; on the other side was a blackboard, on which our serious misdeeds were marked with circles and our little ones with crosses. To the left was the corner where we were put on our knees.

How well I remember that corner! I remember the door of the stove, the ventilator in that door, and the noise it made when turned. One used to kneel and kneel in the corner until one's knees and back ached and used to think, "Karl Iványch has forgotten me; he no doubt is comfortable sitting in his soft arm-chair, and reading his hydrostatics, but what of me?" And to remind him of oneself one would begin softly to open and shut the stove door, or to pick bits of plaster off the wall, but if too big a piece of plaster fell noisily on the floor the fright alone was, truly, worse than any punishment. One would turn to look at Karl Iványch, and there he sat, book in hand, as if he noticed nothing.

In the middle of the room stood a table covered with torn black oilcloth under which in many places one saw the edges of the table all cut with penknives. Round the table stood several wooden stools, unpainted, but polished by long use. The last wall was taken up by three windows. The view from those windows was this: just in front of them was a road, every hole, every stone, every rut of which had long been familiar and dear to me; beyond the road was a clipped lime-tree avenue, behind which here and there a wattle-fence was visible; across the avenue one could see the meadow, on one side of which was a threshing-floor, and opposite to this a wood. Deep in the wood one could see the watchman's hut. From the window to the right, part of the verandah was visible on which the grown-up people generally sat before dinner. Sometimes while Karl Iványch was correcting a page of dictation one would glance that way and see mamma's dark head, somebody's back, and

[5] "Dear Karl Iványch."

faintly hear sounds of voices and laughter coming from there, and one would be cross that one could not be there and would think, "When shall I be big, finish learning, and always sit, not over 'Dialogues,' but with those I love?" Vexation would turn to sadness and one would ponder so deeply, heaven only knows why and what, that one did not notice Karl Iványch getting angry about the mistakes.

Karl Iványch took off his dressing-gown, put on his blue, swallow-tail coat with the padding and gathers on the shoulders, adjusted his cravat before the looking-glass, and took us downstairs to say "good morning" to our mother.

II
MAMMA

Mamma was in the drawing-room pouring out tea. In one hand she held the teapot and with the other the tap of the samovar, from which the water poured over the top of the teapot on to the tray. But though she was looking fixedly at it she did not notice this, nor did she notice our coming in.

So many past memories arise when one tries to recall the features of a beloved being that one sees those features dimly through the memories as if through tears. They are the tears of imagination. When I try to recall my mother as she was at that time I can only picture her brown eyes, always expressing the same kindness and love, the mole on her neck just below the place where the short curls grew, her embroidered white collar, and the delicate dry hand which so often caressed me and I so often kissed, but her general expression escapes me.

To the left of the sofa stood an old, English, grand piano, at which sat my dark-haired sister Lyúba, with rosy fingers just washed in cold water playing with evident effort Clementi's exercises. She was eleven. She wore a short gingham frock and white, lace-trimmed drawers, and could only take an octave as an arpeggio. Beside her, half turned towards her, sat Márya Ivánovna, wearing a cap with pink ribbons and a blue gown; her face was red and cross and became even more stern as soon as Karl Iványch entered. She looked severely at him and, without returning his bow, tapped the floor with her foot and went on counting, "*Un,*

deux, trois; un, deux, trois" yet louder and more impera-
tively than before.

Karl Iványch, without taking the least notice of this, as
usual in his German way approached my mother to kiss
her hand. She roused herself, shook her head as if to drive
away sad thoughts, gave Karl Iványch her hand, and kissed
him on his wrinkled temple while he kissed her hand.

"*Ich danke, lieber Karl Iványch,*"[1] and continuing to
speak German, she asked: "Did the children sleep well?"

Karl Iványch was deaf on one ear and now from the
noise of the piano heard nothing. He stooped nearer to the
sofa, and leaning with one hand on the table and standing
on one leg, raised his skull-cap above his head with a smile,
which then appeared to me the height of refinement, and
said: "You will excuse me, Natálya Nikolávna?"

Karl Iványch, for fear of catching cold in his bald head,
always wore his red cap, but every time he entered the
drawing room, he asked permission to do so.

"Put it on, Karl Iványch. . . . I was asking you whether
the children slept well," said mamma, moving towards him
and speaking rather loudly.

But he again heard nothing, covered his bald head with
the red cap, and smiled even more pleasantly.

"Wait a moment, Mimi!" mamma said to Márya
Ivánovna with a smile, "One can't hear anything."

When mamma smiled, beautiful as her face was it grew
incomparably more lovely, and everything around seemed
brighter. If in life's sad moments I could but have had a
glimpse of that smile I should not have known what sorrow
is. It seems to me that what we call beauty in a face lies in
the smile. If a smile adds charm to a face, the face is
beautiful, if it does not change it, the face is ordinary, and
if it is spoilt by a smile, it is ugly.

When she had said good morning, mamma took my
head in both her hands and tilted it back, then looked
intently at me and said: "Have you cried this morning?"

I did not answer. She kissed my eyes and asked in
German: "What did you cry about?"

When she had a friendly talk with us she always spoke
in that language, which she knew perfectly.

---

[1] "I thank you, dear Karl Iványch."

"I cried in my sleep, mamma," I said, remembering my invented dream in all its details and involuntarily shuddering at the thought.

Karl Iványch confirmed my words but kept silent about the dream. After speaking of the weather—a conversation in which Mimi also took part—mamma put six lumps of sugar on a tray for certain specially esteemed servants, got up, and moved to the embroidery-frame which stood by the window.

"Now go to papa, children, and tell him to be sure to come to me before he goes to the threshing-ground."

The music, the counting, and the stern glances were resumed, and we went to papa. Having passed through the room which still retained from grandpapa's time the name of "the steward's room," we entered the study.

III

PAPA

He stood at his writing table and pointing to some envelopes, papers, and piles of money, spoke angrily—heatedly explaining something to the steward, Jacob Mikháylov, who stood in his usual place between the door and the barometer with his hands behind his back, rapidly moving his fingers in all directions.

The more vehement papa became the more rapidly the fingers twitched, and when papa paused the fingers too became still; but when Jacob himself spoke they were exceedingly restless and twitched desperately this way and that; by their movements one could, I think, have guessed Jacob's secret thoughts, but his face was always calm—expressing consciousness of his own worth, and at the same time subservience, saying as it were: "I am right, but let it be as you decide!"

On seeing us, papa only said, "Wait a minute," and indicated by a movement of his head that one of us should shut the door.

"Oh, gracious heavens! What is the matter with you to-day, Jacob?" he said to the steward, shrugging one shoulder (it was a habit of his). "This envelope with 800 rubles enclosed in it . . ."

Jacob drew the abacus nearer, moved the balls on it to

show 800, and, fixing his eyes on an indefinite spot, awaited what would come next.

". . . is for general expenses during my absence. You understand? You must get 1,000 rubles for the mill—is that right or not?—you must get back from the Treasury 8,000 rubles; for the hay, of which by your own reckoning there should be 7,000 puds for sale—reckon it at 45 kopeks— you will get 3,000 rubles; so altogether you will have . . . how much? 12,000 . . . is that so or not?"

"Just so, sir," said Jacob.

But by the movement of his fingers I saw that he wanted to make some objection; papa stopped him.

"Well, of this money you will send 10,000 rubles to the Council for the Petróvsk estate. Now as to the money that is in the office—" continued papa (Jacob pushed back the 12,000 he had shown on the abacus and cast on 21,000)— "you will bring it to me, and will show it as paid out to-day." (Jacob again disarranged the abacus and turned it over, no doubt to intimate that the 21,000 would also disappear.) "This envelope with the money in it you will deliver to the address on it."

I was standing near the table and glanced at the address. It was to "Karl Iványch Mauer."

Probably noticing that I had read what I ought not to know, papa placed his hand on my shoulder and with a slight movement turned me away from the table. I did not understand whether this was a caress or a rebuke, but in any case I kissed the large, muscular hand that lay on my shoulder.

"Yes, sir!" said Jacob. "And what are your orders about the Khabárovka money?"

Khabárovka was mamma's estate.

"Keep it in the office and do not use it on any account without my order."

Jacob remained silent for a few seconds, then suddenly his fingers began to move with increased rapidity, and changing the look of stolid obedience with which he had listened to his master's orders to his natural expression of roguish shrewdness, he drew the abacus nearer and began to speak.

"Permit me to report to you, Peter Alexándrych, it's just as you please, but the money can't be paid to the Council

by the due date. . . . You were pleased to say," he went on
with deliberation, "that the money due from the deposits
for the mill, and for the hay, must come in. . . ." (As he
mentioned these items he cast them up on the abacus.)
"But I am afraid we may be wrong in our reckoning," he
added after a pause and with a thoughtful look at papa.

"Why?"

"Permit me to explain. As to the mill—the miller has
twice been to see me begging for a delay and swearing by
Christ the Lord that he has no money. . . . Why, he is here
even now—perhaps you would please speak to him yourself?"

"What does he say?" asked papa, making a sign with his
head that he did not wish to speak to the miller.

"Why, that's quite plain! He says there has been nothing
to grind and what little money he had has all been spent
on the dam. And suppose we turn him out, sir, shall we gain
anything? You were pleased to mention the deposits. I think
I already reported that our money is sunk there and we
shan't soon get it back. I sent a load of flour to town the
other day for Iván Afanásich and with it a note about this
business, and the answer is again the same: 'I should be
glad to do anything I could for Peter Alexándrych but the
matter does not depend on me' and everything indicates
that you will hardly get the receipts for another two
months. . . . You were pleased to mention the hay—let us
say it will sell for 3,000."

He cast 3,000 on the abacus and was silent for about a
minute, looking now at the abacus and now into papa's
eyes, as much as to say: "You see yourself that it is too
little! And the hay, again, must first be sold; if we sell it
now, you know yourself . . ."

He evidently still had a large supply of arguments, and
probably for that reason papa interrupted him.

"I am not going to change my orders," he said, "but if
there should really be a delay in receiving these sums it
can't be helped, you will have to take as much from the
Khabárovka money as will be necessary."

"Yes, sir."

One could see by Jacob's face and fingers that this last
order afforded him great satisfaction.

Jacob was a serf, a very zealous and devoted man, and

like all good stewards extremely close-fisted for his master, and he had the queerest notions as to what was advantageous for his master. He was always working to increase his master's property at the expense of his mistress's and tried to prove that it was absolutely necessary to use the income from her estate for Petróvsk—the estate where we lived. At that moment he was triumphant because he had quite succeeded in this.

Having wished us "good morning," papa said we had kicked our heels in the country long enough, that we were no longer little children, and that it was time for us to learn seriously.

"I think you know that I am going to Moscow to-night, and I am taking you with me," he said. "You will live with grandmamma, and mamma will remain here with the girls; and you know her only pleasure will be to hear that you learn well and give satisfaction."

Though from the preparations that had been going on for the last few days we were expecting something unusual, yet this news gave us a terrible shock. Volódya grew red and in a trembling voice gave papa our mother's message.

"So that is what my dream foreboded!" I thought. "God grant that nothing worse happens."

I felt very, very sorry for mamma and at the same time was very pleased at the thought that we were now really big boys.

"If we are going to-day, I expect there will be no lessons. That's splendid!" I thought. "However, I am sorry for Karl Iványch. He, no doubt, will be dismissed, or otherwise they would not have prepared that envelope for him. . . . It would be better to go on learning for ever than to go away, leave mamma, and offend poor Karl Iványch. He is very unhappy as it is!"

These thoughts flashed through my mind; I did not move, but stood looking at the black bows on my shoes.

After saying a few words to Karl Iványch about a fall in the barometer, and ordering Jacob not to feed the dogs, so that before leaving he might go out after dinner and try the young hounds, papa, contrary to my expectations, told us to go and do our lessons, comforting us however with a promise to take us to the hunt.

On my way upstairs I ran out on to the verandah. At

the door, with her eyes closed in the sun, lay my father's favourite borzoi, Mílka.

"Mílka dear," I said patting her and kissing her on the muzzle, "we are going away to-day. Good-bye! We shall never see one another again," and I gave way to my feelings and began to cry.

◇◇◇

V

THE SIMPLETON

A man of about fifty, with a pale, long, deeply pock-marked face, long grey hair, and a scanty reddish beard, entered the room. He was so tall that to come in at the door he not only had to bow his head but to bend his whole body. He was wearing a tattered garment, something between a peasant coat and a cassock, and he held an enormous staff in his hand. He struck the floor with it with all his might as he entered the room and, lifting his eyebrows and opening his mouth extremely wide, burst into a terrible and unnatural laugh. He was blind in one eye, and the white iris of that eye moved incessantly and gave his face, already ill-favoured, a still more repulsive expression.

"Aha, caught!" he shouted, and running with short steps up to Volódya seized him by the head and began carefully examining the crown of it, and then with a perfectly serious face he left Volódya, came up to the table, and began blowing under the oil-cloth and making the sign of the cross over it. "O-oh, a pity! O-oh, painful! . . . the dears . . . will fly away," he then said in a voice trembling with tears, looking at Volódya with emotion and wiping on his sleeve the tears that were really falling.

His voice was rough and hoarse, his movements hasty and jerky, his speech senseless and incoherent (he never used any pronouns), but his intonation was so touching and his yellow, misshapen face sometimes took on such a frankly sorrowful expression, that when listening to him it was impossible to repress a mingled feeling of compassion, fear, and sadness.

He was the saintly fool and pilgrim, Grísha.

Where he came from, who his parents had been, what induced him to take up this wandering life, no one knew. All I know is that from the age of fifteen he had been known as a saintly fool who went barefoot summer and winter, visited monasteries, gave small icons to those he took a fancy to, and uttered enigmatic sayings which some people regarded as prophecies—that no one had ever known him in a different condition, that he had sometimes come to my grandmother's house and that some people said he was the unfortunate son of rich parents, and a pure soul, while others said that he was simply a lazy peasant.

At last the long-wished-for and punctual Fóka appeared and we went downstairs. Grísha, sobbing and continuing to utter incoherent phrases, followed us, thumping the steps with his staff. Papa and mamma were walking up and down the drawing-room arm in arm, talking in low tones. Márya Ivánovna sat stiffly in one of the arm-chairs that stood symmetrically at right-angles near to the sofa, and in a stern but subdued voice imparted information to the girls, who sat near her. As soon as Karl Iványch entered the room she glanced at him and turned away, and her face assumed an expression which might be interpreted to mean, "I do not notice you, Karl Iványch." One could see by the girls' eyes that they were impatient to tell us some very important news, but to jump up and come to us would have been an infringement of Mimi's rules. We had first to approach her and say, "*Bonjour, Mimi!*" with a bow and a scrape, and only then might we begin a conversation.

What an unendurable person that Mimi was! One could not talk about anything in her presence: she considered everything improper. In addition she continually nagged us, "*Parlez donc français,*"[1] just when, as ill luck would have it, one wanted to chatter in Russian. Or at dinner when one had just got the taste of some dish and did not wish to be disturbed, she would be sure to come out with her, "*Mangez donc avec du pain*"[2] or "*Comment est-ce que vous tenez votre fourchette?*"[3] "And what has she to do with

[1] "Do speak French."
[2] "Eat bread with it."
[3] "How are you holding your fork?"

us?" one would think. . . . "Let her teach the girls; we have Karl Iványch for that." I fully shared his dislike for *certain people*.

"Ask mamma to get us taken to the hunt," Kátya said to me in a whisper, catching hold of my jacket, while the grown-up people went into the dining-room before us.

"All right, we'll try."

Grísha ate in the dining-room, but at a separate table; he did not lift his eyes from his plate, occasionally sighed, made terrible faces, and kept saying, as if to himself, "A pity! . . . flown, the dove will fly to heaven. . . . Oh, there is a stone on the grave . . .!" and so on.

Mamma had been upset ever since the morning; Grísha's presence, words, and actions evidently intensified this.

"Oh yes, I almost forgot to ask you something," she said, handing my father a plate of soup.

"What is it?"

"Please have your dreadful dogs locked up; they nearly bit poor Grísha as he crossed the yard. They might attack the children too."

Hearing himself mentioned, Grísha turned towards the table and showed the torn skirts of his garment and, continuing to chew, he muttered: "Wished to bite to death. . . . God did not permit. Sin to set dogs on one! A great sin! Don't beat, elder,[4] why beat? . . . God will forgive . . . the days are not such."

"What is he saying?" asked papa, scrutinizing him sharply and severely. "I understand nothing of it."

"But I do," answered mamma, "he told me how one of the hunt-servants set the dogs at him on purpose, so he says, 'Wished them to bite to death, but God did not permit,' and he asks you not to have the servant punished."

"Oh, that's it!" said papa. "How does he know that I want to punish the hunt-servant? You know I am not very fond of such fellows in general," he continued in French, "but this one I particularly dislike, and no doubt . . ."

"Oh, don't say that, my dear!" said mamma as if frightened at something. "How do you know?"

"I should think I have had opportunities to study this

---

[4] He called all men this, without distinction.—L.T.

species of folk—such a lot of them come to see you, and they are all of one pattern. It's everlastingly the same story . . ."

It was evident that my mother was of quite a different opinion but did not want to dispute.

"Please give me a pie!" she said. "Are they good to-day?"

"But it makes me angry," continued papa, taking up a pie but holding it at such a distance that mamma could not reach it, "it makes me angry when I see intelligent and educated people yielding to such deception."

And he struck the table with his fork.

"I asked you to give me a pie," she repeated, holding out her hand.

"And they do well," papa continued, drawing his hand back, "who put such people in prison. The only thing they can do is to upset those whose nerves are not strong as it is," he added with a smile, noticing that this conversation was very disagreeable to mamma, and he handed her the pie.

"I will only say one thing to that: it is hard to believe that a man who, though he is sixty, goes barefoot summer and winter and always under his clothes wears chains weighing seventy pounds and who has more than once declined a comfortable life offered him with everything found—it is hard to believe that such a man does all this merely because he is lazy. As for predictions," she added after a pause and sighed, "*je suis payée pour y croire*;[5] I think I told how Kiryúshka foretold my father's death to him to the very day and very hour."

"Oh, what have you done with me?" said papa, smiling and putting his hand up to his mouth on the side where Mimi was sitting (when he did this I always listened with keen attention, expecting something funny). "Why did you remind me of his feet? I have looked at them, and now I shan't be able to eat anything."

The dinner was drawing to an end. Lyúba and Kátya kept winking at us, fidgeting in their chairs, and in general showing great restlessness. This winking meant, "Why don't you ask them to take us to the hunt?" I nudged Volódya with my elbow. Volódya nudged me and finally, taking

[5] "I have good cause to believe in them."

courage, explained, first timidly, then firmly and louder, that as we had to leave to-day we should like the girls to go with us to the hunt, in the carriage. After a little discussion among the grown-ups the question was decided in our favour, and what was still better, mamma said she would herself come with us.

VI
PREPARATION FOR THE HUNT

During the sweets-course Jacob was sent for, and orders were given about the carriage, the dogs, and the saddle-horses—all in great detail, mentioning each horse by name. Volódya's horse was lame, and papa ordered one of the hunters to be saddled for him. The word "hunter" sounded strange to mamma's ears: it seemed to her that a hunter must be something in the nature of a ferocious beast that would certainly bolt and kill Volódya. Despite the assurances of papa and of Volódya, who said with wonderful pluck that it was nothing, and that he liked it very much when a horse bolted, poor mamma went on saying that she would be upset during the whole outing.

The dinner was over: the grown-ups went to the study to drink coffee, and we ran out into the garden to rustle our feet along the paths which were covered with fallen yellow leaves and to talk. We began talking about Volódya's riding a hunter, about it being a shame that Lyúba could not run so fast as Kátya, about how interesting it would be to see Grísha's chains, and so on; but about our having to part we did not say a word. Our conversation was interrupted by the clatter of the approaching trap, at each corner of which sat a serf-boy. Behind the trap rode the hunt-servants with the dogs, and behind them the coach-man, Ignát, on the horse intended for Volódya, and leading my ancient Kleper by the bridle. At first we all rushed to the fence through which one could see all these interesting things, and then, squealing and stamping, we ran up-stairs to dress, and to dress so as to look as much like huntsmen as possible. One of the principal ways of doing this was to tuck our trousers into our high boots. We set to work without losing a moment, hurrying to get ready and to run to the porch to enjoy the sight of the dogs and the horses and to have a talk with the hunt servants.

It was a hot day. White, fantastic clouds had appeared on the horizon ever since morning; then a light breeze drove them nearer and nearer together so that at times they hid the sun. But many as were the clouds that passed and darkened, they were evidently not fated to gather into a storm and spoil our parting pleasure. Towards evening they began to disperse again: some grew paler, lengthened out, and ran down towards the horizon; others, just over-head, turned into transparent white fleeciness; only one large black cloud settled in the east. Karl Iványch always knew where any cloud would go; he declared that that cloud would go to Máslovka, that there would be no rain and the weather would be beautiful.

Fóka, despite his advanced age, ran very nimbly and rapidly downstairs, called out, "Drive up!" and, with his feet apart, took his stand at the middle of the entrance between the place where the coachman would bring the carriage and the threshold, in the attitude of one whom it was not necessary to remind of his duty. The ladies came down and after a little discussion as to which side to sit and to whom each was to hold on (though I don't think there was any need to hold on), they took their seats, opened their parasols, and started. When the trap moved off, mamma, pointing to the hunter, asked the coach-man in a trembling voice: "Is that horse for Vladímir Petróvich?"

When the coachman said it was, she waved her hand and turned away. I felt very impatient, mounted my horse, looked out between its ears, and made various evolutions in the yard.

"Please don't step on the dogs," said one of the men.

"Never fear, I am not out for the first time!" I replied proudly.

Volódya mounted the "hunter," but in spite of his firm-ness of character not without a certain tremor, and, patting it, he asked several times: "Is she quiet?"

He looked very well on horseback, just like a man. His thighs in his tight trousers lay so well on the saddle that I felt envious, especially as, so far as I could judge by my shadow, I was far from having as fine an appearance.

And now we heard papa's footsteps on the stairs. The dog-keeper collected the hounds that were running about, the huntsmen with the borzoi dogs called them in and mounted their horses, the groom led a horse up to the porch, and the hounds of papa's pack, which had been lying in various picturesque attitudes beside it, rushed to him. After him Mílka, in her beaded collar, jingling its ring, ran out merrily. When she came out she always greeted the kennel-dogs: with some she would play, at others she would sniff or growl, and on some she would hunt for fleas.

Papa mounted his horse and we set off.

VII
THE HUNT

Túrka, the huntsman, with a shaggy cap on his head, a huge horn behind his shoulders, and a hunting knife in his belt, rode ahead of us all on a mouse-grey, hook-nosed horse. From that man's gloomy and fierce appearance one might have thought he was riding to mortal combat rather than to a hunt. At the hind legs of his horse ran the pack of hounds in an excited, mottled group. It was pitiful to see the fate of an unlucky dog that took it into its head to lag behind. When after great effort it succeeded in holding back the companion to which it was leashed, one of the dog-tenders riding behind would be sure to hit it with his whip, exclaiming: "Back to the pack!" When we came out of the gate papa ordered the huntsmen and us to keep to the road, while he himself turned into the rye-field.

Harvesting was in full swing. The limitless, brilliantly yellow field was bound only on one side by the tall, bluish forest, which then seemed to me a most distant, mysterious place beyond which either the world came to an end or uninhabited countries began. The whole field was full of sheaves and peasants. Here and there among the thick, high rye where a strip had been reaped, one saw the bent back of a woman reaping, the swing of the ears as she grasped the stalks, a woman bending over a cradle in the shade, and bundles of rye scattered over the reaped parts of the field which was all covered with cornflowers. In another place peasants in their shirts and trousers stood on the carts loading up the sheaves and raising the dust on the dry scorched field. The village elder, in boots, and with a coat thrown over his shoulders and tallysticks in his hand, took off his felt hat when he saw papa in the distance, wiped his red-haired head and beard with a towel, and shouted at the women. The little roan papa rode went with a light, playful step, sometimes bending his head to his chest, pulling at the reins, and brushing off with his thick tail the gadflies and gnats that settled greedily on him. Two borzois with tense tails raised sickle-wise, and lifting their feet high, leapt gracefully over the tall stubble, behind the horse's feet. Mílka ran in front and with head lifted awaited the quarry. The peasants' voices, the tramp of horses and creaking of carts, the merry whistle of quail, the hum of insects hovering in the air in steady swarms, the odour of wormwood, straw, and horses' sweat, the thousands of different colours and shadows with which the burning sun flooded the light yellow stubble, the dark blue of the distant forest, the light lilac clouds, and the white cobwebs that floated in the air or stretched across the stubble—all this I saw, heard, and felt.

When we arrived at the Kalína wood we found the carriage already there and, surpassing our highest expectations, a one-horse cart in the middle of which sat the butler. From under the hay in it peeped a samovar, a pail with an ice-cream mould, and some other attractive bundles and boxes. There could be no mistake: it meant tea in the open air, with ices and fruit. At the sight of the cart we loudly expressed our delight, for to drink tea in the woods, on the grass, and in general somewhere where no one had ever drunk tea before was considered a great treat.

Túrka rode up to the chase, stopped, listened attentively to papa's detailed instructions as to where to line up and where to come out (though he never conformed to such instructions but followed his own devices), unleashed the dogs, strapped the leashes deliberately to his saddle, remounted his horse, and disappeared, whistling, behind the young birch-trees. The unleashed dogs first expressed their pleasure by wagging their tails, then shook themselves, pulled themselves together, and only after that, sniffing and wagging their tails, moved off in different directions at a slow trot.

"Have you a handkerchief?" asked papa.

I drew one out of my pocket and showed it.

"Well, tie that grey dog to it."

"Zhirán?" I said, with the air of an expert.

"Yes, and run along the road. When you come to the glade, stop. And mind, don't come back to me without a hare!"

I tied the handkerchief round Zhirán's shaggy neck and rushed headlong towards the appointed place. Papa laughed and shouted after me: "Quick, quick, or you'll be too late!"

Zhirán kept stopping, pricking his ears, and listening to the halloing of the huntsmen. I had not the strength to drag him from the spot and began to shout "Atóu!" Then he would pull so hard that I could hardly hold him back and fell more than once, before reaching the appointed place. Having chosen a shady, level spot at the foot of a tall oak, I lay down in the grass, made Zhirán sit beside me, and waited. My fancy, as always happens under such circumstances, far outstripped reality: I imagined that I was hunting my third hare, when the voice of the first hound came from the wood, from where Túrka's voice reverberated even louder and with more animation. A dog gave a cry, and its voice was heard more and more frequently. Another deeper voice chimed in, and then a third, and a fourth. . . . These voices sometimes fell and sometimes overlapped one another. The sounds grew gradually louder and more continuous and were at last blent into a ringing, clamorous din. The chase was filled with sound and the hounds bayed in chorus.

When I heard this I seemed rooted to the spot. With my eyes fixed on the outskirts of the chase, I smiled inanely while perspiration poured down my face, and though the drops tickled me as they ran down my chin I did not wipe them off. It seemed to me that there could be nothing more decisive than this moment. This strained condition was too unnatural to last long. The dogs now bayed close to the outskirts of the chase, now gradually receded from me; there was no hare. I began looking around me. It was just the same with Zhirán: at first he tugged and yelped but then lay down, put his head on my lap, and was quiet.

By the bare roots of the oak under which I was sitting, the dry grey earth, the dead oak-leaves, the acorns, the dry bare twigs, the yellowish-green moss, and the green grass-blades that sprouted here and there, teemed with swarms of ants. One after another they hurried along the paths they had made, some of them loaded, others not. I took up a twig and barred their way. It was a sight to see how, despising the danger, some crawled under the twig, others over it, and some, especially those carrying loads, seemed quite bewildered and did not know what to do: they stopped, looked for a way round, or turned back, or came up the twig to my hand and, I think, intended to crawl up the sleeve of my jacket. My intention was diverted from these interesting observations by a butterfly with yellow wings that fluttered very enticingly before me. As soon as it had drawn my attention it flew a couple of paces from me, circled a few times round an almost withered white clover-flower, and alighted on it. I do not know whether it felt the warmth of the sun or was drinking juice from that flower, but it evidently felt very well satisfied. It now and then moved its wings and pressed close to the flower, and at last it became quite motionless. I rested my head on both hands and watched the butterfly with pleasure.

Suddenly Zhirán began to whine and gave such a violent tug that I nearly fell over. I turned round. At the edge of the chase leaped a hare, with one ear flat and the other erect. The blood rushed to my head and, forgetting everything for the moment, I shouted frantically, let the dog loose, and began to run myself. Hardly had I done so than I began to regret it—the hare squatted, gave a leap, and I saw no more of it.

But what was my shame when, following the hounds who came into the open in full cry, Túrka appeared from behind the bushes. He had seen my mistake (which was that I did not control myself) and, looking contemptuously at me, only said: "Eh, master!" But you should have heard how he said it! It would have been pleasanter for me had he hung me from his saddle like a hare.

I stood on that spot for a long time in despair, did not call the dog, and only kept saying as I slapped my thighs: "Oh God, what have I done!"

I heard the hounds run farther, a clattering at the other side of the chase, how they caught a hare, and how Túrka with his huge horn called the dogs back, but still I did not budge.

⚬⚬⚬

X
THE KIND OF MAN MY FATHER WAS

He was a man of the past age and had the indefinable character common among those who were young then: a compound of chivalry, enterprise, self-confidence, amiability, and licentiousness. He regarded the people of our day contemptuously, and his opinion resulted as much from innate pride as from secret regret that he could not in our time have either the influence or the success he had had in his own. The two chief passions of his life were cards and women; he had won several million rubles in the course of his life and had had affairs with innumerable women of all classes.

A tall, stately figure, a strange way of walking with short steps, a habit of jerking one shoulder, small ever-smiling eyes, a large aquiline nose, irregular lips that closed in an awkward but pleasing way, a defective enunciation—a kind of lisp—and a quite bald head—such was my father's exterior as far back as I can remember him, and with which he managed not only to be reputed, but to be, a man *à bonnes fortunes*[1] and to be liked by all without exception—by people of every class and position, and especially by those he wished to please.

He knew how to gain the upper hand in his relations with any one. Without having ever belonged to the very highest circles he was always in touch with people of those circles, and in such a way as to be respected by them. He knew just the limits of pride and self-confidence which, without offending others, raised him in the world's opinion. He was original, but not always so, and he used his originality as a means which sometimes served instead of social standing or wealth. Nothing in the world could arouse astonishment in him: in however brilliant a position he

[1] A lady-killer.

found himself, he always seemed born to it. He could so well hide from others and put away from himself the dark side of life, full of the small vexations and mortifications known to every one, that one could not but envy him. He was an expert in all that conduced to comfort and enjoyment, and knew how to avail himself of them. He was specially proud of the brilliant connexions he possessed, partly through my mother's family and partly through the comrades of his youth with whom in his heart he was angry for having risen high in rank while he had always remained a retired lieutenant of the Guards. Like all retired military men, he did not know how to dress fashionably; but then he dressed with originality and elegance. He always wore very wide and light clothes and beautiful linen with large turn-down cuffs and collars. . . . Anything, however, seemed to suit his tall figure and powerful build, bald head, and quiet self-assured movements. He was emotional and even easily moved to tears. Often when in reading aloud he came to a pathetic place, his voice would falter, tears would show themselves in his eyes and he would put down the book in vexation. He was fond of music and, accompanying himself on the piano, sang songs by his friend A———, gipsy songs, or some arias from operas, but he did not like classical music, and regardless of the accepted opinion, frankly said that Beethoven's sonatas made him feel sleepy and dull, and that he knew nothing better than "Wake me not, while young," as Semënova used to sing it, or "Not Alone," as the gipsy girl Tanyúsha sang it. His nature was one that needed a public for a good action, and he only thought that good which the public considered so. Heaven knows whether he had any moral convictions. His life was so full of distractions of all kinds that he had no time to form convictions, and, besides that, he was so fortunate in life that he saw no need for them.

In old age he formed settled opinions and immutable rules, but all founded on an entirely practical basis. Those actions and that way of life which gave him happiness or pleasure he considered good and thought that everybody should always act so. He spoke very convincingly, and that capacity, it seemed to me, enhanced the elasticity of his principles: he could describe the selfsame action as a very charming bit of mischief or as the meanest rascality.

XI
WHAT WENT ON IN THE STUDY AND
THE DRAWING-ROOM

It was getting dusk when we reached home. Mamma sat down to the piano, and we children brought paper, pencils, and paints and arranged ourselves at the round table to draw. I had only blue paint; but for all that I took it into my head to draw the hunt. Having very vividly depicted a blue boy on a blue horse, and blue dogs, I was in doubt whether one could paint a blue hare and ran into papa's study to consult him. Papa was reading something, and in answer to my question whether there were blue hares, replied, "Yes, my dear, there are," without raising his head. I returned to the round table and painted a blue hare but then found it necessary to change the hare into a bush. I did not like the bush either and made it into a tree, then the tree into a cornstack, and the stack into a cloud, and finally I so smeared my whole sheet of paper with blue paint that I tore it up in vexation and sat down to dream in the lounge chair.

Mamma was playing the second concerto of Field, her music-master. I was dreaming, and there awoke in my fancy light, bright and translucent memories. She started playing Beethoven's Sonata Pathétique, and I remembered something sad, oppressive, and gloomy. Mamma often played those two pieces, and so I well remember the feeling they aroused in me. That feeling resembled memories, but memories of what? It was as if I were recalling something that had never been.

Opposite to me was the door of the study, and I saw how Jacob and some other men, bearded and in peasant coats, entered it. The door immediately closed behind them. "Now business has begun!" I thought. It seemed to me that nothing in the world could be more important than what was being done in the study. That idea was strengthened by the fact that generally everybody who approached that door spoke in whispers and walked on tiptoe, while from it came the sound of papa's loud voice and the smell of his cigar, which always, I don't know why, attracted me.

While half asleep I was suddenly struck by a familiar creaking of boots in the steward's room. Karl Iványch, with some notes in his hand, approached the door on tiptoe but with a gloomy and determined look, and knocked lightly at it. He was admitted and the door again closed.

"If only some misfortune does not happen," I thought. "Karl Iványch is angry: he is ready for anything. . . ."

Again I dozed off.

No misfortune however occurred. An hour later I was again awakened by the creaking of the same boots. Karl Iványch, wiping with his handkerchief tears which I noticed on his cheeks, came out of the study and, muttering something to himself, went upstairs. Papa followed him out and came into the drawing-room.

"Do you know what I have just decided?" he said in a cheerful voice, putting his hand on mamma's shoulder.

"What, my dear?"

"I am taking Karl Iványch with the children. There is room in the trap. They are used to him, he seems to be really attached to them, and 700 rubles a year won't make any difference to us, *et puis au fond c'est un très bon diable.*"[1]

I could not at all grasp why papa was abusing Karl Iványch.

"I am very glad both for the children and for him," said mamma; "he is an excellent old man."

"You should have seen how touched he was when I told him to keep the five hundred rubles as a gift . . . but what was most amusing was the bill he brought to me. It is worth looking at," he added with a smile, as he gave her a note in Karl Iványch's hand. "It's lovely!"

This is what the note contained:

For the children, two fishing-rods	0 r.	70 kopeks
Coloured paper, gold border, and paste for boxes, as presents	6 r.	55 kopeks
Book and a bow, presents to the children	8 r.	16 kopeks
Trousers for Nicholas	4 r.	0 kopeks
Promised by Peter Alexándrych from Moscow in the year 18— a gold watch	140 r.	0 kopeks
Total to be received by Karl Iványch Mauer, besides his salary	159 r.	41 kopeks

[1] "And then at bottom he is a very good devil."

On reading this note, in which Karl Iványch demanded payment for all he had spent on presents, and even for a present promised to him, every one would conclude that Karl Iványch was merely an unfeeling and mercenary egotist, and every one would be mistaken.

On entering the study with the note in his hand and a speech he had prepared in his head, he intended to show papa eloquently all the injustice he had endured in our house; but when he began to speak in the touching voice and with the pathetic intonations he used when dictating to us, his eloquence acted chiefly on himself, so that when he reached the place where he said, "Sad as it will be for me to part from the children—" he became quite confused, his voice trembled, and he had to get his chequered handkerchief out of his pocket. "Yes, Peter Alexándrych," he said through his tears (there was nothing of this in his prepared speech), "I have grown so used to the children that I don't know what I shall do without them. I would rather serve you without salary," he added, wiping his eyes with one hand and handing in the bill with the other.

That Karl Iványch was speaking sincerely at that moment I can affirm, for I know what a kind heart he had; but how to reconcile the bill with his words remains a mystery to me.

"If you are sad at leaving, I should be still sadder to part from you," said papa, patting him on the shoulder. "I have changed my mind now."

Not long before supper Grísha came into the room. From the moment he had entered our house he had never left off sighing and weeping, which in the opinion of those who believed in his power of prophecy foreboded some calamity to our houses. He began to take leave and said he would start on his way next morning. I winked at Volódya and went out of the room.

"What is it?"

"If you want to see Grísha's chains, let us go upstairs at once to the men-serfs' quarters. Grísha sleeps in the second room, and we can sit capitally in the cupboard and see everything."

"Excellent! Wait here and I will call the girls."

The girls came running, and we went upstairs. Having

decided, not without some dispute, who should first enter the dark cupboard, we settled down and waited.

XII
GRÍSHA

We all felt rather scared in the dark cupboard; we pressed close to one another and did not say a word. Almost immediately after us Grísha entered the room with soft steps. In one hand he held his staff, in the other a tallow candle in a brass candlestick. We did not dare to breathe.

"Lord Jesus Christ! Most Holy Mother of God! To the Father, the Son, and the Holy Ghost . . ." said he, breathing heavily and with different intonations and abbreviations natural only to one who often repeated those words.

After placing his staff in a corner of the room, with a prayer, he began to undress. Having untied his old black girdle he slowly took off his tattered nankeen coat, folded it carefully, and hung it over the back of a chair. His face now had not its usual hurried and inane expression; on the contrary he was calm, pensive, and even dignified. His movements were slow and considered.

When he was in his underclothes, he slowly let himself down on to the bed, made the sign of the cross on every side of it, and with an effort, as was evident from his frown, readjusted the chains under his shirt. After sitting still for a while and carefully examining his linen, which was torn in several places, he arose, and lifting the candle, with a prayer, to the level of the glass case in which were several icons, he crossed himself before them and turned the candle upside down. It crackled and went out.

Through the windows which looked out towards the forest the moon, which was almost full, shone in. The long white figure of the simpleton was lit up on one side by its pale silvery beams, and on the other its shadow, together with that of the window-frames, fell on the floor, on the walls, and reached up to the ceiling. In the yard outside the watchman was striking a copper plate.

Folding his huge hands on his breast, Grísha stood with bowed head, sighing heavily and continually before the

icons, and then sank with difficulty to his knees and began
to pray.

At first he softly said familiar prayers, only accentuating
certain words, then he repeated them, but louder and with
more animation. Then he began to pray in his own words,
trying, with evident difficulty, to express himself in Church-
Slavonic. His words were awkward but pathetic. He prayed
for all his benefactors (so he termed those who received
him), among them for my mother and ourselves; he prayed
for himself, asking God to forgive him his grievous sins,
and he kept repeating: "Lord, forgive my enemies!" He
rose groaning and again and again repeating the same
words, fell on the floor and rose again despite the weight
of his chains, which gave a hard, sharp sound as they
struck the floor.

Volódya pinched my leg very painfully, but I did not
even turn around. I only rubbed the place with my hand,
following all Grísha's movements and words with a child's
surprise, pity, and emotion.

Instead of the fun and laughter I had expected when I
entered the cupboard, I trembled and felt a sinking of
the heart.

Grísha remained long in that state of religious exalta-
tion, improvising prayers. Now he would repeat several
times, "Lord, have mercy," but each time with new strength
and expression; then he said, "Forgive, Lord, teach what to
do . . . teach what to do, O Lord!" with an expression as
if he expected an immediate answer to his words; then
piteous sobs were all one heard. . . . He raised himself to
his knees, folded his hands on his breast, and grew silent.

I softly thrust my head out of the door and held my
breath. Grísha did not move; deep sighs broke from his
breast; a tear stood in the dim pupil of his sightless eye
which was lit up by the moon.

"Thy will be done!" exclaimed he suddenly, in an
inimitable tone, sank with his forehead on the ground, and
sobbed like a child.

Much water has flowed by since then, many memories
of the past have lost their meaning for me and become
dim recollections, even pilgrim Grísha has long since completed his last pilgrimage; but the impression he made on

me and the feeling he evoked will never die in my memory.

Oh, great Christian, Grísha! Your faith was so strong that you felt the nearness of God; your love was so great that the words flowed of themselves from your lips— you did not test them by your reason. . . . And what lofty praise you gave to His Majesty when, unable to find words, you fell weeping to the ground! . . .

The emotion with which I listened to Grísha could not last long; in the first place because my curiosity was satisfied, and secondly because I had pins and needles in my legs from sitting so long in one position, and I wished to join in the general whimpering and commotion I heard behind me in the dark cupboard. Some one touched my hand and whispered, "Whose hand is this?" It was quite dark in the cupboard, but I knew at once by the touch and by the voice whispering just above my ear, that it was Kátya.

Quite unconsciously I took hold of her bare elbow and pressed by lips on her arm. Kátya was no doubt surprised at this action and she drew away her arm; this movement of hers upset a broken chair that stood in the cupboard: Grísha lifted his head, looked slowly round and, repeating a prayer, made the sign of the cross towards all the corners of the room. Talking in whispers we ran noisily out of the cupboard.

XIII
NATÁLYA SÁVISHNA

In the middle of the last century in the homesteads of the village of Khabárovka, there used to run about in a coarse linen dress a bare-footed, plump, and red-cheeked girl, Natásha. As a reward for the faithful services of her father, the clarionet-player, Sávva, and at his request, my grandfather took her "upstairs" and gave her a place among my grandmother's female servants. As a housemaid Natásha distinguished herself by her meekness and zeal. When my mother was born and a nursemaid was needed, this duty was put upon Natásha. In that new post she earned praise and rewards for her activity, fidelity, and attachment to her young mistress. However, the powdered head and the stockings and buckles of the brisk young footman, Fóka, who came much across her in the course of his work, captivated her rude but loving heart. She even braced herself to go and ask my grandfather's permission to marry Fóka. Grandpapa regarded her wish as a sign of ingratitude. He was angry with her, and as a punishment sent poor Natásha to a cattle-farm on a property of his in the steppes. Six months later however, as no one could be found to replace her, Natásha was brought back to the estate and restored to her former position. Having returned from her exile in her coarse linen dress, she went to grandpapa, fell at his feet and begged him to restore her to his favour and kindness and to forget the folly that had possessed her and which, she swore, would never return. And she really kept her word.

After that she was no longer called Natásha, but by the more respectful name of Natálya Sávishna, and wore a cap like a married woman: the whole store of her love she transferred to her young lady

When a governess took her place with my mother, she was given the keys of the store-room and all the household linen and provisions were placed under her charge. She fulfilled these new duties with the same zeal and love. She put her whole life into care for her master's belongings; saw waste, damage, and pilfering everywhere; and tried by all means to counteract them.

When mamma married, anxious to show her gratitude in some way to Natálya Sávishna for her twenty years' work and devotion, she called her in and, having expressed her gratitude and affection in most flattering terms, handed her a paper with a government stamp, granting her her freedom, and said that whether she remained in our service or not, she should always have a pension of 300 rubles a year. Natálya Sávishna heard all this in silence, then took the document, looked at it, angrily muttered something, and ran out of the room slamming the door behind her. Not understanding such strange behaviour, mamma went a little later into Natálya Sávishna's room. She was sitting on her trunk with tear-stained eyes, fingering her handkerchief and looking fixedly at the torn bits of the deed of emancipation which lay on the floor before her.

"What is the matter, my dear Natálya Sávishna?" mamma asked, taking her by the hand.

"Nothing, ma'am," Natálya Sávishna answered. "Evidently I have displeased you in some way, that you are turning me out of the house. . . . Well, I shall go."

She pulled away her hand and, hardly able to restrain her tears, was going out of the room. Mamma held her back, embraced her, and they both began to cry.

Ever since I can remember myself, I remember Natálya Sávishna, her love and her caresses; but it is only now that I know how to value them; it never then entered my head to realize what a rare, wonderful being that old woman was. She not only never spoke, but it seems that she never even thought, of herself; her whole life consisted of love and self-sacrifice. I was so accustomed to her disinterested and tender affection for us that I did not imagine it could have been otherwise. I was not in the least grateful to her and never asked myself whether she were happy or satisfied.

Sometimes on the plea of necessity I would escape from lessons to her room, would sit down and begin to day-dream aloud, quite unabashed by her presence. She was always busy, either knitting a stocking, rummaging in the chests which filled her room, or making a list of the linen, while she listened to all the nonsense I was talking.—"So when I am a general I will marry a wonderful beauty, will buy myself a roan horse, build a glass house, and send for Karl Iványch's relatives from Saxony—" etc., and she kept saying, "Yes, my dear, yes." Generally when I got up to go she would open a blue chest, inside the lid of which—I remember as if I had seen it yesterday—were pasted a coloured picture of an hussar, a picture off a pomatum pot, and a drawing of Volódya's; would take out a piece of pastille, light it, and, waving it about, would say: "This, my dear, is still one of the Ochákov pastilles. When your sainted grandfather—may the Kingdom of Heaven be his—went against the Turk, he brought it back from there. This is the last piece left," she would add with a sigh.

The chests that filled her room contained absolutely everything. No matter what was wanted, it was usually said: "We must ask Natálya Sávishna for it," and really, after rummaging awhile, she would find the thing that was wanted and would remark: "It's lucky I put it away." In those chests there were thousands of articles about which no one in the house, but she, either knew or cared.

Once I got angry with her. This is what happened. One day at dinner when pouring myself out a glass of kvas,[1] I dropped the decanter and spilt the kvas over the tablecloth.

"Call Natálya Sávishna to admire what her darling has done!" said mamma.

Natálya Sávishna came in, saw the puddle I had made, and shook her head. Then mamma said something in her ear, and shaking her finger at me she left the room.

After dinner when in the highest spirits I went bounding into the dancing-room, Natálya Sávishna suddenly jumped from behind the door with the tablecloth in her hands, caught me, and despite my desperate resistance began rubbing my face with the wet cloth, saying, "Don't soil tablecloths, don't soil tablecloths!" I was so offended that I howled with anger.

"What!" said I to myself, pacing up and down the room and choking with tears, "Natálya Sávishna—no, simply Natálya—speaks so rudely to me and even strikes me in the face with a wet cloth as if I were a serf-boy. No, this is awful!"

When Natálya Sávishna saw me sobbing she ran away at once, and I continued to walk up and down, considering how I could pay out the impertinent Natálya for the insult she had offered me.

In a few minutes she returned, came timidly up to me, and began to console me: "Don't, my dear, don't cry . . . forgive me, old fool that I am . . . I have done wrong . . . but forgive me, my pet . . . here you are. . . ."

She took from under her shawl a screw of red paper in which there were two caramels and a fig and with trembling hand gave it me. I could not look the kind

---

[1] A drink made of rye malt, generally non-intoxicating.

old woman in the face, but accepting her present I turned away and my tears flowed still faster, no longer from anger but from love and shame.

The narrator's mother dies, attended by her old servant Natálya Sávishna.

XXVII
GRIEF

Late in the evening of the following day I felt a wish to look at her again. Having mastered an involuntary feeling of dread, I softly opened the door and entered the music-room on tiptoe.

On a table in the middle of the room stood the coffin; around it were candles that had burnt low in their tall silver candle-sticks; in the far corner of the room sat the chanter reading the psalter in a soft monotonous voice.

I stopped at the door and looked, but my eyes were so swollen from weeping and my nerves so unstrung that I could not distinguish anything. Everything seemed to run strangely together: the light, the gold brocade, the velvet, the tall candle-sticks, the pink, lace-trimmed pillow, a frontlet, her ribbon-trimmed cap, and something else of a translucent wax-colour. I got up on a chair to look at her face, but in its place I again saw the same pale-yellow, translucent object. I could not believe that it was her face. I gazed at it more intently and little by little began to recognize in it her dear, familiar features. I shuddered with terror when I realized that this was she. But why were the closed eyes so sunken? Why that dreadful pallor and that dark spot under the transparent skin on one of the cheeks? Why was the expression of her whole face so cold and severe? Why were the lips so pale and their shape so beautiful, so majestic, and expressive of such unearthly calm that a cold shudder ran over my spine and hair when I looked at them?

I gazed, and felt that an incomprehensible, irresistible

power drew my eyes to that lifeless face. I did not take my eyes off it, yet my fancy drew pictures of blooming life and happiness. I kept forgetting that the dead body which lay before me, and at which I gazed unreasoningly as at an object that had nothing in common with my memories, was *she*. I imagined her now in one situation and now in another: alive, gay, and smiling; then I was suddenly struck by some feature of the pale face on which my eyes were resting: I recalled the terrible reality and shuddered, but continued to look. And again dreams replaced the reality, and again a consciousness of the reality destroyed the dreams. At last my imagination was tired out, it ceased to deceive me. The consciousness of the reality also vanished and I became quite unconscious. I do not know how long I remained in that condition, nor what it was; I only know that for a time I ceased to be aware of my existence and experienced a lofty, inexpressibly delightful and sad enjoyment.

Maybe as she flew towards a better world her lovely spirit turned sadly to look at the one in which she had left us; she saw my sorrow, pitied it, and with a heavenly smile of compassion came down to earth on the wings of love to console and bless me.

The door creaked and another chanter entered the room to relieve the first one. The noise roused me, and the first thought that came to me was that, as I was not crying but stood on a chair in an attitude not at all touching, the chanter might take me for a heartless boy who had climbed on to the chair out of pity or curiosity, and I made the sign of the cross, bowed, and began to cry.

Recalling my impression of that time I find that only that momentary self-forgetfulness was true grief. Before and after the funeral I did not cease crying and felt sad, but I am ashamed to remember that sadness, for it was always mingled with some selfish feeling: now a desire to show that I grieved more than any one else, now anxiety as to the effect I was producing on others, now an aimless curiosity, which made me observe Mimi's cap or the faces of those present. I despised myself because I did not experience exclusively a feeling of sorrow, and I tried to conceal all other feelings: this made my grief insincere and unnatural. Besides this, I felt a kind of enjoyment at knowing myself to be unhappy, and tried to stimulate my consciousness of unhappiness, and this egotistic feeling, more than any other, stifled real sorrow in me.

Having slept soundly and calmly that night, as is always the case after great distress, I awoke with my eyes dry and my nerves soothed. At ten o'clock we were called to the service, which was held before the coffin was carried out. The room was filled with domestic and peasant serfs, who all came with tears in their eyes to take leave of their mistress. During the service I wept, crossed myself, and bowed to the ground in the proper way but did not pray with my soul and was rather indifferent. I was concerned about the fact that the new jacket they had put on me was very tight under the arms; I was thinking how to keep my trousers clean when I knelt down, and stealthily observed all who were present. My father stood at the head of the coffin, was as pale as a handkerchief, and restrained his tears with evident difficulty. His tall figure in a black dress-coat, his pale expressive face, and his movements, graceful and confident as ever when he crossed himself and bowed touching the ground with his fingers, took a candle from the priest's hand, or went up to the coffin, were extremely effective; but, I don't know why, I did not like his being able to be so effective at that moment. Mimi stood leaning against the wall and seemed hardly able to stand on her feet, her dress was crumpled and had bits of down sticking to it, her cap was on one side, her swollen eyes were red, her head shook, she did not cease sobbing in a heart-rending manner, and she kept covering her face with her handkerchief and her hands. It seemed to me that she did this to hide her face from the spectators and to rest a moment from feigned sobbing. I remembered that, the day before, she told papa that mamma's death was such a terrible blow for her that she could never hope to recover from it, that it had deprived her of everything, that this angel (as she called mamma) had not forgotten her at the last and had expressed her wish to secure her and Katya's future. She shed bitter tears while saying this and perhaps her sorrow was sincere, but it was not pure and exclusive. Lyúba, in a black frock trimmed with weepers, all wet with tears, hung her head and occasionally glanced at the coffin. Her face expressed nothing but childish fear. Kátya stood beside her mother and, despite her long-drawn face, looked as rosy as ever. Volódya's frank nature was frank in its sorrow: now he stood deep in thought his eyes fixed on some object, now his lips suddenly quivered and he hurriedly crossed himself and bowed down. All the outsiders who attended the funeral seemed insufferable to me. The words of condolence they addressed to my father about her being happier there and not having been for this world evoked a kind of vexation in me

What right had they to talk about her and to weep for her? Some of them spoke of us as *"orphans."* Just as if we did not know ourselves that children who have no mother are called so! They seemed to like being the first to call us by that name, just as people generally are in a hurry to call a newly married girl *Madame* for the first time.

In a far corner of the room, almost hidden by the open door of the butler's pantry, knelt a bent, greyhaired, old woman. With folded hands, raised to heaven, she did not weep but prayed. Her soul went out to God and she asked Him to unite her with the one she had loved more than anything on earth, and she firmly believed that this would happen soon.

"There is one who loved her truly!" I thought, and I felt ashamed of myself.

The service was over; the face of the deceased was uncovered, and all present, excepting ourselves, went up to the coffin one after another to kiss her.

One of the last to walk up and take leave of her was a peasant woman with a pretty five-year-old girl in her arms, whom she had brought there heavens knows why. At that moment I dropped my wet handkerchief and was on the point of picking it up; but just as I stooped, I was struck by a piercing cry of such horror that I shall never forget it were I to live to be a hundred; whenever I think of it, a cold shudder runs down my body. I raised my head: on a stool by the coffin stood that peasant woman, with difficulty holding in her arms the little girl who was pushing with her little hands, throwing back her frightened face, fixing her staring eyes on the dead face, and screaming in a dreadful, frenzied voice. I cried out in a voice that, I think, was even more dreadful than the one that had so staggered me, and ran out of the room.

It was only then that I understood what the strong, oppressive smell was that mingling with the incense filled the whole room; and the thought that the face that but a few days before had been so full of beauty and tenderness, the face of her I loved more than anything on earth, could evoke horror, seemed to reveal the bitter truth to me for the first time, and filled my soul with despair.

XXVIII
LAST SAD MEMORIES

Mamma was no more, yet our life continued on the old lines: we went to bed and got up at the same hours and in the same rooms; morning and evening tea, dinner, supper—all took place at the usual time; tables and chairs stood in the same places, nothing had changed in the house or in our way of life—only she was not there.

It seemed to me that after such a misfortune everything ought to be changed; our ordinary course of life seemed to me an affront to her memory and too vividly reminded me of her absence.

On the day before the funeral, after dinner, I felt sleepy and went to Natálya Sávishna's room, meaning to lie down on her soft feather-bed under her warm quilt. When I entered Natálya Sávishna was lying on her bed, probably asleep. Hearing the sound of my footsteps she sat up, threw back the woollen shawl with which she had protected her head from the flies, straightened her cap, and seated herself on the side of her bed.

As I had often before happened to come to have an after-dinner nap in her room, she guessed why I had come, and rising from the bed, said: "I suppose you have come to have a rest, my pet? Lie down!"

"Oh no, Natálya Sávishna!" said I, holding her back

by her arm, "I did not come at all for that . . . I've come just to . . . and you are tired yourself, you'd better lie down."

"No, my dear, I am quite rested," she said (I knew she had not slept for three days). "Besides, this is no time for sleeping," she added with a deep sigh.

I wanted to speak of our misfortune with Natálya Sávishna: I knew her sincerity and love, and so it would be a consolation for me to weep with her.

"Natálya Sávishna," I asked after a pause, as I sat down on her bed, "did you expect it?"

The old woman gave me a perplexed and surprised look, probably not understanding why I put that question to her.

"Who could have expected it?" I said.

"Oh, my dear," she replied, giving me a look of the tenderest sympathy, "not only did I not expect it but I can't even think of it now. Now for an old woman like me it has long been time to lay my old bones to rest—but see what I have had to survive. My old master, your grandfather—blessed be his memory! Prince Nicholas Mikháylovich, two brothers, sister Anna: I have followed them all to the grave, and they were all younger than I, my dear, and now—for my sins no doubt—I have had to outlive her too. It's His holy will! He has taken her because she was worthy, and He needs the good there, too."

This simple thought struck me as comforting, and I moved closer to Natálya Sávishna. She folded her hands on her bosom and looked upwards; her sunken and moist eyes expressed a great but tranquil sorrow. She firmly trusted that God had not parted her for long from the one on whom all her power of love had been centred for so many years.

"Yes, my dear, it does not seem long since I dandled her and swaddled her, and since she called me 'Násha.' She would come running to me, put her tiny arms round me and kiss me, saying: 'Násha mine, beauty mine, you my little turkey-hen!' and I would say in fun: 'Not at all, madam, you don't love me; only wait a little, when you grow up and get married you'll forget your Násha!' And she would become thoughtful and say: 'No, I'd rather not marry if I can't take Násha with me; I shall never leave Násha.' And now she has left me and did not wait for me. And how she did love me! But, to tell the truth, whom did she not love? Yes, my dear, you must not forget your mother; she was not human, but an angel from heaven. When her soul is in the kingdom of heaven she will still love you there and still rejoice in you."

"Why do you say, 'When she will be in the kingdom of heaven,' Natálya Sávishna?" I asked. "I should think she is there now."

"No, my dear," said Nátalya Sávishna, lowering her voice and settling closer to me in the bed, "her soul is here now."

She pointed upward. She spoke almost in a whisper and with such feeling and conviction that I involuntarily raised my eyes and looked at the cornice, searching for something there.

"Before a righteous soul goes to paradise it must pass through forty trials, my dear, for forty days, and may remain in its own home. . . ."

She continued to speak for a long time in this way, and so simply and with such conviction—as if telling about quite ordinary things she had seen herself and about which it could never enter any one's head to have the least doubt—that I listened to her, holding my breath and, though without quite understanding what she said, fully believing her.

"Yes, my dear, she is here now looking at us, and perhaps hearing what we are saying," concluded Natálya Sávishna, and lowering her head she became silent.

She wanted a handkerchief to dry her falling tears; rose, looked me straight in the face, and in a voice trembling with emotion said: "The Lord has drawn me many steps closer to Himself through this. What is there left for me here? Whom have I to live for? Whom to love?"

"But don't you love us?" I said reproachfully and hardly refraining from tears.

"God knows how I love you, my darlings, but I have never loved, nor can love, any one as I loved her."

She could not say any more, turned away from me, and sobbed aloud.

I no longer thought of sleep, and we sat silently opposite one another and wept.

Fóka entered the room and, seeing our condition and probably unwilling to disturb us, silently and timidly stopped at the door looking round.

"What do you want, Fóka dear?" asked Natálya Sávishna, drying her face.

"A pound and a half of raisins, four pounds of sugar, and three pounds of rice for the *kutyá*."[1]

"Directly, directly, Fóka," said Natálya Sávishna hurriedly taking a pinch of snuff and going with rapid steps to the provision bin. The last traces of sorrow occasioned by our conversation vanished when she set about her duty, which she considered most important.

"Why four pounds?" she said in a grumbling tone, getting out the sugar and weighing it on the balance, "three and a half will be sufficient," and she took a few lumps from the balance.

"And what do they mean by asking for more rice, when I let them have eight pounds yesterday? You may do as you please, Fóka Demídych, but I won't let them have any more rice. That Vánka is glad of the turmoil in the house: perhaps he thinks things will pass unnoticed. No, I won't overlook anything concerning the master's property. Now who ever saw such a thing? Eight pounds!"

"What's to be done? He says it's all used up."

"Oh well, here it is, take it. Let him have it!"

I was at the time surprised by this change from the touching emotion with which she had been speaking to me to querulousness and petty economy. When considering it later I understood that, in spite of what was passing in her soul, she had sufficient presence of mind to carry on her work and that force of habit drew her to her usual occupations. Sorrow had acted on her so powerfully that she did not find it necessary to disguise the fact that she could attend to other things; she would not even have understood how such an idea could occur to any one.

---

[1] *Kutyá* is a dish made of rice, sugar, raisins, and such things, placed on a table in church at services for the dead.

Vanity is a feeling quite incompatible with true sorrow, and yet that feeling is so firmly grafted into man's nature that even the deepest sorrow rarely banishes it. Vanity in sorrow expresses itself by a desire to appear either stricken with grief, or unhappy, or firm, and these mean desires which we do not confess, but which hardly ever leave us even in our deepest sorrow, rob it of its strength, dignity, and sincerity. But Natálya Sávishna was so deeply stricken by her misfortune that she had not a single desire left in her soul and lived on only from habit.

When she had let Fóka have the provisions asked for and had reminded him about the pie which had to be made to set before the clergy, she let him go, took up her knitting, and again once more sat down beside me.

We again began talking about the same things, we wept again, and again dried our tears.

My talks with Natálya Sávishna were repeated every day; her quiet tears and calm, pious words gave me comfort and relief.

But we were soon separated: three days after the funeral we all moved to Moscow, and I was not destined ever to see her again.

Grandmamma received the terrible news only on our arrival, and her grief was extreme. We were not admitted to her, because for a whole week she was not in her right mind; the doctors feared for her life, the more so as she not only would not take any medicine but did not speak to anybody, did not sleep, and took no food. Sometimes, sitting alone in the room in her easy chair, she suddenly began to laugh, then to sob without any tears, had convulsions, and in a frenzied voice shouted meaningless or terrible words. It was the first great sorrow she had experienced and it brought her to despair. She wanted to blame some one for her misfortune, and she uttered dreadful words, threatened some one, jumped up from the chair with extraordinary violence, paced the room with large, rapid strides, and then fell down unconscious.

Once I went to her room; she was sitting as usual in her armchair and appeared calm, but I was struck by her expression. Her eyes were wide open but her look seemed vague and dull: she gazed straight at me but probably did not see me. Her lips stretched slowly into a smile and she began to speak in a pathetic and tender tone: "Come here, my pet; come, my angel!"

I thought she was addressing me, and I drew nearer, but she was not looking at me. "Oh, if you knew, my treasure, how I have suffered and how glad I am now that you have come. . . ." I understood that she imagined that she saw mamma, and I stopped. "And I was told you were no more," she continued, with a frown. "What nonsense! As if you could die before me!" and she burst into terrible hysterical laughter.

Only people capable of loving deeply can experience deep grief, but that same necessity of loving acts as an antidote to grief and cures them. In consequence of this, man's moral nature is more tenacious of life than his physical nature. Grief never kills.

After a week grandmamma was able to weep, and she got better. Her first thoughts after she came to herself were of us, and her love for us increased. We kept near her chair; she wept softly, spoke of mamma, and caressed us tenderly.

No one who saw her grief could think that she exaggerated it, and the expressions of that grief were vehement and touching; but I, without knowing why, sympathized more with Natálya Sávishna, and am still convinced that no one loved mamma so sincerely and purely and mourned her loss so deeply as that simple-hearted and loving creature.

With my mother's death the happy period of childhood ended for me and a new period began—that of boyhood, but since my recollections of Natálya Sávishna, whom I never saw again and who had such a powerful and good influence on my disposition and the development of my sensibility, belong to the first period, I will say a few more words about her and her death.

After we had left, as I was afterwards told by persons who had remained in the country, she fretted very much for want of occupation. Though all the chests were still in her charge and she kept rummaging them, arranging, airing, and unfolding their contents, she missed the noise and bustle of a country residence inhabited by the family, to which she had from childhood been accustomed. Grief, the changed manner of life, and the absence of household cares, soon developed in her a senile ailment to which she had a tendency. Just a year after my mother's death she became affected with dropsy and took to her bed.

It must have been hard for Natálya Sávishna to live alone, and still harder to die alone, in the great, empty house at Petróvskoe, without relatives or friends. Every one in the house was fond of Natálya Sávishna and respected her, but she was not intimate with any of them and prided herself on this. She considered that in her position of housekeeper, enjoying her master's confidence and in charge of so many chests full of all sorts of goods, intimacy with any one would inevitably involve her in partiality and guilty connivance; for this reason, or perhaps because she had nothing in common with the other servants, she kept aloof from them all and used to say that she had neither gossips nor connexions in the house and that no one would have her connivance in matters concerning the master's property.

She sought and found consolation in the confession of her feelings to God in ardent prayers, but sometimes in the moments of weakness to which every one is subject, when man finds the best consolation in the love and sympathy of a living being, she would take on to her bed her little pug dog (which fixed its yellow eyes on her and licked her hands), speak to it, and weep gently as she caressed it. When the dog began to whimper piteously she would try to quieten it and say: "Don't I know without that, that I shall die soon?"

A month before her death she took some white calico, white muslin, and pink ribbons out of her trunk and with her maid's help made herself a white gown and cap and arranged all that would be needed for her funeral to the last detail. She also sorted out everything in her master's chests and with the greatest exactitude gave it over, with a written inventory, into the care of the steward's wife. Then she got out two silk gowns and an ancient shawl that had once been given her by my grandmother, and my grandfather's gold-embroidered military uniform, which had also been given her to dispose of as she liked. Thanks to her care, the gold embroidery and lace on the uniform had remained quite fresh and the cloth untouched by moth. Before her death she expressed her wish that one of these gowns, a pink one, should be given to Volódya for a dressing-gown or a *beshmet*[2] and the other, a brown, chequered one, to me for the same purpose, and the shawl to Lyúba. She bequeathed the uniform to whichever of us should first become an officer. All the rest of her goods and money, except forty rubles which she set aside for her funeral and for prayers for her soul, she left to her brother. Her brother, who had been granted his freedom long before, was living in some distant province and led a most dissolute life, so she had had no intercourse with him during her lifetime.

When this brother came to receive his legacy, and her whole property proved to be worth only twenty-five assignation rubles,[3] he did not wish to believe it and declared that it was impossible that an old woman who had lived with a wealthy family for sixty years and had charge of everything in it and who was penurious all her life and trembled over every rag, should have left nothing. But it really was so.

Natálya Sávishna's illness lasted two months, and she bore her sufferings with truly Christian patience, did not grumble or complain, but only kept calling on God, as was her wont. An hour before her death she confessed with peaceful joy and received the sacrament and extreme unction.

She begged forgiveness of every one in the household for any wrong she might have done them, asked Father Basil, her confessor, to tell us all that she did not know how to thank us for our kindness, and that she asked us to forgive her if, through her stupidity, she had offended any one,—"but I have never been a thief, and I can say that I never filched so much as a thread from my master!" That was the one virtue she valued herself upon.

[2] A Tartar under-tunic.

[3] The assignation rubles were the depreciated currency in use after the Napoleonic wars, eventually converted at the rate of 3½ assignation rubles for one silver ruble of the value of about 38 pence.

Having put on the dress and cap she had prepared, and leaning her elbows on her pillow, she talked with the priest to the very last, remembered that she had left nothing for the poor, got out ten rubles, and asked him to distribute them in the parish: then she crossed herself, lay down, sighed deeply for the last time, and uttered the name of God with a joyous smile.

She left this life without regret, did not fear death, and accepted it as a boon. This is often said, but how seldom it really is so! Natálya Sávishna was able not to fear death because she died in stedfast faith and having fulfilled the gospel commandments. Her whole life had been pure unselfish love and self-sacrifice.

What if her beliefs might have been more lofty and her life devoted to higher aims—was that pure soul therefore less worthy of love and admiration?

She accomplished the best and greatest thing in life —she died without regrets or fear.

She was buried, according to her own wish, not far from the chapel that stands over our mother's grave. The little mound, overgrown with nettles and thistles, under which she lies, is surrounded by a black railing, and I never forget to go from the chapel to that fence and bow down to the ground.

Sometimes I stop in silence between the chapel and the black railing. Painful memories suddenly awaken in my soul. The question occurs to my mind: "Can Providence have united me with those two beings only that I should eternally regret them?"

1852

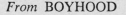

From BOYHOOD

I
TRAVELLING TO TOWN

Once more two vehicles are drawn up at the porch of the Petróvskoe house—the one a closed carriage in which Mimi, Kátya, Lyúba, and a maid-servant take their seats, and the steward, Jacob, takes his place on the box; the other the brichka, in which Volódya, I, and the footman, Vasíli— not long since recalled from commuted labour—are to travel.

Papa, who is to come to Moscow a few days later, stands bare-headed in the porch and makes the sign of the cross over the carriage window and the brichka.

"Well, Christ be with you! Drive on!" Jacob and the coachman (we are travelling with our own horses) take off their caps and cross themselves. "Gee up! God be with us!" The carriages begin to jolt over the uneven road and the birches of the avenue one after the other run past us. I am not at all sad; my mental vision is directed not to what I am leaving behind but to what awaits me. The farther I am parted from the objects connected with the depressing memories that till now have filled my imagination, the more they lose their power and are rapidly replaced by a cheerful consciousness of life full of vigour, freshness, and hope.

I have seldom spent days—I won't say so merrily, for I still felt ashamed to yield to merriment—but so pleasantly, so contentedly, as the four days of our journey. I had not before my eyes the closed doors of my mother's bedroom which I could not pass without a tremor, nor the closed piano, never approached by any one and even looked at with a kind of dread, nor mourning garments (we were all dressed in ordinary travelling clothes), nor any of the things that, vividly reminding me of my irreparable loss, made me shun any manifestation of life for fear in some way of offending *her* memory. Here, on the contrary, new, picturesque places and objects continually arrested and diverted my attention, and the freshness of spring aroused in my soul joyful feelings of contentment with the present and bright hopes for the future.

Very, very early in the morning the pitiless and—like all holders of new posts—over-zealous Vasíli, pulls off my blanket and declares that everything is ready and it is time to start. Shrink, pretend, or get angry as you may, in order to prolong your sweet morning slumber for another quarter of an hour, you see by Vasíli's resolute face that he is inflexible and is prepared to pull off the blanket another twenty times, and you jump up and run out into the yard to have a wash.

In the passage a samovar into which Mítka, the postilion, flushed red as a lobster, is blowing, is already on the boil. It is damp and misty outside, as if steam were rising from the odorous manure heap; the sun lights with its bright gay beams the eastern part of the sky and the thatched roofs, shiny with dew, of the roomy pent-houses that surround the yard. Under these one can see our horses tethered to the mangers and hear their steady chewing. A shaggy mongrel that has had a nap before dawn on a dry heap of manure stretches itself lazily and, wagging its tail, starts at a jog-trot for the opposite side of the yard. An active peasant-woman opens some creaking gates and drives the dreamy cows into the street, where the tramping, the lowing, and the bleating of the herd is already audible, and she exchanges a few words with a sleepy neighbour. Philip, his shirt-sleeves rolled up, winds up a bucket from the deep well and, splashing the clear water, pours it into an oak trough beside which the awakened ducks are already plashing in a puddle; and I look with pleasure at Philip's impressive face with its broad beard, and at the thick sinews and muscles standing out sharply on his powerful bare arms when he makes any effort.

Behind the partition where Mimi slept with the girls and through which we had exchanged remarks in the evening, there is a sound of movement. Másha, the maid, runs past us more and more frequently with different articles she tries to hide from our curiosity with her dress, and at last the door opens and we are called in to tea.

Vasíli, in a superfluous fit of zeal, keeps continually running into the room, carrying out first one thing and then another, winking at us, and in all manner of ways imploring Márya Ivánovna to make an early start. The horses are harnessed and manifest their impatience by occasionally jingling the bells on their harness. Portmanteaux, trunks, boxes large and small are again packed in, and we take our places. But every time this occurs we find a hill instead of a seat in the brichka, so that we cannot make out how all the things previously got packed in, or how we are now to sit. In particular a walnut tea-caddy with a three-cornered lid, which is put into the brichka and placed under me, arouses me to great indignation. But Vasíli declares that it will all settle down, and I have no choice but to believe him.

The sun has only just risen above the dense white cloud which had covered the eastern horizon, and all about us is brightened by a calm, cheerful light. All around me is so beautiful, and my heart is so light and calm. . . . The road winds in front like a broad, greyish ribbon between fields of dry stubble and verdure gleaming with dew. Here and there we come across a gloomy willow or a young birch-tree with small, sticky leaves that throws a long shadow on the dry clayey ruts and the small green grass of the road. . . . The monotonous rumble of our wheels and the tinkling of the bells do not drown the songs of the larks which circle around close to the road. The odour of moth-eaten cloth, dust, and acid of some kind which distinguishes our brichka is overpowered by the fragrance of the morning, and I feel within me a joyful unrest, a wish to do something—which is the sign of true enjoyment.

I had not time to say my prayers at the inn, but as I had noticed more than once that when, for any reason, I forgot to perform that duty I met with some mishap, I try to make good the omission: I take off my cap, turn towards the corner of the brichka, say my prayers, and cross myself under my jacket so that nobody shall notice it. But thousands of different objects distract my attention and I absent-mindedly repeat the same words of the prayer several times over.

There on the foot-path that winds beside the road, some slowly moving figures appear: they are women-pilgrims. Their heads are wrapped in dirty shawls, on their backs they carry knapsacks of birch-bark, their legs are swathed in dirty, ragged leg-bands, and they wear heavy bast shoes. With measured swing of their staffs, and scarcely turning to look at us, one after another they move forward with slow heavy steps, and I am interested by the questions: where, and why, are they going? Will their journey be a long one, and how soon will the elongated shadows they throw on the road join the shadow of the willow near which they must pass? Here is a calash with four post-horses, rushing quickly towards us. Two seconds more, and faces looking at us affably and with curiosity from two yards off have flashed past, and it seems strange that those faces have nothing in common with me and I shall perhaps never see them again.

Then at one side of the road run two sweating, shaggy horses with collars on and with traces tucked under their harness; and behind them, his legs in enormous boots hanging astride a horse on whose neck hangs a bow[1] with a bell that occasionally tinkles slightly, rides a post-boy—his felt hat stuck over one ear—singing a drawling song. His face and attitude indicate so much lazy and careless content, that it seems to me the height of happiness to be a post-boy and to ride on a return journey, singing sad songs. There, far beyond the ravine, a village church with a green roof shows up against the light-blue sky; here is the village, and the red roof of the squire's house with its green garden. Who lives in that house? Are there children, a father, a mother, or a teacher in it? Why should we not drive up to that house and get to know its owners? Here comes a long row of enormous loaded carts, each drawn by three well-fed, stout-legged horses, to pass which we must keep to the side of the road. "What are you carting?" Vasíli asks the first carter, who, dangling his huge legs down from the cart and flourishing his little whip, turns an intent and inane look on us for a long time, and only

---

[1] Part of the Russian harness to which the shafts are fixed.

replies when too far off to be heard. "What goods are you carting?" Vasíli asks another carter, who is lying, covered with new matting, in the railed-in front of a cart. A brown head with a red face and a small russet beard thrusts itself from under the matting, casts a look of contemptuous indifference at our brichka and again hides itself—and it occurs to me that probably these carters don't know who we are, where we come from, or where we are going.

For an hour and a half, absorbed in various observations, I pay no heed to the slanting figures on the mileposts, but now the sun begins to shine more fiercely on my head and back, the road grows more dusty, the triangular lid of the tea-caddy begins to disturb me seriously, and I change my position several times and grow hot, uncomfortable, and dull. My whole attention turns to the mileposts and the figures on them; and I do various calculations as to when we can reach the next station. Twelve versts are one-third of thirty-six, and there are forty-one versts to Líptsi, so we have done one-third, and how much more? and so on.

"Vasíli," I say, when I see he is beginning to nod on the box, "let me sit on the box, there's a dear." Vasíli agrees. We change places; he at once begins to snore and stretches out so that there is no room left for anybody else in the brichka, while from the height I occupy there opens out before me an extremely pleasant picture—our four horses, Neruchínskaya, Sexton, Left-Shaft, and Apothecary, whom I knew down to the minutest details and shades of all their characteristics.

"Why is it, Philip, that Sexton is on the off-side and not on the near-side to-day?" I ask rather timidly.

"Sexton?"

"And Neruchínskaya is not pulling at all!" say I.

"Sexton can't be harnessed on the near-side," says Philip, disregarding my last remark. "He is not that kind of horse to be harnessed on the near-side. On the near-side one wants a horse that, in a word, *is* a horse, and he is not that kind of horse."

With these words Philip leans over to his right and, jerking the rein with all his might, begins to whip poor Sexton on his legs and tail in a peculiar upward manner, and though Sexton tries as hard as he can, and pulls the whole brichka to one side, Philip only abandons that proceeding when he feels it necessary to rest and pull his hat, for some unknown reason, on one side, though till then it had sat very firmly and well on his head. I take advantage of that propitious moment and ask Philip to let me drive. He first gives me one rein, then another, and at last all six reins and the whip pass into my hands and I am perfectly happy. I try to imitate Philip in every way and ask him whether it's all right, but it generally ends by his being dissatisfied with me, saying that one horse pulls too hard and another does not pull at all, and finally he thrusts his elbow in front of me and deprives me of the reins. The heat continually increases; fleecy clouds like soap-bubbles begin to be blown upwards higher and higher, run together, and assume dark-grey shades. A hand holding a bottle and a small bundle is thrust out of the carriage window, and Vasíli, with surprising agility, jumps down from the moving brichka and brings us a bottle of kvas and some cheese-cakes.

At a steep downward slope we all get out of the vehicles and sometimes race down to the bridge, while Vasíli and Jacob, after putting a drag on the wheels, hold the carriage on both sides with their hands, as if they could support it should it fall. Then, with Mimi's permission, Volódya or I get into the carriage, and Lyúba or Kátya into the brichka. This change affords great pleasure to the girls because as they rightly say, it is much jollier in the brichka. At times, while passing through a grove during the heat of the day, we lag behind the carriage, gather some green branches, and construct with them an arbour over the brichka. The moving arbour races full speed after the carriage, and then Lyúba shrieks in a most piercing voice, as she never fails to do on every occasion that gives her great pleasure.

But here is the village where we are to dine and rest. The smells of the village are already noticeable—smells of smoke, tar, and cracknels; we hear the sound of voices, of footsteps, and of wheels, and our harness-bells do not sound as they did in the open fields; on both sides we catch glimpses of thatched huts, with their small, carved, wooden porches and green or red shutters to their little windows, out of which here and there the head of an inquisitive woman is thrust. Here are little peasant boys and girls with nothing on but their smocks: with wide-open eyes and out-stretched arms they stand motionless on one spot or run bare-foot through the dust after our vehicles with quick little steps, and, regardless of Philip's threatening gestures, try to climb on the portmanteaux that are strapped on behind. And now two red-haired inn-keepers come running, one each side of our vehicles, and with inviting words and gestures vie with each other in enticing the travellers. "Whoa!" The gates creak, the cross-bars to which the traces of the side-horses are attached scrape the gateposts, and we drive into the yard of an inn. Four hours of rest and freedom!

II
THE STORM

The sun was sinking to the west and burnt my neck and cheeks intolerably with its slanting rays; it was impossible to touch the scorching edges of the brichka; dense clouds of dust rose from the road and filled the air. There was not a breath of air to carry it away. At a regular distance in front of us swung, with a rhythmic motion, the tall dusty body of our carriage, with luggage on its roof, and beyond this now and then appeared the whip the coachman was flourishing, his hat, and Jacob's cap. I did not know what to do with myself; neither Volódya's face black with dust, as he dozed by my side, nor the movements of Philip's back, nor the long shadow of our brichka which followed us at an oblique angle afforded me any diversion. My whole attention was concentrated on the mile-posts which I noticed from afar, and on the clouds, which had been scattered over the horizon but, with threatening black hues, now gathered into one gloomy storm-cloud. Now and then there came a roll of distant thunder. This latter fact above all increased my impatience to reach the inn. Thunderstorms produced in me an indescribable feeling of depression and dread.

It was yet some ten versts to the nearest village, and the large, dark-purple cloud, appearing from heaven knows where, was approaching swiftly though there was no wind. The sun, not yet hidden by the clouds, brightly lit up its sombre form and the grey streaks that ran from it to the very horizon. At times lightning flashed in the distance, and a feeble rumble, which gradually grew stronger, came nearer and passed into an intermittent thunder that resounded through the whole heaven.

Vasíli rose from the box-seat and lifted the hood of the brichka; the coachmen put on their overcoats and, taking off their caps, crossed themselves at each clap of thunder; the horses pricked up their ears and distended their nostrils, as if smelling the fresh air which came from the approaching storm-cloud; and the brichka travelled faster over the dusty road. I felt ill at ease and the blood flowed faster through my veins.

But now the nearest cloud begins to obscure the sun, which peeps out for the last time, lights up the terribly gloomy part of the horizon, and disappears. Everything around suddenly changes and takes on a sombre aspect. Here the aspen grove begins to quiver, its leaves turn a kind of dim whitish colour clearly outlined against the purple background of the cloud, and they rustle and twirl about; the tops of the tall birches begin to sway and tufts of dry grass fly across the road. Martens and white-breasted swallows, as if intending to stop us, sweep round the brichka and fly under the very breasts of the horses; jackdaws with ruffled wings fly sideways to the wind, the flaps of the leather apron we have fastened over ourselves begin to lift, let in gusts of damp wind, and, blowing about, flap against the body of the brichka. The lightning seems to flash right into the brichka, blinds me, and lights up for an instant the grey cloth, its braiding, and Volódya's figure crouching in the corner. Just above my head at that very moment a majestic peal resounds, which, seeming to rise higher and higher and wider and wider in a huge spiral, gradually strengthens and changes into a deafening roar— forcing one involuntarily to tremble and hold one's breath. "The wrath of God!" How much poetry there is in that popular conception!

The wheels revolve faster and faster; by the backs of Vasíli and of Philip, who impatiently shakes the reins, I notice that they too are frightened. The brichka rolls rapidly downhill and rattles on to a wooden bridge. I fear to move, and every moment expect that we shall all perish.

"Whoa!" A swingle-tree has come off, and despite the continuous and deafening peals of thunder we are obliged to stop on the bridge.

Leaning my head against the edge of the brichka, I hopelessly watch with sinking heart and bated breath the movements of Philip's thick black fingers, while he slowly ties a loop and adjusts the traces, pushing the side horse now with the palm of his hand, now with the whip-handle.

Anxious feelings of depression and fear increase in me with the intensity of the storm, but when the solemn momentary lull arrives which usually precedes a violent outbreak, these feelings reach such a pitch that if that condition had lasted another quarter of an hour I feel sure I should have died of the agitation.

At that very moment from under the bridge, a human creature suddenly appears in a dirty tattered shirt, with a swollen meaningless countenance, with a shaking, close-cropped, bare head, crooked muscleless legs, and in place of a hand a red shiny stump, which he thrusts straight into the brichka.

"Ma-a-ster! Give something to a cripple for Christ's sake!" he says in a suffering voice and at each word crosses himself and bows down to his waist.

I cannot express the chill of horror which seized my soul at that moment. A shiver ran through my hair, and my eyes were fixed with blank dread upon the beggar.

Vasíli, who distributes the alms on our journey, gives Philip instructions how to re-attach the swingle-tree, and only when everything is ready, and Philip, gathering up the reins, is climbing back on to the box, begins to take something out of his side pocket. But we have hardly started before a blinding flash of lightning, that for an instant fills the whole hollow with fiery light, causes the horses to stop and is immediately followed by such a deafening clap of thunder that it seems as if the whole vault of heaven will crash down upon us. The wind still increases; the manes and tails of the horses, Vasíli's cloak, and the flaps of the leather apron are blown in the same direction and spread out boisterously in the wind. A raindrop falls heavily on the leather hood of the brichka . . . another, a third, a fourth, and suddenly, as if some one had begun drumming over our heads, the whole country resounds with the regular pattering of falling rain. By the motion of Vasíli's elbows I see that he is untying his purse; the beggar, still crossing himself and bowing, runs so close to our wheels that he may be run over at any moment. "Give, in Chist's name!" At last a copper coin flies past us, and the pitiful creature in his coarse rags, that are wet through and cling to his thin limbs, stops bewildered in the middle of the road, swaying in the wind, and is lost to my sight.

The slanting rain, driven by the violent wind, pours down as from a bucket; from the back of Vasíli's frieze coat streams run down into the pool of turbid water that has gathered on the apron. The dust, at first beaten into little pellets, changes into liquid mud which is kneaded by the wheels; the jolting becomes less violent, and turbid streams run in the clayey ruts. The lightning flashes become wider and paler, and the rolling of the thunder is now less startling amid the regular patter of the rain.

But now the rain becomes finer, the black cloud, beginning to break into fleecy cloudlets, grows lighter where the sun should be—and between the light-grey edges of the cloud a patch of clear azure just shows itself. A minute later a timid ray of sunshine glistens in the puddles of the road, in the straight streaks of fine rain that fall as if coming through a sieve, and on the bright rain-washed grass along the road. A black cloud still covers the opposite horizon just as threateningly, but I no longer fear it. I experience an inexpressible, joyful feeling of hope in life, which rapidly replaces my heavy feeling of terror. My soul smiles in accord with refreshed and rejoicing nature. Vasíli turns down the collar of his cloak, takes off his cap and shakes it; Volódya throws back the apron; I lean out of the brichka and eagerly inhale the fresh and fragrant air. The bright, well-washed body of the carriage, with its boxes and portmanteaux, sways in front of us; the backs of the horses, the harness, the reins, and the tyres are all wet and glisten in the sun as if freshly varnished. On one side of the road a boundless field of winter grain, divided here and there by shallow hollows, gleams with its wet earth and vegetation and stretches away like a shadowy carpet to the very horizon. On the other side an aspen grove with hazel and wild cherry undergrowth stands motionless as if in an excess of joy and slowly sheds bright raindrops from its clean-washed branches onto last year's leaves. On all sides crested skylarks circle with glad songs and swoop swiftly down. In the wet bushes one hears the busy movements of small birds, and from the middle of the wood distinctly comes the voice of a cuckoo. The delicious scent of the wood after the spring storm, the odour of the birches, of the violets, the rotting leaves, the mushrooms, and the wild cherry, is so enthralling that I cannot stay in the brichka but jump down from its step, run to the bushes, and, though I get sprinkled with the rain-drops that shower down on me, break off wet branches of the flowering wild cherry, stroke my face with them, and revel in their exquisite aroma. Heedless even of the fact that large lumps of mud stick to my boots and that my stockings have long been wet, I run splashing through the mud to the carriage window.

"Lyúba! Kátya!" I shout, handing in some branches of wild cherry, "look how nice it is!"

The girls squeal and exclaim; Mimi shouts to me to go away or I shall certainly be run over.

"But just smell what a scent it has!" I cry.

∽∾∽∾

They go to Moscow.

VI
MÁSHA

But no change that took place in my outlook on things was so startling to myself as the one which made me cease to regard one of our housemaids as a servant of the feminine gender and begin to see in her a *woman*, on whom might depend, to some extent, my peace of mind and happiness.

As far back as I can remember myself, I remember Másha in our house, and never till the occurrence that entirely changed my view of her, and which I will relate presently, had I paid the slightest attention to her. Másha was about twenty-five when I was fourteen. She was very good-looking, but I am afraid to describe her lest my fancy should again present to me the enchanting and delusive image it formed at the time of my passion for her. Not to blunder, I will only say that she had a remarkably white skin, was voluptuously developed, and was a woman— while I was fourteen.

In one of those moods when, lesson-book in hand, you pace up and down the room trying to step only on the cracks between the boards, or sing some senseless air, or smear the edge of the table with ink, or quite unthinkingly repeat some saying: in short, when your mind refuses to work and your imagination, taking the upper hand, seeks impressions, I left the classroom and aimlessly went on to the landing.

Some one in house-shoes was ascending the lower flight of the staircase. Of course I wanted to know who it was, but suddenly the sound of the steps ceased, and I heard Másha's voice: "Now then, what are you fooling for? If Márya Ivánovna comes, will it be nice?"

"She won't come," Volódya's voice whispered, and something rustled as if he were trying to hold her back.

"Now, where are you putting your hands? For shame!" and Másha, with her kerchief pulled awry exposing her plump white neck, ran up past me.

I cannot express my amazement at this discovery, but the feeling of astonishment was soon replaced by one of sympathy with Volódya's act—I no longer marvelled at his action itself, but only at his having discovered that it was pleasant to behave so, and I involuntarily wished to imitate him.

I sometimes spent hours on the landing, not thinking at all but listening with the closest attention to the slightest movement upstairs, but I could never bring myself to imitate Volódya, though I wished to do that more than anything else in the world. Sometimes, hidden behind a door, I listened with a painful feeling of envy and jealousy to a commotion beginning in the maids' room, and the thought occurred to me what my position would be if I were to go upstairs and, like Volódya, try to kiss Másha. What should I, with my broad nose and bristling tufts of hair, reply if she asked me what I wanted? At times I heard Másha say to Volódya: "Well, this is horrid! Really, why have you come bothering? Go away, you naughty boy! Why does Nicholas Petróvich never come here and play the fool?" . . . She did not know that Nicholas Petróvich was under the stairs at that moment, and was ready to give anything in the world to be in naughty Volódya's place.

I was bashful by nature, but my bashfulness was still further increased by the conviction that I was ugly. I am convinced that nothing has so marked an influence on the direction of a man's mind as his appearance, and not his appearance itself so much as his conviction that it is attractive or unattractive.

I was too egotistic to get used to my position and comforted myself as the fox did when it persuaded itself that the grapes were sour; that is, I tried to despise all the pleasures afforded by attractive looks, which it seemed to me Volódya availed himself of and which I envied him with all my soul, and I exerted all my powers of mind and imagination to find pleasure in haughty solitude.

∽∽∽

XVIII
THE MAIDS' ROOM

I felt more and more lonely, and my chief pleasures were solitary reflections and observations. Of the subject of my reflections I will tell in the next chapter, but the chief scene of my observations was the maids' room, in which what was for me a very interesting and touching romance was proceeding. The heroine of that romance, needless to say, was Másha. She was in love with Vasíli, who had known her when she was still at home and had then already promised to marry her. Fate, which had separated them five years before, had brought them together again in grandmamma's house but had set a barrier to their mutual affection in the person of Nicholáy, Másha's uncle, who would not hear of his niece marrying Vasíli, whom he spoke of as an "unsuitable and uncontrolled man."

This barrier had the effect of making Vasíli, formerly rather cool and careless in the matter, suddenly fall in love with Másha—as much in love as ever a domestic serf in a pink shirt, with pomaded hair, and trained as a tailor, is capable of being in love.

Though the manifestations of his love were very strange and inappropriate (for instance, on meeting Másha he always tried to hurt her: either pinched her, slapped her with the palm of his hand, or squeezed her so tightly that she could hardly draw her breath), yet his love was sincere, as was proved by the fact that, when Nicholáy definitely refused him the hand of his niece, Vasíli started drinking, began loafing about in public houses, kicked up rows, and in a word, behaved so badly that he more than once underwent the humiliation of being locked up in the police-station. But all these actions of his and their consequences were, it seemed, meritorious in Másha's eyes and only increased her love for him. When Vasíli was locked up, Másha's eyes were not dry for days on end; she wept, complained of her bitter fate to Gásha who took a lively interest in the unfortunate lovers' affairs, and regardless of her uncle's scoldings and beatings, ran secretly to the police-station to visit and console her friend.

Do not disdain, reader, the company into which I am introducing you. If the chords of love and sympathy have not slackened in your soul, sounds will be met with in the maids' room to which they can respond. Whether you care to follow me or not, I am going to the staircase landing from which I can see all that goes on in the maids' room. There is the ledge of the stove on which stand a flat-iron, a dressmaker's papier-mâché dummy with a broken nose, a wash-tub, and a jug; there is the window-sill on which lie in disorder a bit of black wax, a skein of silk, a half-eaten green cucumber, and a sweetmeat box; and there is the large red table on which, on an unfinished piece of needlework, lies a weight-cushion made of a chintz-covered brick. At that table *she* sits in the pink gingham dress that I like, and with a blue kerchief which particularly attracts my attention. She is sewing, occasionally stopping to scratch her head with her needle or to trim the candle, and I look on and think. "Why was she not born a lady, with those bright blue eyes, that immense plait of auburn hair and full bust? How well it would suit her to sit in the drawing-room with pink ribbons on her head and in a crimson silk gown——not like Mimi's, but like one I saw on the Tverskóy Boulevard. She would then have worked at an embroidery-frame, and I should have been looking at her in the mirror and doing whatever she wanted: helping her on with her cloak or handing her her meals myself.

And what a drunken face and repulsive figure that Vasíli has, in his tight coat put on over the dirty pink shirt he wears outside his trousers! In every movement of his body, in every curve of his back, I seem to see clear indications of the horrid punishment he had undergone. . . .

"What, again, Vásya?" said Másha, sticking her needle into the cushion and not looking up at Vasíli as he entered.

"And what d'you think? As if any good could come from *him!*" answered Vasíli. "If only he had settled it one way or other. As it is I'm going to ruin for nothing, and all through *him.*"

"Will you have some tea?" asked Nadëzha, another housemaid.

"Thank you kindly. . . . And why does he hate me, that thief, your uncle, what for? Because I have proper clothes, for my smartness, for my way of walking, in a word. . . . Oh, gracious!" Vasíli said, flourishing his arm.

"One should be submissive," said Másha, biting off a thread, "but you always . . ."

"I can't bear it any longer, that's what it is!"

At that moment I heard the sound of grandmamma's door and the voice of Gásha, grumbling as she came up the stairs.

"Give satisfaction indeed, when she doesn't herself know what she wants. . . . What a confounded life, a prisoner's life! God forgive me!" she muttered, swinging her arms.

"My respects, Agatha Mikháylovna!" said Vasíli to her, rising as she entered.

"Oh, get along! I have other things than your respects to think of!" she replied, looking at him angrily. "And why do you come here? Is the maids' room the place for a man?"

"I wanted to ask about your health," said Vasíli timidly.

"I shall die soon—that's what my health is!" shouted Agatha Mikháylovna at the top of her voice and still more angrily.

Vasíli began to laugh.

"There's nothing to laugh about—when I tell you to be off, get away! Look at the dirty lout! Wants to marry—the villain! Now then, be off, quick march!"

And Agatha Mikháylovna, stamping her feet, went to her own room, banging the door so that the window-panes rattled.

She could be heard for a long time behind the partition, abusing everything and everybody and cursing her life. She threw her things about, pulled the ears of her pet cat, and at last the door opened a little way and the cat, piteously miaowing, was flung out by her tail.

"It looks as if I had better come some other time for a cup of tea," said Vasíli in a whisper. "Good-bye till the next pleasant meeting."

"Never mind," said Nadëzha with a wink, "I'll just go and see if the samovar is boiling."

"Yes, I'll make an end of it somehow," continued Vasíli, seating himself closer to Másha, as soon as Nadëzha had left the room. "Either I'll go straight to the countess and tell her so and so, or I'll throw everything up and run away to the end of the world. I swear I will."

"And how shall I be left . . .?"

"It's only you I am sorry to leave, or else I'd have been free lo-o-ong ago, really, really!"

"Why don't you bring me your shirts to wash, Vásya?" said Másha, after a short pause. "Just look how dirty it is," she added, taking hold of his shirt-collar.

At the moment grandmamma's bell rang, and Gásha came out of her room.

"Now then you wretched fellow, what are you trying to get from her?" she said, pushing Vasíli, who had risen hurriedly at sight of her, to the door. "See what you've brought the girl to, and you go on bothering her. . . . It seems you think it fun to look at her tears, you starveling. Get out! Don't leave a trace of yourself here! And what have you found in him?" she went on, turning to Másha. "Hasn't your uncle beaten you enough to-day on his account? No, it's always your own way! 'I won't have any one but Vasíli Grúskov.' Fool!"

"Yes, I won't have any one else. I don't love any one else, even if you killed me!" said Másha, suddenly bursting into tears.

I looked long at Másha as she lay on a trunk, wiping her tears with her kerchief, and I tried by all manner of means to change my opinion of Vasíli, and sought for a point of view from which it was possible for him to appear to her so attractive. But though I sincerely sympathized with Másha in her sorrow, I could not at all understand how so charming a creature as, in my eyes, she was, could love Vasíli.

When I am grown up, I thought to myself, after I had gone to my room, Petróvskoe will belong to me, and Vasíli and Másha will be my serfs. I shall be sitting in my study and smoking my pipe. Másha will pass with a flat-iron on her way to the kitchen. I shall say: "Call Másha here." She will come, and nobody else will be in the room. . . . Suddenly Vasíli will enter and, seeing Másha, will say: "It's all up with me!" and Másha also will begin to cry, and I shall say: "Vasíli, I know you love her and she loves you. Here are a thousand rubles for you. Marry her, and God grant you happiness!" And I myself shall go into the sitting-room. . . .

Among the innumerable thoughts and fancies that pass through the mind and the imagination without any trace, there are some which leave a deep, pronounced groove, so that often when you no longer remember the essence of the thought, you are conscious that something good has been in your mind, you feel the trace left by the thought and try to reproduce it. A deep trace of that kind was left in my soul by the thought of sacrificing my own feeling in favour of Másha's happiness, which she could find only in marriage with Vasíli.

XIX
BOYHOOD

It will hardly be believed what were my favourite and most constant subjects of reflection during boyhood—so incompatible were they with my age and position. But in my opinion the incompatibility of a man's position with his moral activity is the surest indication of his searching for truth.

For a year, during which I led a solitary, self-concentrated mental life, all the abstract questions con-

cerning man's destiny, future life, and the immortality of
the soul had presented themselves to me, and my feeble,
childish mind, with all the ardour of inexperience, tried to
clear up these questions the formulation of which is the
highest stage the human mind can reach, but the solution
of which is not granted to it.

It seems to me that the human mind in each separate
individual follows in its development the same road along
which it has developed during many generations and that
the thoughts which serve as basis for various philosophic
theories are indivisible parts of that mind, but that each man
more or less clearly realized them before he knew of the
existence of the philosophic theories.

These thoughts presented themselves to my mind so
clearly and definitely that I even tried to apply them to life,
imagining that I was the first discoverer of such great and
useful truths.

At one time the idea occurred to me that happiness does
not depend on external causes but on our relation to those
causes, and that a man accustomed to endure sufferings
cannot be unhappy—and to inure myself to hardship, regardless of the severe pain I felt, I used to hold Tatishchev's
dictionaries out at arm's length for five minutes at a time
or go into the box-room and lash my bare back with a rope
so painfully that tears involuntarily appeared in my eyes.

At another time, remembering that death awaited me at
any hour and at any moment, I understood, wondering that
people had not understood it before, that one can only be
happy by enjoying the present and not thinking of the
future, and, for three days, under the influence of this
idea, I neglected to learn my lessons and did nothing but
lie on my bed, enjoying myself by reading a novel, and
eating gingerbread made with honey, on which I spent my
last coins.

Another time, standing before a blackboard and drawing
various figures on it with chalk, I was suddenly struck by
the thought: "Why does symmetry please the eye? What is
symmetry?" "It is an innate feeling," I replied to myself.
"On what is it based? Is there symmetry in everything in
life?" "On the contrary—this is life"; and I drew an oval
figure on the board—"when life ends the soul passes into

eternity—this is eternity"; and I drew a line from one side of the oval figure right to the edge of the board. "Why is there no such line on the other side? Yes, indeed, how can eternity be only on one side? We must have existed before this life, though we have lost the recollection of it."

This reflection, which seemed to me exceedingly novel and clear, and whose logic I can now perceive only with difficulty, pleased me extremely, and taking a sheet of paper I intended to expound it in writing, but thereupon such a host of ideas suddenly collected in my head that I was obliged to get up and walk about the room. When I came to the window my attention was attracted to the horse used for carrying water, which the coachman was just then harnessing, and my thoughts all centred on the question: what animal or man that horse's soul would enter when it died? Just then Volódya, as he passed through the room, smiled on seeing me pondering over something, and that smile was sufficient for me to understand that all I was thinking about was awful nonsense.

I have only related this case, which for some reason seemed to me memorable, in order to let the reader see what my reflections were like.

But by none of my philosophical tendencies was I so carried away as by skepticism, which at one time led me to the verge of insanity. I imagined that besides myself nobody and nothing existed in the universe, that objects were not objects at all but images which appeared only when I paid attention to them, and that as soon as I left off thinking of them, these images immediately disappeared. In a word, I coincided with Schelling in the conviction that not objects exist but my relation to them. There were moments when, under the influence of this *idée fixe*, I reached such a state of insanity that I sometimes looked rapidly round to one side, hoping to catch emptiness (*néant*) unawares where I was not.

A pitiful, trivial spring of mental action is the mind of man! My feeble mind could not penetrate the impenetrable and in that effort lost, one by one, the convictions which, for my life's happiness, I ought never to have dared to disturb.

From all this heavy moral toil I obtained nothing except

a flexibility of mind that weakened my will-power, and a habit of constant moral analysis, destructive to freshness of feeling and clarity of reason.

Abstract thoughts form as a result of man's capacity to seize a consciousness of the state of his soul at a given moment and to transfer that perception to his memory. My fondness for abstract reasoning developed consciousness in me so unnaturally that often when I began thinking about the simplest things, I fell into the vicious circle of analysis of my thoughts, and I no longer thought about the original question that had occupied me but thought about what I was thinking about. I asked myself: "What am I thinking about?" and answered: "I am thinking about what I am thinking. And now what am I thinking about? I am thinking that I think about what I am thinking about," and so on. I had thought myself out of my wits.

However, the philosophical discoveries I made flattered my vanity extremely: I often imagined myself a great man, discovering new truths for the benefit of mankind, and regarded the rest of humanity with a proud consciousness of my own worth; but strangely enough when I encountered those other mortals I felt shy of each of them, and the higher I set myself in my own estimation, the less was I capable not only of exhibiting the consciousness of my own dignity, but even of accustoming myself to avoid being ashamed of my simplest words and movements.

XX
VOLÓDYA

Yes, the farther I advance in the description of this period of my life, the more painful and difficult it becomes for me. Very rarely among the memories of this time do I find moments of genuine warm feeling such as brightly and constantly lit up the commencement of my life. Involuntarily I wish to pass quickly over the desert of my boyhood, and to reach the happy time when the truly tender and noble feeling of friendship brighly lit up the end of that period and formed the beginning of a new one full of delight and poetry—the period of adolescence.

I will not follow my reminiscences hour by hour but will cast a rapid glance at the chief of them, from the time to

which I have brought my story to the time of my coming
in touch with the exceptional man who had a definite and
beneficent influence on my character and tendencies.

Volódya is just entering the University. Masters already
come to him separately, and I listen with envy and involuntary respect when he, briskly tapping the blackboard with
the chalk, talks of functions, sines, co-ordinates, and so on,
which seem to me the expressions of an unattainable
wisdom. At last, one Sunday after dinner, all the masters
and two professors assemble in grandmamma's room, and
in the presence of papa and several visitors have a rehearsal
of the University's examination in which, to grandmamma's
great delight, Volódya evinces extraordinary knowledge.
Some questions are put to me too, but I cut a very poor
figure, and the professors evidently try to hide my ignorance
from grandmamma, which confuses me still more. However, little attention is paid to me: I am only fifteen, so
there is still a year before my examination. Volódya only
comes down to dinner and spends whole days and even
evenings upstairs studying—not compulsorily, but at his
own wish. He is extremely ambitious and wants to pass his
examination not just moderately, but excellently.

And now the day of the first examination has arrived;
Volódya puts on a blue dress-coat with gilt buttons, a gold
watch, and patent-leather boots. Papa's phaeton drives up
to the door; Nicholáy throws back the apron, and Volódya
and St. Jérôme drive to the University. The girls, especially
Kátya, look out of the window with joyful, ecstatic faces at
Volódya's graceful figure, as he gets into the phaeton. Papa
says: "God grant it, God grant it!" and grandmamma has
also dragged herself to the window and with tears in her
eyes makes the sign of the cross towards Volódya and
murmurs something until the phaeton turns the corner of
the street.

Volódya returns. Everybody questions him impatiently:
"Well? Was it all right? What were your marks?" but by
Volódya's happy face one sees that it is all right. He has
got a "five." Next day he is seen off with the same wishes
for his success and the same fears and is met with the same
impatience and joy. Nine days pass in that manner. On the
tenth day the last and most difficult examination, in
Scripture, takes place. Every one stands by the window and

awaits Volódya with yet greater impatience. It is already two o'clock, and he is not back yet.

"Oh, Lord! Gracious goodness!! Here they are, here they are!" shouts Lyúba, pressing her face to the window.

And actually in the phaeton beside St. Jérôme sits Volódya, but no longer in his blue dress-suit and grey cap but in a student's uniform, with a blue embroidered collar, a three-cornered hat, and a short gilt sword at his side.[1]

"Oh, that you were alive!" exclaims grandmamma, seeing Volódya in his uniform, and she faints away and falls.

Volódya, with a radiant face runs into the hall, kisses and embraces me, Lyúba, Mimi, and Kátya, who blushes up to her ears. Volódya is beside himself with joy. And how handsome he looks in that uniform! How well the blue collar goes with his faintly appearing little black moustache! What a long, thin waist he has, and what a noble bearing! On that memorable day everybody dines in grandmamma's room, and all faces shine with joy. With the pudding-course the butler, with a decorously majestic and yet jovial countenance, brings in a bottle of champagne wrapped in a napkin. Grandmamma for the first time since mamma's death drinks champagne and empties a full glass, as she congratulates Volódya, and again she weeps with joy as she looks at him.

Volódya now drives out alone in his own equipage, receives his own acquaintances, smokes, goes to balls, and I myself even see how he and his friends once drink two bottles of champagne in his room and hear them toast some mysterious persons at each glass and dispute to whom should accrue *"le fond de la bouteille."*[2] However, he dines regularly at home and after dinner makes himself comfortable in the sitting-room as of old and always converses mysteriously with Kátya, but from what I, a non-participator in their conversation, can hear, they talk only of the heroes and heroines of novels they have read, about jealousy, and love, and I can't at all make out what they can find interesting in such conversations, and why they smile so subtly and dispute so warmly.

In general I notice that besides the understandable

---

[1] This was the proper uniform of a University student at the time.
[2] The last of the bottle.

friendship between companions of childhood, certain peculiar relations exist between them, which separate them from us, and mysteriously unite them with each other.

XXI
KÁTYA AND LYÚBA

Kátya is sixteen; she is grown up. The angularity of her figure, her shyness, and the awkwardness of movement natural to the age of transition have given place to the harmonious freshness and grace of a budding flower, but she has not changed. She has the same light-blue eyes and smiling look, the same straight nose almost in line with her forehead and with firm nostrils, the same brightly smiling lips, the same tiny dimples in the clear, rosy cheeks, the same white little hands . . . and, I don't know why, to be called a *clean little girl* still suits her extremely well. The only new things about her are her thick plait of light-brown hair which she wears like a grown-up person, and her young bosom, the development of which evidently pleases and confuses her.

Though Lyúba has always grown up and been educated with her, she is in all respects quite a different girl.

Lyúba is not tall, and as a result of rickets her feet still turn in and she has a horrid figure. There is nothing beautiful about her whole person except her eyes, but they are really beautiful—large, black, and with such an irresistibly pleasant expression of importance and naïveté that they cannot fail to arrest one's attention. Lyúba is simple and natural in everything, while Kátya seems to be trying to resemble some one else. Lyúba always looks straight at you, and sometimes, when she fixes her large black eyes on some one, she does not lower them for so long that she gets scolded for being impolite. Kátya, on the contrary, droops her lashes, screws up her eyes, and declares that she is short-sighted, though I know very well that she sees excellently. Lyúba does not like to show off before strangers, and when any one kisses her before visitors, she pouts and says she can't bear *sentimentality*. Kátya on the other hand always grows particularly affectionate to Mimi in the presence of visitors and likes walking up and down the ball-room with her arms about some other girl. Lyúba is a terrible laugher and sometimes in a fit of laughter swings her arms and runs about the room; Kátya on the contrary covers her mouth with her handkerchief or her hands when she begins to laugh. Lyúba always sits straight and walks with her arms hanging down; Kátya holds her head a little on one side and walks with her arms folded. Lyúba is always extremely pleased when she manages to have a talk with a grown-up man and says she will certainly marry a hussar; Kátya says all men are disgusting to her, that she will never marry, and she completely changes, as if frightened, when a man speaks to her. Lyúba is always indignant with Mimi for lacing her up in tight corsets "so that one can't breathe," and she is fond of eating; Kátya on the contrary often thrusts a finger under the peak of her bodice to show us how much too wide it is, and she eats remarkably little. Lyúba likes drawing heads, but Kátya draws only flowers and butterflies. Lyúba plays Field's concertos and some of Beethoven's sonatas with great clearness; Kátya plays variations and valses, confusing the time, thumping, and using the pedal continually, and before beginning to play anything takes three arpeggios very feelingly.

But Kátya, as I then thought, more resembled a grown-up woman and therefore pleased me most.

∽∾∾

XXV
VOLÓDYA'S FRIENDS

Though in the company of Volódya's acquaintances I played an humiliating part which hurt my vanity, I liked to sit in his room when he had visitors and silently to watch all that happened there.

Adjutant Dubkóv and Prince Nekhyúdov came to see him oftener than any one else. Dubkóv was small, sinewy, and dark, no longer in his first youth and had rather short legs, but he was not bad-looking and was always high-spirited. He was one of those limited men who are particularly attractive just because of their limitations; they cannot see things from different sides and are always being carried away. Such men's judgments are one-sided and faulty, but always sincere and attractive. Even their narrow egotism somehow appears excusable and attractive. Besides this, Dubkóv had for Volódya and me a twofold charm— his military appearance and still more his age, which young people are apt to confuse with *le comme il faut,* which is very highly valued in youth. And in fact, Dubkóv, really was what is called *un homme comme il faut.* One thing which pained me was that in his presence Volódya seemed ashamed of me for my most innocent actions, and most of all for my youth.

Nekhlyúdov was not good-looking: his small grey eyes, low straight forehead, and disproportionately long arms and legs could not be considered handsome. His only handsome features were his unusually tall figure, his delicate complexion, and his beautiful teeth, but his face received so original and energetic a character from his narrow, brilliant eyes and changeable smile—now severe, now child-like and indefinite—that one could not but notice it.

He seemed very bashful, for every trifle made him blush to his ears, but his bashfulness did not resemble mine. The more he blushed the more resolute became the expression of his face, as if he were angry with himself for his own weakness.

Though he seemed very friendly with Dubkóv and Volódya, it was evident that it was only chance that had brought them together. Their inclinations were quite different: Volódya and Dubkóv seemed afraid of anything resembling serious discussion or sentiment; Nekhlyúdov on the contrary was an enthusiast in the highest degree and in spite of ridicule often plunged into the discussion of philosophic questions and of sentiments. Volódya and Dubkóv liked to talk about the objects of their love (and were in love with several women at a time and both of them with the same woman). Nekhlyúdov, on the contrary, was always seriously angry when they hinted at his love of some "red-haired girl." Volódya and Dubkóv often allowed themselves to make affectionate fun of their relations, but Nekhlyúdov was beside himself if one said anything to the disadvantage of his aunt, for whom he had a kind of ecstatic adoration. Volódya and Dubkóv used to drive somewhere after supper without Nekhlyúdov, whom they called "a beauteous maiden."

Prince Nekhlyúdov struck me from the first both by his conversation and by his appearance. But though I saw in his bent of mind much that resembled my own—or perhaps on that very account—the feeling with which he inspired me when I first saw him was far from friendly.

I did not like his quick glance, firm voice, proud look, and above all the complete indifference with which he regarded me. Often during a conversation I felt a strong desire to contradict him; to punish his pride I wished to get the better of him in an argument—to prove to him that I was clever in spite of the fact that he did not wish to pay any attention to me. My shyness however restrained me.

∽∽∽

II
SPRING

The year I entered the university, Easter came rather late in April, so the examinations were fixed for the week after Easter, and in Passion week I had both to prepare myself for the Sacrament and to make final preparations for my examination.

The weather, after a fall of sleet—which Karl Iványch used to call "the son coming after his father"—had been calm, warm, and bright for three days. There was not a speck of snow left in the streets, the dirty sludge on the roads had given place to a wet glistening surface and to swift-running rivulets. In the sun the last drops were falling from the roofs, the buds were swelling on the trees in the garden, in the yard there was a dry path to the stables past a frozen heap of manure, and beside the porch green mossy grass appeared between the stones. It was that peculiar period of spring which most affects the human soul—everything glittering in the bright, not yet hot, sunshine; rivulets and wet places where the snow had thawed; a scented freshness in the air, and a delicately blue sky with long transparent clouds. I do not know why, but it seems to me as if the effect of this first period of new-born spring is more perceptible and stronger on the soul in a big city—one sees less but feels more. I stood at the window, into which the morning sun threw dusty rays through the double panes on to the floor of the classroom, of which I was unendurably weary and where I was trying to solve a long algebraical equation on the blackboard. In one hand I held a limp, tattered copy of Franker's *Algebra*, in the other a small piece of chalk, with which I had already soiled both hands, my face, and the elbows of my jacket. Nicholáy,[1] with his apron on and his sleeves rolled up, was breaking off the putty with a pair of pincers and bending back the nails holding the frame of the window that looked out on to the garden. His occupation and the noise he made distracted my attention. I was moreover in a very bad, dissatisfied mood. Nothing seemed to succeed: I had made a mistake at the beginning of my calculation, so that it had to be done all over again; I had twice dropped the chalk; I felt that my face and hands were smeared, the sponge had vanished somewhere, and Nicholáy's knocking affected my nerves painfully. I wanted to get into a temper and to grumble. I threw down the chalk and the *Algebra* and began pacing up and down the room. Then I remembered that we had to go to confession that day and must avoid everything evil, and suddenly a peculiarly mild mood came over me and I went up to Nicholáy.

"Let me help you, Nicholáy," I said, trying to speak in the mildest tone possible. The thought that I was acting well by repressing my vexation and helping him increased that meek frame of mind still more.

The putty was knocked away and the nails bent back, but though Nicholáy tugged at the frame with all his might it would not yield.

"If the frame comes out at once when I pull with him," I thought, "that will mean that it would be a sin to learn any more to-day." The frame moved forward on one side and came out.

"Where shall I take it to?" I asked.

"Allow me, I can manage it myself," replied Nicholáy, evidently surprised and seemingly not pleased by my zeal. "They must not be mixed up, and I have them all numbered in the box-room."

"I will mark this one," I said, lifting the frame.

I think that if the box-room had been two miles away and the frame twice as heavy I should have been very well satisfied. I wanted to exhaust myself helping Nicholáy. When I returned to the room the little bricks and salt

---

[1] Nicholáy was removing the inner frame of the window, all the windows having double frames, in winter, to keep out the cold.

pyramids[2] had already been moved on to the window-sill and Nicholáy was sweeping the sand and the sleepy flies out of the open window with a goose-wing. The fresh fragrant air had already penetrated into the room and filled it. From the window one could hear the din of the city, and the sparrows chirping in the garden.

Everything was brilliantly illumined; the room had grown gayer; a light spring breeze moved the leaves of my *Algebra* and the hair on Nicholáy's head. I went to the window, sat down on the sill, leaned over into the garden, and mused.

An extremely powerful and pleasant feeling, quite new to me, suddenly penetrated my soul. The wet earth through which here and there bright-green blades of grass with yellow stems were pushing up; the rills glistening in the sunlight and bearing whirling bits of earth and chips of wood; the reddening twigs of lilac with their swelling buds swaying just under the window; the busy twitter of birds bustling about in the bush; the dark fence wet with melting snow; and above all, that moist aromatic air and joyous sunshine spoke distinctly and clearly to me of something new and beautiful, which, though I cannot render as it revealed itself to me, I will try to tell of as I conceived it. Everything spoke to me of beauty, happiness, and virtue; told me that each of these was quite easy and attainable for me, that the one could not be without the others, and even that beauty, happiness, and virtue were one and the same thing. "How could I have failed to understand this? How bad I have been till now! How good and happy I might have been, and how good and happy I can be in future!" I said to myself. "I must quickly, quickly, this very moment, become a different being and begin to live differently." Regardless of this, however, I continued to sit on the window-sill for a long time dreaming and doing nothing. Has it ever happened to you to lie down and fall asleep on a dull rainy day in summer and waking up at sunset to open your eyes and see in the broadening square of the window, from under the linen blind which bulges out and beats with

2 Salt, sand, and other substances are placed between the inner and the outer window-frames to absorb any moisture there may be.

its rod against the window-sill, the shady, purple side of a lime avenue wet with rain and a moist garden path lit by the brilliant slanting rays of the sun and suddenly to hear the merry life of the birds in the garden and see the insects which, translucent in the sunshine, whirl about in the open window; to smell the fragrance of the air after the rain, and to think, "How is it I was not ashamed to waste such an evening in sleep?" and hurriedly to jump up to go into the garden and rejoice in life? If it has happened to you, it may serve as an example of the powerful feelings I experienced at this time.

◇◇◇

V
RULES

I took a sheet of paper and at first wanted to start on the list of duties and occupations for the coming year. I had to rule the sheet, but as I could not find the ruler, I used the Latin dictionary for the purpose. By drawing my pen along the side of the dictionary, which I then moved away, it turned out that I had made an inky smear instead of a line, besides this the dictionary was not large enough to cover the whole length of the paper and on reaching its soft corner the line went crooked. I took another sheet of paper and by moving the dictionary along managed to rule the paper in a sort of way. Having divided my duties into three kinds—duties to myself, to my neighbours, and to God—I began to set down the first; but I found so many of them, and so many kinds and subdivisions, that it was necessary first to write down the "Rules of Life," and then set to work on the list. I took six sheets of paper, sewed them together, and wrote on the cover, "Rules of Life." These words were so crookedly and unevenly written that I long considered whether I should not rewrite them, and for some considerable time tormented myself looking at the list I had torn up and at that ill-written heading. "Why is it all so beautiful and clear in my soul and comes out so misshapen on paper and in life in general, when I wish to practice anything I have planned . . .?"

"The Father-confessor has arrived; please come down to hear the precepts read," Nicholáy came and announced.

I hid my papers in the table drawer, looked in the glass, brushed my hair upwards, which I was convinced gave me a pensive air, and went down into the sitting-room, where a table was placed ready covered with a cloth, and with an icon and burning wax-tapers upon it. Papa entered at the same time by another door. The confessor, a grey-haired monk with a stern, aged face, gave papa his blessing. Papa kissed his small, broad, dry hand, and I did the same.

"Call Vóldemar!" said papa. "Where is he? No, don't; he will of course do his devotions at the university."

"He is busy with the prince," said Kátya, and glanced at Lyúba. Lyúba suddenly blushed about something, puckered up her face pretending to be in pain, and left the room. I followed her. She had stopped in the drawing-room and was again writing something with pencil on her paper.

"What! Have you committed another sin?" I asked.

"No, it's nothing, only . . ." she replied and blushed.

At that moment Dmítri's voice was heard in the hall bidding good-bye to Volódya.

"There now you get temptations everywhere," said Kátya, coming into the room and addressing Lyúba.

I could not make out what was happening to my sister: she was so confused that tears rose to her eyes, and her confusion, reaching its utmost limits, turned into vexation with herself and with Kátya who was evidently teasing her.

"There, one can see at once you are a *foreigner*." (Nothing offended Kátya more than to be called a *foreigner* —that was why Lyúba had used the word.) "Before such a sacrament!" she continued in a solemn tone—"and you upset me on purpose . . . you ought to understand . . . it is not a trifling matter."

"Do you know, Nicholas, what she has put down?" said Kátya, greatly offended at being called a *foreigner*. "She has written . . ."

"I did not expect you to be so spiteful," said Lyúba, now quite tearful, as she went away. "At such a moment and on purpose, always to lead one into sin. I don't bother you about your feelings and sufferings!"

〜◦〜

He goes to confession.

VII
VISIT TO THE MONASTERY

I woke several times during the night, afraid of oversleeping myself, and was up before six. Only a little light showed through the window. I put on my clothes and boots, that lay crumpled and unbrushed beside my bed as Nicholáy had not yet come for them, and, without saying my prayers or washing, I went out into the street alone for the first time in my life.[1]

On the opposite side, beyond the green roof of a high house, the rosy gleam of dawn gleamed through the cold mist. A fairly sharp spring morning frost had hardened the mud and fettered the streams of water; it made my feet tingle and pinched my face and hands. There was not a single cabman as yet in our street, though I had counted on finding one to take me to the Monastery and back quickly. Only some loaded carts were moving down the Arbát street, and two bricklayers passed along the pavement chatting. After I had gone about a thousand paces I began to met people—women on their way to market with their baskets, water-carts going to fetch water in their barrels, and a pieman who appeared at the crossroads; a bakery shop was opening, and at the Arbát gates I came across an old cabman dozing and swaying as he jolted along on his shabby, patched, light-blue *calíberny drózhki*.[2] Still probably half asleep, he asked only twenty kopeks to drive to the Monastery and back, then he came to his senses suddenly and, just as I was going to take my seat, began whipping his horse with the ends of the reins and very nearly drove away. "Must feed my horse! I can't, sir," he muttered.

With difficulty I persuaded him to stop, and offered him forty kopeks. He stopped, looked at me attentively, and said: "Get in, sir." I own I was rather afraid he might take me into some out-of-the-way lane and rob me. Catching

---

[1] Lads of good family were kept under strict supervision till they were grown up.

[2] A primitive vehicle with a very narrow seat.

hold of the collar of his tattered coat, and so pitiably exposing the wrinkled neck above his very bent back, I mounted the lumpy, ricketty, light-blue seat, and we went rattling up the Vozdvízhenka street. On the way I noticed that the back of the vehicle was covered with a bit of the same greenish cloth of which the cabman's coat was made, and this circumstance somehow quieted me, and I no longer feared that he would drive me into an out-of-the-way street and rob me.

The sun had already risen pretty high and was brightly gilding the domes of the churches when we reached the Monastery. In the shade the ground was still frozen, but rapid and turbid streams flowed all over the road and the horse splashed through the thawing mud. When I had entered the Monastery enclosure I asked the first person I met for the Father-confessor.

"That is his cell," said the monk who was passing by, pointing to a small house with a porch.

"Thank you very much," I said.

But what could the monks, who looked at me as one by one they came out of church, think of me? I was not grown up, nor a child; my face was not washed, my hair not combed, fluff was sticking to my clothes, my boots were muddy and not blacked. To what class of people would the observant monks mentally assign me? And they were looking at me attentively. However, I went on in the direction the young monk had indicated.

An old man in black garments and with thick grey eyebrows met me on the narrow path leading to the cells and asked me what I wanted.

For a moment I wished to say, "Nothing," run back to the cab, and drive home; but despite his overhanging eyebrows the old man's face inspired confidence. I said I wanted to see the Confessor, and gave his name.

"Come, young gentleman, I will show you the way," said he turning back, and apparently at once guessing my situation. "The Father is at matins; he will come soon."

He opened the door and led me through a neat passage and anteroom over a clean linen floor-cloth into the cell.

"You can wait here," he said to me with a kindly comforting look, and went away.

The room in which I found myself was very small and

most neatly arranged. Its whole furniture consisted of a small table covered with oilcloth, which stood between two casement windows with two geraniums in pots on the window-sills, a stand with icons and a lamp hanging before them, one arm-chair and two others. In the corner hung a clock with a floral design on its face and two brass weights hanging from its chains; on the partition, which was connected with the ceiling by small whitewashed wooden crosspieces, and behind which no doubt was a bed, two cassocks hung on a nail.

The windows faced a white wall some five feet from them. Between it and them grew a small lilac bush. Not a sound from outside reached the room, so that the pleasant rhythmic tick of the pendulum sounded loud in that stillness.

As soon as I was alone in that quiet little nook, all my former thoughts and recollections left my head as if they had never been there and I fell into a kind of inexpressibly pleasant musing. That faded nankeen cassock with its threadbare lining, the worn black leather bindings and brass clasps of the books, those dull green plants with their washed leaves, the carefully watered earth, and especially the monotonous recurring sound of the pendulum spoke to me clearly of some new hitherto unknown life, a life of solitude, prayer, and quiet peaceful happiness. . . .

"Months pass, years pass," I thought, "and he is always alone, always calm, and always feels his conscience clean before God and that his prayers are heard by Him." I sat for about half an hour on a chair trying not to move and not to breathe audibly, lest I should disturb the harmony of the sounds that told me so much. And the pendulum continued ticking, more loudly to the right, less loudly to the left.

VIII

MY SECOND CONFESSION

The steps of the Confessor roused me from my musings.

"Good morning," he said, smoothing his grey hair with his hand. "What is it you want?"

I asked him to bless me and kissed his small yellowish hand with peculiar pleasure.

When I explained my request to him, he said nothing but went up to the icons and began the confession.

When the confession was over and, mastering my shame, I had told him all that was on my mind, he placed his hands on my head and said in his soft resounding voice: "The blessing of the Heavenly Father be upon thee, my son, and may He ever preserve thee in faith, meekness, and humility. Amen."

I was completely happy; tears of joy choked me. I kissed a fold of his cloth cassock and raised my head. The monk's countenance was quite calm.

I felt that I was enjoying my emotion, and fearing to disturb it in any way I hurriedly took leave of the Confessor, and without looking to either side for fear of letting it evaporate, I passed through the enclosure and again mounted the jolting, motley, swaying vehicle. But its jolting, and the variety of objects that flitted before my eyes, soon dispersed that feeling, and I was already thinking that the Confessor was probably now saying to himself that he had never in his whole life met, nor would meet, a young man with so beautiful a soul as mine, and even that there were none such. I felt convinced of this, and it gave me a sense of joy of the kind one must communicate to somebody.

I had a terrible desire to talk to some one, and as I had no one at hand except the cabman, I addressed myself to him.

"Was I gone long?" I asked.

"A good long while, and my horse should have had a feed long ago; you see I am a night-cabman," answered the old man, who seemed more cheerful than he had been, now that the sun was up.

"But to me it seemed only a minute," I said. "Do you know why I went to the Monastery?" I added, moving into the hollow nearer to the old man.

"What's our business? To drive our fare where he tells us to go," he answered.

"But all the same, what do you think?" I continued.

"I dare say you have to bury some one and went to buy a plot for the grave," he answered.

"No, friend; but do you know why I went?"

"Can't say, sir," he replied.

The cabman's voice seemed to me so kindly that, as an

example to him, I decided to tell him the object of my visit and even the feeling I had experienced.

"Shall I tell you? Well, you see . . ."

I told him everything and described all my beautiful feelings to him. I blush even now at the recollection.

"Indeed, sir?" he said sceptically.

For a long time after that, he remained silent and sat immovable, except that he occasionally tucked in the skirt of his coat, which kept slipping from under his striped trousers as his leg, in his enormous boot, jolted on the step of the vehicle. I was beginning to imagine that he thought the same about me as the Confessor—namely, that there was not another such splendid young man as I in the whole world; but he suddenly turned towards me.

"I say, sir, you belong to the gentry?"

"What?" I asked.

"To the gentry, the gentry?" he repeated, mumbling with his toothless mouth.

"No," I thought, "he has not understood me," and I said nothing more to him till I got home.

Not the emotional and devout feeling itself, but my satisfaction at having experienced it, remained with me all the way, despite the people dotting the streets in the brilliant sunlight—but as soon as I got home that feeling vanished completely. I had not got the forty kopeks for the cabman, and Gabriel, the butler, to whom I was already in debt, would not lend me anything more. The cabman, having seen me run twice across the yard to find some money, and probably guessing what I was about, got down from his seat and, though he had seemed so kind, began saying in a loud voice—with evident intent to sting me—that there were swindlers around who did not pay their fares.

Everybody at home was still asleep, so that except the servants, there was no one from whom I could borrow the forty kopeks. At last Vasíli, on my giving him my most solemn word of honour to repay him—which, as I saw by his face, he did not at all believe in—because he liked me and remembered the service I had done him, paid the cabman for me. So the feeling I had had dispersed like smoke. When I began to dress for church to go with all the others to receive communion, and it turned out that my suit had not been mended and I could not wear it, I committed

many sins. Having put on another suit, I went to communion in a strange condition of mental flurry and entire
distrust of my fine inclinations.

∽∽∽

X

THE EXAMINATION IN HISTORY

On the 16th of April, under the guidance of St. Jérôme, I
entered the large university hall for the first time. We had
come in our rather smart phaeton. For the first time in my
life I wore a dress-coat, and all my clothes, even my linen
and my stockings, were quite new and of the best. When
the doorkeeper downstairs helped me off with my overcoat
and I stood before him in all the beauty of my attire, I
even felt a little ashamed to be so dazzling. But when I
entered the bright parquet-floored hall, full of people, and
saw hundreds of young men in high-school uniforms, or
dress-coats, some of whom glanced at me with indifference,
and the solemn professors at the farther end walking freely
about between the tables or sitting in large arm-chairs, I
at once felt disappointed in my hopes of attracting general
attention, and the expression of my face, which at home
and even at the entrance had denoted some regret that I
involuntarily presented so noble and important an appearance, changed to one of much timidity and some dejection.
I even went to the opposite extreme and was very glad to
see, near me, a very badly and not cleanly dressed man,
who though not old was almost completely grey, and who
sat apart from the rest on the last bench. I immediately sat
down near him and began to scrutinize the candidates and
form conclusions about them. There were many figures
and faces there, but according to my ideas at that time they
could all be divided into three classes.

There were some like myself, who had come to the
examination accompanied by tutors or parents, and among
these was the younger Ívin with Frost, whom I knew, and
Ílinka Grap with his old father. All these had fluffy chins,
displayed clean linen, and sat quietly without opening the
books and papers they had brought with them, looking

with evident timidity at the professors and the examination tables. The second class of candidates wore high-school uniforms, and many of them already shaved. Most of them knew one another, spoke loudly, used the professors' Christian names, prepared answers to various examination questions, passed their note-books to one another, stepped across the benches, brought pies and sandwiches from outside and ate them then and there, only bending their heads to the level of the benches. And finally a third class of candidates, of whom however there were not many, were quite old; some in dress-coats, but more in long coats and shewing no linen. These were very serious, sat separately, and looked very dismal.

The student who had comforted me by being certainly worse dressed than myself, belonged to this third category. Leaning on his elbows with his head between his hands and with his greyish hair sticking out between his fingers, he was reading a book and, giving me only a momentary and not very friendly glance with his glittering eyes, frowned morosely and protruded a shiny elbow to prevent my coming closer. The high-school pupils on the contrary were too sociable, and I was a bit afraid of them. One, pushing a book into my hand, said, "Hand it on to him, there." Another, as he passed me, said, "Let me pass, lad." A third, as he climbed across a bench, leant his hand on my shoulder as if it were a desk. All this seemed strange and unpleasant to me; I regarded myself as far superior to these high-school pupils and considered that they ought not to allow themselves such familiarities with me. At last names were called out. The high-school pupils went forward boldly and generally answered well and came back cheerful; our set were much more timid and, it seemed, did not answer so well. Of the older ones some answered excellently, others very badly.

When the name Seménov was called, my neighbour with the greyish hair and glittering eyes pushed by me roughly, stepped across my legs, and went up to the table. One could see by the professors' looks that he answered excellently and confidently. When he returned to his place he quietly gathered up his notebook and left without waiting to hear what mark he had received. I had already shuddered several times at the sound of the voice that called out the names, but my turn in the alphabetical order had not yet come, though some names beginning with an "I" were already being called. "Ikónin and Tényev!" some one suddenly called out from the professors' corner. A chill ran down my back and hair.

"Who was called? Who is 'Bartényev'?" people said near me.

"Ikónin, go; you are being called. But who 'Bartényev' or 'Mordényev' is, I don't know. Own up!" said a tall, red-cheeked, high-school student standing beside me.

"It's you," said St. Jérôme.

"My name is Irtényev," I said to the red-cheeked high-school student. "Did they call Irtényev?"

"Why, yes! Why don't you go? . . . Just see what a dandy!" he said, not loud but so that I heard his words as I passed between the benches. In front of me walked Ikónin, a tall young man of about twenty-five, who belonged to the third category—the old ones. He wore a tight olive dress-coat and a blue satin cravat, over which his long, fair hair was carefully combed behind, *à la moujhik*. I had noticed his appearance while we were still sitting on the benches. He was not bad-looking and was talkative, but what struck me most was the strange red hair which he had allowed to grow on his throat, and the yet stranger habit he had of continually unbuttoning his waistcoat and scratching his chest under his shirt.

Three professors were sitting at the table to which Ikónin and I went up; not one of them acknowledged our bow. A young professor was shuffling the question slips like a pack of cards; another, with a star attached to his coat, was looking at a high-school student who was rapidly saying something about Charlemagne, adding "finally" after every sentence, and the third professor, an old man, sat with bowed head, looked at us over his spectacles, and pointed to the question slips. I felt that his look was directed collectively to Ikónin and to me and that something about us displeased him—possibly Ikónin's red hair —for, again looking at us both, he made an impatient gesture with his head for us to hurry us and draw our tickets. I was vexed and offended, first that no one had answered our bow, and secondly that I was evidently coupled with Ikónin as the same sort of candidate and that there should already be a prejudice against me on account of Ikónin's red hair. I drew a ticket without timidity and was about to answer the question on it, but the professor indicated Ikónin by a look. I read the question on my ticket. It was one I knew, and quietly awaiting my turn I watched what went on before me. Ikónin was not at all intimidated and, with his side to the table, even moved too boldly to draw a ticket, shook back his hair, and briskly read the question written on the slip. He opened his mouth to begin to answer, I supposed, when the professor who wore the star, having dismissed the high-school pupil with commendation, suddenly looked at Ikónin. The latter seemed to remember something and stopped. There was a general silence for about two minutes.

"Well?" said the professor in spectacles.

Ikónin opened his mouth and again said nothing.

"You are not the only one here, you know! Will you please answer or not?" asked the young professor, but Ikónin did not even look at him. He gazed intently at the ticket and did not utter a word. The spectacled professor looked at him through his glasses, and over his glasses, and without his glasses, for he had had time to take them off, wipe them carefully, and to put them on again. Ikónin had not uttered a word. Suddenly a smile flashed across his face; he shook back his hair and, again turning his whole side to the table, put down his ticket, looked at each of the professors in turn, then at me, turned round, and swinging his arms went back with brisk strides to the bench. The professors exchanged looks.

"He's a nice one . . ." said the young professor, "a paying pupil!"[1]

I moved up to the table, but the professors continued to talk almost in whispers among themselves as if none of them even suspected that I was there. I was, at the time, firmly convinced that all three professors were deeply interested in the question whether I should pass my examination and whether I should pass it well but that just to give themselves airs they pretended it did not matter to them at all and that they did not notice me.

[1] A large number of pupils had their fees, and even their board and lodging, paid out of university funds, and those well enough off to pay their own way were regarded as rather exceptional.

When the spectacled professor addressed me in a tone of indifference and asked me to reply to the question I had drawn, I looked into his eyes and felt a little ashamed for him, on account of his duplicity towards me, and I became a little confused when I began to answer; but it soon became easier and easier, and as the question was one in Russian history, which I knew excellently, I finished brilliantly and even got into the swing of it so that, wishing to make the professors feel that I was not Ikónin and could not be mixed up with him, I offered to draw another ticket; but the professor gave me a nod, said, "That's all right," and put something down in his book. As soon as I returned to the benches, I was told by the high-school pupils, who (heaven knows how) seemed to know everything, that I had received the highest mark—a five.

⋘⋙

XV
I AM CONGRATULATED

Dubkóv and Volódya knew everybody at Yar's by name, and everybody from the hall porter to the proprietor showed them great respect. We were immediately given a private room and served with a wonderful dinner, which Dubkóv chose from a French menu. A bottle of iced champagne, at which I tried to look as unconcernedly as possible, was already prepared. The dinner passed off very pleasantly and merrily, though Dubkóv, as was his habit, told the strangest stories as if they were really true—among others, how his grandmother had killed with a blunderbuss three brigands who had waylaid her (which made me blush, lower my eyes, and turn away from him), and though Volódya was evidently uneasy whenever I opened my mouth (which was quite unnecessary, for as far as I remember I said nothing to be much ashamed of). When the champagne was served they all congratulated me, and I crossed hands with Dubkóv and Dmítri, drank "brotherhood" with them, and we kissed each other. As I did not know who had stood the champagne (it was really on our joint account, as was afterwards explained to me), and as I wished to treat my friends with my own money, which I kept feeling in my pocket, I stealthily took out a ten-ruble note, called the waiter, gave him the money, and in a whisper but so that everybody heard for they were all looking at me in silence, asked him to be so good as to bring another half-bottle of champagne. Volódya blushed, jerked his shoulder, and looked in a frightened way at me and at the rest, so that I felt I had made a mistake, but the half-bottle was brought and we drank it with great pleasure. Everything still seemed very jolly. Dubkóv continued to lie unceasingly. Volódya, too, said such funny things and so well—which I never expected of him—that we laughed a great deal. The character of their fun consisted in the imitation and exaggeration of the well-known anecdote: "Have you been abroad?" asks one, and the other answers, "No, I haven't, but my brother plays the violin." They brought this kind of comic inanity to such perfection that telling the original anecdote, they changed the reply into, "But my brother also never played the violin!" In this manner they answered every question the other put and even without waiting for a question tried to unite the most incongruous ideas and uttered this nonsense with serious faces—and the result was very funny. I began to see what the point was and wished to say something funny myself, but they looked embarrassed, or tried not to look at me whilst I was speaking, and my anecdote fell flat. Dubkóv said: "You have muddled it, brother diplomat," but after the champagne I had drunk, and in the company of grown-up people, I had such a pleasant feeling that this remark seemed but a pinprick. Dmítri alone, though he drank as much as we did, remained in his severe, serious frame of mind, which somewhat restrained the general gaiety.

"Now listen," remarked Dubkóv. "After dinner we must take the diplomat in hand. Should we not take him along to *Auntie's*? We would soon dispose of him there."

"Nekhlyúdov won't go, you know," said Volódya.

"Intolerable saint! You are an intolerable saint!" said Dubkóv, addressing Dmítri. "Come with us and you will find that Auntie is a splendid lady."

"Not only will I not go, but I won't let him go either!" answered Dmítri blushing.

"Whom? The diplomat? You want to go, don't you, diplomat? Look at him, he even quite brightened up as soon as Auntie was mentioned!"

"It's not exactly that I won't let him go," continued Dmítri, rising and beginning to pace the room without looking at me—"but I advise him not to go and I don't want him to go. He is not a child now and if he wants to go he can do so without you. But you, Dubkóv, ought to be ashamed of yourself: because you do wrong you want others to do the same."

"What is there wrong in my inviting you all to a cup of tea at Auntie's?" said Dubkóv, winking at Volódya. "But if you don't like to go with us, very well! I will go with Volódya. Volódya, you'll come?"

"H'm h'm," said Volódya affirmatively. "Let's go there and afterwards you will come home with me and we will finish the piquet."

"Do you want to go with them or not?" asked Dmítri, coming up to me.

"No," I answered, moving to make room for him beside me on the sofa, where he sat down, "I really don't want to go and if you advise me not to, nothing will induce me to go. No," I added, "it's not true that I don't want to go with them, but I am glad I am not going."

"That's capital," he said. "Live your own way and don't dance to anyone's fiddle. That's best."

This little dispute did not at all spoil our pleasure but even heightened it. Dmítri's mood suddenly changed to the gentle one I liked best. The consciousness of having acted well, as I afterwards noticed more and more, had this effect on him. He was now pleased with himself for having restrained me. He became very merry, ordered another bottle of champagne (which was against his rules), invited a stranger into our room, made him drink, sang "*Gaudeamus igitur*," invited us all to join in the chorus, and suggested a drive to Sokólniki, to which Dubkóv replied that it would be too sentimental.

"Let us make merry to-day," said Dmítri with a smile. "In honour of his entering the university I will get drunk for the first time. It can't be helped!"

This gaiety seemed very strange in Dmítri. He was like a tutor or a kind father who being satisfied with his children is in high spirits and wishes to give them pleasure and at the same time to prove that it is possible to make merry honestly and decently; but still his unexpected gaiety seemed to act contagiously on me and on the others— the more so since we had each of us drunk nearly half a bottle of champagne.

In this pleasant frame of mind I went out into the large room to light a cigarette which Dubkóv had given me.

When I rose from my seat I noticed that my head felt rather giddy and my arms and legs retained a natural position only as long as I paid special attention to them. Otherwise my legs moved sideways and my arms gesticulated. I fixed my whole attention to these limbs, forced my hands to rise, button my coat and smooth my hair (during which my elbows jerked up terribly high), and compelled my feet to walk to the door, which they did, but they stepped either very firmly or too gently, and the left foot in particular always stepped on tiptoe. A voice called out, "Where are you going? They'll bring a candle!" I guessed it was Volódya's voice and it gave me pleasure to think that after all I had guessed right, but I only gave a slight smile and went on.

XVI
THE QUARREL

In the large room a short, thickset civilian with a red moustache sat eating something at a small table. By him sat a tall, dark, clean-shaven man. They were speaking French. Their looks disturbed me, but nevertheless I decided to light my cigarette at the candle in front of them. Looking about me so as not to meet their eyes, I went up to their table and began lighting my cigarette. When it burnt up I could not resist looking at the man who was dining. His grey eyes were fixed on me attentively and threateningly. I was about to turn away when his red moustache began to move and he said in French, "I don't like people smoking when I am dining, sir!"

I muttered something incomprehensible.

"No, I don't like it," continued the man with the moustache severely, with a rapid glance at the clean-shaven man as if inviting him to see what a dressing-down he would give me. "Nor do I like those who are rude enough to come and smoke under my nose. I do not like them either."

I realized at once that the man was scolding me but at first felt very guilty towards him.

"I did not think it would incommode you," I said.

"Ah, you did not think you were a churl, but I did . . ." shouted the man.

"What right have you to shout?" I said, feeling that he was insulting me and beginning to grow angry myself.

"This right, that I will never allow anyone to fail in respect to me, and will always give such fellows as you a lesson. What is your name, sir, and where do you live?"

I was much enraged, my lips quivered and I gasped for breath. But I still felt myself to blame, no doubt for drinking too much champagne, and I did not say anything rude to him, but on the contrary let my lips utter my name and address very submissively.

"My name is Kólpikov, sir, and you must be more polite in future! You will hear from me (*Vous aurez de mes nouvelles*)," he concluded, as the conversation was carried on in French.

I only said: "Very pleased," trying to render my voice as firm as possible, and I turned away with the cigarette, which had by this time gone out, and went back to our room.

I said nothing of what had happened either to my brother or to my friends, especially as they were warmly discussing something, but I seated myself alone in a corner and began pondering over this strange incident. The words: "You are a churl, sir! (*un mal élevé*)" kept ringing in my ears, and more and more aroused my indignation. My muzziness had quite passed off. As I was considering how I had acted in this affair, the terrible thought suddenly struck me that I had behaved like a coward. What right had he to attack me? Why didn't he simply tell me that I was incommoding him? Certainly he was in the wrong! Why, when he called me a churl, didn't I say to him: "A churl, sir, is one who permits himself to be rude." Or why didn't I simply shout "Shut up!" That would have been excellent. Why didn't I challenge him to a duel? I hadn't done any of these things but had just swallowed the offence like a mean coward. "You are a churl, sir!" rang in my ears continually and irritatingly. "No, it can't be left like that," thought I, and I rose with the firm intention of going back to that gentleman and telling him something terrible, even perhaps knocking him on the head with the candlestick if opportunity occurred. I thought of this last intention with the highest delight, but it was not without considerable fear that I went back to the large room. Fortunately Mr. Kólpikov was no longer there, and a waiter, clearing the table, was the only person in the room. I wanted to inform the waiter of what had happened and explain to him that I was not at all to blame, but somehow I changed my mind and went back to our room in a most dismal frame of mind. "What has happened to our diplomat?" asked Dubkóv. "He is no doubt deciding the fate of Europe!"

"Oh, leave me in peace!" I said morosely, turning away. After that, pacing the room, I began to consider that Dubkóv was not a nice man at all. "And why this everlasting poking and calling me 'diplomat'? There is nothing kindly about it. All he cares for is to win from Volódya at cards and visit some kind of 'Auntie'. . . . There's nothing agreeable about him. Whatever he says is a lie or a commonplace, and he always tries to make fun of me. It seems to me that he is simply stupid, besides being a bad man." I spent about five minutes in such reflections, feeling for some reason a growing hostility to Dubkóv. Dubkóv however took no heed of me, and this irritated me still more. I was even angry with Volódya and Dmítri for talking to him.

"I say, you fellows, we must pour some water on the diplomat!" said Dubkóv suddenly, glancing at me with a smile which seemed to me derisive and even treacherous. "He is very bad! By heavens, he *is* bad."

"One must pour water over you, too. You are bad yourself!" I replied smiling viciously.

This reply must have astonished Dubkóv, but he turned away indifferently and continued his conversation with Volódya and Dmítri.

I tried to join in their conversation, but felt it quite impossible to dissemble, and again betook myself to my corner, where I remained till our departure.

When the bill had been paid and we were putting on

our overcoats, Dubkóv turned to Dmítri and said: "Well, and where will Orestes and Pylades go? Home, I suppose, to talk of *love*. That's not our plan—we'll call on dear 'Auntie'—that's better than your sour friendship."

"How dare you speak so . . . laughing at us?" I suddenly began, going up very close to him and waving my arms. "How dare you laugh at feelings you don't understand? I won't allow you to do it! Hold your tongue!" I shouted, and then held my own, not knowing what more to say, and breathless with agitation. Dubkóv was surprised at first, then he tried to smile and take it as a joke, but finally, to my great amazement, grew frightened and lowered his eyes.

"I do not laugh at you at all, nor at your feelings. I only say . . ." he began evasively.

"I dare say!" I shouted, but at that very moment I felt ashamed of myself and sorry for Dubkóv, whose flushed and disconcerted face expressed real suffering.

"What is the matter with you?" Volódya and Dmítri began both at once. "Nobody wished to hurt your feelings."

"Yes, he wished to affront me."

"What a desperate fellow your brother is!" remarked Dubkóv just as he went out of the room so that he could not hear my rejoinder.

Perhaps I might have run after him and said some more insulting things, but just then the waiter who had been present during my encounter with Kólpikov handed me my overcoat and I at once quieted down, only pretending to Dmítri to be sufficiently angry for my sudden appeasement not to seem strange to him. Next day when Dubkóv and I met in Volódya's room, we did not allude to that incident, but were less intimate, and it was more difficult than ever for us to meet one another's eyes.

The memory of my quarrel with Kólpikov (who however did not send me *de ses nouvelles* either the next day or on any other) remained for many years terribly vivid and painful to me. For perhaps five years after, I shuddered and exclaimed every time I remembered that unavenged insult, but I consoled myself by recalling with satisfaction what a dashing fellow I had shown myself to be in the affair with Dubkóv. Only much later did I begin to see the matter in quite a different light and to recall my quarrel with Kólpikov with comical amusement and regret the undeserved insult to which I had subjected "that *good fellow* Dubkóv."

When that very evening I told Dmítri of my adventure with Kólpikov, whose appearance I minutely described to him, he was extremely surprised.

"Yes, he's the very man!" he said. "Fancy, this Kólpikov is a notorious good-for-nothing and card-sharper, but above all a coward who was expelled from his regiment by his fellow-officers for having had his face smacked and being unwilling to fight a duel. Where did he get the pluck from?" he added, looking at me with a good-natured smile. "But he said nothing worse that 'churl'?"

"No"—I began, and blushed.

"It's impolite, but it's no great matter!" Dmítri consoled me.

Only long after, thinking over the circumstance quietly, I reached the rather probable conclusion that Kólpikov, feeling that it was safe to attack me in the presence of the dark, clean-shaven man, avenged on me after many years the slap he had received, just as I had once avenged his calling me a "churl" on the innocent Dubkóv.

⬿⬿⬿

He goes to pay calls.

XX

THE ÍVINS

It had become still more unpleasant to think of the unavoidable visit before me. But before going to the prince, I had first to call on the Ívins on my way. They lived on the Tverskáya Street in an enormous and fine house. Not without timidity did I pass into the front entrance where a door-keeper stood holding a staff.

I inquired whether anybody was at home.

"Whom do you want to see? The general's son is at home," the door-keeper answered.

"And the general himself?" I asked courageously.

"You must be announced. What shall I say?" said the door-keeper and rang. The gaitered legs of a footman appeared on the staircase. Without knowing why, I was so intimidated that I told the footman not to announce me to the general, but that I would first go to see the general's son. As I ascended that broad staircase I felt as if I had become quite small, not in a figurative but in the literal sense of the word. I had had that same feeling as my drozhki drove up to the main entrance: it had seemed to me that the drozhki, the horse, and the coachman had all grown small. The general's son lay asleep on the sofa, with an open book before him, when I entered the room. His tutor, Frost, who was still with them, followed me into the room with his usual jaunty step and aroused his pupil. Ivin did not evince any particular pleasure at sight of me, and I noticed that he looked at my eyebrows when talking to me. Though he was very polite, it seemed to me that he was entertaining me as the eldest princess had done and that he did not feel particularly attracted to me nor in any need of my acquaintance, since he certainly had a different circle of acquaintances of his own. All this I conjectured chiefly from his gazing at my eyebrows. In short, his attitude towards me, unpleasant as it is to admit it, was almost the same as mine towards Ilinka. I began to feel irritated, watched every one of Ivin's looks, and when his eyes met Frost's I interpreted its meaning to be: "Whatever has he come here for?"

After talking to me for a while, Ivin told me that his father and mother were at home and asked whether I would not like to go down with him to see them.

"Just a minute, I will get dressed," he added, going into another room, though he was already well dressed in this one—in a new coat and a white waistcoat. In a few minutes he returned in a uniform all buttoned up, and we went downstairs together. The reception rooms through which we passed were very large, high, and, I think, luxuriously furnished. There was something made of marble and gold, something wrapped in muslin, and mirrors. Just as we entered a small drawing-room, Ivin's mother came in through another door. She received me in a familiar and friendly manner, made me sit beside her, and questioned me sympathetically about all our family.

I had barely seen her once or twice before, but now I looked at her attentively and liked her very much. She was tall, thin, very pale, and seemed always sad and worn. Her smile was sad but extremely kind, her eyes were large, tired, and squinted a little, which gave her a still sadder and more attractive look. She did not stoop but sat with her whole body relaxed, and all her movements were drooping. She spoke languidly, but her voice and enunciation, with indistinct *r*'s and *l*'s were very pleasant. She did not try to entertain me. My answers to her inquiries about my relations evidently aroused her melancholy interest, as if while hearing me she sadly recalled happier times. Her son had gone out somewhere. She looked at me silently for a minute or two and suddenly burst into tears. I sat before her and could not imagine what to say or do. She continued to weep without looking at me. At first I felt sorry for her, then I wondered whether I ought not to try to console her, and how to do it; but finally I became vexed that she should place me in such an awkward situation. "Can I really be such a pathetic sight?" I thought, "or is she doing this on purpose to see how I shall behave in such circumstances?"

"It would not do to go away now, as if I were running away from her tears," I thought. I turned on my chair to remind her at least of my presence.

"Ah, how stupid I am!" she said, looking at me and trying to smile. "There are days when one cries without any reason."

She began to feel for the handkerchief that was beside her on the sofa and suddenly burst into more intense weeping.

"Oh, God! How absurd it is to keep on crying! I loved your mother so, we were such friends . . . we . . . and . . ."

She found her handkerchief, covered her face with it, and continued to cry. My position was again an awkward one and continued to be so for a good while. I felt vexed and yet sorry for her. Her tears seemed sincere, but I thought that she was not crying so much about my mother as because she herself was not happy now and things had been much better in those days. I do not know how it would have ended, if young Ívin had not returned and said that his father wanted her. She rose and was just going, when Ivin himself came into the room. He was a short sturdy man with thick black eyebrows, closely cropped and quite grey hair, and a very austere and firm expression of mouth.

I rose and bowed to him, but Ívin, who had three decorations on his green dress-coat, not only did not return my greeting but scarcely looked at me, so that I suddenly felt that I was not a human being but some insignificant thing—a chair or a window, or if human, then such a being as in no way differed from a chair or a window.

"You have not yet written to the countess, my dear," he said to his wife in French, with an impassive but firm expression of face.

"Goodbye, M. Irtényev," his wife said to me, suddenly nodding her head haughtily and looking at my eyebrows as her son had done. I bowed again to her and to her husband, and again my bow affected her husband as the opening or shutting of a window might have done. Student Ívin, however, saw me to the door and told me on the way that he was being transferred to the Petersburg University as his father had received an appointment there—mentioning some very important post."

"Well, whatever papa may say," I muttered to myself as I got into my drozhki, "I will never set foot there again; that mope cries when she looks at me as if I were some unfortunate wretch, and that swine Ívin does not acknowledge my bow; but I'll give it him . . .!" How I was going to give it him I certainly did not know, but the remark seemed appropriate.

Often afterwards I had to put up with the injunctions of my father, who said that it was essential to cultivate that acquaintance and that I could not expect a person in such a position as Ívin's to be attentive to such a youngster as myself, but I held to my resolution for a good while.

XVIII
IN THE COUNTRY

The next day Volódya and I set out with post-horses for the country. On the way, going over various Moscow reminiscences, I remembered Sónya Valákhina, but this only towards evening when we had already gone five stages. "It is strange," thought I, "that I am in love and quite forgot to think of it; I must think about her." And I began thinking of her as one thinks when travelling, not connectedly but vividly, and I thought to such effect that for two days after my arrival in the country I considered it necessary to appear sad and pensive before the household —especially before Kátya whom I regarded as a great expert in such matters and to whom I hinted at the state of my heart. But despite all my efforts to deceive others and myself, and despite the intentional adoption of all the symptoms I had noticed in others who were in love, I only remembered for two days—and that not continuously but chiefly in the evenings—that I was in love, and finally as soon as I entered into the new rut of country life and occupations I quite forgot about my love for Sónya.

We arrived in Petróvskoe in the night, and I was so fast asleep that I saw neither the house nor the birch avenue. Nor did we see any of the household, who had all gone to bed and had long been fast asleep. Bent-backed old Fóka came carrying a candle, barefoot, and with his wife's wadded jacket over his shoulders, to open the door. On seeing us he trembled with joy, kissed our shoulders, hurriedly put away the piece of felt on which he had been sleeping, and began to dress himself. I passed through the hall and up the stairs not yet fully awake, but in the ante-room the lock of the door, the latch, a warped floor-board, the settee, the old candlestick covered with grease as of old, the shadows cast by the crooked flame of the freshly lit tallow candle, the ever-dusty double panes of the window that was never opened, and beyond which grew, as I remembered, a mountain ash were all so familiar, so full of memories, so harmonious—as if united by a common idea—that I suddenly seemed to feel that the dear old house was caressing me. Involuntarily the question presented itself to my mind: how we, the house and I, had managed to live so long apart? and I ran hurriedly to see whether the rooms were all still the same. They were just the same, only they had all become smaller and lower and I seemed to have grown taller, heavier, and coarser; but such as I was, the house received me joyfully into its embrace, and every floor-board, every window, each step of the stair-

case, and every sound awoke in me a host of images, feelings, and memories of occurrences in the irrecoverable,
happy past. We came into our nursery—all the terrors of
childhood's days again lurked in the dusk of the corners
and doorways; we went into the drawing-room—the same
quiet tender mother-love seemed spread over all the objects
in the room; we passed through the ball-room—noisy, care-
free, childish mirth seemed to reside there still and only
waited to be revived. In the sitting-room, where Fóka
took us, and where he had made up beds for us, everything
—the looking-glass, the screen, the old wooden icon, each
unevenness of the white-papered wall—spoke of suffering
and death and of what would never be again.

We went to bed and Fóka left us after saying good-
night.

"Why, this is the room in which mama died!" said
Volódya.

I did not reply and pretended to be asleep. Had I said
anything I should have begun to cry. Next morning when
I awoke, papa was sitting in his dressing-gown, wearing
soft boots, with a cigar in his mouth, on Volódya's bed,
talking and laughing with him. With a merry jerk of his
shoulder he jumped up from Volódya's bed, came to me,
slapped me on the back with his large hand, turned his
cheek to me and pressed it to my lips.

"Well, that's excellent. Thank you, diplomat!" he said,
with his peculiar, affectionate banter, gazing at me with his
small sparkling eyes. "Volódya says you passed your exams
like a brick; well, that's fine. When you make up your mind
not to play the fool, you, too, are a fine lad. Thank you,
my dear! Now we shall have a good time here, and in
winter we may perhaps move to Petersburg. It's a pity
though that hunting is over, else I'd have given you a treat;
but can you hunt with a gun, Vóldemar? There's plenty
of game, and I may go out with you myself one day. Then
in winter, please God, we'll move to Petersburg, and you'll
meet people and make acquaintances. I've now got grown-
up fellows in you. As I was just saying to Vóldemar, you
are now on the road and my work is done, you can go by
yourselves, but if you want to consult me, do so. I am no
longer your usher but your friend; at any rate I wish to
be your friend and comrade and adviser as far as I can,

and nothing more. How does that match your philosophy, Nicky, eh? Is it good or bad? Eh?"

Of course I said it was splendid, and I really found it so. Papa seemed particularly attractive, bright, and happy that day. His new relations with me as with an equal, a comrade, made me love him more than ever.

"Well, tell me, have you been to see all our relations? The Ívins? Did you see the old man? What did he say to you?" he went on questioning me. "Did you call on Prince Iván?"

We talked so long without dressing that the sun had already begun to move away from the window and Jacob (who seemed just as old, still twiddled his thumbs behind his back, and still said "on the other hand") came into our room to tell papa that the calash was ready.

"Where are you going?" I asked papa.

"Oh, I almost forgot," said papa with a jerk of vexation and a slight cough, "I promised to go and see the Epifánovs to-day. You remember Mademoiselle Epifánova—*la belle Flamande*? . . . She used to come to see your mama. They are excellent people." And papa, jerking his shoulder, bashfully as it seemed to me, left the room.

While we were talking, Lyúba had come to the door several times and asked whether she might come in, but papa each time had shouted to her through the door, "On no account, we are not dressed."

"What does it matter? I've often seen you in your dressing-gown!"

"You cannot see your brothers without their *inexpressibles*," he called to her, "but they will both of them rap on the door to you. Is that enough? Go and rap! It is not even proper for them to speak to you in such a dishabille."

"Oh, what a nuisance you are! Then at least be quick and come to the drawing-room. Mimi is so anxious to see you," shouted Lyúba through the door.

As soon as papa had gone I dressed quickly in my student's uniform and went to the drawing-room. Volódya on the contrary did not hurry and stayed upstairs a long time talking to Jacob and asking him where snipe and double-snipe were to be found. As I have already intimated, he feared nothing so much as what he called "tenderness"

with his brother, his father, or his sister, and avoiding
every show of sentiment, he went to the opposite extreme
—a coldness that often hurt people who did not understand
its cause. In the anteroom I stumbled on papa, who with
short rapid steps was on his way to take his seat in the
calash. He was wearing his new fashionable Moscow coat
and smelt of perfume. When he saw me he nodded merrily,
as if to say, "You see, it is fine!" and I was again struck
by the happy expression of his eyes, which I had noticed
that morning.

The drawing-room was still the same bright and lofty
room, with the yellow-coloured English grand piano and
large open windows, into which the green trees looked
merrily over the reddish-yellow garden paths. Having kissed
Lyúba and Mimi, on going up to Kátya it suddenly occurred
to me that it would no longer be proper for me to kiss her,
and blushing, I stopped short in silence. Kátya without
being at all confused held out her little white hand and
congratulated me on having entered the university. When
Volódya came into the drawing-room and met Kátya, the
same thing happened to him. It was really difficult to
make up one's mind how we, who had grown up together
and seen each other every day, were to behave now on
meeting again after our first separation. Kátya blushed
more than either of us. Volódya was not at all abashed
but, bowing lightly to her, went over to Lyúba and having
spoken to her for a short time, and not at all seriously,
went out for a walk alone.

XXIX

OUR RELATIONS WITH THE GIRLS

Volódya had such strange opinions of the girls that he
could pay attention to whether they had had enough to
eat, whether they had slept well, whether they were
properly dressed, and whether they made mistakes in
French which would cause him to feel ashamed before
strangers, but he did not admit the thought that they
could think or feel anything human and still less admitted
the possibility of discussing anything with them. If they
happened to ask him some serious question (which, however, they already avoided doing), if they asked his

opinion about some novel or about his work at the university, he made a face at them and went away without speaking, or answered in broken French, such as *"Com ce tri jauli,"*[2] or put on a serious, intentionally stupid expression, and said some word that had no meaning or connexion with their question, uttering with a dull look in his eyes words like *"bun,"* *"gone driving,"* *"cabbage,"* or something like that. If I happened to repeat to him something Lyúba or Kátya had told me he always said, "Hm, so you still discuss with them! No, I see you are not yet up to much."

And one must have heard and seen him then to appreciate the deep unalterable contempt those words expressed. Volódya had now been grown up for two years and was always falling in love with every pretty woman he met, but though he saw Kátya every day, and she had been wearing long dresses for two years already and grew prettier every day, the possibility of falling in love with her never occurred to him. Whether this was the result of prosaic childhood memories—the ruler, the bathsheet, the caprices—still too fresh in his memory, or of the repulsion very young people feel from everything domestic, or of the common human inclination to neglect the good and beautiful they first meet, saying to themselves: "Eh, I shall come across much of that sort in my life!"—whatever the reason, Volódya till then did not regard Kátya as a woman.

Volódya seemed greatly bored all that summer; his boredom resulted from his contempt of us, which as I have mentioned he did not try to conceal. The constant expression of his face said: "Pfu! How dull! And there's no one to talk to!" He would go out with his gun in the morning or would stay in his room without dressing till dinner-time, reading a book. When papa was not at home, Volódya even came to dinner with a book and continued to read it, not speaking to any of us, which made us all feel as if we were guilty towards him. In the evening too he would lie with his feet up on the sofa in the drawing-room and sleep, leaning on his arm,

---

[1] *Comme c'est très joli.* (How very pretty that is!)

or with a serious countenance would talk terrible, sometimes rather improper, nonsense, which made Mimi furious and caused her to flush in spots, while we died with
laughter, but except with papa, and very occasionally with
me, he never deigned to speak seriously to any member
of the household.

In my view of the girls I quite involuntarily followed
my brother, though I did not fear susceptibility as he
did, and my contempt for them was far from being as
deep and decided as his. From dullness that summer I
even tried to get nearer to, and to talk with, Lyúba and
Kátya, but each time I found such a lack of capacity
to think logically and such ignorance of the simplest
and commonest things, such, for instance, as what money
is, what is studied at the university, what war is, and
so on, and such indifference to the explanations of these
things, that my attempts only confirmed my unfavourable
opinion of them.

I remember one evening Lyúba was repeating for the
hundredth time some intolerably tiresome passage on
the piano, while Volódya lay dozing on the drawing-
room sofa, occasionally muttering with a sort of malevolent irony, not speaking to any one in particular. "She
does bang! . . . Musicianess! . . . *Bithoven!*" (he pronounced that name in a tone of particular irony) "Tremendous! . . . Now once again! . . . That's it!" and so on.
Kátya and I remained at the table, and I remember
that she somehow led the conversation to her favourite
subject—love. I was in a mood to philosophize and began
condescendingly to define love as the desire to obtain
from another what one lacks oneself, etc. But Kátya
replied that, on the contrary, it is not love when a girl
thinks of marrying a rich man, and that in her opinion,
possessions were a most unimportant matter, and that it
is real love only if it can endure a separation (I understood this to be a hint at her love for Dubkóv). Volódya,
who no doubt heard our conversation, suddenly raised
himself on his elbow and interrogatively exclaimed,
"Kátya—*the Russians?*"

"Always nonsense," said Kátya.

"*Into the pepper-pot?*" Volódya went on, accentuating

each vowel, and I could not help thinking that he was quite right.

Besides the general mental faculty, more or less developed in different individuals, of sentiment and artistic feeling, there exists, more or less developed in different circles of society and especially in families, a special capacity which I call *understanding*. The gist of this capacity is a conventional sense of proportion and a conventional and particular outlook on things. Two people of the same set or family who have this faculty always permit an expression of feeling up to a certain point beyond which they both see only empty phrases. They both see at the same moment where praise ceases and irony begins, where enthusiasm ends and pretence begins—which may all seem quite different to people having different ideas. People of the same understanding are struck by anything equally, chiefly on its comic, its beautiful, or its nasty side. To help this common understanding between people of the same set or family, a language of their own establishes itself—their own special turns of speech and even words, which indicate shades of meaning non-existent for others. In our family, this understanding was developed in the highest degree between papa and us brothers. Dubkóv, too, fitted well in with our circle and *understood*. Dmítri, however, though far more intelligent, was dull in this respect. But with no one had I developed this capacity to such a point as with Volódya, with whom I had grown up under the same conditions. Papa already lagged far behind us, and much that was as clear to us as twice two was incomprehensible to him. For instance, heaven knows why, the following words were accepted between Volódya and me with their corresponding meaning: *raisins* meant a conceited desire to show that one has money; *shell* (with one finger of each hand touching and a special stress on the *sh*) meant something fresh, healthy, and refined, but not showy; a noun used in the plural indicated a special liking for that object, etc., etc. However, the meaning depended most of all on the expression of one's face and on the general conversation, so that no matter what new word one of us might invent to express a new shade of meaning, the other, at the first hint, understood it the same way. The girls did not have this *understanding* of ours, and that was the chief cause of our mental disunion and of the contempt we felt for them.

They may have had an understanding of their own, but it did not coincide with ours, so that where we already descried empty phrases they saw feeling, and what to us was irony to them was truth, and so on. But at that time I did not understand that they were not to blame for this and that this absence of understanding did not prevent their being pretty and intelligent girls, and I despised them. Then, having taken up with the idea of frankness and carried its application in myself to an extreme, I accused the calm and confiding Lyúba, who saw no necessity for digging up and examining all her thoughts and impulses, of secretiveness and pretence. For instance, the fact that Lyúba made the sign of the cross over papa every night, that she and Kátya wept in the chapel where we went when mass was said for our mother, or that Kátya sighed and rolled her eyes when playing the piano—all seemed to me extreme dissimulation, and I asked myself when had they learnt to pretend like grown-up people, and why were they not ashamed to do it?

∽∾∾

XXXIV
OUR FATHER'S MARRIAGE

My father was forty-eight when he married his second wife, Avdótya Vasílyevna Epifánova.

Having come to the country with only the girls, papa, I imagine, was in the peculiar agitatedly happy and sociable state of mind gamblers usually are in when they stop playing after winning much. He felt that he had still a great store of unspent happiness which, if he no longer wished to spend it on cards, he might devote to general success in life. Besides, it was spring; he had unexpectedly much money and was alone and dull. Talking business affairs over with Jacob and recalling the endless litigation with the Epifánovs, and the beautiful Avdótya Vasílyevna whom he had not seen for a long time, I imagine him saying to Jacob: "Do you know, Jacob Kharlámpych, instead of bothering about that lawsuit I think it would be simpler to let them have that damned land, eh? What do you think?"

I imagine how Jacob's thumbs began to twist negatively behind his back at such a question, and how he argued that: "On the other hand, ours is a just case, sir."

But papa ordered his calash, put on his new-fashioned olive Hungarian coat, brushed the remainder of his hair, sprinkled his handkerchief with scent, and in the gayest spirits, aroused by the conviction that he was behaving like a gentleman and above all by the hope of meeting a good-looking woman, went to call on his neighbours.

I only know that on his first visit papa did not find Peter Epifánov, who was out in the fields, and spent a couple of hours alone with the ladies. I imagine how he launched out into compliments, how he charmed them, tapping the floor with his soft boot, whispering, and looking sentimental. I imagine too how the merry old lady suddenly began to like him, and how her cold, beautiful daughter brightened up.

When a maid ran, panting, to inform Peter Epifánov that old Irtényev himself had arrived, I imagine how Peter crossly replied: "Well, what if he has arrived?" and how in consequence he walked home as slowly as he could, and perhaps also on reaching his room purposely put on his dirtiest coat and sent to tell the cook that if his mistress ordered him to cook anything extra for dinner he should on no account do so.

I often saw papa and Epifánov together afterwards and so can vividly imagine that first meeting. I imagine how, though papa offered to settle their dispute amicably, Peter remained morose and cross, because he had sacrificed his career for his mother while papa had done nothing of the kind; how nothing surprised him, and how papa, as if unaware of that moroseness, was playful, gay, and treated Peter as a wonderful humorist—which Peter sometimes resented, though occasionally against his will he could not help yielding to it. Papa, with his inclination to treat everything as a joke, called Peter "Colonel" for some reason or other, and although the latter once, stammering worse than usual and blushing with vexation, remarked in my presence that he was not a "co-co-co-colonel, but a lieu-lieu-lieu-lieutenant",[1] papa five minutes later, again addressed him as Colonel.

Lyúba told me that before we came to the country they saw the Epifánovs every day and had an extremely good time. Papa, with his skill at arranging everything with originality, humorously, and yet simply and with good taste, got up some hunting, fishing, and some fireworks, at which the Epifánovs were present. "And it would have been still jollier if that insufferable Peter Vasílich had not been present; sulking, stammering, and upsetting everything," Lyúba remarked.

After our arrival the Epifánovs had only been twice to see us, and once we all drove to their house. But after St. Peter's day, papa's name-day, when they and a crowd of visitors came, our intercourse with the Epifánovs for some reason ceased completely and papa alone continued to visit them.

During the short time that I saw papa together with Avdótya—or Dúnichka,[2] as her mother called her—I managed to notice the following: Papa was always in the same happy frame of mind as had struck me on the day of our arrival. He was so gay, young, full of life, and happy that the beams of his happiness spread to all around and involuntarily infected them with the same mood. He did not go a step away from Avdótya Vasílyevna when she was in the room, continually paid her such sickly-sweet compliments that I felt ashamed for him, or, gazing silently at her, twitched his shoulder in a passionate and self-satisfied kind of way, coughed, sometimes smiled, and even whispered to her; but he did it all quite in the jesting way characteristic of him even in very serious matters.

Avdótya Vasílyevna seemed to have assimilated papa's

---

[1] The Russian words for colonel and lieutenant begin with the same syllable, which may furnish some shadow of excuse for Irtényev's confusion of them.

[2] Dúnichka is a diminutive, and a rather contemptuous diminutive, of Avdótya.

happy expression, which at that time shone in her large blue eyes almost continually, except when she was suddenly seized with such shyness that I, who knew that feeling, felt pained and sorry to see her. At such moments she seemed to be afraid of every glance or movement, imagined that every one was looking at her, thinking only of her, and finding everything about her improper. She looked around at everybody in alarm, the colour came and went in her face, and she began to speak loudly and boldly, uttering nonsense for the most part, felt this, and felt that everybody, including papa, had heard her, and then blushed still more. But on such occasions papa did not even notice the nonsense; he continued coughing just as passionately and looking at her with joyous rapture. I noticed that these fits of shyness, though they used to occur without any reason, sometimes immediately followed a mention in papa's presence of some young and beautiful woman. Her frequent transitions from pensiveness to the kind of strange and awkward gaiety to which I have already referred, her use of papa's favourite words and turns of speech, her way of continuing with others a conversation begun with papa—all this, if the person concerned had not been my own father or had I been a little older, would have explained to me what their relations were, but at that time I suspected nothing, even when on receiving in my presence a letter from Peter Epifánov, papa seemed much upset and ceased his visits to the Epifánovs till the end of August.

At the end of August papa again began visiting our neighbours, and the day before Volódya and I left for Moscow he announced to us that he was going to marry Avdótya Vasílyevna Epifánova.

XXXV

HOW WE TOOK THE NEWS

On the day before this official announcement every one in the house knew and discussed the matter from various sides. Mimí did not leave her room all day and wept. Kátya stayed with her and only came out to dinner, with an injured expression on her face evidently borrowed from her mother; Lyúba on the other hand was very cheerful and remarked at dinner that she knew a splendid secret which however she would not tell any one.

"There is nothing splendid in your secret," Volódya said to her, by no means sharing her satisfaction. "If you could think seriously about anything, you would understand that on the contrary it's very bad."

Lyúba looked intently at him with amazement and said no more.

After dinner Volódya was about to take my arm, but probably afraid that this would look like susceptibility, merely touched my elbow and nodded his head towards the ball-room.

"Do you know what secret Lyúba was speaking about?" he asked when he was sure we were alone.

Volódya and I seldom spoke to one another alone and about anything serious, so that when this happened we felt a kind of mutual awkwardness, and "specks began to dance in our eyes," as he phrased it. But that day, in response to my look of confusion, he continued to gaze seriously straight into my eyes with an expression which seemed to say: "There's no need for confusion. After all we are brothers and must consult together on family matters." I understood him, and he continued: "Papa is going to marry the Epifánova, you know."

I nodded, because I had already heard about it.

"You know it's not at all good!" Volódya continued.

"Why?"

"Why?" he replied with vexation. "It's very pleasant to have a stammering uncle like that colonel, and all those connexions. Besides, though she now seems kindly and all right, who knows how she'll turn out later? Granted that it won't matter to us, but Lyúba must soon come out into the world. With a stepmother like that it won't be very pleasant. She even speaks French badly, and what kind of manners can she give her? She's a fishwife, that's all she is—perhaps a kindly one, but nevertheless a fishwife," Volódya concluded, evidently pleased with the term "fishwife."

Strange as it was to me to hear Volódya judging papa's choice so calmly, he seemed to me to be right.

"Why is papa marrying?" I asked.

"That's a queer story. Heaven only knows! All I know

is that Peter Epifánov persuaded him and insisted that he should marry her; that papa did not want to, and then the fancy seized him out of some idea of chivalry. It's a queer story! I am only now beginning to understand father," Volódya continued (that he called him "father" and not "papa" stung me painfully). "He is a fine man, kind and intelligent, but such lightmindedness and flightiness—it's amazing! He can't look at a woman calmly. Why, you know that he has never been acquainted with a woman without falling in love with her. You know Mimí too . . ."

"What do you mean?"

"I tell you it is so. I found it out only a while ago; he was in love with Mimí when she was young, and wrote verses to her, and there was something between them. Mimí suffers till now!" and Volódya laughed.

"Impossible!" I said, with surprise.

"But the chief thing is," Volódya went on, becoming serious again and beginning to speak in French, "how pleased all our relations will be at such a marriage! And she'll be sure to have children."

I was so struck by Volódya's sensible view and foresight that I did not know what to say.

At that moment Lyúba came in.

"So you know?" she said with a happy look.

"Yes," answered Volódya, "but I am surprised, Lyúba —after all you are not a babe in arms—that you should be pleased that papa is marrying some sort of riff-raff!"

Lyúba suddenly looked grave and became thoughtful.

"Why riff-raff, Volódya? How dare you speak so of Avdótya Vasílyevna? If papa is going to marry her, of course she is not riff-raff."

"Well—not riff-raff—I only put it like that, but all the same . . ."

"There's no 'all the same' about it," Lyúba interrupted him warmly. "I did not say that the young lady you are in love with was riff-raff. How can you speak like that about papa and a splendid woman? Though you are my eldest brother, do not say that to me. You must not say it!"

"But why should we not discuss . . .?"

"One must not discuss," Lyúba interrupted again, "one

must not discuss a father like ours. Mimí may discuss him, but not you, our eldest brother."

"No, you don't understand anything yet!" said Volódya contemptuously. "You just think! Will it be nice that some Epifánova—Dúnichka—should take the place of your dead mother?"

Lyúba was silent for a moment and tears suddenly rose to her eyes.

"I knew you were proud, but I did not think you were so spiteful," she said, and went away.

"*Into the bun*," said Volódya, making a serio-comic face and with a vacant look. "There now, just try to argue with them," he continued as if reproaching himself for having so far forgotten himself as to deign to converse with Lyúba.

The weather was bad the next morning, and neither papa nor the ladies had come down to breakfast when I entered the drawing-room. There had been a cold autumnal rain during the night; the remnants of the clouds that had almost emptied themselves during the night were flying across the sky, and the light disk of the sun, already high in the heavens, shone dimly through them. It was windy, damp, and cold. The door was open into the garden, and puddles left by the night's rain were drying on the floor of the verandah, dark with moisture. The open door, fastened back with a cabin-hook, shook in the wind; the paths were damp and muddy; the old birches with their bare white boughs, the bushes, the grass, the nettles, the currant and elder-bushes with the pale linings of their leaves turned outward, swaying in their places, seemed to be trying to tear themselves from their roots. Down the lime-tree avenue, whirling and chasing one another, the round yellow leaves came flying and lay down saturated on the path and on the dark-green aftermath of the meadow. My thoughts were occupied with my father's impending marriage, from the point of view from which Volódya regarded it. My sisters' future, our own, and even our father's did not seem to me to promise anything good. I was filled with indignation at the thought that an outsider, a stranger, and above all a *young* woman without any right to it, should usurp in many ways the place of—whom? An ordinary *young* lady would usurp the place of my dead mother! I felt sad, and my father seemed to me more and more to blame. Just then I heard him talking with Volódya in the pantry. I did not want to see my father at that moment and I passed out through the door, but Lyúba came for me and said that papa was asking for me.

He was standing in the drawing-room leaning with his hand on the piano and looking impatiently and yet solemnly in my direction. There was no longer that look of youth and happiness on his face which I had observed on it all this time. He was sad. Volódya was pacing the room with a pipe in his hand. I came up to my father and wished him good morning.

"Well, my dears," he said with decision, raising his head and in that peculiarly brisk tone in which evidently unpleasant things which it is too late to discuss are spoken of. "I think you know that I am going to marry Avdótya Vasílyevna—" he paused. "I never meant to marry again after your mama . . . but—" he hesitated for a moment "—but it is evidently fate! Dúnya is a good, kind girl and no longer very young. I hope you will learn to love her children, and she already loves you from her heart. She is good. You," he said, turning to me and Volódya and hurrying to speak for fear we might interrupt him, "will soon be going, but I shall remain here till the New Year and will come to Moscow," he hesitated again, "with my wife and Lyúba." It pained me to see my father apparently feeling abashed and guilty towards us, and I went nearer to him, but Volódya, continuing to smoke and hanging his head, still paced up and down the room.

"Ah, yes, my dears, see what your old father has taken into his head!" papa concluded, blushing, coughing, and holding out his hands to Volódya and me. There were tears in his eyes as he said this and I noticed that the hand which he held out to Volódya, who was at the other side of the room just then, trembled a little. The sight of that trembling hand struck me painfully and a strange thought occurred to me and touched me still more, namely, that papa had served in the campaign of 1812 and was well known to be a brave officer. I kept his large, muscular hand in mine and kissed it. He pressed mine closely and, gulping down his tears, suddenly took Lyúba's dark little head in his hands and kissed her on the eyes. Volódya pretended to drop his pipe, bent down, stealthily wiped his eyes with his fist, and, trying not to be noticed, went out of the room.

XXXVI

THE UNIVERSITY

The wedding was to take place in a fortnight; but our lectures at the university were beginning, and Volódya and I went back to Moscow in the first days of September. The Nekhlyúdovs also returned from the country. Dmítri (with whom at parting I had exchanged promises to write, though of course neither of us had written the other a single letter) came to see me at once, and it was arranged that he should take me with him to the university for my first lecture.

It was a bright and sunny day.

As soon as I entered the auditorium I felt my personality disappearing in the throng of gay young people which, in the bright sunshine flowing in through the large windows, surged noisily through all the corridors and doorways.

The consciousness of being a member of that great company was very pleasant. But I knew only a very few of all these people, and my acquaintanceship with them went no farther than a nod and the words: "How d'you do, Irtényev?" Around me there was hand-shaking, pushing—smiles and friendly words and jests showered from all sides. I was conscious everywhere of the bond uniting this youthful company and felt with sorrow that this bond seemed to miss me. But this was only a momentary impression. As a consequence of this and of the vexation born of it, I soon concluded that it was even a very good thing that I did not belong to all that society, that I must have a circle of my own, of decent people, and I took a seat on the third bench, where Count B., Baron Z., Prince R., Ívin, and others of that class sat—of whom I knew Ívin and Count B. But these gentlemen too looked at me so that I felt I did not quite belong to them either. I began noticing all that went on around me.

Semënov with his rumpled grey hair, white teeth, and unbuttoned coat sat not far from me and, leaning on his elbows, gnawed a quill pen. The high-school lad who had been first at the examinations sat on the front bench with a black neck-cloth still tied round his cheek, and played with a silver watch-key that hung on his satin waistcoat. Ikónin, who had after all managed to enter the university, sat on a raised bench, wearing pale-blue trousers with stripes down the seams and that hung quite over his boots, laughing, and shouting out that he was on Parnassus. Ílinka, who to my surprise bowed to me coldly and even contemptuously as if wishing to remind me that we were all equals here, sat in front of me and, throwing his thin legs on to the bench in a very free-and-easy manner (on my account as it seemed to me), talked with another student and occasionally glanced round at me. Beside me the Ívin set were talking French. These gentlemen appeared to me awfully stupid. Every word I heard of their conversation seemed to me not merely senseless but even incorrect, simply not French (*"Ce n'est pas français"* I said to myself), and the attitude, the words, and the actions of Semënov, Ílinka, and the others of their set seemed to me ungenteel, incorrect, and not *comme il faut.*

I did not belong to any group, and feeling myself isolated and incapable of sociability, I chafed. A student on the bench in front of me bit his nails, and his fingers with red hangnails seemed so disgusting that I even moved farther away from him. I was, I remember, sad at heart that first day.

When the Professor entered everybody moved and then became silent. I remember that my satirical observation extended to him and I was struck by his beginning his lecture with an introductory sentence which, in my opinion, did not make sense. I wanted the lecture to be so clever from beginning to end that it would be impossible to omit, or add to it, a single word. Disappointed in this, under the heading "First Lecture" written in a handsomely bound note-book I had brought with me, I immediately sketched eighteen profiles, forming a wreath-like circle, and only occasionally moved my hand across the page that the Professor (who I felt convinced was much interested in me) might think I was taking notes.

Having at this lecture decided that it was unnecessary, and would even be foolish, to take down everything that each of the professors said, I kept to this rule to the end of the course.

At the following lectures I did not feel so isolated; I became acquainted with many of the students, shook hands, and talked, but for some reason real intimacy between me and my comrades was still lacking, and it therefore often happened that I felt sad at heart and pretended. With Ívin's set of "aristocrats," as everybody called them, I could not become intimate because, as I now remember, I was shy and rude with them and only bowed when they had first bowed to me, and they seemed to have very little need of my company. With the majority, however, the cause was quite a different one. As soon as I felt that a fellow-student was becoming well-disposed towards me, I immediately gave him to understand that I dined with Prince Iván and had my own trap. I said all this merely to show myself off to better advantage and that my fellow-student should like me the more for it, but on the contrary almost every time, to my amazement, my comrade, as a result of the information that I was related to Prince Iván and had a trap, suddenly became proud and cold to me.

We had among us a bursar-student, Opérov, a modest, very capable, and industrious young man, who always offered his hand as if it were a board, not bending his fingers or moving them at all, so that the jesters among his comrades also held out theirs "like little boards" as they called it, when they shook hands with him. I almost always took a seat beside him and often talked with him. I specially liked Opérov because of the free opinions he expressed about the professors. He defined the merits and defects of each professor's lecture very clearly and precisely and even occasionally ridiculed them, which seemed to me specially strange and striking when spoken in his quiet voice and coming from his tiny mouth. Nevertheless he carefully noted down, in his minute handwriting, all the lectures without exception. We were already becoming intimate and had decided to prepare for the examinations together, and his small grey short-sighted eyes had already begun to turn towards me with pleasure when I came to sit beside him, when I found it necessary to tell him once in the course of conversation that my mother, when dying, had asked my father not to send us to any institution supported by the crown, and that all crown scholars, though they might be very learned, seemed to me not at all the thing—*"Ce ne sont pas des gens comme il faut,"* I said falteringly and feeling that I was growing red for some reason. Opérov said nothing to me, but at the following lectures he did not greet me first, did not hold out his "board" to me, and when I took my seat, bent his head to one side close to his note-books as if examining them. I was surprised by his causeless coolness, but I considered that *pour un jeune homme de bonne maison*[1] it would not be proper to curry favour with a bursar-student like Opérov, and I left him alone, although I confess that his coolness grieved me. Once I arrived earlier than he, and as the lecture was by a favourite professor to which students came who did not always attend, and all the places were occupied, I took Opérov's place, laid my note-books on the desk, and went out. On returning to the auditorium I saw that my note-books had been moved to a place farther back and Opérov was sitting in my place. I remarked to him that I had put my note-books there.

"I don't know," he said, suddenly flushing up and not looking at me.

"I tell you I put my note-books here," said I, purposely getting heated and thinking to frighten him by my boldness. "Everybody saw it," I added, turning to the other students, but though many looked at me with curiosity no one responded.

"The places here are not purchased; the one who comes first takes the seat," said Opérov, moving in his place and momentarily giving me an indignant glance.

"That shows you are ill-bred," I said.

I think Opérov muttered something. I even thought he said: "and you are a stupid urchin." I did not hear it clearly. Besides, where would have been the use if I had heard?—only to have a quarrel like some *manant* (boor). (I was very fond of that word *manant*, and it served me

---

[1] For a young man of good family.

as an answer to and a solution of many perplexities.) I might have said something more, but at that moment the door slammed and the professor, in his blue dress-coat, bowed and hastily ascended the platform.

Before the examinations, however, when I was in need of the notes, Opérov, remembering his promise, offered me his and invited me to study with him.

⟁⟁⟁

XXXIX
THE CAROUSAL

Though, under the influence of Dmítri, I had not yet taken up the ordinary student amusements called *carousals*, it happened that I took part in one that winter and carried away a not altogether pleasant impression. This is what occurred.

At a lecture at the beginning of the year, Baron Z., a tall, fair-haired young man with a very serious expression on his regular features, invited us all to a comrades' evening. "All" of course meant all the first-year students who were more or less *comme il faut*; among whom, naturally, neither Grap, Semënov, Opérov, nor any of that rather poor lot were included. Volódya smiled contemptuously when he heard that I was going to a carouse of first-year men; but I expected great and unusual pleasure from this, which was still to me a quite unknown pastime, and punctually at eight o'clock I reached Baron Z's.

Baron Z., with his coat unbuttoned over a white waistcoat, received his visitors in the brightly lit ballroom and drawing-room of a small house in which his parents lived; they had let him have the reception-rooms for that evening's festivities. I caught sight of the dresses and heads of inquisitive maids in the passage and once had a glimpse of the dress of a lady, whom I took to be the Baroness herself, in the pantry. There were about twenty guests, all students except Herr Frost, who had come with the Ívins, and a very rosy tall civilian who conducted the festivities and was introduced to every one as a relative of the Baron and a former student of

Dorpat University. The overbright illumination and the usual formal arrangement of the reception rooms had at first such a chilling effect on the youthful company that every one involuntarily kept to the walls, except a few bold spirits and the Dorpat student who, having already unbuttoned his waistcoat, seemed to be in both rooms at once and in every corner of each room, filling the whole apartment with his agreeable, resonant, and never-ceasing tenor voice. But the students either kept silent or modestly conversed about their professors, studies, examinations, and serious and interesting subjects in general. All without exception kept glancing at the pantry door and, though they tried to conceal it, their looks seemed to say: "Well, isn't it time to begin?" I too felt it was time to begin and expected *the beginning* with impatient joy.

After tea, which was served to the visitors by footmen, the Dorpat student asked Frost in Russian: "Can you make punch, Frost?"

"*O ja!*"[1] Frost answered, wriggling his calves, but the Dorpat student said, again in Russian, "well then, take it in hand," (as ex-fellow-students at the Dorpat University they were familiar with one another); and Frost, with big strides of his muscular legs, began moving backwards and forwards from drawing-room to pantry, and from pantry to drawing-room, and soon a large soup-tureen appeared on the table with a ten-pound sugar-loaf poised above it on three crossed students' swords. Baron Z. meanwhile kept approaching all the visitors, who had assembled in the drawing-room looking at the soup-tureen, and with unalterably serious face said to each one almost in the same words: "Let us all pass the glass round student-fashion, and drink *Bruderschaft*,[2] without it there is no comradeship at all in our set. But unbutton your coats, or take them off altogether as he has done!" The Dorpat student had, in fact, taken off his coat and, with his white shirt-sleeves turned up above his elbows and his legs spread resolutely apart, was already setting fire to the rum in the soup-tureen.

---

[1] German for "Oh, yes."

[2] To drink *Bruderschaft* (Brotherhood) is a German custom. They drink with arms interlinked and afterwards address each other in the secon person singular, a sign of intimacy.

"Gentlemen, put out the lights!" he suddenly exclaimed, as loudly and commandingly as though we had all been shouting. But we were all silently gazing at the soup-tureen and the Dorpat student's shirt, and we all felt that the solemn moment had arrived.

"*Löschen sie die Lichter aus,* Frost!"[3] the Dorpat student shouted again, this time in German, probably having become too excited. Frost and all of us began putting out the lights. The room grew dark, only the white sleeves and the hands supporting the sugar-loaf on the swords were lit up by the bluish flame. The Dorpat student's loud tenor was no longer the only voice heard, for talking and laughter came from every corner of the room. Many took off their coats (especially those who had fine and quite clean shirts). I did the same, and realized that it *had begun.* Though nothing jolly had happened, I was firmly convinced all the same that it would be capital when each of us had drunk a glass of the beverage that was being prepared.

The drink was ready. The Dorpat student, soiling the table considerably, filled the glasses and shouted: "Now then, gentlemen, come along!" When each of us had taken one of the full, sticky tumblers, the Dorpat student and Frost began singing a German song in which the exclamation *juche!*[4] was frequently repeated. We all joined in discordantly, began to clink glasses, to shout something, to praise the punch, and with arms linked or not, began drinking the strong, sweet liquor. There was now nothing to wait for—the carouse was in full swing. I had already drunk a whole glass of punch; they refilled my glass. My temples were throbbing, the flame looked blood-red, every one around me was shouting and laughing, but still it not only did not seem gay but I was convinced that I and all the others were dull, and that for some reason or other we all merely thought it necessary to pretend that it was very jolly. The only one perhaps who did not pretend was the Dorpat student; he became ever redder and redder and seemed more than ever omnipresent, filling everybody's empty glass, and

[3] "Put out the lights."
[4] Hurrah!

spilling more and more over the table which had become all sweet and sticky. I do not remember how events followed each other, but I remember that during that evening I was awfully fond of the Dorpat student and Frost and was learning the German song by heart and kissing them both on their sugary lips; I also remember that I hated the Dorpat student that same evening and wished to throw a chair at him but restrained myself. I remember also that besides the feeling of disobedience in all my limbs that I had experienced on the day of the dinner at Yar's, my head so ached and swam that evening that I felt terribly afraid I was going to die then and there; I also recollect that we all sat down on the floor—I don't know why—and swung our arms, pretending to row, and sang, "Adown the river, Mother Volga" and that I thought at the time that it was quite unnecessary to do so. I also remember lying on the floor and wrestling gipsy-fashion with interlocked legs, twisting some one's neck and thinking that this would not have happened had he not been drunk. Then I remember we had supper and drank something else; that I repeatedly went outside to refresh myself, and my head felt cold, and that on leaving I noticed that it was terribly dark, that the step of my trap had become slanting and slippery, and that it was impossible to hold on to Kuzmá because he had become weak and swayed about like a rag. But above all I remember constantly feeling that evening that I was behaving very stupidly, pretending to feel very jolly and to be very fond of drinking a great deal, and that I was not at all tipsy, and that I felt all the time that the others were also behaving very stupidly by pretending the same. It seemed to me that each of them separately was uncomfortable as I was but, imagining that only he had that uncomfortable feeling, each one considered himself bound to pretend to be merry in order not to infringe the general gaiety. Moreover, strange to say, I considered myself obliged to pretend, merely because three bottles of champagne at ten rubles each and ten bottles of rum at four rubles each—which came to seventy rubles—had been poured into the soup-tureen, apart from the cost of the supper. I felt so convinced of this that at the lecture next day I was greatly surprised that my comrades who had been at Baron Z.'s party not only were not ashamed to recall what they had done there but spoke of it so that other students could hear. They said it had been a splendid carouse, that Dorpat students were fine fellows at that sort of thing, and that forty bottles of rum had been drunk by twenty men, and many had been left dead-drunk under the tables. I could not understand why they not only talked of it but even told lies about themselves.

PART TWO

Fiction in
the Years of
War and Peace

〜〜〜〜〜〜〜〜〜〜〜〜〜〜〜〜〜〜〜〜〜

THE RAID
A Volunteer's
Story

The portions of this story enclosed in square brackets are those the Censor suppressed, and are now published in English for the first time. —A.M.

I

[War always interested me: not war in the sense of manoeuvres devised by great generals—my imagination refused to follow such immense movements, I did not understand them—but the reality of war, the actual killing. I was more interested to know in what way and under the influence of what feeling one soldier kills another than to know how the armies were arranged at Austerlitz and Borodinó.

I had long passed the time when, pacing the room alone and waving my arms, I imagined myself a hero instantaneously slaughtering an immense number of men and receiving a generalship as well as imperishable glory for so doing. The question now occupying me was different: under the influence of what feeling does a man, with no apparent advantage to himself, decide to subject himself to danger and, what is more surprising still, to kill his fellow men? I always wished to think that this is done under the influence of anger, but we cannot suppose that all those who fight are angry all the time, and I had to postulate feelings of self-preservation and duty.

What is courage—that quality respected in all ages and among all nations? Why is this good quality—contrary to all others—sometimes met with in vicious men? Can it be that to endure danger calmly is merely a physical capacity and that people respect it in the same way that they do a man's tall stature or robust frame? Can a horse be called brave, which fearing the whip throws itself down a steep place where it will be smashed to pieces; or child who fearing to be punished runs into a forest where it will lose itself; or a woman who for fear of shame kills her baby and has to endure penal prosecution; or a man who from vanity resolves to kill a fellow creature and exposes himself to the danger of being killed?

In every danger there is a choice. Does it not depend on whether the choice is prompted by a noble feeling or a base one whether it should be called courage or cowardice? These were the questions and the doubts that occupied my mind and to decide which I intended to avail myself of the first opportunity to go into action.

In the summer of 184– I was living in the Caucasus at the small fortified post of N————.]

On the twelfth of July Captain Khlópov entered the low door of my earth-hut. He was wearing epaulettes and carrying a sword, which I had never before seen him do since I had reached the Caucasus.

"I come straight from the colonel's," he said in answer to my questioning look. "To-morrow our battalion is to march."

"Where to?" I asked.

"To M. The forces are to assemble there."

"And from there I suppose they will go into action?"

"I expect so."

"In what direction? What do you think?"

"What is there to think about? I am telling you what I know. A Tartar galloped here last night and brought orders from the general for the battalion to march with two days' rations of rusks. But where to, why, and for how long, we do not ask, my friend. We are told to go— and that's enough."

"But if you are to take only two days' rations of rusks it proves that the troops won't be out longer than that."

"It proves nothing at all!"

"How is that?" I asked with surprise.

"Because it is so. We went to Dargo and took one week's rations of rusks, but we stayed there nearly a month."

"Can I go with you?" I asked after a pause.

"You could, no doubt, but my advice is, don't. Why run risks?"

"Oh, but you must allow me not to take your advice. I have been here a whole month solely on the chance of seeing an action, and you wish me to miss it!"

"Well, you must please yourself. But really you had better stay behind. You could wait for us here and might go hunting—and we would go our way, and it would be splendid," he said with such conviction that for a moment it really seemed to me too that it would be "splendid." However, I told him decidedly that nothing would induce me to stay behind.

"But what is there for you to see?" the captain went on, still trying to dissuade me. "Do you want to know what battles are like? Read Mikháylovski Danílevski's *Description of War*. It's a fine book; it gives a detailed account of everything. It gives the position of every corps and describes how battles are fought."

"All that does not interest me," I replied.

"What is it then? Do you simply wish to see how people are killed? In 1832 we had a fellow here, also a civilian, a Spaniard I think he was. He took part with us in two campaigns, wearing some kind of blue mantle. Well, they did for the fine fellow. You won't astonish anyone here, friend!"

Humiliating though it was that the captain so misjudged my motives, I did not try to disabuse him.

"Was he brave?" I asked.

"Heaven only knows: he always used to ride in front, and where there was firing there he always was."

"Then he must have been brave," said I.

"No. Pushing oneself in where one is not needed does not prove one to be brave."

"Then what do you call brave?"

"Brave? . . . brave?" repeated the captain with the air

of one to whom such a question presents itself for the first time. "He who does what he ought to do is brave," he said after thinking awhile.

I remembered that Plato defines courage as "The knowledge of what should and what should not be feared," and despite the looseness and vagueness of the captain's definition I thought that the fundamental ideas of the two were not so different as they might appear and that the captain's definition was even more correct than that of the Greek philosopher. For if the captain had been able to express himself like Plato he would no doubt have said that, "He is brave who fears only what should be feared and not what should not be feared."

I wished to explain my idea to the captain.

"Yes," said I, "it seems to me that in every danger there is a choice, and a choice made under the influence of a sense of duty is courage, but a choice made under the influence of a base motive is cowardice. Therefore a man who risks his life from vanity, curiosity, or greed cannot be called brave; while on the other hand he who avoids a danger from honest consideration for his family, or simply from conviction, cannot be called a coward."

The captain looked at me with a curious expression while I was speaking.

"Well, that I cannot prove to you," he said, filling his pipe, "but we have a cadet here who is fond of philosophizing. You should have a talk with him. He also writes verses."

I had known of the captain before I left Russia, but I had only made his acquaintance in the Caucasus. His mother, Mary Ivánovna Khlópova, a small and poor landowner, lives within two miles of my estate. Before I left for the Caucasus I had called on her. The old lady was very glad to hear that I should see her "Páshenka," by which pet name she called the grey-haired elderly captain, and that I, "a living letter," could tell him all about her and take him a small parcel from her. Having treated me to excellent pie and smoked goose, Mary Ivánovna went into her bedroom and returned with a black bag to which a black silk ribbon was attached.

"Here, this is the icon of our Mother Mediatress of the Burning Bush," said she, crossing herself and kissing the icon of the Virgin and placing it in my hands. "Please let him have it. You see, when he went to the Caucasus I had a Mass said for him and promised, if he remained alive and safe, to order this icon of the Mother of God for him. And now for eighteen years the Mediatress and the Holy Saints have had mercy on him, he has not been wounded once, and yet in what battles has he not taken part? . . . What Michael who went with him told me was enough, believe me, to make one's hair stand on end. You see, what I know about him is only from others. He, my pet, never writes me about his campaigns for fear of frightening me."

(After I reached the Caucasus I learnt, and then not from the captain himself, that he had been severely wounded four times and of course never wrote to his mother either about his wounds or his campaigns.)

"So let him now wear this holy image," she continued. "I give it him with my blessing. May the Most Holy Mediatress guard him. Especially when going into battle let him wear it. Tell him so, dear friend. Say 'Your mother wishes it.' "

I promised to carry out her instructions carefully.

"I know you will grow fond of my Páshenka," continued the old lady. "He is such a splendid fellow. Will you believe it, he never lets a year pass without sending me some money, and he also helps my daughter Ánnushka a good deal, and all out of his pay! I thank God for having given me such a child," she continued with tears in her eyes.

"Does he often write to you?" I asked.

"Seldom, my dear: perhaps once a year. Only when he sends the money, not otherwise. He says, 'If I don't write to you, mother, that means I am alive and well. Should anything befall me, which God forbid, they'll tell you without me.' "

When I handed his mother's present to the captain (it was in my own quarters) he asked for a bit of paper, carefully wrapped it up, and then put it away. I told him many things about his mother's life. He remained silent, and when I had finished speaking he went to a corner of the room and busied himself for what seemed a long time, filling his pipe.

"Yes, she's a splendid old woman!" he said from there

in a rather muffled voice. "Will God ever let me see her again?"

These simple words expressed much love and sadness.

"Why do you serve here?" I asked.

"One has to serve," he answered with conviction.

["You should transfer to Russia. You would then be nearer to her."

"To Russia? To Russia?" repeated the captain, dubiously swaying his head and smiling mournfully. "Here I am still of some use, but there I should be the least of the officers. And besides, the double pay we get here also means something to a poor man."

"Can it be, Pável Ivánovich, that living as you do the ordinary pay would not suffice?"

"And does the double pay suffice?" interjected the captain. "Look at our officers! Have any of them a brass farthing? They all go on tick at the sutler's and are all up to their ears in debt. You say 'living as I do'. . . . Do you really think that living as I do I have anything over out of my salary? Not a farthing! You don't yet know what prices are like here; everything is three times dearer. . . ."]

The captain lived economically, did not play cards, rarely went carousing, and smoked the cheapest tobacco (which for some reason he called home-grown tobacco). I had liked him before—he had one of those simple, calm, Russian faces which are easy and pleasant to look straight in the eyes—and after this talk I felt a sincere regard for him.

II

Next morning at four o'clock the captain came for me. He wore an old threadbare coat without epaulettes, wide Caucasian trousers, a white sheepskin cap the wool of which had grown yellow and limp, and had a shabby Asiatic sword strapped round his shoulder. The small white horse he rode ambled along with short strides, hanging its head down and swinging its thin tail. Although the worthy captain's figure was not very martial or even good-looking, it expressed such equanimity towards everything around him that it involuntarily inspired respect.

I did not keep him waiting a single moment but mounted

my horse at once, and we rode together through the gates of the fort.

The battalion was some five hundred yards ahead of us and looked like a dense, oscillating, black mass. It was only possible to guess that it was an infantry battalion by the bayonets, which looked like needles standing close together, and by the sound of the soldiers' songs which occasionally reached us, the beating of a drum, and the delightful voice of the Sixth Company's second tenor, which had often charmed me at the fort. The road lay along the middle of a deep and broad ravine by the side of a stream which had overflowed its banks. Flocks of wild pigeons whirled above it, now alighting on the rocky banks, now turning in the air in rapid circles and vanishing out of sight. The sun was not yet visible, but the crest of the right side of the ravine was just beginning to be lit up. The grey and whitish rock, the yellowish-green moss, the dew-covered bushes of Christ's Thorn, dogberry, and dwarf elm appeared extraordinarily distinct and salient in the golden morning light, but the other side and the valley, wrapped in thick mist which floated in uneven layers, were damp and gloomy and presented an indefinite mingling of colours: pale purple, almost black, dark green, and white. Right in front of us, strikingly distinct against the dark-blue horizon, rose the bright, dead-white masses of the snowy mountains, with their shadows and outlines fantastic and yet exquisite in every detail. Crickets, grasshoppers, and thousands of other insects awoke in the tall grasses and filled the air with their clear and ceaseless sounds: it was as if innumerable tiny bells were ringing inside our very ears. The air was full of the scent of water, grass, and mist: the scent of a lovely early summer morning. The captain struck a light and lit his pipe, and the smell of his cheap tobacco and of the tinder seemed to me extraordinarily pleasant.

To overtake the infantry more quickly we left the road. The captain appeared more thoughtful than usual, did not take his Daghestan pipe from his mouth, and at every step touched with his heels his horse, which swaying from side to side left a scarcely perceptible green track in the tall wet grass. From under its very feet, with the cry and the whirr of wings which involuntarily sends a thrill through every sportsman, a pheasant rose, and flew slowly upwards. The captain did not take the least notice of it.

We had nearly overtaken the battalion when we heard the thud of a horse galloping behind us, and that same moment a good-looking youth in an officer's uniform and white sheepskin cap galloped past us. He smiled in passing, nodded to the captain, and flourished his whip. I only had time to notice that he sat his horse and held his reins with peculiar grace, that he had beautiful black eyes, a fine nose, and only the first indications of a moustache. What specially pleased me about him was that he could not repress a smile when he noticed our admiration. This smile alone showed him to be very young.

"Where is he galloping to?" muttered the captain with a dissatisfied air, without taking the pipe from his mouth.

"Who is he?" I replied.

"Ensign Alánin, a subaltern in my company. He came from the Cadet Corps only a month ago."

"I suppose he is going into action for the first time," I said.

"That's why he is so delighted," answered the captain, thoughtfully shaking his head. "Youth!"

"But how could he help being pleased? I can fancy how interesting it must be for a young officer."

The captain remained silent for a minute or two.

"That is just why I say 'youth'," he added in a deep voice. "What is there to be pleased at without ever having seen the thing? When one has seen it many times one is not so pleased. There are now, let us say, twenty of us officers here: one or other is sure to be killed or wounded, that is quite certain. To-day it may be I, to-morrow he, the next day a third. So what is there to be pleased about?"

III

As soon as the bright sun appeared above the hill and lit up the valley along which we were marching, the wavy clouds of mist cleared and it grew hot. The soldiers, with muskets and sacks on their shoulders, marched slowly along the dusty road. Now and then Ukrainian words and laughter could be heard in their ranks. Several old soldiers in white blouses (most of them non-commissioned officers) walked together by the roadside, smoking their pipes and conversing gravely. Heavily laden wagons drawn by three horses moved steadily along, raising thick clouds of dust that hung motionless in the air. The officers rode in front: some of them caracoled—whipping their horses, making them take three or four leaps and then, pulling their heads round, stopping abruptly. Others were occupied with the singers, who in spite of the heat and sultriness sang song after song.

With the mounted Tartars, about two hundred yards ahead of the infantry, rode a tall handsome lieutenant in Asiatic costume on a large white horse. He was known in the regiment as a desperate dare-devil who would spit the truth out at anybody. He wore a black tunic trimmed with gold braid, leggings to match, soft closely fitting gold-braided oriental shoes, a yellow coat, and a tall sheepskin cap pushed back from his forehead. Fastened to the silver strap that lay across his chest and back, he carried a powder-flask, and a pistol behind him. Another pistol and a silver-mounted dagger hung from his girdle, and above these a sword in a red leather sheath and a musket in a black cover, were slung over his shoulder. By his clothing, by the way he sat his horse, by his general bearing, in fact by his every movement, one could see that he tried to re-semble a Tartar. He even spoke to the Tartars with whom he was riding in a language I did not know, and from the bewildered and amused looks with which they glanced at one another I surmised that they did not understand him either. He was one of our young officers, dare-devil braves who shape their lives on the model of Lérmontov's and Marlínsky's heroes. These officers see the Caucasus only through the prism of such books as *A Hero of Our Time*, and *Mullah-Nur*,[1] and are guided in their actions not by their own inclinations but by the examples of their models.

The lieutenant, for instance, may perhaps have liked the company of well-bred women and men of rank: generals, colonels, and aides-de-camp (it is even my conviction that he liked such society very much, for he was exceedingly ambitious), but he considered it his imperative duty to turn his roughest side to all important men, though he was

[1] Novels by the authors mentioned.

strictly moderate in his rudeness to them; and when any lady came to the fort he considered it his duty to walk before her window with his bosom friends, in a red shirt and with slippers on his bare feet, and shout and swear at the top of his voice. But all this he did not so much with the intention of offending her as to let her see what beautiful white feet he had, and how easy it would be to fall in love with him should he desire it. Or he would often go with two or three friendly Tartars to the hills at night to lie in ambush by the roadside to watch for passing hostile Tartars and kill them: and though his heart told him more than once that there was nothing valiant in this, he considered himself bound to cause suffering to people with whom he affected to be disillusioned and whom he chose to hate and despise. He always carried two things: a large icon hanging round his neck and a dagger which he wore over his shirt even when in bed. He sincerely believed that he had enemies. To persuade himself that he must avenge himself on someone and wash away some insult with blood was his greatest enjoyment. He was convinced that hatred, vengeance, and contempt for the human race were the noblest and most poetic of emotions. But his mistress (a Circassian of course) whom I happened to meet subsequently, used to say that he was the kindest and mildest of men, and that every evening he wrote down his dismal thoughts in his diary, as well as his accounts on ruled paper, and prayed to God on his knees. And how much he suffered merely to appear in his own eyes what he wished to be! For his comrades and the soldiers could never see him as he wished to appear. Once on one of his nocturnal expeditions on the road with his bosom friends he happened to wound a hostile Chechen with a bullet in the leg and took him prisoner. After that, the Chechen lived for seven weeks with the lieutenant, who attended to him and nursed him as he would have nursed his dearest friend, and when the Chechen recovered he gave him presents and set him free. After that, during one of our expeditions when the lieutenant was retreating with the soldiers of the cordon and firing to keep back the foe, he heard someone among the enemy call him by name, and the man he had wounded rode forward and made signs to the lieutenant to do the same. The lieutenant rode up to his friend and pressed his hand. The hillsmen stood some way back and did not fire, but scarcely had the lieutenant turned his horse to return before several men shot at him and a bullet grazed the small of his back. Another time, at night, when a fire had broken out in the fort and two companies of soldiers were putting it out, I myself saw how the tall figure of a man mounted on a black horse and lit up by the red glow of the fire suddenly appeared among the crowd and, pushing through, rode up to the very flames. When quite close the lieutenant jumped from his horse and rushed into the house, one side of which was burning. Five minutes later he came out with singed hair and scorched elbow, carrying in his bosom two pigeons he had rescued from the flames.

His name was Rosenkranz, yet he often spoke of his descent, deducing it somehow from the Varángians (the first rulers of Russia), and clearly demonstrated that he and his ancestors were pure Russians.

IV

The sun had done half its journey and cast its hot rays through the glowing air onto the dry earth. The dark blue sky was perfectly clear, and only the base of the snowy mountains began to clothe itself in lilac-tinged white clouds. The motionless air seemed full of transparent dust; the heat was becoming unbearable.

Half-way on their march the troops reached a small stream and halted. The soldiers stacked their muskets and rushed to the stream; the commander of the battalion sat down in the shade of a drum, his full face assuming the correct expression denoting the greatness of his rank. He, together with some other officers, prepared to have a snack. The captain lay down on the grass under his company's wagon. The brave Lieutenant Rosenkranz and some other young officers disposed themselves on their outspread cloaks and got ready for a drinking-bout, as could be gathered from the bottles and flasks arranged round them, as well as from the peculiar animation of the singers who, standing before them in a semicircle, sang a Caucasian dance-song with a whistling obbligato interjected:

> Shamyl, he began to riot
> In the days gone by,
> Try-ry-rataty,
> In the days gone by!

Among these officers was the young ensign who had overtaken us in the morning. He was very amusing: his eyes shone, he spoke rather thickly, and he wished to kiss and declare his love to everyone. Poor boy! He did not know that he might appear funny in such a situation, that the frankness and tenderness with which he assailed every one predisposed them not to the affection he so longed for, but to ridicule; nor did he know that when, quite heated, he at last threw himself down on the cloak and rested on his elbow with his thick black hair thrown back, he looked uncommonly charming.

[In a word, everyone was cheerful, except perhaps one officer who, sitting under his company's cart, had lost the horse he was riding to another officer at cards and had agreed to hand it over when they reached head-quarters. He was vainly trying to induce the other to play again, offering to stake a casket which everyone could confirm he had bought for thirty rubles from a Jew, but which—merely because he was in difficulties—he was now willing to stake for fifteen. His opponent looked casually into the distance and persistently remained silent, till at last he remarked that he was terribly anxious to have a doze.

I confess that from the time I started from the fort and decided to take part in this action, gloomy reflections involuntarily rose in my mind, and so—since one has a tendency to judge of others by oneself] I listened with curiosity to the conversation of the soldiers and officers and attentively watched the expression of their faces but could find absolutely no trace of the anxiety I myself experienced: jokes, laughter and anecdotes, gambling and drunkenness, expressed the general carelessness and indifference to the impending danger [as if all these people had long ago finished their affairs in this world. What was this—firmness, habituation to danger, or carelessness and indifference to life? Or was it all these things together as well as others I did not know, forming a complex but powerful moral motive of human nature termed *esprit de corps*—a subtle code embracing within itself a general expression of all the virtues and vices of men banded together in any permanent condition, a code each new member involuntarily submits to unmurmuringly and which does not change with the individuals, since whoever they may be the sum total of human tendencies everywhere and always remains the same?]

V

Towards seven that evening, dusty and tired, we entered the wide fortified gate of Fort M. The sun was already setting and threw its rosy slanting rays on the picturesque little batteries, on the gardens with their tall poplars which surrounded the fortress, on the yellow gleaming cultivated fields, and on the white clouds that crowding round the snowy peaks had, as if trying to imitate them, formed a range not less fantastic and beautiful. On the horizon the new moon appeared delicate as a little cloud. In the Tartar village, from the roof of a hut, a Tartar was calling the faithful to prayer, and our singers raised their voices with renewed energy and vigour.

After a rest and after tidying myself up a bit, I went to an adjutant of my acquaintance to ask him to let the general know of my intention. On my way from the suburb where I had put up I noticed in Fort M. something I did not at all expect: a pretty little brougham overtook me, in which I caught sight of a fashionable bonnet and from which I overheard some French words. The sounds of some "Lizzie" or "Kátenka" polka, played on a bad ramshackle piano, reached me through the windows of the commander's house. In a little grocery and wine shop which I passed, some clerks with cigarettes in their fingers sat drinking wine, and I heard one of them say to another, "No, excuse me, as to politics, Mary Gregórevna is first of our ladies." A Jew in a worn-out coat, with a bent back and sickly countenance, was dragging along a wheezy barrel-organ and the whole suburb resounded to the tones of the finale of *Lucia*. Two women in rustling dresses with silk kerchiefs on their heads and carrying bright-coloured parasols passed by along the planks that did duty for a pavement. Two girls, one in a pink, the other in a blue dress stood bareheaded beside the earth-embankments of a low-roofed house, and shrieked with high-pitched, forced laughter, evidently to attract the attention of passing officers. Officers, dressed in new uniforms with glittering epaulettes and white gloves, flaunted along the street and on the boulevard.

I found my acquaintance on the ground floor of the general's house. I had scarcely had time to explain my wish to him and to get his reply that it could easily be fulfilled, when the pretty little brougham I had noticed outside rattled past the window we were sitting at. A tall, well-built man in an infantry major's uniform and epaulettes got out and entered the house.

"Oh, please excuse me," said the adjutant, rising, "I must go and announce them to the general."

"Who is it?" I asked.

"The countess," he replied, and buttoning his uniform he rushed upstairs.

A few minutes later a very handsome man in a frock coat without epaulettes and with a white cross in his buttonhole went out into the porch. He was not tall but remarkably good-looking. He was followed by the major, an adjutant, and a couple of other officers. The general's gait, voice, and all his movements showed him to be a man well aware of his own value.

"*Bonsoir, madame la comtesse,*"[1] he said, offering his hand through the carriage window.

A small hand in a kid glove pressed his, and a pretty smiling face in a yellow bonnet appeared at the carriage window.

Of the conversation which lasted several minutes I only overheard the general say laughingly as I passed by: "*Vouz savez que j'ai fait voeu de combattres les infidèles; prenez donc garde de la devenir.*"[2]

A laugh replied from inside the carriage.

---

[1] "Good evening, Countess."

[2] "You know I have sworn to fight the infidels (the unfaithful), so beware of becoming one."

"*Adieu donc, cher général!*"[3]

"*Non, au revoir,*" said the general, ascending the steps of the porch. "*N'oubliez pas, que je m'invite pour la soirée de demain.*"[4]

The carriage rattled off [and the general went into the sitting-room with the major. Passing by the open window of the adjutant's room, he noticed my un-uniformed figure and turned his kind attention to me. Having heard my request he announced his complete agreement with it and passed on into his room.]

"There again," I thought as I walked home, "is a man who possesses all that Russians strive after: rank, riches, distinction; and this man, the day before an engagement the outcome of which is known only to God, jokes with a pretty woman and promises to have tea with her next day, just as if they had met at a ball!"

[I remembered a reflection I had heard a Tartar utter, to the effect that only a pauper can be brave. "*Become rich, become a coward,*" said he, not at all to offend his comrade but as a common and unquestionable rule. But the general could lose, together with his life, much more than anyone else I had had an opportunity of observing and, contrary to the Tartar's rule, no one had shown such a pleasant, graceful indifference and confidence as he. My conception of courage became completely confused.]

At that same adjutant's I met a young man who surprised me even more. He was a young lieutenant of the K. regiment who was noted for his almost feminine meekness and timidity and who had come to the adjutant to pour out his vexation and resentment against those who, he said, had intrigued against him to keep him from taking part in the impending action. He said it was mean to behave in that way, that it was unfriendly, that he would not forget it, and so forth. Intently as I watched the expression of his face and listened to the sound of his voice, I could not help feeling convinced that he was not pretending but was genuinely filled with indignation and grief at not being allowed to go and shoot Circassians and expose himself to

---

[3] "Good-bye then, dear general."

[4] "No, *au revoir*. Don't forget that I am inviting myself for to-morrow's soirée."

their fire. He was grieving like a little child who has been unjustly birched . . . I could make nothing at all of it.

VI

The troops were to start at ten in the evening. At half-past eight I mounted and rode to the general's, but thinking that he and his adjutant were busy I tied my horse to the fence and sat down on an earth-bank intending to catch the general when he came out.

The heat and glare of the sun were now replaced by the coolness of night and the soft light of the young moon, which had formed a pale glimmering semi-circle around itself on the deep blue of the starry sky and was already setting. Lights appeared in the windows of the houses and shone through cracks in the shutters of the earth huts. The stately poplars, beyond the white moonlit earth huts with their rush-thatched roofs, looked darker and taller than ever against the horizon.

The long shadows of the houses, the trees, and the fences stretched out daintily on the dusty road. . . . From the river came the ringing voices of frogs;[1] along the street came the sound of hurried steps and voices talking, or the gallop of a horse, and from the suburb the tones of a barrel-organ playing now "The winds are blowing," now some "Aurora Waltz."

I will not say in what meditations I was absorbed: first, because I should be ashamed to confess the gloomy waves of thought that insistently flooded my soul while around me I noticed nothing but gaiety and joy, and secondly, because it would not suit my story. I was so absorbed in thought that I did not even notice the bell strike eleven and the general with his suite ride past me.

[Hastily mounting my horse I set out to overtake the detachment.]

The rear-guard was still within the gates of the fort. I had great difficulty in making my way across the bridge among the guns, ammunition wagons, carts of different

[1] Frogs in the Caucasus make a noise quite different from the croaking of frogs elsewhere.—L. T.

companies, and officers noisily giving orders. Once outside the gates I trotted past the troops who, stretching out over nearly three-quarters of a mile, were silently moving on amid the darkness, and I overtook the general. As I rode past the guns drawn out in single file, and the officers who rode between them, I was hurt as by a discord in the quiet and solemn harmony by the German accents of a voice shouting, "A linstock, you devil!" and the voice of a soldier hurriedly exclaiming, "Schévchenko, the lieutenant wants a light!"

The greater part of the sky was now overcast by long strips of dark grey clouds; it was only here and there that a few stars twinkled dimly among them. The moon had already sunk behind the near horizon of the black hills visible to the right and threw a faint trembling light on their peaks, in sharp contrast to the impenetrable darkness enveloping their base. The air was so warm and still that it seemed as if not a single blade of grass, not a single cloudlet, was moving. It was so dark that even objects close at hand could not be distinguished. By the sides of the road I seemed to see now rocks, now animals, now some strange kind of men, and I discovered that they were merely bushes only when I heard them rustle or felt the dew with which they were sprinkled.

Before me I saw a dense heaving wall followed by some dark moving spots; this was the cavalry vanguard and the general with his suite. Another similar dark mass, only lower, moved beside us; this was the infantry.

The silence that reigned over the whole division was so great that all the mingling sounds of night with their mysterious charm were distinctly audible: the far-off mournful howling of jackals, now like agonized weeping, now like chuckling; the monotonous resounding song of crickets, frogs, and quails; a sort of rumbling I could not at all account for but which seemed to draw nearer; and all those scarcely audible motions of Nature which can neither be understood nor defined, mingled into one beautiful harmony which we call the stillness of night. This stillness was interrupted by, or rather combined with, the dull thud of hoofs and the rustling of the tall grass caused by the slowly advancing detachment.

Only very occasionally could the clang of a heavy gun,

the sound of bayonets touching one another, hushed voices, or the snorting of a horse, be heard. [By the scent of the wet juicy grass which sank under our horses' feet, by the light steam rising from the ground and by the horizons seen on two sides of us, it was evident that we were moving across a wide, luxuriant meadow.] Nature seemed to breathe with pacifying beauty and power.

Can it be that there is not room for all men on this beautiful earth under those immeasurable starry heavens? Can it be possible that in the midst of this entrancing Nature feelings of hatred, vengeance, or the desire to exterminate their fellows can endure in the souls of men? All that is unkind in the hearts of men should, one would think, vanish at contact with Nature—that most direct expression of beauty and goodness.

[War! What an incomprehensible phenomenon! When one's reason asks: "Is it just, is it necessary?" an inner voice always replies, "No." Only the persistence of this unnatural occurrence makes it seem natural, and a feeling of self-preservation makes it seem just.

Who will doubt that in the war of the Russians against the mountain-tribes, justice—resulting from a feeling of self-preservation—is on our side? Were it not for this war, what would secure the neighbouring rich and cultured Russian territories from robbery, murder, and raids by wild and warlike tribes? But consider two private persons. On whose side is the feeling of self-preservation and consequently of justice? Is it on the side of this ragamuffin— some Djemi or other—who hearing of the approach of the Russians snatches down his old gun from the wall, puts three or four charges (which he will only reluctantly discharge) in his pouch, and runs to meet the giaours, and on seeing that the Russians still advance, approaching the fields he has sown which they will tread down and his hut which they will burn, and the ravine where his mother, his wife, and his children have hidden themselves, shaking with fear—seeing that he will be deprived of all that constitutes his happiness—in impotent anger and with a cry of despair tears off his tattered jacket, flings down his gun, and drawing his sheepskin cap over his eyes sings his death-song and flings himself headlong onto the Russian bayonets with only a dagger in his hand? Is justice on his side or on that of this officer on the general's staff who is singing French chansonettes so well just as he rides past us? He has a family in Russia, relations, friends, serfs, and obligations towards them but has no reason or desire to be at enmity with the hillsmen and has come to the Caucasus just by chance and to show his courage. Or is it on the side of my acquaintance the adjutant, who only wishes to obtain a captaincy and a comfortable position as soon as possible and for that reason has become the hillsmen's enemy? Or is it on the side of this young German who, with a strong German accent, is demanding a linstock from the artillerymen? What devil has brought him from his fatherland and set him down in this distant region? Why should this Saxon, Kaspar Lavréntich, mix himself up in our blood-thirsty conflict with these turbulent neighbours?]

VII

We had been riding for more than two hours. I was beginning to shiver and feel drowsy. Through the gloom I still seemed to see the same indefinite forms; a little way in front the same black wall and the moving spots. Close in front of me I could see the crupper of a white horse which swung its tail and threw its hind legs wide apart, the back of a white Circassian coat on which could be discerned a musket in a black case and the glimmering butt of a pistol in an embroidered holster; the glow of a cigarette lit up a fair moustache, a beaver collar and a hand in a chamois glove. Every now and then I leant over my horse's neck, shutting my eyes and forgetting myself for a few minutes, then startled by the familiar tramping and rustling I glanced round and felt as if I were standing still and the black wall in front was moving towards me, or that it had stopped and I should in a moment ride into it. At one such moment the rumbling which increased and seemed to approach, and the cause of which I could not guess, struck me forcibly: it was the sound of water. We were entering a deep gorge and approaching a mountain-stream that was overflowing its banks.[1] The rumbling increased, the damp grass became

---

[1] In the Caucasus rivers are apt to overflow in July.—L. T.

thicker and taller and the bushes closer, while the horizon gradually narrowed. Now and then bright lights appeared here and there against the dark background of the hills and vanished instantly.

"Tell me, please, what are those lights?" I asked in a whisper of a Tartar riding beside me.

"Don't you know?" he replied.

"No."

"The hillsmen have tied straw to poles and are waving it about alight."

"Why are they doing that?"

"So that everyone should know that the Russians have come. Oh, oh! What a bustle is going on now in the *aouls*! Everybody's dragging his belongings into the ravine," he said laughing.

"Why, do they already know in the mountains that a detachment is on its way?" I asked him.

"How can they help knowing? They always know. Our people are like that."

"Then Shamyl[2] too is preparing for action?" I asked.

"No," he answered, shaking his head, "Shamyl won't go into action; Shamyl will send his *naibs*,[3] and he himself will look on through a telescope from above."

"Does he live far away?"

"Not far. Some eight miles to the left."

"How do you know?" I asked. "Have you been there?"

"I have. Our people have all been."

"Have you seen Shamyl?"

"Such as we don't see Shamyl! There are a hundred, three hundred, a thousand *murids*[4] all round him, and Shamyl is in the centre," he said, with an expression of servile admiration.

Looking up, it was possible to discern that the sky, now cleared, was beginning to grow lighter in the east and the Pleiades to sink towards the horizon, but the ravine through which we were marching was still damp and gloomy.

---

[2] Shamyl was the leader (in 1834–59) of the Caucasian hill-tribes in their resistance of Russia.

[3] A *naib* was a man to whom Shamyl had entrusted some administrative office.—L. T.

[4] The word *murid* has several meanings, but here it denotes something between an adjutant and a bodyguard.

Suddenly a little way in front of us several lights flashed through the darkness; at the same moment some bullets flew whizzing past amid the surrounding silence [and sharp abrupt firing could be heard and loud cries, as piercing as cries of despair but expressing instead of fear such a passion of brutal audacity and rage that one could not but shudder at hearing it]. It was the enemy's advanced picket. The Tartars who composed it whooped, fired at random, and then ran in different directions.

All became silent again. The general called up an interpreter. A Tartar in a white Circassian coat rode up to him and, gesticulating and whispering, talked with him for some time.

"Colonel Khasánov! Order the cordon to take open order," commanded the general with a quiet but distinct drawl.

The detachment advanced to the river, the black hills and gorges were left behind, the dawn appeared. The vault of the heavens, in which a few pale stars were still dimly visible, seemed higher; the sunrise glow beyond shone brightly in the east, a fresh penetrating breeze blew from the west, and the white mists rose like steam above the rushing stream.

VIII

Our guide pointed out a ford and the cavalry vanguard, followed by the general, began crossing the stream. The water which reached to the horses' chests rushed with tremendous force between the white boulders which here and there appeared on a level with its surface and formed foaming and gurgling ripples round the horses' legs. The horses, surprised by the noise of the water, lifted their heads and pricked their ears but stepped evenly and carefully against the current on the uneven bottom of the stream. Their riders lifted their feet and their weapons. The infantry, literally in nothing but their shirts, linked arm in arm by twenties and holding above the water their muskets to which their bundles of clothing were fastened, made great efforts (as the strained expression of their faces showed) to resist the force of the current. The mounted artillerymen with loud shouts drove their horses into the water at a trot.

The guns and green ammunition wagons, over which the water occasionally splashed, rang against the stony bottom, but the sturdy little horses, churning the water, pulled at the traces in unison and with dripping manes and tails clambered out on the opposite bank.

As soon as the crossing was accomplished the general's face suddenly assumed a meditative and serious look and he turned his horse and, followed by the cavalry, rode at a trot down a broad glade which opened out before us in the midst of the forest. A cordon of mounted Cossacks was scattered along the skirts of the forest.

In the woods we noticed a man on foot dressed in a Circassian coat and wearing a tall cap—then a second and a third. One of the officers said: "Those are Tartars." Then a puff of smoke appeared from behind a tree, a shot, and another. . . . Our rapid fire drowns the enemy's. Only now and then a bullet, with a slow sound like the buzzing of a bee's wings, passes by and proves that the firing is not all ours. Now the infantry at a run and the guns at a trot pass into the cordon. You can hear the boom of the guns, the metallic sounds of flying grape-shot, the hissing of rockets, and the crackle of musketry. Over the wide glade on all sides you can see cavalry, infantry, and artillery. Puffs of smoke mingle with the dew-covered verdure and the mist. Colonel Khasánov, approaching the general at full gallop, suddenly reins in his horse.

"Your Excellency, shall we order the cavalry to charge?" he says, raising his hand to his cap. "The enemy's colours[1] are in sight," and he points with his whip to some mounted Tartars in front of whom ride two men on white horses with bits of blue and red stuff fastened to poles in their hands.

"Go, and God be with you, Iván Mikháylovich!" says the general.

The colonel turns his horse sharply round, draws his sword, and shouts "Hurrah!"

"Hurrah! Hurrah! Hurrah!" comes from the ranks, and the cavalry gallop after him. . . .

[1] The colours among the hillsmen correspond to those of our troops, except that every *dzhigit* or "brave" among them may make his own colours and carry them.—L. T.

Everyone looks on with interest: there is a colour, another, a third, and a fourth. . . .

The enemy not waiting for the attack, hides in the wood and thence opens a small-arms fire. Bullets come flying more and more frequently.

"Quel charmant coup d'oeil!"[2] says the general, rising slightly, English fashion, in his saddle on his slim-legged black horse.

"Charmant!" answers the major, rolling his *r*'s and striking his horse he rides up to the general: *"C'est un vrai plaisir que la guerre dans un aussi beau pays,"*[3] he says.

"Et surtout en bonne compagnie,"[4] replies the general with a pleasant smile.

The major bows.

At that moment a hostile cannon-ball flies past with a disagreeable whiz and strikes something. We hear behind us the moan of a wounded man.

This moaning strikes me so strangely that the warlike scene instantly loses all its charm for me. But no one except myself seems to notice it: the major laughs with apparently greater gusto, another officer repeats with perfect calm the first words of a sentence he had just been saying, the general looks the other way and with the quietest smile says something in French.

"Shall we reply to their fire?" asks the commander of the artillery, galloping up.

"Yes, frighten them a bit!" carelessly replies the general, lighting a cigar.

The battery takes up its position and the firing begins. The earth groans under the shots, the discharges flash out incessantly, and smoke, through which it is scarcely possible to distinguish the artillerymen moving round their guns, veils your sight.

The *aoul* has been bombarded. Colonel Khasánov rides up again and at the general's command gallops towards the *aoul*. The war-cry is again heard and the cavalry disappears in the cloud of dust it has raised.

---

[2] "What a charming view."
[3] "Charming . . . , War in such beautiful country is a real pleasure."
[4] "Especially in good company."

The spectacle was truly magnificent. The one thing that spoilt the general impression for me—who took no part in the affair and was unaccustomed to it—was that this movement and the animation and the shouting appeared unnecessary. The comparison involuntarily suggested itself to me of a man swinging his arms vigorously to cut the air with an axe.

IX

Our troops had taken possession of the village and not a single soul of the enemy remained in it when the general and his suite, to which I had attached myself, rode up to it.

The long clean huts, with their flat earthen roofs and shapely chimneys, stood on irregular stony mounds between which flowed a small stream. On one side were green gardens with enormous pear and small plum trees brightly lit up by the sun, on the other strange upright shadows, the perpendicular stones of the cemetery, and long poles with balls and many-coloured flags fastened to their ends. (These marked the graves of *dzhigits*.)

The troops were drawn up outside the gates.

["Well, how about it, Colonel?" said the general. "Let them loot. I see they are terribly anxious to," he added with a smile, pointing at the Cossacks.

You cannot imagine how striking was the contrast between the carelessness with which the general uttered these words and their import and the military surroundings.]

A moment later, dragoons, Cossacks, and infantry spread with evident delight through the crooked lanes and in an instant the empty village was animated again. Here a roof crashes, an axe rings against the hard wood of a door that is being forced open, here a stack of hay, a fence, a hut, is set on fire and a pillar of thick smoke rises up in the clear air. Here is a Cossack dragging along a sack of flour and a carpet, there a soldier, with a delighted look on his face, brings a tin basin and some rag out of a hut, another is trying with outstretched arms to catch two hens that struggle and cackle beside a fence, a third has somewhere discovered an enormous pot of milk and after drinking some of it throws the rest on the ground with a loud laugh.

The battalion with which I had come from Fort N. was

also in the *aoul*. The captain sat on the roof of a hut and sent thin whiffs of cheap tobacco smoke through his short pipe with such an expression of indifference on his face that on seeing him I forgot that I was in a hostile *aoul* and felt quite at home.

"Ah, you are here too?" he said when he noticed me.

The tall figure of Lieutenant Rosenkranz flitted here and there in the village. He gave orders unceasingly and appeared exceedingly engrossed in his task. I saw him with a triumphant air emerge from a hut followed by two soldiers leading an old Tartar. The old man, whose only clothing consisted of a mottled tunic all in rags and patch-work trousers, was so frail that his arms, tightly bound behind his bent back, seemed scarcely to hold onto his shoulders, and he could scarcely drag his bare crooked legs along. His face and even part of his shaven head were deeply furrowed. His wry toothless mouth kept moving beneath his close-cut moustache and beard, as if he were chewing something; but a gleam still sparkled in his red lashless eyes which clearly expressed an old man's indiffer-ence to life.

Rosenkranz asked him, through an interpreter, why he had not gone away with the others.

"Where should I go?" he answered, looking quietly away.

"Where the others have gone," someone remarked.

"The *dzhigits* have gone to fight the Russians, but I am an old man."

"Are you not afraid of the Russians?"

"What will the Russians do to me? I am old," he re-peated, again glancing carelessly round the circle that had formed about him.

Later, as I was returning, I saw that old man, bare-headed, with his arms tied, being jolted along behind the saddle of a Cossack, and he was looking round with the same expression of indifference on his face. He was needed for the exchange of prisoners.

I climbed onto the roof and sat down beside the captain.

[A bugler who had vodka and provisions was sent for. The captain's calmness and equanimity involuntarily pro-duced an effect on me. We ate roasted pheasant and chatted, without at all reflecting that the owners of that hut had not merely no desire to see us there but could hardly have imagined our existence.]

"There don't seem to have been many of the enemy," I said, wishing to know his opinion of the action that had taken place.

"The enemy?" he repeated with surprise. "The enemy was not there at all! Do you call those the enemy? . . . Wait till the evening when we go back, and you will see how they will speed us on our way: what a lot of them will pour out from there," he said, pointing to a thicket we had passed in the morning.

"What is that?" I asked anxiously, interrupting the captain and pointing to a group of Don Cossacks who had collected round something not far from us.

A sound of something like a child's cry came from there, and the words: "Stop . . . don't hack it . . . you'll be seen . . . Have you a knife, Evstignéich. . . . Lend me a knife. . . ."

"They are up to something, the scoundrels ." replied the captain calmly.

But at that moment the young ensign, his comely face flushed and frightened, came suddenly running from behind a corner and rushed towards the Cossacks waving his arms.

"Don't touch it! Don't kill it!" he cried in a childish voice.

Seeing the officer, the Cossacks stepped apart and released a little white kid. The young ensign was quite abashed, muttered something, and stopped before us with a confused face. Seeing the captain and me on the roof he blushed still more and ran leaping towards us.

"I thought they were killing a child," he said with a bashful smile.

X

The general went ahead with the cavalry. The battalion with which I had come from Fort N. remained in the rearguard. Captain Khlópov's and Lieutenant Rosenkranz's battalions retired together.

The captain's prediction was fully justified. No sooner had we entered the narrow thicket he had mentioned than on both sides of us we caught glimpses of hillsmen mounted and on foot, and so near were they that I could distinctly see how some of them ran stooping, rifle in hand, from one tree to another.

The captain took off his cap and piously crossed himself; some of the older soldiers did the same. From the wood were heard war-cries and the words *"Iay giaour," "Urus! iay!"* Sharp short rifle-shots, following one another fast, whizzed on both sides of us. Our men answered silently with a running fire, and only now and then remarks like the following were made in the ranks: "See where *he*[1] fires from! It's all right for him inside the wood. We ought to use cannon," and so forth.

Our ordnance was brought out, and after some grape-shot had been fired the enemy seemed to grow weaker, but a moment later and at every step taken by our troops, the enemy's fire again grew hotter and the shouting louder.

We had hardly gone seven hundred yards from the village before enemy cannon-balls began whistling over our heads. I saw a soldier killed by one. . . . But why should I describe the details of that terrible picture which I would myself give much to be able to forget!

Lieutenant Rosenkranz kept firing and incessantly shouted in a hoarse voice at the soldiers and galloped from one end of the cordon to the other. He was rather pale and this suited his martial countenance very well.

The good-looking young ensign was in raptures: his beautiful dark eyes shone with daring, his lips were slightly smiling, and he kept riding up to the captain and begging permission to charge.

"We will repel them," he said persuasively. "We certainly will."

"It's not necessary," replied the captain abruptly. "We must retreat."

The captain's company held the skirts of the wood, the men lying down and replying to the enemy's fire. The captain in his shabby coat and shabby cap sat silent on his white horse, with loose reins, bent knees, his feet in the stirrups, and did not stir from his place. (The soldiers knew and did their work so well that there was no need to give

[1] He is a collective noun by which the soldiers indicate the enemy. —L. T.

them any orders.) Only at rare intervals he raised his voice to shout at those who exposed their heads. There was nothing at all martial about the captain's appearance, but there was something so sincere and simple in it that I was unusually struck by it. "It is he who is really brave," I involuntarily said to myself.

He was just the same as I had always seen him: the same calm movements, the same guileless expression on his plain but frank face, only his eyes, which were brighter than usual, showed the concentration of one quietly engaged on his duties. "As I had always seen him" is easily said, but how many different shades have I noticed in the behaviour of others; one wishing to appear quieter, another sterner, a third merrier, than usual, but the captain's face showed that he did not even see why he should appear anything but what he was.

The Frenchman at Waterloo who said, "*La garde meurt, mais ne se rend pas*,"[2] and other, particularly French, heroes who uttered memorable sayings were brave, and really uttered remarkable words, but between their courage and the captain's there was this difference, that even if a great saying had in any circumstance stirred in the soul of my hero, I am convinced that he would not have uttered it: first because by uttering a great saying he would have feared to spoil a great deed, and secondly because when a man feels within himself the capacity to perform a great deed, no talk of any kind is needed. That, I think, is a peculiar and a lofty characteristic of Russian courage, and that being so, how can a Russian heart help aching when our young Russian warriors utter trivial French phrases intended to imitate antiquated French chivalry?

Suddenly from the side where our young ensign stood with his platoon we heard a not very hearty or loud "Hurrah!" Looking round to where the shout came from, I saw some thirty soldiers with sacks on their shoulders and muskets in their hands managing with very great difficulty to run across a ploughed field. They kept stumbling, but nevertheless ran on and shouted. In front of them, sword in hand, galloped the young ensign.

They all disappeared into the wood. . . .

---

[2] "The Guard dies, but does not surrender."

After a few minutes of whooping and clatter a frightened horse ran out of the wood, and soldiers appeared bringing back the dead and wounded. Among the latter was the young ensign. Two soldiers supported him under his arms. He was as pale as a sheet, and his pretty head, on which only a shadow remained of the warlike enthusiasm that had animated him a few minutes before, was dreadfully sunk between his shoulders and drooped on his chest. There was a small spot of blood on the white shirt beneath his unbuttoned coat.

"Ah, what a pity!" I said, involuntarily turning away from this sad spectacle.

"Of course it's a pity," said an old soldier, who stood leaning on his musket beside me with a gloomy expression on his face. "He's not afraid of anything. How can one do such things?" he added, looking intently at the wounded lad. "He was still foolish and now he has paid for it!"

"And you?" I asked. "Are you afraid?"

"What do you expect?"

XI

Four soldiers were carrying the ensign on a stretcher and behind them an ambulance soldier was leading a thin, broken-winded horse with two green boxes on its back containing surgical appliances. They waited for the doctor. Some officers rode up to the stretcher and tried to cheer and comfort the wounded lad.

"Well, friend Alánin, it will be some time before you will dance again with castanets," said Lieutenant Rosenkranz, riding up to the stretcher with a smile.

He probably supposed that these words would raise the young ensign's spirits, but as far as one could judge by the latter's coldly sad look the words had not the desired effect.

The captain rode up too. He looked intently at the wounded man and his usually calm and cold face expressed sincere sympathy. "Well, my dear Anatól Ivánich," he said, in a voice of tender sympathy such as I never expected from him, "evidently it was God's will."

The wounded lad looked round and his pale face lit up with a sad smile. "Yes, I disobeyed you."

"Say rather, it was God's will," repeated the captain.

The doctor when he arrived [as far as could be judged by the shakiness of his legs and the redness of his eyes, was in no fit condition to bandage the patient: however, he] took from his assistant bandages, a probe, and another instrument, rolled up his sleeves, and stepped up to the ensign with an encouraging smile.

"So it seems they have made a hole in a sound spot for you too," he said in a carelessly playful tone. "Let me see."

The ensign obeyed, but the look he gave the merry doctor expressed astonishment and reproof which the inebriated practitioner did not notice. He touched the wound so awkwardly, quite unnecessarily pressing on it with his unsteady fingers, that the wounded ensign, driven beyond the limits of endurance, pushed away his hand with a deep groan.

"Let me alone!" he said in a scarcely audible voice. "I shall die anyway."

[Then, addressing the captain, he said with difficulty: "Please, Captain . . . yesterday I lost . . . twenty rubles to Drónov. . . . When my things are sold . . . let him be paid."]

With those words he fell back, and five minutes later when I passed the group that had formed around him, and asked a soldier, "How is the ensign?" the answer was, "Passing away."

XII

It was late in the day when the detachment, formed into a broad column and singing, approached the Fort.

[The general rode in front and by his merry countenance one could see that the raid had been successful. In fact, with little loss, we had that day been in Mukay *aoul*— where from immemorial times no Russian foot had trod.

The Saxon, Kaspar Lavréntich, narrated to another officer that he had himself seen how three Chechens had aimed straight at his breast. In the mind of Lieutenant Rosenkranz a complete story of the day's action had formulated itself. Captain Khlópov walked with thoughtful face in front of his company, leading his little white horse by its bridle.]

The sun had hidden behind the snowy mountain range and threw its last rosy beams on a long thin cloud stretching motionless across the clear horizon. The snow peaks began to disappear in purple mist and only their top outline was visible, wonderfully distinct in the crimson sunset glow. The delicate moon, which had risen long since, began to grow pale against the deep azure. The green of the grass and trees was turning black and becoming covered with dew. The dark masses of troops moved with measured sounds over the luxuriant meadows. Tambourines, drums, and merry songs were heard from various sides. The voice of the second tenor of the Sixth Company rang out with full force and the sounds of his clear chest-notes, full of feeling and power, floated through the clear evening air.

1852

THE
WOOD-FELLING
A Cadet's Story

I

In the middle of the winter of 185– a division of one battery was on service with the detachment operating in that part of the Térek Territory[1] called the Great Chéchnya. On the evening of February 14, knowing that the platoon, which I, in the absence of any officer was commanding, was to join a column told off to fell wood next day and having given and received the necessary orders, I retired to my tent earlier than usual. As I had not contracted the bad habit of warming my tent with hot charcoal, I lay down without undressing on my bed, which was supported on stakes driven into the ground, drew my fur cap over my eyes, tucked myself up in my sheepskin cloak, and fell into that peculiar, heavy, and deep sleep which comes at times of anxiety and when one is awaiting danger. The expectation of the next day's affair had this effect on me.

At three next morning, while it was still quite dark, the warm sheepskin was pulled off me and my eyes, heavy with sleep, were unpleasantly struck by the red light of a candle.

"Get up, please," said a voice. I shut my eyes, unconsciously pulled the sheepskin back over myself, and again fell asleep. "Get up, please," said Dmítry once more, remorselessly shaking me by the shoulder; "the infantry are starting." The reality suddenly flashed on my mind; I sat up and jumped to my feet. After hurriedly drinking a glass of tea and washing myself with icy water I crept out of the tent and went to the "park" (the place where the cannon

[1] The Térek Territory lies to the north-east of the Caucasian Mountains. The Great and Little Chéchnya are districts in the southern part of it.

were). It was dark, misty, and cold. The dim red light of the night-fires, which gleaming here and there in the camp showed up the figures of the sleepy soldiers who lay near them, seemed only to make the darkness more intense.

Near by, quiet regular snoring could be heard, and from farther off, sounds of movements, voices, and the clatter of the muskets of the infantry preparing to start. There was a smell of smoke, manure, torches, and mist; the morning air caused cold shivers to run down one's back, and one's teeth chattered involuntarily.

It was only by the snorting and occasional stamping of the horses harnessed to them that we could tell where the limbers and ammunition wagons stood in the impenetrable darkness, and only the fiery dots of the linstocks showed where the guns were. "God be with us!" With these words came the clanging sound of the first gun moving, then the noise of the ammunition wagon—and the platoon started. We all took off our caps and crossed ourselves. Having occupied the interval between the infantry companies, the platoon stopped and waited a quarter of an hour for the whole column to collect and for the commander to appear.

"One of our men is missing, Nicholas Petróvich." With these words a black figure approached me, whom I only knew by the voice to be the gun-sergeant of the platoon, Maksímov.

"Who is it?"

"Velenchúk is missing. He was there all the time they were harnessing—I saw him myself—but now he's gone."

As the column could not be expected to start at once, we decided to send Corporal Antónov to look for Velenchúk. Directly after that, several horsemen trotted past us in the dark. They were the commander and his suite; and immediately the head of the column moved and started and so at last did we also, but Antónov and Velenchúk were still absent. We had, however, hardly gone a hundred yards before they both overtook us.

"Where was he?" I asked Antónov.

"Asleep in the 'park'."

"Why, has he had a drop too much?"

"Oh, no."

"Then how is it he fell asleep?"

"I can't make out."

For about three hours we moved slowly on in silence and darkness over some unploughed fields bare of snow and over low bushes that crackled under the wheels of the gun-carriages. At last, after we had crossed a shallow but extremely rapid stream, we were stopped, and we heard the abrupt reports of *vintóvkas*[2] in the direction of the vanguard.

These sounds as usual had a most exhilarating effect on everyone. The detachment seemed to wake up: sounds of talking, movement, and laughter were heard in the ranks. Here a soldier wrestled with a comrade, there another hopped from foot to foot. Here was one chewing hard-tack or, to while away the time, shouldering and grounding arms. Meanwhile the mist began to grow distinctly whiter in the east, the damp became more intense, and the surrounding objects gradually emerged from the gloom. I could already discern the green gun-carriages and ammunition wagons, the brass of the guns covered with moisture by the mist, the familiar figures of my soldiers, every minute detail of which I had involuntarily studied, the bay horses, and the lines of infantry with their bright bayonets, their bags, their ramrods, and the kettles they carried on their backs.

We were soon again moved forward a few hundred yards where there was no road, and then we were shown our position. To the right one could see the steep bank of a winding stream and the high wooden posts of a Tartar cemetery; to the left and in front a black strip was visible through the mist. The platoon unlimbered. The Eighth Company, which covered us, piled their muskets, and a battalion with axes and muskets went to the forest.

Before five minutes were over fires were crackling and smoking in all directions. The soldiers dispersed, blew the fires and stirred them with hands and feet, dragged logs and branches, while the forest resounded with the unceasing noise of hundreds of axes and the crashing of falling trees.

The artillery, with a certain rivalry of the infantry,

2 The *vintóvka* was a long Asiatic rifle used by the Circassians (Cherkéses). When firing, they rested the barrel on a support formed by two thin spiked sticks tied at the top by a strap.

heaped their pile high, and though it was already burning
so that one could hardly come within two paces of it and
thick black smoke was rising through the frozen branches,
which the soldiers pressed down into the fire (and from
which drops fell sizzling into the flames), and though the
charcoal was glowing beneath and the grass was scorched
all around, the soldiers were not satisfied but kept throwing
great logs on to the pile, feeding it with dry grass beneath and heaping it higher and higher.

When I came up to the fire to smoke a cigarette,
Velenchúk, always officious, but to-day feeling guilty and
bustling about more than any one, in a fit of zeal snatched
a piece of charcoal from the fire with his bare hand and,
after tossing it from hand to hand a couple of times,
dropped it on the ground.

"Light a twig and hold it up," said a soldier.

"No, better get a linstock, lad," said another.

When I had at length lit my cigarette without the aid
of Velenchúk, who was again trying to take a piece of
charcoal in his hand, he rubbed his burnt fingers on the
skirts of his sheepskin coat and then, probably for want of
something else to do, lifted a large piece of plane-tree
wood and swung it into the fire. When at last he felt free
to rest a bit, he came close up to the fire, threw open his
cloak which he wore like a mantle fastened by one button,
spread out his legs, held out his big, black hands, and drawing his mouth a bit to one side, screwed up his eyes.

II

In Russia there are three predominant types of soldier under
which the men of all our forces—whether line, guards, infantry, cavalry, artillery, army of the Caucasus, or what
not—may be classified.

These principal types, including many sub-divisions and
combinations, are:

1. The submissive;
2. The domineering;
3. The reckless.

The submissive are divided into (*a*) the calmly submissive and (*b*) the bustlingly submissive.

The domineering are divided into (*a*) the sternly domineering and (*b*) the diplomatically domineering.

The reckless are divided into (*a*) the amusingly reckless and (*b*) the viciously reckless.

The type most often met with—a type more lovable and attractive than the others and generally accompanied by the best Christian virtues: meekness, piety, patience, and devotion to the will of God—is the submissive type in general. The distinctive feature of the calmly submissive is his invincible resignation to and contempt for all the reverses of fate which may befall him; the distinctive features of the submissive drunkard are a mild, poetic disposition and sensibility; the distinctive feature of the bustlingly submissive is limited mental capacity combined with purposeless industry and zeal.

The domineering type in general is found chiefly among the higher grade of soldiers: the corporals, sergeants, sergeant-majors, and so on. The first sub-division, the sternly domineering, is a noble, energetic, pre-eminently military type and does not exclude high poetic impulses (Corporal Antónov, with whom I wish to acquaint the reader, belonged to this type). The second sub-division, formed by the diplomatically domineering, has for some time past been increasing largely. A man of this type is always eloquent and literate,[1] wears pink shirts, won't eat out of the common pot, sometimes smokes tobacco of Mousátov's brand, and thinks himself much superior to the common soldier but is rarely himself as good a soldier as the domineering of the first sub-division.

The reckless type, like the domineering type, is good in its first sub-division, the amusingly reckless, whose characteristic traits are irresistible mirth, great capacity of all kinds, and a highly gifted and daring nature. As with the domineering class, the second sub-division is bad; the viciously reckless are terribly bad, but to the honour of the Russian army it must be said that this type is very rare, and when found it is excluded from companionship by the public opinion of the soldiers themselves. Unbelief and a

[1] A distinction very frequently met with in Russian is between *literate* and *illiterate* people—that is, between those who can and those who cannot read and write.

kind of boldness in vice are the chief traits characteristic of this class.

Velenchúk belonged to the bustlingly submissive. He was an Ukranian by birth, had already served for fifteen years, and although not a showy or smart soldier he was simple-minded, kindly, extremely though often inopportunely zealous, and also exceedingly honest. I say exceedingly honest, because an incident had occurred the year before which made this characteristic quality of his very evident. It must be remembered that almost every soldier knows a trade. The most usual trades are tailoring and boot-making. Velenchúk taught himself the former, and judging from the fact that even Michael Doroféich, the sergeant-major, ordered clothes from him, he must have attained some proficiency at his craft. Last year, in camp, Velenchúk undertook to make a fine cloth coat for Michael Doroféich; but that very night after he had cut out the coat and measured out the trimmings and put them all under his pillow in the tent, a misfortune befell him: the cloth that had cost *seven rubles*, disappeared during the night! Velen-chúk, with tears in his eyes, trembling white lips and suppressed sobs, informed the sergeant-major of the occurrence. Michael Doroféich was enraged. In the first moment of irritation he threatened the tailor; but after-wards, being a man with means and kindly, he just waved his hand and did not demand from Velenchúk payment of the value of the cloth. In spite of all the fuss made by the fussy Velenchúk, in spite of all the tears he shed when telling of his mishap, the thief was not found. A strong suspicion fell on the viciously reckless soldier Chernóv, who slept in the same tent; but there were no positive proofs. The diplomatically domineering Michael Doroféich, being a man with means and having some little business transactions with the master-at-arms and the caterer of the mess (the aristocracy of the battery), very soon forgot all about the loss of his mufti coat. Not so Velenchúk. He did not forget his misfortune. The soldiers said they feared at the time that he might commit suicide or run away into the mountains, so great was the effect of his mishap upon him. He neither ate nor drank and could not even work, but was continually crying. When three days had passed he appeared, quite pale, before Michael Doroféich, took with trembling fingers a gold coin from under his cuff, and gave it him. "Heaven's my witness, Michael Doroféich, that it's all I have, and even that I borrowed from Zhdánov," said he, sobbing again; "and the other two rubles I swear I will also return as soon as I have earned them. He" (whom "he" meant Velenchúk did not himself know) "has made me appear like a rascal before you. He—with his loathsome, viper soul—he takes the last morsel from his brother soldier, after I have served for fifteen years. . . ." To the honour of Michael Doroféich be it said, he did not take the remaining two rubles, though Velenchúk brought them to him two months later.

III

Besides Velenchúk, five other soldiers of my platoon sat warming themselves by our fire.

In the best place, on a butt with his back to the wind, sat Maksímov, the gun-sergeant of the platoon, smoking a pipe. The habit of commanding and the consciousness of his dignity were betrayed by the pose, the look, and by every movement of this man, not to mention his nankeen-covered sheepskin coat and the butt he was sitting on, which latter is an emblem of power at a halting-place.

When I came up he turned his head towards me without removing his eyes from the fire, and his look, following the direction his head had taken, only fell on me some time later. Maksímov was not a serf but a peasant-yeoman; he had some money, had qualified to take a class in the school-brigade, and had stuffed his head with erudition. He was awfully rich and awfully learned, so the soldiers said. I remember how once, when we were practising plunging fire with a quadrant, he explained to the soldiers gathered round that a spirit level *is nothing but as it occurs that atmospheric mercury has its motion*. In reality, Maksímov was far from being stupid and understood his work thoroughly, but he had the unfortunate peculiarity of sometimes purposely speaking so that there was no possibility of understanding him and so that, I am convinced, he did not understand his own words. He was particularly fond of the words "as it occurs" and "continues," so that when

I heard him say "as it occurs" or "continues," I knew beforehand that I should understand nothing of what followed. The soldiers on the other hand, as far as I could judge, liked to hear his "as it occurs" and suspected it of being fraught with deep meaning, though they did not understand a word of it any more than I did. This they attributed entirely to their own stupidity, and respected Theodor Maksímov all the more. In a word, Maksímov was one of the diplomatically domineering.

The soldier next to him, who had bared his sinewy red legs and was putting on his boots again by the fire, was Antónov—that same Corporal Antónov who in 1837, remaining with only two others in charge of an exposed gun, persisted in firing back at a powerful enemy and, with two bullets in his leg, continued to serve his gun and to reload it.

The soldiers used to say that he would have been made a gun-sergeant long ago but for his character. And his character really was very peculiar. No one could have been calmer, gentler, or more accurate that he was when sober; but when he had a fit of drinking he became quite another man: he would not submit to authority, fought, brawled, and became a perfectly good-for-nothing soldier. Only the week before this, during the Carnival, he had had a drinking-bout, and in spite of all threats, persuasions, and being tied to a cannon, he went on drinking and brawling up to the first day of Lent. During the whole of Lent, though the division had been ordered not to fast, he fed on dried bread, and during the first week would not even drink the regulation cup of vodka. But one had to see his sturdy thick-set figure, as of wrought iron, on its stumpy bandy legs, and his shiny moustached visage when in a tipsy mood he took the *balaláyka* in his sinewy hands and looking carelessly round played "Lady," or walked down the street with his cloak thrown loosely over his shoulders, his medals dangling, his hands in the pockets of his blue nankeen trousers, and a look on his countenance of soldierly pride and of contempt for all that was not of the artillery—one had to see all this in order to understand how impossible it was for him at such a moment to abstain from fighting an orderly, a Cossack, an infantry-man, a peasant (in fact, anyone not of the artillery) who was rude to him or happened merely to be in his way. He fought and rioted not so much for his own pleasure as to maintain the spirit of soldiership in general, of which he felt himself to be the representative.

The third soldier, who sat on his heels smoking a clay pipe, was the artillery driver Chíkin. He had an ear-ring in one of his ears, bristling little moustaches, and the physiognomy of a bird. "Dear old Chíkin," as the soldiers called him, was a wit. During the bitterest frost, or up to his knees in mud, or after going two days without food, on the march, on parade, or at drill, the "dear fellow" was always and everywhere making faces, twisting his legs about, or cracking jokes that convulsed the whole platoon with laughter. At every halting-place, and in the camp, there was always a circle of young soldiers collected round Chíkin, who played *Fílka*[1] with them, told them stories about the cunning soldier and the English *milord*, personated a Tartar or a German, or simply made remarks of his own at which everyone roared with laughter. It is true that his reputation as a wit was so well established in the battery that it was sufficient for him to open his mouth and wink in order to produce a general guffaw, but really there was much in him that was truly humorous and surprising. He saw something special, something that never entered anybody else's head, in everything, and above all, this capacity for seeing the funny side of things was proof against any and every trial.

The fourth soldier was an insignificant-looking boy re- cruited the year before and this was his first campaign. He stood surrounded by the smoke and so near the flames that his threadbare cloak seemed in danger of catching fire, yet judging by the way he extended the skirts of his cloak and bent out his calves, and by his quiet self-satisfied pose, he was feeling highly contented.

The fifth and last of the soldiers was Daddy Zhdánov. He sat a little way off, cutting a stick. Zhdánov had been serving in the battery longer than anyone else, had known all the others as recruits, and they were all in the habit of calling him "daddy." It was said of him that he never drank, smoked, or played cards (not even "noses"), and never used bad language. He spent all his spare time boot-making,

---

[1] A soldier's card game.—L. T.

went to church on holidays where that was possible, or else put a farthing taper before his icon and opened the book of psalms, the only book he could read. He seldom kept company with the other soldiers. To those who were his seniors in rank though his juniors in years he was coldly respectful; with his equals he had few opportunities of mixing, not being a drinker. He liked the recruits and the youngest soldiers best: he always took them under his protection, admonished them, and often helped them. Everyone in the battery considered him a capitalist because he had some twenty-five rubles, out of which he was always ready to lend something to a soldier in real need.

The same Maksímov who was now gun-sergeant told me that ten years ago, when he first came as a recruit and drank all he had with the old soldiers who were in the habit of drinking, Zhdánov, noticing his unfortunate position, called him up, severely reprimanded him for his conduct and even beat him, delivered a lecture on how one should live in the army, and sent him away after giving him a shirt (which Maksímov lacked) and half-a-ruble in money. "He made a man of me," Maksímov always used to say with respect and gratitude. He also helped Velen-chúk (whom he had taken under his protection since he was a recruit) at the time of his misfortune. When the coat was stolen he helped him as he had helped many and many another during the twenty-five years of his service.

One could not hope to find a man in the service who knew his work more thoroughly or was a better or more conscientious soldier than he; but he was too meek and insignificant-looking to be made a gun-sergeant, though he had been bombardier for fifteen years. Zhdánov's one enjoyment and passion was song. He had a few favourite songs, always collected a circle of singers from among the younger soldiers, and though he could not sing himself he would stand by them, his hands in the pockets of his cloak, his eyes closed, showing sympathy by the movements of his head and jaw. I don't know why, but that regular movement of the jaws below the ears, which I never noticed in anyone else, seemed to me extremely expressive. His snow-white head, his blackened moustaches, and his sunburnt, wrinkled face, gave him at first sight a stern and harsh expression, but on looking closer into his large round eyes, especially when they smiled (he never laughed with his lips), you were suddenly struck by something remarkable in their unusually mild, almost childlike look.

IV

"I'll be blowed! I've gone and forgot my pipe. Here's a go, lads!" repeated Velenchúk.

"You should smoke *cikars*, old fellow!" began Chíkin, drawing his mouth to one side and winking. "There, now, I always smoke *cikars* when I'm at home—them's sweeter."

Of course everybody burst out laughing.

"Forgot your pipe, indeed!" interrupted Maksímov, without heeding the general mirth, and beating the tobacco out of his pipe into the palm of his left hand with the proud air of a superior; "where did you vanish to—eh, Velenchúk?"

Velenchúk, half turning round to him, was about to raise his hand to his cap, but dropped it again.

"Seems to me you hadn't your sleep out after yesterday —falling asleep when you are once up! It's not thanks the likes of you get for such goings on."

"May I die, Theodor Maksímov, if a drop has passed my lips; I don't myself know what happened to me," answered Velenchúk. "Much cause I had for revelling," he muttered.

"Just so; but we have to answer to the authorities because of the likes of you, and you continue—it's quite scandalous!" the eloquent Maksímov concluded in a calmer tone.

"It's quite wonderful, lads," Velenchúk went on after a moment's silence, scratching his head and addressing no one in particular, "really quite wonderful, lads! Here have I been serving for the last sixteen years and such a thing never happened to me. When we were ordered to appear for muster I was all right, but at the 'park,' there *it* suddenly clutches hold of me, and clutches and clutches, and down it throws me, down on the ground and no more ado —and I did not myself know how I fell asleep, lads! That must have been the trances," he concluded.

"True enough, I hardly managed to wake you," said Antónov as he pulled on his boot. "I had to push and push just as if you'd been a log!"

"Fancy now," said Velenchúk, "if I'd been drunk now! . . ."

"That's just like a woman we had at home," began Chíkin; "she hardly got off the stove for two years. Once they began waking her—they thought she was asleep—and she was already dead. She used to be taken sleepy that way. That's what it is, old fellow!"

"Now then, Chíkin, won't you tell us how you set the tone during your leave of absence?" said Maksímov, looking at me with a smile as if to say, "Would you, too, like to hear the stupid fellow?"

"What tone, Theodor Maksímov?" said Chíkin, giving me a rapid side-glance. "In course I told them what sort of a *Caw-cusses* we'd got here."

"Well, yes, how did you do it? There! don't give yourself airs; tell us how you *administrated* it to them."

"How should I administrate it? In course they asked me how we live," Chíkin began rapidly with the air of a man recounting something he had repeated several times before. " 'We live well, old fellow,' says I. 'Provisions in plenty we get: morning and night a cup of *chokelad* for every *soldier lad*, and at noon barley broth before us is set, such as gentlefolks get, and instead of vodka we get a pint of Modera wine from Devirier, such as costs forty-four—with the bottle ten more!' "

"Fine Modera," Velenchúk shouted louder than anyone, rolling with laughter; "that's Modera of the right sort!"

"Well, and what did you tell them about the Asiaites?" Maksímov went on to ask when the general mirth had subsided a little.

Chíkin stooped over the fire, poked out a bit of charcoal with a stick, put it to his pipe, and long continued puffing at his shag as though not noticing the silent curiosity awakened in his hearers. When he had at last drawn enough smoke he threw the bit of charcoal away, pushed his cap yet farther back, and, stretching himself, continued with a slight smile.

"Well, so they asked, 'What's that Cherkés fellow or Turk as you've got down in your Cawcusses,' they say 'as fights?' and so I says 'Them's not all of one sort; there's different Cherkéses, old fellow. There's the Wagabones, them as lives in the stony mountains and eat stones instead of bread. They're big,' says I, 'as big as a good-sized beam, they've one eye in the forehead and wear burning red caps,' just such as yours, old fellow," he added, turning to the young recruit, who really wore an absurd cap with a red crown.

At this unexpected sally the recruit suddenly collapsed, slapped his knees, and burst out laughing and coughing so that he hardly managed to utter in a stifled voice, "Them Wagabones is the right sort!"

" 'Then,' says I, 'there's also the Mopingers,' " continued Chíkin, making his cap slip onto his forehead with a movement of his head: " 'These others are little twins, so big . . . all in pairs,' says I, 'they run about hand in hand at such a rate,' says I, 'that you couldn't catch 'em on a horse!' —'Then how's it, lad,' they say, 'how's them Mopingers, be they born hand in hand?' " He said this in a hoarse bass, pretending to imitate a peasant. " 'Yes,' says I, 'he's naturally like that. Tear their hands apart and they'll bleed just like a Chinaman: take a Chinaman's cap off and it'll bleed.'—'And tell us, lad, how do they fight?'—'That's how,' says I, 'they catch you and rip your belly up and wind your bowels round your arm, and wind and wind. They go on winding and you go on laughing till your breath all goes.' "

"Well, and did they believe you, Chíkin?" said Maksímov with a slight smile, while all the rest were dying with laughter.

"Such queer people, Theodor Maksímych, they believe everything. On my word they do. But when I told them about Mount Kazbéc and said that the snow didn't melt on it all the summer, they mocked at me! 'What are you bragging for, lad,' they says; 'a big mountain and the snow on it don't melt? Why, lad, when the thaw sets in here every tiny bit of a hillock thaws first while the snow still lies in the hollows.' There now!" Chíkin concluded with a wink.

V

The bright disk of the sun shining through the milky-white mist had already risen to a considerable height. The purple-grey horizon gradually widened, but though it had receded considerably it was still as sharply outlined by a deceptive white wall of mist.

Beyond the felled wood a good-sized plain now opened in front of us. The black or milky-white or purple smoke of the fires expanded and fantastic shapes of white mist-clouds floated above the plain. An occasional group of mounted Tartars appeared far in the distance before us and at rare intervals the reports of our rifles[1] and of their *vintóvkas* and cannon were to be heard.

This, as Captain Khlópov said, was "not yet business, but only play."

The commander of the 9th Company of Chasseurs, that formed our support, came up to our guns, pointed to three Tartars[2] on horseback skirting the forest some 1,400 yards from us, and with the fondness for artillery fire common among infantry officers in general asked me to let off a ball or bomb at them.

"Do you see?" he said with a kind and persuasive smile, as he stretched his hand from behind my shoulder, "in front of those big trees there . . . one on a white horse and in a black Circassian cloak and two others behind. Do you see? Could you not, please?"

"And there are three more riding at the outskirt of the forest," said Antónov, who had astonishingly sharp eye-sight, coming up to us, and hiding behind his back the pipe he had been smoking. "There, the one in front has taken his gun out of its case. They can be seen distinctly, y'r honor!"

"Look there! he's fired, lads. D'ye see the white smoke?" said Velenchúk, who was one of a group of soldiers standing a little behind us.

"At our line surely, the blackguard!" remarked another.

"See what a lot of 'em come streaming out of the forest. Must be looking round . . . want to place a gun," said a third.

[1] Most of the Russian army at that time were armed with smooth-bore muskets, but a few had wide-calibred muzzle-loading rifles (*stútzers*), which were difficult to handle and slow to load. *Vintóvkas* were also rifles.

[2] Russians in the Caucasus used the word "Tartar" loosely for any of the native Mohammedan tribes (Circassians, Kabardáns, etc.), much as among ourselves the word "Niggers" is used to denote almost any dark race.

"Supposing now a bomb was sent right into that lot, wouldn't they spit!"

"And what d'ye think, old fellow—that it would just reach 'em?" said Chíkin.

"Twelve hundred or twelve hundred and fifty yards: not more than that," said Maksímov calmly, and as if speaking to himself, though it was evident he was just as anxious to fire as the rest; "if we were to give an elevation of forty-five lines to our 'unicorn'[3] we could hit the very point, that is to say, perfectly."

"D'ye know, if you were now to aim at that group you would be sure to hit somebody. There now, they are all together—please be quick and give the order to fire," the company commander continued to entreat me.

"Are we to point the gun?" suddenly asked Antónov in an abrupt bass with a look as if of gloomy anger.

I must admit that I also felt a strong wish to fire, so I ordered the second gun to be trained.

I had hardly given the order before the shell was charged and rammed in and Antónov, leaning against the cheek of the gun-carriage and holding two of his thick fingers to the base-ring, was directing the movement of the tail of the gun. "Right, left—a bit to the left, a wee bit —more—more—right!" he said, stepping from the gun with a look of pride.

The infantry officer, I, and Maksímov, one after the other, approached, put our heads to the sights, and expressed our various opinions.

"By Heavens, it will shoot over," remarked Velenchúk, clicking his tongue, though he was only looking over Antónov's shoulder and therefore had no grounds for this supposition. "By Hea-vens it will shoot over; it will hit that there tree, my lads!"

I gave the order: "Two."

The men stepped away from the gun. Antónov ran aside to watch the flight of the shot. The touch-hole flashed and the brass rang. At the same moment we were enveloped in a cloud of powder-smoke and, emerging from the overpowering boom of the discharge, the humming, metallic

---

[3] The "unicorn" was a type of gun, narrowing towards the muzzle, used in the Russian artillery at that time.

sound of the flying shot receded with the swiftness of lightning and died away in the distance amid general silence.

A little beyond the group of horsemen a white cloudlet appeared, the Tartars galloped away in all directions, and the report of the explosion reached us. "That was very fine!" "Ah, how they galloped!" "The devils don't like that!" came the words of approval and ridicule from the ranks of the artillery and infantry.

"If we had had the gun pointed only a touch lower we should just have caught him. I said it would hit the tree and sure enough it did go to the right," remarked Velenchúk.

VI

Leaving the soldiers to discuss how the Tartars galloped off when they saw the shell, why they had been riding there, and whether there were many of them in the forest, I went and sat down with the company commander under a tree a few steps off to wait while the cutlets he had invited me to share were being warmed up. The company commander, Bólkhov, was one of the officers nicknamed "bon-jourists" in the regiment. He was a man of some means, had formerly served in the Guards, and spoke French. But in spite of all this his comrades liked him. He was clever enough, and had tact enough, to wear a coat of Petersburg make, to eat a good dinner, and to speak French, without too much offending his fellow officers. After talking about the weather, the military operations, our mutual acquaintances among the officers, and having assured ourselves of the satisfactory state of each other's ideas by questions and answers and the views expressed, we involuntarily passed to more intimate conversation. And when people belonging to the same circle meet in the Caucasus a very evident, even if unspoken, question arises: "Why are you here?" and it was to this silent question of mine that, as it seemed to me, my companion wished to reply.

"When will this expedition end?" he said lazily. "It is so dull."

"I don't think it dull," said I. "It's much worse on the staff."

"Oh, it's ten thousand times worse on the staff," he said irascibly. "No, I mean when will the whole thing end?"

"What is it you want to end?" I asked.

"Everything—the whole affair! . . . Are the cutlets ready, Nikoláyev?"

"Then why did you come to serve here if you so dislike the Caucasus?" I said.

"Do you know why?" he answered with resolute frankness. "In obedience to tradition! You know there exists in Russia a most curious tradition about the Caucasus, making it out to be a "promised land" for all unfortunates."

"Yes, that is almost true," said I. "Most of us—"

"But the best of it is," he said, interrupting me, "that all of us who came to the Caucasus in obedience to the tradition made a terrible mistake in our calculations and I can't for the life of me see why one should, in consequence of an unfortunate love affair or of financial troubles, choose to go and serve in the Caucasus rather than in Kazán or Kalúga. Why in Russia they imagine the Caucasus to be something majestic: eternal virgin ice, rushing torrents, daggers, mantles, fair Circassians, and an atmosphere of terror and romance; but in reality there is nothing amusing in it. If they only realized that we never get to the virgin ice, that it would not be at all amusing if we did, and that the Caucasus is divided into governments— Stavrópol, Tiflís, and so on."

"Yes," said I, laughing, "we look very differently at the Caucasus when we are in Russia and when we are here. It is like what you may have experienced when reading verses in a language you are not familiar with; you imagine them to be much better than they are."

"I really don't know; but I dislike this Caucasus awfully," he said, interrupting me.

"Well, no; I still like the Caucasus, only in a different way."

"Perhaps it is all right," he continued irritably; "all I know is that I'm not all right in the Caucasus."

"Why is that?" I asked, to say something.

"Well, first because it has deceived me. All that I, in obedience to tradition, came to the Caucasus to be cured of has followed me here, only with the difference that there it was all on a big scale and now it is on a little dirty one where at each step I find millions of petty anxieties, shabbinesses, and insults; and next because I feel that I am sinking, morally, lower and lower every day; but chiefly, because I do not feel fit for the service here. I can't stand running risks. The fact of the matter is simply that I am not brave."

He stopped and looked at me, not joking.

Though this unasked-for confession surprised me very much, I did not contradict him as he evidently wished me to do but waited for his own refutation of his words, which always follows in such cases.

"Do you know, in coming on this expedition I am taking part in an action for the first time," he continued, "and you can't think what was going on in me yesterday. When the sergeant-major brought the order that my company was to join the column, I turned as white as a sheet and could not speak for excitement. And if you only knew what a night I had! If it were true that one's hair turns white from fear, mine ought to be perfectly white to-day, because I don't think any one condemned to death ever suffered more in a night than I did; and even now, though I feel a bit easier than in the night, this is what goes on inside!" he added, turning his fist about before his chest. "And what is funny is that while a most fearful tragedy is being enacted, here one sits eating cutlets and onions and making believe that it is great fun. Have we any wine, Nikoláyev?" he added, yawning.

"That's *him*, my lads!" came the excited voice of one of the soldiers, and all eyes turned towards the border of the distant forest.

In the distance a puff of bluish smoke expanded and rose, blown about by the wind. When I had understood that this was a shot fired at us by the enemy, all before my eyes at the moment assumed a sort of new and majestic character. The piles of arms, the smoke of the fires, the blue sky, the green gun-carriages, Nikoláyev's sunburnt, moustached face—all seemed telling me that the ball that had already emerged from the smoke and was at that moment flying through space might be directed straight at my breast.

"Where did you get the wine?" I asked Bólkhov lazily, while deep in my soul two voices spoke with equal clearness. One said, "Lord receive my soul in peace," the other, "I hope I shall not stoop, but smile, while the ball is passing," and at that moment something terribly unpleasant whistled past our heads and a cannon ball crashed down a couple of paces from us.

"There now, had I been a Napoleon or a Frederick I should certainly have paid you a compliment," Bólkhov remarked, turning towards me quite calmly.

"You have done so as it is," I answered, with difficulty hiding the excitement produced in me by the danger just passed.

"Well, what if I have?—no one will write it down."

"Yes, I will."

"Well, if you do put it down, it will only be 'for criticism,' as Míschenkov says," he added with a smile.

"Ugh! the damned thing!" just then remarked Antónov behind us, as he spat over his shoulder with vexation, "just missed my legs!"

All my attempts to seem calm, and all our cunning phrases, suddenly seemed to me insufferably silly after that simple exclamation.

VII

The enemy had really placed two guns where we had seen the Tartars riding, and they fired a shot every twenty or thirty minutes at our men who were felling the wood. My platoon was ordered forward to the plain to answer the enemy's fire. A puff of smoke appeared on the outskirts of the forest, then followed a report and a whistle, and a ball fell in front or behind us. The enemy's shots fell fortunately for us and we sustained no losses.

The artillery men behaved splendidly as they always do; loaded quickly, pointed carefully at the spots where the puffs of smoke were, and quietly joked with one another.

The infantry supports lay near in silent inaction awaiting their turn. The wood-fellers went on with their work, the axes rang faster and more unintermittently through the forest; but when the whistle of a shot became audible all were suddenly silent and, in the midst of the deathly stillness, voices not quite calm exclaimed, "Scatter, lads!" and all eyes followed the ball ricochetting over wood piles and strewn branches.

The mist had now risen quite high and, turning into clouds, gradually disappeared into the dark-blue depths of the sky; the unveiled sun shone brightly, throwing sparkling reflections from the steel bayonets, the brass of the guns, the thawing earth, and the glittering hoar-frost. In the air one felt the freshness of the morning frost together with the warmth of the spring sunshine; thousands of different hues and tints mingled in the dry leaves of the forest, and the shining, beaten track plainly showed the traces left by wheels and the marks of rough-shod horses' feet.

The movement became greater and more noticeable between the two forces. On all sides the blue smoke of the guns appeared more and more frequently. Dragoons rode forward, the streamers of their lances flying; from the infantry companies one heard songs, and the carts laden with firewood formed into a train in our rear. The general rode up to our platoon and ordered us to prepare to retire. The enemy settled in the bushes on our left flank and their snipers began to molest us seriously. A bullet came humming from the woods to the left and struck a gun-carriage, then came another, and a third. . . . The infantry supports that had been lying near us rose noisily, took up their muskets and formed into a line.

The small-arm firing increased and bullets flew more and more frequently. The retreat commenced and consequently the serious part of the action, as is usual in the Caucasus.

Everything showed that the artillerymen like the bullets as little as the infantry had liked the cannon-balls. Antónov frowned, Chíkin imitated the bullets and joked about them, but it was easy to see he did not like them. "It's in a mighty hurry," he said of one of them; another he called "little bee"; a third, which seemed to fly slowly past overhead with a kind of piteous wail, he called an "orphan," which caused general laughter.

The recruit, who, unaccustomed to such scenes, bent his head to one side and stretched his neck every time a bullet passed, also made the soldiers laugh. "What, is that a friend of yours you're bowing to?" they said to him. Velenchúk also, usually quite indifferent to danger, was now excited: he was evidently vexed that we did not fire case-shot in the direction whence the bullets came. He repeated several times in a discontented tone, "Why is *he* allowed to go for us and gets nothing in return? If we turned a gun that way and gave them a taste of case-shot they'd hold their noise, no fear!"

It was true that it was time to do this, so I ordered them to fire a last bomb and then to load with case-shot.

"Case-shot!" Antónov called out briskly as he went through the thick of the smoke to sponge out the gun as soon as it was discharged.

At that moment I heard just behind me the rapid whiz of a bullet suddenly stopped by something, with a dull thud. My heart ceased beating. "Someone of the men had been hit," I thought, while a sad presentiment made me afraid to turn round. And really that sound was followed by the heavy fall of a body, and the heart-rending "Oh-o-oh" of someone who had been wounded. "I'm hit, lads!" a voice I knew exclaimed with an effort. It was Velenchúk. He was lying on his back between the limbers and a cannon. The cartridge-bag he had been carrying was thrown to one side. His forehead was covered with blood, and a thick red stream was running down over his right eye and nose. He was wounded in the stomach but hardly bled at all there; his forehead he had hurt against a log in falling.

All this I made out much later; the first moment I could only see an indistinct mass and, as it seemed to me, a tremendous quantity of blood.

Not one of the soldiers who were loading said a word; only the young recruit muttered something that sounded like "Dear me! he's bleeding;" and Antónov, frowning, gave an angry grunt; but it was clear that the thought of death passed through the soul of each. All set to work very actively and the gun was loaded in a moment, but the ammunition-bearer bringing the case-shot went two or

three steps round the spot where Velenchúk still lay
groaning.

VIII

Everyone who has been in action undoubtedly knows that
strange and though illogical yet powerful feeling of aversion
for the spot where some one has been killed or wounded.
It was evident that for a moment my men gave way to this
feeling when Velenchúk had to be taken to the cart that
came up to fetch him. Zhdánov came up angrily to the
wounded man and, taking him under the arms, lifted him
without heeding his loud screams. "Now then, what are
you standing there for? take hold!" he shouted, and about
ten assistants, some of them superfluous, immediately
surrounded Velenchúk. But hardly had they moved him
when he began screaming and struggling terribly.

"What are you screaming like a hare for?" said
Antónov roughly, holding his leg; "mind, or we'll just
leave you."

And the wounded man really became quiet and only
now and then uttered, "Oh, it's my death! Oh, oh, oh, lads!"

When he was laid in the cart he even stopped moaning
and I heard him speak to his comrades in low clear tones,
probably saying farewell to them.

No one likes to look at a wounded man during an
action and, instinctively hurrying to end this scene, I
ordered him to be taken quickly to the ambulance and
returned to the guns. But after a few minutes I was told
that Velenchúk was asking for me, and I went up to the
cart.

The wounded man lay at the bottom of the cart holding
on to the sides with both hands. His broad healthy face
had completely changed during those few moments; he
seemed to have grown thinner and years older; his lips were
thin and pale and pressed together with an evident strain.
The hasty and dull expression of his glance was replaced
by a kind of bright clear radiance, and on the bloody forehead and nose already lay the impress of death. Though
the least movement caused him excruciating pain, he

nevertheless asked to have a small *chérez*[1] with money taken from his left leg.

The sight of his bare, white, healthy leg, when his jackboot had been taken off and the purse untied, produced on me a terribly sad feeling.

"Here are three rubles and a half," he said, as I took the purse: "you'll take care of them."

The cart was starting, but he stopped it.

"I was making a cloak for Lieutenant Sulimóvsky. He gave me two rubles. I bought buttons for one and a half, and half a ruble is in my bag with the buttons. Please let him have it."

"All right! all right!" said I. "Get well again, old fellow."

He did not answer; the cart started and he again began to groan and cry out in a terrible, heart-rending voice. It was as if, having done with the business of this life, he did not think it necessary to restrain himself and considered it permissible to allow himself this relief.

IX

"Where are you off to? Come back! Where are you going?" I shouted to the recruit, who with his reserve linstock under his arm and a stick of some sort in his hand was, in the coolest manner, following the cart that bore the wounded man.

But the recruit only looked at me lazily, muttered something or other, and continued his way, so that I had to send a soldier to bring him back. He took off his red cap and looked at me with a stupid smile.

"Where were you going?" I asked.

"To the camp."

"Why?"

"Why? . . . Velenchúk is wounded," he said, again smiling.

"What's that to you? You must stay here."

He looked at me with surprise, then turned quietly round, put on his cap, and went back to his place.

---

[1] The *chérez* is a purse in the form of a garter, usually worn by soldiers below the knee.—L. T.

The affair in general was successful. The Cossacks, as we heard, had made a fine charge and brought back three dead Tartars;[1] the infantry had provided itself with firewood and had only half-a-dozen men wounded; the artillery had lost only Velenchúk and two horses. For that, two miles of forest had been cut down and the place so cleared as to be unrecognizable. Instead of the thick outskirts of the forest you saw before you a large plain covered with smoking fires and cavalry and infantry marching back to camp.

Though the enemy continued to pursue us with artillery and small-arms fire up to the cemetery by the little river we had crossed in the morning, the retirement was successfully accomplished. I was already beginning to dream of the cabbage-soup and mutton-ribs with buckwheat that were awaiting me in camp, when a message came from the general ordering a redoubt to be constructed by the river, and the 3rd battalion of the K—— Regiment and the platoon of the 4th Battery to remain there till next day.

The carts with the wood and the wounded, the Cossacks, the artillery, the infantry with muskets and faggots on their shoulders, all passed us with noise and songs. Every face expressed animation and pleasure caused by the escape from danger and the hope of rest. Only we and the 3rd battalion had to postpone those pleasant feelings till to-morrow.

X

While we of the artillery were busy with the guns—parking the limbers and the ammunition wagons and arranging the picket-ropes—the infantry had already piled their muskets, made up camp-fires, built little huts of branches and maize straw, and begun boiling their buckwheat.

The twilight had set in. Bluish white clouds crept over

[1] The "Tartars," being Mohammedans, made a point of not letting the bodies of their slain fall into the hands of the "unbelievers," but removed them and buried them as heroes. The capture of three bodies therefore indicates the vigour of the attack and the demoralization of the enemy.

the sky. The mist, turning into fine dank drizzle, wetted the earth and the soldiers' cloaks; the horizon narrowed and all the surroundings assumed a gloomier hue. The damp I felt through my boots and on my neck, the ceaseless movement and talk in which I took no part, the sticky mud on which my feet kept slipping, and my empty stomach, all combined to put me into the dreariest, most unpleasant frame of mind after the physical and moral weariness of the day. I could not get Velenchúk out of my head. The whole simple story of his soldier-life depicted itself persistently in my imagination.

His last moments were as clear and calm as his whole life had been. He had lived too honestly and been too artless for his simple faith in a future heavenly life to be shaken at the decisive moment.

"Your honour!" said Nikoláyev, coming up to me, "the captain asks you to come and have tea with him."

Having scrambled through, as best I could, between the piles of arms and the camp-fires, I followed Nikoláyev to where Bólkhov was, thinking with pleasure of a tumbler of hot tea and a cheerful conversation which would disperse my gloomy thoughts.

"Have you found him?" I heard Bólkhov's voice say from inside a maize-hut in which a light was burning.

"I've brought him, y'r honour," answered Nikoláyev's bass voice.

Inside the hut Bólkhov was sitting on a dry mantle, with unbuttoned coat and no cap. A samovar stood boiling by his side and on a drum were light refreshments. A bayonet holding a candle was stuck into the ground.

"What do you think of it?" he asked, looking proudly round his cosy establishment. It really was so nice inside the hut that at tea I quite forgot the damp, the darkness, and Velenchúk's wound. We talked of Moscow and of things that had not the least relation to the war or to the Caucasus.

After a moment of silence such as sometimes occurs in the most animated conversation, Bólkhov looked at me with a smile.

"I think our conversation this morning struck you as being very strange," he said.

"No, why do you think so? It only seemed to me that

you were too frank; there are things which we all know, but which should never be mentioned."

"Why not? If there were the least possibility of changing this life for the lowest and poorest without danger and without service. I should not hesitate a moment."

"Then why don't you return to Russia?" I asked.

"Why?" he repeated. "Oh, I have thought about that long ago. I can't return to Russia now until I have the Anna and Vladímir orders: an Anna round my neck and the rank of major, as I planned when I came here."

"Why?—if, as you say, you feel unfit for the service here."

"But what if I feel still more unfit to go back to Russia to the same position that I left? That is also one of the traditions in Russia, confirmed by Pássek, Sleptsóv, and others, that one need only go to the Caucasus to be laden with rewards. Everyone expects and demands it of us; and I have been here for two years, have been on two expeditions, and have got nothing. But still I have so much ambition that I won't leave on any account until I am a major with a Vladímir and Anna round my neck. I have become so concerned about it that it upsets me when Gnilokíshkin gets a reward and I don't. And then how am I to show myself in Russia, to the village elder, to the merchant Kotélnikov to whom I sell my corn, to my Moscow aunt, and to all those good people, if after two years spent in the Caucasus I return without any reward? It is true I don't at all wish to know all those people, and they no doubt care very little about me either; but man is so made that, though I don't want to know them, yet on account of them I'm wasting the best years of my life, all my life's happiness, and am ruining my future."

XI

Just then we heard the voice of the commander of the battalion outside, addressing Bólkhov.

"Who is with you, Nicholas Fëdorovich?"

Bólkhov gave him my name, and then three officers scrambled into the hut—Major Kirsánov; the adjutant of his battalion; and Captain Trosénko.

Kirsánov was not tall but stout; he had black moustaches, rosy cheeks, and oily little eyes. These eyes were his most remarkable feature. When he laughed nothing remained of them but two tiny moist stars, and these little stars together with his wide-stretched lips and outstretched neck often gave him an extraordinarily senseless look. In the regiment Kirsánov behaved himself and bore himself better than anyone else; his subordinates did not complain of him and his superiors respected him—though the general opinion was that he was very limited. He knew the service, was exact and zealous, always had ready money, kept a carriage and a man-cook, and knew how to make an admirable pretence of being proud.

"What were you talking about, Nicholas Fëdorovich?"

"Why, about the attractions of the service here."

But just then Kirsánov noticed me, a cadet, and to impress me with his importance he paid no attention to Bólkhov's reply but looked at the drum and said, "Are you tired, Nicholas Fëdorovich?"

"No, you see we—" Bólkhov began.

But again the dignity of the commander of the battalion seemed to make it necessary to interrupt and to ask another question.

"That was a famous affair to-day, was it not?"

The adjutant of the battalion was a young ensign recently promoted from being a cadet, a modest, quiet lad with a bashful and kindly pleasant face. I had met him at Bólkhov's before. The lad would often come here, bow, sit down in a corner, and remain silent for hours making cigarettes and smoking them; then he would rise, bow, and go away. He was the type of a poor Russian nobleman's son who had chosen the military career as the only one possible to him with his education and who esteemed his position as an officer above everything else in the world—a simple-minded and lovable type notwithstanding the comical appurtenances inseparable from it: the tobacco-pouch, dressing-gown, guitar, and little moustache-brush we are accustomed to associate with it. It was told of him in the regiment that he bragged about being just but strict with his orderly and that he used to say, I punish seldom, but when I am compelled to do it it's no joke," but that when his tipsy orderly robbed him outrageously and even began to insult him, he, the master, took him to the guard-house and ordered everything to be prepared for a flogging but was so upset at the sight of the preparations that he could only say, "There now, you see, I could—" and becoming quite disconcerted, ran home in great confusion and was henceforth afraid to look his man Chernóv in the eyes. His comrades gave the simple-minded boy no rest but teased him continually about this episode, and more than once I heard how he defended himself, and blushing to the tips of his ears assured them that it was not true, but just the contrary.

The third visitor, Captain Trosénko, was a thorough-going old Caucasian—that is, a man for whom the company he commanded had become his family; the fortress where the staff was, his home; and the soldiers' singing his only pleasure in life. He was a man for whom everything unconnected with the Caucasus was contemptible and scarcely worthy of being considered probable, and everything connected with the Caucasus was divided into two halves: ours and not ours. The first he loved, the second he hated with all the power of his soul; but above all he was a man of steeled, calm courage, wonderfully kind in his behaviour to his comrades and subordinates and desperately frank and even rude to aides-de-camp and "bonjourists," for whom for some reason he had a great dislike. On entering the hut he nearly caved the roof in with his head, then suddenly sank down and sat on the ground.

"Well?" he said, and then suddenly remarking me whom he did not know, he stopped and gazed at me with a dull, fixed look.

"Well, and what have you been conversing about?" asked the major, taking out his watch and looking at it, though I am perfectly certain he had no need to.

"Why, I've been asked my reasons for serving here—"

"Of course, Nicholas Fëdorovich wishes to distinguish himself here, and then to return home," said the major.

"Well, and you, Abram Ilých," said Bólkhov, addressing Kirsánov, "tell me why you are serving in the Caucasus."

"I serve because in the first place, as you know, it is everyone's duty to serve. . . . What?" he then added, though no one had spoken. "I had a letter from Russia yesterday, Nicholas Fëdorovich," he continued, evidently wishing to change the subject. "They write that . . . they ask such strange questions."

"What questions?" asked Bólkhov.

The major began laughing.

"Very queer questions. . . . They ask, can jealousy exist where there is no love. . . . What?" he asked, turning round and glancing at us all.

"Dear me!" said Bólkhov, with a smile.

"Yes, you know, it is nice in Russia," continued the major, just as if his sentences flowed naturally from one another. "When I was in Tambóv in '52 they received me everywhere as if I had been some emperor's aide-de-camp. Will you believe it that at a ball at the governor's, when I came in, you know . . . well, they received me very well. The general's wife herself, you know, talked to me and asked me about the Caucasus, and everybody was . . . so that I hardly knew. . . . They examined my gold sabre as if it were some curiosity; they asked for what I had received the sabre, for what the Anna, for what the Vladímir . . . so I just told them. . . . What? That's what the Caucasus is good for, Nicholas Fëdorovich!" he continued without waiting for any reply. "There they think very well of us Caucasians. You know a young man that's a staff-officer and has an Anna and a Vladímir . . . that counts for a good deal in Russia. . . . What?"

"And you, no doubt, piled it on a bit, Abram Ilých?" said Bólkhov.

"He—he!" laughed the major stupidly. "You know one has to do that. And didn't I feed well those two months!"

"And tell me, is it nice there in Russia?" said Trosénko, inquiring about Russia as though it were China or Japan.

"Yes, and the champagne we drank those two months, it was awful!"

"Eh, nonsense! You'll have drunk nothing but lemonade. There now, I'd have burst to let them see how Caucasians drink. I'd have given them something to talk about. I'd have shown them how one drinks; eh, Bólkhov?" said Trosénko.

"But you, Daddy, have been more than ten years in the Caucasus," said Bólkhov, "and you remember what

Ermólov[1] said? . . . And Abram Ilých has been only six."

"Ten indeed! . . . nearly sixteen. . . . Well, Bólkhov, let us have some sage-vodka. It's damp, b-r-r-r! . . . Eh?" said Trosénko, smiling, "Will you have a drink, Major?"

But the major had been displeased by the old captain's first remarks to him and plainly drew back and sought refuge in his own grandeur. He hummed something and again looked at his watch.

"For my part I shall never go there!" Trosénko continued without heeding the major's frowns. "I have lost the habit of speaking and walking in the Russian way. They'd ask, 'What curious creature is this coming here? Asia, that's what it is.' Am I right, Nicholas Fëdorovich? Besides, what have I to go to Russia for? What does it matter? I shall be shot here some day. They'll ask, 'Where's Trosénko?' 'Shot!' What will you do with the 8th Company then, eh?" he added, always addressing the major.

"Send the officer on duty!" shouted the major, without answering the captain, though I again felt sure there was no need for him to give any orders.

"And you, young man, are glad, I suppose, to be drawing double pay?"[2] said the major, turning to the adjutant of the battalion after some moments of silence.

"Yes sir, very glad of course."

"I think our pay now very high, Nicholas Fëdorovich," continued the major; "a young man can live very decently and even permit himself some small luxuries."

"No, really, Abram Ilých," said the adjutant bashfully. "Though it's double it's barely enough. You see one must have a horse."

"What are you telling me, young man? I have been an ensign myself and know. Believe me, one can live very well with care. But there! count it up," added he, bending the little finger of his left hand.

"We always draw our salaries in advance; isn't that

<hr />

[1] General A. P. Ermólov (1772–1861), who was renowned for his firmness and justness as a ruler in the Caucasus, and who subdued Chéchnya and Daghestán, used to say that after ten years in the Caucasus an officer "either takes to drink or marries a loose woman."

[2] An officer's allowance in Russia proper was very small, but when on service in Poland, the Caucasus, Siberia, etc., they received a higher rate of pay.

account enough for you?" said Trosénko, emptying a glass of vodka.

"Well, yes, but what do you expect. . . . What?"

Just then a white head with a flat nose thrust itself into the opening of the hut and a sharp voice said with a German accent, "Are you there, Abram Ilých? The officer on duty is looking for you."

"Come in, Kraft!" said Bólkhov.

A long figure in the uniform of the general staff crept in at the door and began shaking hands all round with peculiar fervour.

"Ah, dear Captain, are you here too?" said he, turning to Trosénko.

In spite of the darkness the new visitor made his way to the captain and to the latter's extreme surprise and dismay, as it seemed to me, kissed him on the lips.

"This is a German trying to be hail fellow well met," thought I.

XII

My surmise was at once confirmed. Captain Kraft asked for vodka, calling it a "warmer," croaked horribly, and throwing back his head emptied the glass.

"Well, gentlemen, we have scoured the plains of Chéchnya to-day, have we not?" he began, but seeing the officer on duty, stopped at once to allow the major to give his orders.

"Have you been round the lines?"

"Yes, sir."

"Have the ambuscades been placed?"

"Yes, sir."

"Then give the company commanders orders to be as cautious as possible."

"Yes, sir."

The major screwed up his eyes in profound contemplation.

"Yes, and tell the men they may now boil their buckwheat."

"They are already boiling it, sir."

"All right! you may go, sir."

"Well, we were just reckoning up how much an officer needs," continued the major, turning to us with a condescending smile. "Let us count. You want a uniform and a pair of trousers, don't you?"

"Certainly."

"That, let us say, is 50 rubles for two years; therefore 25 rubles a year for clothes. Then for food, 40 kopeks a day—is that right?"

"Oh yes, that is even too much."

"Well, never mind, I'll leave it so. Then for a horse and repair of harness and saddle—30 rubles. And that is all. So it's 25, and 120, and 30—that's 175 rubles. So you have for luxuries—tea, sugar, tobacco—a matter of 20 rubles left. So you see . . . Isn't it so, Nicholas Fëdorovich?"

"No, but excuse me, Abram Ilých," said the adjutant timidly, "nothing remains for tea and sugar. You allow one suit in two years; but it's hardly possible to keep oneself in trousers with all this marching. And boots? I wear out a pair almost every month. Then underclothing— shirts, towels, leg-bands,[1]—it all has to be bought. When one comes to reckon it all up nothing remains over. That's really so, Abram Ilých."

"Ah, it's splendid to wear leg-bands," Kraft suddenly remarked after a moment's silence, uttering the word "leg-bands" in specially tender tones. "It's so simple, you know; quite Russian!"

"I'll tell you something," Trosénko remarked. "Reckon what way you like and you'll find we might as well put our teeth away on a shelf, and yet here we are all alive, drinking tea, smoking tobacco, and drinking vodka. When you've served as long as I have," he went on, turning to the ensign, "you'll have also learned how to live. Why, gentlemen, do you know how he treats the orderlies?"

And Trosénko, dying with laughter, told us the whole story about the ensign and his orderly, though we had all heard it hundreds of times.

"Why do you look so like a rose, old chap?" continued he, addressing the ensign, who blushed, perspired, and

---

[1] It is customary, especially among the peasants and soldiers, to wrap long strips of linen round the feet and legs instead of wearing stockings.

smiled, so that it was pitiful to see him. "Never mind, old chap! I was just like you once and now look what a fine fellow I am. You let a young fellow straight from Russia in here—haven't we seen them?—and he gets spasms or rheumatism or something; and here am I settled here, and it's my house and my bed and all, d'you see?"

And thereupon he drank another glass of vodka and looking fixedly at Kraft, said, "Eh?"

"That is what I respect! Here's a genuine old Caucasian! Permit me to shake hands."

And Kraft, pushing us all aside, forced his way to Trosénko and catching hold of his hand shook it with peculiar emotion.

"Yes," continued Kraft, "we may say we have gone through every kind of experience here. In '45—you were present, Captain, were you not?—you remember the night between the 12th and 13th, when we spent the night knee-deep in mud and next day captured the barricades they had made of felled trees. I was attached to the commander-in-chief at the time and we took fifteen barricades that one day—you remember, Captain?"

Trosénko nodded affirmatively, stuck out his nether lip, and screwed up his eyes.

"You see . . ." began Kraft with great animation, making unsuitable gestures with his hands and addressing the major.

But the major, who had in all probability heard the story more than once, suddenly looked at the speaker with such dim, dull eyes that Kraft turned away from him and addressed me and Bólkhov, looking alternately at one and the other. But he did not give a single glance at Trosénko during the whole of his narration.

"Well then, you see, when we went out in the morning the commander-in-chief said to me, 'Kraft, take those barricades!' Well, you know, a soldier's duty is not to reason—it's hand to cap, and 'Yes, your Excellency!' and off. Only as we drew near the first barricade I turned and said to the soldiers, 'Now then, lads, don't funk it but look sharp. If anyone hangs back I'll cut him down myself!' With Russian soldiers, you know, one has to speak straight out. Suddenly a bomb . . . I look, one soldier down, another, a third, . . then bullets came whizzing . . .

vzin! . . . vzin! . . . vzin . . . 'On!' I cry, 'On, follow me!' Just as we got there I look and see a . . . a . . . you know . . . what do you call it?" and the narrator flourished his arms, trying to find the word he wanted.

"A scarp?" suggested Bólkhov.

"No . . . Ach! what is the word? Good heavens, what is it? . . . A scarp!" he said quickly. "So, 'fix bayonets! Hurrah! ta-ra, ta-ta-ta!' not a sign of the enemy! Everybody was surprised, you know. Well, that's all right; we go on to the second barricade. Ah, that was a totally different matter. Our mettle was now up, you know. Just as we reached it I look and see the second barricade, and we could not advance. There was a what's-its-name . . . now what do you call it? Ach, what is it? . . ."

"Another scarp, perhaps," I suggested.

"Not at all," he said crossly, "not a scarp but—oh dear, what do you call it?" and he made an awkward gesture with his hands. "Oh, good heavens, what is it?" He seemed so distressed that one involuntarily wished to help him.

"A river, perhaps," said Bólkhov.

"No, only a scarp! Hardly had we got down, when, will you believe it, such a hell of fire . . ."

At this moment someone outside the tent asked for me. It was Maksímov. And as after having heard the different histories of these two barricades there were still thirteen left, I was glad to seize the excuse to return to my platoon. Trosénko came out with me.

"It's all lies," he said to me when we were a few steps from the hut; "he never was near those barricades at all," and Trosénko laughed so heartily that I, too, enjoyed the joke.

XIII

It was already dark and only the watch-fires dimly lit up the camp when, after the horses were groomed, I rejoined my men. A large stump lay smouldering on the charcoal. Only three men sat round it: Antónov, who was turning a little pot of *ryábco*[1] on the fire; Zhdánov, who was dreamily poking the embers with a stick, and Chíkin, with

[1] *Ryábco*, soldier's food, made of soaked hard-tack and dripping. —L. T.

his pipe, which never would draw well. The rest had already lain down to sleep—some under the ammunition wagons, some on the hay, some by the camp-fires. By the dim light of the charcoal I could distinguish familiar backs, legs, and heads, and among the latter that of the young recruit who, drawn close to the fire, seemed to be already sleeping. Antónov made room for me. I sat down by him and lit a cigarette. The smell of mist and the smoke of damp wood filled the air and made one's eyes smart and, as before, a dank drizzle kept falling from the dismal sky.

One could hear the regular sound of snoring near by, the crackling of branches in the fire, a few words now and then, and the clattering of muskets among the infantry. The camp watch-fires glowed all around, lighting up within narrow circles the dark shadows of the soldiers near them. Where the light fell by the nearest fires I could distinguish the figures of naked soldiers waving their shirts close over the fire. There were still many who had not lain down but moved and spoke, collected on a space of some eighty square yards; but the gloomy dull night gave a peculiar mysterious character to all this movement as if each one felt the dark silence and feared to break its calm monotony.

When I began to speak I felt that my voice sounded strange, and I discerned the same frame of mind reflected in the faces of all the soldiers sitting near me. I thought that before I joined them they had been talking about their wounded comrade, but it had not been so at all. Chíkin had been telling them about receiving supplies at Tiflís and about the scamps there.

I have noticed always and everywhere, but especially in the Caucasus, the peculiar tact with which our soldiers avoid mentioning anything that might have a bad effect on a comrade's spirits. A Russian soldier's spirit does not rest on easily inflammable enthusiasm which cools quickly, like the courage of southern nations; it is as difficult to inflame him as it is to depress him. He does not need scenes, speeches, war-cries, songs, and drums; on the contrary he needs quiet, order, and an absence of any affection. In a Russian, a real Russian, soldier you will never find any bragging, swagger, or desire to befog or excite himself in time of danger; on the contrary, modesty, simplicity, and a capacity for seeing in peril something quite else than the

danger are the distinctive features of his character. I have
seen a soldier wounded in the leg, who in the first instant
thought only of the hole in his new sheepskin cloak, and
an artillery outrider who, creeping from beneath a horse
that was killed under him, began unbuckling the girths to
save the saddle. Who does not remember the incident at
the siege of Gergebel when the fuse of a loaded bomb
caught fire in the laboratory and an artillery sergeant
ordered two soldiers to take the bomb and run to throw
it into the ditch, and how the soldiers did not run to the
nearest spot by the colonel's tent, which stood over the
ditch, but took it farther on so as not to wake the gentlemen asleep in the tent and were consequently both blown
to pieces? I remember also how, in the expedition of 1852,
something led a young soldier while in action to say he
thought the platoon would never escape, and how the
whole platoon angrily attacked him for such evil words
which they did not like even to repeat. And now, when the
thought of Velenchúk must have been in the mind of each
one and when we might expect Tartars to steal up at any
moment and fire a volley at us, everyone listened to
Chíkin's sprightly stories and no one referred either to
the day's action, or to the present danger, or to the wounded
man; as if it had all happened goodness knows how long
ago or had never happened at all. But it seemed to me
that their faces were rather sterner than usual, that they
did not listen to Chíkin so very attentively, and that even
Chíkin himself felt he was not being listened to but talked
for the sake of talking.

Maksímov joined us at the fire and sat down beside me.
Chíkin made room for him, stopped speaking, and started
sucking at his pipe once more.

"The infantry have been sending to the camp for vodka,"
said Maksímov after a considerable silence; "they have
just returned." He spat into the fire. "The sergeant says
they saw our man."

"Is he alive?" asked Antónov, turning the pot.

"No, he's dead."

The young recruit suddenly raised his head in the little
red cap, looked intently for a minute over the fire at
Maksímov and at me, then quickly let his head sink again
and wrapped himself in his cloak.

"There now, it wasn't for naught that death had laid its hand on him when I had to wake him in the 'park' this morning," said Antónov.

"Nonsense!" said Zhdánov, turning the smouldering log, and all were silent.

Then, amid the general silence, came the report of a gun from the camp behind us. Our drummers beat an answering tattoo. When the last vibration ceased Zhdánov rose first, taking off his cap. We all followed his example.

Through the deep silence of the night rose an harmonious choir of manly voices:

"Our Father which art in heaven, hallowed be Thy name. Thy kingdom come. Thy will be done as in heaven so on earth. Give us day by day our daily bread. And forgive us our debts as we forgive our debtors. And lead us not into temptation; but deliver us from the evil one."

"We had a man in '45 who was wounded in the same place," said Antónov when we had put on our caps and again sat down by the fire. "We carried him about with us on a gun for two days—do you remember Shévchenko, Zhdánov?—and then we just left him there under a tree."

At this moment an infantryman with tremendous whiskers and moustaches came up to our fire, carrying a musket and pouch.

"Give me a light for my pipe, comrades," said he.

"All right, smoke away: there's fire enough," remarked Chíkin.

"I suppose it's about Dargo[2] you are telling, comrade," said the infantry soldier to Antónov.

"Yes, about Dargo in '45," Antónov replied.

The infantryman shook his head, screwed up his eyes, and sat down on his heels near us.

"Yes, all sorts of things happened there," he remarked.

"Why did you leave him behind?" I asked Antónov.

"He was suffering a lot with his stomach. As long as we halted it was all right, but as soon as we moved on he screamed aloud and asked for God's sake to be left behind—but we felt it a pity. But when *he* began to give it us hot, killed three of our men from the guns and an officer besides, and we somehow got separated from our

2 Dargo, in the Térek Territory, was the headquarters of Shamyl until 1845.

battery. . . . It was such a go! We thought we shouldn't get our guns away. It was muddy and no mistake!"

"The mud was worst under the Indéysky[3] Mountain," remarked one of the soldiers.

"Yes, it was there he got more worse! So we considered it with Anóshenka—he was an old artillery sergeant. 'Now really he can't live and he's asking for God's sake to be left behind; let us leave him here.' So we decided. There was a tree, such a branchy one, growing there. Well, we took some soaked hard-tack Zhdánov had, and put it near him, leant him against the tree, put a clean shirt on him, and said good-bye—all as it should be—and left him."

"And was he a good soldier?"

"Yes, he was all right as a soldier," remarked Zhdánov.

"And what became of him God only knows," continued Antónov; "many of the likes of us perished there."

"What, at Dargo?" said the infantryman as he rose, scraping out his pipe and again half-closing his eyes and shaking his head. "All sorts of things happened there."

And he left us.

"And have we many still in the battery who were at Dargo?" I asked.

"Many? Why, there's Zhdánov, myself, Patsán who is now on furlough, and there may be six others, not more."

"And why's our Patsán holiday-making all this time?" said Chíkin, stretching out his legs and lying down with his head on a log. "I reckon he's been away getting on for a year."

"And you, have you had your year at home?" I asked Zhdánov.

"No, I didn't go," he answered unwillingly.

"You see, it's all right to go," said Antónov, "if they're well off at home or if you are yourself fit to work; then it's tempting to go and they're glad to see you."

"But where's the use of going when one's one of two brothers?" continued Zhdánov. "It's all they can do to get their bread; how should they feed a soldier like me? I'm no help to them after twenty-five years' service. And who knows whether they're alive still?"

"Haven't you ever written?" I asked.

[3] The soldier miscalls the Andíysky chain of mountains 'Indéysky,' apparently connecting them with India.

"Yes, indeed! I wrote two letters, but never had an answer. Either they're dead or simply won't write because they're living in poverty themselves; so where's the good?"

"And is it long since you wrote?"

"I wrote last when we returned from Dargo . . . Won't you sing us 'The Birch-Tree'?" he said, turning to Antónov, who sat leaning his elbows on his knees and humming a song.

Antónov began to sing "The Birch-Tree."

"This is the song Daddy Zhdánov likes most best of all," said Chíkin to me in a whisper, pulling at my cloak. "Sometimes he right down weeps when Philip Antónych sings it."

Zhdánov at first sat quite motionless with eyes fixed on the glimmering embers, and his face, lit up by the reddish light, seemed very gloomy; then his jaws below his ears began to move faster and faster, and at last he rose and, spreading out his cloak, lay down in the shadow behind the fire. Either it was his tossing and groaning as he settled down to sleep, or it may have been the effect of Velenchúk's death and of the dull weather, but it really seemed to me that he was crying.

The bottom of the charred log, bursting every now and then into flames, lit up Antónov's figure with his grey moustaches, red face, and the medals on the cloak that he had thrown over his shoulders, or it lit up someone's boots, head, or back. The same gloomy drizzle fell from above, the air was still full of moisture and smoke, all around were the same bright spots of fires, now dying down, and amid the general stillness came the mournful sound of Antónov's song, and when that stopped for an instant the faint nocturnal sounds of the camp—snoring, clanking of sentries' muskets, voices speaking in low tones—took part.

"Second watch! Makatyúk and Zhdánov!" cried Maksímov.

Antónov stopped singing. Zhdánov rose, sighed, stepped across the log, and went slowly towards the guns.

15 June 1855

SEVASTOPOL

The early dawn is just beginning to colour the horizon above the Sapún Hill. The dark blue surface of the sea has already thrown off the gloom of night and is only awaiting the first ray of the sun to begin sparkling merrily. A current of cold misty air blows from the bay; there is no snow on the hard black ground, but the sharp morning frost crunches under your feet and makes your face tingle. The distant, incessant murmur of the sea, occasionally interrupted by the reverberating boom of cannon from Sevastopol, alone infringes the stillness of the morning. All is quiet on the ships. It strikes eight bells.

On the north side the activity of day is beginning gradually to replace the quiet of night: here some soldiers with clanking muskets pass to relieve the guard, there a doctor is already hurrying to the hospital, and there a soldier, having crept out of his dug-out, washes his weather-beaten face with icy water and then turning to the reddening horizon says his prayers, rapidly crossing himself; a creaking Tartar cart drawn by camels crawls past on its way to the cemetery to bury the blood-stained dead with which it is loaded almost to the top. As you approach the harbour you are struck by the peculiar smell of coal-smoke, manure, dampness, and meat. Thousands of different objects are lying in heaps by the harbour: firewood, meat, gabions, sacks of flour, iron, and so on. Soldiers of various regiments, some carrying bags and muskets and others empty-handed, are crowded together here, smoking, quarrelling, and hauling heavy loads onto the steamer which lies close to the wharf, its funnel smoking. Private boats crowded with all sorts of people—soldiers, sailors, merchants, and women—keep arriving at the landing stage or leaving it.

"To the Gráfskaya, your Honour? Please to get in!" two or three old salts offer you their services, getting out of their boats.

You choose the one nearest to you, step across the half-decayed carcass of a bay horse that lies in the mud close to the boat, and pass on towards the rudder. You push off from the landing stage, and around you is the sea, now glittering in the morning sunshine. In front of you the old sailor, in his camel-hair coat, and a flaxen-haired boy silently and steadily ply the oars. You gaze at the enormous striped ships scattered far and wide over the bay, at the ships' boats that move about over the sparkling azure like small black dots, at the opposite bank where the handsome light-coloured buildings of the town are lit up by the rosy rays of the morning sun, at the foaming white line by the breakwater and around the sunken vessels, the black tops of whose masts here and there stand mournfully out of the water, at the enemy's fleet looming on the crystal horizon of the sea, and at the foaming and bubbling wash of the oars. You listen to the steady sound of voices that reaches you across the water and to the majestic sound of firing from Sevastopol, which as it seems to you is growing more intense.

It is impossible for some feeling of heroism and pride not to penetrate your soul at the thought that you, too, are in Sevastopol, and for the blood not to run faster in your veins.

"Straight past the *Kistentin*,[1] your Honour!" the old sailor tells you, turning round to verify the direction towards the right in which you are steering.

"And she's still got all her guns!"[2] says the flaxen-headed boy, examining the ship in passing.

"Well, of course. She's a new one. Kornílov lived on her," remarks the old seaman, also looking up at the ship.

"Look where it's burst!" the boy says after a long silence,

---

[1] The vessel, the *Constantine*.

[2] The guns were removed from most of the ships for use on the fortifications.

watching a small white cloud of dispersing smoke that has suddenly appeared high above the South Bay accompanied by the sharp sound of a bursting bomb.

"That's *him* firing from the new battery to-day," adds the old seaman, calmly spitting on his hand. "Now then, pull away, Míshka! Let's get ahead of that long-boat." And your skiff travels faster over the broad swell of the road-stead, gets ahead of the heavy long-boat laden with sacks and unsteadily and clumsily rowed by soldiers, and making its way among all sorts of boats moored there is made fast to the Gráfsky landing.

Crowds of grey-clad soldiers, sailors in black, and gaily dressed women throng noisily about the quay. Here are women selling buns, Russian peasants with samo-vars are shouting, "Hot sbíten!³," ⁴ and here too on the very first steps lie rusty cannon-balls, bombs, grape-shot, and cannon of various sizes. A little farther on is a large open space where some enormous beams are lying, together with gun carriages and sleeping soldiers. Horses, carts, cannon, green ammunition wagons, and stacked muskets are standing there. Soldiers, sailors, officers, women, children, and tradespeople are moving about, carts loaded with hay, sacks, and casks are passing, and now and then a Cossack, a mounted officer, or a general in a vehicle. To the right is a street closed by a barricade on which some small guns are mounted in embrasures and beside which sits a sailor smoking a pipe. To the left is a handsome building with Roman figures engraved on its frontage and before which soldiers are standing with blood-stained stretchers. Everywhere you will see the unpleasant indications of a war camp. Your first impressions will certainly be most disagreeable: the strange mixture of camp-life and town-life—of a fine town and a dirty bivouac—is not only ugly but looks like horrible disorder: it will even seem to you that every one is scared, in a commotion, and at a loss what to do. But look more closely at the faces of these people moving about around you and you will get a very different impression. Take for instance this convoy soldier

³ The samovar, or "self-boiler," is an urn in which water can be boiled and kept hot without any other fire having to be lit.

⁴ A hot drink made with treacle and lemon, or honey and spice.

muttering something to himself as he goes to water those three bay horses, and doing it all so quietly that he evidently will not get lost in this motley crowd, which does not even exist as far as he is concerned, but will do his job, be it what it may—watering horses or hauling guns—as calmly, self-confidently, and unconcernedly as if it were all happening in Túla or Saránsk. You will read the same thing on the face of this officer passing by in immaculate white gloves, on the face of the sailor who sits smoking on the barricade, on the faces of the soldiers waiting in the portico of what used to be the Assembly Hall, and on the face of that girl who, afraid of getting her pink dress muddy, is jumping from stone to stone as she crosses the street.

Yes, disenchantment certainly awaits you on entering Sevastopol for the first time. You will look in vain in any of these faces for signs of disquiet, perplexity, or even of enthusiasm, determination, or readiness for death—there is nothing of the kind. What you see are ordinary people quietly occupied with ordinary activities, so that perhaps you may reproach yourself for having felt undue enthusiasm and may doubt the justice of the ideas you had formed of the heroism of the defenders of Sevastopol, based on the tales and descriptions and sights and sounds and heard from the North Side. But before yielding to such doubts go to the bastions and see the defenders of Sevastopol at the very place of the defence, or better still go straight into that building opposite which was once the Sevastopol Assembly Rooms and in the portico of which stand soldiers with stretchers. There you will see the defenders of Sevastopol and will see terrible and lamentable, solemn and amusing, but astounding and soul-elevating sights.

You enter the large Assembly Hall. As soon as you open the door you are struck by the sight and smell of forty or fifty amputation and most seriously wounded cases, some in cots but most of them on the floor. Do not trust the feeling that checks you at the threshold; it is a wrong feeling. Go on, do not be ashamed of seeming to have come to *look* at the sufferers, do not hesitate to go up and speak to them. Sufferers like to see a sympathetic human face, like to speak of their sufferings and to hear words of love and sympathy. You pass between the rows of beds and look for a face less stern and full of suffering, which you feel you can approach and speak to.

"Where are you wounded?" you inquire hesitatingly and timidly of an emaciated old soldier who is sitting up in his cot and following you with a kindly look as if inviting you to approach him. I say "inquire timidly" because, besides strong sympathy, sufferings seem to inspire a dread of offending, as well as a great respect for him who endures them.

"In the leg," the soldier replies, and at the same moment you yourself notice from the fold of his blanket that one leg is missing from above the knee. "Now, God be thanked," he adds, "I am ready to leave the hospital."

"Is it long since you were wounded?"

"Well, it's over five weeks now, your Honour."

"And are you still in pain?"

"No, I'm not in any pain now; only when it's bad weather I seem to feel a pain in the calf, else it's all right."

"And how did it happen that you were wounded?"

"It was on the Fifth Bastion, your Honour, at the first *bondbarment*. I trained the gun and was stepping across to the next embrasure, when *he* hits me in the leg, just as if I had stumbled into a hole. I look—and the leg is gone."

"Do you mean to say you felt no pain the first moment?"

"Nothing much, only as if something hot had shoved against my leg."

"And afterwards?"

"And nothing much afterwards except when they began to draw the skin together, then it did seem to smart. The chief thing, your Honour, is *not to think*; if you don't think it's nothing much. It's most because of a man thinking."

At this moment a woman in a grey striped dress and with a black kerchief tied round her head comes up to you and enters into your conversation with the sailor. She begins telling you about him, about his sufferings, the desperate condition he was in for four weeks, and of how when he was wounded he stopped his stretcher-bearers that he might see a volley fired from our battery; and how the Grand Duke spoke to him and gave him twenty-five rubles, and how he had told them he wanted to go back to the bastion to teach the young ones, if he could not himself work any longer. As she says all this in a breath, the woman keeps looking now at you and now at the sailor, who having turned away is picking lint on his pillow as if not listening, and her eyes shine with a peculiar rapture.

"She's my missus, your Honour!" he remarks with a look that seems to say, "You must excuse her. It's a woman's way to talk nonsense."

You begin now to understand the defenders of Sevastopol and for some reason begin to feel ashamed of yourself in the presence of this man. You want to say too much, in order to express your sympathy and admiration, but you can't find the right words and are dissatisfied with those that occur to you, and so you silently bow your head before this taciturn and unconscious grandeur and firmness of spirit—which is ashamed to have its worth revealed.

"Well, may God help you to get well soon," you say to him, and turn to another patient who is lying on the floor apparently awaiting death in unspeakable torment.

He is a fair-haired man with a puffy pale face. He is lying on his back with his left arm thrown back in a position that indicates cruel suffering. His hoarse breathing comes with difficulty through his parched, open mouth, his leaden blue eyes are rolled upwards, and what remains of his bandaged right arm is thrust out from under his tumbled blanket. The oppressive smell of mortified flesh assails you yet more strongly, and the feverish inner heat in all the sufferer's limbs seems to penetrate you also.

"Is he unconscious?" you ask the woman who follows you and looks at you kindly as at someone akin to her.

"No, he can still hear, but not at all well," and she adds in a whisper, "I gave him some tea to drink to-day—what if he is a stranger, one must have pity—but he hardly drank any of it."

"How do you feel?" you ask him.

The wounded man turns his eyes at the sound of your voice but neither sees nor understands you.

"My heart's on fire," he mumbles.

A little farther on you see an old soldier who is changing his shirt. His face and body are a kind of reddish brown and as gaunt as a skeleton. Nothing is left of one of his arms. It has been amputated at the shoulder. He sits up firmly, he is convalescent, but his dull, heavy look, his terrible emaciation and the wrinkles on his face, show that the best part of this man's life has been consumed by his sufferings.

In a cot on the opposite side you see a woman's pale, delicate face, full of suffering, a hectic flush suffusing her cheek.

"That's the wife of one of our sailors: she was hit in the leg by a bomb on the 5th,"[5] your guide will tell you. "She was taking her husband's dinner to him at the bastion."

"Amputated?"

"Yes, cut off above the knee."

Now, if your nerves are strong, go in at the door to the left; it is there they bandage and operate. There you will see doctors with pale, gloomy faces, and arms red with blood up to the elbows, busy at a bed on which a wounded man lies under chloroform. His eyes are open and he utters, as if in delirium, incoherent but sometimes simple and pathetic words. The doctors are engaged on the horrible but beneficent work of amputation. You will see the sharp curved knife enter the healthy white flesh; you will see the wounded man come back to life with terrible, heart-rending screams and curses. You will see the doctor's assistant toss the amputated arm into a corner, and in the same room you will see another wounded man on a stretcher watching the operation, and writhing and groaning not so much from physical pain as from the mental torture of anticipation. You will see ghastly sights that will rend your soul; you will see war not with its orderly beautiful and brilliant ranks, its music and beating drums, its waving banners, its generals on prancing horses, but war in its real aspect of blood, suffering, and death. . . .

On coming out of this house of pain you will be sure to experience a sense of relief, you will draw deeper breaths of the fresh air and rejoice in the consciousness of your own health. Yet the contemplation of those sufferings will have made you realize your own insignificance, and you will go calmly and unhesitatingly to the bastions.

"What matters the death and suffering of so insignificant a worm as I, compared to so many deaths, so much suffer-

---

[5] The first bombardment of Sevastopol was on the 5th of October 1854, Old Style (O.S.—that is) the 17th of October, New Style (N.S.).

ing?" But the sight of the clear sky, the brilliant sun, the beautiful town, the open church, and the soldiers moving in all directions will soon bring your spirit back to its normal state of frivolity, its pretty cares and absorption in the present. You may meet the funeral procession of an officer as it leaves the church, the pink coffin accompanied by waving banners and music, and the sound of firing from the bastions may reach your ears. But these things will not bring back your former thoughts. The funeral will seem a very beautiful military pageant, the sounds very beautiful warlike sounds, and neither to these sights nor these sounds will you attach the clear and personal sense of suffering and death that came to you in the hospital.

Passing the church and the barricade you enter that part of the town where everyday life is most active. On both sides of the street hang the signboards[6] of shops and restaurants. Tradesmen, women with bonnets or kerchiefs on their heads, dandified officers—everything speaks of the firmness, self-confidence, and security of the inhabitants.

If you care to hear the conversation of army and navy officers, enter the restaurant on the right. There you are sure to hear them talk about last night, about Fanny, about the affair of the 24th,[7] about how dear and badly served the cutlets are, and how such and such of their comrades have been killed.

"Things were confoundedly bad at our place to-day!" a fair beardless little naval officer with a green knitted scarf round his neck says in a bass voice.

"Where was that?" asks another.

"Oh, in the Fourth Bastion," answers the young officer, and at the words "Fourth Bastion" you will certainly look more attentively and even with a certain respect at this fair-complexioned officer. The excessive freedom of his manner, his gesticulations, and his loud voice and laugh, which had appeared to you impudent before, now seem to indicate that peculiarly combative frame of mind noticeable in some young men after they have been in danger, but all the same

---

[6] Among a population largely illiterate, the signboards were usually pictorial. The bakers showed loaves and rolls, the bootmakers boots and shoes, and so on.

[7] The 24th of October o.s. = 5th November n.s., the date of the Battle of Inkerman.

you expect him to say how bad the bombs and bullets made things in the Fourth Bastion. Not at all! It was the mud that made things so bad. "One can scarcely get to the battery," he continues, pointing to his boots, which are muddy even above the calves. "And I have lost my best gunner," says another, "hit right in the forehead." "Who's that? Mitúkhin?" "No . . . but am I ever to have my veal, you rascal?" he adds, addressing the waiter. "Not Mitúkhin but Abrámov—such a fine fellow. He was out in six sallies."

At another corner of the table sit two infantry officers with plates of cutlets and peas before them and a bottle of sour Crimean wine called "Bordeaux." One of them, a young man with a red collar and two little stars on his cloak, is talking to the other, who has a black collar and no stars, about the Alma affair. The former has already been drinking and the pauses he makes, the indecision in his face—expressive of his doubt of being believed—and especially the fact that his own part in the account he is giving is too important and the thing is too terrible show that he is diverging considerably from the strict truth. But you do not care much for stories of this kind, which will long be current all over Russia; you want to get quickly to the bastions, especially to that Fourth Bastion about which you have been told so many and such different tales. When anyone says: "I am going to the Fourth Bastion" he always betrays a slight agitation or too marked an indifference; if anyone wishes to chaff you, he says: "You should be sent to the Fourth Bastion." When you meet someone carried on a stretcher and ask, "Where from?" the answer usually is, "From the Fourth Bastion." Two quite different opinions are current concerning this terrible bastion[8]: that of those who have never been there and who are convinced it is a certain grave for any one who goes, and that of those who, like the fair-complexioned midshipman, live there and who when speaking of the Fourth Bastion will tell you whether it is dry or muddy, whether it is cold or warm in the dugouts, and so forth.

During the half-hour you have spent in the restaurant the weather has changed. The mist that spread over the sea has gathered into dull grey moist clouds which hide the

[8] Called by the English the "Flagstaff Bastion."

sun, and a kind of dismal sleet showers down and wets the roofs, the pavements, and the soldiers' overcoats.

Passing another barricade you go through some doors to the right and up a broad street. Beyond this barricade the houses on both sides of the street are unoccupied: there are no sign-boards, the doors are boarded up, the windows smashed, here a corner of the wall is knocked down and there a roof is broken in. The buildings look like old veterans who have borne much sorrow and privation; they even seem to gaze proudly and somewhat contemptuously at you. On the road you stumble over cannon-balls that lie about, and into holes made in the stony ground by bombs and full of water. You meet and overtake detachments of soldiers, Cossacks, officers, and occasionally a woman or a child; only it will not be a woman wearing a bonnet, but a sailor's wife wearing an old cloak and soldiers' boots. After you have descended a little slope farther down the same street you will no longer see any houses but only ruined walls amid strange heaps of bricks, boards, clay, and beams, and before you, up a steep hill, you see a black untidy space cut up by ditches. This space you are approaching is the Fourth Bastion. . . . Here you will meet still fewer people and no women at all, the soldiers walk briskly by, there are traces of blood on the road, and you are sure to meet four soldiers carrying a stretcher and on the stretcher probably a pale yellow face and a blood-stained overcoat. If you ask, "Where is he wounded?" the bearers without looking at you will answer crossly, "in the leg" or "in the arm" if the man is not severely wounded or will remain sternly silent if no head is raised on the stretcher and the man is either dead or seriously wounded.

The whiz of cannon-ball or bomb near by impresses you unpleasantly as you ascend the hill, and the meaning of the sounds is very different from what it seemed to be when they reached you in the town. Some peaceful and joyous memory will suddenly flash through your mind; self-consciousness begins to supersede the activity of your observation: you are less attentive to all that is around you and a disagreeable feeling of indecision suddenly seizes you. But silencing this despicable little voice that has suddenly made itself heard within you at the sight of danger—especially after seeing a soldier run past you laughing, waving his arms and slipping downhill through the yellow mud—you involuntarily expand your chest, raise your head higher, and clamber up the slippery clay hill. You have climbed only a little way before bullets begin to whiz past you to the right and left, and you will perhaps consider whether you had not better walk inside the trench which runs parallel to the road, but the trench is full of such yellow liquid stinking mud, more than knee deep, that you are sure to choose the road, especially as *everybody* does so. After walking a couple of hundred yards you come to a muddy place much cut up, surrounded by gabions, cellars, platforms, and dug-outs, and on which large cast-iron cannon are mounted and cannon-balls lie piled in orderly heaps. It all seems placed without any plan, aim, connexion, or order. Here a group of sailors are sitting in the battery; here in the middle of the open space, half sunk in mud, lies a shattered cannon; and there a foot-soldier is crossing the battery, drawing his feet with difficulty out of the sticky mud. Everywhere, on all sides and all about, you see fragments of bombs, unexploded bombs, cannon-balls, and various traces of an encampment, all sunk in the liquid, sticky mud. You think you hear the thud of a cannon-ball not far off and you seem to hear the different sounds of bullets all around, some humming like bees, some whistling, and some rapidly flying past with a shrill screech like the string of some instrument. You hear the dreadful boom of a shot that sends a shock all through you and seems most terrible.

"So this is Fourth Bastion! This is that terrible, truly dreadful spot!" So you think, experiencing a slight feeling of pride and a strong feeling of suppressed fear. But you are mistaken, this is not the Fourth Bastion yet. This is only Yazónovsky Redoubt—comparatively a very safe and not at all dreadful place. To get to the Fourth Bastion you must turn to the right along that narrow trench where a foot-soldier has just passed, stooping down. In this trench you may again meet men with stretchers and perhaps a sailor or a soldier with a spade. You will see the mouths of mines, dug-outs into which only two men can crawl, and there you will see the Cossacks of the Black Sea battalions changing their boots, eating, smoking their pipes, and, in short, living. And again you will see the same stinking mud, the traces of camp life and cast-iron refuse of every shape and form. When you have gone some three hundred steps more you will come out at another battery—a flat space with many holes, surrounded with gabions filled with earth and cannons on platforms, and the whole walled in with earthworks. Here you will perhaps see four or five soldiers playing cards under shelter of the breastworks, and a naval officer, noticing that you are a stranger and inquisitive, will be pleased to show you his "household" and everything that can interest you. This officer sits on a cannon rolling a yellow cigarette so composedly, walks from one embrasure to another so quietly, talks to you so calmly and with such an absence of affectation that in spite of the bullets whizzing around you oftener than before you yourself grow cooler, question him carefully, and listen to his stories. He will tell you (but only if you ask) about the bombardment on the 5th of October; will tell you that only one gun of his battery remained usable and only eight gunners of the crew were left, and that nevertheless he fired all his guns next morning, the 6th. He will tell you how a bomb dropped into one of the dug-outs and knocked over eleven sailors; from an embrasure he will show you the enemy's batteries and trenches which are here not more than seventy-five to eighty-five yards distant. I am afraid, though, that when you lean out of the embrasure to have a look at the enemy, the whiz of the flying bullets will hinder you from seeing anything, but if you do see anything you will be much surprised to find that this whitish stone wall—which is so near you and from which puffs of white smoke keep bursting—is the enemy: *he*, as the soldiers and sailors say.

It is even very likely that the naval officer, from vanity or merely for a little recreation, will wish to show you some firing. "Call the gunner and crew to the cannon!" and fourteen sailors—their hob-nailed boots clattering on the platform, one putting his pipe in his pocket, another still chewing a rusk—will quickly and cheerfully man the gun and begin loading. Look well into these faces and note the bearing and carriage of these men. In every wrinkle of that tanned face with its high cheek-bones, in every muscle, in the breadth of those shoulders, the thickness of those legs in their enormous boots, in every movement, quiet, firm, and deliberate, can be seen the chief characteristic of the strength of the Russian—his simplicity and obstinacy.

Suddenly the most fearful roar strikes not only your ears but your whole being and makes you shudder all over. It is followed by the whistle of the departing ball, and a thick cloud of powder-smoke envelops you, the platform, and the black moving figures of the sailors. You will hear various comments made by the sailors concerning this shot of ours and you will notice their animation, the evidences of a feeling you had not perhaps expected: the feeling of animosity and thirst for vengeance which lies hidden in each man's soul. You will hear joyful exclamations: "It's gone right into the embrasure! It's killed two, I think. . . . There, they're carrying them off!" "And now *he's* riled and will send one this way," some one remarks; and really, soon after, you will see before you a flash and some smoke; the sentinel standing on the breastwork will call out "Ca-n-non!" and then a ball will whiz past you and bury itself in the earth, throwing out a circle of stones and mud. The commander of the battery will be irritated by this shot and will give orders to fire another and another cannon, the enemy will reply in like manner, and you will experience interesting sensations and see interesting sights. The sentinel will again call "Cannon!" and you will have the same sound and shock, and the mud will be splashed around as before. Or he will call out "Mortar!" and you will hear the regular and rather pleasant whistle—which it is difficult to connect with the thought of anything dreadful —of a bomb; you will hear this whistle coming nearer and faster towards you, then you will see a black ball, feel the shock as it strikes the ground, and will hear the ringing explosion. The bomb will fly apart into whizzing and shrieking fragments, stones will rattle in the air, and you will be bespattered with mud.

At these sounds you will experience a strange feeling of mingled pleasure and fear. At the moment you know the shot is flying towards you, you are sure to imagine that it will kill you, but a feeling of pride will support you and no one will know of the knife that cuts at your heart. But when the shot has flown past without hitting you, you revive and are seized, though only for a moment, by an inexpressibly joyful emotion, so that you feel a peculiar delight in the danger—in this game of life and death—and wish the bombs and balls to fall nearer and nearer to you.

But again the sentinel in his loud gruff voice shouts "Mortar!" again a whistle, a fall, an explosion; and mingled with this last you are startled by a man's groans. You approach the wounded sailor just as the stretchers are brought. Covered with blood and dirt he presents a strange, scarcely human appearance. Part of his breast has been torn away. For the first few moments only terror and the kind of feigned, premature look of suffering, common to men in this state, appear on his mud-besprinkled face, but when the stretcher is brought and he himself lies down on it on his healthy side you notice that his expression changes. His eyes shine more brightly, his teeth are clenched, he raises his head higher with difficulty, and when the stretcher is lifted he stops the bearers for a moment and turning to his comrades says with an effort, in a trembling voice, "Forgive me, brothers!"[9] He wishes to say more, something pathetic, but only repeats, "Forgive me, brothers!" At this moment a sailor approaches him, places the cap on the head the wounded man holds up towards him, and then placidly swinging his arms returns quietly to his cannon.

"That's the way with seven or eight every day," the naval officer remarks to you, answering the look of horror on your face, and he yawns as he rolls another yellow cigarette.

So now you have seen the defenders of Sevastopol where they are defending it, and somehow you return with a tranquil heightened spirit, paying no heed to the balls and bombs whose whistle accompanies you all the way to the ruined theatre. The principal thought you have brought away with you is a joyous conviction of the strength of the Russian people, and this conviction you have gained not by looking at all those traverses, breastworks, cunningly inter-

[9] "Forgive me" and "farewell" are almost interchangeable expressions in Russian. "Good-bye" (*prostcháyte*) etymologically means "forgive." The form (*prostíte*) here used, however, means primarily "forgive me."

laced trenches, mines, cannon, one after another, of which you could make nothing, but from the eyes, words, and actions—in short from seeing what is called the "spirit"— of the defenders of Sevastopol. What they do is all done so simply, with so little effort, that you feel convinced that they could do a hundred times as much. . . . You understand that the feeling which actuates them is not that petty ambition or forgetfulness which you yourself experienced, but something more powerful, which has made them able to live so quietly under the flying balls, exposed to a hundred chances of death besides the one all men are subject to—and this amid conditions of constant toil, lack of sleep, and dirt. Men could not accept such terrible conditions of life for the sake of a cross, or promotion, or because of a threat: there must be some other and higher motive power.

It is only now that the tales of the early days of the siege of Sevastopol are no longer beautiful historical legends for you but have become realities: the tales of the time when it was not fortified, when there was no army to defend it, when it seemed a physical impossibility to retain it and yet there was not the slightest idea of abandoning it to the enemy—of the time when Kornílov, that hero worthy of ancient Greece, making his round of the troops, said, "Lads, we will die, but will not surrender Sevastopol!" and our Russians, incapable of phrase-making, replied, "We will die! Hurrah!" You will clearly recognize in the men you have just seen those heroes who gladly prepared for death and whose spirits did not flag during those dismal days, but rose.

The evening is closing in. Just before setting, the sun emerges from behind the grey clouds that covered the sky and suddenly lights up with its bright red glow the purple clouds, the greenish sea with the ships and boats rocking on its broad even swell, the white buildings of the town, and the people moving in the streets. The sound of some old valse played by a military band on the boulevard is carried across the water and mingles strangely with the sound of firing on the bastions.

Sevastopol, 25 April o.s. 1855

SEVASTOPOL IN MAY 1855

I

Six months have passed since the first cannon-ball went whistling from the bastions of Sevastopol and threw up the earth of the enemy's entrenchments. Since then bullets, balls, and bombs by the thousand have flown continually from the bastions to the entrenchments and from the entrenchments to the bastions, and above them the angel of death has hovered unceasingly.

Thousands of human ambitions have had time to be mortified, thousands to be gratified and extend, thousands to be lulled to rest in the arms of death. What numbers of pink coffins and linen palls! And still the same sounds from the bastions fill the air; the French still look from their camp with involuntary trepidation and fear at the yellowy earth of the bastions of Sevastopol and count the embrasures from which the iron cannon frown fiercely; as before, through the fixed telescope on the elevation of the signal-station the pilot still watches the bright-coloured figures of the French, their batteries, their tents, their columns on the green hill, and the puffs of smoke that rise from the entrenchments; and as before, crowds of different men, with a still greater variety of desires, stream with the same ardour from many parts of the world to this fatal spot. But the question the diplomatists did not settle still remains unsettled by powder and blood.

2

A regimental band was playing on the boulevard near the pavilion in the besieged town of Sevastopol, and crowds of women and military men strolled along the paths making holiday. The bright spring sun had risen in the morning above the English entrenchments, had reached the bastions, then the town and the Nicholas Barracks, shining with equal joy on all, and was now sinking down to the distant blue sea which, rocking with an even motion, glittered with silvery light.

A tall infantry officer with a slight stoop, drawing on

a presentable though not very white glove, passed out of the gate of one of the small sailors' houses built on the left side of the Morskáya Street and gazing thoughtfully at the ground ascended the hill towards the boulevard. The expression of his plain face did not reveal much intellectual power, but rather good-nature, common sense, honesty, and an inclination to respectability. He was badly built and seemed rather shy and awkward in his movements. His cap was nearly new, a gold watch-chain showed from under his thin cloak of a rather peculiar lilac shade, and he wrote trousers with foot-straps and clean, shiny calf-skin boots. He might have been a German (but that his features indicated his purely Russian origin), an adjutant, or a regimental quartermaster (but in that case he would have worn spurs), or an officer transferred from the cavalry or the Guards for the duration of the war. He was in fact an officer who had exchanged from the cavalry, and as he ascended the hill towards the boulevard he was thinking of a letter he had received from a former comrade now retired from the army, a landed proprietor in the government of T———, and of his great friend, the pale, blue-eyed Natásha, that comrade's wife. He recalled a part of the letter where his comrade wrote:

"When we receive the *Invalide*,[1] Púpka" (so the retired Uhlan called his wife) "rushes headlong into the hall, seizes the paper, and runs with it to a seat in the arbour or the drawing-room in which, you remember, we spent such jolly winter evenings when your regiment was stationed in our town—and reads of *your* heroic deeds with an ardour you cannot imagine. She often speaks of you. 'There now,' she says, 'Mikháylov is a *darling*. I am ready to cover him with kisses when I see him. He [is fighting on the bastions and] is certain to receive a St. George's Cross, and they'll write about him in the papers,' etc., etc., so that I am beginning to be quite jealous of you."

In another place he wrote: "The papers reach us awfully late, and though there are plenty of rumours one cannot believe them all. For instance, those [young ladies with music] you know of were saying yesterday that

[1] The Army and Navy Gazette.

Napoleon has been captured by our Cossacks and sent to St. Petersburg, but you can imagine how much of this I believe. One fresh arrival from Petersburg tells us for certain (he is a capital fellow, sent by the Minister on special business—and now there is no one in the town you can't think what a *resource* he is to us), that we have taken Eupatoria [so that the French are cut off from Balaclava], and that we lost two hundred in the affair and the French as many as fifteen thousand. My wife was in such raptures that she *caroused* all night and said that a presentiment assured her that you distinguished yourself in that affair."

In spite of the words and expressions I have purposely italicized, and the whole tone of the letter, Lieutenant-Captain Mikháylov thought with an inexpressibly melancholy pleasure about his pale-faced provincial friend and how he used to sit with her of an evening in the arbour, talking *sentiment.* He thought of his kind comrade the Uhlan: how the latter used to get angry and lose when they played cards in the study for kopek points and how his wife used to laugh at him. He recalled the friendship these people had for him (perhaps he thought there was something more on the side of the pale-faced friend): these people and their surroundings flitted through his memory in a wonderfully sweet, joyously rosy light and, smiling at the recollection, he put his hand to the pocket where this *dear* letter lay.

From these recollections Lieutenant-Captain Mikháylov involuntarily passed to dreams and hopes. "How surprised and pleased Natásha will be," he thought as he passed along a narrow side-street, "when she reads in the *Invalide* of my being the first to climb on the cannon, and receiving the St. George! I ought to be made full captain on that former recommendation. Then I may easily become a major this year by seniority, because so many of our fellows have been killed and no doubt many more will be killed this campaign. Then there'll be more fighting and I, as a well-known man, shall be entrusted with a regiment . . . then a lieutenant-colonel, the order of St. Anna . . . a colonel" . . . and he was already a general, honouring with a visit Natásha, the widow of his comrade (who would be dead by that time according to his daydream), when the sounds of the music on the boulevard reached his ears more distinctly, a crowd of people appeared before his eyes, and he realized that he was on the boulevard and a lieutenant-captain of infantry as before.

3

He went first to the pavilion, beside which stood the band with soldiers of the same regiment acting as music-stands and holding open the music books, while around them clerks, cadets, nursemaids, and children formed a circle, looking on rather than listening. Most of the people who were standing, sitting, and sauntering round the pavilion were naval officers, adjutants, and white-gloved army officers. Along the broad avenue of the boulevard walked officers of all sorts and women of all sorts—a few of the latter in hats, but the greater part with kerchiefs on their heads, and some with neither kerchiefs nor hats—but it was remarkable that there was not a single old woman amongst them—all were young. Lower down, in the scented alleys shaded by the white acacias, isolated groups sat or strolled.

No one was particularly glad to meet Lieutenant-Captain Mikháylov on the boulevard, except perhaps Captain Obzhógov of his regiment and Captain Súslikov who pressed his hand warmly, but the first of these wore camel-hair trousers, no gloves, and a shabby overcoat, and his face was red and perspiring, and the second shouted so loud and was so free and easy that one felt ashamed to be seen walking with him, especially by those white-gloved officers—to one of whom, an adjutant, Mikháylov bowed, and he might have bowed to another, a Staff officer whom he had twice met at the house of a mutual acquaintance. Besides, what was the fun of walking with Obzhógov and Súslikov when as it was he met them and shook hands with them six times a day? Was this what he had come to hear *the music* for?

He would have liked to accost the adjutant whom he had bowed to and to talk with those gentlemen, not at all that he wanted Captains Obzhógov and Súslikov and Lieutenant Pashtétski and others to see him talking to them, but simply because they were pleasant people who knew all the news and might have told him something.

But why is Lieutenant-Captain Mikháylov afraid and unable to muster courage to approach them? "Supposing they don't return my greeting," he thinks, "or merely bow and go on talking among themselves as if I were not there, or simply walk away and leave me standing among the aristocrats?" The word aristocrats (in the sense of the highest and most select circle of any class) has lately gained great popularity in Russia, where one would think it ought not to exist. It has made its way to every part of the country, and into every grade of society which can be reached by vanity—and to what conditions of time and circumstance does this pitiful propensity not penetrate? You find it among merchants, officials, clerks, officers—in Sarátov, Mamadíshi, Vínnitza, in fact wherever men are to be found. And since there are many men, and consequently much vanity, in the besieged town of Sevastopol, aristocrats are to be found here too, though death hangs over everyone, be he aristocrat or not.

To Captain Obzhógov, Lieutenant-Captain Mikháylov was an aristocrat, and to Lieutenant-Captain Mikháylov, Adjutant Kalúgin was an aristocrat, because he was an adjutant and intimate with another adjutant. To Adjutant Kalúgin, Count Nórdov was an aristocrat, because he was aide-de-camp to the Emperor.

Vanity! vanity! vanity! everywhere, even on the brink of the grave and among men ready to die for a noble cause. Vanity! It seems to be the characteristic feature and special malady of our time. How is it that among our predecessors no mention was made of this passion, as of small-pox and cholera? How is it that in our time there are only three kinds of people: those who, considering vanity an inevitably existing fact and therefore justifiable, freely submit to it; those who regard it as a sad but unavoidable condition; and those who act unconsciously and slavishly under its influence? Why did the Homers and Shakespeares speak of love, glory, and suffering, while the literature of to-day is an endless story of snobbery and vanity?

Twice the lieutenant-captain passed irresolutely by the group of his aristocrats, but drawing near them for the third time he made an effort and walked up to them. The group consisted of four officers: Adjutant Kalúgin, Mikháylov's acquaintance, Adjutant Prince Gáltsin, who was rather an aristocrat even for Kalúgin himself, Lieutenant-Colonel Nefërdov, one of the so-called two hundred and twenty-two society men who being on the retired list re-entered the army for this war; and Cavalry-Captain Praskúkhin, also of the "two hundred and twenty-two." Luckily for Mikháylov, Kalúgin was in splendid spirits (the general had just spoken to him in a very confidential manner, and Prince Gáltsin who had arrived from Petersburg was staying with him), so he did not think it beneath his dignity to shake hands with Mikháylov, which was more than Praskúkhin did, though he had often met Mikháylov on the bastion, had more than once drunk his wine and vodka, and even owed him twelve and a half rubles lost at cards. Not being yet well acquainted with Prince Gáltsin he did not like to appear to be acquainted with a mere lieutenant-captain of infantry. So he only bowed slightly.

"Well, Captain," said Kalúgin, "when will you be visiting the bastion again? Do you remember our meeting at the Schwartz Redoubt? Things were hot, weren't they, eh?"

"Yes, very," said Mikháylov, and he recalled how when making his way along the trench to the bastion he had met Kalúgin walking bravely along, his sabre clanking smartly.

"My turn's to-morrow by rights, but we have an officer ill," continued Mikháylov, "so—"

He wanted to say that it was not his turn but as the Commander of the 8th Company was ill and only the ensign was left in the company, he felt it his duty to go in place of Lieutenant Nepshisétski and would therefore be at the bastion that evening. But Kalúgin did not hear him out.

"I feel sure that something is going to happen in a day or two," he said to Prince Gáltsin.

"How about to-day? Will nothing happen to-day?" Mikháylov asked shyly, looking first at Kalúgin and then at Gáltsin.

No one replied. Prince Gáltsin only puckered up his

face in a curious way and looking over Mikháylov's cap said after a short silence: "Fine girl that, with the red kerchief. You know her, don't you, Captain?"

"She lives near my lodgings; she's a sailor's daughter," answered the lieutenant-captain.

"Come, let's have a good look at her."

And Prince Gáltsin gave one of his arms to Kalúgin and the other to the lieutenant-captain, being sure he would confer great pleasure on the latter by so doing, which was really quite true.

The lieutenant-captain was superstitious and considered it a great sin to amuse himself with women before going into action, but on this occasion he pretended to be a *roué*, which Prince Gáltsin and Kalúgin evidently did not believe and which greatly surprised the girl with the red kerchief, who had more than once noticed how the lieutenant-captain blushed when he passed her window. Praskúkhin walked behind them, and kept touching Prince Gáltsin's arm and making various remarks in French, but as four people could not walk abreast on the path he was obliged to go alone until, on the second round, he took the arm of a well-known brave naval officer, Servyágin, who came up and spoke to him, being also anxious to join the aristocrats. And the well-known hero gladly passed his honest muscular hand under the elbow of Praskúkhin, whom everybody, including Servyágin himself, knew to be no better than he should be. When, wishing to explain his acquaintance with this sailor, Praskúkhin whispered to Prince Gáltsin—who had been in the Fourth Bastion the day before and seen a shell burst at some twenty yards' distance—considering himself not less courageous than the newcomer, and believing that many reputations are obtained by luck, paid not the slightest attention to Servyágin.

Lieutenant-Captain Mikháylov found it so pleasant to walk in this company that he forgot the nice letter from T——— and his gloomy forebodings at the thought of having to go to the bastion. He remained with them till they began talking exclusively among themselves, avoiding his eyes to show that he might go, and at last walked away from him. But all the same the lieutenant-captain was contented, and when he passed Cadet Baron Pesth—who was particularly conceited and self-satisfied since the previous night, when for the first time in his life he had been in the bomb-proof of the Fifth Bastion and had consequently become a hero in his own estimation—he was not at all hurt by the suspiciously haughty expression with which the cadet saluted him.

4

But the lieutenant-captain had hardly crossed the threshold of his lodgings before very different thoughts entered his head. He saw his little room with its uneven earth floor, its crooked windows, the broken panes mended with paper, his old bedstead with two Túla pistols and a rug (showing a lady on horseback) nailed to the wall beside it,[2] as well as the dirty bed of the cadet who lived with him, with its cotton quilt. He saw his man Nikíta, with his rough greasy hair, rise from the floor scratching himself, he saw his old cloak, his common boots, a little bundle tied in a handkerchief ready for him to take to the bastion, from which peeped a bit of cheese and the neck of a porter bottle containing vodka— and he suddenly remembered that he had to go with his company to spend the whole night at the lodgements.

"I shall certainly be killed to-night," thought he, "I feel I shall. And there was really no need for me to go—I offered to do it of my own accord. And it always happens that the one who offers himself gets killed. And what is the matter with that confounded Nepshisétski? He may not be ill at all, and they'll go and kill me because of him—they're sure to. Still, if they don't kill me I shall certainly be recommended for promotion. I saw how pleased the regimental commander was when I said: 'Allow me to go if Lieutenant Nepshisétski is ill.' If I'm not made a major then I'll get the Order of Vladímir for certain. Why, I am going to the bastion for the thirteenth time. Oh dear, the thirteenth! Unlucky number! I am

[2] A common way in Russia of protecting a bed from the damp or cold of a wall, is to nail a rug or carpet to the wall by the side of the bed.

certain to be killed. I feel I shall . . . but somebody had to go: the company can't go with only an ensign. Supposing something were to happen. . . . Why, the honour of the regiment, the honour of the army, is at stake. It is my *duty* to go. Yes, my sacred duty. . . . But I have a presentiment."

The lieutenant-captain forgot that it was not the first time he had felt this presentiment: that in a greater or lesser degree he had it whenever he was going to the bastion, and he did not know that before going into action everyone has such forebodings more or less strongly. Having calmed himself by appealing to his sense of duty—which was highly developed and very strong—the lieutenant-captain sat down at the table and began writing a farewell letter to his father. Ten minutes later, having finished his letter, he rose from the table, his eyes wet with tears, and repeating mentally all the prayers he knew he began to dress. His rather tipsy and rude servant lazily handed him his new cloak—the old one which the lieutenant-captain usually wore at the bastion not being mended.

"Why isn't my cloak mended? You do nothing but sleep," said Mikháylov angrily.

"Sleep indeed!" grumbled Nikíta, "I do nothing but run about like a dog the whole day, and when I get fagged I mayn't even go to sleep!"

"I see you are drunk again."

"It's not at your expense if I am, so you needn't complain."

"Hold your tongue, you dolt!" shouted the lieutenant-captain, ready to strike the man.

Already upset, he now quite lost patience and felt hurt by the rudeness of Nikíta, who had lived with him for the last twelve years and whom he was fond of and even spoilt.

"Dolt? Dolt?" repeated the servant. "And why do you, sir, abuse me and call me a dolt? You know in times like these it isn't right to abuse people."

Recalling where he was about to go, Mikháylov felt ashamed.

"But you know, Nikíta, you would try anyone's

patience!" he said mildly. "That letter to my father on the table you may leave where it is. Don't touch it," he added reddening.

"Yes sir," said Nikita, becoming sentimental under the influence of the vodka he had drunk, as he said, at his own expense, and blinking with an evident inclination to weep.

But at the porch, when the lieutenant-captain said, "Good-bye, Nikíta," Nikíta burst into forced sobs and rushed to kiss his master's hand, saying, "Good-bye, sir," in a broken voice. A sailor's widow who was also standing in the porch could not, as a woman, help joining in this tender scene and began wiping her eyes on her dirty sleeve, saying something about people who, though they were gentlefolk, took such sufferings upon themselves while she, poor woman, was left a widow. And she told the tipsy Nikíta for the hundredth time about her sorrows: how her husband had been killed in the first *bondbarment*, and how her hut had been shattered (the one she lived in now was not her own), and so on. After his master was gone Nikíta lit his pipe, asked the landlady's little girl to get some vodka, very soon left off crying, and even had a quarrel with the old woman about a pail he said she had smashed for him.

"But perhaps I shall only be wounded," reasoned the lieutenant-captain as he drew near the bastion with his company when twilight had already begun to fall. "But where, and how? Here or here?" he said to himself, mentally passing his chest, his stomach, and his thighs in review. "Supposing it's here' (he thought of his thighs) 'and goes right round. . . . Or goes here with a piece of a bomb, then it will be all up."

The lieutenant-captain passed along the trenches and reached the lodgements safely. In perfect darkness he and an officer of Engineers set the men to their work, after which he sat down in a pit under the breastwork. There was little firing; only now and again there was a lightning flash on our side or *his*, and the brilliant fuse of a bomb formed a fiery arc on the dark, star-speckled sky. But all the bombs fell far beyond or far to the right of the lodgement where the lieutenant-captain sat

in his pit. He drank some vodka, ate some cheese, smoked
a cigarette, said his prayers, and felt inclined to sleep for
a while.

5

Prince Gáltsin, Lieutenant-Colonel Nefërdov, and
Praskúkhin—whom no one had invited and to whom no
one spoke, but who still stuck to them—went to Kalúgin's
to tea.

"But you did not finish telling me about Váska
Méndel," said Kalúgin, when he had taken off his cloak
and sat in a soft easy chair by the window unbuttoning
the collar of his clean starched shirt. "How did he get
married?"

"It was a joke, my boy! . . . *Je vous dis, il y avait un
temps, on ne parlait que de ça à Pétersbourgh,*"[3] said Prince
Gáltsin, laughing as he jumped up from the piano-stool
and sat down near Kalúgin on the window-sill,[4] "a capital
joke. I know all about it."

And he told, amusingly, cleverly, and with animation,
a love story which, as it has no interest for us, we will
omit.

It was noticeable that not only Prince Gáltsin but each
of these gentlemen who established themselves, one on
the window-sill, another with his legs in the air, and
a third by the piano, seemed quite different people now
from what they had been on the boulevard. There was
none of the absurd arrogance and haughtiness they had
shown towards the infantry officers; here among themselves they were natural, and Kalúgin and Prince Gáltsin
in particular showed themselves very pleasant, merry, and
good-natured young fellows. Their conversation was about
their Petersburg fellow officers and acquaintances.

"What of Máslovski?"

"Which one—the Leib-Uhlan, or the Horse Guard?"

"I know them both. The one in the Horse Guards I

---

[3] "I tell you, at one time it was the only thing talked of in
Petersburg."

[4] The thick walls of Russian houses allow ample space to sit or
lounge at the windows.

knew when he was a boy just out of school. But the eldest—is he a captain yet?"

"Oh yes, long ago."

"Is he still fussing about with his gipsy?"

"No, he has dropped her. . . ." And so on in the same strain.

Later on Prince Gáltsin went to the piano and gave an excellent rendering of a gipsy song. Praskúkhin, chiming in unasked, put in a second and did it so well that he was invited to continue, and this delighted him.

A servant brought tea, cream, and cracknels on a silver tray.

"Serve the prince," said Kalúgin.

"Isn't it strange to think that we're in a besieged town," said Gáltsin, taking his tea to the window, "and here's a *pianerforty*, tea with cream, and a house such as I should really be glad to have in Petersburg?"

"Well, if we hadn't even that much," said the old and ever-dissatisfied lieutenant-colonel, "the constant uncertainty we are living in—seeing people killed day after day and no end to it—would be intolerable. And to have dirt and discomfort added to it—"

"But our infantry officers live at the bastions with their men in the bomb-proofs and eat the soldiers' soup," said Kalúgin, "what of them?"

"What of them? Well, though it's true they don't change their shirts for ten days at a time, they are heroes all the same—wonderful fellows."

Just then an infantry officer entered the room.

"I . . . I have orders . . . may I see the Gen . . . his Excellency? I have come with a message from General N.," he said with a timid bow.

Kalúgin rose and without returning the officer's greeting asked with an offensive, affected, official smile if he would not have the goodness to wait, and without asking him to sit down or taking any further notice of him he turned to Gáltsin and began talking French, so that the poor officer left alone in the middle of the room did not in the least know what to do with himself.

"It is a matter of the utmost urgency, sir," he said after a short silence.

"Ah! Well then, please come with me," said Kalúgin,

putting on his cloak and accompanying the officer to the door.

"Eh bien, messieurs, je crois que cela chauffera cette nuit,"[5] said Kalúgin when he returned from the general's.

"Ah! What is it—a sortie?" asked the others.

"That I don't know. You will see for yourselves," replied Kalúgin with a mysterious smile.

"And my commander is at the bastion, so I suppose I must go too," said Praskúkhin, buckling on his sabre.

No one replied, it was his business to know whether he had to go or not.

Praskúkhin and Nefërdov left to go to their appointed posts.

"Good-bye gentlemen. *Au revoir!* We'll meet again before the night is over," shouted Kalúgin from the window as Praskúkhin and Nefërdov, stooping on their Cossack saddles, trotted past. The tramp of their Cossack horses soon died away in the dark street.

"Non, dites-moi, est-ce qu'il y aura véritablement quelque chose cette nuit?"[6] said Gáltsin as he lounged in the window-sill beside Kalúgin and watched the bombs that rose above the bastions.

"I can tell *you*, you see . . . you have been to the bastions?" (Gáltsin nodded, though he had only been once to the Fourth Bastion.) "You remember just in front of our lunette there is a trench"—and Kalúgin, with the air of one who without being a specialist considers his military judgement very sound, began, in a rather confused way and misusing the technical terms, to explain the position of the enemy, and of our own works, and the plan of the intended action.

"But I say, they're banging away at the lodgements! Oho! I wonder if that's ours or *his*? . . . Now it's burst," said they, as they lounged on the window-sill looking at the fiery trails of the bombs crossing one another in the air, at flashes that for a moment lit up the dark sky, at puffs of white smoke, and listened to the more and more rapid reports of the firing.

---

[5] "Well, gentlemen, I think there will be warm work to-night."

[6] "No, tell me, will there really be anything to-night?"

"*Quel charmant coup d'œil! a?*"[7] said Kalúgin, drawing his guest's attention to the really beautiful sight. "Do you know, you sometimes can't distinguish a bomb from a star."

"Yes, I thought that was a star just now and then saw it fall . . . there! it's burst. And that big star—what do you call it?—looks just like a bomb."

"Do you know I am so used to these bombs that I am sure when I'm back in Russia I shall fancy I see bombs every starlight night—one gets so used to them."

"But hadn't I better go with this sortie?" said Prince Gáltsin after a moment's pause.

"Humbug, my dear fellow! Don't think of such a thing. Besides, I won't let you," answered Kalúgin. "You will have plenty of opportunities later on."

"Really? You think I need not go, eh?"

At that moment, from the direction in which these gentlemen were looking, amid the boom of the cannon came the terrible rattle of musketry, and thousands of little fires flaming up in quick succession flashed all along the line.

"There! Now it's the real thing!" said Kalúgin, "I can't keep cool when I hear the noise of muskets. It seems to seize one's very soul, you know. There's an *hurrah!*" he added, listening intently to the distant and prolonged roar of hundreds of voices—"Ah—ah—ah" —which came from the bastions.

"Whose *hurrah* was it? Theirs or ours?"

"I don't know, but it's hand-to-hand fighting now, for the firing has ceased."

At that moment an officer followed by a Cossack galloped under the window and alighted from his horse at the porch.

"Where are you from?"

"From the bastion. I want the general."

"Come along. Well, what's happened?"

"The lodgements have been attacked—and occupied. The French brought up tremendous reserves—attacked us—we had only two battalions," said the officer, panting. He was the same officer who had been there that evening,

---

[7] "What a charming sight, eh?"

but though he was now out of breath he walked to the door with full self-possession.

"Well, have we retired?" asked Kalúgin.

"No," angrily replied the officer, "another battalion came up in time—we drove them back, but the colonel is killed and many officers. I have orders to ask for reinforcements."

And saying this he went with Kalúgin to the general's, where we shall not follow him.

Five minutes later Kalúgin was already on his Cossack horse (again in the semi-Cossack manner which I have noticed that all adjutants, for some reason, seem to consider the proper thing) and rode off at a trot towards the bastion to deliver some orders and await the final result of the affair. Prince Gáltsin, under the influence of that oppressive excitement usually produced in a spectator by proximity to an action in which he is not engaged, went out and began aimlessly pacing up and down the street.

6

Soldiers passed carrying the wounded on stretchers or supporting them under their arms. It was quite dark in the streets, lights could be seen here and there, but only in the hospital windows or where some officers were sitting up. From the bastions still came the thunder of cannon and the rattle of muskets,[8] and flashes kept on lighting up the dark sky as before. From time to time the tramp of hoofs could be heard as an orderly galloped past, or the groans of a wounded man, the steps and voices of stretcher-bearers, or the words of some frightened women who had come out onto their porches to watch the cannonade.

Among the spectators were our friend Nikíta, the old sailor's widow with whom he had again made friends, and her ten-year-old daughter.

---

[8] Rifles, except some clumsy *stutzers*, had not been introduced into the Russian army, but were used by the besiegers, who had a still greater advantage in artillery. It is characteristic of Tolstóy that, occupied with men rather than mechanics, he does not in these sketches dwell on this disparity of equipment.

"O Lord God! Holy Mary, Mother of God!" said the old woman, sighing as she looked at the bombs that kept flying across from side to side like balls of fire; "What horrors! What horrors! Ah, ah! Oh, oh! Even at the first *bondbarment* it wasn't like that. Look now where the cursed thing has burst just over our house in the suburb."

"No, that's further, they keep tumbling into Aunt Irene's garden," said the girl.

"And where, where, is master now?" drawled Nikíta, who was not quite sober yet. "Oh! You don't know how I love that master of mine! I love him so that if he were killed in a sinful way, which God forbid, then would you believe it, granny, after that I myself don't know what I wouldn't do to myself! I don't! . . . My master is that sort, there's only one word for it. Would I change him for such as them there, playing cards? What are they? Ugh! There's only one word for it!" concluded Nikíta, pointing to the lighted window of his master's room, to which, in the absence of the lieutenant-captain, Cadet Zhvadchévski had invited Sub-Lieutenants Ugróvich and Nepshisétski—the latter suffering from face-ache—and where he was having a spree in honour of a medal he had received.

"Look at the stars! Look how they're rolling!" the little girl broke the silence that followed Nikíta's words as she stood gazing at the sky. "There's another rolled down. What is it a sign of, mother?"

"They'll smash up our hut altogether," said the old woman with a sigh, leaving her daughter unanswered.

"As we went there to-day with uncle, mother," the little girl continued in a sing-song tone, becoming loquacious, "there was such a b-i-g cannon-ball inside the room close to the cupboard. Must have smashed in through the passage and right into the room! Such a big one—you couldn't lift it."

"Those who had husbands and money all moved away," said the old woman, "and there's the hut, all that was left me, and that's been smashed. Just look at *him* blazing away! The fiend! . . . O Lord! O Lord!"

"And just as we were going out, comes a bomb fly-ing,

and goes and bur-sts and co-o-vers us with dust. A bit of it nearly hit me and uncle."

<h1 style="text-align:center">7</h1>

Prince Gáltsin met more and more wounded, carried on stretchers or walking supported by others who were talking loudly.

"Up they sprang, friends," said the bass voice of a tall soldier with two guns slung from his shoulder, "up they sprang, shouting 'Allah! Allah!'[9] and just climbing one over another. You kill one and another's there, you couldn't do anything; no end of 'em——"

But at this point in the story Gáltsin interrupted him.

"You are from the bastion?"

"Yes, your Honour."

"Well, what happened? Tell me."

"What happened? Well, your Honour, such a force of 'em poured down on us over the rampart, it was all up. They quite overpowered us, your Honour!"

"Overpowered? . . . But you repulsed them?"

"How could we repulse them when *his* whole force came on, killed all our men, and no re'forcements were given us?"

The soldier was mistaken, the trench had remained ours; but it is a curious fact, which anyone may notice, that a soldier wounded in action always thinks the affair lost and imagines it to have been a very bloody fight.

"How is that? I was told they had been repulsed," said Gáltsin irritably. "Perhaps they were driven back after you left? Is it long since you came away?"

"I am straight from there, your Honour," answered the soldier; "it is hardly possible. They must have kept the trench, *he* quite overpowered us."

"And aren't you ashamed to have lost the trench? It's terrible!" said Gáltsin, provoked by such indifference.

"Why, if the strength is on their side . . ." muttered the soldier.

"Ah, your Honour," began a soldier from a stretcher which had just come up to them, "how could we help

---

[9] Our soldiers fighting the Turks have become so accustomed to this cry of the enemy that they now always say that the French also shout "Allah!"—L. T.

giving up when *he* had killed almost all our men? If we'd had the strength we wouldn't have given it up, not on any account. But as it was, what could we do? I stuck one, and then something hits me. Oh, oh-h! Steady, lads, steady! Oh, oh!" groaned the wounded man.

"Really, there seem to be too many men returning," said Gáltsin, again stopping the tall soldier with the two guns. "Why are you retiring? You there, stop!"

The soldier stopped and took off his cap with his left hand.

'Where are you going, and why?" shouted Gáltsin severely, "you scoun—"

But having come close up to the soldier, Gáltsin noticed that no hand was visible beneath the soldier's right cuff and that the sleeve was soaked in blood to the elbow.

"I am wounded, your Honour."

"Wounded? How?"

"Here. Must have been with a bullet," said the man, pointing to his arm, "but I don't know what struck my head here," and bending his head he showed the matted hair at the back stuck together with blood.

"And whose is this other gun?"

"It's a French rifle I took, your Honour. But I wouldn't have come away if it weren't to lead this fellow—he may fall," he added, pointing to a soldier who was walking a little in front leaning on his gun and painfully dragging his left leg.

Prince Gáltsin suddenly felt horribly ashamed of his unjust suspicions. He felt himself blushing, turned away, and went to the hospital without either questioning or watching the wounded men any more.

Having with difficulty pushed his way through the porch among the wounded who had come on foot and the bearers who were carrying in the wounded and bringing out the dead, Gáltsin entered the first room, gave a look round, and involuntarily turned back and ran out into the street: it was too terrible.

8

The large, lofty, dark hall, lit up only by the four or five candles with which the doctors examined the wounded, was quite full. Yet the bearers kept bringing in more wounded —laying them side by side on the floor which was already so packed that the unfortunate patients were jostled together, staining one another with their blood—and going to fetch more wounded. The pools of blood visible in the unoccupied spaces, the feverish breathing of several hundred men, and the perspiration of the bearers with the stretchers filled the air with a peculiar, heavy, thick, fetid mist, in which the candles burnt dimly in different parts of the hall. All sorts of groans, sighs, death-rattles, now and then interrupted by shrill screams, filled the whole room. Sisters with quiet faces, expressing no empty feminine tearful pity but active practical sympathy, stepped here and there across the wounded with medicines, water, bandages, and lint, flitting among the blood-stained coats and shirts. The doctors, kneeling with rolled-up sleeves beside the wounded, by the light of the candles their assistants held, examined, felt, and probed their wounds, heedless of the terrible groans and entreaties of the sufferers. One doctor sat at a table near the door and at the moment Gáltsin came in was already entering No. 532.

"Iván Bogáev, Private, Company Three, S———— Regiment, *fractura femuris complicata!*" shouted another doctor from the end of the room, examining a shattered leg. "Turn him over."

"Oh, oh, fathers! Oh, you're our fathers!" screamed the soldier, beseeching them not to touch him.

"Perforatio capitis!"

"Simon Nefërdov, Lieutenant-Colonel of the N———— Infantry Regiment. Have a little patience, Colonel, or it is quite possible: I shall give it up!" said a third doctor, poking about with some kind of hook in the unfortunate colonel's skull.

"Oh, don't! Oh, for God's sake be quick! Be quick! Ah——!"

"Perforatio pectoris . . . Sebastian Seredá, Private . . . what regiment? But you need not write that: *moritur.* Carry him away," said the doctor, leaving the soldier, whose eyes turned up and in whose throat the death-rattle already sounded.

About forty soldier stretcher-bearers stood at the door

waiting to carry the bandaged to the wards and the dead to the chapel. They looked on at the scene before them in silence, only broken now and then by a heavy sigh.

9

On his way to the bastion Kalúgin met many wounded, but knowing by experience that in action such sights have a bad effect on one's spirits, he did not stop to question them but tried on the contrary not to notice them. At the foot of the hill he met an orderly-officer galloping fast from the bastion.

"Zóbkin! Zóbkin! Wait a bit!"

"Well, what is it?"

"Where are you from?"

"The lodgements."

"How are things there—hot?"

"Oh, awful!"

And the orderly galloped on.

In fact, though there was now but little small-arm firing, the cannonade had recommenced with fresh heat and persistence.

"Ah, that's bad!" thought Kalúgin with an unpleasant sensation, and he too had a presentiment—a very usual thought, the thought of death. But Kalúgin was ambitious and blessed with nerves of oak—in a word, he was what is called brave. He did not yield to the first feeling but began to nerve himself. He recalled how an adjutant, Napoleon's he thought, having delivered an order, galloped with bleeding head full speed to Napoleon. "*Vous êtes blessé?*"[10] said Napoleon. "*Je vous demande pardon, sire, je suis mort,*"[11] and the adjutant fell from his horse, dead.

That seemed to him very fine, and he pictured himself for a moment in the role of that adjutant. Then he whipped his horse, assuming a still more dashing Cossack seat, looked back at the Cossack who, standing up in his stirrups, was trotting behind, and rode quite gallantly up to the spot where he had to dismount. Here he found four soldiers sitting on some stones smoking their pipes.

[10] "You are wounded?"
[11] "Excuse me, sire, I am dead."

"What are you doing there?" he shouted at them.

"Been carrying off a wounded man and sat down to rest a bit, your Honour," said one of them, hiding his pipe behind his back and taking off his cap.

"Resting, indeed! . . . To your places, march!"

And he went up the hill with them through the trench, meeting wounded men at every step.

After ascending the hill he turned to the left and a few steps farther on found himself quite alone. A splinter of a bomb whizzed near him and fell into the trench. Another bomb rose in front of him and seemed flying straight at him. He suddenly felt frightened, ran a few steps at full speed, and lay down flat. When the bomb burst a considerable distance off he felt exceedingly vexed with himself and rose, looking round to see if anyone had noticed his downfall, but no one was near.

But when fear has once entered the soul it does not easily yield to any other feeling. He, who always boasted that he never even stooped, now hurried along the trench almost on all fours. He stumbled, and thought, "Oh, it's awful! They'll kill me for certain!" His breath came with difficulty, and perspiration broke out over his whole body. He was surprised at himself but no longer strove to master his feelings.

Suddenly he heard footsteps in front. Quickly straightening himself he raised his head and boldly clanking his sabre went on more deliberately. He felt himself quite a different man. When he met an officer of the Engineers and a sailor, and the officer shouted to him to lie down, pointing to a bright spot which growing brighter and brighter approached more and more swiftly and came crashing down close to the trench, he only bent a little, involuntarily influenced by the frightened cry, and went on.

"That's a brave one," said the sailor, looking quite calmly at the bomb and with experienced eye deciding at once that the splinters could not fly into the trench, "he won't even lie down."

It was only a few steps across open ground to the bomb-proof shelter of the commander of the bastion, when Kalúgin's mind again became clouded and the same stupid terror seized him: his heart beat more violently, the blood rushed to his head, and he had to make an effort to force himself to run to the bomb-proof.

"Why are you so out of breath?" said the general, when Kalúgin had reported his instructions.

'I walked very fast, your Excellency!"

"Won't you have a glass of wine?"

Kalúgin drank a glass of wine and lit a cigarette. The action was over; only a fierce cannonade still continued from both sides. In the bomb-proof sat General N———, the commander of the bastion, and some six other officers among whom was Praskúkhin. They were discussing various details of the action. Sitting in this comfortable room with blue wall-paper, a sofa, a bed, a table with papers on it, a wall-clock with a lamp burning before it, and an icon[12]— looking at these signs of habitation, at the beams more than two feet thick that formed the ceiling, and listening to the shots that sounded faint here in the shelter, Kalúgin could not understand how he had twice allowed himself to be overcome by such unpardonable weakness. He was angry with himself and wished for danger in order to test his nerve once more.

"Ah! I'm glad you are here, Captain," said he to a naval officer with big moustaches who wore a staff-officer's coat with a St. George's Cross and had just entered the shelter and asked the general to give him some men to repair two embrasures of his battery which had become blocked. When the general had finished speaking to the captain, Kalúgin said: "The commander-in-chief told me to ask if your guns can fire case-shot into the trenches."

"Only one of them can," said the captain sullenly.

"All the same, let us go and see."

The captain frowned and gave an angry grunt.

"I have been standing there all night and have come in to get a bit of rest—couldn't you go alone?" he added. "My assistant, Lieutenant Kartz, is there and can show you everything."

The captain had already been more than six months in

---

[12] The Russian icons are paintings in Byzantine style of God, the Holy Virgin, Christ, or some saint, martyr, or angel. They are usually on wood and often covered over, except the face and hands, with an embossed gilt cover.

command of this, one of the most dangerous batteries. From the time the siege began, even before the bomb-proof shelters were constructed, he had lived continuously on the bastion and had a great reputation for courage among the sailors. That is why his refusal struck and surprised Kalúgin. "So much for reputation," thought he.

"Well then, I will go alone if I may," he said in a slightly sarcastic tone to the captain, who however paid no attention to his words.

Kalúgin did not realize that whereas he had spent some fifty hours all in all at different times on the bastions, the captain had lived there for six months. Kalúgin was still actuated by vanity, the wish to shine, the hope of rewards, of gaining a reputation, and the charm of running risks. But the captain had already lived through all that: at first he had felt vain, had shown off his courage, had been fool-hardy, had hoped for rewards and reputation and had even gained them, but now all these incentives had lost their power over him and he saw things differently. He fulfilled his duty exactly, but quite understanding how much the chances of life were against him after six months at the bastion, he no longer ran risks without serious need, and so the young lieutenant who had joined the battery a week ago and was now showing it to Kalúgin, with whom he vied in uselessly leaning out of the embrasures and climb-ing out on the banquette, seemed ten times braver than the captain.

Returning to the shelter after examining the battery, Kalúgin in the dark came upon the general, who accom-panied by his staff officers was going to the watch-tower.

"Captain Praskúkhin," he heard the general say, "please go to the right lodgement and tell the second battalion of the M——— Regiment which is at work there to cease their work, leave the place, and noiselessly rejoin their regiment which is stationed in reserve at the foot of the hill. Do you understand? Lead them yourself to the regiment."

"Yes, sir."

And Praskúkhin started at full speed towards the lodge-ments.

The firing was now becoming less frequent.

10

"Is this the second battalion of the M———— Regiment?" asked Praskúkhin, having run to his destination and coming across some soldiers carrying earth in sacks.

"It is, your Honour."

"Where is the Commander?"

Mikháylov, thinking that the commander of the company was being asked for, got out of his pit and taking Praskúkhin for a commanding officer saluted and approached him.

"The general's orders are . . . that you . . . should go . . . quickly . . . and above all quietly . . . back—no not back, but to the reserves," said Praskúkhin, looking askance in the direction of the enemy's fire.

Having recognized Praskúkhin and made out what was wanted, Mikháylov dropped his hand and passed on the order. The battalion became alert, the men took up their muskets, put on their cloaks, and set out.

No one without experiencing it can imagine the delight a man feels when, after three hours' bombardment, he leaves so dangerous a spot as the lodgements. During those three hours Mikháylov, who more than once and not without reason had thought his end at hand, had had time to accustom himself to the conviction that he would certainly be killed and that he no longer belonged to this world. But in spite of that he had great difficulty in keeping his legs from running away with him when, leading the company with Praskúkhin at his side, he left the lodgement.

"*Au revoir!*" said a major with whom Mikháylov had eaten bread and cheese sitting in the pit under the breastwork and who was remaining at the bastion in command of another battalion. "I wish you a lucky journey."

"And I wish you a lucky defence. It seems to be getting quieter now."

But scarcely had he uttered these words before the enemy, probably observing the movement in the lodgment, began to fire more and more frequently. Our guns replied and a heavy firing recommenced.

The stars were high in the sky but shone feebly. The night was pitch dark, only the flashes of the guns and the bursting bombs made things around suddenly visible. The soldiers walked quickly and silently, involuntarily outpacing one another; only their measured footfalls on the dry road was heard besides the incessant roll of the guns, the ringing of bayonets when they touched one another, a sigh, or the prayer of some poor soldier lad: "Lord, O Lord! What does it mean?" Now and again the moaning of a man who was hit could be heard, and the cry, "Stretchers!" (In the company Mikháylov commanded artillery fire alone carried off twenty-six men that night.) A flash on the dark and distant horizon, the cry, "Can-n-on!" from the sentinel on the bastion, and a ball flew buzzing above the company and plunged into the earth, making the stones fly.

"What the devil are they so slow for?" thought Praskúkhin, continually looking back as he marched beside Mikháylov. "I'd really better run on. I've delivered the order. . . . But no, they might afterwards say I'm a coward. What must be will be. I'll keep beside him."

"Now why is he walking with me?" thought Mikháylov on his part. "I have noticed over and over again that he always brings ill luck. Here it comes, I believe, straight for us."

After they had gone a few hundred paces they met Kalúgin, who was walking briskly towards the lodgements clanking his sabre. He had been ordered by the general to find out how the works were progressing there. But when he met Mikháylov he thought that instead of going there himself under such a terrible fire—which he was not ordered to do—he might just as well find out all about it from an officer who had been there. And having heard from Mikháylov full details of the work and walked a little way with him, Kalúgin turned off into a trench leading to the bomb-proof shelter.

"Well, what news?" asked an officer who was eating his supper there all alone.

"Nothing much. It seems that the affair is over."

"Over? How so? On the contrary, the general has just gone again to the watch-tower and another regiment has arrived. Yes, there it is. Listen! The muskets again! Don't you go—why should you?" added the officer, noticing that Kalúgin made a movement.

"I certainly ought to be there," thought Kalúgin, "but I have already exposed myself a great deal today: the firing is awful!"

"Yes, I think I'd better wait here for him," he said.

And really about twenty minutes later the general and the officers who were with him returned. Among them was Cadet Baron Pesth but not Praskúkhin. The lodgements had been retaken and occupied by us.

After receiving a full account of the affair, Kalúgin, accompanied by Pesth, left the bomb-proof shelter.

II

"There's blood on your coat! You don't mean to say you were in the hand-to-hand fight?" asked Kalúgin.

"Oh, it was awful! Just fancy—"

And Pesth began to relate how he had led his company, how the company-commander had been killed, how he himself had stabbed a Frenchman, and how if it had not been for him we should have lost the day.

This tale was founded on fact: the company-commander had been killed and Pesth had bayoneted a Frenchman, but in recounting the details the cadet invented and bragged.

He bragged unintentionally, because during the whole of the affair he had been as it were in a fog and so bewildered that all he remembered of what had happened seemed to have happened somewhere, at some time, and to somebody. And very naturally he tried to recall the details in a light advantageous to himself. What really occurred was this:

The battalion the cadet had been ordered to join for the sortie stood under fire for two hours close to some low wall. Then the battalion-commander in front said something, the company-commanders became active, the battalion advanced from behind the breastwork, and after going about a hundred paces stopped to form into company columns. Pesth was told to take his place on the right flank of the second company.

Quite unable to realize where he was and why he was there, the cadet took his place and involuntarily holding his breath while cold shivers ran down his back he gazed into the dark distance expecting something dreadful. He was however not so much frightened (for there was no firing) as disturbed and agitated at being in the field beyond the fortifications.

Again the battalion-commander in front said something. Again the officers spoke in whispers passing on the order, and the black wall, formed by the first company, suddenly sank out of sight. The order was to lie down. The second company also lay down and in lying down Pesth hurt his hand on a sharp prickle. Only the commander of the second company remained standing. His short figure brandishing a sword moved in front of the company and he spoke incessantly.

"Mind lads! Show them what you're made of! Don't fire, but give it them with the bayonet—the dogs!—when I cry 'Hurrah!' Altogether, mind, that's the thing! We'll let them see who we are. We won't disgrace ourselves, eh lads? For our father the Tsar!"

"What's your company-commander's name?" asked Pesth of a cadet lying near him. "How brave he is!"

"Yes, he always is, in action," answered the cadet. "His name is Lisinkóvski."

Just then a flame suddenly flashed up right in front of the company, who were deafened by a resounding crash. High up in the air stones and splinters clattered. (Some fifty seconds later a stone fell from above and severed a soldier's leg.) It was a bomb fired from an elevated stand, and the fact that it reached the company showed that the French had noticed the column.

"You're sending bombs, are you? Wait a bit till we get at you, then you'll taste a three-edged Russian bayonet, damn you!" said the company-commander so loud that the battalion-commander had to order him to hold his tongue and not make so much noise.

After that the first company got up, then the second. They were ordered to fix bayonets and the battalion advanced. Pesth was in such a fright that he could not in the least make out how long it lasted, where he went, or who was who. He went on as if he were drunk. But suddenly a million fires flashed from all sides, and something whistled and clattered. He shouted and ran somewhere, because everyone shouted and ran. Then he stumbled and fell over something. It was the company-commander, who had been wounded at the head of his company, and who taking the cadet for a Frenchman had seized him by the leg. Then when Pesth had freed his leg and got up, someone else ran against him from behind in the dark and nearly knocked him down again. "Run him through!" someone else shouted. "What are you stopping for?" Then someone seized a gun and stuck it into something soft. "*Ah Dieu!*" came a dreadful, piercing voice and Pesth only then understood that he had bayoneted a Frenchman. A cold sweat covered his whole body; he trembled as in a fever and threw down his musket. But this lasted only a moment; the thought immediately entered his head that he was a hero. He again seized his musket, and shouting "Hurrah!" ran with the crowd away from the dead Frenchman. Having run twenty paces he came to a trench. Some of our men were there with the battalion-commander.

"And I have killed one!" said Pesth to the commander.

"You're a fine fellow, Baron!"

12

"Do you know Praskúkhin is killed?" said Pesth, while accompanying Kalúgin on his way home.

"Impossible!"

"It is true. I saw him myself."

"Well, good-bye . . . I must be off."

"This is capital!" thought Kalúgin, as he came to his lodgings. "It's the first time I have had such luck when on duty. It's first-rate. I am alive and well and shall certainly get an excellent recommendation and am sure of a gold sabre. And I really have deserved it."

After reporting what was necessary to the general he went to his room, where Prince Gáltsin, long since returned, sat awaiting him, reading a book he had found on Kalúgin's table.

It was with extraordinary pleasure that Kalúgin found himself safe at home again, and having put on his nightshirt and got into bed he gave Gáltsin all the details of the affair, telling them very naturally from a point of view where those details showed what a capable and brave officer he, Kalúgin, was (which it seems to me it was hardly necessary to allude to, since everybody knew it and had no right or reason to question it, except perhaps the deceased Captain Praskúkhin who, though he had considered it an honour to walk arm in arm with Kalúgin, had privately told a friend only yesterday that though Kalúgin was a first-rate fellow, yet, "between you and me, he was awfully disinclined to go to the bastions").

Praskúkhin, who had been walking beside Mikháylov after Kalúgin had slipped away from him, had scarcely begun to revive a little on approaching a safer place, than he suddenly saw a bright light flash up behind him and heard the sentinel shout "Mortar!" and a soldier walking behind him say: "That's coming straight for the bastion!"

Mikháylov looked round. The bright spot seemed to have stopped at its zenith, in the position which makes it absolutely impossible to define its direction. But that only lasted a moment: the bomb, coming faster and faster, nearer and nearer, so that the sparks of its fuse were already visible and its fatal whistle audible, descended towards the centre of the battalion.

"Lie down!" shouted someone.

Mikháylov and Praskúkhin lay flat on the ground. Praskúkhin, closing his eyes, only heard the bomb crash down on the hard earth close by. A second passed which seemed an hour: the bomb had not exploded. Praskúkhin was afraid. Perhaps he had played the coward for nothing. Perhaps the bomb had fallen far away and it only seemed to him that its fuse was fizzling close by. He opened his eyes and was pleased to see Mikháylov lying immovable at his feet. But at that moment he caught sight of the glowing fuse of the bomb which was spinning on the ground not a yard off. Terror, cold terror excluding every other thought and feeling, seized his whole being. He covered his face with his hands.

Another second passed—a second during which a whole world of feelings, thoughts, hopes, and memories flashed before his imagination.

"Whom will it hit—Mikháylov or me? Or both of us? And if it's me, where? In the head? Then I'm done for. But if it's the leg, they'll cut it off (I'll certainly ask for chloroform) and I may survive. But perhaps only Mikháy-lov will be hit. Then I will tell how we were going side by side and how he was killed and I was splashed with his blood. No, it's nearer to me . . . it will be I."

Then he remembered the twelve rubles he owed Mikháy-lov, remembered also a debt in Petersburg that should have been paid long ago, and the gipsy song he had sung that evening. The woman he loved rose in his imagination wear-ing a cap with lilac ribbons. He remembered a man who had insulted him five years ago and whom he had not yet paid out. And yet, inseparable from all these and thousands of other recollections, the present thought, the expectation of death, did not leave him for an instant. "Perhaps it won't explode," and with desperate decision he resolved to open his eyes. But at that instant a red flame pierced through the still closed lids and something struck him in the middle of his chest with a terrible crash. He jumped up and began to run, but stumbling over the sabre that got between his legs he fell on his side.

"Thank God, I'm only bruised!" was his first thought, and he was about to touch his chest with his hand, but his arms seemed tied to his sides and he felt as if a vice were squeezing his head. Soldiers flitted past him and he counted them unconsciously: "One, two, three soldiers! And there's an officer with his cloak tucked up," he thought. Then lightning flashed before his eyes and he wondered whether the shot was fired from a mortar or a cannon. "A cannon, probably. And there's another shot and here are more soldiers—five, six, seven soldiers. . . . They all pass by!" He was suddenly seized with fear that they would crush him. He wished to shout that he was hurt, but his mouth was so dry that his tongue clove to the roof of his mouth and a terrible thirst tormented him. He felt a wetness about his chest and this sensation of being wet made him think of water, and he longed to drink even this that made him feel wet. "I suppose I hit myself in falling and made myself bleed," thought he, and giving way more and more to fear lest the soldiers who kept flitting past might trample on him, he gathered all his strength and tried to shout, "Take me with you!" but instead of that he uttered such a terrible groan that the sound frightened him. Then some other red fires began dancing before his eyes and it seemed to him that the soldiers put stones on him. The fires danced less and less but the stones they put on him pressed more and more heavily. He made an effort to push off the stones, stretched himself, and saw and heard and felt nothing more. He had been killed on the spot by a bomb-splinter in the middle of his chest.

13

When Mikháylov dropped to the ground on seeing the bomb he too, like Praskúkhin, lived through an infinitude of thoughts and feelings in the two seconds that elapsed before the bomb burst. He prayed mentally and repeated, "Thy will be done." And at the same time he thought, "Why did I enter the army? And why did I join the infantry and take part in this campaign? Wouldn't it have been better to have remained with the Uhlan regiment at T——— and spent my time with my friend Natásha? And now here I am . . ." and he began to count, "One, two, three, four," deciding that if the bomb burst at an even number he would live but if at an odd number he would be killed. "It's all over, I'm killed!" he thought when the bomb burst (he did not remember whether at an odd or even number) and he felt a blow and a cruel pain in his head. "Lord, forgive me my trespasses!" he muttered, folding his hands. He rose but fell on his back senseless.

When he came to, his first sensations were that of blood trickling down his nose, and the pain in his head which had become much less violent. "That's the soul passing," he thought. "How will it be *there*? Lord, receive my soul in peace. . . . Only it's strange," thought he, "that while dying I should hear the steps of the soldiers and the sounds of the firing so distinctly."

"Bring stretchers! Eh, the captain has been hit!" shouted a voice above his head, which he recognized as the voice of the drummer Ignátyev.

Someone took him by the shoulders. With an effort he opened his eyes and saw above him the sky, some groups of stars, and two bombs racing one another as they flew over him. He saw Ignátyev, soldiers with stretchers and

guns, the embankment, the trenches, and suddenly realized
that he was not yet in the other world.

He had been slightly wounded in the head by a stone.
His first feeling was one almost of regret: he had prepared
himself so well and so calmly to go *there* that the return
to reality, with its bombs, stretchers, and blood, seemed
unpleasant. The second feeling was unconscious joy at
being alive, and the third a wish to get away from the
bastion as quickly as possible. The drummer tied a handkerchief round his commander's head and taking his arm
led him towards the ambulance station.

"But why and where am I going?" thought the lieutenant-
captain when he had recollected his senses. "My duty is to
remain with the company and not leave it behind—
especially," whispered a voice, "as it will soon be out of
range of the guns."

"Don't trouble about me, my lad," said he, drawing his
hand away from the attentive drummer. "I won't go to the
ambulance station: I'll stay with the company."

And he turned back.

"It would be better to have it properly bandaged, your
honour," said Ignátyev. "It's only in the heat of the
moment that it seems nothing. Mind it doesn't get worse.
. . . And just see what warm work it is here. . . . Really,
your honour—"

Mikháylov stood for a moment undecided and would
probably have followed Ignátyev's advice had he not
reflected how many severely wounded there must be at the
ambulance station. "Perhaps the doctors will smile at my
scratch," thought the lieutenant-captain, and in spite of
the drummer's arguments he returned to his company.

"And where is the orderly officer Praskúkhin, who was
with me?" he asked when he met the ensign who was leading the company.

"I don't know. Killed, I think," replied the ensign unwillingly.

"Killed? Or only wounded? How is it you don't know?
Wasn't he going with us? And why didn't you bring him
away?"

"How could we, under such a fire?"

"But how could you do such a thing, Michael Iványch?"

said Mikháylov angrily. "How could you leave him supposing he is alive? Even if he's dead his body ought to have been brought away."

"Alive indeed, when I tell you I went up and saw him myself!" said the ensign. "Excuse me. . . . It's hard enough to collect our own. There, those villains are at it again!" he added. "They're sending up cannon-balls now."

Mikháylov sat down and lifted his hands to his head, which ached terribly when he moved.

"No, it is absolutely necessary to go back and fetch him," he said. "He may still be alive. It is our *duty*, Michael Iványch."

Michael Iványch did not answer.

"O Lord! Just because he didn't bring him in at the time, soldiers will have to be sent back alone now . . . and yet can I possibly send them under this terrible fire? They may be killed for nothing," thought Mikháylov.

"Lads! Someone will have to go back to fetch the officer who was wounded out there in the ditch," said he, not very loudly or peremptorily, for he felt how unpleasant it would be for the soldiers to execute this order. And he was right. Since he had not named any one in particular no one came forward to obey the order.

"And after all he may be dead already. It isn't worth exposing men uselessly to such danger. It's all my fault, I ought to have seen to it. I'll go back myself and find out whether he is alive. It is my *duty*," said Mikháylov to himself.

"Michael Iványch, you lead the company, I'll catch you up," said he, and holding up his cloak with one hand while with the other he kept touching a small icon of St. Metrophanes than hung round his neck and in which he had great faith, he ran quickly along the trench.

Having convinced himself that Praskúkhin was dead he dragged himself back panting, holding the bandage that had slipped on his head, which was beginning to ache very badly. When he overtook the battalion it was already at the foot of the hill and almost beyond the range of the shots. I say "almost," for a stray bomb reached even here now and then.

"To-morrow I had better go and be entered at the ambulance station," thought the lieutenant-captain, while a medical assistant, who had turned up, was bandaging his head.

14

Hundreds of bodies, which a couple of hours before had been men full of various lofty or trivial hopes and wishes, were lying with fresh bloodstains on their stiffened limbs in the dewy, flowery valley which separated the bastions from the trenches and on the smooth floor of the mortuary chapel in Sevastopol. Hundreds of men with curses or prayers on their parched lips, crawled, writhed, and groaned, some among the dead in the flowery valley, some on stretchers, or beds, or on the blood-stained floor of the ambulance station. Yet the dawn broke behind the Sapún hill, the twinkling stars grew pale, and the white mists spread from the dark roaring sea just as on other days, and the rosy morning glow lit up the east, long streaks of red clouds spread along the pale-blue horizon, and just as in the old days the sun rose in power and glory, promising joy, love, and happiness to all the awakening world.

15

Next evening the Chasseurs' band was again playing on the boulevard, and officers, cadets, soldiers, and young women again promenaded round the pavilion and along the side-walks under the acacias with their sweet-scented white blossoms.

Kalúgin was walking arm in arm with Prince Gáltsin and a colonel near the pavilion and talking of last night's affair. The main theme of their conversation, as usual in such cases, was not the affair itself, but the part each of the speakers had taken in it. Their faces and the tone of their voices were serious, almost sorrowful, as if the losses of the night had touched and saddened them all. But to tell the truth, as none of them had lost any one very dear to him, this sorrowful expression was only an official one they considered it their duty to exhibit.

Kalúgin and the colonel in fact, though they were first-rate fellows, were ready to see such an affair every day if they could gain a gold sword and be made major-general each time. It is all very well to call some conqueror a monster because he destroys millions to gratify his ambition, but go and ask any Ensign Petrúshev or Sub-Lieutenant Antónov on their conscience, and you will find that everyone of us is a little Napoleon, a petty monster ready to start a battle and kill a hundred men merely to get an extra medal or one-third additional pay.

"No, I beg your pardon," said the colonel. "It began first on the left side. I was there myself."

"Well, perhaps," said Kalúgin. " I spent more time on the right. I went there twice: first to look for the general, and then just to see the lodgements. It was hot there, I can tell you!"

"Kalúgin ought to know," said Gáltsin. "By the way, V——— told *me* to-day that you are a trump—"

"But the losses, the losses are terrible!" said the colonel. "In my regiment we had four hundred casualties. It is astonishing that I'm still alive."

Just then the figure of Mikháylov, with his head bandaged, appeared at the end of the boulevard walking towards these gentlemen.

"What, are you wounded, captain?" said Kalúgin.

"Yes, slightly, with a stone," answered Mikháylov.

"*Est-ce que le pavillon est baissé déjà?*"[13] asked Prince Gáltsin, glancing at the lieutenant-captain's cap and not addressing anyone in particular.

"*Non, pas encore,*"[14] answered Mikháylov, wishing to show that he understood and spoke French.

"Do you mean to say the truce still continues?" said Gáltsin, politely addressing him in Russian and thereby (so it seemed to the lieutenant-captain) suggesting: "It must no doubt be difficult for you to have to speak French, so hadn't we better simply . . ." and with that the adjutants went away. The lieutenant-captain again felt exceedingly lonely, just as he had done the day before. After bowing to various people—some of whom he did not wish and some of whom he did not venture to join—he sat down near the Kazárski monument and smoked a cigarette.

Baron Pesth also turned up on the boulevard. He men-

---

[13] "Is the flag (of truce) lowered already?"
[14] "No, not yet."

tioned that he had been at the parley and had spoken to the French officers. According to his account one of them had said to him: *"S'il n'avait pas fait clair encore pendant une demi-heure, les ambuscades auraient été reprises,"*[15] and he replied, *"Monsieur, je ne dis pas non, pour ne pas vous donner un démenti,"*[16] and he told how pat it had come out, and so on.

But though he had been at the parley he had not really managed to say anything in particular, though he much wished to speak with the French ("for it's awfully jolly to speak to those fellows"). He had paced up and down the line for a long time asking the Frenchmen near him: *"De quel régiment êtes-vous?"*[17] and had got his answer and nothing more. When he went too far beyond the line, the French sentry, not suspecting that "that soldier" knew French, abused him in the third person singular: *"Il vient regarder nos travaux, ce sacré* ————."[18] in consequence of which Cadet Baron Pesth, finding nothing more to interest him at the parley, rode home, and on his way back composed the French phrases he now repeated.

On the boulevard was Captain Zóbov talking very loud, and Captain Obzhógov, the artillery captain who never curried favour with anyone, was there too, in a dishevelled condition, and also the cadet who was always fortunate in his love affairs, and all the same people as yesterday, with the same motives as always. Only Praskúkhin, Neferdov, and a few more were missing, and hardly anyone now remembered or thought of them, though there had not yet been time for their bodies to be washed, laid out, and put into the ground.

16

White flags are hung out on our own bastions and on the French trenches, and in the flowery valley between them lie heaps of mangled corpses without boots, some clad in blue and others in grey, which workmen are removing and piling

---

[15] "Had it remained dark for another half hour, the ambuscades would have been recaptured."

[16] "Sir, I will not say no, lest I give you the lie."

[17] "What regiment do you belong to?"

[18] "He's come to look at our works, the confounded ————."

onto carts. The air is filled with the smell of decaying flesh. Crowds of people have poured out from Sevastopol and from the French camp to see the sight, and with eager and friendly curiosity draw near to one another.

Listen to what these people are saying.

Here, in a circle of Russians and Frenchmen who have collected round him, a young officer, who speaks French badly but sufficiently to be understood, is examining a guardsman's pouch.

"*Eh sussy, poor quah se waso lié?*"[19]

"*Parce que c'est une giberne d'un régiment de la garde, monsieur, qui porte l'aigle impérial.*"[20]

"*Eh voo de la guard?*"[21]

"*Pardon, monsieur, du 6-ème de ligne.*"[22]

"*Eh sussy oo ashtay?*"[23] pointing to a cigarette-holder of yellow wood, in which the Frenchman is smoking a cigarette.

"*A Balaclava, monsieur. C'est tout simple en bois de palme.*"[24]

"*Joli,*"[25] say the officer, guided in his remarks not so much by what he wants to say as by the French words he happens to know.

"*Si vous voulez bien garder cela comme souvenir de cette rencontre, vous m'obligerez.*"[26] . . . .

And the polite Frenchman puts out his cigarette and presents the holder to the officer with a slight bow. The officer gives him his, and all present, both French and Russian, smile and seem pleased.

Here is a bold infantryman in a pink shirt with his cloak thrown over his shoulders, accompanied by other

[19] "And what is this tied bird for?"

[20] "Because this is a cartridge pouch of a guard regiment, monsieur, and bears the Imperial eagle."

[21] "And do you belong to the Guards?"

[22] "No, monsieur, to the 6th regiment of the line."

[23] "And where did you buy this?"

[24] "At Balaclava, monsieur. It's only made of palm wood."

[25] "Pretty."

[26] "If you will be so good as to keep it as a souvenir of this meeting you will do me a favour."

soldiers standing near him with their hands folded behind their backs and with merry inquisitive faces. He has approached a Frenchman and asked for a light for his pipe. The Frenchman draws at and stirs up the tobacco in his own short pipe and shakes a light into that of the Russian.

"*Tabac boon?*" says the soldier in the pink shirt, and the spectators smile. "*Oui, bon tabac, tabac turc,*" says the Frenchman. "*Chez vous autres tabac—Russe? Bon?*"[27]

"*Roos boon,*" says the soldier in the pink shirt while the onlookers shake with laughter. "*Fransay* not *boon. Bongjour, mossier!*" and having let off his whole stock of French at once, he slaps the Frenchman on the stomach and laughs. The French also laugh.

"*Ils ne sont pas jolis ces b——— de Russes,*"[28] says a Zouave among the French.

"*De quoi est-ce qu'ils rient donc?*"[29] says another with an Italian accent, a dark man, coming up to our men.

"Coat *boon,*" says the cheeky soldier, examining the embroidery of the Zouave's coat, and everybody laughs again.

"*Ne sors pas de ta ligne; à vos places, sacré nom!*"[30] cries a French corporal, and the soldiers separate with evident reluctance.

And here, in the midst of a group of French officers, one of our young cavalry officers is gushing. They are talking about some Count Sazónof, "*que j'ai beaucoup connu, monsieur,*" says a French officer with only one epaulette. "*C'est un de ces vrais comtes russes, comme nous les aimons.*"[31]

"*Il y a un Sazónoff, que j'ai connu,*" says the cavalry officer, "*mais il n'est pas comte, à moins que je sache, un petit brun de votre âge à peu près.*"[32]

[27] "Yes, good tobacco, Turkish tobacco . . . You others have Russian tobacco. Is it good?"

[28] "They are not handsome, these d——— Russians."

[29] "What are they laughing about?"

[30] "Don't leave your ranks; to your places, damn it!"

[31] "Whom I knew very intimately, monsieur. He is one of those real Russian counts of whom we are so fond."

[32] "I am acquainted with a Sazónoff, but he is not a count, as far as I know—a small dark man, of about your age."

"*C'est ça, monsieur, c'est lui. Oh! que je voudrais le voir, ce cher comte. Si vous le voyez, je vous prie bien de lui faire mes compliments — Capitaine Latour,*"[33] he said, bowing.

"*N'est-ce pas terrible la triste besogne que nous faisons? Ça chauffait cette nuit, n'est-ce pas?*"[34] said the cavalry officer, wishing to maintain the conversation and pointing to the corpses.

"*Oh, monsieur, c'est affreux! Mais quels gaillards vos soldats, quels gaillards! C'est un plaisir que de se battre avec des gaillards comme eux.*"[35]

"*Il faut avouer que les vôtres ne se mouchent pas du pied non plus,*"[36] said the cavalry officer, bowing and imagining himself very agreeable.

But enough.

Let us rather look at this ten-year-old boy in an old cap (probably his father's), with shoes on his stockingless feet and nankeen trousers held up by one brace. At the very beginning of the truce he came over the entrenchments and has been walking about the valley ever since, looking with dull curiosity at the French and at the corpses that lie on the ground and gathering the blue flowers with which the valley is strewn. Returning home with a large bunch of flowers he holds his nose to escape the smell that is borne towards him by the wind and stopping near a heap of corpses gazes for a long time at a terrible headless body that lies nearest to him. After standing there some time he draws nearer and touches with his foot the stiff out-stretched arm of the corpse. The arm trembles a little. He touches it again more boldly; it moves and falls back to its old position. The boy gives a sudden scream, hides his face in his flowers, and runs towards the fortifications as fast as his legs can carry him.

---

[33] "Just so, monsieur, that is he. Oh, how I should like to meet the dear count. If you should see him, please be so kind as to give him my compliments—Captain Latour."

[34] "Isn't it terrible, this sad duty we are engaged in? It was warm work last night, wasn't it?"

[35] "Ah, monsieur, it is terrible! But what fine fellows your men are, what fine fellows! It is a pleasure to fight with such fellows!"

[36] "It must be admitted that yours are no fools either." (Literally, "don't wipe their noses with their feet.")

Yes, there are white flags on the bastions and the trenches but the flowery valley is covered with dead bodies. The glorious sun is sinking towards the blue sea, and the undulating blue sea glitters in the golden light. Thousands of people crowd together, look at, speak to, and smile at one another. And these people—Christians professing the one great law of love and self-sacrifice—on seeing what they have done do not at once fall repentant on their knees before Him who has given them life and laid in the soul of each a fear of death and a love of the good and the beautiful and do not embrace like brothers with tears of joy and gladness.

The white flags are lowered, the engines of death and suffering are sounding again, innocent blood is flowing, and the air is filled with moans and curses.

There, I have said what I wished to say this time. But I am seized by an oppressive doubt. Perhaps I ought to have left it unsaid. What I have said perhaps belongs to that class of evil truths that lie unconsciously hidden in the soul of each man and should not be uttered lest they become harmful, as the dregs in a bottle must not be disturbed for fear of spoiling the wine. . . .

Where in this tale is the evil that should be avoided, and where the good that should be imitated? Who is the villain and who the hero of the story? All are good and all are bad.

Not Kalúgin, with his brilliant courage—*bravoure de gentilhomme*—and the vanity that influences all his actions, not Praskúkhin, the empty harmless fellow (though he fell in battle for faith, throne, and fatherland), not Mikháylov with his shyness, nor Pesth, a child without firm principles or convictions, can be either the villain or the hero of the tale.

The hero of my tale—whom I love with all the power of my soul, whom I have tried to portray in all his beauty, who has been, is, and will be beautiful—is Truth.

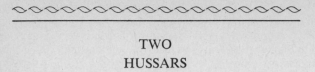

TWO
HUSSARS
A Story

Jomini and Jomini—
Not half a word of vodka.—D. DAVÝDOV.[1]

Early in the nineteenth century, when there were as yet no
railways or macadamized roads, no gaslight, no stearine
candles, no low couches with sprung cushions, no un-
varnished furniture, no disillusioned youths with eye-
glasses, no liberalizing women philosophers, nor any
charming *dames aux camélias* of whom there are so many
in our times, in those naïve days, when leaving Moscow
for Petersburg in a coach or carriage provided with a
kitchenful of home-made provisions one travelled for eight
days along a soft, dusty or muddy road and believed in
chopped cutlets, sledge-bells, and plain rolls; when in the
long autumn evenings the tallow candles, around which
family groups of twenty or thirty people gathered, had to
be snuffed; when ball-rooms were illuminated by candelabra
with wax or spermaceti candles, when furniture was arranged symmetrically, when our fathers were still young
and proved it not only by the absence of wrinkles and
grey hair but by fighting duels for the sake of a woman
and rushing from the opposite corner of a room to pick
up a bit of a handkerchief purposely or accidentally
dropped; when our mothers wore short-waisted dresses
and enormous sleeves and decided family affairs by drawing lots, when the charming *dames aux camélias* hid from
the light of day—in those naïve days of Masonic lodges,[2]

---

[1] From *The Song of an Old Hussar*, in which the great days of the
past are contrasted with the trivial present. D. V. Davýdov is referred to in *War and Peace*.

[2] Freemasonry in Russia was a secret association, the original purpose
of which was the moral perfecting of people on the basis of equality

Martinists,[3] and Tugendbunds,[4] the days of Milorádoviches[5] and Davýdovs[6] and Púshkins—a meeting of landed proprietors was held in the Government town of K———, and the nobility elections[7] were being concluded.

I

"Well, never mind, the saloon will do," said a young officer in a fur cloak and hussar's cap, who had just got out of a post-sledge and was entering the best hotel in the town of K———.

"The assembly, your Excellency, is enormous," said the boots, who had already managed to learn from the orderly that the hussar's name was Count Túrbin, and therefore addressed him as "your Excellency."

"The proprietress of Afrémovo with her daughters has said she is leaving this evening, so No. 11 will be at your disposal as soon as they go," continued the boots, stepping softly before the count along the passage and continually looking round.

In the general saloon at a little table under the dingy full-length portrait of the Emperor Alexander the First,

---

and universal brotherhood. Commencing as a mystical-religious movement in the eighteenth century, it became political during the reign of Alexander I and was suppressed in 1822.

[3] The Martinists were a society of Russian Freemasons founded in 1780 and named after the French theosophist, Louis Claude Saint-Martin.

[4] The Tugendbund (League of Virtue) was a German association founded in 1808 with the acknowledged purpose of cultivating patriotism, reorganizing the army, and encouraging education, and with the secret aim of throwing off the French yoke. Dissolved on Napoleon's demand in 1809, it continued to exist secretly and exerted great influence in 1812. It was suspected of having revolutionary tendencies and was in very bad odor with the Russian government at the time of the Holy Alliance.

[5] M. H. Milorádovich (1770–1825) distinguished himself in the Napoleonic war, became Governor-General of Petersburg, and was killed when suppressing the "Decembrist" mutiny in 1825. He appears in *War and Peace*.

[6] D. V. Davýdov (1784–1839), a popular poet, and leader of a guerrilla force in the war of 1812. A. S. Púshkin (1799–1837), the greatest of Russian poets, was his contemporary.

[7] The *nobility* included not merely those who had titles, but all who in England would be called the gentry.

several men, probably belonging to the local nobility, sat drinking champagne, while at another side of the room sat some travellers—tradesmen in blue, fur-lined cloaks.

Entering the room and calling in Blücher, a gigantic grey mastiff he had brought with him, the count threw off his cloak, the collar of which was still covered with hoar-frost, called for vodka, sat down at the table in his blue-satin Cossack jacket, and entered into conversation with the gentlemen there.

The handsome open countenance of the newcomer immediately predisposed them in his favour and they offered him a glass of champagne. The count first drank a glass of vodka and then ordered another bottle of champagne to treat his new acquaintances. The sledge-driver came in to ask for a tip.

"Sáshka!" shouted the count. "Give him something!"

The driver went out with Sáshka but came back again with the money in his hand.

"Look here, y'r 'xcelence, haven't I done my very best for y'r honour? Didn't you promise me half a ruble, and he's only given me a quarter!"

"Give him a ruble, Sáshka."

Sáshka cast down his eyes and looked at the driver's feet.

"He's had enough!" he said, in a bass voice. "And besides, I have no more money."

The count drew from his pocket-book the two five-ruble notes which were all it contained and gave one of them to the driver, who kissed his hand and went off.

"I've run it pretty close!" said the count. "These are my last five rubles."

"Real hussar fashion, Count," said one of the nobles who from his moustache, voice, and a certain energetic freedom about his legs, was evidently a retired cavalryman. "Are you staying here some time, Count?"

"I must get some money. I shouldn't have stayed here at all but for that. And there are no rooms to be had, devil take them, in this accursed pub."

"Permit me, Count," said the cavalryman. "Will you not join me? My room is No. 7 . . . If you do not mind, just for the night. And then you'll stay a couple of days with us? It happens that the *Maréchal de la Noblesse* is giving a ball to-night. You would make him very happy by going."

"Yes, Count, do stay," said another, a handsome young man. "You have surely no reason to hurry away! You know this only comes once in three years—the elections, I mean. You should at least have a look at our young ladies, Count!"

"Sáshka, get my clean linen ready. I am going to the bath,"[8] said the count, rising, 'and from there perhaps I may look in at the Marshal's."

Then, having called the waiter and whispered something to him to which the latter replied with a smile, "That can all be arranged," he went out.[9]

"So I'll order my trunk to be taken to your room, old fellow," shouted the count from the passage.

"Please do, I shall be most happy," replied the cavalryman, running to the door. "No. 7—don't forget."

When the count's footsteps could no longer be heard the cavalryman returned to his place and sitting close to one of the group—a government official—and looking him straight in the face with smiling eyes, said: "It is the very man, you know!"

"No!"

"I tell you it is! It is the very same duellist hussar—the famous Túrbin. He knew me—I bet you anything he knew me. Why, he and I went on the spree for three weeks without a break when I was at Lebedyáni[10] for remounts. There was one thing he and I did together. . . . He's a fine fellow, eh?"

"A splendid fellow. And so pleasant in his manner! Doesn't show a grain of—what d'you call it?" answered the handsome young man. "How quickly we became intimate. . . . He's not more than twenty-five, is he?"

"Oh no, that's what he looks but he is more than that. One has to get to know him, you know. Who abducted Migúnova? He. It was he who killed Sáblin. It was he who dropped Matnëv out of the window by his legs. It was he

[8] For a Russian bath, as for a Turkish bath, one goes to a public establishment and subjects oneself to heat that produces profuse perspiration.

[9] It was not unusual at the bath to associate with a woman.

[10] A town in the Tambóv province noted for its horse fair.

who won three hundred thousand rubles from Prince Néstorov. He is a regular dare-devil, you know: a gambler, a duellist, a seducer, but a jewel of an hussar—a real jewel. The rumours that are afloat about us are nothing to the reality—if anyone knew what a true hussar is! Ah yes, those were times!"

And the cavalryman told his interlocutor of such a spree with the count in Lebedyáni as not only never had, but never even could have, taken place.

It could not have done so, first because he had never seen the count till that day and had left the army two years before the count entered it; and secondly because the cavalryman had never really served in the cavalry at all but had for four years been the humblest of cadets in the Belévski regiment and retired as soon as ever he became ensign. But ten years ago he had inherited some money and had really been in Lebedyáni where he squandered seven hundred rubles with some officers who were there buying remounts. He had even gone so far as to have an uhlan uniform made with orange facings, meaning to enter an uhlan regiment. This desire to enter the cavalry, and the three weeks spent with the remount officers at Lebedyáni, remained the brightest and happiest memories of his life, so he transformed the desire first into a reality and then into a reminiscence and came to believe firmly in his past as a cavalry officer—all of which did not prevent his being, as to gentleness and honesty, a most worthy man.

"Yes, those who have never served in the cavalry will never understand us fellows."

He sat astride a chair and thrusting out his lower jaw began to speak in a bass voice. "You ride at the head of your squadron, not a horse but the devil incarnate prancing about under you, and you just sit in devil-may-care style. The squadron commander rides up to review: 'Lieutenant,' he says. 'We can't get on without you—please lead the squadron to parade.' 'All right,' you say, and there you are: you turn round, shout to your moustached fellows. . . . Ah, devil take it, those were times!"

The count returned from the bath-house very red and with wet hair, and went straight to No. 7, where the cavalryman was already sitting in his dressing-gown smoking a pipe and considering with pleasure, and not without some apprehension, the happiness that had befallen him of sharing a room with the celebrated Túrbin. "Now suppose," he thought, "that he suddenly takes me, strips me naked, drives me to the town gates, and sets me in the snow, or .. tars me, or simply. . . . But no," he consoled himself, "I e wouldn't do that to a comrade."

"Sáshka, feed Blücher!" shouted the count.

Sáshka, who had taken a tumbler of vodka to refresh himself after the journey and was decidedly tipsy, came in.

"What, already! You've been drinking, you rascal! . . . Feed Blücher!"

"He won't starve anyway: see how sleek he is!" answered Sáshka, stroking the dog.

"Silence! Be off and feed him!"

"You want the dog to be fed, but when a man drinks a glass you reproach him."

"Hey! I'll thrash you!" shouted the count in a voice that made the window-panes rattle and even frightened the cavalryman a bit.

"You should ask if Sáshka has had a bite to-day! Yes, beat me if you think more of a dog than of a man," muttered Sáshka.

But here he received such a terrible blow in the face from the count's fist that he fell, knocked his head against the partition, and clutching his nose fled from the room and fell on a settee in the passage.

"He's knocked my teeth out," grunted Sáshka, wiping his bleeding nose with one hand while with the other he scratched the back of Blücher, who was licking himself. "He's knocked my teeth out, Blüchy, but still he's my count and I'd go through fire for him —I would! Because he—is my count. Do you understand, Blüchy? Want your dinner, eh?"

After lying still for a while he rose, fed the dog and then, almost sobered, went in to wait on his count and to offer him some tea.

"I shall really feel hurt," the cavalryman was saying meekly, as he stood before the count who was lying on the other's bed with his legs up against the partition. "You see I also am an old army man and, if I may say so, a comrade. Why should you borrow from anyone else when

I shall be delighted to lend you a couple of hundred rubles? I haven't got them just now—only a hundred rubles—but I'll get the rest to-day. You would really hurt my feelings, Count."

"Thank you, old man," said the count, instantly discerning what kind of relations had to be established between them, and slapping the cavalryman on the shoulder. "Thanks! Well then, we'll go to the ball if it must be so. But what are we to do now? Tell me what you have in your town. What pretty girls? What men fit for a spree? What gaming?"

The cavalryman explained that there would be an abundance of pretty creatures at the ball, that Kólkov, who had been re-elected captain of police, was the best hand at a spree, only he lacked the true hussar go—otherwise he was a good sort of a chap, that the Ilyúshin gipsy chorus had been singing in the town since the elections began, Stëshka leading, and that everybody meant to go to hear them after leaving the marshal's that evening.

"And there's a devilish lot of card-playing too," he went on. "Lúkhnov plays. He has money and is staying here to break his journey, and Ilyín, an uhlan cornet who has room No. 8, has lost a lot. They have already begun in his room. They play every evening. And what a fine fellow that Ilyín is! I tell you, Count, he's not mean—he'll let his last shirt go."

"Well then, let us go to his room. Let's see what sort of people they are," said the count.

"Yes do—pray do. They'll be devilish glad."

II

The uhlan cornet, Ilyín, had not long been awake. The evening before he had sat down to cards at eight o'clock and had lost pretty steadily for fifteen hours on end—till eleven in the morning. He had lost a considerable sum but did not know exactly how much, because he had about three thousand rubles of his own, and fifteen thousand of Crown money which had long since got mixed up with his own, and he feared to count lest his fears that some of the Crown money was already gone should be confirmed. It was nearly noon when he fell asleep and he had slept that heavy dreamless sleep which only very young men sleep after a heavy loss. Waking at six o'clock (just when Count Túrbin arrived at the hotel), and seeing the floor all around strewn with cards and bits of chalk, and the chalk-marked tables in the middle of the room, he recalled with horror last night's play, and the last card— a knave on which he lost five hundred rubles; but not yet quite convinced of the reality of all this, he drew his money from under the pillow and began to count it. He recognized some notes which had passed from hand to hand several times with "corners" and "transports," and he recalled the whole course of the game. He had none of his own three thousand rubles left, and some two thousand five hundred of the government money was also gone.

Ilyín had been playing for four nights running.

He had come from Moscow where the Crown money had been entrusted to him and at K——— had been detained by the superintendent of the post-house on the pretext that there were no horses, but really because the superintendent had an agreement with the hotel-keeper to detain all travellers for a day. The uhlan, a bright young lad who had just received three thousand rubles from his parents in Moscow for his equipment on entering his regiment, was glad to spend a few days in the town of K——— during the elections and hoped to enjoy himself thoroughly. He knew one of the landed gentry there who had a family, and he was thinking of looking them up and flirting with the daughters, when the cavalryman turned up to make his acquaintance. Without any evil intention the cavalryman introduced him that same evening, in the general saloon or common room of the hotel, to his acquaintances, Lúkhnov and other gamblers. And ever since then the uhlan had been playing cards, not asking at the post-station for horses, much less going to visit his acquaintance the landed proprietor, and not even leaving his room for four days on end.

Having dressed and drunk tea he went to the window. He felt that he would like to go for a stroll to get rid of the recollections that haunted him, and he put on his cloak and went out into the street. The sun was already hidden behind the white houses with their red roofs and it was getting dusk. It was warm for winter. Large wet snowflakes were falling slowly into the muddy street. Suddenly at the thought that he had slept all through the day now ending, a feeling of intolerable sadness overcame him.

"This day, now past, can never be recovered," he thought.

"I have ruined my youth!" he suddenly said to himself, not because he really thought he had ruined his youth— he did not even think about it—but because the phrase happened to occur to him.

"And what am I to do now?" thought he. "Borrow from someone and go away?" A lady passed him along the pavement. "There's a stupid woman," thought he for some reason. "There's no one to borrow from . . . I have ruined my youth!" He came to the bazaar. A tradesman in a fox-fur cloak stood at the door of his shop touting for customers. "If I had not withdrawn that eight I should have recovered my losses." An old beggar-woman followed him whimpering. "There's no one to borrow from." A man drove past in a bearskin cloak; a policeman was standing at his post. "What unusual thing could I do? Fire at them? No, it's dull . . . I have ruined my youth! . . . Ah, those are fine horse-collars and trappings hanging there! Ah, if only I could drive in a tróyka: Gee-up, beauties! . . . I'll go back. Lúkhnov will come soon, and we'll play."

He returned to the hotel and again counted his money. No, he had made no mistake the first time: there were still two thousand five hundred rubles of Crown money missing. "I'll stake twenty-five rubles, then make a 'corner' . . . seven-fold it, fifteen-fold thirty, sixty . . . three thousand rubles. Then I'll buy the horse-collars and be off. He won't let me, the rascal! I have ruined my youth!"

That is what was going on in the uhlan's head when Lúkhnov actually entered the room.

"Have you been up long, Michael Vasílich?" asked Lúkhnov, slowly removing the gold spectacles from his skinny nose and carefully wiping them with a red silk handkerchief.

"No, I've only just got up—I slept uncommonly well."

"Some hussar or other has arrived. He has put up with Zavalshévski—had you heard?"

"No, I hadn't. But how is it no one else is here yet?"

"They must have gone to Pryákhin's. They'll be here directly."

And sure enough a little later there came into the room a garrison officer who always accompanied Lúkhnov, a Greek merchant with an enormous brown hooked nose and sunken black eyes, and a fat puffy landowner, the proprietor of a distillery, who played whole nights, always staking "simples" of half a ruble each. Everybody wished to begin playing as soon as possible, but the principal gamesters, especially Lúkhnov who was telling about a robbery in Moscow in an exceedingly calm manner, did not refer to the subject.

"Just fancy," he said, "a city like Moscow, the historic capital, a metropolis, and men dressed up as devils go about there with crooks, frighten stupid people, and rob the passers by—and that's the end of it! What are the police about? That's the question."

The uhlan listened attentively to the story about the robbers, but when a pause came he rose and quietly ordered cards to be brought. The fat landowner was the first to speak out.

"Well, gentlemen, why lose precious time? If we mean business let's begin."

"Yes, you walked off with a pile of half-rubles last night so you like it," said the Greek.

"I think we might start," said the garrison officer.

Ilyín looked at Lúkhnov. Lúkhnov looking him in the eye quietly continued his story about robbers dressed up like devils with claws.

"Will you keep the bank?" asked the uhlan.

"Isn't it too early?"

"Belóv!" shouted the uhlan, blushing for some unknown reason, "bring me some dinner—I haven't had anything to eat yet, gentlemen—and a bottle of champagne and some cards."

At this moment the count and Zavalshévski entered the room. It turned out that Túrbin and Ilyín belonged to the same division. They took to one another at once, clinked glasses, drank champagne together, and were on intimate terms in five minutes. The count seemed to like Ilyín very much; he looked smilingly at him and teased him about his youth.

"There's an uhlan of the right sort!" he said. "What moustaches! Dear me, what moustaches!"

Even what little down there was on Ilyín's lip was quite white.

"I suppose you are going to play?" said the count. "Well, I wish you luck, Ilyín! I should think you are a master at it," he added with a smile.

"Yes, they mean to start," said Lúkhnov, tearing open a bundle of a dozen packs of cards," and you'll join in too, Count, won't you?"

"No, not to-day. I should clear you all out if I did. When I begin 'cornering' in earnest the bank begins to crack! But I have nothing to play with—I was cleaned out at a station near Volochók. I met some infantry fellow there with rings on his fingers—a sharper I should think—and he plucked me clean."

"Why, did you stay at that station long?" asked Ilyín.

"I sat there for twenty-two hours. I shan't forget that accursed station! And the superintendent won't forget me either . . ."

"How's that?"

"I drive up, you know; out rushes the superintendent looking a regular brigand. 'No horses!' says he. Now I must tell you that it's my rule, if there are no horses I don't take off my fur cloak but go into the superintendent's own room—not into the public room but into his private room—and I have all the doors and windows opened on the ground that it's smoky. Well, that's just what I did there. You remember what frosts we had last month? About twenty degrees![1] The superintendent began to argue; I punched his head. There was an old woman there, and girls and other women; they kicked up a row, snatched up their pots and pans, and were rushing off to the village. . . . I went to the door and said, 'Let me have horses and I'll be off.' If not, no one shall go out: I'll freeze you all' "

"That's an infernally good plan!" said the puffy squire, rolling with laughter. "Its the way they freeze out cockroaches . . ."

"But I didn't watch carefully enough and the superintendent got away with the women. Only one old woman

---

[1] Réaumur = thirteen below zero Fahrenheit.

remained in pawn on the top of the stove; she kept sneezing and saying prayers. Afterwards we began negotiating: the superintendent came and from a distance began persuading me to let the old woman go, but I set Blücher at him a bit. Blücher's splendid at tackling superintendents! But still the rascal didn't let me have horses until the next morning. Meanwhile that infantry fellow came along. I joined him in another room, and we began to play. You have seen Blücher? . . . Blücher! . . ." and he gave a whistle.

Blücher rushed in, and the players condescendingly paid some attention to him though it was evident that they wished to attend to quite other matters.

"But why don't you play, gentlemen? Please don't let me prevent you. I am a chatterbox, you see," said Túrbin. "Play is play whether one likes it or not."

III

Lúkhnov drew two candles nearer to him, took out a large brown pocket-book full of paper money, and slowly, as if performing some rite, opened it on the table, took out two one-hundred ruble notes and placed them under the cards.

"Two hundred for the bank, the same as yesterday," said he, adjusting his spectacles and opening a pack of cards.

"Very well," said Ilyín, continuing his conversation with Túrbin without looking at Lúknov.

The game[1] started. Lúkhnov dealt the cards with machine-like precision, stopping now and then and deliberately jotting something down, or looking sternly over his spectacles and saying in low tones, "Pass up!" The fat landowner spoke louder than anyone else, audibly deliberating with himself and wetting his plump fingers

[1] The game referred to was *shtos*. The players selected cards for themselves from packs on the table and placed their stakes on or under their cards. The banker had a pack from which he dealt to right and left alternately. Cards dealt to the right won for him, those dealt to the left won for the players. "Pass up" was a reminder to the players to hand up stakes due to the bank. "Simples" were single stakes. By turning down "corners" of his card a player increased his stake two- or three-fold. A "transport" increased it sixfold. *Shtos* has long gone out of fashion and been replaced by other forms of gambling.

when he turned down the corner of a card. The garrison officer silently and neatly noted the amount of his stake on his card and bent down small corners under the table. The Greek sat beside the banker, watching the game attentively with his sunken black eyes, and seemed to be waiting for something. Zavalshévski, standing by the table, would suddenly begin to fidget all over, take a red or blue bank-note[2] out of his trouser pocket, lay a card on it, slap it with his palm, and say: "Little seven, pull me through!" Then he would bite his moustache, shift from foot to foot, and keep fidgeting till his card was dealt. Ilyín sat eating veal and pickled cucumbers, which were placed beside him on the horsehair sofa, and hastily wiping his hands on his coat laid down one card after another. Túrbin, who at first was sitting on the sofa, quickly saw how matters stood. Lúkhnov did not look at or speak to Ilyín, only now and then his spectacles would turn for a moment towards the latter's hand, but most of Ilyín's cards lost.

"There now, I'd like to beat that card," said Lúkhnov of a card the fat landowner, who was staking half-rubles, had put down.

"You beat Ilyín's, never mind me!" remarked the squire.

And indeed Ilyín's cards lost more often than any of the others. He would tear up the losing card nervously under the table and choose another with trembling fingers. Túrbin rose from the sofa and asked the Greek to let him sit by the banker. The Greek moved to another place; the count took his chair and began watching Lúkhnov's hands attentively, not taking his eyes off them.

"Ilyín!" he suddenly said in his usual voice, which quite unintentionally drowned all the others. "Why do you keep to a routine? You don't know how to play."

"It's all the same how one plays."

"But you're sure to lose that way. Let me play for you."

"No, please excuse me. I always do it myself. Play for yourself if you like."

"I said I should not play for myself, but I should like to play for you. I am vexed that you are losing."

"I suppose it's my fate."

2 Five-ruble notes were blue and ten-ruble notes red.

The count was silent, but leaning on his elbows he again gazed intently at the banker's hands.

"Abominable!" he suddenly said in a loud, long-drawn tone.

Lúkhnov glanced at him.

"Abominable, quite abominable!" he repeated still louder, looking straight into Lúkhnov's eyes.

The game continued.

"It is not right!" Túrbin remarked again, just as Lúkhnov beat a heavily backed card of Ilyín's.

"What is it you don't like, Count?" inquired the banker with polite indifference.

"This!—that you let Ilyín win his simples and beat his corners. That's what's bad."

Lúkhnov made a slight movement with his brows and shoulders, expressing the advisability of submitting to fate in everything, and continued to play.

"Blücher!" shouted the count, rising and whistling to the dog. "At him!" he added quickly.

Blücher, bumping his back against the sofa as he leapt from under it and nearly upsetting the garrison officer, ran to his master and growled, looking around at everyone and moving his tail as if asking, "Who is misbehaving here, eh?"

Lúkhov put down his cards and moved his chair to one side.

"One can't play like that," he said. "I hate dogs. What kind of a game is it when you bring a whole pack of hounds in here?"

"Especially a dog like that. I believe they are called 'leeches,'" chimed in the garrison officer.

"Well, are we going to play or not, Michael Vasílich?" said Lúkhov to their host.

"Please don't interfere with us, Count," said Ilyín, turning to Túrbin.

"Come here a minute," said Túrbin, taking Ilyín's arm and going behind the partition with him.

The count's words, spoken in his usual tone, were distinctly audible from there. His voice always carried across three rooms.

"Are you daft, eh? Don't you see that that gentleman in spectacles is a sharper of the first water?"

"Come now, enough! What are you saying?"

"No enough about it! Stop playing, I tell you. It's nothing to me. Another time I'd pluck you myself, but somehow I'm sorry to see you fleeced. And maybe you have Crown money too?"

"No . . . why do you imagine such things?"

"Ah, my lad, I've been that way myself so I know all those sharpers' tricks. I tell you the one in spectacles is a sharper. Stop playing! I ask you as a comrade."

"Well then, I'll only finish this one deal."

"I know what 'one deal' means. Well, we'll see."

They went back. In that one deal Ilyín put down so many cards and so many of them were beaten that he lost a large amount.

Túrbin put his hands in the middle of the table "Now stop it! Come along."

"No, I can't. Leave me alone, do!" said Ilyín, irritably shuffling some bent cards without looking at Túrbin.

"Well, go to the devil! Go on losing for certain, if that pleases you. It's time for me to be off. Let's go to the Marshal's, Zavalshévski."

They went out. All remained silent and Lúkhnov dealt no more cards until the sound of their steps and of Blücher's claws on the passage floor had died away.

"What a devil of a fellow!" said the landowner, laughing.

"Well, he won't interfere now," remarked the garrison officer hastily, and still in a whisper.

And the play continued.

IV

The band, composed of some of the marshal's serfs standing in the pantry—which had been cleared out for the occasion —with their coat-sleeves turned up already, had at a given signal struck up the old polonaise, "Alexander, 'Lizabeth," and under the bright soft light of the wax-candles a Governor-general of Catherine's days, with a star on his breast, arm-in-arm with the marshal's skinny wife, and the rest of the local grandees with their partners, had begun slowly gliding over the parquet floor of the large dancing-room in various combinations and variations, when

Zavalshévski entered, wearing stockings and pumps and a blue swallow-tail coat with an immense and padded collar, and exhaling a strong smell of the frangipane with which the facings of his coat, his handkerchief, and his moustaches, were abundantly sprinkled. The handsome hussar who came with him wore tight-fitting light-blue riding-breeches and a gold-embroidered scarlet on which a Vladímir cross and an 1812 medal[1] were fastened. The count was not tall but remarkably well built. His clear blue and exceedingly brilliant eyes, and thick, closely curling, dark-brown hair, gave a remarkable character to his beauty. His arrival at the ball was expected, for the handsome young man who had seen him at the hotel had already prepared the Marshal for it. Various impressions had been produced by the news, for the most part not altogether pleasant.

"It's not unlikely that this youngster will hold us up to ridicule," was the opinion of the men and of the older women. "What if he should run away with me?" was more or less in the minds of the younger ladies, married or unmarried.

As soon as the polonaise was over and the couples after bowing to one another had separated—the women into one group and the men into another—Zavalshévski, proud and happy, introduced the count to their hostess.

The marshal's wife, feeling an inner trepidation lest this hussar should treat her in some scandalous manner before everybody, turned away haughtily and contemptuously as she said, "Very pleased, I hope you will dance," and then gave him a distrustful look that said, "Now, if you offend a woman it will show me that you are a perfect villain." The count however soon conquered her prejudices by his amiability, attentive manner, and handsome gay appearance, so that five minutes later the expression on the face of the Marshal's wife told the company: "I know how to manage such gentlemen. He immediately understood with whom he had to deal, and now he'll be charming to me for the rest of the evening." Moreover at that moment the governor of the town, who had known the count's father,

---

[1] That is to say, a medal gained in the defence of his country against Napoleon.

came up to him and very affably took him aside for a talk, which still further calmed the provincial public and raised the count in its estimation. After that Zavalshévski introduced the count to his sister, a plump young widow whose large black eyes had not left the count from the moment he entered. The count asked her to dance the waltz the band had just commenced, and the general prejudice was finally dispersed by the masterly way in which he danced.

"What a splendid dancer!" said a fat landed proprietress, watching his legs in their blue riding-breeches as they flitted across the room, and mentally counting "one, two, three—one, two three—splendid!"

"There he goes—jig, jig, jig," said another, a visitor in the town whom local society did not consider genteel. "How does he manage not to entangle his spurs? Wonderfully clever!"

The count's artistic dancing eclipsed the three best dancers of the province: the tall fair-haired adjutant of the governor, noted for the rapidity with which he danced and for holding his partner very close to him; the cavalryman, famous for the graceful swaying motion with which he waltzed and for the frequent but light tapping of his heels; and a civilian, of whom everybody said that though he was not very intellectual he was a first-rate dancer and the soul of every ball. In fact, from its very commencement this civilian would ask all the ladies in turn to dance, in the order in which they were sitting,[2] and never stopped for a moment except occasionally to wipe the perspiration from his weary but cheerful face with a very wet cambric handkerchief. The count eclipsed them all and danced with the three principal ladies: the tall one, rich, handsome, stupid; the one of middle height, thin and not very pretty but splendidly dressed; and the little one, who was plain but very clever. He danced with others too—with all the pretty ones, and there were many of these—but it was Zavalshévski's sister, the little widow, who pleased him best. With her he danced a quadrille, an *écossaise*, and a mazurka. When they were sitting down during the quadrille he began paying her many compliments; comparing her to

[2] The custom was, not to dance a whole dance with one lady but to take a few turns round the room, conduct her to her seat, bow to her, thank her and seek a fresh partner.

Venus and Diana, to a rose, and to some other flower. But all these compliments only made the widow bend her white neck, lower her eyes and look at her white muslin dress, or pass her fan from hand to hand. But when she said, "Don't, you're only joking, Count," and other words to that effect, there was a note of such naïve simplicity and amusing silliness in her slightly guttural voice that looking at her it really seemed that this was not a woman but a flower, and not a rose, but some gorgeous scentless rosy-white wild flower that had grown all alone out of a snowdrift in some very remote land.

This combination of naïveté and unconventionality with her fresh beauty created such a peculiar impression on the count that several times during the intervals of conversation, when gazing silently into her eyes or at the beautiful outline of her neck and arms, the desire to seize her in his arms and cover her with kisses assailed him with such force that he had to make a serious effort to resist it. The widow noticed with pleasure the effect she was producing, yet something in the count's behaviour began to frighten and excite her, though the young hussar, despite his insinuating amiability, was respectful to a degree that in our days would be considered cloying. He ran to fetch almond-milk for her, picked up her handkerchief, snatched a chair from the hands of a scrofulous young squire who danced attendance on her to hand it her more quickly, and so forth.

When he noticed that the society attentions of the day had little effect on the lady he tried to amuse her by telling her funny stories and assured her that he was ready to stand on his head, to crow like a cock, to jump out of the window or plunge into the water through a hole in the ice, if she ordered him to do so. This proved quite a success. The widow brightened up and burst into peals of laughter, showing her lovely white teeth, and was quite satisfied with her cavalier. The count liked her more and more every minute, so that by the end of the quadrille he was seriously in love with her.

When, after the quadrille, her eighteen-year-old adorer of long standing came up to the widow (he was the same scrofulous young man from whom Túrbin had snatched the chair—a son of the richest local landed proprietor and not yet in government service) she received him with extreme coolness and did not show one-tenth of the confusion she had experienced with the count.

"Well, you are a fine fellow!" she said, looking all the time at Túrbin's back and unconsciously considering how many yards of gold cord it had taken to embroider his whole jacket. "You are a good one! You promised to call and fetch me for a drive and bring me some comfits."

"I did come, Anna Fëdorovna, but you had already gone, and I left some of the very best comfits for you," said the young man, who—despite his tallness—spoke in a very high-pitched voice.

"You always find excuses! . . . I don't want your bonbons. Please don't imagine—"

"I see, Anna Fëdorovna, that you have changed towards me and I know why. But it's not right," he added, evidently unable to finish his speech because a strong inward agitation caused his lips to quiver in a very strange and rapid manner.

Anna Fëdorovna did not listen to him but continued to follow Túrbin with her eyes.

The master of the house, the stout, toothless, stately old marshal, came up to the count, took him by the arm, and invited him into the study for a smoke and a drink. As soon as Túrbin left the room Anna Fëdorovna felt that there was absolutely nothing to do there and went out into the dressing-room arm-in-arm with a friend of hers, a bony, elderly, maiden lady.

"Well, is he nice?" asked the maiden lady.

"Only he bothers so!" Anna Fëdorovna replied walking up to the mirror and looking at herself.

Her face brightened, her eyes laughed, she even blushed, and suddenly imitating the ballet-dancers she had seen during the elections, she twirled round on one foot, then laughed her guttural but pleasant laugh and even bent her knees and gave a jump.

"Just fancy, what a man! He actually asked me for a keepsake," she said to her friend, "but he will get no-o-o-thing." She sang the last word and held up one finger in her kid glove which reached to her elbow.

In the study, where the marshal had taken Túrbin, stood bottles of different sorts of vodka, liqueurs, champagne, and *zakúska.*[3] The nobility, walking about or sitting in a cloud of tobacco smoke, were talking about the elections.

"When the whole worshipful society of our nobility has honoured him by their choice," said the newly elected Captain of Police who had already imbibed freely, "he should on no account transgress in the face of the whole society—he ought never . . ."

The count's entrance interrupted the conversation. Everybody wished to be introduced to him, and the Captain of Police especially kept pressing the count's hand between his own for a long time and repeatedly asked him not to refuse to accompany him to the new restaurant where he was going to treat the gentlemen after the ball, and where the gipsies were going to sing. The count promised to come without fail, and drank some glasses of champagne with him.

"But why are you not dancing, gentlemen?" said the count, as he was about to leave the room.

"We are not dancers," replied the Captain of Police, laughing. "Wine is more in our line, Count. . . . And besides, I have seen all those young ladies grow up, Count! But I can walk through an *écossaise* now and then, Count . . . I can do it, Count."

"Then come and walk through one now," said Túrbin. "It will brighten us up before going to hear the gipsies."

"Very well, gentlemen! Let's come and gratify our host."

And three or four of the noblemen who had been drinking in the study since the commencement of the ball, put on gloves of black kid or knitted silk and with red faces were just about to follow the count into the ball-room when they were stopped by the scrofulous young man who, pale and hardly able to restrain his tears, accosted Túrbin.

"You think that because you are a count you can jostle people about as if you were in the market-place," he said, breathing with difficulty, "but that is impolite . . ."

---

[3] The *zakúska* ("little bite") consists of a choice of snacks: caviare, salt-fish, cheese, radishes, or what not, with small glasses of vodka or other spirits. It is sometimes served alone but usually forms an appetizer laid out on a side table and partaken of immediately before dinner or supper. It answers somewhat to the *hors-d'œuvre* of an English dinner.

And again, do what he would, his quivering lips checked the flow of his words.

"What?" cried Túrbin, suddenly frowning. "What? . . . You brat!" he cried, seizing him by the arms and squeezing them so that the blood rushed to the young man's head not so much from vexation as from fear. "What? Do you want to fight? I am at your service!"

Hardly had Túrbin released the arms he had been squeezing so hard than two nobles caught hold of them and dragged the young man towards the back door.

"What! Are you out of your mind? You must be tipsy! Suppose we were to tell your papa! What's the matter with you?" they said to him.

"No, I'm not tipsy, but he jostles one and does not apologize. He's a swine, that's what he is!" squealed the young man, now quite in tears.

But they did not listen to him and someone took him home.

On the other side the Captain of Police and Zavalshévski were exhorting Túrbin: "Never mind him, Count, he's only a child. He still gets whipped, he's only sixteen. . . . What can have happened to him? What bee has stung him? And his father such a respectable man—and our candidate."

"Well, let him go to the devil if he does not wish . . ."

And the count returned to the ball-room and danced the *écossaise* with the pretty widow as gaily as before, laughed with all his heart as he watched the steps performed by the gentlemen who had come with him out of the study, and burst into peals of laughter that rang across the room when the Captain of Police slipped and measured his full length in the midst of the dancers.

V

While the count was in the study Anna Fëdorovna had approached her brother, and supposing that she ought to pretend to be very little interested in the count, began by asking: "Who is that hussar who was dancing with me? Can you tell me, brother?"

The cavalryman explained to his sister as well as he could what a great man the hussar was and told her at the same time that the count was only stopping in the town

because his money had been stolen on the way, and that he
himself had lent him a hundred rubles, but that that was
not enough, so that perhaps "sister" would lend another
couple of hundred. Only Zavalshévski asked her on no
account to mention the matter to anyone— especially not
to the count. Anna Fëdorovna promised to send her brother
the money that very day and to keep the affair secret, but
somehow during the *écossaise* she felt a great longing herself to offer the count as much money as he wanted. She
took a long time making up her mind, and blushed, but at
last with a great effort broached the subject as follows.

"My brother tells me that a misfortune befell you on the
road, Count, and that you have no money by you. If you
need any, won't you take it from me? I should be so glad."

But having said this, Anna Fëdorovna suddenly felt
frightened of something and blushed. All gaiety instantly
left the count's face.

"Your brother is a fool!" he said abruptly. "You know
when a man insults another man they fight; but when a
woman insults a man, what does he do then—do you
know?"

Poor Anna Fëdorovna's neck and ears grew red with
confusion. She lowered her eyes and said nothing.

"He kisses the woman in public," said the count in a
low voice, leaning towards her ear. "Allow me at least to
kiss your little hand," he added in a whisper after a prolonged silence, taking pity on his partner's confusion.

"But not now!" said Anna Fëdorovna, with a deep sigh.

"When then? I am leaving early to-morrow and you owe
it me."

"Well then it's impossible," said Anna Fëdorovna with
a smile.

"Only allow me a chance to meet you to-night to kiss
your hand. I shall not fail to find an opportunity."

"How can you find it?"

"That is not your business. In order to see you everything is possible. . . . It's agreed?"

"Agreed."

The *écossaise* ended. After that they danced a mazurka
and the count was quite wonderful: catching handkerchiefs,
kneeling on one knee, striking his spurs together in a quite
special Warsaw manner, so that all the old people left their

game of boston and flocked into the ball-room to see, and the cavalryman, their best dancer, confessed himself eclipsed.Then they had supper after which they danced the "Grandfather," and the ball began to break up. The count never took his eyes off the little widow. It was not pretence when he said he was ready to jump through a hole in the ice for her sake. Whether it was whim, or love, or obstinacy, all his mental powers that evening were concentrated on the one desire—to meet and love her. As soon as he noticed that Anna Fëdorovna was taking leave of her hostess he ran out to the footmen's room, and thence— without his fur cloak—into the courtyard to the place where the carriages stood.

"Anna Fëdorovna Záytseva's carriage!" he shouted.

A high four-seated closed carriage with lamps burning moved from its place and approached the porch.

"Stop!" he called to the coachman and plunging knee-deep into the snow ran to the carriage.

"What do you want?" said the coachman.

"I want to get into the carriage," replied the count, opening the door and trying to get in while the carriage was moving. "Stop, I tell you, you fool!"

"Stop, Váska!" shouted the coachman to the postilion and pulled up the horses. "What are you getting into other people's carriages for? This carriage belongs to my mistress, to Anna Fëdorovna, and not to your honour."

"Shut up, you blockhead! Here's a ruble for you; get down and close the door," said the count. But as the coachman did not stir he lifted the steps himself and, lowering the window, managed somehow to close the door. In the carriage, as in all old carriages, especially in those in which yellow galloon is used, there was a musty odour something like the smell of decayed and burnt bristles. The count's legs were wet with snow up to the knees and felt very cold in his thin boots and riding-breeches; in fact the winter cold penetrated his whole body. The coachman grumbled on the box and seemed to be preparing to get down. But the count neither heard nor felt anything. His face was aflame and his heart beat fast. In his nervous tension he seized the yellow window strap and leant out of the side window, and all his being merged into one feeling of expectation.

This expectancy did not last long. Someone called from

the porch: "Záytseva's carriage!" The coachman shook the reins, the body of the carriage swayed on its high springs, and the illuminated windows of the house ran one after another past the carriage windows.

"Mind, fellow," said the count to the coachman, putting his head out of the front window, "if you tell the footman I'm here, I'll thrash you, but hold your tongue and you shall have another ten rubles."

Hardly had he time to close the window before the body of the carriage shook more violently and then stopped. He pressed close into the corner, held his breath, and even shut his eyes, so terrified was he lest anything should balk his passionate expectation. The door opened, the carriage steps fell noisily one after the other, he heard the rustle of a woman's dress, a smell of frangipane perfume filled the musty carriage, quick little feet ran up the carriage steps, and Anna Fëdorovna, brushing the count's leg with the skirt of her cloak which had come open, sank silently onto the seat behind him breathing heavily.

Whether she saw him or not no one could tell, not even Anna Fëdorovna herself, but when he took her hand and said, "Well, now I will kiss your little hand,"[1] she showed very little fear, gave no reply, but yielded her arm to him, which he covered much higher than the top of her glove with kisses. The carriage started.

"Say something! Art thou angry?" he said.

She silently pressed into her corner, but suddenly something caused her to burst into tears and of her own accord she let her head fall on his breast.

VI

The newly elected Captain of Police and his guests the cavalryman and other nobles had long been listening to the gipsies and drinking in the new restaurant when the count, wearing a blue cloth cloak lined with bearskin which had belonged to Anna Fëdorovna's late husband, joined them.

"Sure, your excellency, we have been awaiting you impatiently!" said a dark cross-eyed gipsy, showing his white teeth, as he met the count at the very entrance and rushed

[1] The same word (*ruká*) stands for hand or arm in Russian.

to help him off with his cloak. "We have not seen you since the fair at Lebedyáni . . . Stëshka is quite pining away for you."

Stëshka, a young, graceful little gipsy with a brick-red glow on her brown face and deep, sparkling black eyes shaded by long lashes, also ran out to meet him.

"Ah, little Count! Dearest! Jewel! This is a joy!" she murmured between her teeth, smiling merrily.

Ilyúshka himself ran out to greet him, pretending to be very glad to see him. The old women, matrons, and maids jumped from their places and surrounded the guest, some claiming him as a fellow godfather, some as brother by baptism.[1]

Túrbin kissed all the young gipsy girls on their lips; the old women and the men kissed him on his shoulder or hand. The noblemen were also glad of their visitor's arrival, especially as the carousal, having reached its zenith, was beginning to flag, and everyone was beginning to feel satiated. The wine having lost its stimulating effect on the nerves merely weighed on the stomach. Each one had already let off his store of swagger, and they were getting tired of one another; the songs had all been sung and had got mixed in everyone's head, leaving a noisy, dissolute impression behind. No matter what strange or dashing thing anyone did, it began to occur to everyone that there was nothing agreeable or funny in it. The Captain of Police, who lay in a shocking state on the floor at the feet of an old woman, began wriggling his legs and shouting: "Champagne . . . The Count's come! . . . Champagne! . . . He's come . . . now then, champagne! . . . I'll have a champagne bath and bathe in it! Noble gentlemen! . . . I love the society of our brave old nobility . . . Stëshka, sing 'The Pathway.' "

The cavalryman was also rather tipsy, but in another way. He sat on a sofa in the corner very close to a tall handsome gipsy girl, Lyubásha; and feeling his eyes misty with drink he kept blinking and shaking his head and, repeating the same words over and over again in a whisper, besought the gipsy to fly with him somewhere. Lyubásha,

---

[1] In Russia god-parents and their god-children, and people having the same god-father or god-mother, were considered to be related.

smiling and listening as if what he said were very amusing
and yet rather sad, glanced occasionally at her husband—
the cross-eyed Sáshka who was standing behind the chair
opposite her—and in reply to the cavalryman's declarations
of love, stooped and whispering in his ear asked him to buy
her some scent and ribbons on the quiet, so that the others
should not notice.

"Hurrah!" cried the cavalryman when the count entered.

The handsome young man was pacing up and down the
room with laboriously steady steps and a careworn expression on his face, warbling an air from *Il Seraglio*.

An elderly paterfamilias, who had been tempted by the
persistent entreaties of the nobles to come and hear the
gipsies, as they said that without him the thing would be
worthless and it would be better not to go at all, was lying
on a sofa where he had sunk as soon as he arrived, and no
one was taking any notice of him. Some official or other
who was also there had taken off his swallow-tail coat and
was sitting up on the table, feet and all, ruffling his hair,
and thereby showing that he was very much on the spree.
As soon as the count entered, this official unbuttoned the
collar of his shirt and got still farther onto the table. In
general, on Túrbin's arrival the carousal revived.

The gipsy girls, who had been wandering about the
room, again gathered and sat down in a circle. The count
took Stëshka, the leading singer, on his knee, and ordered
more champagne.

Ilyúshka came and stood in front of Stëshka with his
guitar, and the "dance" commenced—that is, the gipsy
songs, "When you go along the Street," "O Hussars!," "Do
you hear, do you know?," and so on in a definite order.
Stëshka sang admirably. The flexible sonorous contralto
that flowed from her very chest, her smiles while singing,
her laughing passionate eyes, and her foot that moved
involuntarily in measure with the song, her wild shriek at
the commencement of the chorus—all touched some powerful but rarely-reached chord. It was evident that she lived
only in the song she was singing. Ilyúshka accompanied her
on the guitar—his back, legs, smile, and whole being expressing sympathy with the song—and eagerly watching
her, raised and lowered his head as attentive and engrossed
as though he heard the song for the first time. Then at the

last melodious note he suddenly drew himself up and, as if feeling himself superior to everyone in the world, proudly and resolutely threw up his guitar with his foot, twirled it about, stamped, tossed back his hair, and looked round at the choir with a frown. His whole body from neck to heels began dancing in every muscle—and twenty energetic, powerful voices each trying to chime in more strongly and more strangely than the rest, rang through the air. The old women bobbed up and down on their chairs waving their handkerchiefs, showing their teeth, and vying with one another in their harmonious and measured shouts. The basses with strained necks and heads bent to one side boomed while standing behind the chairs.

When Stëshka took a high note Ilyúshka brought his guitar closer to her as if wishing to help her, and the handsome young man screamed with rapture, saying that now they were beginning the *bémols*.[2]

When a dance was struck up and Dunyásha, advancing with quivering shoulders and bosom, twirled round in front of the count and glided onwards, Túrbin leapt up, threw off his jacket, and in his red shirt stepped jauntily with her in precise and measured step, accomplishing such things with his legs that the gipsies smiled with approval and glanced at one another.

The Captain of Police sat down like a Turk, beat his breast with his fist and cried "*Vivat!*" and then, having caught hold of the count's leg, began to tell him that of two thousand rubles he now had only five hundred left, but that he could do anything he liked if only the count would allow it. The elderly paterfamilias awoke and wished to go away but was not allowed to do so. The handsome young man began persuading a gipsy to waltz with him. The cavalryman, wishing to show off his intimacy with the count, rose and embraced Túrbin. "Ah, my dear fellow," he said, "why didst thou leave us, eh?" The count was silent, evidently thinking of something else. "Where did you go to? Ah, you rogue of a count, I know where you went to!"

For some reason this familiarity displeased Túrbin.

---

[2] *Bémol* is French for a flat; but in Russia many people knowing nothing of musical technicalities imagined it to have something to do with excellence in music.

Without a smile he looked silently into the cavalryman's face and suddenly launched at him such terrible and rude abuse that the cavalryman was pained and for a while could not make up his mind whether to take the offence as a joke or seriously. At last he decided to take it as a joke, smiled, and went back to his gipsy, assuring her that he would certainly marry her after Easter. They sang another song and another, danced again, and "hailed the guests," and everyone continued to imagine that he was enjoying it. There was no end to the champagne. The count drank a great deal. His eyes seemed to grow moist, but he was not unsteady. He danced even better than before, spoke firmly, even joined in the chorus extremely well, and chimed in when Stëshka sang "Friendship's Tender Emotions." In the midst of a dance the landlord came in to ask the guests to return to their homes as it was getting on for three in the morning.

The count seized the landlord by the scruff of his neck and ordered him to dance the Russian dance. The landlord refused. The count snatched up a bottle of champagne and having stood the landlord on his head and had him held in that position, amidst general laughter, slowly emptied the bottle over him.

It was beginning to dawn. Everyone looked pale and exhausted except the count.

"Well, I must be starting for Moscow," said he, suddenly rising, "Come along, all of you! Come and see me off . . . and we'll have some tea together."

All agreed except the paterfamilias (who was left behind asleep), and crowding into three large sledges that stood at the door, they all drove off to the hotel.

VII

"Get horses ready!" cried the count as he entered the saloon of his hotel, followed by the guests and gipsies. "Sáshka!—not gipsy Sáshka but my Sáshka—tell the superintendent I'll thrash him if he gives me bad horses. And get us some tea. Zavalshévski, look after the tea: I'm going to have a look at Ilyín and see how he's getting on . . ." added Túrbin and went along the passage towards the uhlan's room.

Ilyín had just finished playing and having lost his last kopék was lying face downwards on the sofa, pulling one hair after another from its torn horsehair cover, putting them in his mouth, biting them in two and spitting them out again.

Two tallow candles, one of which had burnt down to the paper in the socket, stood on the card-strewn table and feebly wrestled with the morning light that crept in through the window. There were no ideas in Ilyín's head: a dense mist of gambling passion shrouded all his faculties; he did not even feel penitent. He made one attempt to think of what he should do now: how being penniless he could get away, how he could repay the fifteen thousand rubles of Crown money, what his regimental commander would say, what his mother and his comrades would say, and he felt such terror and disgust with himself that wishing to forget himself he rose and began pacing up and down the room trying to step only where the floor-boards joined, and began, once more, vividly to recall every slightest detail of the course of play. He vividly imagined how he had begun to win back his money, how he withdrew a nine and placed the king of spades over two thousand rubles. A queen was dealt to the right, an ace to the left, then the king of diamonds to the right and all was lost; but if, say, a six had been dealt to the right and the king of diamonds to the left, he would have won everything back, would have played once more double or quits, would have won fifteen thousand rubles, and would then have bought himself an ambler from his regimental commander and another pair of horses besides, and a phaeton. Well, and what then? Well, it would have been a splendid, splendid thing!

And he lay down on the sofa again and began chewing the horse-hair.

"Why are they singing in No. 7?" thought he. "There must be a spree on at Túrbin's. Shall I go in and have a good drink?"

At this moment the count entered.

"Well, old fellow, cleaned out, are you? Eh?" cried he.

"I'll pretend to be asleep," thought Ilyín, "or else I shall have to speak to him, and I want to sleep."

Túrbin, however, came up and stroked his head.

"Well, my dear friend, cleaned out—lost everything? Tell me."

Ilyín gave no answer.

The count pulled his arm.

"I have lost. But what is that to you?" muttered Ilyín in a sleepy, indifferent, discontented voice, without changing his position.

"Everything?"

"Well—yes. What of it? Everything. What is it to you?"

"Listen. Tell me the truth as to a comrade," said the count, inclined to tenderness by the influence of the wine he had drunk and continuing to stroke Ilyín's hair. "I have really taken a liking to you. Tell me the truth. If you have lost Crown money I'll get you out of your scrape: it will soon be too late. . . . Had you Crown money?"

Ilyín jumped up from the sofa.

"Well then, if you wish me to tell you, don't speak to me, because . . . please don't speak to me. . . . To shoot myself is the only thing!" said Ilyín, with real despair, and his head fell on his hands and he burst into tears, though but a moment before he had been calmly thinking about amblers.

"What pretty girlishness! Where's the man who has not done the like? It's not such a calamity; perhaps we can mend it. Wait for me here."

The count left the room.

"Where is Squire Lúkhnov's room?" he asked the boots.

The boots offered to show him the way. In spite of the valet's remark that his master had only just returned and was undressing, the count went in. Lúkhnov was sitting at a table in his dressing-gown counting several packets of paper money that lay before him. A bottle of Rhine wine, of which he was very fond, stood on the table. After winning he permitted himself that pleasure. Lúkhnov looked coldly and sternly through his spectacles at the count as though not recognizing him.

"You don't recognize me, I think?" said the count, resolutely stepping up to the table.

Lúkhnov made a gesture of recognition, and said, "What is it you want?"

"I should like to play with you," said Túrbin, sitting down on the sofa.

"Now?"

"Yes."

"Another time with pleasure, Count! But now I am tired and am going to bed. Won't you have a glass of wine? It is famous wine."

"But I want to play a little—now."

"I don't intend to play any more to-night. Perhaps some of the other gentlemen will, but I won't. You must please excuse me, Count."

"Then you won't?"

Lúkhnov shrugged his shoulders to express his regret at his inability to comply with the count's desire.

"Not on any account?"

The same shrug.

"But I particularly request it. . . . Well, will you play?"

Silence.

"Will you play?" the count asked again. "Mind!"

The same silence and a rapid glance over the spectacles at the count's face which was beginning to frown.

"Will you play?" shouted the count very loud, striking the table with his hand so that the bottle toppled over and the wine was spilt. "You know you did not win fairly. . . . Will you play? I ask you for the third time."

"I said I would not. This is really strange, Count! And it is not at all proper to come and hold a knife to a man's throat," remarked Lúkhnov, not raising his eyes. A momentary silence followed during which the count's face grew paler and paler. Suddenly a terrible blow on the head stupefied Lúkhnov. He fell on the sofa trying to seize the money and uttered such a piercingly despairing cry as no one could have expected from so calm and imposing a person. Túrbin gathered up what money lay on the table, pushed aside the servant who ran in to his master's assistance, and left the room with rapid strides.

"If you want satisfaction I am at your service! I shall be in my room for another half-hour," said the count, returning to Lúkhnov's door.

"Thief! Robber! I'll have the law on you . . ." was all that was audible from the room.

Ilyín, who had paid no attention to the count's promise to help him, still lay as before on the sofa in his room choking with tears of despair. Consciousness of what had really happened, which the count's caresses and sympathy had evoked from behind the strange tangle of feelings, thoughts, and memories filling his soul, did not leave him. His youth, rich with hope, his honour, the respect of society, his dreams of love and friendship—all were utterly lost. The source of his tears began to run dry, a too passive feeling of hopelessness overcame him more and more, and thoughts of suicide, no longer arousing revulsion or horror, claimed his attention with increasing frequency. Just then the count's firm footsteps were heard.

In Túrbin's face traces of anger could still be seen, his hands shook a little, but his eyes beamed with kindly merriment and self-satisfaction.

"Here you are, it's won back!" he said, throwing several bundles of paper money on the table. "See if it's all there and then make haste and come into the saloon. I am just leaving," he added, as though not noticing the joy and gratitude and extreme agitation on Ilyín's face, and whistling a gipsy song he left the room.

VIII

Sáshka, with a sash tied round his waist, announced that the horses were ready but insisted that the count's cloak, which, he said, with its fur collar was worth three hundred rubles, should be recovered, and the shabby blue one returned to the rascal who had changed it for the count's at the Marshal's; but Túrbin told him there was no need to look for the cloak, and went to his room to change his clothes.

The cavalryman kept hiccoughing as he sat silent beside his gipsy girl. The Captain of Police called for vodka and invited everyone to come at once and have breakfast with him, promising that his wife would certainly dance with the gipsies. The handsome young man was profoundly explaining to Ilyúshka that there is more soulfulness in pianoforte music and that it is not possible to play *bémols* on a guitar. The official sat in a corner sadly drinking his tea and in the daylight seemed ashamed of his debauchery. The gipsies were disputing among themselves in their own tongue as to "hailing the guests" again, which Stëshka opposed, saying that the *baroráy* (in gipsy language, count or prince or, more literally, "great gentleman") would be angry. In general the last embers of the debauch were dying down in everyone.

"Well, one farewell song, and then off home!" said the count, entering the parlour in travelling dress, fresh, merry, and handsomer than ever.

The gipsies again formed their circle and were just ready to begin when Ilyín entered with a packet of paper money in his hand and took the count aside.

"I only had fifteen thousand rubles of Crown money and you have given me sixteen thousand three hundred," he said, "so this is yours."

"That's a good thing. Give it here!"

Ilyín gave him the money and, looking timidly at the count, opened his lips to say something, but only blushed till tears came into his eyes and seizing the count's hand began to press it.

"You be off! . . . Ilyúshka! Here's some money for you, but you must accompany me out of the town with songs!" and he threw onto the guitar the thirteen hundred rubles Ilyín had brought him. But the count quite forgot to repay the hundred rubles he had borrowed of the cavalryman the day before.

It was already ten o'clock in the morning. The sun had risen above the roofs of the houses. People were moving about in the streets. The tradesmen had long since opened their shops. Noblemen and officials were driving through the streets and ladies were shopping in the bazaar, when the whole gipsy band, with the Captain of Police, the cavalryman, the handsome young man, Ilyín, and the count in the blue bearskin cloak came out into the hotel porch.

It was a sunny day and a thaw had set in. The large post-sledges, each drawn by three horses with their tails tied up tight, drove up to the porch splashing through the mud and the whole lively party took their places. The count, Ilyín, Stëshka, and Ilyúshka, with Sáshka the count's orderly, got into the first sledge. Blücher was beside himself

and wagged his tail, barking at the shaft-horse. The other
gentlemen got into the two other sledges with the rest
of the gipsy men and women. The tróykas got abreast
as they left the hotel and the gipsies struck up in chorus.
The tróykas with their songs and bells—forcing every
vehicle they met right onto the pavements—dashed through
the whole town right to the town gates.

The tradesmen and passers-by who did not know them,
and especially those who did, were not a little astonished
when they saw the noblemen driving through the streets
in broad daylight with gipsy girls and tipsy gipsy men,
singing.

When they had passed the town gates the tróykas stopped
and everyone began bidding the count farewell.

Ilyín, who had drunk a good deal at the leave-taking
and had himself been driving the sledge all the way, suddenly became very sad, begged the count to stay another
day, and, when he found that this was not possible, rushed
quite unexpectedly at his new friend, kissed him, and
promised with tears to try to exchange into the hussar
regiment the count was serving in as soon as he got
back. The count was particularly gay; he tumbled the
cavalryman, who had become very familiar in the morning, into a snowdrift, set Blücher at the Captain of Police,
took Stëshka in his arms and wished to carry her off
to Moscow, and finally jumped into his sledge and made
Blücher, who wanted to stand up in the middle, sit down
by his side. Sáshka jumped on the box after having
again asked the cavalryman to recover the count's cloak
from *them* and to send it on. The count cried, "Go!,"
took off his cap, waved it over his head, and whistled to
the horses like a post-boy. The tróykas drove off in their
different directions.

A monotonous snow-covered plain stretched far in front
with a dirty yellowish road winding through it. The bright
sunshine—playfully sparkling on the thawing snow which
was coated with a transparent crust of ice—was pleasantly
warm to one's face and back. Steam rose thickly from
the sweating horses. The bell tinkled merrily. A peasant,
with a loaded sledge that kept gliding to the side of the
road, got hurriedly out of the way, jerking his rope reins
and plashing with his wet bast shoes as he ran along

the thawing road. A fat red-faced peasant woman, with a baby wrapped in the bosom of her sheepskin cloak, sat in another laden sledge, urging on a thin-tailed, jaded white horse with the ends of the reins. The count suddenly thought of Anna Fëdorovna.

"Turn back!" he shouted.

The driver did not at once understand.

"Turn back! Back to town! Be quick!"

The tróyka passed the town gates once more, and drove briskly up to the wooden porch of Anna Fëdorovna's house. The count ran quickly up the steps, passed through the vestibule and the drawing-room, and having found the widow still asleep, took her in his arms, lifted her out of bed, kissed her sleepy eyes, and ran quickly back. Anna Fëdorovna, only half awake, licked her lips and asked, "What has happened?" The count jumped into his sledge, shouted to the driver, and with no further delay and without even a thought of Lúkhnov, or the widow, or Stëshka, but only of what awaited him in Moscow, left the town of K——— for ever.

IX

More than twenty years had gone by. Much water had flowed away, many people had died, many been born, many had grown up or grown old; still more ideas had been born and had died, much that was old and beautiful and much that was old and bad had perished; much that was beautiful and new had grown up and still more that was immature, monstrous, and new, had come into God's world.

Count Fëdor Túrbin had been killed long ago in a duel by some foreigner he had horse-whipped in the street. His son, physically as like him as one drop of water to another, was a handsome young man already twenty-three years old and serving in the Horse Guards. But morally the young Túrbin did not in the least resemble his father. There was not a shade of the impetuous, passionate, and, to speak frankly, depraved propensities of the past age. Together with his intelligence, culture, and the gifted nature he had inherited a love of propriety and the comforts of life; a practical way of looking at men and affairs, reasonableness, and prudence were his distinguishing characteristics. The young count had got on well in the service and at twenty-three was already a lieutenant. At the commencement of the war he made up his mind that he would be more likely to secure promotion if he exchanged into the active army, and so he entered an hussar regiment as captain and was soon in command of a squadron.

In May 1848[1] the S——— hussar regiment was marching to the campaign through the province of K———, and the very squadron young Count Túrbin commanded had to spend the night in the village of Morózovka, Anna Fëdorovna's estate.

Anna Fëdorovna was still living but was already so far from young that she did not even consider herself young, which means a good deal for a woman. She had grown very fat, which is said to make a woman look younger, but deep soft wrinkles were apparent on her white plumpness. She never went to town now, it was an effort for her even to get into her carriage, but she was still just as kind-hearted and as silly as ever (now that her beauty no longer biases one, the truth may be told). With her lived her twenty-three-year-old daughter Lisa, a Russian country belle, and her brother—our acquaintance the cavalryman—who had good-naturedly squandered the whole of his small fortune and had found a home for his old age with Anna Fëdorovna. His hair was quite grey and his upper lip had fallen in, but the moustache above it was still carefully blackened. His back was bent, and not only his forehead and cheeks but even his nose and neck were wrinkled, yet in the movements of his feeble crooked legs the manner of a cavalryman was still perceptible.

The family and household sat in the small drawing-room of the old house, with an open door leading out onto the verandah, and open windows overlooking the ancient star-shaped garden with its lime trees. Grey-haired Anna Fëdorovna, wearing a lilac jacket, sat on the sofa laying out cards on a round mahogany table. Her old brother in his clean white trousers and a blue coat had settled

[1] Tolstóy seems here to antedate Russia's intervention in the Hungarian insurrection. The Russian army did not enter Hungary till May 1849 and the war lasted till the end of September that year.

himself by the window and was plaiting a cord out of
white cotton with the aid of a wooden fork—a pastime his
niece had taught him and which he liked very much, as
he could no longer do anything and his eyes were too
weak for newspaper reading, his favourite occupation.
Pímochka, Anna Fëdorovna's ward, sat by him learning
a lesson—Lisa helping her and at the same time making
a goat's-wool stocking for her uncle with wooden knitting
needles. The last rays of the setting sun, as usual at
that hour, shone through the lime-tree avenue and threw
slanting gleams on the farthest window and the what-not
standing near it. It was so quiet in the garden and the
room that one could hear the swift flutter of a swallow's
wings outside the window and Anna Fëdorovna's soft sigh
or the old man's slight groan as he crossed his legs.

"How do they go? Show me, Lisa! I always forget,"
said Anna Fëdorovna, at a standstill in laying out her
cards for patience.

Without stopping her work Lisa went to her mother
and glanced at the cards.

"Ah, you've muddled them all, mamma dear!" she
said, rearranging them. "That's the way they should go.
And what you are trying your fortune about will still come
true," she added, withdrawing a card so that it was not
noticed.

"Ah yes, you always deceive me and say it has come
out."

"No, really, it means . . . you'll succeed. It has come
out."

"All right, all right, you sly puss! But isn't it time
we had tea?"

"I have ordered the samovar to be lit. I'll see to it
at once. Do you want to have it here? . . . Be quick and
finish your lesson, Pímochka, and let's have a run."

And Lisa went to the door.

"Lisa, Lizzie!" said her uncle, looking intently at his
fork. "I think I've dropped a stitch again—pick it up
for me, there's a dear."

"Directly, directly! But I must give out a loaf of sugar
to be broken up."

And really, three minutes later she ran back, went to
her uncle and pinched his ear.

"That's for dropping your stitches!" she said, laughing, "and you haven't done your task!"

"Well, well, never mind, never mind. Put it right— there's a little knot or something."

Lisa took the fork, drew a pin out of her tippet— which thereupon the breeze coming in at the door blew slightly open—and managing somehow to pick up the stitch with the pin pulled two loops through, and returned the fork to her uncle.

"Now give me a kiss for it," she said, holding out her rosy cheek to him and pinning up her tippet. "You shall have rum with your tea to-day. It's Friday, you know."

And she again went into the tea-room.

"Come here and look, uncle, the hussars are coming!" she called from there in her clear voice.

Anna Fëdorovna came with her brother into the tea-room, the windows of which overlooked the village, to see the hussars. Very little was visible from the windows —only a crowd moving in a cloud of dust.

"It's a pity we have so little room, sister, and that the wing is not yet finished," said the old man to Anna Fëdorovna. "We might have invited the officers. Hussar officers are such splendid, gay young fellows, you know. It would have been good to see something of them."

"Why of course, I should have been only too glad, brother; but you know yourself we have no room. There's my bedroom, Lisa's room, the drawing-room, and this room of yours, and that's all. Really now, where could we put them? The village elder's hut has been cleaned up for them: Michael Matvéev says it's quite clean now."

"And we could have chosen a bridgegroom for you from among them, Lizzie—a fine hussar!"

"I don't want an hussar; I'd rather have an uhlan. Weren't you in the uhlans, uncle? . . . I don't want to have anything to do with these hussars. They are all said to be desperate fellows." And Lisa blushed a little but again laughed her musical laugh.

"Here comes Ustyúshka running; we must ask her what she has seen," she added.

Anna Fëdorovna told her to call Ustyúshka.

"It's not in you to keep to your work, you must needs

run off to see the soldiers," said Anna Fëdorovna. "Well, where have the officers put up?"

"In Erómkin's house, mistress. There are two of them, such handsome ones. One's a count, they say!"

"And what's his name?"

"Kazárov or Turbínov. . . . I'm sorry—I've forgotten."

"What a fool; can't so much as tell us anything. You might at least have found out the name."

"Well, I'll run back."

"Yes, I know you're first-rate at that sort of thing. . . . No, let Daniel go. Tell him to go and ask whether the officers want anything, brother. One ought to show them some politeness after all. Say the mistress sent to inquire."

The old people again sat down in the tea-room and Lisa went to the servants' room to put into a box the sugar that had been broken up. Ustyúshka was there telling about the hussars.

"Darling miss, what a handsome man that count is!" she said. "A regular cherubim with black eyebrows. There now, if you had a bridegroom like that you would be a couple of the right sort."

The other maids smiled approvingly; the old nurse sighed as she sat knitting at a window and even whispered a prayer, drawing in her breath.

"So you liked the hussars very much?" said Lisa. "And you're a good one at telling what you've seen. Go, please, and bring some of the cranberry juice, Ustyúshka, to give the hussars something sour to drink."

And Lisa, laughing, went out with the sugar basin in her hands.

"I should really like to have seen what that hussar is like," she thought, "brown or fair? And he would have been glad to make our acquaintance I should think. . . . And if he goes away he'll never know that I was here and thought about him. And how many such have already passed me by? Who sees me here except uncle and Ustyúshka? Whichever way I do my hair, whatever sleeves I put on, no one looks at me with pleasure," she thought with a sigh as she looked at her plump white arm. "I suppose he is tall, with large eyes, and certainly small black moustaches. . . . Here am I, more than twenty-two, and no one has fallen in love with me except pock-marked Iván Ipátich, and four years ago I was even prettier. . . . And so my girlhood has passed without gladdening anyone. Oh, poor, poor country lass that I am!''

Her mother's voice, calling her to pour out tea, roused the country lass from this momentary meditation. She lifted her head with a start and went into the tea-room.

The best results are often obtained accidentally, and the more one tries the worse things turn out. In the country, people rarely try to educate their children and therefore unwittingly usually give them an excellent education. This was particularly so in Lisa's case. Anna Fëdorovna, with her limited intellect and careless temperament, gave Lisa no education—did not teach her music or that very useful French language—but having accidentally borne a healthy pretty child by her deceased husband she gave her little daughter over to a wet-nurse and a dry-nurse, fed her, dressed her in cotton prints and goat-skin shoes, sent her out to walk and gather mushrooms and wild berries, engaged a student from the seminary to teach her reading, writing, and arithmetic, and when sixteen years had passed she casually found in Lisa a friend, an ever-kind-hearted, ever-cheerful soul, and an active housekeeper. Anna Fëdorovna, being kind-hearted, always had some children to bring up—either serf children or foundlings. Lisa began looking after them when she was ten years old: teaching them, dressing them, taking them to church, and checking them when they played too many pranks. Later on the decrepit kindly uncle, who had to be tended like a child, appeared on the scene. Then the servants and peasants came to the young lady with various requests and with their ailments, which latter she treated with elderberry, peppermint, and camphorated spirits. Then there was the household management which all fell on her shoulders of itself. Then an unsatisfied longing for love awoke and found its outlet only in Nature and religion. And Lisa accidentally grew into an active, good-natured, cheerful, self-reliant, pure, and deeply religious woman. It is true that she suffered a little from vanity when she saw neighbours standing by her in church wearing fashionable bonnets brought from K———, and sometimes she was vexed to tears by her old mother's whims and grumbling. She had dreams of love, too, in most absurd and sometimes crude forms, but these were dispersed by her useful activity which had grown into a necessity, and at the age of twenty-two there was not one spot or sting of remorse in the clear calm soul of the physically and morally beautifully developed maiden. Lisa was of medium height, plump rather than thin; her eyes were hazel, not large, and had slight shadows on the lower lids; and she had a long light-brown plait of hair. She walked with big steps and with a slight sway —a "duck's waddle" as the saying is. Her face, when she was occupied and not agitated by anything in particular, seemed to say to everyone who looked into it: "It is a joy to live in the world when one has someone to love and a clear conscience." Even in moments of vexation, perplexity, alarm, or sorrow, in spite of herself there shone—through the tear in her eye, her frowning left eyebrow, and her compressed lips—a kind straightforward spirit unspoilt by the intellect; it shone in the dimples of her cheeks, in the corners of her mouth, and in her beaming eyes accustomed to smile and to rejoice in life.

X

The air was still hot though the sun was setting when the squadron entered Morózovka. In front of them along the dusty village street trotted a brindled cow separated from its herd, looking around and now and then stopping and lowing, but never suspecting that all she had to do was to turn aside. The peasants—old men, women, and children—and the servants from the manor-house, crowded on both sides of the street and eagerly watched the hussars as the latter rode through a thick cloud of dust, curbing their horses which occasionally stamped and snorted. On the right of the squadron were two officers who sat their fine black horses carelessly. One was Count Túrbin, the commander, the other a very young man recently promoted from cadet, whose name was Pólozov.

An hussar in a white linen jacket came out of the best of the huts, raised his cap, and went up to the officers.

"Where are the quarters assigned us?"

"For your Excellency?" answered the quartermaster-sergeant, with a start of his whole body. "The village elder's hut has been cleaned out. I wanted to get quarters at the manor-house, but they say there is no room there. The proprietress is such a vixen."

"All right!" said the count, dismounting and stretching his legs as he reached the village elder's hut. "And has my phaeton arrived?"

"It has deigned to arrive, your Excellency!" answered the quartermaster-sergeant, pointing with his cap to the leather body of a carriage visible through the gateway and rushing forward to the entrance of the hut, which was thronged with members of the peasant family collected to look at the officer. He even pushed one old women over as he briskly opened the door of the freshly cleaned hut and stepped aside to let the count pass.

The hut was fairly large and roomy but not very clean. The German valet, dressed like a gentleman, stood inside sorting the linen in a portmanteau after having set up an iron bedstead and made the bed.

"Faugh, what filthy lodgings!" said the count with vexation. "Couldn't you have found anything better at some gentleman's house, Dyádenko?"

"If your Excellency desires it I will try at the manor-house," answered the quartermaster-sergeant, "but it isn't up to much—doesn't look much better than a hut."

"Never mind now. Go away."

And the count lay down on the bed and threw his arms behind his head.

"Johann!" he called to his valet. "You've made a lump in the middle again! How is it you can't make a bed properly?"

Johann came up to put it right.

"No, never mind now. But where is my dressing-gown?" said the count in a dissatisfied tone.

The valet handed him the dressing-gown. Before putting it on the count examined the front.

"I thought so, that spot is not cleaned off. Could anyone be a worse servant than you?" he added, pulling the dressing-gown out of the valet's hands and putting it on. "Tell me, do you do it on purpose? . . . Is the tea ready?"

"I have not had time," said Johann.

"Fool!"

After that the count took up the French novel placed ready for him and read for some time in silence: Johann went out into the passage to prepare the samovar. The count was obviously in a bad temper, probably caused by fatigue, a dusty face, tight clothing, and an empty stomach.

"Johann!" he cried again, "bring me the account for those ten rubles. What did you buy in the town?"

He looked over the account handed him, and made some dissatisfied remarks about the dearness of the things purchased.

"Serve rum with my tea."

"I didn't buy any rum," said Johann.

"That's good! . . . How many times have I told you to have rum?"

"I hadn't enough money."

"Then why didn't Pólozov buy some? You should have got some from his man."

"Cornet Pólozov? I don't know. He bought the tea and the sugar."

"Idiot! . . . Get out! . . . You are the only man who knows how to make me lose my patience. . . . You know that on a march I always have rum with my tea."

"Here are two letters for you from the staff," said the valet.

The count opened his letters and began reading them without rising. The cornet, having quartered the squadron, came in with a merry face.

"Well, how is it, Túrbin? It seems very nice here. But I must confess I'm tired. It was hot."

"Very nice! . . . A filthy stinking hut, and thanks to your lordship no rum; your blockhead didn't buy any, nor did this one. You might at least have mentioned it."

And he continued to read his letter. When he had finished he rolled it into a ball and threw it on the floor.

In the passage the cornet was meanwhile saying to his orderly in a whisper: "Why didn't you buy any rum? You had money enough, you know."

"But why should we buy everything? As it is I pay for everything, while his German does nothing but smoke his pipe."

It was evident that the count's second letter was not unpleasant, for he smiled as he read it.

"Who is it from?" asked Pólozov, returning to the room and beginning to arrange a sleeping-place for himself on some boards by the oven.

"From Mina," answered the count gaily, handing him the letter, "Do you want to see it? What a delightful woman she is! . . . Really she's much better than our young ladies. . . . Just see how much feeling and wit there is in that letter. Only one thing is bad—she's asking for money."

"Yes, that's bad," said the cornet.

"It's true I promised her some, but then this campaign came on, and besides. . . However if I remain in command of the squadron another three months I'll send her some. It's worth it, really; such a charming creature, eh?" said he, watching the expression on Pólozov's face as he read the letter.

"Dreadfully ungrammatical, but very nice, and it seems as if she really loves you," said the cornet.

"H'm . . . I should think so! It's only women of that kind who love sincerely when once they do love."

"And who was the other letter from?" asked the cornet, handing back the one he had read.

"Oh, that . . . there's a man, a nasty beast who won from me at cards, and he's reminding me of it for the third time. . . . I can't let him have it at present. . . . A stupid letter!" said the count, evidently vexed at the recollection.

After this both officers were silent for a while. The cornet, who was evidently under the count's influence, glanced now and then at the handsome though clouded countenance of Túrbin—who was looking fixedly through the window—and drank his tea in silence, not venturing to start a conversation.

"But d'you know, it may turn out capitally," said the count, suddenly turning to Pólozov with a shake of his head. "Supposing we get promotions by seniority this year and take part in an action besides, I may get ahead of my own captains in the Guards."

The conversation was still on the same topic and they were drinking their second tumblers of tea when old Daniel entered and delivered Anna Fëdorovna's message.

"And I was also to inquire if you are not Count Fëdor Iványch Túrbin's son?" added Daniel on his own account, having learnt the count's name and remembering the deceased count's sojourn in the town of K————. "Our mistress, Anna Fëdorovna, was very well acquainted with him."

"He was my father. And tell your mistress I am very much obliged to her. We want nothing but say we told you to ask whether we could not have a cleaner room somewhere—in the manor-house, or anywhere."

"Now, why did you do that?" asked Pólozov when Daniel had gone. "What does it matter? Just for one night—what does it matter? And they will be inconveniencing themselves."

"What an idea! I think we've had our share of smoky huts! . . . It's easy to see you're not a practical man. Why not seize the opportunity when we can, and live like human beings for at least one night? And on the contrary they will be very pleased to have us. . . . The worst of it is, if this lady really knew my father . . ." continued the count with a smile which displayed his glistening white teeth. "I always have to feel ashamed of my departed papa. There is always some scandalous story or other, or some debt he has left. That's why I hate meeting these acquaintances of my father's. However, that was the way in those days," he added, growing serious.

"Did I ever tell you," said Pólozov, "I once met an uhlan brigade-commander, Ilyín? He was very anxious to meet you. He is awfully fond of your father."

"That Ilyín is an awful good-for-nothing, I believe. But the worst of it is that these good people, who assure me that they knew my father in order to make my acquaintance, while pretending to be very pleasant, relate such tales about my father as make me ashamed to listen. It is true—I don't deceive myself, but look at things dispassionately—that he had too ardent a nature and sometimes did things that were not nice. However, that was the way in those times. In our days he might have turned out a very successful man, for to do him justice he had extraordinary capacities."

A quarter of an hour later the servant came back

with a request from the proprietress that they would be
so good as to spend the night at her house.

XI

Having heard that the hussar officer was the son of Count
Fëdor Túrbin, Anna Fëdorovna was all in a flutter.

"Oh, dear me! The darling boy! . . . Daniel, run quickly
and say your mistress asks them to her house!" she began,
jumping up and hurrying with quick steps to the servants'
room. "Lizzie! Ustyúshka! . . . Your room must be got
ready, Lisa, you can move into your uncle's room. And
you, brother, you won't mind sleeping in the drawing-
room, will you? It's only for one night."

"I don't mind, sister. I can sleep on the floor."

"He must be handsome if he's like his father. Only to
have a look at him, the darling. . . . You must have a
good look at him, Lisa! The father *was* handsome. . . .
Where are you taking that table to? Leave it here," said
Anna Fëdorovna, bustling about. "Bring two beds—take
one from the foreman's—and get the crystal candlestick,
the one my brother gave me on my birthday—it's on the
what-not—and put a stearine candle in it."

At last everything was ready. In spite of her mother's
interference Lisa arranged the room for the two officers
her own way. She took out clean bed-clothes scented with
mignonette, made the beds, had candles and a bottle
of water placed on a small table near by, fumigated the
servants' room with scented paper, and moved her own
little bed into her uncle's room. Anna Fëdorovna quieted
down a little, settled in her own place, and even took up
the cards again, but instead of laying them out she leaned
her plump elbow on the table and grew thoughtful.

"Ah, time, time, how it flies!" she whispered to herself.
"Is it so long ago? It is as if I could see him now. Ah,
he was a madcap! . . ." and tears came into her eyes.
"And now there's Lizzie . . . but still, she's not what I
was at her age—she's a nice girl but she's not like that . . ."

"Lisa, you should put on your *mousseline-de-laine* dress
for the evening."

"Why, mother, you are not going to ask them in to

see us? Better not," said Lisa, unable to master her excitement at the thought of meeting the officers. "Better not, mamma!"

And really her desire to see them was less strong than her fear of the agitating joy she imagined awaited her.

"Maybe they themselves will wish to make our acquaintance, Lizzie!" said Anna Fëdorovna, stroking her head and thinking, "No, her hair is not what mine was at her age. . . . Oh, Lizzie, how I should like you to . . ." And she really did very earnestly desire something for her daughter. But she could not imagine a marriage with the count, and she could not desire for her daughter relations such as she had had with the father; but still she did desire something very much. She may have longed to relive in the soul of her daughter what she had experienced with him who was dead.

The old cavalryman was also somewhat excited by the arrival of the count. He locked himself into his room and emerged a quarter of an hour later in a Hungarian jacket and pale-blue trousers, and entered the room prepared for the visitors with the bashfully pleased expression of a girl who puts on a ball-dress for the first time in her life.

"I'll have a look at the hussars of to-day, sister! The late count was indeed a true hussar. I'll see, I'll see!"

The officers had already reached the room assigned to them through the back entrance.

"There, you see! Isn't this better than that hut with the cockroaches?" said the count, lying down as he was, in his dusty boots, on the bed that had been prepared for him.

"Of course it's better; but still, to be indebted to the proprietress . . ."

"Oh, what nonsense! One must be practical in all things. They're awfully pleased, I'm sure . . . Eh, you there!" he cried. "Ask for something to hang over this window, or it will be draughty in the night."

At this moment the old man came in to make the officers' acquaintance. Of course, though he did it with a slight blush, he did not omit to say that he and the old count had been comrades, that he had enjoyed the count's favour, and he even added that he had more than once been under obligations to the deceased. What obligations he referred to, whether it was the count's omission to repay the hundred rubles he had borrowed, or his throwing him into a snow-heap, or swearing at him, the old man quite omitted to explain. The young count was very polite to the old cavalryman and thanked him for the night's lodging.

"You must excuse us if it is not luxurious, Count," (he very nearly said "your Excellency," so unaccustomed had he become to conversing with important persons), "my sister's house is so small. But we'll hang something up there directly and it will be all right," added the old man, and on the plea of seeing about a curtain, but mainly because he was in a hurry to give an account of the officers, he bowed and left the room.

The pretty Ustyúshka came in with her mistress's shawl to cover the window, and besides, the mistress had told her to ask if the gentlemen would not like some tea.

The pleasant surroundings seemed to have a good influence on the count's spirits. He smiled merrily, joked with Ustyúshka in such a way that she even called him a scamp, asked whether her young lady was pretty, and in answer to her question whether they would have any tea he said she might bring them some tea, but the chief thing was that, their own supper not being ready yet, perhaps they might have some vodka and something to eat, and some sherry if there was any.

The uncle was in raptures over the young count's politeness and praised the new generation of officers to the skies, saying that the present men were incomparably superior to the former generation.

Anna Fëdorovna did not agree—no one could be superior to Count Fëdor Iványch Túrbin—and at last she grew seriously angry and drily remarked, "The one who has last stroked you, brother, is always the best. . . . Of course people are cleverer nowadays, but Count Fëdor Iványch danced the *écossaise* in such a way and was so amiable that everybody lost their heads about him, though he paid attention to no one but me. So you see, there were good people in the old days too."

Here came the news of the demand for vodka, light refreshments, and sherry.

"There now, brother, you never do the right thing; you should have ordered supper," began Anna Fëdorovna. "Lisa, see to it, dear!"

Lisa ran to the larder to get some pickled mushrooms and fresh butter, and the cook was ordered to make rissoles.

"But how about sherry? Have you any left, brother?"

"No, sister, I never had any."

"How's that? Why, what is it you take with your tea?"

"That's rum, Anna Fëdorovna."

"Isn't it all the same? Give me some of that—it's all the same. But wouldn't it after all be best to ask them in here, brother? You know all about it—I don't think they would take offence."

The cavalryman declared he would warrant that the count was too good-natured to refuse and that he would certainly fetch them. Anna Fëdorovna went and put on a silk dress and a new cap for some reason, but Lisa was so busy that she had no time to change her pink gingham dress with the wide sleeves. Besides, she was terribly excited; she felt as if something wonderful was awaiting her and as if a low black cloud hung over her soul. It seemed to her that this handsome hussar count must be a perfectly new, incomprehensible, but beautiful being. His character, his habits, his speech must all be so unusual, so different from anything she had ever met. All he thinks or says must be wise and right; all he does must be honourable; his whole appearance must be beautiful. She never doubted that. Had he asked not merely for refreshments and sherry but for a bath of sage-brandy and perfume, she would not have been surprised and would not have blamed him but would have been firmly convinced that it was right and necessary.

The count at once agreed when the cavalryman informed them of his sister's wish. He brushed his hair, put on his uniform, and took his cigar-case.

"Come along," he said to Pólozov.

"Really it would be better not to go," answered the cornet. "*Ils feront des frais pour nous recevoir.*"[1]

"Nonsense, they will be only too happy! Besides, I have

[1] They will be putting themselves to expense on our account.

made some inquiries: there is a pretty daughter. . . . Come along!" said the count, speaking in French.

"*Je vous en prie, messieurs!*"[2] said the cavalryman, merely to make the officers feel that he also knew French and had understood what they had said.

XII

Lisa, afraid to look at the officers, blushed and cast down her eyes and pretended to be busy filling the teapot when they entered the room. Anna Fëdorovna on the contrary jumped up hurriedly, bowed, and not taking her eyes off the count, began talking to him—now saying how unusually like his father he was, now introducing her daughter to him, now offering him tea, jam, or home-made sweetmeats. No one paid any attention to the cornet because of his modest appearance, and he was very glad of it, for he was, as far as propriety allowed, gazing at Lisa and minutely examining her beauty which evidently took him by surprise. The uncle, listening to his sister's conversation with the count, awaited, with the words ready on his lips, an opportunity to narrate his cavalry reminiscences. During tea the count lit a cigar and Lisa found it difficult to prevent herself from coughing. He was very talkative and amiable, at first slipping his stories into the intervals of Anna Fëdorovna's ever-flowing speech, but at last monopolizing the conversation. One thing struck his hearers as strange; in his stories he often used words not considered improper in the society he belonged to, but which here sounded rather too bold and somewhat frightened Anna Fëdorovna and made Lisa blush to her ears, but the count did not notice it and remained calmly natural and amiable.

Lisa silently filled the tumblers, which she did not give into the visitors' hands but placed on the table near them, not having quite recovered from her excitement, and she listened eagerly to the count's remarks. His stories, which were not very deep, and the hesitation in his speech gradually calmed her. She did not hear from him the very clever things she had expected, nor did she see that elegance in everything which she had vaguely expected to find in

[2] "If you please, gentlemen."

him. At the third glass of tea, after her bashful eyes had once met his and he had not looked down but had continued to look at her too quietly and with a slight smile, she even felt rather inimically disposed towards him and soon found that not only was there nothing especial about him but that he was in no wise different from other people she had met, that there was no need to be afraid of him though his nails were long and clean, and that there was not even any special beauty in him. Lisa suddenly relinquished her dream, not without some inward pain, and grew calmer, and only the gaze of the taciturn cornet which she felt fixed upon her, disquieted her.

"Perhaps it's not this one, but that one!" she thought.

XIII

After tea the old lady asked the visitors into the drawing-room and again sat down in her old place.

"But wouldn't you like to rest, Count?" she asked, and after receiving an answer in the negative continued, "What can I do to entertain our dear guests? Do you play cards, Count? There now, brother, you should arrange something; arrange a set—"

"But you yourself play *préférence*,"[1] answered the cavalryman. "Why not all play? Will you play, Count? And you too?"

The officers expressed their readiness to do whatever their kind hosts desired.

Lisa brought her old pack of cards which she used for divining when her mother's swollen face would get well, whether her uncle would return the same day when he went to town, whether a neighbour would call to-day, and so on. These cards, though she had used them for a

[1] In *préférence* partners play together as in whist. There is a method of scoring "with tables" which increases the gains and losses of the players. The players compete in declaring the number of tricks the cards they hold will enable them to make. The highest bidder decides which suit is to be trumps and has to make the number of tricks he has declared, or be fined. A player declaring *misère* undertakes to make no tricks and is fined (puts on a *remise*) for each trick he or she takes. "Ace and king blank" means that a player holds the two highest cards and no others of a given suit.

couple of months, were cleaner than those Anna Fëdorovna used to tell fortunes.

"But perhaps you won't play for small stakes?" inquired the uncle. "Anna Fëdorovna and I play for half-kopeks. . . . And even so she wins all our money."

"Oh, any stakes you like—I shall be delighted," replied the count.

"Well then, one-kopek 'assignats'[2] just for once, in honour of our dear visitors! Let them beat me, an old woman!" said Anna Fëdorovna, settling down in her armchair and arranging her mantilla. "And perhaps I'll win a ruble or so from them," thought she, having developed a slight passion for cards in her old age.

"If you like, I'll teach you to play with 'tables' and '*misère*,'" said the count. "It is capital."

Everyone liked the new Petersburg way. The uncle was even sure he knew it; it was just the same as "boston" used to be, only he had forgotten it a bit. But Anna Fëdorovna could not understand it at all and failed to understand it for so long that at last, with a smile and nod of approval, she felt herself obliged to assert that now she understood it and that all was quite clear to her. There was not a little laughter during the game when Anna Fëdorovna, holding ace and king blank, declared *misère* and was left with six tricks. She even became confused and began to smile shyly and hurriedly explain that she had not got quite used to the new way. But they scored against her all the same, especially as the count, being used to playing a careful game for high stakes, was cautious, skilfully played through his opponents' hands, and refused to understand the shoves the cornet gave him under the table with his foot or the mistakes the latter made when they were partners.

[2] At the time of this story two currencies were in use simultaneously —the depreciated "assignats" and the "silver rubles," which like the assignats were usually paper. The assignats had been introduced in Russia in 1768 and by the end of the Napoleonic wars were much depreciated. They fluctuated till 1841, when a new silver ruble was introduced, the value of which was about 38 pence. Paper silver rubles were exchangeable for coin at par, and it was decreed that the assignats would be redeemed at the rate of 3½ assignats for one silver ruble. In out-of-the-way provincial districts the assignats were still in general use.

Lisa brought more sweets, three kinds of jam, and some specially prepared apples that had been kept since last season and stood behind her mother's back watching the game and occasionally looking at the officers and especially at the count's white hands with their rosy well-kept nails, which threw the cards and took up the tricks in so practised, assured, and elegant a manner.

Again Anna Fëdorovna, rather irritably out-bidding the others, declared seven tricks, made only four, and was fined accordingly, and having very clumsily noted down, on her brother's demand, the points she had lost, became quite confused and fluttered.

"Never mind, mamma, you'll win it back!" smilingly remarked Lisa, wishing to help her mother out of the ridiculous situation. "Let uncle make a forfeit, and then he'll be caught."

"If you would only help me, Lisa dear!" said Anna Fëdorovna, with a frightened glance at her daughter. "I don't know how this is . . ."

"But I don't know this way either," Lisa answered, mentally reckoning up her mother's losses. "You will lose a lot that way, mamma! There will be nothing left for Pímochka's new dress," she added in jest.

"Yes, this way one may easily lose ten silver rubles," said the cornet looking at Lisa and anxious to enter into conversation with her.

"Aren't we playing for assignats?" said Anna Fëdorovna, looking round at them all.

"I don't know how we are playing, but I can't reckon in assignats," said the count. "What is it? I mean, what are assignats?"

"Why, nowadays nobody counts in assignats any longer," remarked the uncle, who had played very cautiously and had been winning.

The old lady ordered some sparkling home-made wine to be brought, drank two glasses, became very red, and seemed to resign herself to any fate. A lock of her grey hair escaped from under her cap and she did not even put it right. No doubt it seemed to her as if she had lost millions and it was all up with her. The cornet touched the count with his foot more and more often. The count scored down the old lady's losses. At last the game ended, and in spite of Anna Fëdorovna's attempts to add to her score by pretending to make mistakes in adding it up, in spite of her horror at the amount of her losses, it turned out at last that she had lost 920 points. "That's nine assignats?" she asked several times and did not comprehend the full extent of her loss until her brother told her, to her horror, that she had lost more than thirty-two assignats and that she must certainly pay.

The count did not even add up his winnings but rose immediately the game was over, went over to the window at which Lisa was arranging the *zakúshka* and turning pickled mushrooms out of a jar onto a plate for supper, and there quite quietly and simply did what the cornet had all that evening so longed, but failed, to do—entered into conversation with her about the weather.

Meanwhile the cornet was in a very unpleasant position. In the absence of the count, and more especially of Lisa, who had been keeping her in good humour, Anna Fëdorovna became frankly angry.

"Really, it's too bad that we should win from you like this," said Pólozov in order to say something. "It is a real shame!"

"Well, of course, if you go and invent some kind of 'tables' and '*misères*' and I don't know how to play them. . . . Well then, how much does it come to in assignats?" she asked.

"Thirty-two rubles, thirty-two and a quarter," repeated the cavalryman, who under the influence of his success was in a playful mood. "Hand over the money, sister; pay up!"

"I'll pay it all, but you won't catch me again. No! . . . I shall not win this back as long as I live."

And Anna Fëdorovna went off to her room, hurriedly swaying from side to side, and came back bringing nine assignats. It was only on the old man's insistent demand that she eventually paid the whole amount.

Pólozov was seized with fear lest Anna Fëdorovna should scold him if he spoke to her. He silently and quietly left her and joined the count and Lisa who were talking at the open window.

On the table spread for supper stood two tallow candles. Now and then the soft fresh breath of the May night caused the flames to flicker. Outside the window, which opened onto the garden, it was also light but it was a quite different light. The moon, which was almost full and already losing its golden tinge, floated above the tops of the tall lindens and more and more lit up the thin white clouds which veiled it at intervals. Frogs were croaking loudly by the pond, the surface of which, silvered in one place by the moon, was visible through the avenue. Some little birds fluttered slightly or lightly hopped from bough to bough in a sweet-scented lilac-bush whose dewy branches occasionally swayed gently close to the window.

"What wonderful weather!" the count said as he approached Lisa and sat down on the low window-sill. "I suppose you walk a good deal?"

"Yes," said Lisa, not feeling the least shyness in speaking with the count. "In the morning about seven o'clock I look after what has to be attended to on the estate and take my mother's ward, Pímochka, with me for a walk."

"It is pleasant to live in the country!" said the count, putting his eye-glass to his eye and looking now at the garden, now at Lisa. "And don't you ever go out at night, by moonlight?"

"No. But two years ago uncle and I used to walk every moonlight night. He was troubled with a strange complaint—insomnia. When there was a full moon he could not fall asleep. His little room—that one—looks straight out into the garden, the window is low but the moon shines straight into it."

"That's strange: I thought that was your room," said the count.

"No, I only sleep there to-night. You have my room."

"Is it possible? Dear me, I shall never forgive myself for having disturbed you in such a way!" said the count, letting the monocle fall from his eye in proof of the sincerity of his feelings. "If I had known that I was troubling you . . ."

"It's no trouble! On the contrary I am very glad: uncle's is such a charming room, so bright, and the window is so low. I shall sit there till I fall asleep, or else I shall climb out into the garden and walk about a bit before going to bed."

"What a splendid girl!" thought the count, replacing his eyeglass and looking at her and trying to touch her foot

with his own while pretending to seat himself more comfortably on the window-sill. "And how cleverly she has let
me know that I may see her in the garden at the window
if I like!" Lisa even lost much of her charm in his eyes—
the conquest seemed so easy.

"And how delightful it must be," he said, looking
thoughtfully at the dark avenue of trees, "to spend a night
like this in the garden with a beloved one."

Lisa was embarrassed by these words and by the repeated, seemingly accidental touch of his foot. Anxious to
hide her confusion she said without thinking, "Yes, it is
nice to walk in the moonlight." She was beginning to feel
rather uncomfortable. She had tied up the jar out of which
she had taken the mushrooms and was going away from the
window, when the cornet joined them and she felt a wish to
see what kind of man he was.

"What a lovely night!" he said.

"Why, they talk of nothing but the weather," thought
Lisa.

"What a wonderful view!" continued the cornet. "But
I suppose you are tired of it," he added, having a curious
propensity to say rather unpleasant things to people he
liked very much.

"Why do you think so? The same kind of food or the
same dress one may get tired of, but not of a beautiful
garden if one is fond of walking—especially when the moon
is still higher. From uncle's window the whole pond can
be seen. I shall look at it to-night."

"But I don't think you have any nightingales?" said
the count, much dissatisfied that the cornet had come and
prevented his ascertaining more definitely the terms of
the rendezvous.

"No, but there always were until last year when some
sportsman caught one, and this year one began to sing
beautifully only last week but the police-officer came here
and his carriage-bells frightened it away. Two years ago
uncle and I used to sit in the covered alley and listen to
them for two hours or more at a time."

"What is this chatterbox telling you?" said her uncle,
coming up to them. "Won't you come and have something
to eat?"

After supper, during which the count by praising the

food and by his appetite had somewhat dispelled the
hostess's ill humour, the officers said good-night and went
into their room. The count shook hands with the uncle,
and to Anna Fëdorovna's surprise shook her hand also
without kissing it, and even shook Lisa's, looking straight
into her eyes the while and slightly smiling his pleasant
smile. This look again abashed the girl.

"He is very good-looking," she thought, "but he thinks
too much of himself."

XIV

"I say, aren't you ashamed of yourself?" said Pólozov when
they were in their room. "I purposely tried to lose and
kept touching you under the table. Aren't you ashamed?
The old lady was quite upset, you know."

The count laughed very heartily.

"She was awfully funny, that old lady. . . . How offended
she was! . . ."

And he again began laughing so merrily that even
Johann, who stood in front of him, cast down his eyes and
turned away with a slight smile.

"And with the son of a friend of the family! Ha-ha-
ha! . . ." the count continued to laugh.

"No, really it was too bad. I was quite sorry for her,"
said the cornet.

"What nonsense! How young you still are! Why, did you
wish me to lose? Why should one lose? I used to lose before
I knew how to play! Ten rubles may come in useful, my
dear fellow. You must look at life practically or you'll
always be left in the lurch."

Pólozov was silenced; besides, he wished to be quiet and
to think about Lisa, who seemed to him an unusually pure
and beautiful creature. He undressed and lay down in the
soft clean bed prepared for him.

"What nonsense all this military honour and glory is!"
he thought, looking at the window curtained by the shawl
through which the white moonbeams stole in. "It would
be happiness to live in a quiet nook with a dear, wise,
simple-hearted wife—yes, that is true and lasting
happiness!"

But for some reason he did not communicate these reflections to his friend and did not even refer to the country lass, though he was convinced that the count too was thinking of her.

"Why don't you undress?" he asked the count who was walking up and down the room.

"I don't feel sleepy yet, somehow. You can put out the candle if you like. I shall lie down as I am."

And he continued to pace up and down.

"Don't feel sleepy yet somehow," repeated Pólozov, who after this last evening felt more dissatisfied than ever with the count's influence over him and was inclined to rebel against it. "I can imagine," he thought, addressing himself mentally to Túrbin, "what is now passing through that well-brushed head of yours! I saw how you admired her. But you are not capable of understanding such a simple honest creature: you want a Mina and a colonel's epaulettes. . . . I really must ask him how he liked her."

And Pólozov turned towards him—but changed his mind. He felt he would not be able to hold his own with the count, if the latter's opinion of Lisa were what he supposed it to be, and that he would even be unable to avoid agreeing with him, so accustomed was he to bow to the count's influence, which he felt more and more every day to be oppressive and unjust.

"Where are you going?" he asked, when the count put on his cap and went to the door.

"I'm going to see if things are all right in the stables."

"Strange!" thought the cornet, but put out the candle and turned over on his other side, trying to drive away the absurdly jealous and hostile thoughts that crowded into his head concerning his former friend.

Anna Fëdorovna meanwhile, having as usual kissed her brother, daughter, and ward and made the sign of the cross over each of them, had also retired to her room. It was long since the old lady had experienced so many strong impressions in one day and she could not even pray quietly: she could not rid herself of the sad and vivid memories of the deceased count and of the young dandy who had plundered her so unmercifully. However, she undressed as usual, drank half a tumbler of *kvas*[1] that stood ready for her on a little table by her bed, and lay down. Her favourite cat crept softly into the room. Anna Fëdorovna called her up and began to stroke her and listen to her purring but could not fall asleep.

"It's the cat that keeps me awake," she thought and drove her away. The cat fell softly on the floor and gently moving her bushy tail leapt onto the stove. And now the maid, who always slept in Anna Fëdorovna's room, came and spread the piece of felt that served her for a mattress, put out the candle, and lit the lamp before the icon. At last the maid began to snore, but still sleep would not come to soothe Anna Fëdorovna's excited imagination. When she closed her eyes the hussar's face appeared to her, and she seemed to see it in the room in various guises when she opened her eyes and by the dim light of the lamp looked at the chest of drawers, the table, or a white dress that was hanging up. Now she felt very hot on the feather bed, now her watch ticked unbearably on the little table, and the maid snored unendurably through her nose. She woke her up and told her not to snore. Again thoughts of her daughter, of the old count and the young one, and of the *préférence*, became curiously mixed in her head. Now she saw herself waltzing with the old count, saw her own round white shoulders, felt someone's kisses on them, and then saw her daughter in the arms of the young count. Ustyúshka again began to snore.

"No, people are not the same nowadays. The other one was ready to leap into the fire for me—and not without cause. But this one is sleeping like a fool, no fear, glad to have won—no love-making about him. . . . How the other one said on his knees, 'What do you wish me to do? I'll kill myself on the spot, or do anything you like!' And he would have killed himself had I told him to."

Suddenly she heard a patter of bare feet in the passage and Lisa, with a shawl thrown over her, ran in pale and trembling and almost fell onto her mother's bed.

After saying good-night to her mother that evening Lisa had gone alone to the room her uncle generally slept

[1] *Kvas* is a non-intoxicating drink usually made from rye-malt and rye-flour.

in. She put on a white dressing-jacket and covered her long thick plait with a kerchief, extinguished the candle, opened the window, and sat down on a chair, drawing her feet up and fixing her pensive eyes on the pond now all glittering in the silvery light.

All her accustomed occupations and interests suddenly appeared to her in a new light: her capricious old mother, uncritical love for whom had become part of her soul; her decrepit but amiable old uncle; the domestic and village serfs who worshipped their young mistress; the milch cows and the calves, and all this Nature which had died and been renewed so many times and amid which she had grown up loving and beloved—all this that had given such light and pleasant tranquillity to her soul suddenly seemed unsatisfactory; it seemed dull and unnecessary. It was as if someone had said to her: "Little fool, little fool, for twenty years you have been trifling, serving someone without knowing why, and without knowing what life and happiness are!" As she gazed into the depths of the moon-lit, motionless garden she thought this more intensely, far more intensely, than ever before. And what caused these thoughts? Not any sudden love for the count as one might have supposed. On the contrary, she did not like him. She could have been interested in the cornet more easily, but he was plain, poor fellow, and silent. She kept involuntarily forgetting him and recalling the image of the count with anger and annoyance. "No, that's not it," she said to herself. Her ideal had been so beautiful. It was an ideal that could have been loved on such a night amid this Nature without impairing its beauty—an ideal never abridged to fit it to some coarse reality.

Formerly, solitude and the absence of anyone who might have attracted her attention had caused the power of love, which Providence has given impartially to each of us, to rest intact and tranquil in her bosom, and now she had lived too long in the melancholy happiness of feeling within her the presence of this something, and of now and again opening the secret chalice of her heart to contemplate its riches, to be able to lavish its contents thoughtlessly on anyone. God grant she may enjoy to her grave this chary bliss! Who knows whether it be not the best and strongest, and whether it is not the only true and possible happiness?

"O Lord my God," she thought, "can it be that I have lost my youth and happiness in vain and that it will never be . . . never be? Can that be true?" And she looked into the depths of the sky lit up by the moon and covered by light fleecy clouds that, veiling the stars, crept nearer to the moon. "If that highest white cloudlet touches the moon it will be a sign that it is true," thought she. The mist-like smoky strip ran across the bottom half of the bright disk and little by little the light on the grass, on the tops of the limes, and on the pond, grew dimmer and the black shadows of the trees grew less distinct. As if to harmonize with the gloomy shadows that spread over the world outside, a light wind ran through the leaves and brought to the window the odour of dewy leaves, of moist earth, and of blooming lilacs.

"But it is not true," she consoled herself. "There now, if the nightingale sings to-night it will be a sign that what I'm thinking is all nonsense, and that I need not despair," thought she. And she sat a long while in silence waiting for something, while again all became bright and full of life and again and again the cloudlets ran across the moon making everything dim. She was beginning to fall asleep as she sat by the window, when the quivering trills of a nightingale came ringing from below across the pond and awoke her. The country maiden opened her eyes. And once more her soul was renewed with fresh joy by its mysterious union with Nature which spread out so calmly and brightly before her. She leant on both arms. A sweet, languid sensation of sadness oppressed her heart, and tears of pure wide-spreading love, thirsting to be satisfied —good comforting tears—filled her eyes. She folded her arms on the window-sill and laid her head on them. Her favourite prayer rose to her mind and she fell asleep with her eyes still moist.

The touch of someone's hand aroused her. She awoke. But the touch was light and pleasant. The hand pressed hers more closely. Suddenly she became alive to reality, screamed, jumped up, and trying to persuade herself that she had not recognized the count who was standing under the window bathed in the moonlight, she ran out of the room. . . .

XV

And it really was the count. When he heard the girl's cry and a husky sound from the watchman behind the fence, who had been roused by that cry, he rushed headlong across the wet dewy grass into the depths of the garden feeling like a detected thief. "Fool that I am!" he repeated unconsciously, "I frightened her. I ought to have aroused her gently by speaking to her. Awkward brute that I am!" He stopped and listened: the watchman came into the garden through the gateway, dragging his stick along the sandy path. It was necessary to hide and the count went down by the pond. The frogs made him start as they plumped from beneath his feet into the water. Though his boots were wet through, he squatted down and began to recall all he had done: how he had climbed the fence, looked for her window, and at last espied a white shadow; how, listening to the faintest rustle, he had several times approached the window and gone back again; how at one moment he felt sure she was waiting, vexed at his tardiness, and the next, that it was impossible she should so readily have agreed to a rendezvous; how at last, persuading himself that it was only the bashfulness of a country-bred girl that made her pretend to be asleep, he went up resolutely and distinctly saw how she sat but then for some reason ran away again and only after severely taunting himself for cowardice boldly drew near to her and touched her hand.

The watchman again made a husky sound and the gate creaked as he left the garden. The girl's window was slammed to and a shutter fastened from inside. This was very provoking. The count would have given a good deal for a chance to begin all over again; he would not have acted so stupidly now. . . . "And she is a wonderful girl— so fresh—quite charming! And I have let her slip through my fingers. . . . Awkward fool that I am!" He did not want to sleep now and went at random, with the firm tread of one who has been crossed, along the covered lime-tree avenue.

And here the night brought to him also its peaceful gifts of soothing sadness and the need of love. The straight pale beams of the moon threw spots of light through the thick foliage of the limes onto the clay path, where a few blades of grass grew or a dead branch lay here and there. The light falling on one side of a bent bough made it seem as if covered with white moss. The silvered leaves whispered now and then. There were no lights in the house and all was silent; the voice of the nightingale alone seemed to fill the bright, still, limitless space. "O God, what a night! What a wonderful night!" thought the count, inhaling the fragrant freshness of the garden. "Yet I feel a kind of regret—as if I were discontented with myself and with others, discontented with life generally. A splendid, sweet girl! Perhaps she was really hurt. . . ." Here his dreams became mixed: he imagined himself in this garden with the country-bred girl in various extraordinary situations. Then the role of the girl was taken by his beloved Mina. "Eh, what a fool I was! I ought simply to have caught her round the waist and kissed her." And regretting that he had not done so, the count returned to his room.

The cornet was still awake. He at once turned in his bed and faced the count.

"Not asleep yet?" asked the count.

"No."

"Shall I tell you what has happened?"

"Well?"

"No, I'd better not, or . . . all right, I'll tell you—draw in your legs."

And the count, having mentally abandoned the intrigue that had miscarried, sat down on his comrade's bed with an animated smile.

"Would you believe it, that young lady gave me a rendezvous!"

"What are you saying?" cried Pólozov, jumping out of bed.

"No, but listen."

"But how? When? It's impossible!"

"Why, while you were adding up after we had played *préférence*, she told me she would sit at the window in the night and that one could get in at the window. There, you see what it is to be practical! While you were calculating with the old woman, I arranged that little matter. Why, you heard her say in your presence that she would sit by the window to-night and look at the pond."

"Yes, but she didn't mean anything of the kind."

"Well, that's just what I can't make out: did she say it intentionally or not? Maybe she didn't really wish to agree so suddenly, but it looked very like it. It turned out horribly. I quite played the fool," he added, smiling contemptuously at himself.

"What do you mean? Where have you been?"

The count, omitting his manifold irresolute approaches, related everything as it had happened.

"I spoilt it myself: I ought to have been bolder. She screamed and ran from the window."

"So she screamed and ran away," said the cornet, smiling uneasily in answer to the count's smile, which for such a long time had had so strong an influence over him.

"Yes, but it's time to go to sleep."

The cornet again turned his back to the door and lay silent for about ten minutes. Heavens knows what went on in his soul, but when he turned again, his face bore an expression of suffering and resolve.

"Count Túrbin!" he said abruptly.

"Are you delirious?" quietly replied the count. "What is it, Cornet Pólozov?"

"Count Túrbin, you are a scoundrel!" cried Pólozov and again jumped out of bed.

XVI

The squadron left next day. The two officers did not see their hosts again and did not bid them farewell. Neither did they speak to one another. They intended to fight a duel at the first halting-place. But Captain Schulz, a good comrade and splendid horseman, beloved by everyone in the regiment and chosen by the count to act as his second, managed to settle the affair so well that not only did they not fight but no one in the regiment knew anything about the matter, and Túrbin and Pólozov, though no longer on the old friendly footing, still continued to speak in familiar terms to one another and to meet at dinners and card-parties.

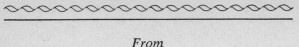

From
THE COSSACKS
A Tale of 1852

I

All is quiet in Moscow. The squeak of wheels is seldom heard in the snow-covered street. There are no lights left in the windows and the street lamps have been extinguished. Only the sound of bells, borne over the city from the church towers, suggests the approach of morning. The streets are deserted. At rare intervals a night-cabman's sledge kneads up the snow and sand in the street as the driver makes his way to another corner where he falls asleep while waiting for a fare. An old woman passes by on her way to church, where a few wax candles burn with a red light reflected on the gilt mountings of the icons. Workmen are already getting up after the long winter night and going to their work—but for the gentlefolk it is still evening.

From a window in Chevalier's Restaurant a light—illegal at that hour—is still to be seen through a chink in the shutter. At the entrance a carriage, a sledge, and a cabman's sledge stand close together with their backs to the curbstone. A three-horse sledge from the post-station is there also.[1] A yard-porter muffled up and pinched with cold is sheltering behind the corner of the house.

"And what's the good of all this jawing?" thinks the footman who sits in the hall weary and haggard. "This always happens when I'm on duty." From the adjoining room are heard the voices of three young men, sitting there at a table on which are wine and the remains of supper. One, a rather plain, thin, neat little man, sits looking with

[1] In those pre-rail days travellers usually relied on vehicles hired at the posting-stations.

tired kindly eyes at his friend, who is about to start on a journey. Another, a tall man, lies on a sofa beside a table on which are empty bottles and plays with his watch-key. A third, wearing a short, fur-lined coat, is pacing up and down the room, stopping now and then to crack an almond between his strong, rather thick, but well-tended fingers. He keeps smiling at something and his face and eyes are all aglow. He speaks warmly and gesticulates but evidently does not find the words he wants and those that occur to him seem to him inadequate to express what has risen to his heart.

"Now I can speak out fully," said the traveller. "I don't want to defend myself, but I should like you at least to understand me as I understand myself and not look at the matter superficially. You say I have treated her badly," he continued, addressing the man with the kindly eyes who was watching him.

"Yes, you are to blame," said the latter, and his look seemed to express still more kindliness and weariness.

"I know why you say that," rejoined the one who was leaving. "To be loved is in your opinion as great a happiness as to love, and if a man obtains it, it is enough for his whole life."

"Yes, quite enough, my dear fellow, more than enough!" confirmed the plain little man, opening and shutting his eyes.

"But why shouldn't the man love too?" said the traveller thoughtfully, looking at his friend with something like pity. "Why shouldn't one love? Because love doesn't come. . . . No, to be beloved is a misfortune. It is a misfortune to feel guilty because you do not give something you cannot give. O my God!" he added, with a gesture of his arm. "If it all happened reasonably, and not all topsy-turvy—not in our way but in a way of its own! Why, it's as if I had stolen that love! You think so too, don't deny it. You must think so. But will you believe it, of all the horrid and stupid things I have found time to do in my life—and there are many—this is one I do not and cannot repent of. Neither at the beginning nor afterwards did I lie to myself or to her. It seemed to me that I had at last fallen in love, but then I saw that it was an involuntary falsehood, and that

that was not the way to love, and I could not go on, but she did. Am I to blame that I couldn't? What was I to do?"

"Well, it's ended now!" said his friend, lighting a cigar to master his sleepiness. "The fact is that you have not yet loved and do not know what love is."

The man in the fur-lined coat was going to speak again, and put his hands to his head, but could not express what he wanted to say.

"Never loved! . . . Yes, quite true, I never have! But after all, I have within me a desire to love, and nothing could be stronger than that desire! But then, again, does such love exist? There always remains something incomplete. Ah well! What's the use of talking? I've made an awful mess of life! And I feel that I am beginning a new life."

"Which you will again make a mess of," said the man who lay on the sofa playing with his watch-key. But the traveller did not listen to him.

"I am sad and yet glad to go," he continued. "Why I am sad I don't know."

And the traveller went on talking about himself, without noticing that this did not interest the others as much as it did him. A man is never such an egotist as at moments of spiritual ecstasy. At such times it seems to him that there is nothing on earth more splendid and interesting than himself.

"Dmítri Andréich! The coachman won't wait any longer!" said a young serf, entering the room in a sheepskin coat, with a scarf tied round his head. "The horses have been standing since twelve, and it's now four o'clock!"

Dmítri Andréich looked at his serf, Vanyúsha. The scarf round Vanyúsha's head, his felt boots and sleepy face, seemed to be calling his master to a new life of labour, hardship, and activity.

"True enough! Good-bye!" said he, feeling for the unfastened hook and eye on his coat.

In spite of advice to mollify the coachman by another tip, he put on his cap and stood in the middle of the room. The friends kissed once, then again, and after a pause a third time. The man in the fur-lined coat approached the table and emptied a champagne glass, then took the plain little man's hand and blushed.

"Ah well, I will speak out all the same. . . . I must and will be frank with you because I am fond of you. . . . Of course you love her—I always thought so—don't you?"

"Yes," answered his friend, smiling still more gently.

"And perhaps . . ."

"Please sir, I have orders to put out the candles," said the sleepy attendant, who had been listening to the last part of the conversation and wondering why gentlefolk always talk about one and the same thing. "To whom shall I make out the bill? To you sir?" he added, knowing whom to address and turning to the tall man.

"To me," replied the tall man. "How much?"

"Twenty-six rubles."

The tall man considered for a moment but said nothing and put the bill in his pocket.

The other two continued their talk.

"Good-bye, you are a capital fellow!" said the short plain man with the mild eyes.

Tears filled the eyes of both. They stepped into the porch.

"Oh, by the by," said the traveller, turning with a blush to the tall man, "will you settle Chevalier's bill and write and let me know?"

"All right, all right!" said the tall man, pulling on his gloves. "How I envy you!" he added quite unexpectedly when they were out in the porch.

The traveller got into his sledge, wrapped his coat about him, and said: "Well then, come along!" He even moved a little to make room in the sledge for the man who said he envied him—his voice trembled.

"Good-bye, Mítya! I hope that with God's help you . . ." said the tall one. But his wish was that the other would go away quickly, and so he could not finish the sentence.

They were silent a moment. Then someone again said, "Good-bye," and a voice cried, "Ready," and the coachman touched up the horses.

Hy, Elisár!" one of the friends called out, and the other coachman and the sledge-drivers began moving, clicking their tongues and pulling at the reins. Then the stiffened carriage-wheels rolled squeaking over the frozen snow.

"A fine fellow, that Olénin!" said one of the friends. "But what an idea to go to the Caucasus—as a cadet, too!

I wouldn't do it for anything. . . . Are you dining at the club to-morrow?"

"Yes."

They separated.

The traveller felt warm, his fur coat seemed too hot. He sat on the bottom of the sledge and unfastened his coat, and the three shaggy post-horses dragged themselves out of one dark street into another, past houses he had never before seen. It seemed to Olénin that only travellers starting on a long journey went through those streets. All was dark and silent and dull around him, but his soul was full of memories, love, regrets, and a pleasant tearful feeling.

II

"I'm fond of them, very fond! . . . First-rate fellows! . . . Fine!" he kept repeating, and felt ready to cry. But why he wanted to cry, who were the first-rate fellows he was fond of, was more than he quite knew. Now and then he looked round at some house and wondered why it was so curiously built; sometimes he began wondering why the post-boy and Vanyúsha, who were so different from himself, sat so near and together with him were being jerked about and swayed by the tugs the side-horses gave at the frozen traces, and again he repeated: "First rate . . . very fond!" and once he even said, "And how it seizes one . . . excellent" and wondered what made him say it. "Dear me, am I drunk?" he asked himself. He had had a couple of bottles of wine, but it was not the wine alone that was having this effect on Olénin. He remembered all the words of friendship heartily, bashfully, spontaneously (as he believed) addressed to him on his departure. He remembered the clasp of hands, glances, the moments of silence, and the sound of a voice saying, "Good-bye, Mítya!" when he was already in the sledge. He remembered his own deliberate frankness. And all this had a touching significance for him. Not only friends and relatives, not only people who had been indifferent to him, but even those who did not like him seemed to have agreed to become fonder of him, or to forgive him, before his departure, as people do before confession or death. "Perhaps I shall not return from the Caucasus," he thought. And he felt that he loved his friends and some one besides. He was sorry for himself. But it was not love for his friends that so stirred and up- lifted his heart that he could not repress the meaningless words that seemed to rise of themselves to his lips; nor was it love for a woman (he had never yet been in love) that had brought on this mood. Love for himself, love full of hope—warm young love for all that was good in his own soul (and at that moment it seemed to him that there was nothing but good in it)—compelled him to weep and to mutter incoherent words.

Olénin was a youth who had never completed his uni- versity course, never served anywhere (having only a nominal post in some government office or other), who had squandered half his fortune and had reached the age of twenty-four without having done anything or even chosen a career. He was what in Moscow society is termed *un jeune homme.*

At the age of eighteen he was free—as only rich young Russians in the 'forties who had lost their parents at an early age could be. Neither physical nor moral fetters of any kind existed for him; he could do as he liked, lacking nothing and bound by nothing. Neither relatives, nor fatherland, nor religion nor wants existed for him. He believed in nothing and admitted nothing. But although he believed in nothing he was not a morose or blasé young man, nor self-opinionated, but on the contrary continually let himself be carried away. He had come to the con- clusion that there is no such thing as love, yet his heart always overflowed in the presence of any young and at- tractive woman. He had long been aware that honours and position were nonsense, yet involuntarily he felt pleased when at a ball Prince Sergius came up and spoke to him affably. But he yielded to his impulses only in so far as they did not limit his freedom. As soon as he had yielded to any influence and became conscious of its leading on to labour and struggle, he instinctively hastened to free himself from the feeling or activity into which he was being drawn and to regain his freedom. In this way he experi- mented with society-life, the civil service, farming, music— to which at one time he intended to devote his life—and even with the love of women in which he did not believe.

He meditated on the use to which he should devote that power of youth which is granted to many only once in a lifetime: that force which gives a man the power of making himself, or even—as it seemed to him—of making the universe, into anything he wishes: should it be to art, to science, to love of woman, or to practical activities? It is true that some people are devoid of this impulse, and on entering life at once place their necks under the first yoke that offers itself and honestly labour under it for the rest of their lives. But Olénin was too strongly conscious of the presence of that all-powerful God of Youth—of the capacity to be entirely transformed into an aspiration or idea—the capacity to wish and to do—to throw oneself headlong into a bottomless abyss without knowing why or wherefore. He bore this consciousness within himself, was proud of it, and without knowing it, was happy in that consciousness. Up to that time he had loved only himself and could not help loving himself, for he expected nothing but good of himself and had not yet had time to be disillusioned. On leaving Moscow he was in that happy state of mind in which a young man, conscious of past mistakes, suddenly says to himself, "That was not the real thing." All that had gone before was accidental and unimportant. Till then he had not really tried to live, but now with his departure from Moscow a new life was beginning—a life in which there would be no mistakes, no remorse, and certainly nothing but happiness.

It is always the case on a long journey that till the first two or three stages have been passed imagination continues to dwell on the place left behind, but with the first morning on the road it leaps to the end of the journey and there begins building castles in the air. So it happened to Olénin.

After leaving the town behind, he gazed at the snowy fields and felt glad to be alone in their midst. Wrapping himself in his fur coat, he lay at the bottom of the sledge, became tranquil, and fell into a doze. The parting with his friends had touched him deeply, and memories of that last winter spent in Moscow and images of the past, mingled with vague thoughts and regrets, rose unbidden in his imagination.

He remembered the friend who had seen him off and his relations with the girl they had talked about. The girl was rich. "How could he love her knowing that she loved me?" thought he, and evil suspicions crossed his mind. "There is much dishonesty in men when one comes to reflect." Then he was confronted by the question: "But really, how is it I have never been in love? Every one tells me that I never have. Can it be that I am a moral monstrosity?" And he began to recall all his infatuations. He recalled his entry into society, and a friend's sister with whom he spent several evenings at a table with a lamp on it which lit up her slender fingers busy with needlework, and the lower part of her pretty delicate face. He recalled their conversations that dragged on like the game in which one passes on a stick which one keeps alight as long as possible, and the general awkwardness and restraint and his continual feeling of rebellion at all that conventionality. Some voice had always whispered: "That's not it, that's not it," and so it had proved. Then he remembered a ball and the mazurka he danced with the beautiful D———. "How much in love I was that night and how happy! And how hurt and vexed I was next morning when I woke and felt myself still free! Why does not love come and bind me hand and foot?" thought he. "No, there is no such thing as love! That neighbour who used to tell me, as she told Dubróvin and the Marshal, that she loved the stars, was not *it* either." And now his farming and work in the country recurred to his mind, and in those recollections also there was nothing to dwell on with pleasure. "Will they talk long of my departure?" came into his head; but who "they" were he did not quite know. Next came a thought that made him wince and mutter incoherently. It was the recollection of M. Cappele the tailor and the six hundred and seventy-eight rubles he still owed him, and he recalled the words in which he had begged him to wait another year, and the look of perplexity and resignation which had appeared on the tailor's face. "Oh, my God, my God!" he repeated, wincing and trying to drive away the intolerable thought. "All the same and in spite of everything she loved me," thought he of the girl they had talked about at the farewell supper. "Yes, had I married her I should not now be owing anything, and as it is I am in debt to Vasílyev." Then he remembered the last night he had played with Vasílyev at the club (just after leaving her), and he recalled his humiliating requests for another game and the other's cold refusal. "A year's economizing and they will all be paid, and the devil take them! . . ." But despite this assurance he again began calculating his outstanding debts, their dates, and when he could hope to pay them off. "And I owe something to Morell as well as to Chevalier," thought he, recalling the night when he had run up so large a debt. It was at a carousal at the gipsies arranged by some fellows from Petersburg: Sáshka B———, an aide-de-camp to the Tsar, Prince D———, and that pompous old ———. "How is it those gentlemen are so self-satisfied?" thought he, "and by what right do they form a clique to which they think others must be highly flattered to be admitted? Can it be because they are on the emperor's staff? Why, it's awful what fools and scoundrels they consider other people to be! But I showed them that I at any rate, on the contrary, do not at all want their intimacy. All the same, I fancy Andrew, the steward, would be amazed to know that I am on familiar terms with a man like Sáshka B———, a colonel and an aide-de-camp to the Tsar! Yes, and no one drank more than I did that evening, and I taught the gipsies a new song and everyone listened to it. Though I have done many foolish things, all the same I am a very good fellow," thought he.

Morning found him at the third post-stage. He drank tea, and himself helped Vanyúsha to move his bundles and trunks, and sat down among them, sensible, erect, and precise, knowing where all his belongings were, how much money he had and where it was, where he had put his passport and the post-horse requisition and toll-gate papers, and it all seemed to him so well arranged that he grew quite cheerful and the long journey before him seemed an extended pleasure-trip.

All that morning and noon he was deep in calculations of how many versts he had travelled, how many remained to the next stage, how many to the next town, to the place where he would dine, to the place where he would drink tea, and to Stavrópol, and what fraction of the whole journey was already accomplished. He also calculated how much money he had with him, how much would be left over, how much would pay off all his debts, and what proportion of his income he would spend each month.

Towards evening, after tea, he calculated that to Stavrópol there still remained seven-elevenths of the whole journey, that his debts would require seven months' economy and one-eighth of his whole fortune; and then, tranquillized, he wrapped himself up, lay down in the sledge, and again dozed off. His imagination was now turned to the future: to the Caucasus. All his dreams of the future were mingled with pictures of Amalat-Beks,[1] Circassian women, mountains, precipices, terrible torrents, and perils. All these things were vague and dim, but the love of fame and the danger of death furnished the interest of that future. Now, with unprecedented courage and a strength that amazed everyone, he slew and subdued an innumerable host of hillsmen; now he was himself a hillsman and with them was maintaining their independence against the Russians. As soon as he pictured anything definite, familiar Moscow figures always appeared on the scene. Sáshka B——— fights with the Russians or the hillsmen against him. Even the tailor Cappele in some strange ways takes part in the conqueror's triumph. Amid all this he remembered his former humiliations, weaknesses, and mistakes, and the recollection was not disagreeable. It was clear that there among the mountains, waterfalls, fair Circassians, and dangers, such mistakes could not recur. Having once made full confession to himself there was an end of it all. One other vision, the sweetest of them all, mingled with the young man's every thought of the future—the vision of a woman. And there, among the mountains, she appeared to his imagination as a Circassian slave, a fine figure with a long plait of hair and deep submissive eyes. He pictured a lonely hut in the mountains, and on the threshold *she* stands awaiting him when, tired and covered with dust, blood, and fame, he returns to her. He is conscious of her kisses, her shoulders, her sweet voice, and her submissiveness. She is enchanting, but uneducated, wild, and rough. In the long winter evenings he begins her education. She is clever and gifted and quickly acquires all the knowledge essential. Why not? She can quite easily learn foreign languages, read the French

---

[1] Amalet-Bek is a character in a Russian novel of the Caucasus by Bestúzhev-Marlínsky.

masterpieces and understand them: *Notre Dame de Paris,* for instance, is sure to please her. She can also speak French. In a drawing-room she can show more innate dignity than a lady of the highest society. She can sing, simply, powerfully, and passionately. . . . "Oh, what nonsense!" said he to himself. But here they reached a post-station and he had to change into another sledge and give some tips. But his fancy again began searching for the "nonsense" he had relinquished, and again fair Circassians, glory, and his return to Russia with an appointment as aide-de-camp and a lovely wife rose before his imagination. "But there's no such thing as love," said he to himself. "Fame is all rubbish. But the six hundred and seventy-eight rubles? . . . And the conquered land that will bring me more wealth than I need for a lifetime? It will not be right though to keep all that wealth for myself. I shall have to distribute it. But to whom? Well, six hundred and seventy-eight rubles to Cappele and then we'll see." Quite vague visions now cloud his mind, and only Vanyúsha's voice and the interrupted motion of the sledge break his healthy youthful slumber. Scarcely conscious, he changes into another sledge at the next stage and continues his journey.

Next morning everything goes on just the same: the same kind of post-stations and tea-drinking, the same moving horses' cruppers, the same short talks with Vanyúsha, the same vague dreams and drowsiness, and the same tired, healthy, youthful sleep at night.

III

The farther Olénin travelled from Central Russia the farther he left his memories behind, and the nearer he drew to the Caucasus the lighter his heart became. "I'll stay away for good and never return to show myself in society," was a thought that sometimes occurred to him. "These people whom I see here are *not* people. None of them know me and none of them can ever enter the Moscow society I was in or find out about my past. And no one in that society will ever know what I am doing, living among these people." And quite a new feeling of freedom from his whole past came over him among the rough beings he met on the road whom he did not consider to be *people* in the sense that his Moscow acquaintances were. The rougher the people and the fewer the signs of civilization the freer he felt. Stavrópol, through which he had to pass, irked him. The signboards, some of them even in French, ladies in carriages, cabs in the market-place, and a gentleman wearing a fur cloak and tall hat who was walking along the boulevard and staring at the passers-by quite upset him. "Perhaps these people know some of my acquaintances," he thought; and the club, his tailor, cards, society . . . came back to his mind. But after Stavrópol everything was satisfactory—wild and also beautiful and warlike, and Olénin felt happier and happier. All the Cossacks, post-boys, and post-station masters seemed to him simple folk with whom he could jest and converse simply, without having to consider to what class they belonged. They all belonged to the human race which, without his thinking about it, all appeared dear to Olénin, and they all treated him in a friendly way.

Already in the province of the Don Cossacks his sledge had been exchanged for a cart, and beyond Stavrópol it became so warm that Olénin travelled without wearing his fur coat. It was already spring—an unexpected joyous spring for Olénin. At night he was no longer allowed to leave the Cossack villages, and they said it was dangerous to travel in the evening. Vanyúsha began to be uneasy, and they carried a loaded gun in the cart. Olénin became still happier. At one of the post-stations the post-master told of a terrible murder that had been committed recently on the high road. They began to meet armed men. "So this is where it begins!" thought Olénin, and kept expecting to see the snowy mountains of which mention was so often made. Once, towards evening, the Nogáy driver pointed with his whip to the mountains shrouded in clouds. Olénin looked eagerly, but it was dull and the mountains were almost hidden by the clouds. Olénin made out something grey and white and fleecy, but try as he would he could find nothing beautiful in the mountains of which he had so often read and heard. The mountains and the clouds appeared to him quite alike, and he thought the special beauty of the snow peaks, of which he had so often been told, was as much an invention as Bach's music and the love of women, in which he did not believe. So he gave up looking forward to seeing the mountains. But early next morning, being awakened in his cart by the freshness of the air, he glanced carelessly to the right. The morning was perfectly clear. Suddenly he saw, about twenty paces away as it seemed to him at first glance, pure white gigantic masses with delicate contours, the distinct fantastic outlines of their summits showing sharply against the far-off sky. When he had realized the distance between himself and them and the sky and the whole immensity of the mountains and felt the infinitude of all that beauty, he became afraid that it was but a phantasm or a dream. He gave himself a shake to rouse himself, but the mountains were still the same.

"What's that! What is it?" he said to the driver.

"Why, the mountains," answered the Nogáy driver with indifference.

"And I too have been looking at them for a long while," said Vanyúsha. "Aren't they fine? They won't believe it at home."

The quick progress of the three-horsed cart along the smooth road caused the mountains to appear to be running along the horizon, while their rosy crests glittered in the light of the rising sun. At first Olénin was only astonished at the sight, then gladdened by it; but later on, gazing more and more intently at that snow-peaked chain that seemed to rise not from among other black mountains, but straight out of the plain, and to glide away into the distance, he began by slow degrees to be penetrated by their beauty and at length to *feel* the mountains. From that moment all he saw, all he thought, and all he felt acquired for him a new character, sternly majestic like the mountains! All his Moscow reminiscences, shame, and repentance, and his trivial dreams about the Caucasus, vanished and did not return. "Now it has begun," a solemn voice seemed to say to him. The road and the Térek, just becoming visible in the distance, and the Cossack villages and the people, all no longer appeared to him as a joke. He looked at himself or Vanyúsha and again thought of the mountains. . . . Two Cossacks ride by, their guns in their cases swinging rhythmically behind their backs, the white and bay legs of their horses mingling confusedly . . . and the mountains! Beyond the Térek rises the smoke from a

Tartar village . . . and the mountains! The sun has risen
and glitters on the Térek, now visible beyond the reeds . . .
and the mountains! From the village comes a Tartar
wagon, and women, beautiful young women, pass by . . .
and the mountains! "*Abreks*[1] canter about the plain, and
here am I driving along and do not fear them! I have a
gun, and strength, and youth . . . and the mountains!"

IV

That whole part of the Térek line (about fifty miles) along
which lie the villages of the Grebénsk Cossacks is uniform
in character both as to country and inhabitants. The Térek,
which separates the Cossacks from the mountaineers, still
flows turbid and rapid though already broad and smooth,
always depositing greyish sand on its low reedy right bank
and washing away the steep, though not high, left bank,
with its roots of century-old oaks, its rotting plane trees,
and young brushwood. On the right bank lie the villages
of pro-Russian, though still somewhat restless, Tartars.
Along the left bank, back half a mile from the river and
standing five or six miles apart from one another, are
Cossack villages. In olden times most of these villages
were situated on the banks of the river, but the Térek,
shifting northward from the mountains year by year,
washed away those banks and now there remain only the
ruins of the old villages and of the gardens of pear and
plum trees and poplars, all overgrown with blackberry
bushes and wild vines. No one lives there now, and one
only sees the tracks of the deer, the wolves, the hares, and
the pheasants, who have learned to love these places. From
village to village runs a road cut through the forest as a
cannon-shot might fly. Along the roads are cordons of
Cossacks and watch-towers with sentinels in them. Only a
narrow strip about seven hundred yards wide of fertile
wooded soil belongs to the Cossacks. To the north of it
begin the sand-drifts of the Nogáy or Mozdók steppes,
which stretch far to the north and run, Heaven knows
where, into the Trukhmén, Astrakhán, and Kirghíz-

---

[1] Hostile Chéchens who cross over to the Russian bank of the Térek
to thieve and plunder.

Kaisátsk steppes. To the south, beyond the Térek, are the Great Chéchnya river, the Kochkálov range, the Black Mountains, yet another range, and at last the snowy mountains, which can just be seen but have never yet been scaled. In this fertile wooded strip, rich in vegetation, has dwelt as far back as memory runs the fine warlike and prosperous Russian tribe belonging to the sect of Old Believers,[1] and called the Grebénsk Cossacks.

Long, long ago their Old Believer ancestors fled from Russia and settled beyond the Térek among the Chéchens on the Grében, the first range of wooded mountains of Chéchnya. Living among the Chéchens the Cossacks intermarried with them and adopted the manners and customs of the hill tribes, though they still retained the Russian language in all its purity, as well as their old faith. A tradition, still fresh among them, declares that Tsar Iván the Terrible came to the Térek, sent for their elders, and gave them the land on this side of the river, exhorting them to remain friendly to Russia and promising not to enforce his rule upon them nor oblige them to change their faith. Even now the Cossack families claim relationship with the Chéchens, and the love of freedom, of leisure, of plunder, and of war still form their chief characteristics. Only the harmful side of Russian influence is apparent—by interference at election, by confiscation of church bells, and by the troops who are quartered in the country or march through it. A Cossack is inclined to hate less the *dzhigit*[2] hillsman who maybe has killed his brother than the soldier who is quartered on him to defend his village, but who has defiled his hut with tobacco-smoke. He respects his enemy the hillsman and despises the soldier, who is in his eyes an alien and an oppressor. In reality, from a Cossack's point of view a Russian peasant is a foreign, savage, despicable creature, of whom he sees a sample in the hawkers who come to the country and in the Ukraínian immigrants whom the Cossack contemptuously calls "wool-beaters."

[1] Old Believer is a general name for the sects that separated from the Russo-Greek Church in the seventeenth century. Tobacco is one of the things prohibited by their rules.

[2] Among the Chéchens a *dzhigit* is much the same as a *brave* among the Indians, but the word is inseparably connected with the idea of skilful horsemanship.

For him, to be smartly dressed means to be dressed like a
Circassian. The best weapons are obtained from the hillsmen and the best horses are bought, or stolen, from them.
A dashing young Cossack likes to show off his knowledge
of Tartar, and when carousing talks Tartar even to his
fellow Cossack. In spite of all these things this small
Christian clan stranded in a tiny corner of the earth, surrounded by half-savage Mohammedan tribes and by
soldiers, considers itself highly advanced, acknowledges
none but Cossacks as human beings, and despises everybody
else. The Cossack spends most of his time in the cordon,
in action, or in hunting and fishing. He hardly ever works
at home. When he stays in the village it is an exception to
the general rule and then he is holiday-making. All Cossacks make their own wine, and drunkenness is not so much
a general tendency as a rite, the non-fulfillment of which
would be considered apostasy. The Cossack looks upon
a woman as an instrument for his welfare; only the unmarried girls are allowed to amuse themselves. A married
woman has to work for her husband from youth to very
old age: his demands on her are the Oriental ones of submission and labour. In consequence of this outlook women
are strongly developed both physically and mentally, and
though they are —as everywhere in the East—nominally in
subjection, they possess far greater influence and importance in family-life than Western women. Their exclusion
from public life and inurement to heavy male labour give
the women all the more power and importance in the
household. A Cossack, who before strangers considers it
improper to speak affectionately or needlessly to his wife,
when alone with her is involuntarily conscious of her
superiority. His house and all his property, in fact the
entire homestead, has been acquired and is kept together
solely by her labour and care. Though firmly convinced
that labour is degrading to a Cossack and is only proper
for a Nogáy labourer or a woman, he is vaguely aware of
the fact that all he makes use of and calls his own is the
result of that toil, and that it is in the power of the woman
(his mother or his wife) whom he considers his slave to
deprive him of all he possesses. Besides, the continuous
performance of man's heavy work and the responsibilities
entrusted to her have endowed the Grebénsk woman with

a peculiarly independent masculine character and have remarkably developed her physical powers, common sense, resolution, and stability. The women are in most cases stronger, more intelligent, more developed, and handsomer than the men. A striking feature of a Grebénsk woman's beauty is the combination of the purest Circassian type of face with the broad and powerful build of Northern women. Cossack women wear the Circassian dress—a Tartar smock, *beshmet*,[3] and soft slippers—but they tie their kerchiefs round their heads in the Russian fashion. Smartness, cleanliness, and elegance in dress and in the arrangement of their huts are with them a custom and a necessity. In their relations with men, the women, and especially the unmarried girls, enjoy perfect freedom.

Novomlínsk village was considered the very heart of Grebénsk Cossackdom. In it more than elsewhere the customs of the old Grebénsk population have been preserved, and its women have from time immemorial been renowned all over the Caucasus for their beauty. A Cossack's livelihood is derived from vineyards, fruit-gardens, water-melon and pumpkin plantations, from fishing, hunting, maize and millet growing, and from war plunder. Novomlínsk village lies about two and a half miles away from the Térek, from which it is separated by a dense forest. On one side of the road which runs through the village is the river; on the other, green vineyards and orchards, beyond which are seen the drift-sands of the Nogáy Steppe. The village is surrounded by earth-banks and prickly bramble hedges and is entered by tall gates hung between posts and covered with little reed-thatched roofs. Beside them on a wooden gun-carriage stands an unwieldy cannon captured by the Cossacks at some time or other, and which has not been fired for a hundred years. A uniformed Cossack sentinel with dagger and gun sometimes stands, and sometimes does not stand, on guard beside the gates and sometimes presents arms to a passing officer and sometimes does not. Below the roof of the gateway is written in black letters on a white board: "Houses 266: male inhabitants 897: female 1012." The Cossacks' houses are all raised on pillars two and a half

---

[3] *Beshmet*, a Tartar garment with sleeves.

feet from the ground. They are carefully thatched with reeds and have large carved gables. If not new they are at least all straight and clean, with high porches of different shapes; and they are not built close together, but have ample space around them, and are all picturesquely placed along broad streets and lanes. In front of the large bright windows of many of the houses, beyond the kitchen gardens, dark green poplars and acacias with their delicate pale verdure and scented white blossoms overtop the houses, and beside them grow flaunting yellow sunflowers, creepers, and grape vines. In the broad open square are three shops where drapery, sunflower and pumpkin seeds, locust beans, and gingerbreads are sold; and surrounded by a tall fence, loftier and larger than the other houses, stands the Regimental Commander's dwelling with its casement windows, behind a row of tall poplars. Few people are to be seen in the streets of the village on week-days, especially in summer. The young men are on duty in the cordons or on military expeditions; the old ones are fishing or helping the women in the orchards and gardens. Only the very old, the sick, and the children remain at home.

V

It was one of those wonderful evenings that occur only in the Caucasus. The sun had sunk behind the mountains but it was still light. The evening glow had spread over a third of the sky, and against its brilliancy the dull white immensity of the mountains was sharply defined. The air was rarefied, motionless, and full of sound. The shadow of the mountains reached for several miles over the steppe. The steppe, the opposite side of the river, and the roads were all deserted. If very occasionally mounted men appeared, the Cossacks in the cordon and the Chéchens in their *aouls* (villages) watched them with surprised curiosity and tried to guess who those questionable men could be. At nightfall people from fear of one another flock to their dwellings, and only birds and beasts fearless of man prowl in those deserted spaces. Talking merrily, the women who have been tying up the vines hurry away from the gardens before sunset. The vineyards, like all the surrounding district, are deserted, but the villages become very animated at that time of the evening. From all sides, walking, riding, or driving in their creaking carts, people move towards the village. Girls with their smocks tucked up and twigs in their hands run chatting merrily to the village gates to meet the cattle that are crowding together in a cloud of dust and mosquitoes which they bring with them from the steppe. The well-fed cows and buffaloes disperse at a run all over the streets, and Cossack women in coloured *beshmets* go to and fro among them. You can hear their merry laughter and shrieks mingling with the lowing of the cattle. There an armed and mounted Cossack, on leave from the cordon, rides up to a hut and, leaning towards the window, knocks. In answer to the knock the handsome head of a young woman appears at the window and you can hear caressing, laughing voices. There a tattered Nogáy labourer, with prominent cheekbones, brings a load of reeds from the steppes, turns his creaking cart into the Cossack captain's broad and clean courtyard, and lifts the yoke off the oxen that stand tossing their heads while he and his master shout to one another in Tartar. Past a puddle that reaches nearly across the street, a barefooted Cossack woman with a bundle of firewood on her back makes her laborious way by clinging to the fences, holding her smock high and exposing her white legs. A Cossack returning from shooting calls out in jest; "Lift it higher, shameless thing!" and points his gun at her. The woman lets down her smock and drops the wood. An old Cossack, returning home from fishing with his trousers tucked up and his hairy grey chest uncovered, has a net across his shoulder containing silvery fish that are still struggling; and to take a short cut climbs over his neighbour's broken fence and gives a tug to his coat which has caught on the fence. There a woman is dragging a dry branch along and from round the corner comes the sound of an axe. Cossack children, spinning their tops wherever there is a smooth place in the street, are shrieking; women are climbing over fences to avoid going round. From every chimney rises the odorous *kisyak*[1] smoke. From every homestead comes the sound of increased bustle, precursor to the stillness of night.

---

[1] *Kisyak*, fuel made of straw and manure.

Granny Ulítka, the wife of the Cossack cornet who is also teacher in the regimental school, goes out to the gates of her yard like the other women and waits for the cattle which her daughter Maryánka is driving along the street. Before she has had time fully to open the wattle gate in the fence, an enormous buffalo cow surrounded by mosquitoes rushes up bellowing and squeezes in. Several well-fed cows slowly follow her, their large eyes gazing with recognition at their mistress as they swish their sides with their tails. The beautiful and shapely Maryánka enters at the gate and throwing away her switch quickly slams the gate to and rushes with all the speed of her nimble feet to separate and drive the cattle into their sheds. "Take off your slippers, you devil's wench!" shouts her mother, "You've worn them into holes!" Maryánka is not at all offended at being called a devil's wench but accepting it as a term of endearment cheerfully goes on with her task. Her face is covered with a kerchief tied round her head. She is wearing a pink smock and a green *beshmet*. She disappears inside the lean-to shed in the yard, following the big fat cattle, and from the shed comes her voice as she speaks gently and persuasively to the buffalo: "Won't she stand still? What a creature! Come now, come old dear!" Soon the girl and the old woman pass from the shed to the dairy carrying two large pots of milk, the day's yield. From the dairy chimney rises a thin cloud of *kisyak* smoke: the milk is being used to make into clotted cream. The girl makes up the fire while her mother goes to the gate. Twilight has fallen on the village. The air is full of the smell of vegetables, cattle, and scented *kisyak* smoke. From the gates and along the streets Cossack women come running, carrying lighted rags. From the yards one hears the snorting and quiet chewing of the cattle eased of their milk, while in the street only the voices of women and children sound as they call to one another. It is rare on a week-day to hear the drunken voice of a man.

One of the Cossack wives, a tall, masculine old woman, approaches Granny Ulítka from the homestead opposite and asks her for a light. In her hand she holds a rag.

"Have you cleared up, Granny?"

"The girl is lighting the fire. Is it fire you want?" says Granny Ulítka, proud of being able to oblige her neighbour.

Both women enter the hut, and coarse hands unused to dealing with small articles tremblingly lift the lid of a match-box, which is a rarity in the Caucasus. The masculine-looking new-comer sits down on the doorstep with the evident intention of having a chat.

"And is your man at the school, Mother?" she asked.

"He's always teaching the youngsters, Mother. But he writes that he'll come home for the holidays," said the cornet's wife.

"Yes, he's a clever man, one sees; it all comes useful."

"Of course it does."

"And my Lukáshka is at the cordon; they won't let him come home," said the visitor, though the cornet's wife had known all this long ago. She wanted to talk about her Lukáshka whom she had lately fitted out for service in the Cossack regiment, and whom she wished to marry to the cornet's daughter, Maryánka.

"So he's at the cordon?"

"He is, Mother. He's not been home since last holidays. The other day I sent him some shirts by Fómushkin. He says he's all right, and that his superiors are satisfied. He says they are looking out for *abreks* again. Lukáshka is quite happy, he says."

"Ah well, thank God," said the cornet's wife. " 'Snatcher' is certainly the only word for him." Lukáshka was surnamed "the Snatcher" because of his bravery in snatching a boy from a watery grave, and the cornet's wife alluded to this, wishing in her turn to say something agreeable to Lukáshka's mother.

"I thank God, Mother, that he's a good son! He's a fine fellow, everyone praises him," says Lukáshka's mother. "All I wish is to get him married; then I could die in peace."

"Well, aren't there plenty of young women in the village?" answered the cornet's wife slyly as she carefully replaced the lid of the match-box with her horny hands.

"Plenty, Mother, plenty," remarked Lukáshka's mother, shaking her head. "There's your girl now, your Maryánka— that's the sort of girl! You'd have to search through the whole place to find such another!"

The cornet's wife knows what Lukáshka's mother is after, but though she believes him to be a good Cossack she hangs back: first because she is a cornet's wife and rich, while Lukáshka is the son of a simple Cossack and fatherless; secondly because she does not want to part with her daughter yet; but chiefly because propriety demands it.

"Well when Maryánka grows up she'll be marriageable too," she answers soberly and modestly.

"I'll send the matchmakers to you—I'll send them! Only let me get the vineyard done, and then we'll come and make our bows to you, says Lukáshka's mother. "And we'll make our bows to Elias Vasílich too."

"Elias, indeed!" says the cornet's wife proudly. "It's to me you must speak! All in its own good time."

Lukáshka's mother sees by the stern face of the cornet's wife that it is not the time to say anything more just now, so she lights her rag with the match and says, rising, "Don't refuse us, think of my words. I'll go, it is time to light the fire."

As she crosses the road swinging the burning rag, she meets Maryánka, who bows.

"Ah, she's a regular queen, a splendid worker, that girl!" she thinks, looking at the beautiful maiden. "What need for her to grow any more? It's time she was married and to a good home; married to Lukáshka!"

But Granny Ultíka had her own cares and she remained sitting on the threshold thinking hard about something, till the girl called her.

VI

The male population of the village spend their time on military expeditions and in the cordon—or "at their posts" as the Cossacks say. Towards evening, that same Lukáshka the Snatcher, about whom the old women had been talking, was standing on a watch-tower of the Nízhni-Protótsk post situated on the very banks of the Térek. Leaning on the railing of the tower and screwing up his eyes, he looked now far into the distance beyond the Térek, now down at his fellow Cossacks, and occasionally he addressed the latter. The sun was already approaching the snowy range that gleamed white above the fleecy clouds. The clouds undulating at the base of the mountains grew darker and darker. The clearness of evening was noticeable in the air.

A sense of freshness came from the woods, though round the port it was still hot. The voices of the talking Cossacks vibrated more sonorously than before. The moving mass of the Térek's rapid brown waters contrasted more vividly with its motionless banks. The waters were beginning to subside and here and there the wet sands gleamed drab on the banks and in the shallows. The other side of the river, just opposite the cordon, was deserted; only an immense waste of low-growing reeds stretched far away to the very foot of the mountains. On the low bank, a little to one side, could be seen the flat-roofed clay houses and the funnel-shaped chimneys of a Chéchen village. The sharp eyes of the Cossack who stood on the watch-tower followed, through the evening smoke of the pro-Russian village, the tiny moving figures of the Chéchen women visible in the distance in their red and blue garments.

Although the Cossacks expected *abreks* to cross over and attack them from the Tartar side at any moment, especially as it was May when the woods by the Térek are so dense that it is difficult to pass through them on foot and the river is shallow enough in places for a horseman to ford it, and despite the fact that a couple of days before a Cossack had arrived with a circular from the commander of the regiment announcing that spies had reported the intention of a party of some eight men to cross the Térek, and ordering special vigilance—no special vigilance was being observed in the cordon. The Cossacks unarmed and with their horses unsaddled just as if they were at home, spent their time, some in fishing, some in drinking, and some in hunting. Only the horse of the man on duty was saddled and with its feet hobbled was moving about by the brambles near the wood, and only the sentinel had his Circassian coat on and carried a gun and sword. The corporal, a tall thin Cossack with an exceptionally long back and small hands and feet, was sitting on the earth-bank of a hut with his *beshmet* unbuttoned. On his face was the lazy, bored expression of a superior, and having shut his eyes he dropped his head upon the palm first of one hand then of the other. An elderly Cossack with a broad greyish-black beard was lying in his shirt, girdled with a black strap, close to the river and gazing lazily at the waves of the Térek as they monotonously foamed and swirled. Others, also overcome by the heat and half naked, were rinsing clothes in the Térek, plaiting a fishing line, or humming tunes as they lay on the hot sand of the river bank. One Cossack, with a thin face much burnt by the sun, lay near the hut evidently dead drunk, by a wall which though it had been in shadow some two hours previously was now exposed to the sun's fierce slanting rays.

Lukáshka, who stood on the watch-tower, was a tall handsome lad about twenty years old and very like his mother. His face and whole build, in spite of the angularity of youth, indicated great strength, both physical and moral. Though he had only lately joined the Cossacks at the front, it was evident from the expression of his face and the calm assurance of his attitude that he had already acquired the somewhat proud and warlike bearing peculiar to Cossacks and to men generally who continually carry arms, and that he felt he was a Cossack and fully knew his own value. His ample Circassian coat was torn in some places, his cap was on the back of his head Chéchen fashion, and his leggings had slipped below his knees. His clothing was not rich, but he wore it with that peculiar Cossack foppishness which consists in imitating the Chéchen brave. Everything on a real brave is ample, ragged, and neglected, only his weapons are costly. But these ragged clothes and these weapons are belted and worn with a certain air and matched in a certain manner, neither of which can be acquired by everybody and which at once strike the eye of a Cossack or a hillsman. Lukáshka had this resemblance to a brave. With his hands folded under his sword, and his eyes nearly closed, he kept looking at the distant Tartar village. Taken separately his features were not beautiful, but anyone who saw his stately carriage and his dark-browed intelligent face would involuntarily say "What a fine fellow!"

"Look at the women, what a lot of them are walking about in the village," said he in a sharp voice, languidly showing his brilliant white teeth and not addressing anyone in particular.

Nazárka who was lying below immediately lifted his head and remarked, "They must be going for water."

"Supposing one scared them with a gun?" said Lukáshka, laughing. "Wouldn't they be frightened?"

"It wouldn't reach."

"What! Mine would carry beyond. Just wait a bit, and when their feast comes round I'll go and visit Giréy Khan and drink *buza*[1] there," said Lukáshka, angrily swishing away the mosquitoes which attached themselves to him.

A rustling in the thicket drew the Cossack's attention. A pied mongrel half-setter, searching for a scent and violently wagging its scantily furred tail, came running to the cordon. Lukáshka recognized the dog as one belonging to his neighbour, Uncle Eróshka, a hunter, and saw, following it through the thicket, the approaching figure of the hunter himself.

Uncle Eróshka was a gigantic Cossack with a broad, snow-white beard and such broad shoulders and chest that in the wood, where there was no one to compare him with, he did not look particularly tall, so well proportioned were his powerful limbs. He wore a tattered coat and, over the bands with which his legs were swathed, sandals made of undressed deer's hide tied on with strings; while on his head he had a rough little white cap. He carried over one shoulder a screen to hide behind when shooting pheasants, and a bag containing a hen for luring hawks, and a small falcon; over the other shoulder, attached by a strap, was a wild cat he had killed; and stuck in his belt behind were some little bags containing bullets, gun-powder, and bread, a horse's tail to swish away the mosquitoes, a large dagger in a torn scabbard smeared with old bloodstains, and two dead pheasants. Having glanced at the cordon he stopped.

"Hi, Lyam!" he called to the dog in such a ringing bass that it awoke an echo far away in the wood; and throwing over his shoulder his big gun, of the kind the Cossacks call a "flint," he raised his cap.

"Had a good day, good people, eh?" he said, addressing the Cossacks in the same strong and cheerful voice, quite without effort, but as loudly as if he were shouting to someone on the other bank of the river.

"Yes, yes, Uncle!" answered from all sides the voices of the young Cossacks.

"What have you seen? Tell us!" shouted Uncle Eróshka, wiping the sweat from his broad red face with the sleeve of his coat.

---

[1] Tartar beer made of millet.

"Ah, there's a vulture living in the plane tree here, Uncle. As soon as night comes he begins hovering round," said Nazárka, winking and jerking his shoulder and leg.

"Come, come!" said the old man incredulously.

"Really, Uncle! You must keep watch," replied Nazárka with a laugh.

The other Cossacks began laughing.

The wag had not seen any vulture at all, but it had long been the custom of the young Cossacks in the cordon to tease and mislead Uncle Eróshka every time he came to them.

"Eh, you fool, always lying!" exclaimed Lukáshka from the tower to Nazárka.

Nazárka was immediately silenced.

"It must be watched. I'll watch," answered the old man to the great delight of all the Cossacks. "But have you seen any boars?"

"Watching for boars, are you?" said the corporal, bending forward and scratching his back with both hands, very pleased at the chance of some distraction. "It's *abreks* one has to hunt here and not boars! You've not heard anything, Uncle, have you?" he added, needlessly screwing up his eyes and showing his close-set white teeth.

"*Abreks,*" said the old man. "No, I haven't. I say, have you any *chikhir*?[2] Let me have a drink, there's a good man. I'm really quite done up. When the time comes I'll bring you some fresh meat, I really will. Give me a drink!" he added.

"Well, and are you going to watch?" inquired the corporal, as though he had not heard what the other said.

"I did mean to watch to-night," replied Uncle Eróshka. "Maybe, with God's help, I shall kill something for the holiday. Then you shall have a share, you shall indeed!"

"Uncle! Hallo, Uncle!" called out Lukáshka sharply from above, attracting everybody's attention. All the Cossacks looked up at him. "Just go to the upper watercourse, there's a fine herd of boars there. I'm not inventing, really! The other day one of our Cossacks shot one there. I'm telling you the truth," added he, readjusting the musket at his back and in a tone that showed he was not joking.

[2] Home-made Caucasian wine.

"Ah! Lukáshka the Snatcher is here!" said the old man, looking up. "Where has he been shooting?"

"Haven't you seen? I suppose you're too young!" said Lukáshka. "Close by the ditch," he went on seriously with a shake of the head. "We were just going along the ditch when all at once we heard something crackling, but my gun was in its case. Elias fired suddenly. . . . But I'll show you the place, it's not far. You just wait a bit. I know every one of their footpaths. . . . Daddy Mósev," said he, turning resolutely and almost commandingly to the corporal, "it's time to relieve guard!" and holding aloft his gun he began to descend from the watch-tower without waiting for the order.

"Come down!" said the corporal, after Lukáshka had started, and glanced round. "Is it your turn, Gúrka? Then go. . . . True enough your Lukáshka has become very skilful," he went on, addressing the old man. "He keeps going about just like you, he doesn't stay at home. The other day he killed a boar."

VII

The sun had already set and the shades of night were rapidly spreading from the edge of the wood. The Cossacks finished their task round the cordon and gathered in the hut for supper. Only the old man still stayed under the plane tree watching for the vulture and pulling the string tied to the falcon's leg, but though a vulture was really perching on the plane tree it declined to swoop down on the lure. Lukáshka, singing one song after another, was leisurely placing nets among the very thickest brambles to trap pheasants. In spite of his tall stature and big hands, every kind of work, both rough and delicate, prospered under Lukáshka's fingers.

"Hallo, Luke!" came Nazárka's shrill, sharp voice calling him from the thicket close by. "The Cossacks have gone in to supper."

Nazárka, with a live pheasant under his arm, forced his way through the brambles and emerged on the footpath.

"Oh!" said Lukáshka, breaking off in his song, "where did you get that cock pheasant? I suppose it was in my trap?"

Nazárka was of the same age as Lukáshka and had also only been at the front since the previous spring.

He was plain, thin, and puny, with a shrill voice that rang in one's ears. They were neighbours and comrades. Lukáshka was sitting on the grass cross-legged like a Tartar, adjusting his nets.

"I don't know whose it was—yours, I expect."

"Was it beyond the pit by the plane tree? Then it is mine! I set the nets last night."

Lukáshka rose and examined the captured pheasant. After stroking the dark burnished head of the bird, which rolled its eyes and stretched out its neck in terror, Lukáshka took the pheasant in his hands.

"We'll have it in a pilau[1] to-night. You go and kill and pluck it."

"And shall we eat it ourselves or give it to the corporal?"

"He has plenty!"

"I don't like killing them," said Nazárka.

"Give it here!"

Lukáshka drew a little knife from under his dagger and gave it a swift jerk. The bird fluttered, but before it could spread its wings the bleeding head bent and quivered.

"That's how one should do it!" said Lukáshka, throwing down the pheasant. "It will make a fat pilau."

Nazárka shuddered as he looked at the bird.

"I say, Lukáshka, that fiend will be sending us to the ambush again to-night," he said, taking up the bird. (He was alluding to the corporal.) "He has sent Fómushkin to get wine, and it ought to be his turn. He always puts it on us."

Lukáshka went whistling along the cordon.

"Take the string with you," he shouted.

Nazárka obeyed.

"I'll give him a bit of my mind to-day, I really will," continued Nazárka. "Let's say we won't go; we're tired out and there's an end of it! No, really, you tell him, he'll listen to you. It's too bad!"

"Get along with you! What a thing to make a fuss about!" said Lukáshka, evidently thinking of something else. "What bosh! If he made us turn out of the village at

---

[1] A kind of stew, made with boiled rice.

night now, that would be annoying: there one can have some fun, but here what is there? It's all one whether we're in the cordon or in ambush. What a fellow you are!"

"And are you going to the village?"

"I'll go for the holidays."

"Gúrka says your Dunáyka is carrying on with Fómushkin," said Nazárka suddenly.

"Well, let her go to the devil," said Lukáshka, showing his regular white teeth, though he did not laugh. "As if I couldn't find another!"

"Gúrka says he went to her house. Her husband was out and there was Fómushkin sitting and eating pie. Gúrka stopped awhile and then went away, and passing by the window he heard her say, 'He's gone, the fiend. . . . Why don't you eat your pie, my own? You needn't go home for the night,' she says. And Gúrka under the window says to himself, 'That's fine!' "

"You're making it up."

"No, quite true, by Heaven!"

"Well, if she's found another let her go to the devil," said Lukáshka, after a pause. "There's no lack of girls and I was sick of her anyway."

"Well, see what a devil you are!" said Nazárka. "You should make up to the cornet's girl, Maryánka. Why doesn't she walk out with any one?"

Lukáshka frowned. "What of Maryánka? They're all alike," said he.

"Well, you just try . . ."

"What do you think? Are girls so scarce in the village?"

And Lukáshka recommenced whistling, and went along the cordon pulling leaves and branches from the bushes as he went. Suddenly, catching sight of a smooth sapling, he drew the knife from the handle of his dagger and cut it down. "What a ramrod it will make," he said, swinging the sapling till it whistled through the air.

The Cossacks were sitting round a low Tartar table on the earthen floor of the clay-plastered outer room of the hut, when the question of whose turn it was to lie in ambush was raised. "Who is to go to-night?" shouted one of the Cossacks through the open door to the corporal in the next room.

"Who is to go?" the corporal shouted back. "Uncle Burlák has been and Fómushkin too," said he, not quite confidently. "You two had better go, you and Nazárka," he went on, addressing Lukáshka. "And Ergushóv must go too; surely he has slept it off?"

"You don't sleep it off yourself, so why should he?" said Nazárka in a subdued voice.

The Cossacks laughed.

Ergushóv was the Cossack who had been lying drunk and asleep near the hut. He had only that moment staggered into the room rubbing his eyes.

Lukáshka had already risen and was getting his gun ready.

"Be quick and go! Finish your supper and go!" said the corporal; and without waiting for an expression of consent he shut the door, evidently not expecting the Cossack to obey. "Of course," thought he, "if I hadn't been ordered to I wouldn't send anyone, but an officer might turn up at any moment. As it is, they say eight *abreks* have crossed over."

"Well, I suppose I must go," remarked Ergushóv, "it's the regulation. Can't be helped! The times are such. I say, we must go."

Meanwhile Lukáshka, holding a big piece of pheasant to his mouth with both hands and glancing now at Nazárka, now at Ergushóv, seemed quite indifferent to what passed and only laughed at them both. Before the Cossacks were ready to go into ambush, Uncle Eróshka, who had been vainly waiting under the plane tree till night fell, entered the dark outer room.

"Well, lads," his loud bass resounded through the low-roofed room drowning all the other voices, "I'm going with you. You'll watch for Chéchens and I for boars!"

VIII

It was quite dark when Uncle Eróshka and the three Cossacks, in their cloaks and shouldering their guns, left the cordon and went towards the place on the Térek where they were to lie in ambush. Nazárka did not want to go at all, but Lukáshka shouted at him and they soon started.

After they had gone a few steps in silence the Cossacks turned aside from the ditch and went along a path almost hidden by reeds till they reached the river. On its bank lay a thick black log cast up by the water. The reeds around it had been recently beaten down.

"Shall we lie here?" asked Nazárka.

"Why not?" answered Lukáshka. "Sit down here and I'll be back in a minute. I'll only show Daddy where to go."

"This is the best place; here we can see and not be seen," said Ergushóv, "so it's here we'll lie. It's a first-rate place!"

Nazárka and Ergushóv spread out their cloaks and settled down behind the log, while Lukáshka went on with Uncle Eróshka.

"It's not far from here, Daddy," said Lukáshka, stepping softly in front of the old man; "I'll show you where they've been—I'm the only one that knows, Daddy."

"Show me! You're a fine fellow, a regular Snatcher!" replied the old man, also whispering.

Having gone a few steps Lukáshka stopped, stooped down over a puddle, and whistled. "That's where they come to drink, d'you see?" He spoke in a scarcely audible voice, pointing to fresh hoof-prints.

"Christ bless you," answered the old man. "The boar will be in the hollow beyond the ditch," he added. "I'll watch, and you can go."

Lukáshka pulled his cloak up higher and walked back alone, throwing swift glances now to the left at the wall of reeds, now to the Térek rushing by below the bank. "I daresay he's watching or creeping along somewhere," thought he of a possible Chéchen hillsman. Suddenly a loud rustling and a splash in the water made him start and seize his musket. From under the bank a boar leapt up—his dark outline showing for a moment against the glassy surface of the water and then disappearing among the reeds. Lukáshka pulled out his gun and aimed, but before he could fire the boar had disappeared in the thicket. Lukáshka spat with vexation and went on. On approaching the ambuscade he halted again and whistled softly. His whistle was answered and he stepped up to his comrades.

Nazárka, all curled up, was already asleep. Ergushóv

sat with his legs crossed and moved slightly to make room
for Lukáshka.

"How jolly it is to sit here! It's really a good place,"
said he. "Did you take him there?"

"Showed him where," answered Lukáshka, spreading
out his cloak. "But what a big boar I roused just now close
to the water! I expect it was the very one! You must have
heard the crash?"

"I did hear a beast crashing through. I knew at once it
was a beast. I thought to myself: 'Lukáshka has roused a
beast,' " Ergushóv said, wrapping himself up in his cloak.
"Now I'll go to sleep," he added. "Wake me when the
cocks crow. We must have discipline. I'll lie down and
have a nap, and then you will have a nap and I'll watch—
that's the way."

"Luckily I don't want to sleep," answered Lukáshka.

The night was dark, warm, and still. Only on one side
of the sky the stars were shining, the other and greater
part was overcast by one huge cloud stretching from the
mountain-tops. The black cloud, blending in the absence
of any wind with the mountains, moved slowly onwards, its
curved edges sharply defined against the deep starry sky.
Only in front of him could the Cossack discern the Térck
and the distance beyond. Behind and on both sides he was
surrounded by a wall of reeds. Occasionally the reeds
would sway and rustle against one another apparently without cause. Seen from down below, against the clear part of
the sky, their waving tufts looked like the feathery branches
of trees. Close in front at his very feet was the bank, and
at its base the rushing torrent. A little farther on was the
moving mass of glassy brown water which eddied rhythmically along the bank and round the shallows. Farther still,
water, banks, and cloud all merged together in impenetrable
gloom. Along the surface of the water floated black
shadows, in which the experienced eyes of the Cossack
detected trees carried down by the current. Only very rarely
sheet-lightning, mirrored in the water as in a black glass,
disclosed the sloping bank opposite. The rhythmic sounds
of night—the rustling of the reeds, the snoring of the
Cossacks, the hum of mosquitoes, and the rushing water—
were every now and then broken by a shot fired in the dis-

tance, or by the gurgling of water when a piece of bank slipped down, the splash of a big fish, or the crashing of an animal breaking through the thick undergrowth in the wood. Once an owl flew past along the Térek, flapping one wing against the other rhythmically at every second beat. Just above the Cossack's head it turned towards the wood, and then, striking its wings no longer after every other flap but at every flap, it flew to an old plane tree where it rustled about for a long time before settling down among the branches. At every one of these unexpected sounds the watching Cossack listened intently, straining his hearing, and screwing up his eyes while he deliberately felt for his musket.

The greater part of the night was past. The black cloud that had moved westward revealed the clear starry sky from under its torn edge, and the golden upturned crescent of the moon shone above the mountains with a reddish light. The cold began to be penetrating. Nazárka awoke, spoke a little, and fell asleep again. Lukáshka, feeling bored, got up, drew the knife from his dagger-handle, and began to fashion his stick into a ramrod. His head was full of the Chéchens who lived over there in the mountains, and of how their brave lads came across and were not afraid of the Cossacks, and might even now be crossing the river at some other spot. He thrust himself out of his hiding-place and looked along the river but could see nothing. And as he continued looking out at intervals upon the river and at the opposite bank, now dimly distinguishable from the water in the faint moonlight, he no longer thought about the Chéchens but only of when it would be time to wake his comrades, and of going home to the village. In the village he imagined Dunáyka, his "little soul," as the Cossacks call a man's mistress, and thought of her with vexation. Silvery mists, a sign of coming morning, glittered white above the water, and not far from him young eagles were whistling and flapping their wings. At last the crowing of a cock reached him from the distant village, followed by the long-sustained note of another, which was again answered by yet other voices.

"Time to wake them," thought Lukáshka, who had finished his ramrod and felt his eyes growing heavy. Turning to his comrades he managed to make out which pair of legs belonged to whom, when it suddenly seemed to him that he heard something splash on the other side of the Térek. He turned again towards the horizon beyond the hills, where day was breaking under the upturned crescent, glanced at the outline of the opposite bank, at the Térek, and at the now distinctly visible driftwood upon it. For one instant it seemed to him that he was moving and that the Térek with the drifting wood remained stationary. Again he peered out. One large black log with a branch particularly attracted his attention. The tree was floating in a strange way right down the middle of the stream, neither rocking nor whirling. It even appeared not to be floating altogether with the current, but to be crossing it in the direction of the shallows. Lukáshka stretching out his neck watched it intently. The tree floated to the shallows, stopped, and shifted in a peculiar manner. Lukáshka thought he saw an arm stretched out from beneath the tree. "Supposing I killed an *abrek* all by myself!" he thought and seized his gun with a swift, unhurried movement, putting up his gun-rest, placing the gun upon it, and holding it noiselessly in position. Cocking the trigger, with bated breath he took aim, still peering out intently. "I won't wake them," he thought. But his heart began beating so fast that he remained motionless, listening. Suddenly the trunk gave a plunge and again began to float across the stream towards our bank. "Only not to miss . . ." thought he, and now by the faint light of the moon he caught a glimpse of a Tartar's head in front of the floating wood. He aimed straight at the head which appeared to be quite near—just at the end of his rifle's barrel. He glanced across. "Right enough it is an *abrek*!" he thought joyfully, and suddenly rising to his knees he again took aim. Having found the sight, barely visible at the end of the long rifle, he said: "In the name of the Father and of the Son," in the Cossack way learnt in his childhood, and pulled the trigger. A flash of lightning lit up for an instant the reeds and the water, and the sharp, abrupt report of the shot was carried across the river, changing into a prolonged roll somewhere in the far distance. The piece of driftwood now floated not across, but with the current, rocking and whirling.

"Stop, I say!" exclaimed Ergushóv, seizing his musket

and raising himself behind the log near which he was lying.

"Shut up, you devil!" whispered Lukáshka, grinding his teeth. *"Abreks!"*

"Whom have you shot?" asked Nazárka. "Who was it, Lukáshka?"

Lukáshka did not answer. He was reloading his gun and watching the floating wood. A little way off it stopped on a sand-bank, and from behind it something large that rocked in the water came into view.

"What did you shoot? Why don't you speak?" insisted the Cossacks.

"Abreks, I tell you!" said Lukáshka.

"Don't humbug! Did the gun go off?"

"I've killed an *abrek,* that's what I fired at," muttered Lukáshka in a voice choked by emotion, as he jumped to his feet. "A man was swimming . . ." he said, pointing to the sand-bank. "I killed him. Just look there."

"Have done with your humbugging!" said Ergushóv again, rubbing his eyes.

"Have done with what? Look there," said Lukáshka, seizing him by the shoulders and pulling him with such force that Ergushóv groaned.

He looked in the direction in which Lukáshka pointed and discerning a body immediately changed his tone.

"O Lord! But I say, more will come! I tell you the truth," said he softly and began examining his musket. "That was a scout swimming across: either the others are here already or are not far off on the other side— I tell you for sure!"

Lukáshka was unfastening his belt and taking off his Circassian coat.

"What are you up to, you idiot?" exclaimed Ergushóv. "Only show yourself and you're lost all for nothing, I tell you true! If you've killed him he won't escape. Let me have a little powder for my musket-pan—you have some? Nazárka, you go back to the cordon and look alive; but don't go along the bank or you'll be killed,—I tell you true."

"Catch me going alone! Go yourself!" said Nazárka angrily.

Having taken off his coat, Lukáshka went down to the bank.

"Don't go in, I tell you!" said Ergushóv, putting some powder on the pan. "Look, he's not moving. I can see. It's nearly morning; wait till they come from the cordon. You go, Nazárka. You're afraid! Don't be afraid, I tell you."

"Luke, I say, Lukáshka! Tell us how you did it!" said Nazárka.

Lukáshka changed his mind about going into the water just then. "Go quick to the cordon and I will watch. Tell the Cossacks to send out the patrol. If the *abreks* are on this side they must be caught," said he.

"That's what I say. They'll get off," said Ergushóv, rising. "True, they must be caught!"

Ergushóv and Nazárka rose and, crossing themselves, started off for the cordon—not along the river bank but breaking their way through the brambles to reach a path in the wood.

"Now mind, Lukáshka—they may cut you down here, so you'd best keep a sharp look-out, I tell you!"

"Go along; I know," muttered Lukáshka; and having examined his gun again he sat down behind the log.

He remained alone and sat gazing at the shallows and listening for the Cossacks; but it was some distance to the cordon and he was tormented by impatience. He kept thinking that the other *abreks* who were with the one he had killed would escape. He was vexed with the *abreks* who were going to escape just as he had been with the boar that had escaped the evening before. He glanced round and at the opposite bank, expecting every moment to see a man, and having arranged his gun-rest he was ready to fire. The idea that he might himself be killed never entered his head.

IX

It was growing light. The Chéchen's body which was gently rocking in the shallow water was now clearly visible. Suddenly the reeds rustled not far from Luke and he heard steps and saw the feathery tops of the reeds moving. He set his gun at full cock and muttered: "In the name of the Father and of the Son," but when the cock clicked the sound of steps ceased.

"Hullo, Cossacks! Don't kill your Daddy!" said a deep bass voice calmly; and moving the reeds apart Daddy Eróshka came up close to Luke.

"I very nearly killed you, by God I did!" said Lukáshka.

"What have you shot?" asked the old man.

His sonorous voice resounded through the wood and downward along the river, suddenly dispelling the mysterious quiet of night around the Cossack. It was as if everything had suddenly become lighter and more distinct.

"There now, Uncle, you have not seen anything, but I've killed a beast," said Lukáshka, uncocking his gun and getting up with unnatural calmness.

The old man was staring intently at the white back, now clearly visible, against which the Térek rippled.

"He was swimming with a log on his back. I spied him out! . . . Look there. There! He's got blue trousers, and a gun I think. . . . Do you see?" inquired Luke.

"How can one help seeing?" said the old man angrily, and a serious and stern expression appeared on his face. "You've killed a brave," he said, apparently with regret.

"Well, I sat here and suddenly saw something dark on the other side. I spied him when he was still over there. It was as if a man had come there and fallen in. Strange! And a piece of driftwood, a good-sized piece, comes floating, not with the stream but across it; and what do I see but a head appearing from under it! Strange! I stretched out of the reeds but could see nothing; then I rose and he must have heard, the beast, and crept out into the shallow and looked about. 'No, you don't!' I said, as soon as he landed and looked round, 'you won't get away!' Oh, there was something choking me! I got my gun ready but did not stir, and looked out. He waited a little and then swam out again; and when he came into the moonlight I could see his whole back. 'In the name of the Father and of the Son and of the Holy Ghost' . . . and through the smoke I see him struggling. He moaned, or so it seemed to me. 'Ah,' I thought, 'the Lord be thanked, I've killed him!' And when he drifted on to the sand-bank I could see him distinctly: he tried to get up but couldn't. He struggled a bit and then lay down. Everything could be seen. Look, he does not move—he must be dead! The Cossacks have gone back to the cordon in case there should be any more of them."

"And so you got him!" said the old man. "He is far away now, my lad!" And again he shook his head sadly.

Just then the sound reached them of breaking bushes and the loud voices of Cossacks approaching along the bank on horseback and on foot. "Are you bringing the skiff?" shouted Lukáshka.

"You're a trump, Luke! Lug it to the bank!" shouted one of the Cossacks.

Without waiting for the skiff Lukáshka began to undress, keeping an eye all the while on his prey.

"Wait a bit, Nazárka is bringing the skiff," shouted the corporal.

"You fool! Maybe he is alive and only pretending! Take your dagger with you!" shouted another Cossack.

"Get along," cried Luke, pulling off his trousers. He quickly undressed and, crossing himself, jumped, plunging with a splash into the river. Then with long strokes of his white arms, lifting his back high out of the water and breathing deeply, he swam across the current of the Térek towards the shallows. A crowd of Cossacks stood on the bank talking loudly. Three horsemen rode off to patrol. The skiff appeared round a bend. Lukáshka stood up on the sand-bank, leaned over the body, and gave it a couple of shakes. "Quite dead!" he shouted in a shrill voice.

The Chéchen had been shot in the head. He had on a pair of blue trousers, a shirt, and a Circassian coat, and a gun and dagger were tied to his back. Above all these a large branch was tied, and it was this which at first had misled Lukáshka.

"What a carp you've landed!" cried one of the Cossacks who had assembled in a circle, as the body, lifted out of the skiff, was laid on the bank, pressing down the grass.

"How yellow he is!" said another.

"Where have our fellows gone to search? I expect the

rest of them are on the other bank. If this one had not been a scout he would not have swum that way. Why else should he swim alone?" said a third.

"Must have been a smart one to offer himself before the others; a regular brave!" said Lukáshka mockingly, shivering as he wrung out his clothes that had got wet on the bank.

"His beard is dyed and cropped."

"And he has tied a bag with a coat in it to his back."

"That would make it easier for him to swim," said some one.

"I say, Lukáshka," said the corporal, who was holding the dagger and gun taken from the dead man. "Keep the dagger for yourself and the coat too; but I'll give you three rubles for the gun. You see it has a hole in it," said he, blowing into the muzzle. "I want it just for a souvenir."

Lukáshka did not answer. Evidently this sort of begging vexed him but he knew it could not be avoided.

"See, what a devil!" said he, frowning and throwing down the Chéchen's coat. "If at least it were a good coat, but it's a mere rag."

"It'll do to fetch firewood in," said one of the Cossacks.

"Mósev, I'll go home," said Lukáshka, evidently forgetting his vexation and wishing to get some advantage out of having to give a present to his superior.

"All right, you may go!"

"Take the body beyond the cordon, lads," said the corporal, still examining the gun, "and put a shelter over him from the sun. Perhaps they'll send from the mountains to ransom it."

"It isn't hot yet," said someone.

"And supposing a jackal tears him? Would that be well?" remarked another Cossack.

"We'll set a watch; if they should come to ransom him it won't do for him to have been torn."

"Well, Lukáshka, whatever you do you must stand a pail of vodka for the lads," said the corporal gaily.

"Of course! That's the custom," chimed in the Cossacks. "See what luck God has sent you! Without ever having seen anything of the kind before, you've killed a brave!"

"Buy the dagger and coat and don't be stingy, and I'll

let you have the trousers too," said Lukáshka. "They're too tight for me; he was a thin devil."

One Cossack bought the coat for a ruble and another gave the price of two pails of vodka for the dagger.

"Drink, lads! I'll stand you a pail!" said Luke. "I'll bring it myself from the village."

"And cut up the trousers into kerchiefs for the girls!" said Nazárka.

The Cossacks burst out laughing.

"Have done laughing!" said the corporal. "And take the body away. Why have you put the nasty thing by the hut?"

"What are you standing there for? Haul him along, lads!" shouted Lukáshka in a commanding voice to the Cossacks, who reluctantly took hold of the body, obeying him as though he were their chief. After dragging the body along for a few steps the Cossacks let fall the legs, which dropped with a lifeless jerk, and stepping apart they then stood silent for a few moments. Nazárka came up and straightened the head, which was turned to one side so that the round wound above the temple and the whole of the dead man's face were visible. "See what a mark he has made right in the brain," he said. "He won't get lost. His owners will always know him!" No one answered, and again the Angel of Silence flew over the Cossacks.

The sun had risen high and its diverging beams were lighting up the dewy grass. Near by, the Térek murmured in the awakened wood and, greeting the morning, the pheasants called to one another. The Cossacks stood still and silent around the dead man, gazing at him. The brown body, with nothing on but the wet blue trousers held by a girdle over the sunken stomach, was well shaped and handsome. The muscular arms lay stretched straight out by his sides; the blue, freshly shaven, round head with the clotted wound on one side of it was thrown back. The smooth tanned forehead contrasted sharply with the shaven part of the head. The open glassy eyes with lowered pupils stared upwards, seeming to gaze past everything. Under the red trimmed moustache the fine lips, drawn at the corners, seemed stiffened into a smile of good-natured subtle raillery. The fingers of the small hands covered with red hairs were bent inward, and the nails were dyed red.

Lukáshka had not yet dressed. He was wet. His neck

was redder and his eyes brighter than usual, his broad jaws twitched, and from his healthy body a hardly perceptible steam rose in the fresh morning air.

"He too was a man!" he muttered, evidently admiring the corpse.

"Yes, if you had fallen into his hands you would have had short shrift," said one of the Cossacks.

The Angel of Silence had taken wing. The Cossacks began bustling about and talking. Two of them went to cut brushwood for a shelter; others strolled towards the cordon. Luke and Nazárka ran to get ready to go to the village.

Half an hour later they were both on their way homewards, talking incessantly and almost running through the dense woods which separated the Térek from the village.

"Mind, don't tell her I sent you, but just go and find out if her husband is at home," Luke was saying in his shrill voice.

"And I'll go round to Yámka too," said the devoted Nazárka. "We'll have a spree, shall we?"

"When should we have one if not to-day?" replied Luke.

When they reached the village the two Cossacks drank and lay down to sleep till evening.

X

On the third day after the events just described, two companies of a Caucasian infantry regiment arrived at the Cossack village of Novomlínsk. The horses had been unharnessed and the companies' wagons were standing in the square. The cooks had dug a pit, and the logs gathered from various yards (where they had not been sufficiently securely stored) were now cooking the food; the pay-sergeants were settling accounts with the soldiers. The Service Corps men were driving piles in the ground to which to tie the horses, and the quartermasters were going about the streets just as if they were at home, showing officers and men to their quarters. Here were green ammunition boxes in a line, the company's carts, horses, and cauldrons in which buckwheat porridge was being cooked. Here were the captain and the lieutenant and the sergeant-major, Onísim Mikháylovich, and all this was in the Cossack village where it was reported that the companies were ordered to take up their quarters: therefore they were at home here. But why they were stationed there, who the Cossacks were, and whether they wanted the troops to be there, and whether they were Old Believers[1] or not—was all quite immaterial. Having received their pay and been dismissed, tired out and covered with dust, the soldiers noisily and in disorder, like a swarm of bees about to settle, spread over the squares and streets; quite regardless of the Cossacks' ill will, chattering merrily and with their muskets clinking, by twos and threes they entered the huts and hung up their accoutrements, unpacked their bags, and bantered the women. At their favourite spot, round the porridge-cauldrons, a large group of soldiers assembled and with little pipes between their teeth they gazed, now at the smoke which rose into the hot sky, becoming visible when it thickened into white clouds as it rose, and now at the camp fires which were quivering in the pure air like molten glass, and bantered and made fun of the Cossack men and women because they do not live at all like Russians. In all the yards one could see soldiers and hear their laughter and the exasperated and shrill cries of Cossack women defending their houses and refusing to give the soldiers water or cooking utensils. Little boys and girls, clinging to their mothers and to each other, followed all the movements of the troopers (never before seen by them) with frightened curiosity or ran after them at a respectful distance. The old Cossacks came out silently and dismally and sat on the earthen embankments of their huts and watched the soldiers' activity with an air of leaving it all to the will of God without understanding what would come of it.

Olénin, who had joined the Caucasian Army as a cadet three months before, was quartered in one of the best houses in the village, the house of the cornet, Elias Vasílich—that is to say at Granny Ulítka's.

---

[1] As already mentioned, the Old Believers, among other peculiarities, had a strong religious disapproval of the use of tobacco ("Not that which goeth into the mouth defileth a man; but that which cometh out of the mouth, this defileth a man." Matt. xv. 11). This made the presence of Russian soldiers, who smoke, particularly objectionable to Old Believers.

"Goodness knows what it will be like, Dmítri Andréich," said the panting Vanyúsha to Olénin, who, dressed in a Circassian coat and mounted on a Kabardá horse which he had bought in Gróznoe, was after a five-hours' march gaily entering the yard of the quarters assigned to him.

"Why, what's the matter?" he asked, caressing his horse and looking merrily at the perspiring, dishevelled, and worried Vanyúsha, who had arrived with the baggage wagons and was unpacking.

Olénin looked quite a different man. In place of his clean-shaven lips and chin he had a youthful moustache and a small beard. Instead of a sallow complexion, the result of nights turned into day, his cheeks, his forehead, and the skin behind his ears were now red with healthy sunburn. In place of a clean new black suit he wore a dirty white Circassian coat with a deeply pleated skirt, and he bore arms. Instead of a freshly starched collar, his neck was tightly clasped by the red band of his silk *beshmet*. He wore Circassian dress but did not wear it well, and anyone would have known him for a Russian and not a Tartar brave. It was the thing—but not the real thing. But for all that, his whole person breathed health, joy, and satisfaction.

"Yes, it seems funny to you," said Vanyúsha, "but just try to talk to these people yourself: they set themselves against one and there's an end of it. You can't get as much as a word out of them." Vanyúsha angrily threw down a pail on the threshold. "Somehow they don't seem like Russians."

"You should speak to the Chief of the Village!"

"But I don't know where he lives," said Vanyúsha in an offended tone.

"Who has upset you so?" asked Olénin, looking round.

"The devil only knows. Faugh! There is no real master here. They say he has gone to some kind of *kriga*,[2] and the old woman is a real devil. God preserve us!" answered Vanyúsha, putting his hands to his head. "How we shall live here I don't know. They are worse than Tartars, I do declare—though they consider themselves Christians! A Tartar is bad enough, but all the same he is more noble. Gone to the *kriga* indeed! What this *kriga* they have in-

---

[2] A *kriga* is a place on the river-bank fenced in for fishing.

vented is, I don't know!" concluded Vanyúsha and turned aside.

"It's not as it is in the serfs' quarters at home, eh?" chaffed Olénin without dismounting.

"Please sir, may I have your horse?" said Vanyúsha, evidently perplexed by this new order of things but resigning himself to his fate.

"So a Tartar is more noble, eh, Vanyúsha?" repeated Olénin, dismounting and slapping the saddle.

"Yes, you're laughing! You think it funny," muttered Vanyúsha angrily.

"Come, don't be angry, Vanyúsha," replied Olénin, still smiling. "Wait a minute, I'll go and speak to the people of the house; you'll see I shall arrange everything. You don't know what a jolly life we shall have here. Only don't get upset."

Vanyúsha did not answer. Screwing up his eyes he looked contemptuously after his master and shook his head. Vanyúsha regarded Olénin as only his master, and Olénin regarded Vanyúsha as only his servant, and they would both have been much surprised if anyone had told them that they were friends, as they really were without knowing it themselves. Vanyúsha had been taken into his proprietor's house when he was only eleven and when Olénin was the same age. When Olénin was fifteen he gave Vanyúsha lessons for a time and taught him to read French, of which the latter was inordinately proud; and when in specially good spirits he still let off French words, always laughing stupidly when he did so.

Olénin ran up the steps of the porch and pushed open the door of the hut. Maryánka, wearing nothing but a pink smock, as all Cossack women do in the house, jumped away from the door, frightened, and pressing herself against the wall covered the lower part of her face with the broad sleeve of her Tartar smock. Having opened the door wider, Olénin in the semi-darkness of the passage saw the whole tall shapely figure of the young Cossack girl. With the quick and eager curiosity of youth he involuntarily noticed the firm maidenly form revealed by the fine print smock, and the beautiful black eyes fixed on him with childlike terror and wild curiosity. "This is *she*," thought Olénin. "But there will be many others like her" came at once into his head, and he opened the inner door. Old Granny Ulítka, also dressed only in a smock, was stooping with her back turned to him, sweeping the floor.

"Good-day to you, Mother! I've come about my lodgings," he began.

The Cossack woman, without unbending, turned her severe but still handsome face towards him.

"What have you come here for? Want to mock at us, eh? I'll teach you to mock; may the black plague seize you!" she shouted, looking askance from under her frowning brow at the new-comer.

Olénin had at first imagined that the way-worn, gallant Caucasian Army (of which he was a member) would be everywhere received joyfully, and especially by the Cossacks, our comrades in the war, and he therefore felt perplexed by this reception. Without losing presence of mind, however, he tried to explain that he meant to pay for his lodgings, but the old woman would not give him a hearing.

"What have you come for? Who wants a pest like you, with your scraped face? You just wait a bit; when the master returns he'll show you your place. I don't want your dirty money! A likely thing—just as if we had never seen any! You'll stink the house out with your beastly tobacco and want to put it right with money! Think we've never seen a pest! May you be shot in your bowels and your heart!" shrieked the old woman in a piercing voice, interrupting Olénin.

"It seems Vanyúsha was right!" thought Olénin. "A Tartar would be nobler," and followed by Granny Ulítka's abuse he went out of the hut. As he was leaving, Maryánka, still wearing only her pink smock, but with her forehead covered down to her eyes by a white kerchief, suddenly slipped out from the passage past him. Pattering rapidly down the steps with her bare feet she ran from the porch, stopped, and looking round hastily with laughing eyes at the young man, vanished round the corner of the hut.

Her firm youthful step, the untamed look of the eyes glistening from under the white kerchief, and the firm stately build of the young beauty struck Olénin even more powerfully than before. "Yes, it must be *she*," he thought, and troubling his head still less about the lodgings, he kept looking round at Maryánka as he approached Vanyúsha.

"There you see, the girl too is quite savage, just like a wild filly!" said Vanyúsha, who though still busy with the luggage wagon had now cheered up a bit. "*La fame!*" he added in a loud triumphant voice and burst out laughing.

XI

Towards evening the master of the house returned from his fishing and, having learnt that the cadet would pay for the lodging, pacified the old woman and satisfied Vanyúsha's demands.

Everything was arranged in the new quarters. Their hosts moved into the winter hut and let their summer hut to the cadet for three rubles a month. Olénin had something to eat and went to sleep. Towards evening he woke up, washed and made himself tidy, dined, and having lit a cigarette sat down by the window that looked onto the street. It was cooler. The slanting shadow of the hut with its ornamental gables fell across the dusty road and even bent upwards at the base of the wall of the house opposite. The steep reed-thatched roof of that house shone in the rays of the setting sun. The air grew fresher. Everything was peaceful in the village. The soldiers had settled down and become quiet. The herds had not yet been driven home and the people had not returned from their work.

Olénin's lodging was situated almost at the end of the village. At rare intervals, from somewhere far beyond the Térek in those parts whence Olénin had just come (the Chéchen or the Kumýtsk plain), came muffled sounds of firing. Olénin was feeling very well contented after three months of bivouac life. His newly washed face was fresh and his powerful body clean (an unaccustomed sensation after the campaign) and in all his rested limbs he was conscious of a feeling of tranquillity and strength. His mind, too, felt fresh and clear. He thought of the campaign and of past dangers. He remembered that he had faced them no worse than other men and that he was accepted as a comrade among valiant Caucasians. His Moscow recollections were left behind Heaven knows how far! The old life was wiped out and a quite new life had begun in which there were as yet no mistakes. Here as a new man among new men he could gain a new and good reputation. He was conscious of a youthful and unreasoning joy of life. Looking now out of the window at the boys spinning their tops in the shadow of the house, now round his neat new lodging, he thought how pleasantly he would settle down to this new Cossack village life. Now and then he glanced at the mountains and the blue sky, and an appreciation of the solemn grandeur of nature mingled with his reminiscences and dreams. His new life had begun, not as he imagined it would when he left Moscow, but unexpectedly well. "The mountains, the mountains, the mountains!" they permeated all his thoughts and feelings.

"He's kissed his dog and licked the jug! . . . Daddy Eróshka has kissed his dog!" suddenly the little Cossacks who had been spinning their tops under the window shouted, looking towards the side street. "He's drunk his bitch, and his dagger!" shouted the boys, crowding together and stepping backwards.

These shouts were addressed to Daddy Eróshka, who with his gun on his shoulder and some pheasants hanging at his girdle was returning from his shooting expedition.

"I have done wrong, lads, I have!" he said, vigorously swinging his arms and looking up at the windows on both sides of the street. "I have drunk the bitch; it was wrong," he repeated, evidently vexed but pretending not to care.

Olénin was surprised by the boys' behaviour towards the old hunter but was still more struck by the expressive, intelligent face and the powerful build of the man whom they called Daddy Eróshka.

"Here Daddy, here Cossack!" he called. "Come here!"

The old man looked into the window and stopped.

"Good evening, good man," he said, lifting his little cap off his cropped head.

"Good evening, good man," replied Olénin. "What is it the youngsters are shouting at you?"

Daddy Eróshka came up to the window. "Why, they're teasing the old man. No matter, I like it. Let them joke about their old daddy," he said with those firm musical intonations with which old and venerable people speak. "Are you an army commander?" he added.

"No, I am a cadet. But where did you kill those pheasants?" asked Olénin.

"I dispatched these three hens in the forest," answered the old man, turning his broad back towards the window to show the hen pheasants which were hanging with their heads tucked into his belt and staining his coat with blood. "Haven't you seen any?" he asked. "Take a brace if you like! Here you are," and he handed two of the pheasants in at the window. "Are you a sportsman yourself?" he asked.

"I am. During the campaign I killed four myself."

"Four? What a lot!" said the old man sarcastically. "And are you a drinker? Do you drink *chikhir*?"

"Why not? I like a drink."

"Ah, I see you are a trump! We shall be *kunaks*,[1] you and I," said Daddy Eróshka.

"Step in," said Olénin. "We'll have a drop of *chikhir*."

"I might as well," said the old man, "but take the pheasants." The old man's face showed that he liked the cadet. He had seen at once that he could get free drinks from him, and that therefore it would be all right to give him a brace of pheasants.

Soon Daddy Eróshka's figure appeared in the doorway of the hut, and it was only then that Olénin became fully conscious of the enormous size and sturdy build of this man, whose red-brown face with its perfectly white broad beard was all furrowed by deep lines produced by age and toil. For an old man, the muscles of his legs, arms, and shoulders were quite exceptionally large and prominent. There were deep scars on his head under the short-cropped hair. His thick sinewy neck was covered with deep intersecting folds like a bull's. His horny hands were bruised and scratched. He stepped lightly and easily over the threshold, unslung his gun and placed it in a corner, and casting a rapid glance round the room noted the value of the goods and chattels deposited in the hut, and with out-turned toes stepped softly, in his sandals of raw hide, into the middle of the room. He brought with him a penetrating but not unpleasant smell of *chikhir* wine, vodka, gunpowder, and congealed blood.

Daddy Eróshka bowed down before the icons, smoothed

[1] *Kunak*, a sworn friend for whose sake no sacrifice is too great.

his beard, and approaching Olénin held out his thick brown hand. "*Koshkildy*," said he. "That is Tartar for 'Good-day' —'Peace be unto you,' it means in their tongue."

"*Koshkildy*, I know," answered Olénin, shaking hands.

"Eh, but you don't, you won't know the right order! Fool!" said Daddy Eríshka, shaking his head reproachfully. "If anyone says '*Koshkildy*' to you, you must say '*Allah rasi bo sun*'—that is, 'God save you.' That's the way, my dear fellow, and not '*Koshkildy*.' But I'll teach you all about it. We had a fellow here, Elias Mosévich, one of your Russians, he and I were *kunaks*. He was a trump, a drunkard, a thief, a sportsman—and what a sportsman! I taught him everything."

"And what will you teach me?" asked Olénin, who was becoming more and more interested in the old man.

"I'll take you hunting and teach you to fish. I'll show you Chéchens and find a girl for you, if you like—even that! That's the sort I am! I'm a wag!"—and the old man laughed. "I'll sit down. I'm tired. *Karga?*" he added inquiringly.

"And what does '*Karga*' mean?" asked Olénin.

"Why, that means 'All right' in Georgian. But I say it just so. It is a way I have, it's my favourite word. *Karga, Karga*. I say it just so; in fun I mean. Well, lad, won't you order the *chikhir*? You've got an orderly, haven't you? Hey, Iván!" shouted the old man. "All your soldiers are Ivàns. Is yours Iván?"

"True enough, his name is Iván—Vanyúsha.[2] Here Vanyúsha! Please get some *chikhir* from our landlady and bring it here."

"Iván or Vanyúsha, that's all one. Why are all your soldiers Ivàns? Iván, old fellow," said the old man, "You tell them to give you some from the barrel they have begun. They have the best *chikhir* in the village. But don't give more than thirty kopeks for the quart, mind, because that witch would be only too glad. . . . Our people are anathema people; stupid people," Daddy Eróshka continued in a confidential tone after Vanyúsha had gone out. "They do not look upon you as on men, you are worse than a Tartar in their eyes. 'Worldly Russians' they say. But as

[2] Vanyúsha is a diminutive form of Iván.

for me, though you are a soldier you are still a man and have a soul in you. Isn't that right? Elias Mosévich was a soldier, yet what a treasure of a man he was! Isn't that so, my dear fellow? That's why our people don't like me; but I don't care! I'm a merry fellow, and I like everybody. I'm Eróshka; yes, my dear fellow."

And the old Cossack patted the young man affectionately on the shoulder.

XII

Vanyúsha, who meanwhile had finished his housekeeping arrangements and had even been shaved by the company's barber and had pulled his trousers out of his high boots as a sign that the company was stationed in comfortable quarters, was in excellent spirits. He looked attentively but not benevolently at Eróshka, as at a wild beast he had never seen before, shook his head at the floor which the old man had dirtied, and, having taken two bottles from under a bench, went to the landlady.

"Good evening, kind people," he said, having made up his mind to be very gentle. "My master has sent me to get some *chikhir*, will you draw some for me, good folk?"

The old woman gave no answer. The girl, who was arranging the kerchief on her head before a little Tartar mirror, looked round at Vanyúsha in silence.

"I'll pay money for it, honoured people," said Vanyúsha, jingling the coppers in his pocket. "Be kind to us and we too will be kind to you," he aded.

"How much?" asked the old woman abruptly. "A quart."

"Go, my own, draw some for them," said Granny Ulítka to her daughter. "Take it from the cask that's begun, my precious."

The girl took the keys and a decanter and went out of the hut with Vanyúsha.

"Tell me, who is that young woman?" asked Olénin, pointing to Maryánka, who was passing the window. The old man winked and nudged the young man with his elbow.

"Wait a bit," said he and reached out of the window. "Khm," he coughed and bellowed, "Maryánka dear. Hallo, Maryánka, my girlie, won't you love me, darling? I'm a wag," he added in a whisper to Olénin. The girl, not turn-

ing her head and swinging her arms regularly and vigorously, passed the window with the peculiarly smart and
bold gait of a Cossack woman and only turned her dark
shaded eyes slowly towards the old man.

"Love me and you'll be happy," shouted Eróshka, winking, and he looked questioningly at the cadet.

"I'm a fine fellow, I'm a wag!" he added. "She's a
regular queen, that girl. Eh?"

"She is lovely," said Olénin. "Call her here!"

"No, no," said the old man. "For that one a match
is being arranged with Lukáshka, Luke, a fine Cossack, a
brave, who killed an *abrek* the other day. I'll find you a
better one. I'll find you one that will be all dressed up in
silk and silver. Once I've said it I'll do it. I'll get you a
regular beauty!"

"You, an old man—and say such things," replied Olénin.
"Why, it's a sin!"

"A sin? Where's the sin?" said the old man emphatically.
"A sin to look at a nice girl? A sin to have some fun with
her? Or is it a sin to love her? Is that so in your parts? . . .
No, my dear fellow, it's not a sin, it's salvation! God made
you and God made the girl too. He made it all; so it is no
sin to look at a nice girl. That's what she was made for; to
be loved and to give joy. That's how I judge it, my good
fellow."

Having crossed the yard and entered a cool dark store-
room filled with barrels, Maryánka went up to one of them
and repeating the usual prayer plunged a dipper into it.
Vanyúsha standing in the doorway smiled as he looked at
her. He thought it very funny that she had only a smock
on, close-fitting behind and tucked up in front, and still
funnier that she wore a necklace of silver coins. He thought
this quite un-Russian and that they would all laugh in the
serfs' quarters at home if they saw a girl like that. "*La fille
comme c'est très bien*, for a change," he thought. "I'll tell
that to my master."

"What are you standing in the light for, you devil!"
the girl suddenly shouted. "Why don't you pass me the
decanter!"

Having filled the decanter with cool red wine, Maryánka
handed it to Vanyúsha.

"Give the money to Mother," she said, pushing away the hand in which he held the money.

Vanyúsha laughed.

"Why are you so cross, little dear?" he said good-naturedly, irresolutely shuffling with his feet while the girl was covering the barrel.

·She began to laugh.

"And you! Are you kind?"

"We, my master and I, are very kind," Vanyúsha answered decidedly. "We are so kind that wherever we have stayed our hosts were always very grateful. It's because he's generous."

The girl stood listening.

"And is your master married?" she asked.

"No. The master is young and unmarried, because noble gentlemen can never marry young," said Vanyúsha didactically.

"A likely thing! See what a fed-up buffalo he is—and too young to marry! Is he the chief of you all?" she asked.

"My master is a cadet; that means he's not yet an officer, but he's more important than a general—he's an important man! Because not only our colonel, but the Tsar himself, knows him," proudly explained Vanyúsha. "We are not like those other beggars in the line regiment, and our papa himself was a Senator. He had more than a thousand serfs, all his own, and they send us a thousand rubles at a time. That's why everyone likes us. Another may be a captain but have no money. What's the use of that?"

"Go away. I'll lock up," said the girl, interrupting him.

Vanyúsha brought Olénin the wine and announced that "*La fille c'est tres joulie*," and, laughing stupidly, at once went out.

XIII

Meanwhile the tattoo had sounded in the village square. The people had returned from their work. The herd lowed as in clouds of golden dust it crowded at the village gate. The girls and the women hurried through the streets and yards, turning in their cattle. The sun had quite hidden itself behind the distant snowy peaks. One pale bluish shadow spread over land and sky. Above the darkened gardens stars just discernible were kindling, and the sounds were gradually hushed in the village. The cattle having been attended to and left for the night, the women came out and gathered at the corners of the streets and, cracking sunflower seeds with their teeth, settled down on the earthen embankments of the houses. Later on Maryánka, having finished milking the buffalo and the other two cows, also joined one of these groups.

The group consisted of several women and girls and one old Cossack man.

They were talking about the *abrek* who had been killed. The Cossack was narrating and the women questioning him.

"I expect he'll get a handsome reward," said one of the women.

"Of course. It's said that they'll send him a cross."

"Mósev did try to wrong him. Took the gun away from him, but the authorities at Kizlyár heard of it."

"A mean creature that Mósev is!"

"They say Lukáshka has come home," remarked one of the girls.

"He and Nazárka are merry-making at Yámka's." (Yámka was an unmarried, disreputable Cossack woman who kept an illicit pot-house.) "I heard say they had drunk half a pailful."

"What luck that Snatcher has," somebody remarked. "A real snatcher. But there's no denying he's a fine lad, smart enough for anything, a right-minded lad! His father was just such another, Daddy Kiryák was: he takes after his father. When he was killed the whole village howled. Look, there they are," added the speaker, pointing to the Cossacks who were coming down the street towards them. "And Ergushóv has managed to come along with them too! The drunkard!"

Lukáshka, Nazárka, and Ergushóv, having emptied half a pail of vodka, were coming towards the girls. The faces of all three, but especially that of the old Cossack, were redder than usual. Ergushóv was reeling and kept laughing and nudging Nazárka in the ribs.

"Why are you not singing?" he shouted to the girls. "Sing to our merry-making, I tell you!"

They were welcomed with the words, "Had a good day? Had a good day?"

"Why sing? It's not a holiday," said one of the women. "You're tight, so you go and sing."

Ergushóv roared with laughter and nudged Nazárka. "You'd better sing. And I'll begin too. I'm clever, I tell you."

"Are you asleep, fair ones?" said Nazárka. "We've come from the cordon to drink your health. We've already drunk Lukáshka's health."

Lukáshka, when he reached the group, slowly raised his cap and stopped in front of the girls. His broad cheek-bones and neck were red. He stood and spoke softly and sedately, but in his tranquillity and sedateness there was more of animation and strength than in all Nazárka's loquacity and bustle. He reminded one of a playful colt that with a snort and a flourish of its tail suddenly stops short and stands as though nailed to the ground with all four feet. Lukáshka stood quietly in front of the girls, his eyes laughed, and he spoke but little as he glanced now at his drunken companions and now at the girls. When Maryánka joined the group he raised his cap with a firm deliberate movement, moved out of her way, and then stepped in front of her with one foot a little forward and with his thumbs in his belt, fingering his dagger. Maryánka answered his greeting with a leisurely bow of her head, settled down on the earth-bank, and took some seeds out of the bosom of her smock. Lukáshka, keeping his eyes fixed on Maryánka, slowly cracked seeds and spat out the shells. All were quiet when Maryánka joined the group.

"Have you come for long?" asked a woman, breaking the silence.

"Till to-morrow morning," quietly replied Lukáshka.

"Well, God grant you get something good," said the Cossack; "I'm glad of it, as I've just been saying."

"And I say so too," put in the tipsy Ergushóv, laughing. "What a lot of visitors have come," he added, pointing to a soldier who was passing by. "The soldiers' vodka is good—I like it."

"They've sent three of the devils to us," said one of the women. "Grandad went to the village Elders, but they say nothing can be done."

"Ah, ha! Have you met with trouble?" said Ergushóv.

"I expect they have smoked you out with their tobacco?" asked another woman. "Smoke as much as you like in the yard, I say, but we won't allow it inside the hut. Not if the Elder himself comes, I won't allow it. Besides, they may rob you. He's not quartered any of them on himself, no fear, that devil's son of an Elder."

"You don't like it?" Ergushóv began again.

"And I've also heard say that the girls will have to make the soldiers' beds and offer them *chikhir* and honey," said Nazárka, putting one foot forward and tilting his cap like Lukáshka.

Ergushóv burst into a roar of laughter, and seizing the girl nearest to him, he embraced her. "I tell you true."

"Now then, you black pitch!" squealed the girl. "I'll tell your old woman."

"Tell her," shouted he. "That's quite right what Nazárka says; a circular has been sent round. He can read, you know. Quite true!" And he began embracing the next girl.

"What are you up to, you beast?" squealed the rosy, round-faced Ústenka, laughing and lifting her arm to hit him.

The Cossack stepped aside and nearly fell.

"There, they say girls have no strength, and you nearly killed me."

"Get away, you black pitch, what devil has brought you from the cordon?" said Ústenka, and turning away from him she again burst out laughing. "You were asleep and missed the *abrek*, didn't you? Suppose he had done for you it would have been all the better."

"You'd have howled, I expect," said Nazárka, laughing.

"Howled! A likely thing."

"Just look, she doesn't care. She'd howl, Nazárka, eh? Would she?" said Ergushóv.

Lukáshka all this time had stood silently looking at Maryánka. His gaze evidently confused the girl.

"Well, Maryánka! I hear they've quartered one of the chiefs on you?" he said, drawing nearer.

Maryánka, as was her wont, waited before she replied and slowly raising her eyes looked at the Cossack. Lukáshka's eyes were laughing as if something special, apart from what was said, was taking place between himself and the girl.

"Yes, it's all right for them as they have two huts," replied an old woman on Maryánka's behalf, "but at Fómushkin's now they also have one of the chiefs quartered on them and they say one whole corner is packed full with his things, and the family have no room left. Was such a thing ever heard of as that they should turn a whole horde loose in the village?" she said. "And what the plague are they going to do here?"

"I've heard say they'll build a bridge across the Térek," said one of the girls.

"And I've been told that they will dig a pit to put the girls in because they don't love the lads," said Nazárka, approaching Ústenka; and he again made a whimsical gesture which set everybody laughing, and Ergushóv, passing by Maryánka, who was next in turn, began to embrace an old woman.

"Why don't you hug Maryánka? You should do it to each in turn," said Nazárka.

"No, my old one is sweeter," shouted the Cossack, kissing the struggling old woman.

"You'll throttle me," she screamed, laughing.

The tramp of regular footsteps at the other end of the street interrupted their laughter. Three soldiers in their cloaks, with their muskets on their shoulders, were marching in step to relieve guard by the ammunition wagon.

The corporal, an old cavalry man, looked angrily at the Cossacks and led his men straight along the road where Lukáshka and Nazárka were standing, so that they should have to get out of the way. Nazárka moved, but Lukáshka only screwed up his eyes and turned his broad back without moving from his place.

"People are standing here, so you go round," he muttered, half turning his head and tossing it contemptuously in the direction of the soldiers.

The soldiers passed by in silence, keeping step regularly along the dusty road.

Maryánka began laughing and all the other girls chimed in.

"What swells!" said Nazárka. "Just like long-skirted

choristers," and he walked a few steps down the road imitating the soldiers.

Again everyone broke into peals of laughter.

Lukáshka came slowly up to Maryánka.

"And where have you put up the chief?" he asked.

Maryánka thought for a moment.

"We've let him have the new hut," she said.

"And is he old or young," asked Lukáshka, sitting down beside her.

"Do you think I've asked?" answered the girl. "I went to get him some *chikhir* and saw him sitting at the window with Daddy Eróshka. Red-headed he seemed. They've brought a whole cartload of things."

And she dropped her eyes.

"Oh, how glad I am that I got leave from the cordon!" said Lukáshka, moving closer to the girl and looking straight in her eyes all the time.

"And have you come for long?" asked Maryánka, smiling slightly.

"Till the morning. Give me some sunflower seeds," he said, holding out his hand.

Maryánka now smiled outright and, unfastening the neckband of her smock, "Don't take them all," she said.

"Really I felt so dull all the time without you, I swear I did," he said in a calm, restrained whisper, helping himself to some seeds out of the bosom of the girl's smock, and stooping still closer over her he continued with laughing eyes to talk to her in low tones.

"I won't come, I tell you," Maryánka suddenly said aloud, leaning away from him.

"No really . . . what I wanted to say to you . . ." whispered Lukáshka. "By the Heavens! Do come!"

Maryánka shook her head but did so with a smile.

"Nursey Maryánka! Hallo Nursey! Mammy is calling! Supper time!" shouted Maryánka's little brother, running towards the group.

"I'm coming," replied the girl, "Go, my dear, go alone —I'll come in a minute."

Lukáshka rose and raised his cap.

"I expect I had better go home too, that will be best," he said, trying to appear unconcerned but hardly able to repress a smile, and he disappeared behind the corner of the house.

Meanwhile night had entirely enveloped the village. Bright stars were scattered over the dark sky. The streets became dark and empty. Nazárka remained with the women on the earth-bank and their laughter was still heard, but Lukáshka, having slowly moved away from the girls, crouched down like a cat and then suddenly started running lightly, holding his dagger to steady it: not homeward, however, but towards the cornet's house. Having passed two streets he turned into a lane and lifting the skirt of his coat sat down on the ground in the shadow of a fence. "A regular cornet's daughter!" he thought about Maryánka. "Won't even have a lark— the devil! But just wait a bit."

The approaching footsteps of a woman attracted his attention. He began listening and laughed all by himself. Maryánka with bowed head, striking the pales of the fences with a switch, was walking with rapid regular strides straight towards him. Lukáshka rose. Maryánka started and stopped.

"What an accursed devil! You frightened me! So you have not gone home?" she said, and laughed aloud.

Lukáshka put one arm round her and with the other hand raised her face. "What I wanted to tell you, by Heaven!"—his voice trembled and broke.

"What are you talking of, at night time!" answered Maryánka. "Mother is waiting for me, and you'd better go to your sweetheart."

And freeing herself from his arms she ran away a few steps. When she had reached the wattle fence of her home she stopped and turned to the Cossack who was running beside her and still trying to persuade her to stay a while with him.

"Well, what do you want to say, midnight-gadabout?" and she again began laughing.

"Don't laugh at me, Maryánka! By the Heaven! Well, what if I have a sweetheart? May the devil take her! Only say the word and now I'll love *you*—I'll do anything you wish. Here they are!" and he jingled the money in his pocket. "Now we can live splendidly. Others have pleasures, and I? I get no pleasure from you, Maryánka dear!"

The girl did not answer. She stood before him breaking her switch into little bits with a rapid movement of her fingers.

Lukáshka suddenly clenched his teeth and fists.

"And why keep waiting and waiting? Don't I love you, darling? You can do what you like with me," said he suddenly, frowning angrily and seizing both her hands.

The calm expression of Maryánka's face and voice did not change.

"Don't bluster, Lukáshka, but listen to me," she answered, not pulling away her hands but holding the Cossack at arm's length. "It's true I am a girl, but you listen to me! It does not depend on me, but if you love me I'll tell you this. Let go my hands, I'll tell you without. I'll marry you, but you'll never get any nonsense from me," said Maryánka without turning her face.

"What, you'll marry me? Marriage does not depend on us. Love me yourself, Maryánka dear," said Lukáshka, from sullen and furious becoming again gentle, submissive, and tender, and smiling as he looked closely into her eyes.

Maryánka clung to him and kissed him firmly on the lips.

"Brother dear!" she whispered, pressing him convulsively to her. Then, suddenly tearing herself away, she ran into the gate of her house without looking round.

In spite of the Cossack's entreaties to wait another minute to hear what he had to say, Maryánka did not stop.

"Go," she cried, "you'll be seen! I do believe that devil, our lodger, is walking about the yard."

"Cornet's daughter," thought Lukáshka, "She will marry me. Marriage is all very well, but you just love me!"

He found Nazárka at Yámka's house and after having a spree with him went to Dunáyka's house, where, in spite of her not being faithful to him, he spent the night.

XIV

It was quite true that Olénin had been walking about the yard when Maryánka entered the gate, and had heard

her say, "That devil, our lodger, is walking about." He
had spent that evening with Daddy Eróshka in the porch
of his new lodging. He had had a table, a samovar, wine,
and a candle brought out, and over a cup of tea and
a cigar he listened to the tales the old man told seated
on the threshold at his feet. Though the air was still,
the candle dripped and flickered: now lighting up the
post of the porch, now the table and crockery, now the
cropped white head of the old man. Moths circled round
the flame and, shedding the dust of their wings, fluttered
on the table and in the glasses, flew into the candle, flame,
and disappeared in the black space beyond. Olénin and
Eróshka had emptied five bottles of *chikhir*. Eróshka filled
the glasses every time, offering one to Olénin, drinking
his health, and talking untiringly. He told of Cossack life
in the old days: of his father, "The Broad," who alone had
carried on his back a boar's carcass weighing three
hundredweight and drank two pails of *chikhir* at one
sitting. He told of his own days and his chum Gírchik,
with whom during the plague he used to smuggle felt cloaks
across the Térek. He told how one morning he had killed
two deer, and about his "little soul" who used to run to
him at the cordon at night. He told all this so eloquently
and picturesquely that Olénin did not notice how time
passed. "Ah yes, my dear fellow, you did not know me
in my golden days; then I'd have shown you things.
To-day it's 'Eróshka licks the jug,' but then Eróshka was
famous in the whole regiment. Whose was the finest horse?
Who had a Gurda[1] sword? To whom should one go to
get a drink? With whom go on the spree? Who should
be sent to the mountains to kill Ahmet Khan? Why,
always Eróshka! Whom did the girls love? Always Eróshka
had to answer for it. Because I was a real brave: a drinker,
a thief (I used to seize herds of horses in the mountains), a singer; I was a master of every art! There are
no Cossacks like that nowadays. It's disgusting to look
at them. When they're that high (Eróshka held his hand
three feet from the ground) "they put on idiotic boots
and keep looking at them—that's all the pleasure they

---

[1] The swords and daggers most highly valued in the Caucasus are
called by the name of the maker—Gurda.

know. Or they'll drink themselves foolish, not like men but all wrong. And who was I? I was Eróshka, the thief; they knew me not only in this village but up in the mountains. Tartar princes, my *kunaks*, used to come to see me! I used to be everybody's *kunak*. If he was a Tartar—with an Armenian; a soldier—with a soldier; an officer—with an officer! I didn't care as long as he was a drinker. He says you should cleanse yourself from intercourse with the world, not drink with soldiers, not eat with a Tartar."

"Who says all that?" asked Olénin.

"Why, our teacher! But listen to a Mullah or a Tartar Cadi. He says, 'You unbelieving Giaours, why do you eat pig?' That shows that everyone has his own law. But I think it's all one. God has made everything for the joy of man. There is no sin in any of it. Take example from an animal. It lives in the Tartar's reeds or in ours. Wherever it happens to go, there is its home! Whatever God gives it, that it eats! But our people say we have to lick red-hot plates in hell for that. And I think it's all a fraud," he added after a pause.

"What is a fraud?" asked Olénin.

"Why, what the preachers say. We had an army captain in Chervlëna who was my *kunak*: a fine fellow just like me. He was killed in Chéchnya. Well, he used to say that the preachers invent all that out of their own heads. 'When you die the grass will grow on your grave and that's all!'" The old man laughed. "He was a desperate fellow."

"And how old are you?" asked Olénin.

"The Lord only knows! I must be about seventy. When a Tsaritsa reigned in Russia[2] I was no longer very small. So you can reckon it out. I must be seventy."

"Yes, you must, but you are still a fine fellow."

"Well, thank Heaven I am healthy, quite healthy, except that a woman, a witch, has harmed me. . . ."

"How?"

"Oh, just harmed me."

"And so when you die the grass will grow?" repeated Olénin.

[2] Catherine the Great died in 1799.

Eróshka evidently did not wish to express his thought clearly. He was silent for a while.

"And what did you think? Drink!" he shouted suddenly, smiling and handing Olénin some wine.

XV

"Well, what was I saying?" he continued, trying to remember. "Yes, that's the sort of man I am. I am a hunter. There is no hunter to equal me in the whole army. I will find and show you any animal and any bird, and what and where. I know it all! I have dogs, and two guns, and nets, and a screen and a hawk. I have everything, thank the Lord! If you are not bragging but are a real sportsman, I'll show you everything. Do you know what a man I am? When I have found a track—I know the animal. I know where he will lie down and where he'll drink or wallow. I make myself a perch and sit there all night watching. What's the good of staying at home? One only gets into mischief, gets drunk. And here women come and chatter, and boys shout at me—enough to drive one mad. It's a different matter when you go out at nightfall, choose yourself a place, press down the reeds and sit there and stay waiting, like a jolly fellow. One knows everything that goes on in the woods. One looks up at the sky: the stars move; you look at them and find out from them how the time goes. One looks round— the wood is rustling; one goes on waiting, now there comes a crackling—a boar comes to rub himself; one listens to hear the young eaglets screech and then the cocks give voice in the village, or the geese. When you hear the geese you know it is not yet midnight. And I know all about it! Or when a gun is fired somewhere far away, thoughts come to me. One thinks, who is that firing? Is it another Cossack like myself who has been watching for some animal? And has he killed it? Or only wounded it so that now the poor thing goes through the reeds smearing them with its blood all for nothing? I don't like that! Oh, how I dislike it! Why injure a beast? You fool, you fool! Or one thinks, 'Maybe an *abrek* has killed some silly little Cossack.' All this passes through one's mind. And once as I sat watching by the river I saw a cradle floating down. It was sound except for one corner which was broken off. Thoughts did come that time! I thought some of your soldiers, the devils, must have got into a Tartar village and seized the Chéchen women, and one of the devils has killed the little one: taken it by its legs, and hit its head against a wall. Don't they do such things? Sh! Men have no souls! And thoughts came to me that filled me with pity. I thought: they've thrown away the cradle and driven the wife out, and her brave has taken his gun and come across to our side to rob us. One watches and thinks. And when one hears a litter breaking through the thicket, something begins to knock inside one. Dear one, come this way! 'They'll scent me,' one thinks; and one sits and does not stir while one's heart goes dun! dun! dun! and simply lifts you. Once this spring a fine litter came near me, I saw something black. 'In the name of the Father and of the Son,' and I was just about to fire when she grunts to her pigs. 'Danger, children,' she says, 'there's a man here,' and off they all ran, breaking through the bushes. And she had been so close I could almost have bitten her."

"How could a sow tell her brood that a man was there?" asked Olénin.

"What do you think? You think the beast's a fool? No, he is wiser than a man though you do call him a pig! He knows everything. Take this for instance. A man will pass along your track and not notice it; but a pig as soon as it gets onto your track turns and runs at once: that shows there is wisdom in him, since he scents your smell and you don't. And there is this to be said too: you wish to kill it and it wishes to go about the woods alive. You have one law and it has another. It is a pig, but it is no worse than you—it too is God's creature. Ah, dear! Man is foolish, foolish, foolish!" The old man repeated this several times and then, letting his head drop, he sat thinking.

Olénin also became thoughtful and descending from the porch with his hands behind his back began pacing up and down the yard.

Eróshka, rousing himself, raised his head and began

gazing intently at the moths circling round the flickering flame of the candle and burning themselves in it.

"Fool, fool!" he said. "Where are you flying to? Fool, fool!" He rose and with his thick fingers began to drive away the moths.

"You'll burn, little fool! Fly this way, there's plenty of room." He spoke tenderly, trying to catch them delicately by their wings with his thick fingers and then letting them fly again. "You are killing yourself and I am sorry for you!"

He sat a long time chattering and sipping out of the bottle. Olénin paced up and down the yard. Suddenly he was struck by the sound of whispering outside the gate. Involuntarily holding his breath, he heard a woman's laughter, a man's voice, and the sound of a kiss. Intentionally rustling the grass under his feet he crossed to the opposite side of the yard, but after a while the wattle fence creaked. A Cossack in a dark Circassian coat and a white sheepskin cap passed along the other side of the fence (it was Luke), and a tall woman with a white kerchief on her head went past Olénin. "You and I have nothing to do with one another" was what Maryánka's firm step gave him to understand. He followed her with his eyes to the porch of the hut, and he even saw her through the window take off her kerchief and sit down. And suddenly a feeling of lonely depression and some vague longings and hopes, and envy of someone or other, overcame the young man's soul.

The last lights had been put out in the huts. The last sounds had died away in the village. The wattle fences and the cattle gleaming white in the yards, the roofs of the houses, and the stately poplars all seemed to be sleeping the labourers' healthy peaceful sleep. Only the incessant ringing voices of frogs from the damp distance reached the young man. In the east the stars were growing fewer and fewer and seemed to be melting in the increasing light, but overhead they were denser and deeper than before. The old man was dozing with his head on his hand. A cock crowed in the yard opposite, but Olénin still paced up and down thinking of something. The sound of a song sung by several voices reached him and he stepped up to the fence and listened. The voices of several young

Cossacks carolled a merry song, and one voice was distinguishable among them all by its firm strength.

"Do you know who is singing there?" said the old man, rousing himself. "It is the Brave, Lukáshka. He has killed a Chéchen and now he rejoices. And what is there to rejoice at? . . . The fool, the fool!"

"And have you ever killed people?" asked Olénin.

"You devil!" shouted the old man. "What are you asking? One must not talk so. It is a serious thing to destroy a human being. . . . Ah, a very serious thing! Good-bye, my dear fellow. I've eaten my fill and am drunk," he said rising. "Shall I come to-morrow to go shooting?"

"Yes, come!"

"Mind, get up early; if you oversleep you will be fined!"

"Never fear, I'll be up before you," answered Olénin.

The old man left. The song ceased, but one could hear footsteps and merry talk. A little later the singing broke out again but farther away, and Eróshka's loud voice chimed in with the other. "What people, what a life!" thought Olénin with a sigh as he returned alone to his hut.

Olénin falls in love with the Cossack girl Maryánka, who appears to return his love and be ready to marry him.

XL

The next day Olénin awoke earlier than usual, and immediately remembered what lay before him, and he joyfully recalled her kisses, the pressure of her hard hands, and her words, "What white hands you have!" He jumped up and wished to go at once to his hosts' hut to ask for their consent to his marriage with Maryánka. The sun had not yet risen, but it seemed that there was an unusual bustle in the street and side-street: people were moving about on foot and on horseback, and talking. He threw on his Circassian coat and hastened out into the porch. His hosts were not yet up. Five Cossacks were riding past and talking loudly together. In front rode

Lukáshka on his broad-backed Kabardá horse. The Cossacks were all speaking and shouting so that it was impossible to make out exactly what they were saying.

"Ride to the Upper Post," shouted one.

"Saddle and catch us up, be quick," said another.

"It's nearer through the other gate!"

"What are you talking about?" cried Lukáshka. "We must go through the middle gates, of course."

"So we must, it's nearer that way," said one of the Cossacks who was covered with dust and rode a perspiring horse. Lukáshka's face was red and swollen after the drinking of the previous night and his cap was pushed to the back of his head. He was calling out with authority as though he were an officer.

"What is the matter? Where are you going?" asked Olénin, with difficulty attracting the Cossacks' attention.

"We are off to catch *abreks*. They're hiding among the sand-drifts. We are just off, but there are not enough of us yet."

And the Cossacks continued to shout, more and more of them joining as they rode down the street. It occurred to Olénin that it would not look well for him to stay behind; besides he thought he could soon come back. He dressed, loaded his gun with bullets, jumped onto his horse which Vanyúsha had saddled more or less well, and overtook the Cossacks at the villages gates. The Cossacks had dismounted, and filling a wooden bowl with *chikhir* from a little cask which they had brought with them, they passed the bowl round to one another and drank to the success of their expedition. Among them was a smartly dressed young cornet, who happened to be in the village and who took command of the group of nine Cossacks who had joined for the expedition. All these Cossacks were privates, and although the cornet assumed the airs of a commanding officer, they only obeyed Lukáshka. Of Olénin they took no notice at all, and when they had all mounted and started, and Olénin rode up to the cornet, and began asking what was taking place, the cornet, who was usually quite friendly, treated him with marked condescension. It was with great difficulty that Olénin managed to find out from him what was happening. Scouts who had been sent out to search for *abreks* had come upon several hillsmen some six miles from the village. These *abreks* had taken shelter in pits and had fired at the scouts, declaring they would not surrender. A corporal who had been scouting with two Cossacks had remained to watch the *abreks* and had sent one Cossack back to get help.

The sun was just rising. Three miles beyond the village the steppe spread out and nothing was visible except the dry, monotonous, sandy, dismal plain covered with the footmarks of cattle, and here and there with tufts of withered grass, with low reeds in the flats, and rare, little-trodden footpaths, and the camps of the nomad Nogáy tribe just visible far away. The absence of shade and the austere aspect of the place were striking. The sun always rises and sets red in the steppe. When it is windy, whole hills of sand are carried by the wind from place to place. When it is calm, as it was that morning, the silence, uninterrupted by any movement or sound, is peculiarly striking. That morning in the steppe it was quiet and dull, though the sun had already risen. It all seemed specially soft and desolate. The air was hushed, the footfalls and the snorting of the horses were the only sounds to be heard, and even they quickly died away.

The men rode almost silently. A Cossack always carries his weapons so that they neither jingle nor rattle. Jingling weapons are a terrible disgrace to a Cossack. Two other Cossacks from the village caught the party up and exchanged a few words. Lukáshka's horse either stumbled or caught its foot in some grass, and became restive—which is a sign of bad luck among the Cossacks and at such a time was of special importance. The others exchanged glances and turned away, trying not to notice what had happened. Lukáshka pulled at the reins, frowned sternly, set his teeth, and flourished his whip above his head. His good Kabardá horse, prancing from one foot to another not knowing with which to start, seemed to wish to fly upwards on wings. But Lukáshka hit its well-fed sides with his whip once, then again and a third time, and the horse, showing its teeth and spreading out its tail, snorted and reared and stepped on its hind legs a few paces away from the others.

"Ah, a good steed that!" said the cornet.

That he said *steed* instead of *horse* indicated special praise.

"A lion of a horse," assented one of the others, an old Cossack.

The Cossacks rode forward silently, now at a footpace, then at a trot, and these changes were the only incidents that interrupted for a moment the stillness and solemnity of their movements.

Riding through the steppe, for about six miles, they passed nothing but one Nogáy tent, placed on a cart and moving slowly along at a distance of about a mile from them. A Nogáy family was moving from one part of the steppe to another. Afterwards they met two tattered Nogáy women with high cheekbones, who with baskets on their backs were gathering dung left by the cattle that wandered over the steppe. The cornet, who did not know their language well, tried to question them, but they did not understand him and, obviously frightened, looked at one another.

Lukáshka rode up to them both, stopped his horse, and promptly uttered the usual greeting. The Nogáy women were evidently relieved and began speaking to him quite freely as to a brother.

"*Ay-ay, kop abrek!*" they said plaintively, pointing in the direction in which the Cossacks were going. Olénin understood that they were saying, "Many *abreks.*"

Never having seen an engagement of that kind, and having formed an idea of them only from Daddy Eréshka's tales, Olénin wished not to be left behind by the Cossacks but wanted to see it all. He admired the Cossacks and was on the watch, looking and listening and making his own observations. Though he had brought his sword and a loaded gun with him, when he noticed that the Cossacks avoided him he decided to take no part in the action, as in his opinion his courage had already been sufficiently proved when he was with his detachment, and also because he was very happy.

Suddenly a shot was heard in the distance.

The cornet became excited and began giving orders to the Cossacks as to how they should divide and from which side they should approach. But the Cossacks did not

appear to pay any attention to these orders, listening only
to what Lukáshka said and looking to him alone. Lukáshka's
face and figure were expressive of calm solemnity. He put
his horse to a trot with which the others were unable
to keep pace, and screwing up his eyes kept looking ahead.

"There's a man on horseback," he said, reining in his
horse and keeping in line with the others.

Olénin looked intently but could not see anything. The
Cossacks soon distinguished two riders and quietly rode
straight towards them.

"Are those the *abreks*?" asked Olénin.

The Cossacks did not answer his question, which appeared quite meaningless to them. The *abreks* would have
been fools to venture across the river on horseback.

"That's friend Ródka waving to us, I do believe," said
Lukáshka, pointing to the two mounted men who were
now clearly visible. "Look, he's coming to us."

A few minutes later it became plain that the two horsemen were the Cossack scouts. The corporal rode up to
Lukáshka.

XLI

"Are they far?" was all Lukáshka said.

Just then they heard a sharp shot some thirty paces
off. The corporal smiled slightly.

"Our Gúrka is having shots at them," he said, nodding
in the direction of the shot.

Having gone a few paces farther they saw Gúrka
sitting behind a sand-hillock and loading his gun. To while
away the time he was exchanging shots with the *abreks*,
who were behind another sand-heap. A bullet came
whistling from their side.

The cornet was pale and grew confused. Lukáshka dismounted from his horse, threw the reins to one of the
other Cossacks, and went up to Gúrka. Olénin also dismounted and, bending down, followed Lukáshka. They
had hardly reached Gúrka when two bullets whistled above
them. Lukáshka looked around laughing at Olénin and
stooped a little.

"Look out or they will kill you, Dmítri Andréich," he
said. "You'd better go away—you have no business here."

But Olénin wanted absolutely to see the *abreks*.

From behind the mound he saw caps and muskets some two hundred paces off. Suddenly a little cloud of smoke appeared from thence, and again a bullet whistled past. The *abreks* were hiding in a marsh at the foot of the hill. Olénin was much impressed by the place in which they sat. In reality it was very much like the rest of the steppe, but because the *abreks* sat there it seemed to detach itself from all the rest and to have become distinguished. Indeed it appeared to Olénin that it was the very spot for *abreks* to occupy. Lukáshka went back to his horse and Olénin followed him.

"We must get a hay-cart," said Lukáshka, "or they will be killing some of us. There behind that mound is a Nogáy cart with a load of hay."

The cornet listened to him and the corporal agreed. The cart of hay was fetched, and the Cossacks, hiding behind it, pushed it forward. Olénin rode up a hillock from whence he could see everything. The hay-cart moved on and the Cossacks crowded together behind it. The Cossacks advanced, but the Chéchens, of whom there were nine, sat with their knees in a row and did not fire.

All was quiet. Suddenly from the Chéchens arose the sound of a mournful song, something like Daddy Eróshka's "Ay day, dalalay." The Chéchens knew that they could not escape, and to prevent themselves from being tempted to take to flight they had strapped themselves together, knee to knee, had got their guns ready, and were singing their death-song.

The Cossacks with their hay cart drew closer and closer, and Olénin expected the firing to begin at any moment, but the silence was only broken by the *abreks'* mournful song. Suddenly the song ceased; there was a sharp report, a bullet struck the front of the cart, and Chéchen curses and yells broke the silence and shot followed on shot and one bullet after another struck the cart. The Cossacks did not fire and were now only five paces distant.

Another moment passed and the Cossacks with a whoop rushed out on both sides from behind the cart—Lukáshka in front of them. Olénin heard only a few shots, then shouting and moans. He thought he saw smoke and blood, and abandoning his horse and quite beside himself he ran towards the Cossacks. Horror seemed to blind him. He could not make out anything but understood that all was over. Lukáshka, pale as death, was holding a wounded Chéchen by the arms and shouting, "Don't kill him. I'll take him alive!" The Chéchen was the red-haired man who had fetched his brother's body away after Lukáshka had killed him. Lukáshka was twisting his arms. Suddenly the Chéchen wrenched himself free and fired his pistol. Lukáshka fell, and blood began to flow from his stomach. He jumped up but fell again, swearing in Russian and in Tartar. More and more blood appeared on his clothes and under him. Some Cossacks approached him and began loosening his girdle. One of them, Nazárka, before beginning to help, fumbled for some time unable to put his sword in its sheath: it would not go the right way. The blade of the sword was blood-stained.

The Chéchens with their red hair and clipped moustaches lay dead and hacked about. Only the one we know of, who had fired at Lukáshka, though wounded in many places was still alive. Like a wounded hawk all covered with blood (blood was flowing from a wound under his right eye), pale and gloomy, he looked about him with wide-open excited eyes and clenched teeth as he crouched, dagger in hand, still prepared to defend himself. The cornet went up to him as if intending to pass by and with a quick movement shot him in the ear. The Chéchen started up, but it was too late, and he fell.

The Cossacks, quite out of breath, dragged the bodies aside and took the weapons from them. Each of the red-haired Chéchens had been a man, and each one had his own individual expression. Lukáshka was carried to the cart. He continued to swear in Russian and in Tartar.

"No fear, I'll strangle him with my hands. *Anna seni!*" he cried, struggling. But he soon became quiet from weakness.

Olénin rode home. In the evening he was told that Lukáshka was at death's door, but that a Tartar from beyond the river had undertaken to cure him with herbs.

The bodies were brought to the village office. The women and the little boys hastened to look at them.

It was growing dark when Olénin returned, and he

could not collect himself after what he had seen. But towards night memories of the evening before came rushing to his mind. He looked out of the window, Maryánka was passing to and fro from the house to the cowshed, putting things straight. Her mother had gone to the vineyard and her father to the office. Olénin could not wait till she had quite finished her work but went out to meet her. She was in the hut standing with her back towards him. Olénin thought she felt shy.

"Maryánka," said he, "I say, Maryánka! May I come in?"

She suddenly turned. There was a scarcely perceptible trace of tears in her eyes and her face was beautiful in its sadness. She looked at him in silent dignity.

Olénin again said:

"Maryánka, I have come—"

"Leave me alone!" she said. Her face did not change but the tears ran down her cheeks.

"What are you crying for? What is it?"

"What?" she repeated in a rough voice. "Cossacks have been killed, that's what for."

"Lukáshka?" said Olénin.

"Go away! What do you want?"

"Maryánka!" said Olénin, approaching her.

"You will never get anything from me!"

"Maryánka, don't speak like that," Olénin entreated.

"Get away. I'm sick of you!" shouted the girl, stamping her foot, and moved threateningly towards him. And her face expressed such abhorrence, such contempt, and such anger that Olénin suddenly understood that there was no hope for him, and that his first impression of this woman's inaccessibility had been perfectly correct.

Olénin said nothing more, but ran out of the hut.

XLII

For two hours after returning home he lay on his bed motionless. Then he went to his company commander and obtained leave to visit the staff. Without taking leave of anyone, and sending Vanyúsha to settle his accounts with his landlord, he prepared to leave for the fort where his regiment was stationed. Daddy Eróshka was the only one to see him off. They had a drink, and then a second, and then yet another. Again as on the night of his departure from Moscow, a three-horsed conveyance stood waiting at the door. But Olénin did not confer with himself as he had done then and did not say to himself that all he had thought and done here was "not it." He did not promise himself a new life. He loved Maryánka more than ever and knew that he could never be loved by her.

"Well, good-bye, my lad!" said Daddy Eróshka. "When you go on an expedition, be wise and listen to my words— the words of an old man. When you are out on a raid or the like (you know I'm an old wolf and have seen things), and when they begin firing, don't get into a crowd where there are many men. When you fellows get frightened you always try to get close together with a lot of others. You think it is merrier to be with others, but that's where it is worst of all! They always aim at a crowd. Now I used to keep farther away from the others and went alone, and I've never been wounded. Yet what things haven't I seen in my day?"

"But you've got a bullet in your back," remarked Vanyúsha, who was clearing up the room.

"That was the Cossacks fooling about," answered Eróshka.

"Cossacks? How was that?" asked Olénin.

"Oh, just so. We were drinking. Vánka Sítkin, one of the Cossacks, got merry, and puff! he gave me one from his pistol just here."

"Yes, and did it hurt?" asked Olénin. "Vanyúsha, will you soon be ready?" he added.

"Ah, where's the hurry! Let me tell you. When he banged into me, the bullet did not break the bone but remained here. And I say: 'You've killed me, brother. Eh! What have you done to me? I won't let you off! You'll have to stand me a pailful!' "

"Well, but did it hurt?" Olénin asked again, scarcely listening to the tale.

"Let me finish. He stood a pailful, and we drank it, but the blood went on flowing. The whole room was drenched and covered with blood. Grandad Burlák, he says, "The lad will give up the ghost. Stand a bottle of the sweet sort, or we shall have you taken up!" They bought more drink, and boozed and boozed—"

"Yes, but did it hurt you much?" Olénin asked once more.

"Hurt, indeed! Don't interrupt: I don't like it. Let me finish. We boozed and boozed till morning, and I fell asleep on the top of the oven, drunk. When I woke in the morning I could not unbend myself anyhow—"

"Was it very painful?" repeated Olénin, thinking that now he would at least get an answer to his question.

"Did I tell you it was painful? I did not say it was painful, but I could not bend and could not walk."

"And then it healed up?" said Olénin, not even laughing, so heavy was his heart.

"It healed up, but the bullet is still there. Just feel it!" And lifting his shirt he showed his powerful back, where just near the bone a bullet could be felt and rolled about.

"Feel how it rolls," he said, evidently amusing himself with the bullet as with a toy. "There now, it has rolled to the back."

"And Lukáshka, will he recover?" asked Olénin.

"Heaven only knows! There's no doctor. They've gone for one."

"Where will they get one? From Gróznoe?" asked Olénin.

"No, my lad. Were I the Tsar I'd have hung all your Russian doctors long ago. Cutting is all they know! There's our Cossack Baklághka, no longer a real man now that they've cut off his leg! That shows they're fools. What's Baklúshka good for now? No, my lad, in the mountains there are real doctors. There was my chum, Vórchik, he was on an expedition and was wounded just here in the chest. Well, your doctors gave him up, but one of theirs came from the mountains and cured him! They understand herbs, my lad!"

"Come, stop talking rubbish," said Olénin. "I'd better send a doctor from head-quarters."

"Rubbish!" the old man said mockingly. "Fool, fool! Rubbish. You'll send a doctor! If yours cured people, Cossacks and Chéchens would go to you for treatment, but as it is your officers and colonels send to the mountains for doctors. Yours are all humbugs, all humbugs."

Olénin did not answer. He agreed only too fully that all was humbug in the world in which he had lived and to which he was now returning.

"How is Lukáshka? You've been to see him?" he asked.

"He just lies as if he were dead. He does not eat nor drink. Vodka is the only thing his soul accepts. But as long as he drinks vodka it's well. I'd be sorry to lose the lad. A fine lad—a brave, like me. I too lay dying like that once. The old women were already wailing. My head was burning. They had already laid me out under the holy icons. So I lay there and above me on the oven little drummers, no bigger than this, beat the tattoo. I shout at them and they drum all the harder." The old man laughed. The women brought our church elder. They were getting ready to bury me. They said, 'He defiled himself with worldly unbelievers; he made merry with women; he ruined people; he did not fast, and he played the *balaláyka.*' 'I've sinned!' I said. Whatever the priest said, I always answered 'I've sinned.' He began to ask me about the *balaláyka.* 'Where is the accursed thing?' he says. 'Show it me and smash it.' But I say, 'I've not got it.' I'd hidden it myself in a net in the out-house. I knew they could not find it. So they left me. Yet after all I recovered. When I went for my *balaláyka*—What was I saying?" he continued. "Listen to me, and keep farther away from the other men or you'll get killed foolishly. I feel for you, truly: you are a drinker— I love you! And fellows like you like riding up the mounds. There was one who lived here who had come from Russia, he always would ride up the mounds (he called the mounds, so funnily, 'hillocks'). Whenever he saw a mound, off he'd gallop. Once he galloped off that way and rode to the top quite pleased, but a Chéchen fired at him and killed him! Ah, how well they shoot from their gun-rests, those Chéchens! Some of them shoot even better than I do. I don't like it when a fellow gets killed so foolishly! Sometimes I used to look at your soldiers and wonder at them. There's foolishness for you! They go, the poor fellows, all in a clump, and even sew red collars to their coats! How can they help being hit! One gets killed, they drag him away and another takes his place! What foolishness!" the old man repeated, shaking his head. "Why not scatter, and go one by one? So you just go like that and they won't notice you. That's what you must do."

"Well, thank you! Good-bye, Daddy. God willing we may meet again," said Olénin, getting up and moving towards the passage.

The old man, who was sitting on the floor, did not rise.

"Is that the way one says 'Good-bye'? Fool, fool!" he began. "Oh dear, what has come to people? We've kept company, kept company for wellnigh a year, and now 'Good-bye!' and off he goes! Why, I love you, and how I pity you! You are so forlorn, always alone, always alone. You're somehow so unsociable. At times I can't sleep for thinking about you. I am so sorry for you. As the song has it:

> 'It is very hard, dear brother,
> In a foreign land to live.'

So it is with you."

"Well, good-bye," said Olénin again.

The old man rose and held out his hand. Olénin pressed it and turned to go.

"Give us your mug, your mug!"

And the old man took Olénin by the head with both hands and kissed him three times with wet moustaches and lips, and began to cry.

"I love you, good-bye!"

Olénin got into the cart.

"Well, is that how you're going? You might give me something for a remembrance. Give me a gun! What do you want two for?" said the old man, sobbing quite sincerely.

Olénin got out a musket and gave it to him.

"What a lot you've given the old fellow,' murmured Vanyúsha, "he'll never have enough! A regular old beggar. They are all such irregular people," he remarked, as he wrapped himself in his overcoat and took his seat on the box.

"Hold your tongue, swine!" exclaimed the old man, laughing. "What a stingy fellow!"

Maryánka came out of the cowshed, glanced indifferently at the cart, bowed and went towards the hut.

"*La fille!*" said Vanyúsha with a wink and burst out into a silly laugh.

"Drive on!" shouted Olénin, angrily.

"Good-bye, my lad! Good-bye. I won't forget you!" shouted Eróshka.

Olénin turned round. Daddy Eróshka was talking to Maryánka, evidently about his own affairs, and neither the old man nor the girl looked at Olénin.

Finished Dec. 19, 1862

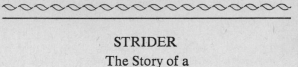

STRIDER
The Story of a
Horse

I

Higher and higher receded the sky, wider and wider spread the streak of dawn, whiter grew the pallid silver of the dew, more lifeless the sickle of the moon, and more vocal the forest. People began to get up, and in the owner's stable-yard the sounds of snorting, the rustling of litter, and even the shrill angry neighing of horses crowded together and at variance about something, grew more and more frequent.

"Hold on! Plenty of time! Hungry?" said the old huntsman, quickly opening the creaking gate. "Where are you going?" he shouted, threateningly raising his arm at a mare that was pushing through the gate.

The keeper, Nester, wore a short Cossack coat with an ornamental leather girdle, had a whip slung over his shoulder, and a hunk of bread wrapped in a cloth stuck in his girdle. He carried a saddle and bridle in his arms.

The horses were not at all frightened or offended at the horseman's sarcastic tone: they pretended that it was all the same to them and moved leisurely away from the gate; only one old brown mare, with a thick mane, laid back an ear and quickly turned her back on him. A small filly standing behind her and not at all concerned in the matter took this opportunity to whinny and kick out at a horse that happened to be near.

"Now then!" shouted the keeper still louder and more sternly, and he went to the opposite corner of the yard.

Of all the horses in the enclosure (there were about a hundred of them, a piebald gelding, standing by himself in a corner under the penthouse and licking an oak post with half-closed eyes, displayed least impatience.

It is impossible to say what flavour the piebald gelding found in the post, but his expression was serious and thoughtful while he licked.

"Stop that!" shouted the groom, drawing nearer to him and putting the saddle and a glossy saddle-cloth on the manure heap beside him.

The piebald gelding stopped licking and without moving gave Nester a long look. The gelding did not laugh, nor grow angry, nor frown, but his whole belly heaved with a profound sigh and he turned away. The horseman put his arm round the gelding's neck and placed the bridle on him.

"What are you sighing for?" said Nester.

The gelding switched his tail as if to say, "Nothing in particular, Nester!" Nester put the saddle-cloth and saddle on him, and this caused the gelding to lay back his ears, probably to express dissatisfaction, but he was only called a "good-for-nothing" for it and his saddle-girths were tightened.

At this the gelding blew himself out, but a finger was thrust into his mouth and a knee hit him in the stomach, so that he had to let out his breath. In spite of this, when the saddle-cloth was being buckled on he again laid back his ears and even looked round. Though he knew it would do no good he considered it necessary to show that it was disagreeable to him and that he would always express his dissatisfaction with it. When he was saddled he thrust forward his swollen off foot and began champing his bit, this too for some reason of his own, for he ought to have known by that time that a bit cannot have any flavour at all.

Nester mounted the gelding by the short stirrup, un-wound his long whip, straightened his coat out from under his knee, seated himself in the manner peculiar to coach-men, huntsmen, and horsemen, and jerked the reins. The gelding lifted his head to show his readiness to go where ordered but did not move. He knew that before starting there would be much shouting and that Nester, from the seat on his back, would give many orders to Váska, the other groom, and to the horses. And Nester did shout: "Váska! Hullo, Váska. Have you let out the brood mares? Where are you going, you devil? Now then! Are you asleep? . . . Open the gate! Let the brood mares get out first!" and so on.

The gate creaked. Váska, cross and sleepy, stood at the gate-post holding his horse by the bridle and letting the other horses pass out. The horses followed one another and stepped carefully over the straw, smelling at it: fillies, yearling colts with their manes and tails cut, suckling foals, and mares in foal carrying their burden heedfully passed one by one through the gateway. The fillies sometimes crowded together in twos and threes, throwing their heads across one another's backs and hitting their hoofs against the gate, for which they received a rebuke from the grooms every time. The foals sometimes darted under the legs of the wrong mares and neighed loudly in response to the short whinny of their own mothers.

A playful filly, directly she had got out at the gate, bent her head sideways, kicked up her hind legs, and squealed, but all the same she did not dare to run ahead of old dappled Zhuldýba who at a slow and heavy pace, swinging her belly from side to side, marched as usual ahead of all the other horses.

In a few minutes the enclosure that had been so animated became deserted, the posts stood gloomily under the empty penthouse, and only trampled straw mixed with manure was to be seen. Used as he was to that desolate sight it probably depressed the piebald gelding. As if making a bow he slowly lowered his head and raised it again, sighed as deeply as the tightly drawn girth would allow, and hobbling along on his stiff and crooked legs shambled after the herd, bearing old Nester on his bony back.

"I know that as soon as we get out on the road he will begin to strike a light and smoke his wooden pipe with its brass mountings and little chain," thought the gelding. "I am glad of it because early in the morning when it is dewy I like that smell, it reminds me of much that was pleasant; but it's annoying that when his pipe is between his teeth the old man always begins to swagger and thinks himself somebody and sits sideways, always sideways—and that side hurts. However, it can't be helped! Suffering for the pleasure of others is nothing new to me. I have even begun to find a certain equine pleasure in it.

Let him swagger, poor fellow! Of course he can only do that when he is alone and no one sees him—let him sit sideways!" thought the gelding, and stepping carefully on his crooked legs he went along the middle of the road.

II

Having driven the horses to the riverside where they were to graze, Nester dismounted and unsaddled. Meanwhile the herd had begun gradually to spread over the untrampled meadow, covered with dew and by the mist that rose from it and the encircling river.

When he had taken the bridle off the piebald gelding, Nester scratched him under the neck, in response to which the gelding expressed his gratitude and satisfaction by closing his eyes. "He likes it, the old dog!" muttered Nester. The gelding however did not really care for the scratching at all and pretended that it was agreeable merely out of courtesy. He nodded his head in assent to Nester's words, but suddenly Nester, quite unexpectedly and without any reason, perhaps imagining that too much familiarity might give the gelding a wrong idea of his importance, pushed the gelding's head away from himself without any warning and, swinging the bridle, struck him painfully with the buckle on his lean leg, and then without saying a word went up the hillock to a tree-stump beside which he generally seated himself.

Though this action grieved the piebald gelding he gave no indication of it, but leisurely switching his scanty tail sniffed at something and, biting off some wisps of grass merely to divert his mind, walked to the river. He took no notice whatever of the antics of the young mares, colts, and foals around him, who were filled with the joy of the morning; and knowing that, especially at his age, it is healthier to have a good drink on an empty stomach and to eat afterwards, he chose a spot where the bank was widest and least steep, and wetting his hoofs and fetlocks, dipped his muzzle in the water and began to suck it up through his torn lips, to expand his filling sides, and from pleasure to switch his scanty tail with its half bald stump.

An aggressive chestnut filly, who always teased the old fellow and did all kinds of unpleasant things to him, now came up to him in the water as if attending to some business of her own but in reality merely to foul the water before his nose. But the piebald gelding, who had already had his fill, as though not noticing the filly's intention quietly drew one foot after the other out of the mud in which they had sunk, jerked his head, and stepping aside from the youthful crowd started grazing. Sprawling his feet apart in different ways and not trampling the grass needlessly, he went on eating without unbending himself for exactly three hours. Having eaten till his belly hung down from his steep skinny ribs like a sack, he balanced himself equally on his four sore legs so as to have as little pain as possible, especially in his off foreleg which was the weakest, and fell asleep.

Old age is sometimes majestic, sometimes ugly, and sometimes pathetic. But old age can be both ugly and majestic, and the gelding's old age was just of that kind.

He was tall, rather over fifteen hands high. His spots were black, or rather they had been black, but had now turned a dirty brown. He had three spots, one on his head, starting from a crooked bald patch on the side of his nose and reaching half-way down his neck. His long mane, filled with burrs, was white in some places and brownish in others. Another spot extended down his off side to the middle of his belly; the third, on his croup, touched part of his tail and went half-way down his quarters. The rest of the tail was whitish and speckled. The big bony head, with deep hollows over the eyes and a black hanging lip that had been torn at some time, hung low and heavily on his neck, which was so lean that it looked as though it were carved of wood. The pendant lip revealed a blackish, bitten tongue and the yellow stumps of the worn lower teeth. The ears, one of which was slit, hung low on either side, and only occasionally moved lazily to drive away the pestering flies. Of the forelock, one tuft which was still long hung back behind an ear; the uncovered forehead was dented and rough, and the skin hung down like bags on his broad jaw-bones. The veins of his neck had grown knotty and twitched and shuddered at every touch of a fly. The expression of his face was one of stern patience, thoughtfulness, and suffering.

His forelegs were crooked to a bow at the knees, there

were swellings over both hoofs, and on one leg, on which the piebald spot reached half-way down, there was a swelling at the knee as big as a fist. The hind legs were in better condition, but apparently long ago his haunches had been so rubbed that in places the hair would not grow again. The leanness of his body made all four legs look disproportionately long. The ribs, though straight, were so exposed and the skin so tightly drawn over them, that it seemed to have dried fast to the spaces between. His back and withers were covered with marks of old lashings, and there was a fresh sore behind, still swollen and festering; the black dock of his tail, which showed the vertebrae, hung down long and almost bare. On his dark-brown croup—near the tail—was a scar, as though of a bite, the size of a man's hand and covered with white hair. Another scarred sore was visible on one of his shoulders. His tail and hocks were dirty because of chronic bowel troubles. The hair on the whole body, though short, stood out straight. Yet in spite of the hideous old age of this horse one involuntarily paused to reflect when one saw him, and an expert would have said at once that he had been a remarkably fine horse in his day. The expert would even have said that there was only one breed in Russia that could furnish such breadth of bone, such immense knees, such hoofs, such slender cannons, such a well-shaped neck, and above all such a skull, such eyes—large, black, and clear — and such a thoroughbred network of veins on head and neck, and such delicate skin and hair.

There was really something majestic in that horse's figure and in the terrible union in him of repulsive indications of decrepitude, emphasized by the motley colour of his hair, and his manner which expressed the self-confidence and calm assurance that go with beauty and strength. Like a living ruin he stood alone in the midst of the dewy meadow, while not far from him could be heard the tramping, snorting and youthful neighing and whinnying of the scattered herd.

III

The sun had risen above the forest and now shone brightly on the grass and the winding river. The dew was drying up and condensing into drops, the last of the morning mist was dispersing like tiny smoke-clouds. The cloudlets were becoming curly but there was as yet no wind. Beyond the river the verdant rye stood bristling, its ears curling into little horns, and there was an odour of fresh verdure and blossom. A cuckoo called rather hoarsely from the forest, and Nester, lying on his back in the grass, was counting the calls to ascertain how many years he still had to live. The larks were rising over the rye and the meadow. A belated hare, finding himself among the horses, leaped into the open, sat down by a bush, and pricked his ears to listen. Váska fell asleep with his head in the grass; the fillies, making a still wider circle about him, scattered over the field below. The old mares went about snorting and made a shiny track across the dewy grass, always choosing a place where no one would disturb them. They no longer grazed but only nibbled at choice tufts of grass. The whole herd was moving imperceptibly in one direction.

And again it was old Zhuldýba who, stepping sedately in front of the others, showed the possibility of going farther. Black Múshka, a young mare who had foaled for the first time, with uplifted tail kept whinnying and snorting at her bluish foal; the young filly Satin, sleek and brilliant, bending her head till her black silky forelock hid her forehead and eyes, played with the grass, nipping off a little and tossing it and stamping her leg with its shaggy fetlock all wet with dew. One of the older foals, probably imagining he was playing some kind of game, with his curly tail raised like a plume, ran for the twenty-sixth time round his mother, who quietly went on grazing, having grown accustomed to her son's ways, and only occasionally glanced askance at him with one of her large black eyes.

One of the very youngest foals, black, with a big head, a tuft sticking up in astonishment between his ears, and a little tail still twisted to one side as it had been in his mother's womb, stood motionless, his ears pricked and his dull eyes fixed, gazing at the frisking and prancing foal—whether admiring or condemning him it is hard to say. Some of the foals were sucking and butting with their noses, some—heaven knows why—despite their mothers' call were running at an awkward little trot in quite the opposite direction as if searching for something and then, for no apparent reason, stopping and neighing with desperate shrillness. Some lay on their sides in a row, some were learning to eat grass, some again were scratching themselves behind their ears with their hind legs. Two mares still in foal were walking apart from the rest and while slowly moving their legs continued to graze. The others evidently respected their condition, and none of the young ones ventured to come near to disturb them. If any saucy youngsters thought of approaching them, the mere movement of an ear or tail sufficed to show them all how improper such behaviour was.

The colts and yearling fillies, pretending to be grown up and sedate, rarely jumped or joined the merry company. They grazed in a dignified manner, curving their close-cropped swan-like necks, and flourished their little broom-like tails as if they also had long ones. Just like the grown-ups they lay down, rolled over, or rubbed one another. The merriest group was composed of the two- and three-year-old fillies and mares not yet in foal. They almost always walked about together like a separate merry virgin crowd. Among them you could hear sounds of tramping, whinnying, neighing, and snorting. They drew close together, put their heads over one another's necks, sniffed at one another, jumped, and sometimes at a semi-trot, semi-amble, with tails lifted like an oriflamme, raced proudly and coquettishly past their companions. The most beautiful and spirited of them was the mischievous chestnut filly. What she devised the others did; wherever she went the whole crowd of beauties followed. That morning the naughty one was in a specially playful mood. She was seized with a joyous fit, just as human beings sometimes are. Already at the riverside she had played a trick on the old gelding, and after that she ran along through the water pretending to be frightened by something, gave a hoarse squeal, and raced full speed into the field so that Váska had to gallop after her and the others who followed her. Then after grazing a little she began rolling, then teasing the old mares by dashing in front of them, then she drove away a small foal from its dam and chased it as if meaning to bite it. Its mother was frightened and stopped grazing, while the little foal cried in a piteous tone, but the mischievous one did not touch him at all, she only wanted to frighten him and give a performance for the benefit of her companions, who watched her escapade approvingly. Then she set out to turn the head of a little roan horse with which a peasant was ploughing in a rye-field far beyond the river. She stopped, proudly lifted her head somewhat to one side, shook herself, and neighed in a sweet, tender, long-drawn voice. Mischief, feeling, and a certain sadness were expressed in that call. There was in it the desire for and the promise of love, and a pining for it.

"There in the thick reeds is a corn-crake running backwards and forwards and calling passionately to his mate; there is the cuckoo, and the quails are singing of love, and the flowers are sending their fragrant dust to each other by the wind. And I too am young and beautiful and strong," the mischievous one's voice said, "but it has not yet been allowed me to know the sweetness of that feeling, and not only to experience it, but no lover—not a single one—has ever seen me!"

And this neighing, sad and youthful and fraught with feeling, was borne over the lowland and the field to the roan horse far away. He pricked up his ears and stopped. The peasant kicked him with his bast shoe, but the little horse was so enchanted by the silvery sound of the distant neighing that he neighed too. The peasant grew angry, pulled at the reins, and kicked the little roan so painfully in the stomach with his bast shoes that he could not finish his neigh and walked on. But the little roan felt a sense of sweetness and sadness, and for a long time the sounds of unfinished and passionate neighing, and of the peasant's angry voice, were carried from the distant rye-field over to the herd.

If the sound of her voice alone so overpowered the little roan that he forgot his duty, what would have happened had he seen the naughty beauty as she stood pricking her ears, breathing in the air with dilated nostrils, ready to run, trembling with her whole beautiful body, and calling to him?

But the mischievous one did not brood long over her impressions. When the neighing of the roan died away she gave another scornful neigh, lowered her head, and began pawing the ground, and then she went to wake and to tease the piebald gelding. The piebald gelding was the constant martyr and butt of those happy youngsters. He suffered more from them than at the hands of men. He did no harm to either. People needed him, but why should these young horses torment him?

IV

He was old, they were young; he was lean, they were sleek; he was miserable, they were gay; and so he was quite alien to them, an outsider, an utterly different creature whom it was impossible for them to pity. Horses only have pity on themselves and very occasionally on those in whose skins they can easily imagine themselves to be. But was it the old gelding's fault that he was old, poor, and ugly?

One might think not, but in equine ethics it was, and only those were right who were strong, young, and happy— those who had life still before them, whose every muscle quivered with superfluous energy, and whose tails stood erect. Maybe the piebald gelding himself understood this and in his quiet moments was ready to agree that it was his fault that he had already lived his life, and that he had to pay for that life, but after all he was a horse and often could not suppress a sense of resentment, sadness, and indignation when he looked at those youngsters who tormented him for what would befall them all at the end of their lives. Another cause of the horses' lack of pity was their aristocratic pride. Every one of them traced back its pedigree, through father or mother, to the famous Creamy, while the piebald was of unknown parentage. He was a chance comer, purchased three years before at a fair for eighty assignat rubles.

The chestnut filly, as if taking a stroll, passed close by the piebald gelding's nose and pushed him. He knew at once what it was, and without opening his eyes laid back his ears and showed his teeth. The filly wheeled round as if to kick him. The gelding opened his eyes and stepped aside. He did not want to sleep any more and began to graze. The mischief-maker, followed by her companions, again approached the gelding. A very stupid two-year-old white-spotted filly who always imitated the chestnut in everything went up with her and, as imitators always do, went to greater lengths than the instigator. The chestnut always went up as if intent on business of her own and passed by the gelding's nose without looking at him, so that he really did not know whether to be angry or not, and that was really funny.

She did the same now, but the white-spotted one, who followed her and had grown particularly lively, bumped right against the gelding with her chest. He again showed his teeth, whinnied, and with an agility one could not have expected of him, rushed after her and bit her flank. The white-spotted one kicked out with all her strength and dealt the old horse a heavy blow on his thin bare ribs. He snorted heavily and was going to rush at her again but bethought himself and drawing a deep sigh stepped aside. The whole crowd of young ones must have taken as a personal affront the impertinence the piebald gelding had permitted himself to offer to the white-spotted one and for the rest of the day did not let him graze in peace for a moment, so that the keeper had to quieten them several times and could not understand what had come over them.

The gelding felt so offended that he went up himself to Nester when the old man was getting ready to drive the horses home and felt happier and quieter when he was saddled and the old man had mounted him.

God knows what the gelding was thinking as he carried old Nester on his back: whether he thought bitterly of the pertinacious and merciless youngsters or forgave his tormenters with the contemptuous and silent pride suited to old age. At all events he did not betray his thoughts till he reached home.

That evening, as Nester drove the horses past the huts of the domestic serfs, he noticed a peasant horse and cart tethered to his porch: some friends had come to see him. When driving the horses in he was in such a hurry that he let the gelding in without unsaddling him and, shouting to Váska to do it, shut the gate and went to his friends. Whether because of the affront to the white-spotted filly—Creamy's great-grand-daughter—by that "mangy trash" bought at the horse fair, who did not know his father or mother, and the consequent outrage to the aristocratic sentiment of the whole herd, or because the gelding with his high saddle and without a rider presented a strangely fantastic spectacle to the horses, at any rate something quite unusual occurred that night in the paddock. All the horses, young and old, ran after the gelding, showing their teeth and driving him all round the yard; one heard the sound of hoofs striking against his bare ribs, and his deep moaning. He could no longer endure this, nor could he avoid the blows. He stopped in the middle of the paddock, his face expressing first the repulsive weak malevolence of helpless old age, and then despair: he dropped his ears, and then something happened that caused all the horses to quiet down. The oldest of the mares, Vyazapúrikha, went up to the gelding, sniffed at him, and sighed. The gelding sighed too. . . .

V

In the middle of the moonlit paddock stood the tall gaunt figure of the gelding, still wearing the high saddle with its prominent peak at the bow. The horses stood motionless and in deep silence around him as if they were learning something new and unexpected. And they had learnt something new and unexpected.

This is what they learnt from him . . .

First Night

Yes, I am the son of Affable I and of Bába. My pedigree name is Muzhík, and I was nicknamed Strider by the crowd because of my long and sweeping strides, the like of which was nowhere to be found in all Russia. There is no more thoroughbred horse in the world. I should never have told you this. What good would it have done? You would never have recognized me: even Vyazapúrikha, who was with me in Khrénovo, did not recognize me till now. You would not have believed me if Vyazapúrikha were not here to be my witness, and I should never have told you this. I don't need equine sympathy. But you wished it. Yes, I am that Strider whom connoisseurs are looking for and cannot find

—that Strider whom the count himself knew and got rid of from his stud because I outran Swan, his favourite.

When I was born I did not know what *piebald* meant—I thought I was just a horse. I remember that the first remark we heard about my colour struck my mother and me deeply.

I suppose I was born in the night; by the morning, having been licked over by my mother, I already stood on my feet. I remember I kept wanting something and that everything seemed very surprising and yet very simple. Our stalls opened into a long warm passage and had latticed doors through which everything could be seen.

My mother offered me her teats but I was still so innocent that I poked my nose now between her forelegs and now under her udder. Suddenly she glanced at the latticed door and lifting her leg over me stepped aside. The groom on duty was looking into our stall through the lattice.

"Why, Bába has foaled!" he said, and began to draw the bolt. He came in over the fresh bedding and put his arms round me. "Just look, Tarás!" he shouted, "what a piebald he is—a regular magpie!"

I darted away from him and fell on my knees.

"Look at him—the little devil!"

My mother became disquieted but did not take my part; she only stepped a little to one side with a very deep sigh. Other grooms came to look at me, and one of them ran to tell the stud groom.

Everybody laughed when they looked at my spots, and they gave me all kinds of strange names, but neither I nor my mother understood those words. Till then there had been no piebalds among all my relatives. We did not think there was anything bad in it. Everybody even praised my strength and my form.

"See what a frisky fellow!" said the groom. "There's no holding him."

Before long the stud groom came and began to express astonishment at my colour; he even seemed aggrieved.

"And who does the little monster take after?" he said. "The general won't keep him in the stud. Oh, Bába, you have played me a trick!" he addressed my mother. "You might at least have dropped one with just a star—but this one is all piebald!"

My mother did not reply but as usual on such occasions drew a sigh.

"And what devil does he take after—he's just like a peasant-horse!" he continued. "He can't be left in the stud —he'd shame us. But he's well built—very well!" said he, and so did everyone who saw me.

A few days later the general himself came and looked at me, and again everyone seemed horrified at something, and abused me and my mother for the colour of my hair. "but he's a fine colt—very fine!" said all who saw me.

Until spring we all lived separately in the brood mares' stable, each with our mother, and only occasionally when the snow on the stable roofs began to melt in the sun were we let out with our mothers into the large paddock strewn with fresh straw. There I first came to know all my dear and my distant relations. Here I saw all the famous mares of the day coming out from different doors with their little foals. There was the old mare Dutch, Fly (Creamy's daughter), Ruddy the riding-horse, Wellwisher—all celebrities at that time. They all gathered together with their foals, walking about in the sunshine, rolling on the fresh straw and sniffing at one another like ordinary horses. I have never forgotten the sight of that paddock full of the beauties of that day. It seems strange to you to think, and hard to believe, that I was ever young and frisky, but it was so. This same Vyazapúrikha was then a yearling filly whose mane had just been cut; a dear, merry, lively little thing, but—and I do not say it to offend her—although among you she is now considered a remarkable thoroughbred she was then among the poorest horses in the stud. She will herself confirm this.

My mottled appearance, which men so disliked, was very attractive to all the horses; they all came round me, admired me, and frisked about with me. I began to forget what men said about my mottled appearance and felt happy. But I soon experienced the first sorrow of my life and the cause of it was my mother. When the thaw had set in, the sparrows twittered under the eaves, spring was felt more strongly in the air, and my mother's treatment of me changed.

Her whole disposition changed: she would frisk about without any reason and run round the yard, which did not at all accord with her dignified age; then she would consider and begin to neigh, and would bite and kick her sister mares, and then begin to sniff at me and snort discontentedly; then on going out into the sun she would lay her head across the shoulder of her cousin, Lady Merchant, dreamily rub her back, and push me away from her teats.

One day the stud groom came and had a halter put on her and she was led out of the stall. She neighed and I answered and rushed after her, but she did not even look back at me. The strapper, Tarás, seized me in his arms while they were closing the door after my mother had been led out.

I bolted and upset the strapper on the straw, but the door was shut and I could only hear the receding sound of my mother's neighing; and that neigh did not sound like a call to me but had another expression. Her voice was answered from afar by a powerful voice—that of Dóbry I, as I learned later, who was being led by two grooms, one on each side, to meet my mother.

I don't remember how Tarás got out of my stall: I felt too sad, for I knew that I had lost my mother's love for ever. "And it's all because I am piebald!" I thought, remembering what people said about my colour, and such passionate anger overcame me that I began to beat my head and knees against the walls of the stall and continued till I was sweating all over and quite exhausted.

After a while my mother came back to me. I heard her run up the passage at a trot and with an unusual gait. They opened the door for her and I hardly knew her—she had grown so much younger and more beautiful. She sniffed at me, snorted, and began to whinny. Her whole demeanour showed that she no longer loved me.

She told me of Dóbry's beauty and her love of him. Those meetings continued and the relations between my mother and me grew colder and colder.

Soon after that we were let out to pasture. I now discovered new joys which made up to me for the loss of my mother's love. I had friends and companions. Together we learnt to eat grass, to neigh like the grown-ups, and to gallop round our mothers with lifted tails. That was a happy time. Everything was forgiven me, everybody loved me, admired me, and looked indulgently at anything I did. But that did not last long.

Soon afterwards something dreadful happened to me. . . .

The gelding heaved a deep sigh and walked away from the other horses.

The dawn had broken long before. The gates creaked. Nester came in, and the horses separated. The keeper straightened the saddle on the gelding's back and drove the horses out.

VI

Second Night

As soon as the horses had been driven in they again gathered round the piebald, who continued:

In August they separated me from my mother and I did not feel particularly grieved. I saw that she was again heavy (with my brother, the famous Usán) and that I could no longer be to her what I had been. I was not jealous but felt that I had become indifferent to her. Besides, I knew that having left my mother I should be put in the general division of foals, where we were kept two or three together and were every day let out in a crowd into the open. I was in the same stall with Darling. Darling was a saddle-horse, who was subsequently ridden by the Emperor and portrayed in pictures and sculpture. At that time he was a mere foal, with a soft glossy coat, a swanlike neck, and straight slender legs taut as the strings of an instrument. He was always lively, good-tempered, and amiable, always ready to gambol, exchange licks, and play tricks on horse or man. Living together as we did we involuntarily made friends, and our friendship lasted the whole of our youth. He was merry and giddy. Even then he began to make love, courted the fillies, and laughed at my guilelessness. To my misfortune vanity led me to imitate him, and I was soon carried away and fell in love. And this early tendency of mine was the cause of the greatest change in my *life* It happened that I was carried away . . . Vyazapúrikha was *a year* older than I, and we were special friends, but towards the autumn I noticed that she began to be shy with me. . . .

But I will not speak of that unfortunate period of *my* first love; she herself remembers my mad passion, which ended for me in the most important change of my life.

The strappers rushed to drive her away and to beat me. That evening I was shut up in a special stall where I neighed all night as if foreseeing what was to happen next.

In the morning the General, the stud groom, the stable-men and the strappers came into the passage where my stall was, and there was a terrible hubbub. The General shouted at the stud groom, who tried to justify himself by saying that he had not told them to let me out but that the grooms had done it of their own accord. The General said that he would have everybody flogged, and that it would not do to keep young stallions. The stud groom promised that he would have everything attended to. They grew quiet and went away. I did not understand anything, but could see that they were planning something concerning me.

The day after that I ceased neighing for ever. I became what I am now. The whole world was changed in my eyes. Nothing mattered any more; I became self-absorbed and began to brood. At first everything seemed repulsive to me. I even ceased to eat, drink, or walk, and there was no idea of playing. Now and then it occurred to me to give a kick, to gallop, or to start neighing, but immediately came the question: Why? What for? and all my energy died away.

One evening I was being exercised just when the horses were driven back from pasture. I saw in the distance a cloud of dust enveloping the indistinct but familiar outlines of all our brood mares. I heard their cheerful snorting and the trampling of their feet. I stopped, though the cord of the halter by which the groom was leading me cut the nape of my neck, and I gazed at the approaching drove as one gazes at happiness that is lost for ever and cannot return. They approached, and I could distinguish one after another all the familiar, beautiful, stately, healthy, sleek figures

Some of them also turned to look at me. I was unconscious of the pain the groom's jerking at my halter inflicted. I forgot myself and from old habit involuntarily neighed and began to trot, but my neighing sounded sad, ridiculous, and meaningless. No one in the drove made sport of me, but I noticed that out of decorum many of them turned away from me. They evidently felt it repugnant, pitiable, indelicate, and above all ridiculous, to look at my thin expressionless neck, my large head (I had grown lean in the meantime), my long, awkward legs, and the silly awkward gait with which by force of habit I trotted round the groom. No one answered my neighing—they all looked away. Suddenly I understood it all, understood how far I was for ever removed from them, and I do not remember how I got home with the groom.

Already before that I had shown a tendency towards gravity and thoughtfulness, but now a decided change came over me. My being piebald, which aroused such curious contempt in men, my terrible and unexpected misfortune, and also my peculiar position in the stud farm which I felt but was unable to explain made me retire into myself. I pondered over the injustice of men, who blamed me for being piebald; I pondered on the inconstancy of mother-love and feminine love in general and on its dependence on physical conditions; and above all I pondered on the characteristics of that strange race of animals with whom we are so closely connected, and whom we call men —those characteristics which were the source of my own peculiar position in the stud farm, which I felt but could not understand.

The meaning of this peculiarity in people and the characteristic on which it is based was shown me by the following occurrence.

It was in winter at holiday time. I had not been fed or watered all day. As I learnt later this happened because the lad who fed us was drunk. That day the stud groom came in, saw that I had no food, began to use bad language about the missing lad, and then went away.

Next day the lad came into our stable with another groom to give us hay. I noticed that he was particularly pale and sad and that in the expression of his long back especially there was something significant which evoked compassion.

He threw the hay angrily over the grating. I made a move to put my head over his shoulder, but he struck me such a painful blow on the nose with his fist that I started back. Then he kicked me in the belly with his boot.

"If it hadn't been for this scurvy beast," he said, "nothing would have happened!"

"How's that?" inquired the other groom.

"You see, he doesn't go to look after the count's horses but visits his own twice a day."

"What, have they given him the piebald?" asked the other.

"Given it, or sold it—the devil only knows! The count's horses might all starve—he wouldn't care—but just dare to leave *his* colt without food! 'Lie down!' he says, and they begin walloping me! No Christianity in it. He has more pity on a beast than on a man. He must be an infidel—he counted the strokes himself, the barbarian! The general never flogged like that! My whole back is covered with wales. There's no Christian soul in him!"

What they said about flogging and Christianity I understood well enough, but I was quite in the dark as to what they meant by the words "*his* colt," from which I perceived that people considered that there was some connexion between me and the head groom. What the connexion was I could not at all understand then. Only much later when they separated me from the other horses did I learn what it meant. At that time I could not at all understand what they meant by speaking of *me* as being a man's property. The words "*my* horse" applied to me, a live horse, seemed to me as strange as to say "my land," "my air," or "my water."

But those words had an enormous effect on me. I thought of them constantly and only after long and varied relations with men did I at last understand the meaning they attach to these strange words, which indicate that men are guided in life not by deeds but by words. They like not so much to do or abstain from doing anything, as to be able to apply conventional words to different objects. Such words, considered very important among them, are *my* and *mine*, which they apply to various things, creatures, or objects: even to land, people, and horses. They have agreed that of any given thing only one person may use the word *mine*, and he who in this game of theirs may use that conventional word about the greatest number of things is considered the happiest. Why this is so I do not know, but it is so. For a long time I tried to explain it by some direct advantage they derive from it, but this proved wrong.

For instance, many of those who called me *their* horse did not ride me, quite other people rode me; nor did they feed me—quite other people did that. Again it was not those who called me *their* horse who treated me kindly, but coachmen, veterinaries, and in general quite other people. Later on, having widened my field of observation, I became convinced that not only as applied to us horses, but in regard to other things, the idea of *mine* has no other basis than a low, mercenary instinct in men, which they call the feeling or right of property. A man who never lives in it says "my house" but only concerns himself with its building and maintenance; and a tradesman talks of "my cloth business" but has none of his clothes made of the best cloth that is in his shop.

There are people who call land theirs, though they have never seen that land and never walked on it. There are people who call other people theirs but have never seen those others, and the whole relationship of the owners to the owned is that they do them harm.

There are men who call women their women or their wives; yet these women live with other men. And men strive in life not to do what they think right but to call as many things as possible *their own*.

I am now convinced that in this lies the essential difference between men and us. Therefore, not to speak of other things in which we are superior to men, on this ground alone we may boldly say that in the scale of living creatures we stand higher than man. The activity of men, at any rate of those I have had to do with, is guided by words, while ours is guided by deeds.

It was this right to speak of me as *my horse* that the stud groom had obtained, and that was why he had the stable lad flogged. This discovery much astonished me and, together with the thoughts and opinions aroused in men by my piebald colour and the thoughtfulness produced in me by my mother's betrayal, caused me to become the serious and thoughtful gelding that I am.

I was thrice unfortunate: I was piebald, I was a gelding, and people considered that I did not belong to God and to myself, as is natural to all living creatures, but that I belonged to the stud groom.

Their thinking this about me had many consequences. The first was that I was kept apart from the other horses, was better fed, oftener taken out on the line, and was broken in at an earlier age. I was first harnessed in my third year. I remember how the stud groom, who imagined I was his, himself began to harness me with a crowd of other grooms, expecting me to prove unruly or to resist. They put ropes round me to lead me into the shafts, put a cross of broad straps on my back and fastened it to the shafts so that I could not kick, while I was only awaiting an opportunity to show my readiness and love of work.

They were surprised that I started like an old horse. They began to brake me and I began to practise trotting. Every day I made greater and greater progress, so that after three months the general himself and many others approved of my pace. But strange to say, just because they considered me not as their own, but as belonging to the head groom, they regarded my paces quite differently.

The stallions who were my brothers were raced, their records were kept, people went to look at them, drove them in gilt sulkies, and expensive horse-cloths were thrown over them. I was driven in a common sulky to Chesménka and other farms on the head groom's business. All this was the result of my being piebald, and especially of my being in their opinion, not the count's, but the head groom's property.

To-morrow, if we are alive, I will tell you the chief consequence for me of this right of property the head groom considered himself to have.

All that day the horses treated Strider respectfully, but Nester's treatment of him was as rough as ever. The peasant's little roan horse neighed again on coming up to the herd, and the chestnut filly again coquettishly replied to him.

VII

Third Night

The new moon had risen and its narrow crescent lit up Strider's figure as he once again stood in the middle of the stable yard. The other horses crowded round him:

The gelding continued:

For me the most surprising consequence of my not being the count's, nor God's, but the head groom's, was that the very thing that constitutes our chief merit—a fast pace—was the cause of my banishment. They were driving Swan round the track, and the head groom, returning from Cheskénka, drove me up and stopped there. Swan went past. He went well, but all the same he was showing off and had not the exactitude I had developed in myself—so that directly one foot touched the ground another instantaneously lifted and not the slightest effort was lost but every atom of exertion carried me forward. Swan went by us. I pulled towards the ring and the head groom did not check me. "Here, shall I try my piebald?" he shouted, and when next Swan came abreast of us he let me go. Swan was already going fast, and so I was left behind during the first round, but in the second I began to gain on him, drew near to his sulky, drew level—and passed him. They tried us again—it was the same thing. I was the faster. And this dismayed everybody. The general asked that I should be sold at once to some distant place, so that nothing more should be heard of me: "Or else the count will get to know of it and there will be trouble!" So they sold me to a horse-dealer as a shaft-horse. I did not remain with him long. An hussar who came to buy remounts bought me. All this was so unfair, so cruel, that I was glad when they took me away from Khrénovo and parted me for ever from all that had been familiar and dear to me. It was too painful for me among them. They had love, honour, freedom, before them! I had labour, humiliation; humiliation, labour, to the end of my life. And why? Because I was piebald, and because of that had to become somebody's horse. . . .

Strider could not continue that evening. An event occurred in the enclosure that upset all the horses. Kupchíkha, a mare big with foal, who had stood listening to the story, suddenly turned away and walked slowly into the shed, and there began to groan so that it drew the attention of all the horses. Then she lay down, then got up again, and again lay down. The old mares understood what was happening to her, but the young ones became excited and, leaving the gelding, surrounded the invalid. Towards morning there was a new foal standing unsteadily on its little legs. Nester shouted to the groom, and the mare and foal were taken into a stall and the other horses driven to the pasture without them.

VIII

Fourth Night

In the evening when the gate was closed and all had quieted down, the piebald continued:

I have had the opportunity to make many observations both of men and horses during the time I passed from hand to hand.

I stayed longest of all with two masters: a prince (an officer of hussars), and later with an old lady who lived near the church of St. Nicholas the Wonder Worker.

The happiest years of my life I spent with the officer of hussars.

Though he was the cause of my ruin, and though he never loved anything or anyone, I loved and still love him for that very reason.

What I liked about him was that he was handsome, happy, rich, and therefore never loved anybody.

You understand that lofty equine feeling of ours. His coldness and my dependence on him gave special strength to my love for him. "Kill me, drive me till my wind is broken!" I used to think in our good days, "and I shall be all the happier."

He bought me from an agent to whom the head groom had sold me for eight hundred rubles, and he did so just because no one else had piebald horses. That was my best time. He had a mistress. I knew this because I took him to her every day and sometimes took them both out.

His mistress was a handsome woman, and he was handsome, and his coachman was handsome, and I loved them all because they were. Life was worth living then. This was how our time was spent: in the morning the groom came to rub me down—not the coachman himself but the groom. The groom was a lad from among the peasants. He would open the door, let out the steam from the horses, throw out the droppings, take off our rugs, and begin to fidget over our bodies with a brush, and lay whitish streaks of dandruff from a curry-comb on the boards of the floor that was dented by our rough horseshoes. I would playfully nip his sleeve and paw the ground. Then we were led out one after another to the trough filled with cold water, and the lad would admire the smoothness of my spotted coat which he had polished, my foot with its broad hoof, my legs straight as an arrow, my glossy quarters, and my back wide enough to sleep on. Hay was piled onto the high racks, and the oak cribs were filled with oats. Then Feofán, the head coachman, would come in.

Master and coachman resembled one another. Neither of them was afraid of anything or cared for anyone but himself, and for that reason everybody liked them. Feofán wore a red shirt, black velveteen knickerbockers, and a sleeveless coat. I liked it on a holiday when he would come into the stable, his hair pomaded, and wearing his sleeveless coat, and would shout, "Now then, beastie, have you forgotten?" and push me with the handle of the stable fork, never so as to hurt me but just as a joke. I immediately knew that it was a joke and laid back an ear, making my teeth click.

We had a black stallion, who drove in a pair. At night they used to put me in harness with him. That Polkán, as he was called, did not understand a joke but was simply vicious as the devil. I was in the stall next to his and sometimes we bit one another seriously. Feofán was not afraid of him. He would come up and give a shout: it looked as if Polkán would kill him, but no, he'd miss, and Feofán would put the harness on him.

Once he and I bolted down Smiths Bridge Street. Neither my master nor the coachman was frightened; they laughed, shouted at the people, checked us, and turned so that no one was run over.

In their service I lost my best qualities and half my life. They ruined me by watering me wrongly, and they foundered me. . . . Still, for all that, it was the best time of my life. At twelve o'clock they would come to harness me, black my hoofs, moisten my forelock and mane, and put me in the shafts.

The sledge was of plaited cane upholstered with velvet; the reins were of silk, the harness had silver buckles, sometimes there was a cover of silken fly-net, and altogether it was such that when all the traces and straps were fastened it was difficult to say where the harness ended and the horse began. We were harnessed at ease in the stable. Feofán would come, broader at his hips than at the shoulders, his red belt up under his arms: he would examine the harness, take his seat, wrap his coat round him, put his foot into the sledge stirrup, let off some joke, and for appearance sake always hung a whip over his arm though he hardly ever hit me, and would say, "Let go!" and playfully stepping from foot to foot I would move out of the gate, and the cook who had come out to empty the slops would stop on the threshold and the peasant who had brought wood into the yard would open his eyes wide. We would come out, go a little way, and stop. Footmen would come out and other coachmen, and a chatter would begin. Everybody would wait: sometimes we had to stand for three hours at the entrance, moving a little way, turning back, and standing again.

At last there would be a stir in the hall: old Tíkhon with his paunch would rush out in his dress coat and cry, "Drive up!" (In those days there was not that stupid way of saying, "Forward!" as if one did not know that we moved forward and not back.) Feofán would cluck, drive up, and the prince would hurry out carelessly, as though there were nothing remarkable about the sledge, or the horse, or Feofán—who bent his back and stretched out his arms so that it seemed it would be impossible for him to keep them long in that position. The prince would have a shako on his head and wear a fur coat with a grey beaver collar hiding his rosy, black-browed, handsome face, that should never have been concealed. He would come out clattering his sabre, his spurs, and the brass backs of the heels of his overshoes, stepping over the carpet as if in a hurry and taking no notice of me or Feofán whom everybody but he looked at and admired. Feofán would cluck, I would tug at the reins, and respectably, at a foot pace, we would draw up to the entrance and stop. I would turn my eyes on the prince and jerk my thoroughbred head with its delicate forelock. . . . The prince would be in good spirits and would sometimes jest with Feofán. Feofán would reply, half turning his handsome head, and without lowering his arms would make a scarcely perceptible movement with the reins which I understand: and then one, two, three . . . with ever wider and wider strides, every muscle quivering, and sending the muddy snow against the front of the sledge, I would go. In those days, too, there was none of the present-day stupid habit of crying, "Oh!" as if the coachman were in pain, instead of the sensible "Be off! Take care!" Feofán would shout, "Be off! Look out there!" and the people would step aside and stand craning their necks to see the handsome gelding, the handsome coachman, and the handsome gentleman. . . .

I was particularly fond of passing a trotter. When Feofán and I saw at a distance a turn-out worthy of the effort, we would fly like a whirlwind and gradually gain on it. Now, throwing the dirt right to the back of the sledge, I would draw level with the occupant of the vehicle and snort above his head: then I would reach the horse's harness and the arch of his troyka, and then would no longer see it but only hear its sounds in the distance behind. And the prince, Feofán, and I, would all be silent, and pretend to be merely going on our own business and not even to notice those with slow horses whom we happened to meet on our way. I liked to pass another horse but also liked to meet a good trotter. An instant, a sound, a glance, and we had passed each other and were flying in opposite directions.

The gate creaked and the voices of Nester and Váska were heard.

Fifth Night

The weather began to break up. It had been dull since morning and there was no dew, but it was warm and the mosquitoes were troublesome. As soon as the horses were driven in they collected round the piebald, and he finished his story as follows:

The happy period of my life was soon over. I lived in that way only two years. Towards the end of the second winter the happiest event of my life occurred, and following it came my greatest misfortune. It was during carnival week. I took the prince to the races. Glossy and Bull were running. I don't know what people were doing in the pavilion, but I know the prince came out and ordered Feofán to drive onto the track. I remember how they took me in and placed me beside Glossy. He was harnessed to a racing sulky and I, just as I was, to a town sledge. I outstripped him at the turn. Roars of laughter and howls of delight greeted me.

When I was led in, a crowd followed me and five or six people offered the prince thousands for me. He only laughed, showing his white teeth.

"No," he said, "this isn't a horse, but a friend. I wouldn't sell him for mountains of gold. *Au revoir*, gentlemen!"

He unfastened the sledge apron and got in.

"To Ostózhenka Street!"

That was where his mistress lived, and off we flew. . . .

That was our last happy day. We reached her home. He spoke of her as *his*, but she loved someone else and had run away with him. The prince learnt this at her lodgings. It was five o'clock, and without unharnessing me he started in pursuit of her. They did what had never been done to me before—struck me with the whip and made me gallop. For the first time I fell out of step and felt ashamed and wished to correct it, but suddenly I heard the prince shout in an unnatural voice: "Get on!" The whip whistled through the air and cut me, and I galloped, striking my foot against the iron front of the sledge. We overtook her after going sixteen miles. I got him there but trembled all night long and could not eat anything. In the morning they gave me water. I drank it and after that was never again the horse that I had been. I was ill, and they tormented me and maimed me—doctoring me, as people call it. My hoofs came off, I had swellings and my legs grew bent; my chest sank in and I became altogether limp and weak. I was sold to a horse-dealer who fed me on carrots and something else and made something of me quite unlike myself, though good enough to deceive one who did not know. My strength and my pace were gone.

When purchasers came the dealer also tormented me by coming into my stall and beating me with a heavy whip to frighten and madden me. Then he would rub down the stripes on my coat and lead me out.

An old woman bought me of him. She always drove to the Church of St. Nicholas the Wonder Worker, and she used to have her coachman flogged. He used to weep in my stall and I learnt that tears have a pleasant, salty taste. Then the old woman died. Her steward took me to the country and sold me to a hawker. Then I overate myself with wheat and grew still worse. They sold me to a peasant. There I ploughed, had hardly anything to eat, my foot got cut by a ploughshare, and I again became ill. Then a gipsy took me in exchange for something. He tormented me terribly and finally sold me to the steward here. And here I am.

All were silent. A sprinkling of rain began to fall.

IX

The Evening After

As the herd returned home the following evening they encountered their master with a visitor. Zhuldýba when nearing the house looked askance at the two male figures: one was the young master in his straw hat, the other a tall, stout, bloated military man. The old mare gave the man a side-glance and, swerving, went near him; the others, the young ones, were flustered and hesitated, especially when the master and his visitor purposely stepped among them, pointing something out to one another and talking.

"That one, the dapple grey, I bought of Voékov," said the master.

"And where did you get that young black mare with the white legs? She's a fine one!" said the visitor. They looked over many of the horses, going forward and stopping them. They noticed the chestnut filly too.

"That is one I kept of Khrénov's saddle-horse breed," said the master.

They could not see all the horses as they walked past, and the master called to Nester, and the old man, tapping the sides of the piebald with his heels, trotted forward. The piebald limped on one leg but moved in a way that showed that as long as his strength lasted he would not murmur on any account, even if they wanted him to run in that way to the end of the world. He was even ready to gallop and tried to do so with his right leg.

"There, I can say for certain that there is no better horse in Russia than this one," said the master, pointing to one of the mares. The visitor admired it. The master walked about excitedly, ran forward, and showed his visitor all the horses, mentioning the origin and pedigree of each.

The visitor evidently found the master's talk dull but devised some questions to show interest.

"Yes, yes," he said absent-mindedly.

"Just look," said the master, not answering a question. "Look at her legs. . . . She cost me a lot but has a third foal already in harness."

"And trots well?" asked the guest.

So they went past all the horses till there were no more to show. Then they were silent.

"Well, shall we go now?"

"Yes, let's go."

They went through the gate. The visitor was glad the exhibition was over and that he could now go to the house where they could eat and drink and smoke, and he grew perceptibly brighter. As he went past Nester, who sat on the piebald waiting for orders, the visitor slapped the piebald's crupper with his big fat hand.

"What an ornamented one!" he said. "I once had a piebald like him; do you remember my telling you of him?"

The master, finding that it was not his horse that was being spoken about, paid no attention but kept looking round at his own herd.

Suddenly above his ear he heard a dull, weak, senile neigh. It was the piebald that had begun to neigh and had broken off as if ashamed.

Neither the visitor nor the master paid any attention to this neighing, but went into the house.

In the flabby old man Strider had recognized his beloved master, the once brilliant, handsome, and wealthy Serpukhovskóy.

X

It kept on drizzling. In the stable yard it was gloomy, but in the master's house it was very different. The table was laid in a luxurious drawing-room for a luxurious evening tea, and at it sat the host, the hostess, and their guest.

The hostess, her pregnancy made very noticeable by her figure, her strained convex pose, her plumpness, and especially by her large eyes with their mild inward look, sat by the samovar.

The host held in his hand a box of special, ten-year-old cigars, such as he said no one else had, and he was preparing to boast about them to his guest. The host was a handsome man of about twenty-five, fresh-looking, well cared for, and well groomed. In the house he was wearing a new loose thick suit made in London. Large expensive pendants hung from his watch-chain. His gold-mounted turquoise shirt studs were also large and massive. He had a beard à la Napoléon III, and the tips of his moustache stuck out in a way that could only have been learned in Paris.

The hostess wore a dress of silk gauze with a large floral pattern of many colours, and large gold hair-pins of a peculiar pattern held up her thick, light-brown hair—beautiful though not all her own. On her arms and hands she wore many bracelets and rings, all of them expensive.

The tea-service was of delicate china and the samovar of silver. A footman, resplendent in dress-coat, white waistcoat and necktie, stood like a statue by the door awaiting orders. The furniture was elegantly carved and upholstered in bright colours, the wall-paper dark with a large flowered pattern. Beside the table, tinkling the silver bells on its collar, was a particularly fine whippet, whose difficult English name its owners, who neither of them knew English, pronounced badly.

In the corner, surrounded by plants, stood an inlaid piano. Everything gave an impression of newness, luxury, and rarity. Everything was good, but it all bore an imprint of superfluity, wealth, and the absence of intellectual interests.

The host, a lover of trotting races, was sturdy and full-blooded—one of that never-dying race which drives about in sable coats, throws expensive bouquets to actresses, drinks the most expensive wines with the most fashionable labels at the most expensive restaurants, offers prizes engraved with the donor's name, and keeps the most expensive mistresses.

Nikíta Serpukhovskóy, their guest, was a man of over forty, tall, stout, bald-headed, with heavy moustaches and whiskers. He must once have been very handsome but had now evidently sunk physically, morally, and financially.

He had such debts that he had been obliged to enter the government service to avoid imprisonment for debt and was now on his way to a provincial town to become the head of a stud farm, a post some important relatives had obtained for him.

He wore a military coat and blue trousers of a kind only a rich man would have had made for himself. His shirt was of similar quality and so was his English watch. His boots had wonderful soles as thick as a man's finger.

Nikíta Serpukhovskóy had during his life run through a fortune of two million rubles, and was now a hundred and twenty thousand in debt. In cases of that kind there always remains a certain momentum of life enabling a man to obtain credit and continue living almost luxuriously for another ten years.

These ten years were however coming to an end, the momentum was exhausted, and life was growing hard for Nikíta. He was already beginning to drink—that is, to get fuddled with wine, a thing that used not to happen, though strictly speaking he had never begun or left off drinking. His decline was most noticeable in the restlessness of his glance (his eyes had grown shifty) and in the uncertainty of his voice and movements. This restlessness struck one the more as it had evidently got hold of him only recently, for one could see that he had all his life been accustomed not to be afraid of anything or anybody and had only recently, through heavy suffering, reached this state of fear so unnatural to him.

His host and hostess noticed this and exchanged glances which showed that they understood one another and were only postponing till bedtime a detailed discussion of the subject, putting up meanwhile with poor Nikíta and even showing him attentions.

The sight of his young host's good fortune humiliated Serpukhovskóy, awakening a painful envy in him as he recalled his own irrecoverable past.

"Do you mind my smoking a cigar, Marie?" he asked, addressing the lady in that peculiar tone acquired only by experience—the tone, polite and friendly but not quite respectful, in which men who know the world speak to kept women in contradistinction to wives. Not that he wished to offend her: on the contrary he now wished rather to curry favour with her and with her keeper, though he would on no account have acknowledged the fact to himself. But he was accustomed to speak in that way to such women. He knew she would herself be surprised and even offended were he to treat her as a lady. Besides he had to retain a certain shade of a respectful tone for his friend's real wife. He always treated his friend's mistresses with respect, not because he shared the so-called convictions promulgated in periodicals (he never read trash of that kind) about the respect due to the personality of every man, about the meaninglessness of marriage, and so forth, but because all decent men do so and he was a decent, though fallen, man.

He took a cigar. But his host awkwardly picked up a whole handful and offered them to him.

"Just see how good these are. Take them!"

Serpukhovskóy pushed aside the hand with the cigars, and a gleam of offence and shame showed itself in his eyes.

"Thank you!" He took out his cigar-case. "Try mine!"

The hostess was sensitive. She noticed his embarrassment and hastened to talk to him.

"I am very fond of cigars. I should smoke myself if everyone about me did not smoke."

And she smiled her pretty, kindly smile. He smiled in return, but irresolutely. Two of his teeth were missing.

"No, take this!" the tactless host continued. "The others are weaker. Fritz, *bringen Sie noch einen Kasten,*" he said; *dort zwei.*"[1]

The German footman brought another box.

"Do you prefer big ones? Strong ones? These are very good. Take them all!" he continued, forcing them on his guest.

He was evidently glad to have someone to boast to of the rare things he possessed, and he noticed nothing amiss. Serpukhovskóy lit his cigar and hastened to resume the conversation they had begun.

"So, how much did you pay for Atlásny?" he asked.

"He cost me a great deal, not less than five thousand, but at any rate I am already safe on him. What colts he gets, I tell you!"

"Do they trot?" asked Serpukhovskóy.

"They trot well! His colt took three prizes this year: in Túla, in Moscow, and in Petersburg; he raced Voékov's Raven. That rascal, the driver, let him make four false steps or he'd have left the other behind the flag."

"He's a bit green. Too much Dutch blood in him, that's what I say," remarked Serpukhovskóy.

"Well, but what about the mares? I'll show Goody to you to-morrow. I gave three thousand for her. For Amiable I gave two thousand."

And the host again began to enumerate his possessions. The hostess saw that this hurt Serpukhovskóy and that he was only pretending to listen.

"Will you have some more tea?" she asked.

"I won't," replied the host and went on talking. She rose, the host stopped her, embraced her, and kissed her.

As he looked at them Serpukhovskóy for their sakes

---

[1] "Bring another box. There are two there."

tried to force a smile, but after the host had got up, embraced her, and led her to the portière, Serpukhovskóy's
face suddenly changed. He sighed heavily, and a look of
despair showed itself on his flabby face. Even malevolence
appeared on it.

The host returned and smilingly sat down opposite him.
They were silent awhile.

XI

"Yes, you were saying you bought him of Voékov," remarked Serpukhovskóy with assumed carelessness.

"Oh yes, that was of Atlásny, you know. I always meant
to buy some mares of Dubovítzki, but he had nothing but
rubbish left."

"He has failed . . ." said Serpukhovskóy, and suddenly
stopped and glanced round. He remembered that he owed
that bankrupt twenty thousand rubles, and if it came to
talking of being bankrupt it was certainly said that he was
one. He laughed.

Both again sat silent for a long time. The host considered
what he could brag about to his guest. Serpukhovskóy was
thinking what he could say to show that he did not consider
himself bankrupt. But the minds of both worked with difficulty, in spite of efforts to brace themselves up with cigars.
"When are we going to have a drink?" thought Serpukhovskóy. "I must certainly have a drink or I shall die of
ennui with this fellow," thought the host.

"Will you be remaining here long?" Serpukhovskóy
asked.

"Another month. Well, shall we have supper, eh? Fritz,
is it ready?"

They went into the dining-room. There under a hanging
lamp stood a table on which were candles and all sorts of
extraordinary things: syphons, and little dolls fastened to
corks, rare wine in decanters, unusual hors-d'oeuvres, and
vodka. They had a drink, ate a little, drank again, ate
again, and their conversation got into swing. Serpukhovskóy
was flushed and began to speak without timidity.

They spoke of women and of who kept this one or that,
a gipsy, a ballet-girl, or a Frenchwoman.

"And have you given up Mathieu?" asked the host. (That was the woman who had ruined Serpukhovskóy.)

"No, she left me. Ah, my dear fellow, when I recall what I have got through in my life! Now I am really glad when I have a thousand rubles, and am glad to get away from everybody. I can't stand it in Moscow. But what's the good of talking!"

The host found it tiresome to listen to Serpukhovskóy. He wanted to speak about himself—to brag. But Serpukhovskóy also wished to talk about himself, about his brilliant past. His host filled his glass for him and waited for him to stop, so that he might tell him about himself and how his stud was now arranged as no one had ever had a stud arranged before. And that his Marie loved him with her heart and not merely for his wealth.

"I wanted to tell you that in my stud . . ." he began, but Serpukhovskóy interrupted him.

"I may say that there was a time," Serpukhovskóy began, "when I liked to live well and knew how to do it. Now you talk about trotting—tell me which is your fastest horse."

The host, glad of an opportunity to tell more about his stud, was beginning, when Serpukhovskóy again interrupted him.

"Yes, yes," he said, "but you breeders do it just out of vanity and not for pleasure, not for the joy of life. It was different with me. You know I told you I had a driving-horse, a piebald with just the same kind of spots as the one your keeper was riding. Oh, what a horse that was! You can't possibly know: it was in 1842, when I had just come to Moscow; I went to a horse-dealer and there I saw a well-bred piebald gelding. I liked him. The price? One thousand rubles. I liked him, so I took him and began to drive with him. I never had, and you have not and never will have, such a horse. I never knew one like him for speed and for strength. You were a boy then and couldn't have known, but you may have heard of him. All Moscow was talking about him."

"Yes, I heard of him," the host unwillingly replied. "But what I wished to say about mine . . ."

"Ah, then you did hear! I bought him just as he was,

without pedigree and without a certificate; it was only afterwards that I got to know Voékov and found out. He was a colt by Affable I. Strider—because of his long strides. On account of his piebald spots he was removed from the Khrénov stud and given to the head keeper, who had him castrated and sold him to a horse-dealer. There are no such horses now, my dear chap. Ah, those were days! Ah, vanished youth!"—and he sang the words of the gipsy song. He was getting tipsy. "Ah, those were good times. I was twenty-five and had eighty thousand rubles a year, not a single grey hair, and all my teeth like pearls. . . . Whatever I touched succeeded, and now it is all ended. . . ."

"But there was not the same mettlesomeness then," said the host, availing himself of the pause. "Let me tell you that my first horses began to trot without . . ."

"Your horses! But they used to be more mettlesome . . ."

"How—more mettlesome?"

"Yes, more mettlesome! I remember as if it were to-day how I drove him once to the trotting races in Moscow. No horse of mine was running. I did not care for trotters, mine were thoroughbreds: General Chaulet, Mahomet. I drove up with my piebald. My driver was a fine fellow, I was fond of him, but he also took to drink. . . . Well, so I got there.

" 'Serpukhovskóy,' I was asked, 'When are you going to keep trotters?' 'The devil take your lubbers!' I replied. 'I have a piebald hack that can outpace all your trotters!' 'Oh no, he won't!' 'I'll bet a thousand rubles!' Agreed, and they started. He came in five seconds ahead and I won the thousand rubles. But what of it? I did a hundred versts[1] in three hours with a troyka of thoroughbreds. All Moscow knows it."

And Serpukhovskóy began to brag so glibly and continuously that his host could not get a single word in and sat opposite him with a dejected countenance, filling up his own and his guest's glass every now and then by way of distraction.

The dawn was breaking and still they sat there. It became intolerably dull for the host. He got up.

"If we are to go to bed, let's go!" said Serpukhovskóy

---

[1] A little over sixty-six miles.

rising, and reeling and puffing he went to the room prepared for him.

The host was lying beside his mistress.

"No, he is unendurable," he said. "He gets drunk and swaggers incessantly."

"And makes up to me."

"I'm afraid he'll be asking for money."

Serpukhovskóy was lying on the bed in his clothes, breathing heavily.

"I must have been lying a lot," he thought. "Well, no matter! The wine was good, but he is an awful swine. There's something cheap about him. And I'm an awful swine," he said to himself and laughed aloud. "First I used to keep women, and now I'm kept. Yes, the Winkler girl will support me. I take money of her. Serves him right. Still, I must undress. Can't get my boots off. Hullo! Hullo!" he called out, but the man who had been told off to wait on him had long since gone to bed.

He sat down, took off his coat and waistcoat and somehow managed to kick off his trousers, but for a long time could not get his boots off—his soft stomach being in the way. He got one off at last, and struggled for a long time with the other, panting and becoming exhausted. And so with his foot in the boot-top he rolled over and began to snore, filling the room with a smell of tobacco, wine, and disagreeable old age.

XII

If Strider recalled anything that night, he was distracted by Váska, who threw a rug over him, galloped off on him, and kept him standing till morning at the door of a tavern, near a peasant horse. They licked one another. In the morning when Strider returned to the herd he kept rubbing himself.

Five days passed. They called in a veterinary, who said cheerfully: "It's the itch; let me sell him to the gipsies."

"What's the use? Cut his throat, and get it done to-day."

The morning was calm and clear. The herd went to pasture, but Strider was left behind. A strange man came— thin, dark, and dirty, in a coat splashed with something black. It was the knacker. Without looking at Strider he took him by the halter they had put on him and led him away. Strider went quietly without looking round, dragging along as usual and catching his hind feet in the straw.

When they were out of the gate he strained towards the well, but the knacker jerked his halter, saying: "Not worth while."

The knacker and Váska, who followed behind, went to a hollow behind the brick barn and stopped as if there were something peculiar about this very ordinary place. The knacker, handing the halter to Váska, took off his coat, rolled up his sleeves, and produced a knife and a whetstone from his boot-leg. The gelding stretched towards the halter meaning to chew it a little from dullness, but he could not reach it. He sighed and closed his eyes. His nether lip hung down, disclosing his worn yellow teeth, and he began to drowse to the sound of the sharpening of the knife. Only his swollen, aching, outstretched leg kept jerking. Suddenly he felt himself being taken by the lower jaw and his head lifted. He opened his eyes. There were two dogs in front of him; one was sniffing at the knacker, the other was sitting and watching the gelding as if expecting something from him. The gelding looked at them and began to rub his jaw against the arm that was holding him.

"Want to doctor me probably—well, let them!" he thought.

And in fact he felt that something had been done to his throat. It hurt, and he shuddered and gave a kick with one foot, but restrained himself and waited for what would follow. . . . Then he felt something liquid streaming down his neck and chest. He heaved a profound sigh and felt much better.

The whole burden of his life was eased.

He closed his eyes and began to droop his head. No one was holding it. Then his legs quivered and his whole body swayed. He was not so much frightened as surprised.

Everything was so new to him. He was surprised and started forward and upward, but instead of this, in moving from the spot his legs got entangled, he began to fall sideways, and trying to take a step fell forward and down on his left side.

The knacker waited till the convulsions had ceased,

drove away the dogs that had crept nearer, took the gelding by the legs, turned him on his back, told Váska to hold a leg, and began to skin the horse.

"It was a horse, too," remarked Váska.

"If he had been better fed the skin would have been fine," said the knacker.

The herd returned down hill in the evening, and those on the left saw down below something red, round which dogs were busy and above which hawks and crows were flying. One of the dogs, pressing its paws against the carcass and swinging his head, with a crackling sound tore off what it had seized hold of. The chestnut filly stopped, stretched out her head and neck, and sniffed the air for a long time. They could hardly drive her away.

At dawn, in a ravine of the old forest, down in an overgrown glade, big-headed wolf cubs were howling joyfully. There were five of them: four almost alike and one with a head bigger than his body. A lean old wolf who was shedding her coat, dragging her full belly with its hanging dugs along the ground, came out of the bushes and sat down in front of the cubs. The cubs came and stood round her in a semi-circle. She went up to the smallest, and bending her knee and holding her muzzle down, made some convulsive movements, and opening her large sharp-toothed jaws disgorged a large piece of horseflesh. The bigger cubs rushed towards her, but she moved threateningly at them and let the little one have it all. The little one, growling as if in anger, pulled the horseflesh under him and began to gorge. In the same way the mother wolf coughed up a piece for the second, the third, and all five of them, and then lay down in front of them to rest.

A week later only a large skull and two shoulder-blades lay behind the barn; the rest had all been taken away. In summer a peasant, collecting bones, carried away these shoulder-blades and skull and put them to use.

The dead body of Serpukhovskóy, which had walked about the earth eating and drinking, was put under ground much later. Neither his skin, nor his flesh, nor his bones, were of any use.

Just as for the last twenty years his body that had walked the earth had been a great burden to everybody, so the putting away of that body was again an additional trouble to people. He had not been wanted by anybody for a long time and had only been a burden, yet the dead who bury their dead found it necessary to clothe that swollen body, which at once began to decompose, in a good uniform and good boots and put it into a new and expensive coffin with new tassels at its four corners, and then to place that coffin in another coffin of lead, to take it to Moscow and there dig up some long buried human bones, and to hide in that particular spot this decomposing maggotty body in its new uniform and polished boots, and cover it all up with earth.

PART THREE
Fiction after
Anna Karenina

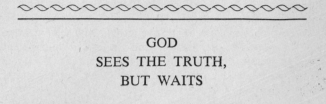

GOD
SEES THE TRUTH,
BUT WAITS

I

In the town of Vladímir lived a young merchant named Iván Dmítrich Aksënov. He had two shops and a house of his own.

Aksënov was a handsome, fair-haired, curly-headed fellow, full of fun and very fond of singing. When quite a young man he had been given to drink and was riotous when he had had too much, but after he married he gave up drinking except now and then.

One summer Aksënov was going to the Nízhny F[air], and as he bade good-bye to his family his wife said to him, "Iván Dmítrich, do not start to-day; I have had a bad dream about you."

Aksënov laughed, and said, "You are afraid that when I get to the fair I shall go on the spree."

His wife replied: "I do not know what I am afraid of; all I know is that I had a bad dream. You returned from the town, and when you took off your cap I saw that your hair was quite grey."

Aksënov laughed. "That's a lucky sign," said he. "See if I don't sell out all my goods, and bring you some presents from the fair."

So he said good-bye to his family, and drove away.

When he had travelled half-way, he met a merchant whom he knew, and they put up at the same inn for the night. They had some tea together and then went to bed in adjoining rooms.

It was not Aksënov's habit to sleep late, and, wishing to travel while it was still cool, he aroused his driver before dawn and told him to put in the horses.

Then he made his way across to the landlord of the inn (who lived in a cottage at the back), paid his bill, and continued his journey.

When he had gone about twenty-five miles he stopped for the horses to be fed. Aksënov rested awhile in the passage of the inn, then he stepped out into the porch and, ordering a samovar to be heated, got out his guitar and began to play.

Suddenly a *trôyka*[1] drove up with tinkling bells, and an official alighted, followed by two soldiers. He came to Aksënov and began to question him, asking him who he was and whence he came. Aksënov answered him fully and said, "Won't you have some tea with me?" But the official went on cross-questioning him and asking him, "Where did you spend last night? Were you alone, or with a fellow-merchant? Did you see the other merchant this morning? Why did you leave the inn before dawn?"

Aksënov wondered why he was asked all these questions, but he described all that had happened, and then added, "Why do you cross-question me as if I were a thief or a robber? I am travelling on business of my own, and there is no need to question me."

Then the official, calling the soldiers, said, "I am the police-officer of this district, and I question you because the merchant with whom you spent last night has been found with his throat cut. We must search your things."

They entered the house. The soldiers and the police-officer unstrapped Aksënov's luggage and searched it. Suddenly the officer drew a knife out of a bag, crying, "Whose knife is this?"

Aksënov, seeing a blood-stained knife taken from his bag, was frightened.

"How is there blood on this knife?"

Aksënov tried to answer but could hardly utter a word, and only stammered: "I—don't know—not mine."

conveyance.

Then the police-officer said, "This morning the merchant was found in bed with his throat cut. You are the only person who could have done it. The house was locked from inside, and no one else was there. Here is this blood-stained knife in your bag, and your face and manner betray you! Tell me how you killed him and how much money you stole?"

Aksënov swore he had not done it; that he had not seen the merchant after they had had tea together; that he had no money except eight thousand rubles[2] of his own, and that the knife was not his. But his voice was broken, his face pale, and he trembled with fear as though he were guilty.

The police-officer ordered the soldiers to bind Aksënov and to put him in the cart. As they tied his feet together and flung him into the cart, Aksënov crossed himself and wept. His money and goods were taken from him, and he was sent to the nearest town and imprisoned there. Enquiries as to his character were made in Vladímir. The merchants and other inhabitants of that town said that in former days he used to drink and waste his time but that he was a good man. Then the trial came on: he was charged with murdering a merchant from Ryazán and robbing him of twenty thousand rubles.

His wife was in despair and did not know what to believe. Her children were all quite small; one was a baby at the breast. Taking them all with her, she went to the town where her husband was in gaol. At first she was not allowed to see him, but, after much begging, she obtained permission from the officials and was taken to him. When she saw her husband in prison-dress and in chains, shut up with thieves and criminals, she fell down and did not come to her senses for a long time. Then she drew her children to her, and sat down near him. She told him of things at home and asked about what had h[appened] to him. He told her all, and she asked, "Wha[t]

"We must petition the Tsar not to let an innocent man perish."

His wife told him that she had sent a petition to the Tsar but that it had not been accepted.

Aksënov did not reply but only looked downcast.

Then his wife said, "It was not for nothing I dreamt your hair had turned grey. You remember? You should not have started that day." And passing her fingers through his hair she said: "Ványa dearest tell your wife the truth; was it not you who did it?"

"So you, too, suspect me!" said Aksënov, and, hiding his face in his hands, he began to weep. Then a soldier came to say that the wife and children must go away, and Aksënov said good-bye to his family for the last time.

When they were gone, Aksënov recalled what had been said, and when he remembered that his wife also had suspected him, he said to himself, "It seems that only God can know the truth; it is to Him alone we must appeal and from Him alone expect mercy."

And Aksënov wrote no more petitions, gave up all hope, and only prayed to God.

Aksënov was condemned to be flogged and sent to the mines. So he was flogged with a knout, and when the wounds caused by the knout were healed, he was driven to Siberia with other convicts.

For twenty-six years Aksënov lived as a convict in Siberia. His hair turned white as snow, and his beard grew long, thin, and grey. All his mirth went; he stooped; he walked slowly, spoke little, and never laughed, but he often prayed.

In prison Aksënov learnt to make boots, and earned a little money, with which he bought *The Lives of the Saints*. He read this book when it was light enough in the prison; nd on Sundays in the prison-church he read the epistle sang in the choir, for his voice was still good.

e prison authorities liked Aksënov for his meekness, s fellow-prisoners respected him: they called him ther," and "The Saint." When they wanted to e prison authorities about anything, they always ov their spokesman, and when there were g the prisoners th

No news reached Aksënov from his home, and he did not even know if his wife and children were still alive.

One day a fresh gang of convicts came to the prison. In the evening the old prisoners collected round the new ones and asked them what towns or villages they came from, and what they were sentenced for. Among the rest Aksënov sat down near the near-comers, and listened with downcast air to what was said.

One of the new convicts, a tall, strong man of sixty, with a closely-cropped grey beard, was telling the others what he had been arrested for.

"Well, friends," he said, "I only took a horse that was tied to a sledge, and I was arrested and accused of stealing. I said I had only taken it to get home quicker, and had then let it go; besides, the driver was a personal friend of mine. So I said, 'It's all right.' 'No,' said they, 'you stole it.' But how or where I stole it they could not say. I once really did something wrong and ought by rights to have come here long ago, but that time I was not found out. Now I have been sent here for nothing at all. . . . Eh, but it's lies I'm telling you; I've been to Siberia before, but I did not stay long."

"Where are you from?" asked some one.

"From Vladímir. My family are of that town. My name is Makár, and they also call me Semënich."

Aksënov raised his head and said: "Tell me, Semënich, do you know anything of the merchants Aksënov, of Vladímir? Are they still alive?"

"Know them? Of course I do. The Aksënovs are rich, though their father is in Siberia: a sinner like ourselves, it seems! As for you, Gran'dad, how did you come here?"

Aksënov did not like to speak of his misfortune. He only sighed, and said, "For my sins I have been in prison these twenty-six years."

"What sins?" asked Makár Semënich.

But Aksënov only said, "Well, well—I must have deserved it!" He would have said no more, but his companions told the new-comer how Aksënov came to b in Siberia: how some one had killed a merchant and h put a knife among Aksënov's things, and he had b unjustly condemned.

When Makár Semënich heard this he looked at Ak

slapped his own knee, and exclaimed, "Well, this is wonderful! Really wonderful! But how old you've grown, Gran'dad!"

The others asked him why he was so surprised, and where he had seen Aksënov before; but Makár Semënich did not reply. He only said: "It's wonderful that we should meet here, lads!"

These words made Aksënov wonder whether this man knew who had killed the merchant; so he said, "Perhaps, Semënich, you have heard of that affair, or maybe you've seen me before?"

"How could I help hearing? The world's full of rumours. But it's long ago, and I've forgotten what I heard."

"Perhaps you heard who killed the merchant?" asked Aksënov.

Makár Semënich laughed, and replied, "It must have been him in whose bag the knife was found! If some one else hid the knife there—'He's not a thief till he's caught,' as the saying is. How could any one put a knife into your bag while it was under your head? It would surely have woke you up?"

When Aksënov heard these words he felt sure this was the man who had killed the merchant. He rose and went away. All that night Aksënov lay awake. He felt terribly unhappy, and all sorts of images rose in his mind. There was the image of his wife as she was when he parted from her to go to the fair. He saw her as if she were present; her face and her eyes rose before him, he heard her speak and laugh. Then he saw his children, quite little, as they were at that time: one with a little cloak on, another at his mother's breast. And then he remembered himself as he used to be—young and merry. He remembered how he sat playing the guitar in the porch of the inn where he was arrested, and how free from care he had been. He saw in his mind the place where he was flogged, the executioner, and the people standing around; he chains, the convicts, all the twenty-six years of his ison life, and his premature old age. The thought of it made him so wretched that he was ready to kill himself.

And it's all that villain's doing!" thought Aksënov. his anger was so great against Makár Semënich that he longed for vengeance, even if he himself should perish for it. He kept saying prayers all night but could get no peace. During the day he did not go near Makár Semënich nor even look at him.

A fortnight passed in this way. Aksënov could not sleep at nights and was so miserable that he did not know what to do.

One night as he was walking about the prison he noticed some earth that came rolling out from under one of the shelves on which the prisoners slept. He stopped to see what it was. Suddenly Makár Semënich crept out from under the shelf, and looked up at Aksënov with frightened face. Aksënov tried to pass without looking at him, but Makár seized his hand and told him that he had dug a hole under the wall, getting rid of the earth by putting it into his high bots and emptying it out every day on the road when the prisoners were driven to their work.

"Just you keep quiet, old man, and you shall get out too. If you blab they'll flog the life out of me, but I will kill you first."

Aksënov trembled with anger as he looked at his enemy. He drew his hand away, saying, "I have no wish to escape, and you have no need to kill me; you killed me long ago! As to telling of you—I may do so or not, as God shall direct."

Next day, when the convicts were led out to work, the convoy soldiers noticed that one or other of the prisoners emptied some earth out of his boots. The prison was searched and the tunnel found. The Governor came and questioned all the prisoners to find out who had dug the hole. They all denied any knowledge of it. Those who knew would not betray Makár Semënich, knowing he would be flogged almost to death. At last the Governor turned to Aksënov, whom he knew to be a just man, and said: "You are a truthful old man; tell me, before God, who dug the hole?"

Makár Semënich stood as if he were quite unconcerned, looking at the Governor and not so much as glancing at Aksënov. Aksënov's lips and hands trembled, and for a long time he could not utter a word. He thought, "Why should I screen him who ruined my life? Let him pay for what I have suffered. But if I tell, they will probably flog the life out of him, and maybe I suspect him wrongly. And, after all, what good would it be to me?"

"Well, old man," repeated the Governor, "tell us the truth: who has been digging under the wall?"

Aksënov glanced at Makár Semënich and said, "I cannot say, your honour. It is not God's will that I should tell! Do what you like with me; I am in your hands."

However much the Governor tried, Aksënov would say no more, and so the matter had to be left.

That night, when Aksënov was lying on his bed and just beginning to doze, some one came quietly and sat down on his bed. He peered through the darkness and recognized Makár.

"What more do you want of me?" asked Aksënov. "Why have you come here?"

Makár Semënich was silent. So Aksënov sat up and said, "What do you want? Go away or I will call the guard!"

Makár Semënich bent close over Aksënov, and whispered, "Iván Dmítrich, forgive me!"

"What for?" asked Aksënov.

"It was I who killed the merchant and hid the knife among your things. I meant to kill you too, but I heard a noise outside; so I hid the knife in your bag and escaped through the window."

Aksënov was silent and did not know what to say. Makár Semënich slid off the bed-shelf and knelt upon the ground. "Iván Dmítrich," said he, "forgive me! For the love of God, forgive me! I will confess that it was I who killed the merchant, and you will be released and can go to your home."

"It is easy for you to talk," said Aksënov, "but I have suffered for you these twenty-six years. Where could I go to now? My wife is dead, and my children have forgotten me. I have nowhere to go . . . ."

Makár Semënich did not rise but beat his head on the floor. "Iván Dmítrich, forgive me!" he cried. "When they flogged me with the knout it was not so hard to bear as it is to see you now . . . yet you had pity on me and did not tell. For Christ's sake forgive me, wretch that I am!" And he began to sob.

When Aksënov heard him sobbing he, too, began to weep.

"God will forgive you!" said he. "Maybe I am a hundred times worse than you." And at these words his heart grew light and the longing for home left him. He no longer had any desire to leave the prison but only hoped for his last hour to come.

In spite of what Aksënov had said, Makár Semënich confessed his guilt. But when the order for his release came, Aksënov was already dead.

Written in 1872

WHAT MEN LIVE BY

"We know that we have passed from death unto life, because
we love the brethren. He that loveth not his brother abideth
in death. . . .

But whoso hath the world's good, and seeth his brother in
need, and shutteth up his bowels of compassion from him,
how dwelleth the love of God in him? My little children, let
us not love in word, neither in tongue; but in deed and
truth. . . .

. . . love is of God; and every one that loveth is born of
God, and knoweth God. He that loveth not knoweth not God;
for God is love. . . .

. . . God is love; and he that dwelleth in love dwelleth in
God, and God dwelleth in him.

If a man say, I love God, and hateth his brother, he is a
liar; for he that loveth not his brother whom he hath seen,
how can he love God whom he hath not seen?"

I John, 3:14, 17–18; 4:7–8, 12, 16, 20

I

A shoemaker named Simon, who had neither house nor
land of his own, lived with his wife and children in a
peasant's hut and earned his living by his work. Work was
cheap but bread was dear, and what he earned he spent
for food. The man and his wife had but one sheep-skin coat
between them for winter wear, and even that was worn to
tatters, and this was the second year he had been wanting
to buy sheep-skins for a new coat. Before winter Simon
saved up a little money: a three-ruble note lay hidden in
his wife's box, and five rubles and twenty kopeks[1] were
owed him by customers in the village.

So one morning he prepared to go to the village to buy
sheep-skins. He put on over his shirt his wife's wadded

hundred kopeks make a ruble. The kopek is worth about a

nankeen jacket, and over that he put his own cloth coat. He took the three-ruble note in his pocket, cut himself a stick to serve as a staff, and started off after breakfast. "I'll collect the five rubles that are due to me," thought he, "add the three I have got, and that will be enough to buy sheep-skins for the winter coat."

He came to the village and called at a peasant's hut, but the man was not at home. The peasant's wife promised that the money should be paid next week, but she would not pay it herself. Then Simon called on another peasant, but this one swore he had no money, and would only pay twenty kopeks which he owed for a pair of boots Simon had mended. Simon then tried to buy the sheep-skins on credit, but the dealer would not trust him.

"Bring your money," said he, "then you may have your pick of the skins. We know what debt-collecting is like."

So all the business the shoemaker did was to get the twenty kopeks for boots he had mended and to take a pair of felt boots a peasant gave him to sole with leather.

Simon felt downhearted. He spent the twenty kopeks on vodka and started homewards without having bought any skins. In the morning he had felt the frost; but now, after drinking the vodka, he felt warm even without a sheep-skin coat. He trudged along, striking his stick on the frozen earth with one hand, swinging the felt boots with the other, and talking to himself.

"I'm quite warm," said he, "though I have no sheep-skin coat. I've had a drop and it runs through my veins. I need no sheep-skins. I go along and don't worry about anything. That's the sort of man I am! What do I care? I can live without sheep-skins. I don't need them. My wife will fret, to be sure. And, true enough, it *is* a shame; one works all day long and then does not get paid. Stop a bit! If you don't bring that money along, sure enough I'll skin you, blessed if I don't. How's that? He pays twenty kopeks at a time! What can I do with twenty kopeks? Drink it—that's all one can do! Hard up, he says he is! So he may be—but what about me? You have house, and cattle, and everything; I've only what I stand up in! You have corn of your own growing, I have to buy every grain. Do what I will, I mus spend three rubles every week for bread alone. I come hor and find the bread all used up and I have to work another ruble and a half. So just you pay up what you owe, and no nonsense about it!"

By this time he had nearly reached the shrine at the bend of the road. Looking up, he saw something whitish behind the shrine. The daylight was fading, and the shoemaker peered at the thing without being able to make out what it was. "There was no white stone here before. Can it be an ox? It's not like an ox. It has a head like a man, but it's too white; and what could a man be doing there?"

He came closer, so that it was clearly visible. To his surprise it really was a man, alive or dead, sitting naked, leaning motionless against the shrine. Terror seized the shoemaker, and he thought, "Some one has killed him, stripped him, and left him here. If I meddle I shall surely get into trouble."

So the shoemaker went on. He passed in front of the shrine so that he could not see the man. When he had gone some way he looked back, and saw that the man was no longer leaning against the shrine but was moving as if looking towards him. The shoemaker felt more frightened than before, and thought, "Shall I go back to him or shall I go on? If I go near him something dreadful may happen. Who knows who the fellow is? He has not come here for any good. If I go near him he may jump up and throttle me, and there will be no getting away. Or if not, he'd still be a burden on one's hands. What could I do with a naked man? I couldn't give him my last clothes. Heaven only help me to get away!"

So the shoemaker hurried on, leaving the shrine behind him—when suddenly his conscience smote him and he stopped in the road.

"What are you doing, Simon?" said he to himself. "The man may be dying of want, and you slip past afraid. Have you grown so rich as to be afraid of robbers? Ah, Simon, shame on you!"

So he turned back and went up to the man.

II

Simon approached the stranger, looked at him and saw that he was a young man, fit, with no bruises on his body, but evidently freezing and frightened, and he sat there leaning back without looking up at Simon, as if too faint to lift his eyes. Simon went close to him and then the man seemed to wake up. Turning his head, he opened his eyes and looked into Simon's face. That one look was enough to make Simon fond of the man. He threw the felt boots on the ground, undid his sash, laid it on the boots, and took off his cloth coat.

"It's not a time for talking," said he. "Come, put this coat on at once!" And Simon took the man by the elbows and helped him to rise. As he stood there, Simon saw that his body was clean and in good condition, his hands and feet shapely, and his face good and kind. He threw his coat over the man's shoulders, but the latter could not find the sleeves. Simon guided his arms into them, and drawing the coat on well, wrapped it closely about him, tying the sash round the man's waist.

Simon even took off his cap to put it on the man's head, but then his own head felt cold and he thought: "I'm quite bald, while he has long curly hair." So he put his cap on his own head again. "It will be better to give him something for his feet," thought he; and he made the man sit down and helped him to put on the felt boots, saying, "There, friend, now move about and warm yourself. Other matters can be settled later on. Can you walk?"

The man stood up and looked kindly at Simon but could not say a word.

"Why don't you speak?" said Simon. "It's too cold to stay here, we must be getting home. There now, take my stick, and if you're feeling weak lean on that. Now step out!"

The man started walking and moved easily, not lagging behind.

As they went along, Simon asked him, "And where do you belong to?"

"I'm not from these parts."

"I thought as much. I know the folks hereabouts. But how did you come to be there by the shrine?"

"I cannot tell."

"Has some one been ill-treating you?"

"No one has ill-treated me. God has punished me."

"Of course God rules all. Still, you'll have to find food and shelter somewhere. Where do you want to go to?"

"It is all the same to me."

Simon was amazed. The man did not look like a rogue, and he spoke gently, but yet he gave no account of himself. Still Simon thought, "Who knows what may have happened?" And he said to the stranger: "Well then, come home with me and at least warm yourself awhile."

So Simon walked towards his home, and the stranger kept up with him, walking at his side. The wind had risen and Simon felt it cold under his shirt. He was getting over his tipsiness by now and began to feel the frost. He went along sniffling and wrapping his wife's coat round him, and he thought to himself: "There now—talk about sheepskins! I went out for sheep-skins and come home without even a coat to my back, and what is more, I'm bringing a naked man along with me. Matrëna won't be pleased!" And when he thought of his wife he felt sad, but when he looked at the stranger and remembered how he had looked up at him at the shrine, his heart was glad.

III

Simon's wife had everything ready early that day. She had cut wood, brought water, fed the children, eaten her own meal, and now she sat thinking. She wondered when she ought to make bread: now or to-morrow? There was still a large piece left.

"If Simon has had some dinner in town," thought she, "and does not eat much for supper, the bread will last out another day."

She weighed the piece of bread in her hand again and again and thought: "I won't make any more to-day. We have only enough flour left to bake one batch. We can manage to make this last out till Friday."

So Matrëna put away the bread and sat down at the table to patch her husband's shirt. While she worked she thought how her husband was buying skins for a winter coat.

"If only the dealer does not cheat him. My good man is much too simple; he cheats nobody, but any child can take him in. Eight rubles is a lot of money—he should get a good coat at that price. Not tanned skins, but still a proper winter coat. How difficult it was last winter to get on without a warm coat. I could neither get down to the river nor go out anywhere. When he went out he put on all we had, and there was nothing left for me. He did not start very early to-day, but still it's time he was back. I only hope he has not gone on the spree!"

Hardly had Matrëna thought this than steps were heard on the threshold and some one entered. Matrëna stuck her needle into her work and went out into the passage. There she saw two men: Simon, and with him a man without a hat and wearing felt boots.

Matrëna noticed at once that her husband smelt of spirits. "There now, he has been drinking," thought she. And when she saw that he was coatless, had only her jacket on, brought no parcel, stood there silent, and seemed ashamed, her heart was ready to break with disappointment. "He has drunk the money," thought she, "and has been on the spree with some good-for-nothing fellow whom he has brought home with him."

Matrëna let them pass into the hut, followed them in, and saw that the stranger was a young, slight man, wearing her husband's coat. There was no shirt to be seen under it, and he had no hat. Having entered, he stood neither moving nor raising his eyes, and Matrëna thought: "He must be a bad man—he's afraid."

Matrëna frowned, and stood beside the stove looking to see what they would do.

Simon took off his cap and sat down on the bench as if things were all right.

"Come, Matrëna; if supper is ready, let us have some."

Matrëna muttered something to herself and did not move but stayed where she was, by the stove. She looked first at the one and then at the other of them and only shook her head. Simon saw that his wife was annoyed, but tried to pass it off. Pretending not to notice anything, he took the stranger by the arm.

"Sit down, friend," said he, "and let us have some supper."

The stranger sat down on the bench.

"Haven't you cooked anything for us?" said Simon.

Matrëna's anger boiled over. "I've cooked, but not for you. It seems to me you have drunk your wits away. You went to buy a sheep-skin coat but come home without so much as the coat you had on and bring a naked vagabond home with you. I have no supper for drunkards like you."

"That's enough, Matrëna. Don't wag your tongue without reason! You had better ask what sort of man—"

"And you tell me what you've done with the money?"

Simon found the pocket of the jacket, drew out the three-ruble note, and unfolded it.

"Here is the money. Trifonov did not pay, but promises to pay soon."

Matrëna got still more angry; he had bought no sheepskins but had put his only coat on some naked fellow and had even brought him to their house.

She snatched up the note from the table, took it to put away in safety, and said: "I have no supper for you. We can't feed all the naked drunkards in the world."

"There now, Matrëna, hold your tongue a bit. First hear what a man has to say—!"

"Much wisdom I shall hear from a drunken fool. I was right in not wanting to marry you—a drunkard. The linen my mother gave me you drank; and now you've been to buy a coat—and have drunk it too!"

Simon tried to explain to his wife that he had only spent twenty kopeks; tried to tell how he had found the man— but Matrëna would not let him get a word in. She talked nineteen to the dozen and dragged in things that had happened ten years before.

Matrëna talked and talked, and at last she flew at Simon and seized him by the sleeve.

"Give me my jacket. It is the only one I have, and you must needs take it from me and wear it yourself. Give it here, you mangy dog, and may the devil take you."

Simon began to pull off the jacket, and turned a sleeve of it inside out; Matrëna seized the jacket and it burst its seams. She snatched it up, threw it over her head, and went to the door. She meant to go out, but stopped undecided— she wanted to work off her anger, but she also wanted to learn what sort of a man the stranger was.

IV

Matrëna stopped and said: "If he were a good man he would not be naked. Why, he hasn't even a shirt on him. If he were all right, you would say where you came across the fellow."

"That's just what I am trying to tell you," said Simon. "As I came to the shrine I saw him sitting all naked and frozen. It isn't quite the weather to sit about naked! God sent me to him or he would have perished. What was I to do? How do we know what may have happened to him? So I took him, clothed him, and brought him along. Don't be so angry, Matrëna. It is a sin. Remember, we must all die one day."

Angry words rose to Matrëna's lips, but she looked at the stranger and was silent. He sat on the edge of the bench, motionless, his hands folded on his knees, his head drooping on his breast, his eyes closed, and his brows knit as if in pain. Matrëna was silent, and Simon said: "Matrëna, have you no love of God?"

Matrëna heard these words, and as she looked at the stranger, suddenly her heart softened towards him. She came back from the door, and going to the stove she got out the supper. Setting a cup on the table, she poured out some kvas. Then she brought out the last piece of bread and set out a knife and spoons.

"Eat, if you want to," said she.

Simon drew the stranger to the table.

"Take your place, young man," said he.

Simon cut the bread, crumbled it into the broth, and they began to eat. Matrëna sat at the corner of the table, resting her head on her hand and looking at the stranger.

And Matrëna was touched with pity for the stranger and began to feel fond of him. And at once the stranger's face lit up; his brows were no longer bent, he raised his eyes and smiled at Matrëna.

When they had finished supper, the woman cleared away the things and began questioning the stranger. "Where are you from?" said she.

"I am not from these parts."

"But how did you come to be on the road?"

"I may not tell."

"Did some one rob you?"

"God punished me."

"And you were lying there naked?"

"Yes, naked and freezing. Simon saw me and had pity on me. He took off his coat, put it on me, and brought me here. And you have fed me, given me drink, and shown pity on me. God will reward you!"

Matrëna rose, took from the window Simon's old shirt she had been patching, and gave it to the stranger. She also brought out a pair of trousers for him.

"There," said she, "I see you have no shirt. Put this on, and lie down where you please, in the loft or on the stove."[1]

The stranger took off the coat, put on the shirt, and lay down in the loft. Matrëna put out the candle, took the coat, and climbed to where her husband lay on the stove.

Matrëna drew the skirts of the coat over her and lay down but could not sleep; she could not get the stranger out of her mind.

When she remembered that he had eaten their last piece of bread and that there was none for to-morrow and thought of the shirt and trousers she had given away, she felt grieved; but when she remembered how he had smiled, her heart was glad.

Long did Matrëna lie awake, and she noticed that Simon also was awake—he drew the coat towards him.

"Simon!"

"Well?"

"You have had the last of the bread and I have not put any to rise. I don't know what we shall do to-morrow. Perhaps I can borrow some of neighbour Martha."

"If we're alive we shall find something to eat."

The woman lay still awhile, and then said, "He seems a good man, but why does he not tell us who he is?"

"I suppose he has his reasons."

"Simon!"

"Well?"

"We give; but why does nobody give us anything?"

---

[1] The brick stove, including the oven, in a Russian peasant's hut is usually built so as to leave a flat top, large enough to lie on, for those who want to sleep in a warm place.

Simon did not know what to say; so he only said, "Let us stop talking" and turned over and went to sleep.

V

In the morning Simon awoke. The children were still asleep; his wife had gone to the neighbour's to borrow some bread. The stranger alone was sitting on the bench, dressed in the old shirt and trousers, and looking upwards. His face was brighter than it had been the day before.

Simon said to him, "Well, friend; the belly wants bread and the naked body clothes. One has to work for a living. What work do you know?"

"I do not know any."

This surprised Simon, but he said, "Men who want to learn can learn anything."

"Men work and I will work also."

"What is your name?"

"Michael."

"Well, Michael, if you don't wish to talk about yourself, that is your own affair; but you'll have to earn a living for yourself. If you will work as I tell you, I will give you food and shelter."

"May God reward you! I will learn. Show me what to do."

Simon took yarn, put it round his thumb and began to twist it.

"It is easy enough—see!"

Michael watched him, put some yarn round his own thumb in the same way, caught the knack, and twisted the yarn also.

Then Simon showed him how to wax the thread. This also Michael mastered. Next Simon showed him how to twist the bristle in, and how to sew, and this, too, Michael learned at once.

Whatever Simon showed him he understood at once, and after three days he worked as if he had sewn boots all his life. He worked without stopping and ate little. When work was over he sat silently, looking upwards. He hardly went into the street, spoke only when necessary, and neither joked nor laughed. They never saw him smile, except that first evening when Matrëna gave him supper.

VI

Day by day and week by week the year went round. Michael lived and worked with Simon. His fame spread till people said that no one sewed boots so neatly and strongly as Simon's workman, Michael; from all the district round people came to Simon for their boots, and he began to be well off.

One winter day, as Simon and Michael sat working, a carriage on sledge-runners, with three horses and with bells, drove up to the hut. They looked out of the window; the carriage stopped at their door; a fine servant jumped down from the box and opened the door. A gentleman in a fur coat got out and walked up to Simon's hut. Up jumped Matrëna and opened the door wide. The gentleman stooped to enter the hut, and when he drew himself up again his head nearly reached the ceiling and he seemed quite to fill his end of the room.

Simon rose, bowed, and looked at the gentleman with astonishment. He had never seen any one like him. Simon himself was lean, Michael was thin, and Matrëna was dry as a bone, but this man was like some one from another world: red-faced, burly, with a neck like a bull's, and looking altogether as if he were cast in iron.

The gentleman puffed, threw off his fur coat, sat down on the bench, and said, "Which of you is the master bootmaker?"

"I am, your Excellency," said Simon, coming forward.

Then the gentleman shouted to his lad, "Hey, Fédka, bring the leather!"

The servant ran in, bringing a parcel. The gentleman took the parcel and put it on the table.

"Untie it," said he. The lad untied it.

The gentleman pointed to the leather.

"Look here, shoemaker," said he, "do you see this leather?"

"Yes, your honour."

"But do you know what sort of leather it is?"

Simon felt the leather and said, "It is good leather."

"Good, indeed! Why, you fool, you never saw such leather before in your life. It's German and cost twenty rubles."

Simon was frightened and said, "Where should I ever see leather like that?' '

"Just so! Now, can you make it into boots for me?"

"Yes, your Excellency, I can."

Then the gentleman shouted at him: "You *can*, can you? Well, remember whom you are to make them for, and what the leather is. You must make me boots that will wear for a year, neither losing shape nor coming unsewn. If you can do it, take the leather and cut it up; but if you can't, say so. I warn you now, if your boots come unsewn or lose shape within a year I will have you put in prison. If they don't burst or lose shape for a year, I will pay you ten rubles for your work."

Simon was frightened and did not know what to say. He glanced at Michael and nudging him with his elbow, whispered: "Shall I take the work?"

Michael nodded his head as if to say, "Yes, take it."

Simon did as Michael advised and undertook to make boots that would not lose shape or split for a whole year.

Calling his servant, the gentleman told him to pull the boot off his left leg, which he stretched out.

"Take my measure!" said he.

Simon stitched a paper measure seventeen inches long, smoothed it out, knelt down, wiped his hands well on his apron so as not to soil the gentleman's sock, and began to measure. He measured the sole, and round the instep, and began to measure the calf of the leg, but the paper was too short. The calf of the leg was as thick as a beam.

"Mind you don't make it too tight in the leg."

Simon stitched on another strip of paper. The gentleman twitched his toes about in his sock looking round at those in the hut, and as he did so he noticed Michael.

"Whom have you there?" asked he.

"That is my workman. He will sew the boots."

"Mind," said the gentleman to Michael, "remember to make them so that they will last me a year."

Simon also looked at Michael and saw that Michael was not looking at the gentleman, but was gazing into the corner behind the gentleman, as if he saw some one there. Michael looked and looked, and suddenly he smiled, and his face became brighter.

"What are you grinning at, you fool?" thundered the

gentleman. "You had better look to it that the boots are ready in time."

"They shall be ready in good time," said Michael.

"Mind it is so," said the gentleman, and he put on his boots and his fur coat, wrapped the latter round him, and went to the door. But he forgot to stoop, and struck his head against the lintel.

He swore and rubbed his head. Then he took his seat in the carriage and drove away.

When he had gone, Simon said: "There's a figure of a man for you! You could not kill him with a mallet. He almost knocked out the lintel, but little harm it did him."

And Matrëna said: "Living as he does, how should he not grown strong? Death itself can't touch such a rock as that."

VII

Then Simon said to Michael: "Well, we have taken the work, but we must see we don't get into trouble over it. The leather is dear, and the gentleman hot-tempered. We must make no mistakes. Come, your eye is truer and your hands have become nimbler than mine, so you take this measure and cut out the boots. I will finish off the sewing of the vamps."

Michael did as he was told. He took the leather, spread it out on the table, folded it in two, took a knife and began to cut out.

Matrëna came and watched him cutting and was surprised to see how he was doing it. Matrëna was accustomed to seeing boots made, and she looked and saw that Michael was not cutting the leather for boots, but was cutting it round.

She wished to say something, but she thought to herself: "Perhaps I do not understand how gentlemen's boots should be made. I suppose Michael knows more about it— and I won't interfere."

When Michael had cut up the leather he took a thread and began to sew not with two ends, as boots are sewn, but with a single end, as for soft slippers.

Again Matrëna wondered, but again she did not interfere. Michael sewed on steadily till noon. Then Simon rose
for dinner, looked around, and saw that Michael had made
slippers out of the gentleman's leather.

"Ah!" groaned Simon, and he thought, "How is it
that Michael, who has been with me a whole year and
never made a mistake before, should do such a dreadful
thing? The gentleman ordered high boots, welted, with
whole fronts, and Michael has made soft slippers with single
soles and has wasted the leather. What am I to say to the
gentleman? I can never replace leather such as this."

And he said to Michael, "What are you doing, friend?
You have ruined me! You know the gentleman ordered
high boots, but see what you have made!"

Hardly had he begun to rebuke Michael, when 'rat-tat'
went the iron ring hung at the door. Some one was knocking. They looked out of the window; a man had come on
horseback and was fastening his horse. They opened the
door, and the servant who had been with the gentleman
came in.

"Good day," said he.

"Good day," replied Simon. "What can we do for you?"

"My mistress has sent me about the boots."

"What about the boots?"

"Why, my master no longer needs them. He is dead."

"Is it possible?"

"He did not live to get home after leaving you but died
in the carriage. When we reached home and the servants
came to help him alight, he rolled over like a sack. He was
dead already, and so stiff that he could hardly be got out
of the carriage. My mistress sent me here, saying: 'Tell the
bootmaker that the gentleman who ordered boots of him
and left the leather for them no longer needs the boots,
but that he must quickly make soft slippers for the corpse.
Wait till they are ready and bring them back with you.'
That is why I have come."

Michael gathered up the remnants of the leather; rolled
them up, took the soft slippers he had made, slapped them
together, wiped them down with his apron, and handed
them and the roll of leather to the servant, who took them
and said: "Good-bye, masters, and good day to you!"

VIII

Another year passed, and another, and Michael was now living his sixth year with Simon. He lived as before. He went nowhere, only spoke when necessary, and had only smiled twice in all those years—one when Matrëna gave him food, and a second time when the gentleman was in their hut. Simon was more than pleased with his workman. He never now asked him where he came from and only feared lest Michael should go away.

They were all at home one day. Matrëna was putting iron pots in the oven; the children were running along the benches and looking out of the window; Simon was sewing at one window and Michael was fastening on a heel at the other.

One of the boys ran along the bench to Michael, leant on his shoulder, and looked out of the window.

"Look, Uncle Michael! There is a lady with little girls! She seems to be coming here. And one of the girls is lame."

When the boy said that, Michael dropped his work, turned to the window, and looked out into the street.

Simon was surprised. Michael never used to look out into the street, but now he pressed against the window, staring at something. Simon also looked out and saw that a well-dressed woman was really coming to his hut, leading by the hand two little girls in fur coats and woolen shawls. The girls could hardly be told one from the other, except that one of them was crippled in her left leg and walked with a limp.

The woman stepped into the porch and entered the passage. Feeling about for the entrance she found the latch, which she lifted and opened the door. She let the two girls go in first, and followed them into the hut.

"Good day, good folk!"

"Pray come in," said Simon. "What can we do for you?"

The woman sat down by the table. The two little girls pressed close to her knees, afraid of the people in the hut.

"I want leather shoes made for these two little girls, for spring."

"We can do that. We never have made such small shoes, but we can make them; either welted or turnover shoes, linen lined. My man, Michael, is a master at the work."

Simon glanced at Michael and saw that he had left his work and was sitting with his eyes fixed on the little girls. Simon was surprised. It was true the girls were pretty, with black eyes, plump, and rosy-cheeked, and they wore nice kerchiefs and fur coats, but still Simon could not understand why Michael should look at them like that— just as if he had known them before. He was puzzled but went on talking with the woman and arranging the price. Having fixed it, he prepared the measure. The woman lifted the lame girl on to her lap and said: "Take two measures from this little girl. Make one shoe for the lame foot and three for the sound one. They both have the same-sized feet. They are twins."

Simon took the measure and, speaking of the lame girl, said: "How did it happen to her? She is such a pretty girl. Was she born so?"

"No, her mother crushed her leg."

Then Matrëna joined in. She wondered who this woman was and whose the children were, so she said: "Are not you their mother, then?"

"No, my good woman; I am neither their mother nor any relation to them. They were quite strangers to me, but I adopted them."

"They are not your children and yet you are so fond of them?"

"How can I help being fond of them? I fed them both at my own breasts. I had a child of my own, but God took him. I was not so fond of him as I now am of these."

"Then whose children are they?"

IX

The woman, having begun talking, told them the whole story.

"It is about six years since their parents died, both in one week: their father was buried on the Tuesday, and their mother died on the Friday. These orphans were born three days after their father's death, and their mother did not live another day. My husband and I were then living as peasants in the village. We were neighbours of theirs, our yard being next to theirs. Their father was a lonely man, a wood-cutter in the forest. When felling trees one day they let one fall on him. It fell across his body and crushed his bowels out. They hardly got him home before his soul went to God; and that same week his wife gave birth to twins—these little girls. She was poor and alone; she had no one, young or old, with her. Alone she gave them birth, and alone she met her death.

"The next morning I went to see her, but when I entered the hut, she, poor thing, was already stark and cold. In dying she had rolled on to this child and crushed her leg. The village folk came to the hut, washed the body, laid her out, made a coffin, and buried her. They were good folk. The babies were left alone. What was to be done with them? I was the only woman there who had a baby at the time. I was nursing my first-born—eight weeks old. So I took them for a time. The peasants came together, and thought and thought what to do with them; and at last they said to me: 'For the present, Mary, you had better keep the girls, and later on we will arrange what to do for them.' So I nursed the sound one at my breast, but at first I did not feed this crippled one. I did not suppose she would live. But then I thought to myself, why should the poor innocent suffer? I pitied her and began to feed her. And so I fed my own boy and these two—the three of them—at my own breast. I was young and strong and had good food, and God gave me so much milk that at times it even overflowed. I used sometimes to feed two at a time, while the third was waiting. When one had had enough I nursed the third. And God so ordered it that these grew up, while my own was buried before he was two years old. And I had no more children, though we prospered. Now my husband is working for the corn merchant at the mill. The pay is good and we are well off. But I have no children of my own, and how lonely I should be without these little girls! How can I help loving them! They are the joy of my life!"

She pressed the lame little girl to her with one hand, while with the other she wiped the tears from her cheeks.

And Matrëna sighed, and said: "The proverb is true

that says, 'One may live without father or mother, but one cannot live without God.' "

So they talked together, when suddenly the whole hut was lighted up as though by summer lightning from the corner where Michael sat. They all looked towards him and saw him sitting, his hands folded on his knees, gazing upwards and smiling.

X

The woman went away with the girls. Michael rose from the bench, put down his work, and took off his apron. Then, bowing low to Simon and his wife, he said: "Farewell, masters. God has forgiven me. I ask your forgiveness, too, for anything done amiss."

And they saw that a light shone from Michael. And Simon rose, bowed down to Michael, and said: 'I see, Michael, that you are no common man, and I can neither keep you nor question you. Only tell me this: how is it that when I found you and brought you home, you were gloomy, and when my wife gave you food you smiled at her and became brighter? Then when the gentleman came to order the boots, you smiled again and became brighter still? And now, when this woman brought the little girls, you smiled a third time and have become as bright as day? Tell me, Michael, why does your face shine so, and why did you smile those three times?"

And Michael answered: "Light shines from me because I have been punished, but now God has pardoned me. And I smiled three times, because God sent me to learn three truths, and I have learnt them. One I learnt when your wife pitied me, and that is why I smiled the first time. The second I learnt when the rich man ordered the boots, and then I smiled again. And now, when I saw those little girls, I learnt the third and last, and I smiled the third time."

And Simon said, "Tell me, Michael, what did God punish you for? and what were the three truths? that I, too, may know them."

And Michael answered: "God punished me for disobeying him. I was an angel in heaven and disobeyed God. God sent me to fetch a woman's soul. I flew to earth and saw a sick woman lying alone who had just given birth to

twin girls. They moved feebly at their mother's side but
she could not lift them to her breast. When she saw me,
she understood that God had sent me for her soul, and
she wept and said: 'Angel of God! My husband has just
been buried, killed by a falling tree. I have neither sister,
nor aunt, nor mother: no one to care for my orphans.
Do not take my soul! Let me nurse my babes, feed them,
and set them on their feet before I die. Children cannot
live without father or mother.' And I hearkened to her. I
placed one child at her breast and gave the other into her
arms, and returned to the Lord in heaven. I flew to the
Lord, and said: 'I could not take the soul of the mother.
Her husband was killed by a tree; the woman has twins
and prays that her soul may not be taken.' She says: 'Let
me nurse and feed my children, and set them on their feet.
Children cannot live without father or mother.' I have not
taken her soul.' And God said: 'Go—take the mother's
soul, and learn three truths: Learn *What dwells in man,
What is not given to man,* and *What men live by.* When
thou hast learnt these things, thou shalt return to heaven.'
So I flew again to earth and took the mother's soul. The
babes dropped from her breasts. Her body rolled over on
the bed and crushed one babe, twisting its leg. I rose above
the village, wishing to take her soul to God, but a wind
seized me and my wings drooped and dropped off. Her
soul rose alone to God, while I fell to earth by the
roadside."

<h1 style="text-align:center">XI</h1>

And Simon and Matrëna understood who it was that had
lived with them and whom they had clothed and fed. And
they wept with awe and with joy. And the angel said: "I
was alone in the field, naked. I had never known human
needs, cold and hunger, till I became a man. I was
famished, frozen, and did not know what to do. I saw,
near the field I was in, a shrine built for God, and I went
to it hoping to find shelter. But the shrine was locked and
I could not enter. So I sat down behind the shrine to shelter
myself at least from the wind. Evening drew on, I was
hungry, frozen, and in pain. Suddenly I heard a man
coming along the road. He carried a pair of boots and was

talking to himself. For the first time since I became a man I saw the mortal face of a man, and his face seemed terrible to me and I turned from it. And I heard the man talking to himself of how to cover his body from the cold in winter, and how to feed wife and children. And I thought: 'I am perishing of cold and hunger and here is a man thinking only of how to clothe himself and his wife, and how to get bread for themselves. He cannot help me.' When the man saw me he frowned and became still more terrible and passed me by on the other side. I despaired; but suddenly I heard him coming back. I looked up and did not recognize the same man: before, I had seen death in his face; but now he was alive and I recognized in him the presence of God. He came up to me, clothed me, took me with him, and brought me to his home. I entered the house; a woman came to meet us and began to speak. The woman was still more terrible than the man had been; the spirit of death came from her mouth; I could not breathe for the stench of death that spread around her. She wished to drive me out into the cold, and I knew that if she did so she would die. Suddenly her husband spoke to her of God, and the woman changed at once. And when she brought me food and looked at me, I glanced at her and saw that death no longer dwelt in her; she had become alive, and in her too I saw God.

"Then I remembered the first lesson God had set me: '*Learn what dwells in man*.' And I understood that in man dwells Love! I was glad that God had already begun to show me what He had promised, and I smiled for the first time. But I had not yet learnt all. I did not yet know *What is not given to man*, and *What men live by*.

"I lived with you and a year passed. A man came to order boots that should wear for a year without losing shape or cracking. I looked at him, and suddenly, behind his shoulder, I saw my comrade—the angel of death. None but me saw that angel; but I knew him, and knew that before the sun set he would take the rich man's soul. And I thought to myself, 'The man is making preparation for a year and does not know that he will die before evening.' And I remembered God's second saying, '*Learn what is not given to man*.'

"What dwells in man I already knew. Now I lear

what is not given him. It is not given to man to know his own needs. And I smiled for the second time. I was glad to have seen my comrade angel—glad also that God had revealed to me the second saying.

"But I still did not know all. I did not know *What men live by*. And I lived on, waiting till God should reveal to me the last lesson. In the sixth year came the girl-twins with the woman; and I recognized the girls and heard how they had been kept alive. Having heard the story, I thought, 'Their mother besought me for the children's sake, and I believed her when she said that children cannot live without father or mother; but a stranger has nursed them and has brought them up.' And when the woman showed her love for the children that were not her own and wept over them, I saw in her the living God, and understood *What men live by*. And I knew that God had revealed to me the last lesson and had forgiven my sin. And then I smiled for the third time."

XII

And the angel's body was bared, and he was clothed in light so that eye could not look on him; and his voice grew louder, as though it came not from him but from heaven above. And the angel said: "I have learnt that all men live not by care for themselves, but by love.

"It was not given to the mother to know what her children needed for their life. Nor was it given to the rich man to know what he himself needed. Nor is it given to any man to know whether, when evening comes, he will need boots for his body or slippers for his corpse.

"I remained alive when I was a man, not by care of myself but because love was present in a passer-by and because he and his wife pitied and loved me. The orphans remained alive not because of their mother's care, but because there was love in the heart of a woman, a stranger to them, who pitied and loved them. And all men live not by the thought they spend on their own welfare, but because love exists in man.

"I knew before that God gave life to men and desires that they should live; now I understood more than that.

"I understood that God does not wish men to live apart,

and therefore he does not reveal to them what each one needs for himself; but he wishes them to live united, and therefore reveals to each of them what is necessary for all.

"I have now understood that though it seems to men that they live by care for themselves, in truth it is love alone by which they live. He who has love, is in God, and God is in him, for God is love."

And the angel sang praise to God, so that the hut trembled at his voice. The roof opened, and a column of fire rose from earth to heaven. Simon and his wife and children fell to the ground. Wings appeared upon the angel's shoulders and he rose into the heavens.

And when Simon came to himself the hut stood as before, and there was no one in it but his own family.

1881

HOW MUCH LAND
DOES A MAN
NEED?

I

An elder sister came to visit her younger sister in the country. The elder was married to a tradesman in town, the younger to a peasant in the village. As the sisters sat over their tea talking, the elder began to boast of the advantages of town life: saying how comfortably they lived there, how well they dressed, what fine clothes her children wore, what good things they ate and drank, and how she went to the theatre, promenades, and entertainments.

The younger sister was piqued, and in turn disparaged the life of a tradesman, and stood up for that of a peasant.

"I would not change my way of life for yours," said she. "We may live roughly, but at least we are free from anxiety. You live in better style than we do, but though you often earn more than you need, you are very likely to lose all you have. You know the proverb, 'Loss and gain are brothers twain.' It often happens that people who are wealthy one day are begging their bread the next. Our way is safer. Though a peasant's life is not a fat one, it is a long one. We shall never grow rich, but we shall always have enough to eat."

The elder sister said sneeringly: "Enough? Yes, if you like to share with the pigs and the calves! What do you know of elegance or manners! However much your goodman may slave, you will die as you are living—on a dung heap—and your children the same."

"Well, what of that?" replied the younger. "Of course our work is rough and coarse. But, on the other hand, it is sure, and we need not bow to any one. But you, in your towns, are surrounded by temptations; to-day all may be right, but to-morrow the Evil One may tempt your husband with cards, wine, or women, and all will go to ruin. Don't such things happen often enough?"

Pahóm, the master of the house, was lying on the top of the stove and he listened to the women's chatter.

"It is perfectly true," thought he. "Busy as we are from childhood tilling mother earth, we peasants have no time to let any nonsense settle in our heads. Our only trouble is that we haven't land enough. If I had plenty of land, I shouldn't fear the Devil himself!"

The women finished their tea, chatted a while about dress, and then cleared away the tea-things and lay down to sleep.

But the Devil had been sitting behind the stove and had heard all that was said. He was pleased that the peasant's wife had led her husband into boasting and that he had said that if he had plenty of land he would not fear the Devil himself.

"All right," thought the Devil. "We will have a tussle. I'll give you land enough; and by means of that land I will get you into my power."

II

Close to the village there lived a lady, a small land-owner, who had an estate of about three hundred acres.[1] She had always lived on good terms with the peasants until she engaged as her steward an old soldier, who took to burdening the people with fines. However careful Pahóm tried to be, it happened again and again that now a horse of his got among the lady's oats, now a cow strayed into her garden, now his calves found their way into her meadows—and he always had to pay a fine.

Pahóm paid up, but grumbled, and going home in a temper, was rough with his family. All through that summer, Pahóm had much trouble because of this steward, and he was even glad when winter came and the cattle had to be stabled. Though he grudged the fodder when

[1] 120 desyatíns. The desyatína is properly 2.7 acres but in this story round numbers are used

they could no longer graze on the pasture-land, at least he was free from anxiety about them.

In the winter the news got about that the lady was going to sell her land and that the keeper of the inn on the high road was bargaining for it. When the peasants heard this they were very much alarmed.

"Well," thought they, "if the innkeeper gets the land, he will worry us with fines worse than the lady's steward. We all depend on that estate."

So the peasants went on behalf of their Commune and asked the lady not to sell the land to the innkeeper, offering her a better price for it themselves. The lady agreed to let them have it. Then the peasants tried to arrange for the Commune to buy the whole estate, so that it might be held by them all in common. They met twice to discuss it, but could not settle the matter; the Evil One sowed discord among them and they could not agree. So they decided to buy the land individually, each according to his means; and the lady agreed to this plan as she had to the other.

Presently Pahóm heard that a neighbour of his was buying fifty acres, and that the lady had consented to accept one half in cash and to wait a year for the other half. Pahóm felt envious.

"Look at that," thought he, "the land is all being sold, and I shall get none of it." So he spoke to his wife.

"Other people are buying," said he, "and we must also buy twenty acres or so. Life is becoming impossible. That steward is simply crushing us with his fines."

So they put their heads together and considered how they could manage to buy it. They had one hundred rubles laid by. They sold a colt and one half of their bees, hired out one of their sons as a labourer and took his wages in advance, borrowed the rest from a brother-in-law, and so scraped together half the purchase money.

Having done this, Pahóm chose out a farm of forty acres, some of it wooded, and went to the lady to bargain for it. They came to an agreement, and he shook hands with her upon it and paid her a deposit in advance. Then they went to town and signed the deeds; he paying half the price down, and undertaking to pay the remainder within two years.

So now Pahóm had land of his own. He borrowed seed, and sowed it on the land he had bought. The harvest was a good one, and within a year he had managed to pay off his debts both to the lady and to his brother-in-law. So he became a landowner, ploughing and sowing his own land, making hay on his own land, cutting his own trees, and feeding his cattle on his own pasture. When he went out to plough his fields, or to look at his growing corn, or at his grass-meadows, his heart would fill with joy. The grass that grew and the flowers that bloomed there seemed to him unlike any that grew elsewhere. Formerly, when he had passed by that land, it had appeared the same as any other land, but now it seemed quite different.

III

So Pahóm was well contented, and everything would have been right if the neighbouring peasants would only not have trespassed on his corn-fields and meadows. He appealed to them most civilly, but they still went on: now the Communal herdsmen would let the village cows stray into his meadows, then horses from the night pasture would get among his corn. Pahóm turned them out again and again and forgave their owners, and for a long time he forbore to prosecute any one. But at last he lost patience and complained to the District Court. He knew it was the peasants' want of land, and no evil intent on their part, that caused the trouble, but he thought: "I cannot go on overlooking it or they will destroy all I have. They must be taught a lesson."

So he had them up, gave them one lesson, and then another, and two or three of the peasants were fined. After a time Pahóm's neighbours began to bear him a grudge for this and would now and then let their cattle on to his land on purpose. One peasant even got into Pahóm's wood at night and cut down five young lime trees for their bark. Pahóm passing through the wood one day noticed something white. He came nearer and saw the stripped trunks lying on the ground, and close by stood the stumps where the trees had been. Pahóm was furious.

"If he had only cut one here and there it would have been bad enough," thought Pahóm, "but the rascal has actually cut down a whole clump. If I could only find out who did this, I would pay him out."

He racked his brains as to who it could be. Finally he decided: "It must be Simon—no one else could have done it." So he went to Simon's homestead to have a look round, but he found nothing and only had an angry scene. However, he now felt more certain than ever that Simon had done it, and he lodged a complaint. Simon was summoned. The case was tried, and retried, and at the end of it all Simon was acquitted, there being no evidence against him. Pahóm felt still more aggrieved, and let his anger loose upon the elder and the judges.

"You let thieves grease your palms," said he. "If you were honest folk yourselves you would not let a thief go free."

So Pahóm quarrelled with the judges and with his neighbours. Threats to burn his building began to be uttered. So though Pahóm had more land, his place in the Commune was much worse than before.

About this time a rumour got about that many people were moving to new parts.

"There's no need for me to leave my land," thought Pahóm. "But some of the others might leave our village and then there would be more room for us. I would take over their land myself and make my estate a bit bigger. I could then live more at ease. As it is, I am still too cramped to be comfortable."

One day Pahóm was sitting at home when a peasant, passing through the village, happened to call in. He was allowed to stay the night, and supper was given him. Pahóm had a talk with this peasant and asked him where he came from. The stranger answered that he came from beyond the Volga, where he had been working. One word led to another, and the man went on to say that many people were settling in those parts. He told how some people from his village had settled there. They had joined the Commune, and had had twenty-five acres per man granted them. The land was so good, he said, that the rye sown on it grew as high as a horse and so thick that five cuts of a sickle made a sheaf. One peasant, he said, had brought nothing with him but his bare hands, and now he had six horses and two cows of his own.

Pahóm's heart kindled with desire. He thought: "Why should I suffer in this narrow hole, if one can live so well elsewhere? I will sell my land and my homestead here, and with the money I will start afresh over there and get everything new. In this crowded place one is always having trouble. But I must first go and find out all about it myself."

Towards summer he got ready and started. He went down the Volga on a steamer to Samára, then walked another three hundred miles on foot, and at last reached the place. It was just as the stranger had said. The peasants had plenty of land: every man had twenty-five acres of communal land given him for his use, and any one who had money could buy, besides, at two shillings an acre[2] as much good freehold land as he wanted.

Having found out all he wished to know, Pahóm returned home as autumn came on and began selling off his belongings. He sold his land at a profit, sold his homestead and all his cattle, and withdrew from membership of the Commune. He only waited till the spring, and then started with his family for the new settlement.

IV

As soon as Pahóm and his family reached their new abode, he applied for admission into the Commune of a large village. He stood treat to the elders and obtained the necessary documents. Five shares of communal land were given him for his own and his sons' use: that is to say, 125 acres (not all together, but in different fields) besides the use of the communal pasture. Pahóm put up the buildings he needed and bought cattle. Of the communal land alone he had three times as much as at his former home, and the land was good cornland. He was ten times better off than he had been. He had plenty of arable land and pasturage and could keep as many head of cattle as he liked.

At first, in the bustle of building and settling down, Pahóm was pleased with it all, but when he got used to it he began to think that even here he had not enough

---

2 Three rubles per desyatína.

land. The first year, he sowed wheat on his share of the communal land and had a good crop. He wanted to go on sowing wheat but had not enough communal land for the purpose, and what he had already used was not available; for in those parts wheat is only sown on virgin soil or on fallow land. It is sown for one or two years, and then the land lies fallow till it is again overgrown with prairie grass. There were many who wanted such land and there was not enough for all; so that people quarrelled about it. Those who were better off wanted it for growing wheat, and those who were poor wanted it to let to dealers, so that they might raise money to pay their taxes. Pahóm wanted to sow more wheat, so he rented land from a dealer for a year. He sowed much wheat and had a fine crop, but the land was too far from the village—the wheat had to be carted more than ten miles. After a time Pahóm noticed that some peasant-dealers were living on separate farms and were growing wealthy, and he thought: "If I were to buy some freehold land and have a homestead on it, it would be a different thing altogether. Then it would all be nice and compact."

The question of buying freehold land recurred to him again and again.

He went on in the same way for three years, renting land and sowing wheat. The seasons turned out well and the crops were good, so that he began to lay money by. He might have gone on living contentedly, but he grew tired of having to rent other people's land every year and having to scramble for it. Wherever there was good land to be had, the peasants would rush for it and it was taken up at once, so that unless you were sharp about it you got none. It happened in the third year that he and a dealer together rented a piece of pasture land from some peasants, and they had already ploughed it up, when there was some dispute and the peasants went to law about it, and things fell out so that the labour was all lost.

"If it were my own land," thought Pahóm, "I should be independent, and there would not be all this unpleasantness."

So Pahóm began looking out for land which he could buy, and he came across a peasant who had bought thirteen hundred acres but having got into difficulties was willing to sell again cheap. Pahóm bargained and haggled with him, and at last they settled the price at 1,500 rubles, part in cash and part to be paid later. They had all but clinched the matter when a passing dealer happened to stop at Pahóm's one day to get a feed for his horses. He drank tea with Pahóm and they had a talk. The dealer said that he was just returning from the land of the Bashkírs, far away, where he had bought thirteen thousand acres of land, all for 1,000 rúbles. Pahóm questioned him further, and the tradesman said: "All one need do is to make friends with the chiefs. I gave away about one hundred rubles worth of silk robes and carpets, besides a case of tea, and I gave wine to those who would drink it; and I got the land for less than a penny an acre."[3]

And he showed Pahóm the title-deeds, saying: "The land lies near a river, and the whole prairie is virgin soil."

Pahóm plied him with questions, and the tradesman said: "There is more land there than you could cover if you walked a year, and it all belongs to the Bashkírs. They are as simple as sheep, and land can be got almost for nothing."

"There now," thought Pahóm, "with my one thousand rúbles, why should I get only thirteen hundred acres, and saddle myself with a debt besides? If I take it out there, I can get more than ten times as much for the money."

V

Pahóm inquired how to get to the place, and as soon as the tradesman had left him, he prepared to go there himself. He left his wife to look after the homestead and started on his journey taking his man with him. They stopped at a town on their way and bought a case of tea, some wine, and other presents, as the tradesman had advised. On and on they went until they had gone more than three hundred miles, and on the seventh day they came to a place where the Bashkírs had pitched their tents. It was all just as the tradesman had said. The people lived on the steppes, by a river, in felt-covered tents. They neither tilled the ground nor ate bread. Their

---

[3] Five kopeks for a desyatína.

cattle and horses grazed in herds on the steppe. The colts were tethered behind the tents, and the mares were driven to them twice a day. The mares were milked and from the milk kumiss was made. It was the women who prepared kumiss, and they also made cheese. As far as the men were concerned, drinking kumiss and tea, eating mutton, and playing on their pipes, was all they cared about. They were all stout and merry, and all the summer long they never thought of doing any work. They were quite ignorant, and knew no Russian, but were good-natured enough.

As soon as they saw Pahóm, they came out of their tents and gathered round their visitor. An interpreter was found, and Pahóm told them he had come about some land. The Bashkírs seemed very glad; they took Pahóm and led him into one of the best tents, where they made him sit on some down cushions placed on a carpet, while they sat round him. They gave him some tea and kumiss and had a sheep killed, and gave him mutton to eat. Pahóm took presents out of his cart and distributed them among the Bashkírs and divided the tea amongst them. The Bashkírs were delighted. They talked a great deal among themselves and then told the interpreter to translate.

"They wish to tell you," said the interpreter, "that they like you and that it is our custom to do all we can to please a guest and to repay him for his gifts. You have given us presents, now tell us which of the things we possess please you best, that we may present them to you."

"What pleases me best here," answered Pahóm, "is your land. Our land is crowded and the soil is exhausted, but you have plenty of land and it is good land. I never saw the like of it."

The interpreter translated. The Bashkírs talked among themselves for a while. Pahóm could not understand what they were saying but saw that they were much amused and that they shouted and laughed. Then they were silent and looked at Pahóm while the interpreter said: "They wish me to tell you that in return for your presents they will gladly give you as much land as you want. You have only to point it out with your hand and it is yours."

The Bashkírs talked again for a while and began to

dispute. Pahóm asked what they were disputing about, and the interpreter told him that some of them thought they ought to ask their Chief about the land and not act in his absence, while others thought there was no need to wait for his return.

VI

While the Bashkírs were disputing, a man in a large fox-fur cap appeared on the scene. They all became silent and rose to their feet. The interpreter said, "This is our Chief himself."

Pahóm immediately fetched the best dressing-gown and five pounds of tea and offered these to the Chief. The Chief accepted them and seated himself in the place of honour. The Bashkírs at once began telling him something. The Chief listened for a while, then made a sign with his head for them to be silent, and addressing himself to Pahóm, said in Russian: "Well, let it be so. Choose whatever piece of land you like; we have plenty of it."

"How can I take as much as I like?" thought Pahóm. "I must get a deed to make it secure, or else they may say, 'It is yours' and afterwards may take it away again."

"Thank you for your kind words," he said aloud. "You have much land, and I only want a little. But I should like to be sure which bit is mine. Could it not be measured and made over to me? Life and death are in God's hands. You good people give it to me, but your children might wish to take it away again."

"You are quite right," said the Chief. "We will make it over to you."

"I heard that a dealer had been here," continued Pahóm," and that you gave him a little land, too, and signed title-deeds to that effect. I should like to have it done in the same way."

The Chief understood.

"Yes," replied he, "that can be done quite easily. We have a scribe, and we will go to town with you and have the deed properly sealed."

"And what will be the price?" asked Pahóm.

"Our price is always the same: one thousand rubles a day."

Pahóm did not understand.

"A day? What measure is that? How many acres would that be?"

"We do not know how to reckon it out," said the Chief. "We sell it by the day. As much as you can go round on your feet in a day is yours, and the price is one thousand rubles a day."

Pahóm was surprised.

"But in a day you can get round a large tract of land," he said.

The Chief laughed.

"It will all be yours!" said he. "But there is one condition: if you don't return on the same day to the spot whence you started, your money is lost."

"But how am I to mark the way that I have gone?"

"Why, we shall go to any spot you like and stay there. You must start from that spot and make your round, taking a spade with you. Wherever you think necessary, make a mark. At every turning, dig a hole and pile up the turf; then afterwards we will go round with a plough from hole to hole. You may make as large a circuit as you please, but before the sun sets you must return to the place you started from. All the land you cover will be yours."

Pahóm was delighted. It was decided to start early next morning. They talked a while, and after drinking some more kumiss and eating some more mutton, they had tea again, and then the night came on. They gave Pahóm a feather-bed to sleep on, and the Bashkirs dispersed for the night, promising to assemble the next morning at daybreak and ride out before sunrise to the appointed spot.

VII

Pahóm lay on the feather-bed, but could not sleep. He kept thinking about the land.

"What a large tract I will mark off!" thought he. "I can easily do thirty-five miles in a day. The days are long now, and within a circuit of thirty-five miles what a lot of land there will be! I will sell the poorer land or let it to peasants, but I'll pick out the best and farm it. I will buy two ox-teams, and hire two more labourers. About a hundred and fifty acres shall be plough-land, and I will pasture cattle on the rest."

Pahóm lay awake all night, and dozed off only just before dawn. Hardly were his eyes closed when he had a dream. He thought he was lying in that same tent and heard somebody chuckling outside. He wondered who it could be, and rose and went out, and he saw the Bashkír Chief sitting in front of the tent holding his sides and rolling about with laughter. Going nearer to the Chief, Pahóm asked, "What are you laughing at?" But he saw that it was no longer the Chief, but the dealer who had recently stopped at his house and had told him about the land. Just as Pahóm was going to ask, "Have you been here long?" he saw that it was not the dealer, but the peasant who had come up from the Volga, long ago, to Pahóm's old home. Then he saw that it was not the peasant either, but the Devil himself with hoofs and horns, sitting there and chuckling, and before him lay a man barefoot, prostrate on the ground, with only trousers and a shirt on. And Pahóm dreamt that he looked more attentively to see what sort of a man it was that was lying there, and he saw that the man was dead and that it was himself! He awoke horror-struck.

"What things one does dream," thought he.

Looking round he saw through the open door that the dawn was breaking.

"It's time to wake them up," thought he. "We ought to be starting."

He got up, roused his man (who was sleeping in his cart), bade him harness, and went to call the Bashkírs.

"It's time to go to the steppe to measure the land," he said.

The Bashkírs rose and assembled, and the Chief came too. Then they began drinking kumiss again, and offered Pahóm some tea, but he would not wait.

"If we are to go, let us go. It is high time," said he.

VIII

The Bashkírs got ready and they all started: some mounted on horses, and some in carts. Pahóm drove in his own small cart with his servant and took a spade with him. When they reached the steppe, the morning red was beginning to kindle. They ascended a hillock (called by the Bashkírs a *shikhan*) and dismounting from their carts and their horses, gathered in one spot. The Chief came up to Pahóm and, stretching out his arm towards the plain, "See," said he, "all this, as far as your eye can reach, is ours. You may have any part of it you like."

Pahóm's eyes glistened: it was all virgin soil, as flat as the palm of your hand, as black as the seed of a poppy, and in the hollows different kinds of grasses grew breast high.

The Chief took off his fox-fur cap, placed it on the ground and said:

"This will be the mark. Start from here, and return here again. All the land you go round shall be yours."

Pahóm took out his money and put it on the cap. Then he took off his outer coat, remaining in his sleeveless under-coat. He unfastened his girdle and tied it tight below his stomach, put a little bag of bread into the breast of his coat, and tying a flask of water to his girdle, he drew up the tops of his boots, took the spade from his man, and stood ready to start. He considered for some moments which way he had better go—it was tempting everywhere.

"No matter," he concluded, "I will go towards the rising sun."

"I must lose no time," he thought, "and it is easier walking while it is still cool."

The sun's rays had hardly flashed above the horizon, before Pahóm, carrying the spade over his shoulder, went down into the steppe.

Pahóm started walking neither slowly nor quickly. After having gone a thousand yards he stopped, dug a hole, and placed pieces of turf one on another to make it more visible. Then he went on, and now that he had walked off his stiffness he quickened his pace. After a while he dug another hole.

Pahóm looked back. The hillock could be distinctly seen in the sunlight, with the people on it, and the glittering tyres of the cart-wheels. At a rough guess Pahóm concluded that he had walked three miles. It was growing warmer; he took off his under-coat, flung it across his shoulder, and went on again. It had grown quite warm now; he looked at the sun, it was time to think of breakfast.

"The first shift is done, but there are four in a day, and it is too soon yet to turn. But I will just take off my boots," said he to himself.

He sat down, took off his boots, stuck them into his girdle, and went on. It was easy walking now.

"I will go on for another three miles," thought he, "and then turn to the left. This spot is so fine that it would be a pity to lose it. The further one goes, the better the land seems."

He went straight on for a while, and when he looked round, the hillock was scarcely visible and the people on it looked like black ants, and he could just see something glistening there in the sun.

"Ah," thought Pahóm, "I have gone far enough in this direction, it is time to turn. Besides I am in a regular sweat, and very thirsty."

He stopped, dug a large hole, and heaped up pieces of turf. Next he untied his flask, had a drink, and then turned sharply to the left. He went on and on; the grass was high, and it was very hot.

Pahóm began to grow tired; he looked at the sun and saw that it was noon.

"Well," he thought, "I must have a rest."

He sat down and ate some bread and drank some water, but he did not lie down, thinking that if he did he might fall asleep. After sitting a little while, he went on again. At first he walked easily: the food had strengthened him, but it had become terribly hot and he felt sleepy, still he went on, thinking: "An hour to suffer, a life-time to live."

He went a long way in this direction also and was about to turn to the left again, when he perceived a damp hollow. "It would be a pity to leave that out," he thought. "Flax would do well there." So he went on past the hollow, and dug a hole on the other side of it before he turned the corner. Pahóm looked towards the hillock. The heat made the air hazy: it seemed to be quivering, and through the haze the people on the hillock could scarcely be seen.

"Ah!" thought Pahóm, "I have made the sides too long; I must make this one shorter." And he went along the third side, stepping faster. He looked at the sun: it was nearly half-way to the horizon, and he had not yet done two miles of the third side of the square. He was still ten miles from the goal.

"No," he thought, "though it will make my land lopsided, I must hurry back in a straight line now. I might go too far, and as it is I have a great deal of land."

So Pahóm hurriedly dug a hole and turned straight towards the hillock.

IX

Pahóm went straight towards the hillock, but he now walked with difficulty. He was done up with the heat, his bare feet were cut and bruised, and his legs began to fail. He longed to rest, but it was impossible if he meant to get back before sunset. The sun waits for no man, and it was sinking lower and lower.

"Oh dear," he thought, "if only I have not blundered trying for too much! What if I am too late?"

He looked towards the hillock and at the sun. He was still far from his goal, and the sun was already near the rim.

Pahóm walked on and on; it was very hard walking but he went quicker and quicker. He pressed on but was still far from the place. He began running, threw away his coat, his boots, his flask, and his cap, and kept only the spade which he used as a support.

"What shall I do?" he thought again. "I have grasped too much and ruined the whole affair. I can't get there before the sun sets."

And this fear made him still more breathless. Pahóm went on running, his soaking shirt and trousers stuck to him and his mouth was parched. His breast was working like a blacksmith's bellows, his heart was beating like a hammer, and his legs were giving way as if they did not belong to him. Pahóm was seized with terror lest he should die of the strain.

Though afraid of death, he could not stop. "After having run all that way, they will call me a fool if I stop now," thought he. And he ran on and on, and drew near and heard the Bashkírs yelling and shouting to him, and their cries inflamed his heart still more. He gathered his last strength and ran on.

The sun was close to the rim, and cloaked in mist looked large, and red as blood. Now, yes now, it was about to set! The sun was quite low, but he was also quite near his aim. Pahóm could already see the people on the hillock waving their arms to hurry him up. He could see the fox-fur cap on the ground and the money on it, and the Chief sitting on the ground holding his sides. And Pahóm remembered his dream.

"There is plenty of land," thought he, "but will God let me live on it? I have lost my life, I have lost my life! I shall never reach that spot!"

Pahóm looked at the sun, which had reached the earth: one side of it had already disappeared. With all his remaining strength he rushed on, bending his body forward so that his legs could hardly follow fast enough to keep him from falling. Just as he reached the hillock it suddenly grew dark. He looked up—the sun had already set! He gave a cry. "All my labour has been in vain," thought he and was about to stop, but he heard the Bashkírs still shouting and remembered that though to him, from below, the sun seemed to have set, they on the hillock could still see it. He took a long breath and ran up the hillock. It was still light there. He reached the top and saw the cap. Before it sat the Chief laughing and holding his sides. Again Pahóm remembered his dream, and he uttered a cry: his legs gave way beneath him, he fell forward and reached the cap with his hands.

"Ah, that's a fine fellow!" exclaimed the Chief. "He has gained much land!"

Pahóm's servant came running up and tried to raise him, but he saw that blood was flowing from his mouth. Pahóm was dead!

The Bashkírs clicked their tongues to show their pity.

His servant picked up the spade and dug a grave long enough for Pahóm to lie in and buried him in it. Six feet from his head to his heels was all he needed.

1886

THE KREUTZER SONATA

But I say unto you, That every one that looketh on a woman to lust after her hath committed adultery with her already in his heart.

The disciples say unto him, If the case of the man must be so with his wife, it is not good to marry. But he said unto them, All men cannot receive this saying, save they to whom it is given. *Matthew, 5:28; 19:10–11*

I

It was early spring, and the second day of our journey. Passengers going short distances entered and left our carriage, but three others, like myself, had come all the way with the train. One was a lady, plain and no longer young, who smoked, had a harassed look, and wore a mannish coat and cap; another was an acquaintance of hers, a talkative man of about forty, whose things looked neat and new; the third was a rather short man who kept himself apart. He was not old, but his curly hair had gone prematurely grey. His movements were abrupt and his unusually glittering eyes moved rapidly from one object to another. He wore an old overcoat, evidently from a first-rate tailor, with an astrakhan collar and a tall astrakhan cap. When he unbuttoned his overcoat a sleeveless Russian coat and embroidered shirt showed beneath it. A peculiarity of this man was a strange sound he emitted, something like a clearing of his throat, or a laugh begun and sharply broken off.

All the way this man had carefully avoided making acquaintance or having any intercourse with his fellow passengers. When spoken to by those near him he gave short and abrupt answers, and at other times read, looked out of the window, smoked, or drank tea and ate something he took out of an old bag.

It seemed to me that his loneliness depressed him, and I made several attempts to converse with him, but whenever our eyes met, which happened often as he sat nearly opposite me, he turned away and took up his book or looked out of the window.

Towards the second evening, when our train stopped at a large station, this nervous man fetched himself some boiling water and made tea. The man with the neat new things—a lawyer as I found out later—and his neighbour, the smoking lady with the mannish coat, went to the refreshment-room to drink tea.

During their absence several new passengers entered the carriage, among them a tall, shaven, wrinkled old man, evidently a tradesman, in a coat lined with skunk fur and a cloth cap with an enormous peak. The tradesman sat down opposite the seats of the lady and the lawyer and immediately started a conversation with a young man who had also entered at that station and, judging by his appearance, was a tradesman's clerk.

I was sitting the other side of the gangway and as the train was standing still I could hear snatches of their conversation when nobody was passing between us. The tradesman began by saying that he was going to his estate which was only one station farther on; then as usual the conversation turned to prices and trade, and they spoke of the state of business in Moscow and then of the Nízhni-Nóvgorod Fair. The clerk began to relate how a wealthy merchant, known to both of them, had gone on the spree at the fair, but the old man interrupted him by telling of the orgies he had been at in former times at Kunávin Fair. He evidently prided himself on the part he had played in them and recounted with pleasure how he and some acquaintances, together with the merchant they had been speaking of, had once got drunk at Kunávin and played such a trick that he had to tell of it in a whisper. The clerk's roar of laughter filled the whole carriage; the old man laughed also, exposing two yellow teeth.

Not expecting to hear anything interesting, I got up

to stroll about the platform till the train should start. At the carriage door I met the lawyer and the lady who were talking with animation as they approached.

"You won't have time," said the sociable lawyer, "the second bell will ring in a moment."[1]

And the bell did ring before I had gone the length of the train. When I returned, the animated conversation between the lady and the lawyer was proceeding. The old tradesman sat silent opposite to them, looking sternly before him, and occasionally mumbled disapprovingly as if chewing something.

"Then she plainly informed her husband," the lawyer was smilingly saying as I passed him, "that she was not able, and did not wish, to live with him since . . ."

He went on to say something I could not hear. Several other passengers came in after me. The guard passed, a porter hurried in, and for some time the noise made their voices inaudible. When all was quiet again the conversation had evidently turned from the particular case to general considerations.

The lawyer was saying that public opinion in Europe was occupied with the question of divorce, and that cases of "that kind" were occurring more and more often in Russia. Noticing that his was the only voice audible, he stopped his discourse and turned to the old man.

"Those things did not happen in the old days, did they?" he said, smiling pleasantly.

The old man was about to reply, but the train moved and he took off his cap, crossed himself, and whispered a prayer. The lawyer turned away his eyes and waited politely. Having finished his prayer and crossed himself three times, the old man set his cap straight, pulled it well down over his forehead, changed his position, and began to speak.

"They used to happen even then, sir, but less often," he said. "As times are now they can't help happening. People have got too educated."

The train moved faster and faster and jolted over

---

[1] It was customary in Russia for a first, second, and third bell to ring before a train left a station.

the joints of the rails, making it difficult to hear, but being interested I moved nearer. The nervous man with the glittering eyes opposite me, evidently also interested, listened without changing his place.

"What is wrong with education?" said the lady, with a scarcely perceptible smile. "Surely it can't be better to marry as they used to in the old days when the bride and bridegroom did not even see one another before the wedding," she continued, answering not what her interlocutor had said but what she thought he would say, in the way many ladies have. "Without knowing whether they loved, or whether they could love, they married just anybody and were wretched all their lives. And you think that was better?" she said, evidently addressing me and the lawyer chiefly and least of all the old man with whom she was talking.

"They've got so very educated," the tradesman reiterated, looking contemptuously at the lady and leaving her question unanswered.

"It would be interesting to know how you explain the connexion between education and matrimonial discord," said the lawyer, with a scarcely perceptible smile.

The tradesman was about to speak, but the lady interrupted him.

"No," she said, "those times have passed." But the lawyer stopped her.

"Yes, but allow the gentleman to express his views."

"Foolishness comes from education," the old man said categorically.

"They make people who don't love one another marry, and then wonder that they live in discord," the lady hastened to say, turning to look at the lawyer, at me, and even at the clerk, who had got up and, leaning on the back of the seat, was smilingly listening to the conversation. "It's only animals, you know, that can be paired off as their master likes; but human beings have their own inclinations and attachments," said the lady, with an evident desire to annoy the tradesman.

"You should not talk like that, madam," said the old man; "animals are cattle, but human beings have a law given them."

"Yes, but how is one to live with a man when there

is no love?" the lady again hastened to express her argument, which probably seemed very new to her.

"They used not to go into that," said the old man in an impressive tone; "it is only now that all this has sprung up. The least thing makes them say: 'I will leave you!' The fashion has spread even to the peasants. 'Here you are!' she says. 'Here, take your shirts and trousers and I will go with Vánka; his head is curlier than yours.' What can you say? The first thing that should be required of a woman is fear!"

The clerk glanced at the lawyer, at the lady, and at me, apparently suppressing a smile and prepared to ridicule or to approve of the tradesman's words according to the reception they met with.

"Fear of what?" asked the lady.

"Why this: let her fear her husband! That fear!"

"Oh, the time for that, sir, has passed," said the lady with a certain viciousness.

"No, madam, that time cannot pass. As she, Eve, was made from the rib of a man, so it will remain to the end of time," said the old man, jerking his head with such sternness and such a victorious look that the clerk at once concluded that victory was on his side and laughed loudly.

"Ah yes, that's the way you men argue," said the lady unyieldingly and turned to us. "You have given yourselves freedom but want to shut women up in a tower.[2] You no doubt permit yourselves everything."

"No one is permitting anything, but a man does not bring offspring into the home, while a woman—a wife— is a leaky vessel," the tradesman continued insistently. His tone was so impressive that it evidently vanquished his hearers, and even the lady felt crushed but still did not give in.

"Yes, but I think you will agree that a woman is a human being and has feelings as a man has. What is she to do then, if she does not love her husband?"

"Does not love!" said the tradesman severely, moving his brows and lips. "She'll love, no fear!" This unexpected

[2] Literally "in the *terem*," the *terem* being the woman's quarter where in olden times the women of a Russian family used to be secluded in oriental fashion.

argument particularly pleased the clerk, and he emitted a sound of approval.

"Oh, no, she won't!" the lady began, "and when there is no love you can't enforce it."

"Well, and supposing the wife is unfaithful, what then?" asked the lawyer.

"That is not admissible," said the old man. "One has to see to that."

"But if it happens, what then? You know it does occur."

"It happens among some, but not among us," said the old man.

All were silent. The clerk moved, came still nearer, and, evidently unwilling to be behindhand, began with a smile.

"Yes, a young fellow of ours had a scandal. It was a difficult case to deal with. It too was a case of a woman who was a bad lot. She began to play the devil, and the young fellow is respectable and cultured. At first it was with one of the office-clerks. The husband tried to persuade her with kindness. She would not stop but played all sorts of dirty tricks. Then she began to steal his money. He beat her, but she only grew worse. Carried on intrigues, if I may mention it, with an unchristened Jew. What was he to do? He turned her out altogether and lives as a bachelor, while she gads about."

"Because he is a fool," said the old man. "If he'd pulled her up properly from the first and not let her have her way, she'd be living with him, no fear! It's giving way at first that counts. Don't trust your horse in the field, or your wife in the house."

At that moment the guard entered to collect the tickets for the next station. The old man gave up his.

"Yes, the female sex must be curbed in time or else all is lost!"

"Yes, but you yourself just now were speaking about the way married men amuse themselves at the Kunávin fair," I could not help saying.

"That's a different matter," said the old man and relapsed into silence.

When the whistle sounded the tradesman rose, got out his bag from under the seat, buttoned up his coat, and slightly lifting his cap went out of the carriage.

II

As soon as the old man had gone several voices were raised.

"A daddy of the old style!" remarked the clerk.

"A living Domostróy!"[1] said the lady. "What barbarous views of women and marriage!"

"Yes, we are far from the European understanding of marriage," said the lawyer.[2]

"The chief thing such people do not understand," continued the lady, "is that marriage without love is not marriage; that love alone sanctifies marriage, and that real marriage is only such as is sanctified by love."

The clerk listened smilingly, trying to store up for future use all he could of the clever conversation.

In the midst of the lady's remarks we heard, behind me, a sound like that of a broken laugh or sob; and on turning round we saw my neighbour, the lonely grey-haired man with the glittering eyes, who had approached unnoticed during our conversation, which evidently interested him. He stood with his arms on the back of the seat, evidently much excited; his face was red and a muscle twitched in his cheek.

"What kind of love . . . love . . . is it that sanctifies marriage?" he asked hesitatingly.

Noticing the speaker's agitation, the lady tried to answer him as gently and fully as possible.

"True love . . . . When such love exists between a man and a woman, then marriage is possible," she said.

"Yes, but how is one to understand what is meant by 'true love'?" said the gentleman with the glittering eyes timidly and with an awkward smile.

"Everybody knows what love is," replied the lady, evidently wishing to break off her conversation with him.

"But I don't," said the man. "You must define what you understand . . ."

"Why? It's very simple," she said but stopped to con-

---

[1] *The Housebuilder*, a sixteenth-century manual, by the monk Silvester, on religion and household management.

[2] One Russian edition adds: "First woman's rights, then civil marriage, and then divorce come as unsettled questions."

sider. "Love? Love is an exclusive preference for one above everybody else," said the lady.

"Preference for how long? A month, two days, or half an hour?" said the grey-haired man and began to laugh.

"Excuse me, we are evidently not speaking of the same thing."

"Oh, yes! Exactly the same."

"She means," interposed the lawyer, pointing to the lady, "that in the first place marriage must be the outcome of attachment—or love, if you please—and only where that exists is marriage sacred, so to speak. Secondly, that marriage when not based on natural attachment— love, if you prefer the word—lacks the element that makes it morally binding. Do I understand you rightly?" he added, addressing the lady.

The lady indicated her approval of his explanation by a nod of her head.

"It follows . . ." the lawyer continued—but the nervous man, whose eyes now glowed as if aflame and who had evidently restrained himself with difficulty, began without letting the lawyer finish: "Yes, I mean exactly the same thing, a preference for one person over everybody else, and I am only asking: a preference for how long?"

"For how long? For a long time; for life sometimes," replied the lady, shrugging her shoulders.

"Oh, but that happens only in novels and never in real life. In real life this preference for one may last for years (that happens very rarely), more often for months, or perhaps for weeks, days, or hours," he said, evidently aware that he was astonishing everybody by his views and pleased that it was so.

"Oh, what are you saying?" "But no . . ." "No, allow me . . ." we all three began at once. Even the clerk uttered an indefinite sound of disapproval.

"Yes, I know," the grey-haired man shouted above our voices; "you are talking about what is supposed to be, but I am speaking of what is. Every man experiences what you call love for every pretty woman."

"Oh, what you say is awful! But the feeling that is called love does exist among people and is given not for months or years, but for a lifetime!"

"No, it does not! Even if we should grant that a man

might prefer a certain woman all his life, the woman in all probability would prefer someone else, and so it always has been and still is in the world," he said, and taking out his cigarette-case he began to smoke.

"But the feeling may be reciprocal," said the lawyer.

"No, sir, it can't!" rejoined the other. "Just as it cannot be that in a cartload of peas two marked peas will lie side by side. Besides, it is not merely this impossibility, but the inevitable satiety. To love one person for a whole lifetime is like saying that one candle will burn a whole life," he said, greedily inhaling the smoke.

"But you are talking all the time about physical love. Don't you acknowledge love based on identity of ideals, on spiritual affinity?" asked the lady.

"Spiritual affinity! Identity of ideals!" he repeated, emitting his peculiar sound. "But in that case why go to bed together? (Excuse my coarseness!) Or do people go to bed together because of the identity of their ideals?" he said, bursting into a nervous laugh.

"But permit me," said the lawyer. "Facts contradict you. We do see that matrimony exists, that all mankind, or the greater part of it, lives in wedlock, and many people honourably live long married lives."

The grey-haired man again laughed.

"First you say that marriage is based on love, and when I express a doubt as to the existence of a love other than sensual, you prove the existence of love by the fact that marriages exist. But marriages in our days are mere deception!"

"No, allow me!" said the lawyer. "I only say that marriages have existed and do exist."

"They do! But why? They have existed and do exist among people who see in marriage something sacramental, a mystery binding them in the sight of God. Among them marriages do exist. Among us, people marry regarding marriage as nothing but copulation, and the result is either deception or coercion. When it is deception it is easier to bear. The husband and wife merely deceive people by pretending to be monogamists, while living polygamously. That is bad, but still bearable. But when, as most frequently happens, the husband and wife have undertaken the external duty of living together all their lives and begin to hate each other after a month, and wish to part but still continue to live together, it leads to that terrible hell which makes people take to drink, shoot themselves, and kill or poison themselves or one another," he went on, speaking more and more rapidly, not allowing anyone to put in a word and becoming more and more excited. We all felt embarrassed.

"Yes, undoubtedly there are critical episodes in married life," said the lawyer, wishing to end this disturbingly heated conversation.

"I see you have found out who I am!" said the grey-haired man softly, and with apparent calm.

"No, I have not that pleasure."

"It is no great pleasure. I am that Pózdnyshev in whose life that critical episode occurred to which you alluded; the episode when he killed his wife," he said, rapidly glancing at each of us.

No one knew what to say and all remained silent.

"Well, never mind," he said with that peculiar sound of his. "However, pardon me. Ah! . . . I won't intrude on you."

"Oh, no, if you please . . ." said the lawyer, himself not knowing "if you please" what.

But Pózdynshev, without listening to him, rapidly turned away and went back to his seat. The lawyer and the lady whispered together. I sat down beside Pózdnyshev in silence, unable to think of anything to say. It was too dark to read, so I shut my eyes pretending that I wished to go to sleep. So we travelled in silence to the next station.

At that station the lawyer and the lady moved into another car, having some time previously consulted the guard about it. The clerk lay down on the seat and fell asleep. Pózdnyshev kept smoking and drinking tea which he had made at the last station.

When I opened my eyes and looked at him he suddenly addressed me resolutely and irritably: "Perhaps it is unpleasant for you to sit with me, knowing who I am? In that case I will go away."

"Oh no, not at all."

"Well then, won't you have some? Only it's very strong."

He poured out some tea for me.

"They talk . . . and they always lie . . ." he remarked.

"What are you speaking about?" I asked.

"Always about the same thing. About that love of theirs and what it is! Don't you want to sleep?"

"Not at all."

"Then would you like me to tell you how that love led to what happened to me?"

"Yes, if it will not be painful for you."

"No, it is painful for me to be silent. Drink the tea . . . or is it too strong?"

The tea was really like beer, but I drank a glass of it.[3] Just then the guard entered. Pózdnyshev followed him with angry eyes, and only began to speak after he had left.

III

"Well then, I'll tell you. But do you really want to hear it?"

I repeated that I wished it very much. He paused, rubbed his face with his hands, and began: "If I am to tell it, I must tell everything from the beginning: I must tell how and why I married, and the kind of man I was before my marriage.

"Till my marriage I lived as everybody does, that is, everybody in our class. I am a landowner and a graduate of the university and was a marshal of the gentry. Before my marriage I lived as everyone does, that is, dissolutely; and while living dissolutely I was convinced, like everybody in our class, that I was living as one has to. I thought I was a charming fellow and quite a moral man. I was not a seducer, had no unnatural tastes, did not make that the chief purpose of my life as many of my associates did, but I practised debauchery in a steady, decent way for health's sake. I avoided women who might tie my hands by having a child or by attachment for me. However, there may have been children and attachments, but I acted as if there were not. And this I not only considered moral, but I was even proud of it."

He paused and gave vent to his peculiar sound, as he evidently did whenever a new idea occurred to him.

"And you know, that is the chief abomination!" he

---

[3] Tea in Russia is usually drunk out of tumblers.

exclaimed. "Dissoluteness does not lie in anything physical
—no kind of physical misconduct is debauchery; real
debauchery lies precisely in freeing oneself from moral
relations with a woman with whom you have physical
intimacy. And such emancipation I regarded as a merit.
I remember how I once worried because I had not had
an opportunity to pay a woman who gave herself to
me (having probably taken a fancy to me) and how I
only became tranquil after having sent her some money
—thereby intimating that I did not consider myself in
any way morally bound to her. . . . Don't nod as if you
agreed with me," he suddenly shouted at me. "Don't I
know these things? We all, and you too unless you are
a rare exception, hold those same views, just as I used
to. Never mind, I beg your pardon, but the fact is that
it's terrible, terrible, terrible!"

"What is terrible?" I asked.

"That abyss of error in which we live regarding women
and our relations with them. No, I can't speak calmly
about it, not because of that 'episode,' as he called it, in
my life, but because since that episode occurred my eyes
have been opened and I have seen everything in quite
a different light. Everything reversed, everything reversed!"

He lit a cigarette and began to speak, leaning his
elbows on his knees.

It was too dark to see his face, but, above the jolting
of the train, I could hear his impressive and pleasant voice.

IV

"Yes, only after such torments as I have endured, only
by their means, have I understood where the root of the
matter lies—understood what ought to be, and therefore
seen all the horror of what is.

"So you will see how and when that which led up
to my 'episode' began. It began when I was not quite
sixteen. It happened when I still went to the grammar
school and my elder brother was a first-year student at
the university. I had not yet known any woman, but, like
all the unfortunate children of our class, I was no longer
an innocent boy. I had been depraved two years before

that by other boys. Already woman, not some particular woman but woman as something to be desired, woman, every woman, woman's nudity, tormented me. My solitude was not pure. I was tormented, as ninety-nine per cent of our boys are. I was horrified, I suffered, I prayed, and I fell. I was already depraved in imagination and in fact, but I had not yet taken the last step. I was perishing, but I had not yet laid hands on another human being. But one day a comrade of my brother's, a jolly student, a so-called good fellow—that is, the worst kind of good-for-nothing—who had taught us to drink and to play cards, persuaded us after a carousal to go *there.* We went. My brother was also still innocent, and he fell that same night. And I, a fifteen-year-old boy, defiled myself and took part in defiling a woman, without at all understanding what I was doing. I had never heard from any of my elders that what I was doing was wrong, you know. And indeed no one hears it now. It is true it is in the Commandments, but then the Commandments are only needed to answer the priest at Scripture examination, and even then they are not very necessary, not nearly as necessary as the commandment about the use of *ut* in conditional sentences in Latin.

"And so I never heard those older persons whose opinions I respected say that it was an evil. On the contrary, I heard people I respected say it was good. I had heard that my struggles and sufferings would be eased after that. I heard this and read it and heard my elders say it would be good for my health, while from my comrades I heard that it was rather a fine, spirited thing to do. So in general I expected nothing but good from it. The risk of disease? But that too had been foreseen. A paternal government[1] saw to that. It sees to the correct working of the brothels[1] and makes profligacy safe for schoolboys. Doctors too deal with it for a consideration. That is proper. They assert that debauchery is good for the health, and they organize proper well-regulated

[1] In Russia, as in other continental countries and formerly in England, the *maisons de tolérance* were under the supervision of the government; doctors were employed to examine the women, and, as far as possible, see they did not continue their trade when diseased.

debauchery. I know some mothers who attend to their sons' health in that sense. And science sends them to the brothels."

"Why do you say 'science'?" I asked.

"Why, who are the doctors? The priests of science. Who deprave youths by maintaining that this is necessary for their health? They do.

"Yet if a one-hundredth part of the efforts devoted to the cure of syphilis were devoted to the eradication of debauchery, there would long ago not have been a trace of syphilis left. But as it is, efforts are made not to eradicate debauchery but to encourage it and to make debauchery safe. That is not the point however. The point is that with me—and with nine-tenths, if not more, not of our class only but of all classes, even the peasants—this terrible thing happens that happened to me; I fell not because I succumbed to the natural temptation of a particular woman's charm—no, I was not seduced by a woman—but I fell because, in the set around me, what was really a fall was regarded by some as a most legitimate function good for one's health, and by others as a very natural and not only excusable but even innocent amusement for a young man. I did not understand that it was a fall, but simply indulged in that half-pleasure, half-need, which, as was suggested to me, was natural at a certain age. I began to indulge in debauchery as I began to drink and to smoke. Yet in that first fall there was something special and pathetic. I remember that at once, on the spot, before I left the room, I felt sad, so sad that I wanted to cry—to cry for the loss of my innocence and for my relationship with women, now sullied for ever. Yes, my natural, simple relationship with women was spoilt for ever. From that time I have not had, and could not have, pure relations with women. I had become what is called a libertine. To be a libertine is a physical condition like that of a morphinist, a drunkard, or a smoker is no longer normal, so too a man who has known several women for his pleasure is not normal but is a man perverted for ever, a libertine. As a drunkard or a morphinist can be recognized at once by his face and manner, so it is with a libertine. A libertine may restrain himself, may struggle, but he will never have those pure, simple, clear, brotherly relations with a woman. By the way he looks at a young woman and examines her, a libertine can always be recognized. And I had become and I remained a libertine, and it was this that brought me to ruin."

V

"Ah yes! After that things went from bad to worse, and there were all sorts of deviations. Oh, God! When I recall the abominations I committed in this respect I am seized with horror! And that is true of me, whom my companions, I remember, ridiculed for my so-called innocence. And when one hears of the 'gilded youths,' of officers, of the Parisians . . .! And when all these gentlemen, and I— who have on our souls hundreds of the most varied and horrible crimes against women—when we thirty-year-old profligates, very carefully washed, shaved, perfumed, in clean linen and in evening dress or uniform, enter a drawing-room or ball-room, we are emblems of purity, charming!

"Only think of what ought to be, and of what is! When in society such a gentleman comes up to my sister or daughter, I, knowing his life, ought to go up to him, take him aside, and say quietly, 'My dear fellow, I know the life you lead, and how and with whom you pass your nights. This is no place for you. That is what ought to be; but what happens is that when such a gentleman comes and dances, embracing our sister or daughter, we are jubilant, if he is rich and well-connected. Maybe after Rigulboche[1] he will honour my daughter! Even if traces of disease remain, no matter! They are clever at curing that nowadays. Oh, yes, I know several girls in the best society whom their parents enthusiastically gave in marriage to men suffering from a certain disease. Oh, oh . . . the abomination of it! But a time will come when this abomination and falsehood will be exposed!"

He made his strange noise several times and again drank tea. It was fearfully strong and there was no water with which to dilute it. I felt that I was much excited by the

---

[1] A notorious Parisian *cancanière*.

two glasses I had drunk. Probably the tea affected him too, for he became more and more excited. His voice grew increasingly mellow and expressive. He continually changed his position, now taking off his cap and now putting it on again, and his face changed strangely in the semi-darkness in which we were sitting.

"Well, so I lived till I was thirty, not abandoning for a moment the intention of marrying and arranging for myself a most elevated and pure family life. With that purpose I observed the girls suitable for that end," he continued. "I weltered in a mire of debauchery and at the same time was on the look-out for a girl pure enough to be worthy of me.

"I rejected many just because they were not pure enough to suit me, but at last I found one whom I considered worthy. She was one of two daughters of a once-wealthy Pénza landowner who had been ruined.

"One evening after we had been out in a boat and had returned by moonlight, and I was sitting beside her admiring her curls and her shapely figure in a tight-fitting jersey, I suddenly decided that it was she! It seemed to me that evening that she understood all that I felt and thought, and that what I felt and thought was very lofty. In reality it was only that the jersey and the curls were particularly becoming to her and that after a day spent near her I wanted to be still closer.

"It is amazing how complete is the delusion that beauty is goodness. A handsome woman talks nonsense, you listen and hear not nonsense but cleverness. She says and does horrid things, and you see only charm. And if a handsome woman does not say stupid or horrid things, you at once persuade yourself that she is wonderfully clever and moral.

"I returned home in rapture, decided that she was the acme of moral perfection, and that therefore she was worthy to be my wife, and I proposed to her next day.

"What a muddle it is! Out of a thousand men who marry (not only among us but unfortunately also among the masses) there is hardly one who has not already been married ten, a hundred, or even, like Don Juan, a thousand times, before his wedding.

"It is true as I have heard and have myself observed that there are nowadays some chaste young men who feel and know that this thing is not a joke but an important matter.

"God help them! But in my time there was not one such in ten thousand. And everybody knows this and pretends not to know it. In all the novels they describe in detail the heroes' feelings and the ponds and bushes beside which they walk, but when their great love for some maiden is described, nothing is said about what has happened to these interesting heroes before: not a word about their frequenting certain houses, or about the servant-girls, cooks, and other people's wives! If there are such improper novels they are not put into the hands of those who most need this information—the unmarried girls.

"We first pretend to these girls that the profligacy which fills half the life of our towns, and even of the villages, does not exist at all.

"Then we get so accustomed to this pretense that at last, like the English, we ourselves really begin to believe that we are all moral people and live in a moral world. The girls, poor things, believe this quite seriously. So too did my unfortunate wife. I remember how, when we were engaged, I showed her my diary, from which she could learn something, if but a little, of my past, especially about my last *liaison*, of which she might hear from others, and about which I therefore felt it necessary to inform her. I remember her horror, despair, and confusion, when she learnt of it and understood it. I saw that she then wanted to give me up. And why did she not do so? . . ."

He again made that sound, swallowed another mouthful of tea, and remained silent for a while.

VI

"No, after all, it is better, better so!" he exclaimed. "It serves me right! But that's not to the point—I meant to say that it is only the unfortunate girls who are deceived.

"The mothers know it, especially mothers educated by their own husbands—they know it very well. While pretending to believe in the purity of men, they act quite differently. They know with what sort of bait to catch men for themselves and for their daughters.

"You see it is only we men who don't know (because we don't wish to know) what women know very well, that the most exalted poetic love, as we call it, depends not on moral qualities but on physical nearness and on the *coiffure* and the colour and cut of the dress. Ask an expert coquette who has set herself the task of captivating a man, which she would prefer to risk: to be convicted in his presence of lying, or cruelty, or even of dissoluteness, or to appear before him in an ugly and badly made dress—she will always prefer the first. She knows that we are continually lying about high sentiments but really only want her body and will therefore forgive any abomination except an ugly tasteless costume that is in bad style.

"A coquette knows that consciously, and every innocent girl knows it unconsciously just as animals do.

"That is why there are those detestable jerseys, bustles, and naked shoulders, arms, almost breasts. A woman, especially if she has passed the male school, knows very well that all the talk about elevated subjects is just talk but that what a man wants is her body and all that presents it in the most deceptive but alluring light, and she acts accordingly. If we only throw aside our familiarity with this indecency, which has become a second nature to us, and look at the life of our upper classes as it is, in all its shamelessness—why, it is simply a brothel . . . You don't agree? Allow me, I'll prove it," he said, interrupting me. "You say that the women of our society have other interests in life than prostitutes have, but I say no and will prove it. If people differ in the aims of their lives, by the inner content of their lives, this difference will necessarily be reflected in externals and their externals will be different. But look at those unfortunate despised women and at the highest society ladies: the same costumes, the same fashions, the same perfumes, the same exposure of arms, shoulders, and breasts, the same tight skirts over prominent bustles, the same passion for little stones, for costly, glittering objects, the same amusements, dances, music, and singing. As the former employ all means to allure, so do these others."

VII

"Well, so these jerseys and curls and bustles caught me!

"It was very easy to catch me for I was brought up in the conditions in which amorous young people are forced like cucumbers in a hot-bed. You see our stimulating super-abundance of food, together with complete physical idleness, is nothing but a systematic excitement of desire. Whether this astonishes you or not, it is so. Why, till quite recently I did not see anything of this myself, but now I have seen it. That is why it torments me that nobody knows this, and people talk such nonsense as that lady did.

"Yes, last spring some peasants were working in our neighbourhood on a railway embankment. The usual food of a young peasant is rye-bread, kvas, and onions; he keeps alive and is vigorous and healthy; his work is light agricultural work. When he goes to railway-work his rations are buckwheat porridge and a pound of meat a day. But he works off that pound of meat during his sixteen hours' work wheeling barrow-loads of half-a-ton weight, so it is just enough for him. But we who every day consume two pounds of meat, and game, and fish and all sorts of heating foods and drinks—where does that go to? Into excesses of sensuality. And if it goes there and the safety-valve is open, all is well; but try and close the safety-valve, as I closed it temporarily, and at once a stimulus arises which, passing through the prism of our artificial life, expresses itself in utter infatuation, sometimes even platonic. And I fell in love as they all do.

"Everything was there to hand: raptures, tenderness, and poetry. In reality that love of mine was the result, on the one hand of her mamma's and the dressmakers' activity, and on the other of the super-abundance of food consumed by me while living an idle life. If on the one hand there had been no boating, no dressmaker with her waists and so forth, and had my wife been sitting at home in a shapeless dressing-gown, and had I on the other hand been in circumstances normal to man—consuming just enough food to suffice for the work I did, and had the safety-valve been open—it happened to be closed at the time—I should not have fallen in love and nothing of all this would have happened."

VIII

"Well, and now it so chanced that everything combined
—my condition, her becoming dress, and the satisfactory
boating. It had failed twenty times but now it succeeded.
Just like a trap! I am not joking. You see nowadays marriages are arranged that way—like traps. What is the
natural way? The lass is ripe, she must be given in marriage. It seems very simple if the girl is not a fright and
there are men wanting to marry. That is how it was done
in olden times. The lass was grown up and her parents
arranged the marriage. So it was done, and is done, among
all mankind—Chinese, Hindus, Mohammedans, and among
our own working class; so it is done among at least
ninety-nine per cent of the human race. Only among one
per cent or less, among us libertines, has it been discovered
that that is not right, and something new has been invented.
And what is this novelty? It is that the maidens sit round
and the men walk about, as at a bazaar, choosing. And
the maidens wait and think, but dare not say: 'Me, please!'
'No, me!' 'Not her, but me!' 'Look what shoulders and
other things I have!' And we men stroll around and look,'
and are very pleased. 'Yes, I know! I won't be caught!'
They stroll about and look and are very pleased that
everything is arranged like that for them. And then in
an unguarded moment—snap! He is caught!"

"Then how ought it to be done?" I asked. "Should the
woman propose?"

"Oh, I don't know how; only if there's to be equality,
let it be equality. If they have discovered that pre-arranged
matches are degrading, why this is a thousand times worse!
Then the rights and chances were equal, but here the
woman is a slave in a bazaar or the bait in a trap. Tell
any mother, or the girl herself, the truth, that she is
only occupied in catching a husband . . . oh dear! what
an insult! Yet they all do it and have nothing else to do.
What is so terrible is to see sometimes quite innocent poor
young girls engaged on it. And again, if it were but
done openly—but it is always done deceitfully. 'Ah, the
origin of species, how interesting!' 'Oh, Lily takes such
an interest in painting! And will you be going to the
exhibition? How instructive!' And the troika-drives, and

shows, and symphonies! 'Oh! how remarkable! My Lily is mad on music.' 'And why don't you share these convictions?' And boating . . . But their one thought is: 'Take me, take me!' 'Take my Lily!' 'Or try—at least!' Oh, what an abomination! What falsehood!" he concluded, finishing his tea and beginning to put away the tea-things.

IX

"You know," he began, while packing the tea and sugar into his bag, "the domination of women from which the world suffers all arises from this."

"What 'domination of women'?" I asked. "The rights, the legal privileges, are on the man's side."

"Yes, yes! That's just it," he interrupted me. "That's just what I want to say. It explains the extraordinary phenomenon that on the one hand woman is reduced to the lowest stage of humiliation, while on the other she dominates. Just like the Jews: as they pay us back for their oppression by a financial domination, so it is with women. 'Ah, you want us to be traders only—all right, as traders we will dominate you!' say the Jews. 'Ah, you want us to be merely objects of sensuality—all right, as objects of sensuality we will enslave you,' say the women. Woman's lack of rights arises not from the fact that she must not vote or be a judge—to be occupied with such affairs is no privilege—but from the fact that she is not man's equal in sexual intercourse and has not the right to use a man or abstain from him as she likes, is not allowed to choose a man at her pleasure instead of being chosen by him. You say that is monstrous. Very well! Then a man must not have those rights either. As it is at present, a woman is deprived of that right while a man has it. And to make up for that right she acts on man's sensuality and through his sensuality subdues him so that he only chooses formally, while in reality it is she who chooses. And once she has obtained these means she abuses them and acquires a terrible power over people."

"But where is this special power?" I inquired.

"Where is it? Why, everywhere, in everything! Go round the shops in any big town. There are goods worth millions and you cannot estimate the human labour expended on them, and look whether in nine-tenths of these shops there is anything for the use of men. All the luxuries of life are demanded and maintained by women.

"Count all the factories. An enormous proportion of them produce useless ornaments, carriages, furniture, and trinkets, for women. Millions of people, generations of slaves, perish at hard labour in factories merely to satisfy woman's caprice. Women, like queens, keep nine-tenths of mankind in bondage to heavy labour. And all because they have been abased and deprived of equal rights with men. And they revenge themselves by acting on our sensuality and catch us in their nets. Yes, it all comes of that.

"Women have made of themselves such an instrument for acting upon our sensuality that a man cannot quietly consort with a woman. As soon as a man approaches a woman he succumbs to her stupefying influence and becomes intoxicated and crazy. I used formerly to feel uncomfortable and uneasy when I saw a lady dressed up for a ball, but now I am simply frightened and plainly see her as something dangerous and illicit. I want to call a policeman and ask for protection from the peril and demand that the dangerous object be removed and put away.

"Ah, you are laughing!" he shouted at me, "but it is not at all a joke. I am sure a time will come, and perhaps very soon, when people will understand this and will wonder how a society could exist in which actions were permitted which so disturb social tranquillity as those adornments of the body directly evoking sensuality, which we tolerate for women in our society. Why, it's like setting all sorts of traps along the paths and promenades—it is even worse! Why is gambling forbidden while women in costumes which evoke sensuality are not forbidden? They are a thousand times more dangerous!"

X

"Well, you see, I was caught that way. I was what is called in love. I not only imagined her to be the height of perfection, but during the time of our engagement I regarded myself also as the height of perfection. You know there is

no rascal who cannot, if he tries, find rascals in some
respects worse than himself, and who consequently cannot
find reasons for pride and self-satisfaction. So it was with
me: I was not marrying for money—covetousness had
nothing to do with it; unlike the majority of my acquaintances who married for money or connexions, I was rich,
she was poor. That was one thing. Another thing I prided
myself on was that while others married intending to continue in future the same polygamous life they had lived
before marriage, I was firmly resolved to be monogamous
after marriage, and there was no limit to my pride on that
score. Yes, I was a dreadful pig and imagined myself to
be an angel.

"Our engagement did not last long. I cannot now think
of that time without shame! What nastiness! Love is supposed to be spiritual and not sensual. Well, if the love is
spiritual, a spiritual communion, then that spiritual communion should find expression in words, in conversations,
in discourse. There was nothing of the kind. It used to be
dreadfully difficult to talk when we were left alone. It was
the labour of Sisyphus. As soon as we thought of something to say and said it, we had again to be silent, devising
something else. There was nothing to talk about. All that
could be said about the life that awaited us, our arrangements and plans, had been said, and what was there more?
Now if we had been animals we should have known that
speech was unnecessary, but here on the contrary it was
necessary to speak, and there was nothing to say, because
we were not occupied with what finds vent in speech. And
moreover there was that ridiculous custom of giving sweets,
of coarse gormandizing on sweets, and all those abominable
preparations for the wedding: remarks about the house,
the bedroom, beds, wraps, dressing-gowns, underclothing,
costumes. You must remember that if one married according to the injunctions of Domostróy, as that old fellow
was saying, then the feather-beds, the trousseau, and the
bedstead are all but details appropriate to the sacrament.
But among us, when of ten who marry there are certainly
nine who not only do not believe in the sacrament but do
not even believe that what they are doing entails certain
obligations; where scarcely one man out of a hundred has
not been married before, and of fifty scarcely one is not

preparing in advance to be unfaithful to his wife at every convenient opportunity; when the majority regard the going to church as only a special condition for obtaining possession of a certain woman—think what a dreadful significance all these details acquire. They show that the whole business is only that; they show that it is a kind of sale. An innocent girl is sold to a profligate, and the sale is accompanied by certain formalities."

XI

"That is how everybody marries and that is how I married, and the much vaunted honeymoon began. Why, its very name is vile!" he hissed viciously. "In Paris I once went to see the sights and noticing a bearded woman and a water-dog on a sign-board, I entered the show. It turned out to be nothing but a man in a woman's low-necked dress, and a dog done up in walrus skin and swimming in a bath. It was very far from being interesting; but as I was leaving, the showman politely saw me out and, addressing the public at the entrance, pointed to me and said, 'Ask the gentleman whether it is not worth seeing! Come in, come in, one franc apiece!' I felt ashamed to say it was not worth seeing, and the showman had probably counted on that. It must be the same with those who have experienced the abomination of a honeymoon and who do not disillusion others. Neither did I disillusion anyone, but I do not now see why I should not tell the truth. Indeed, I think it needful to tell the truth about it. One felt awkward, ashamed, repelled, sorry, and above all dull, intolerably dull! It was something like what I felt when I learnt to smoke—when I felt sick and the saliva gathered in my mouth and I swallowed it and pretended that it was very pleasant. Pleasure from smoking, just as from that, if it comes at all, comes later. The husband must cultivate that vice in his wife in order to derive pleasure from it."

"Why vice?" I said. "You are speaking of the most natural human functions."

"Natural?" he said. "Natural? No, I may tell you that I have come to the conclusion that it is, on the contrary, *un*natural. Yes, quite *un*natural. Ask a child, ask an unperverted girl.

"Natural, you say!

"It is natural to eat. And to eat is, from the very beginning, enjoyable, easy, pleasant, and not shameful; but this is horrid, shameful, and painful. No, it is unnatural! And an unspoilt girl, as I have conceived myself, always hates it."

"But how," I asked, "would the human race continue?"

"Yes, would not the human race perish?" he said, irritably and ironically, as if he had expected this familiar and insincere objection. "Teach abstention from child-bearing so that English lords may always gorge themselves —that is all right. Preach it for the sake of greater pleasure —that is all right; but just hint at abstention from child-bearing in the name of morality—and, my goodness, what a rumpus . . .! Isn't there a danger that the human race may die out because they want to cease to be swine? But forgive me! This light is unpleasant, may I shade it?" he said, pointing to the lamp. I said I did not mind; and with the haste with which he did everything, he got up on the seat and drew the woollen shade over the lamp.

"All the same," I said, "if everyone thought this the right thing to do, the human race would cease to exist."

He did not reply at once.

"You ask how the human race will continue to exist," he said, having again sat down in front of me, and spreading his legs far apart he leant his elbows on his knees. "Why should it continue?"

"Why? If not, we should not exist."

"And why should we exist?"

"Why? In order to live, of course."

"But why live? If life has no aim, if life is given us for life's sake, there is no reason for living. And if it is so, then the Schopenhauers, the Hartmanns, and all the Buddhists as well, are quite right. But if life has an aim, it is clear that it ought to come to an end when that aim is reached. And so it turns out," he said with noticeable agitation, evidently prizing his thought very highly. "So it turns out. Just think: if the aim of humanity is goodness, righteousness, love—call it what you will—if it is what the prophets have said, that all mankind should be united together in love, that the spears should be beaten into pruning-hooks and so forth, what is it that hinders the attainment of this aim? The passions hinder it. Of all the passions the strongest, cruellest, and most stubborn is the sex-passion, physical love; and therefore if the passions are destroyed, including the strongest of them—physical love—the prophecies will be fulfilled, mankind will be brought into a unity, the aim of human existence will be attained, and there will be nothing further to live for. As long as mankind exists the ideal is before it, and of course not the rabbits' and pigs' ideal of breeding as fast as possible, nor that of monkeys or Parisians—to enjoy sex-passion in the most refined manner, but the ideal of good-ness attained by continence and purity. Towards that people have always striven and still strive. You see what follows:

"It follows that physical love is a safety-valve. If the present generation has not attained its aim, it has not done so because of its passions, of which the sex-passion is the strongest. And if the sex-passion endures there will be a new generation and consequently the possibility of attain-ing the aim in the next generation. If the next one does not attain it, then the next after that may, and so on, till the aim is attained, the prophecies fulfilled, and mankind attains unity. If not, what would result? If one admits that God created men for the attainment of a certain aim and created them mortal but sexless, or created them immortal, what would be the result? Why, if they were mortal but without the sex-passion and died without attaining the aim, God would have had to create new people to attain his aim. If they were immortal, let us grant that (though it would be more difficult for the same people to correct their mistakes and approach perfection than for those of another generation) they might attain that aim after many thousands of years, but then what use would they be after-wards? What could be done with them? It is best as it is. . . . But perhaps you don't like that way of putting it? Perhaps you are an evolutionist? It comes to the same thing. The highest race of animals, the human race, in order to main-tain itself in the struggle with other animals ought to unite into one whole like a swarm of bees and not breed con-tinually; it should bring up sexless members as the bees do; that is, again, it should strive towards continence and not towards inflaming desire—to which the whole system of our life is now directed." He paused. "The human race will cease? But can anyone doubt it, whatever his outlook on life may be? Why, it is as certain as death. According to all the teaching of the Church, the end of the world will come, and according to all the teaching of science the same result is inevitable."

XII

"In our world it is just the reverse: even if a man does think of continence while he is a bachelor, once married he is sure to think continence no longer necessary. You know those wedding tours—the seclusion into which, with their parents' consent, the young couple go—are nothing but licensed debauchery. But a moral law avenges itself when it is violated. Hard as I tried to make a success of my honeymoon, nothing came of it. It was horrid, shameful, and dull, the whole time. And very soon I began also to experience a painful, oppressive feeling. That began very quickly. I think it was on the third or fourth day that I found my wife depressed. I began asking her the reason and embracing her, which in my view was all she could want, but she removed my arms and began to cry. What about? She could not say. But she felt sad and distressed. Probably her exhausted nerves suggested to her the truth as to the vileness of our relation but she did not know how to express it. I began to question her, and she said something about feeling sad without her mother. It seemed to me that this was untrue, and I began comforting her without alluding to her mother. I did not understand that she was simply depressed and her mother was merely an excuse. But she immediately took offence because I had not mentioned her mother, as though I did not believe her. She told me she saw that I did not love her. I reproached her with being capricious, and suddenly her face changed entirely and instead of sadness it expressed irritation, and with the most venomous words she began accusing me of selfishness and cruelty. I gazed at her. Her whole face showed complete coldness and hostility, almost hatred. I remember how horror-stricken I was when I saw this. 'How? What?' I thought. 'Love is a union of souls—and instead of that there is this! Impossible, this is not she!' I tried to soften her but encountered such an insuperable wall of cold virulent hostility that before I had time to turn round I too was seized with irritation and we said a great many unpleasant things to one another. The impression of that first quarrel was dreadful. I call it a quarrel, but it was not a quarrel but only the disclosure of the abyss that really existed between us. Amorousness was exhausted by the satisfaction of sensuality and we were left confronting one another in our true relation: that is, as two egotists quite alien to each other who wished to get as much pleasure as possible each from the other. I call what took place between us a quarrel, but it was not a quarrel, only the consequence of the cessation of sensuality—revealing our real relations to one another. I did not understand that this cold and hostile relation was our normal state; I did not understand it because at first this hostile attitude was very soon concealed from us by a renewal of redistilled sensuality—that is, by love-making.

"I thought we had quarrelled and made it up again and that it would not recur. But during that same first month of honeymoon a period of satiety soon returned, we again ceased to need one another, and another quarrel super-vened. This second quarrel struck me even more painfully than the first. 'So the first one was not an accident but was bound to happen and will happen again,' I thought. I was all the more staggered by that second quarrel because it arose from such an impossible pretext. It had something to do with money, which I never grudged and could cer-tainly not have grudged to my wife. I only remember that she gave the matter such a twist that some remark of mine appeared to be an expression of a desire on my part to dominate over her by means of money, to which I was supposed to assert an exclusive right—it was something impossibly stupid, mean, and not natural either to me or to her. I became exasperated, and upbraided her with lack of consideration for me. She accused me of the same thing, and it all began again. In her words and in the expression of her face and eyes I again noticed the cruel hostility that had so staggered me before. I had formerly quarrelled with my brother, my friends, and my father, but there had never, I remember, been the special venomous malice which there was here. But after a while this mutual hatred was screened by amorousness—that is, sensuality, and I still consoled myself with the thought that these two quarrels had been mistakes and could be remedied. But then a third and a fourth quarrel followed and I realized that it was not accidental, but that it was bound to happen and would happen so, and I was horrified at the prospect before me. At the same time I was tormented by the terrible thought that I alone lived on such bad terms with my wife, so unlike what I had expected, whereas this did not happen between other married couples. I did not know then that it is our common fate but that everybody imagines, just as I did, that it is their peculiar misfortune, and everyone conceals this exceptional and shameful misfortune not only from others but even from himself and does not acknowledge it to himself.

"It began during the first days and continued all the time, ever increasing and growing more obdurate. In the depths of my soul I felt from the first weeks that I was lost, that things had not turned out as I expected, that marriage was not only no happiness but a very heavy burden; but like everybody else I did not wish to acknowledge this to myself (I should not have acknowledged it even now but for the end that followed) and I concealed it not only from others but from myself too. Now I am astonished that I failed to see my real position. It might have been seen from the fact that the quarrels began on pretexts it was impossible to remember when they were over. Our reason was not quick enough to *devise* sufficient excuses for the animosity that always existed between us. But more striking still was the insufficiency of the excuses for our reconciliations. Sometimes there were words, explanations, even tears, but sometimes . . . oh! it is disgusting even now to think of it—after the most cruel words to one another came sudden silent glances, smiles, kisses, embraces. . . . Faugh, how horrid! How is it I did not then see all the vileness of it?"

XIII

Two fresh passengers entered and settled down on the farthest seats. He was silent while they were seating themselves but as soon as they had settled down continued, evidently not for a moment losing the thread of his idea.

"You know, what is vilest about it," he began, "is that in theory love is something ideal and exalted, but in practice it is something abominable, swinish, which it is horrid and shameful to mention or remember. It is not for nothing that nature has made it disgusting and shameful. And if it is disgusting and shameful one must understand that it is so. But here, on the contrary, people pretend that what is disgusting and shameful is beautiful and lofty. What were the first symptoms of my love? Why that I gave way to animal excesses, not only without shame but being somehow even proud of the possibility of these physical excesses, and without in the least considering either her spiritual or even her physical life. I wondered what embittered us against one another, yet it was perfectly simple: that animosity was nothing but the protest of our human nature against the animal nature that overpowered it.

"It was surprised at our enmity to one another; yet it could not have been otherwise. That hatred was nothing but the mutual hatred of accomplices in a crime—both for the incitement to the crime and for the part taken in it. What was it but a crime when she, poor thing, became pregnant in the first month and our *swinish* connexion continued? You think I am straying from my subject? Not at all! I am telling you *how* I killed my wife. They asked me at the trial with what and how I killed her. Fools! They thought I killed her with a knife, on the 5th of October. It was not then I killed her, but much earlier. Just as they are all now killing, all, all. . . ."

"But with what?" I asked.

"That is just what is so surprising, that nobody wants to see what is so clear and evident, what doctors ought to know and preach but are silent about. Yet the matter is very simple. Men and women are created like the animals so that physical love is followed by pregnancy and then by suckling—conditions under which physical love is bad for the woman and for her child. There are an equal number of men and women. What follows from this? It seems clear, and no great wisdom is needed to draw the conclusion that animals do—namely, the need of continence. But no. Science has been able to discover some kind of leucocytes that run about in the blood, and all sorts of useless nonsense, but cannot understand that. At least one does not hear of science teaching it!

"And so a woman has only two ways out: one is to make a monster of herself, to destroy and go on destroying within herself to such degree as may be necessary the capacity of being a woman—that is, a mother—in order that a man may quietly and continuously get his enjoyment; the other way out—and it is not even a way out but a simple, coarse, and direct violation of the laws of nature —practised in all so-called decent families—is that, contrary to her nature, the woman must be her husband's mistress even while she is pregnant or nursing—must be what not even an animal descends to, and for which her strength is insufficient. That is what causes nerve troubles and hysteria in our class, and among the peasants causes what they call being 'possessed by the devil'—epilepsy. You will notice that no pure maidens are ever 'possessed,' but only married women living with their husbands. That is so here, and it is just the same in Europe. All the hospitals for hysterical women are full of those who have violated nature's law. The epileptics and Charcot's patients are complete wrecks, you know, but the world is full of half-crippled women. Just think of it, what a great work goes on within a woman when she conceives or when she is nursing an infant. That is growing which will continue us and replace us. And this sacred work is violated—by what? It is terrible to think of it! And they prate about the freedom and the rights of women! It is as if cannibals fattened their captives to be eaten and at the same time declared that they were concerned about their prisoners' rights and freedom."

All this was new to me and startled me.

"What is one to do? If that is so," I said, "it means that one may love one's wife once in two years, yet men . . ."

"Men must!" he interrupted me. "It is again those precious priests of science who have persuaded everybody of that. Imbue a man with the idea that he requires vodka, tobacco, or opium, and all these things will be indispensable to him. It seems that God did not understand what was necessary and therefore, omitting to consult those wizards, arranged things badly. You see matters do not tally. They have decided that it is essential for a man to satisfy his desires, and the bearing and nursing of children comes and interferes with it and hinders the satisfaction of that need. What is one to do then? Consult the wizards! They will arrange it. And they have devised something. Oh! when will those wizards with their deceptions be dethroned? It is high time! It has come to such a point that people go mad and shoot themselves and all because of this. How could it be otherwise? The animals seem to know that their progeny continue their race, and they keep to a certain law in this matter. Man alone neither knows it nor wishes to know but is concerned only to get all the pleasure he can. And who is doing that? The lord of nature—man! Animals, you see, only come together at times when they are capable of producing progeny, but the filthy lord of nature is at it any time if only it pleases him! And as if that were not sufficient, he exalts this apish occupation into the most precious pearl of creation, into love. In the name of this love—that is, this filth—he destroys—what? Why, half the human race! All the women who might help the progress of mankind towards truth and goodness he converts, for the sake of his pleasure, into enemies instead of helpmates. See what it is that everywhere impedes the forward movement of mankind. Women! And why are they what they are? Only because of that. Yes, yes . . ." he repeated several times, and began to move about, and to get out his cigarettes and to smoke, evidently trying to calm himself.

XIV

"I too lived like a pig of that sort," he continued in his former tone. "The worst thing about it was that while living that horrid life I imagined that, because I did not go after other women, I was living an honest family life, that I was a moral man and in no way blameworthy, and if quarrels occurred it was her fault and resulted from her character.

"Of course the fault was not hers. She was like everybody else—like the majority of women. She had been brought up as the position of women in our society requires, and as therefore all women of the leisured classes without exception are brought up and cannot help being brought up. People talk about some new kind of education for women. It is all empty words: their education is exactly what it has to be in view of our unfeigned, real, general opinion about women.

"The education of women will always correspond to men's opinion about them. Don't we know how men regard women: *Wein, Weib, und Gesang*, and what the poets say in their verses? Take all poetry, all pictures and sculpture, beginning with love poems and the nude Venuses and Phrynes, and you will see that woman is an instrument of enjoyment; she is so on the Trubá and the Grachévka,[1] and also at the Court[2] balls. And note the devil's cunning: if they are here for enjoyment and pleasure, let it be known that it is pleasure and that woman is a sweet morsel. But no, first the knights-errant declare that they worship women (worship her, and yet regard her as an instrument of enjoyment), and now people assure us that they respect women. Some give up their places to her, pick up her handkerchief; others acknowledge her right to occupy all positions and to take part in the government, and so on. They do all that, but their outlook on her remains the same. She is a means of enjoyment. Her body is a means of enjoyment. And she knows this. It is just as it is with slavery. Slavery, you know, is nothing else than the exploitation by some of the unwilling labour of many. Therefore to get rid of slavery it is necessary that people should not wish to profit by the forced labour of others and should consider it a sin and a shame. But they go and abolish the external form of slavery and arrange so that one can no longer buy and sell slaves, and they imagine and assure themselves that slavery no longer exists and do not see or wish to see that it does, because people still want and consider it good and right to exploit the labour of others. And as long as they consider that good, there will always be people stronger or more cunning than others who will succeed in doing it. So it is with the emancipation of woman: the enslavement of woman lies simply in

---

[1] Streets in Moscow in which brothels were numerous.
[2] In the printed and censored Russian edition the word "Court" was changed to "most refined."

the fact that people desire, and think it good, to avail themselves of her as a tool of enjoyment. Well, and they liberate woman, give her all sorts of rights equal to man, but continue to regard her as an instrument of enjoyment, and so educate her in childhood and afterwards by public opinion. And there she is, still the same humiliated and depraved slave, and the man still a depraved slave-owner.

"They emancipate women in universities and in law courts but continue to regard her as an object of enjoyment. Teach her, as she is taught among us, to regard herself as such, and she will always remain an inferior being. Either with the help of those scoundrels the doctors she will prevent the conception of offspring—that is, will be a complete prostitute, lowering herself not to the level of an animal but to the level of a thing—or she will be what the majority of women are, mentally diseased, hysterical, unhappy, and lacking capacity for spiritual development. High schools and universities cannot alter that. It can only be changed by a change in men's outlook on women and women's way of regarding themselves. It will change only when woman regards virginity as the highest state and does not, as at present, consider the highest state of a human being a shame and a disgrace. While that is not so, the ideal of every girl, whatever her education may be, will continue to be to attract as many men as possible, as many males as possible, so as to have the possibility of choosing.

"But the fact that one of them knows more mathematics, and another can play the harp, makes no difference. A woman is happy and attains all she can desire when she has bewitched man. Therefore the chief aim of a woman is to be able to bewitch him. So it has been and will be. So it is in her maiden life in our society, and so it continues to be in her married life. For a maiden this is necessary in order to have a choice, for the married woman in order to have power over her husband.

"The one thing that stops this or at any rate suppresses it for a time, is children, and then only if the mother is not a monster—that is, if she nurses them herself. But here the doctors again come in.

"My wife, who wanted to nurse, and did nurse the four later children herself, happened to be unwell after the birth of her first child. And those doctors, who cynically undressed her and felt her all over—for which I had to thank them and pay them money—those dear doctors considered that she must not nurse the child; and that first time she was deprived of the only means which might have kept her from coquetry. We engaged a wet nurse—that is, we took advantage of the poverty, the need, and the ignorance of a woman, tempted her away from her own baby to ours, and in return gave her a fine head-dress with gold lace.[3] But that is not the point. The point is that during that time when my wife was free from pregnancy and from suckling, the feminine coquetry which had lain dormant within her manifested itself with particular force. And coinciding with this the torments of jealousy rose up in me with special force. They tortured me all my married life, as they cannot but torture all husbands who live with their wives as I did with mine, that is, immorally."

XV

"During the whole of my married life I never ceased to be tormented by jealousy, but there were periods when I specially suffered from it. One of these periods was when, after the birth of our first child, the doctors forbade my wife to nurse it. I was particularly jealous at that time, in the first place because my wife was experiencing that unrest natural to a mother which is sure to be aroused when the natural course of life is needlessly violated; and secondly, because seeing how easily she abandoned her moral obligations as a mother, I rightly though unconsciously concluded that it would be equally easy for her to disregard her duty as a wife, especially as she was quite well and in spite of the precious doctors' prohibition was able to nurse her later children admirably."

"I see you don't like doctors," I said, noticing a peculiarly malevolent tone in his voice whenever he alluded to them.

"It is not a case of liking or disliking. They have ruined my life as they have ruined and are ruining the

[3] In Russia wet-nurses were usually provided with an elaborate national costume by their employers.

lives of thousands and hundreds of thousands of human beings, and I cannot help connecting the effect with the cause. I understand that they want to earn money like lawyers and others, and I would willingly give them half my income, and all who realize what they are doing would willingly give them half of their possessions, if only they would not interfere with our family life and would never come near us. I have not collected evidence, but I know dozens of cases (there are any number of them!) where they have killed a child in its mother's womb asserting that she could not give it birth, though she has had children quite safely later on; or they have killed the mother on the pretext of performing some operation. No one reckons these murders any more than they reckoned the murders of the Inquisition, because it is supposed that it is done for the good of mankind. It is impossible to number all the crimes they commit. But all those crimes are as nothing compared to the moral corruption of materialism they introduce into the world, especially through women.

"I don't lay stress on the fact that if one is to follow their instructions, then on account of the infection which exists everywhere and in everything, people would not progress towards greater unity but towards separation; for according to their teaching we ought all to sit apart and not remove the carbolic atomizer from our mouths (though now they have discovered that even that is of no avail). But that does not matter either. The principal poison lies in the demoralization of the world, especially of women.

"To-day one can no longer say: 'You are not living rightly, live better.' One can't say that, either to oneself or to anyone else. If you live a bad life it is caused by the abnormal functioning of your nerves, etc. So you must go to them, and they will prescribe eight penn'orth of medicine from a chemist, which you must take!

"You get still worse: then more medicine and the doctor again. An excellent trick!

"That however is not the point. All I wish to say is that she nursed her babies perfectly well and that only her pregnancy and the nursing of her babies saved me from the torments of jealousy. Had it not been for that it would all have happened sooner. The children saved me and her. In eight years she had five children and nursed all except the first herself."

"And where are your children now?" I asked.

"The children?" he repeated in a frightened voice.

"Forgive me, perhaps it is painful for you to be reminded of them."

"No, it does not matter. My wife's sister and brother have taken them. They would not let me have them. I gave them my estate, but they did not give them up to me. You know I am a sort of lunatic. I have left them now and am going away. I have seen them, but they won't let me have them because I might bring them up so that they would not be like their parents, and they have to be just like them. Oh well, what is to be done? Of course they won't let me have them and won't trust me. Besides, I do not know whether I should be able to bring them up. I think not. I am a ruin, a cripple. Still I have one thing in me. I know! Yes, that is true, I know what others are far from knowing.

"Yes, my children are living and growing up just such savages as everybody around them. I saw them, saw them three times. I can do nothing for them, nothing. I am now going to my place in the south. I have a little house and a small garden there.

"Yes, it will be a long time before people learn what I know. How much of iron and other metal there is in the sun and the stars is easy to find out, but anything that exposes our swinishness is difficult, terribly difficult!

"You at least listen to me, and I am grateful for that."

XVI

"You mentioned my children. There again, what terrible lies are told about children! Children a blessing from God, a joy! That is all a lie. It was so once upon a time, but now it is not so at all. Children are a torment and nothing else. Most mothers feel this quite plainly, and sometimes inadvertently say so. Ask most mothers of our propertied classes and they will tell you that they do not want to have children for fear of their falling ill and dying. They don't want to nurse[1] them if they do have them, for fear of becoming too much attached to them and having to suffer. The pleasure a baby gives them by its loveliness, its little hands and feet, and its whole body, is not as great as the suffering caused by the very fear of its possibly falling ill and dying, not to speak of its actual illness or death. After weighing the advantages and disadvantages it seems disadvantageous, and therefore undesirable, to have children. They say this quite frankly and boldly, imagining that these feelings of theirs arise from their love of children, a good and laudable feeling of which they are proud. They do not notice that by this reflection they plainly repudiate love and only affirm their own selfishness. They get less pleasure from a baby's loveliness than suffering from fear on its account, and therefore the baby they would love is not wanted. They do not sacrifice themselves for a beloved being but sacrifice a being whom they might love, for their own sakes.

"It is clear that this is not love but selfishness. But one has not the heart to blame them—the mothers in well-to-do families—for that selfishness, when one remembers how dreadfully they suffer on account of their children's health, again thanks to the influence of those same doctors among our well-to-do classes. Even now, when I do but remember my wife's life and the condition she was in during the first years when we had three or four children and she was absorbed in them, I am seized with horror! We led no life at all but were in a state of constant danger, of escape from it, recurring danger, again followed by a desperate struggle and another escape—always as if we were on a sinking ship. Sometimes it seemed to me that this was done on purpose and that she pretended to be anxious about the children in order to subdue me. It solved all questions in her favour with such tempting simplicity. It sometimes seemed as if all she did and said on these occasions was pretence. But no! She herself suffered terribly and continually tormented herself about the children and their health and illnesses. It was torture for her and for me too; and it was impossible for her not to suffer.

[1] The practice of employing wet-nurses was very much more general in Russia than in the English-speaking countries.

After all, the attachment to her children, the animal need of feeding, caressing, and protecting them, was there as with most women, but there was not the lack of imagination and reason that there is in animals. A hen is not afraid of what may happen to her chick, does not know all the diseases that may befall it, and does not know all those remedies with which people imagine that they can save from illness and death. And for a hen her young are not a source of torment. She does for them what it is natural and pleasurable for her to do; her young ones are a pleasure to her. When a chick falls ill her duties are quite definite: she warms and feeds it. And doing this she knows that she is doing all that is necessary. If her chick dies she does not ask herself why it died, or where it has gone to; she cackles for a while and then leaves off and goes on living as before. But for our unfortunate women, my wife among them, it was not so. Not to mention illnesses and how to cure them, she was always hearing and reading from all sides endless rules for the rearing and educating of children, which were continually being superseded by others. This is the way to feed a child: feed it in this way, on such a thing; no, not on such a thing, but in this way; clothes, drinks, baths, putting to bed, walking, fresh air—for all these things we, especially she, heard of new rules every week, just as if children had only begun to be born into the world since yesterday. And if a child that had not been fed or bathed in the right way or at the right time fell ill, it appeared that we were to blame for not having done what we ought.

"That was so while they were well. It was a torment even then. But if one of them happened to fall ill, it was all up: a regular hell! It is supposed that illness can be cured and that there is a science about it and people—doctors—who know about it. Ah, but not all of them know—only the very best. When a child is ill one must get hold of the very best one, the one who saves, and then the child is saved; but if you don't get that doctor, or if you don't live in the place where that doctor lives, the child is lost. This was not a creed peculiar to her, it is the creed of all the women of our class, and she heard nothing else from all sides. Catherine Semënovna lost two children because Iván Zakhárych was not called

in in time, but Iván Zakhárych saved Mary Ivánovna's
eldest girl, and the Petróvs moved in time to various hotels
by the doctor's advice, and the children remained alive;
but if they had not been segregated the children would
have died. Another who had a delicate child moved
south by the doctor's advice and saved the child. How can
she help being tortured and agitated all the time, when
the lives of the children for whom she has an animal
attachment depend on her finding out in time what Iván
Zakhárych will say! But what Iván Zakhárych will say
nobody knows, and he himself least of all, for he is well
aware that he knows nothing and therefore cannot be of
any use, but just shuffles about at random so that people
should not cease to believe that he knows something or
other. You see, had she been wholly an animal she would
not have suffered so, and if she had been quite a human
being she would have had faith in God and would have
said and thought, as a believer does: 'The Lord gave
and the Lord hath taken away. One can't escape from God.'

"Our whole life with the children, for my wife and
consequently for me, was not a joy but a torment. How
could she help torturing herself? She tortured herself incessantly. Sometimes when we had just made peace after
some scene of jealousy, or simply after a quarrel, and
thought we should be able to live, to read, and to think
a little, we had no sooner settled down to some occupation than the news came that Vásya was being sick, or
Másha showed symptoms of dysentery, or Andrúsha had
a rash, and there was an end to peace; it was not life
any more. Where was one to drive to? For what doctor?
How isolate the child? And then it's a case of enemas,
temperatures, medicines, and doctors. Hardly is that over
before something else begins. We had no regular settled
family life but only, as I have already said, continual
escapes from imaginary and real dangers. It is like that
in most families nowadays you know, but in my family it
was especially acute. My wife was a child-loving and a
credulous woman.

"So the presence of children not only failed to improve
our life but poisoned it. Besides, the children were a new
cause of dissension. As soon as we had children they

became the means and the object of our discord, and more often the older they grew. They were not only the object of discord but the weapons of our strife. We used our children, as it were, to fight one another with. Each of us had a favourite weapon among them for our strife. I used to fight her chiefly through Vásya, the eldest boy, and she me through Lisa. Besides that, as they grew older and their characters became defined, it came about that they grew into allies whom each of us tried to draw to his or her side. They, poor things, suffered terribly from this, but we, with our incessant warfare, had no time to think of that. The girl was my ally, and the eldest boy, who resembled his mother and was her favourite, was often hateful to me."

XVII

"Well, and so we lived. Our relations to one another grew more and more hostile and at last reached a stage where it was not disagreement that caused hostility but hostility that caused disagreement. Whatever she might say I disagreed with beforehand, and it was just the same with her.

"In the fourth year we both, it seemed, came to the conclusion that we could not understand one another or agree with one another. We no longer tried to bring any dispute to a conclusion. We invariably kept to our own opinions even about the most trivial questions, but especially about the children. As I now recall them the views I maintained were not at all so dear to me that I could not have given them up; but she was of the opposite opinion and to yield meant yielding to her, and that I could not do. It was the same with her. She probably considered herself quite in the right towards me, and as for me I always thought myself a saint towards her. When we were alone together we were doomed almost to silence, or to conversations such as I am convinced animals can carry on with one another: 'What is the time? Time to go to bed. What is to-day's dinner? Where shall we go? What is there in the papers? Send for the doctor; Másha has a sore throat. We only needed to go a hairbreadth beyond this impossibly limited circle of conversation for irritation to flare up.

We had collisions and acrimonious words about the coffee, a tablecloth, a trap, a lead at bridge,[1] all of them things that could not be of any importance to either of us. In me at any rate there often raged a terrible hatred of her. Sometimes I watched her pouring out tea, swinging her leg, lifting a spoon to her mouth, smacking her lips and drawing in some liquid, and I hated her for these things as though they were the worst possible actions. I did not then notice that the periods of anger corresponded quite regularly and exactly to the periods of what we called love. A period of love, then a period of animosity; an energetic period of love, then a long period of animosity; a weaker manifestation of love, and a shorter period of animosity. We did not then understand that this love and animosity were one and the same animal feeling only at opposite poles. To live like that would have been awful had we understood our position; but we neither understood nor saw it. Both salvation and punishment for man lie in the fact that if he lives wrongly he can befog himself so as not to see the misery of his position. And this we did. She tried to forget herself in intense and always hurried occupation with household affairs, busying herself with the arrangements of the house, her own and the children's clothes, their lessons, and their health; while I had my own occupations: wine, my office duties, shooting, and cards. We were both continually occupied, and we both felt that the busier we were the nastier we might be to each other. 'It's all very well for you to grimace," I thought, 'but you have harassed me all night with your scenes, and I have a meeting on.' 'It's all very well for you,' she not only thought but said, 'but I have been awake all night with the baby.' Those new theories of hypnotism, psychic diseases, and hysterics are not a simple folly, but a dangerous and repulsive one. Charcot would certainly have said that my wife was hysterical, and that I was abnormal, and he would no doubt have tried to cure me. But there was nothing to cure.

"Thus we lived in a perpetual fog, not seeing the condition we were in. And if what did happen had not

---

[1] The card-game named in the original, and then much played in Russia, was *vint*, which resembles bridge.

happened, I should have gone on living so to old age and should have thought, when dying, that I had led a good life. I should not have realized the abyss of misery and the horrible falsehood in which I wallowed.

"We were like two convicts hating each other and chained together, poisoning one another's lives and trying not to see it. I did not then know that ninety-nine per cent of married people live in a similar hell to the one I was in and that it cannot be otherwise. I did not then know this either about others or about myself. . . .

"It is strange what coincidences there are in regular, or even in irregular, lives! Just when the parents find life together unendurable, it becomes necessary to move to town for the children's education."

He stopped and once or twice gave vent to his strange sounds, which were now quite like suppressed sobs. We were approaching a station.

"What is the time?" he asked.

I looked at my watch. It was two o'clock.

"You are not tired?" he asked.

"No, but you are?"

"I am suffocating. Excuse me, I will walk up and down and drink some water."

He went unsteadily through the carriage. I remained alone thinking over what he had said, and I was so engrossed in thought that I did not notice when he reentered by the door at the other end of the carriage.

XVIII

"Yes, I keep diverging," he began. "I have thought much over it. I now see many things differently and I want to express it.

"Well, so we lived in town. In town a man can live for a hundred years without noticing that he has long been dead and has rotted away. He has no time to take account of himself, he is always occupied. Business affairs, social intercourse, health, art, the children's health and their education. Now one has to receive so-and-so and so-and-so, go to see so-and-so and so-and-so; now one has to go and look at this, and hear this man or that woman. In town, you know, there are at any given moment one or two, or even three, celebrities whom one must on no account miss seeing. Then one has to undergo a treatment oneself or get someone else attended to, then there are teachers, tutors, and governesses, but one's own life is quite empty. Well, so we lived and felt less the painfulness of living together. Besides at first we had splendid occupations, arranging things in a new place, in new quarters; and we were also occupied in going from the town to the country and back to town again.

"We lived so through one winter, and the next there occurred, unnoticed by anyone, an apparently unimportant thing, but the cause of all that happened later.

"She was not well and the doctors told her not to have children and taught her how to avoid it. To me it was disgusting. I struggled against it, but she with frivolous obstinacy insisted on having her own way and I submitted. The last excuse for our swinish life—children—was then taken away, and life became viler than ever.

"To a peasant, a labouring man, children are necessary; though it is hard for him to feed them, still he needs them, and therefore his marital relations have a justification. But to us who have children, more children are unnecessary; they are an additional care and expense, a further division of property, and a burden. So our swinish life has no justification. We either artifically deprive ourselves of children or regard them as a misfortune, the consequences of carelessness, and that is still worse.

"We have no justification. But we have fallen morally so low that we do not even feel the need of any justification.

"The majority of the present educated world devote themselves to this kind of debauchery without the least qualm of conscience.

"There is indeed nothing that can feel qualms, for conscience in our society is non-existent, unless one can call public opinion and the criminal law a 'conscience.' In this case neither the one nor the other is infringed: there is no reason to be ashamed of public opinion for everybody acts in the same way—Mary Pávlovna, Iván Zakhárych, and the rest. Why breed paupers or deprive oneself of the possibility of social life? There is no need to fear or be ashamed in face of the criminal law either. Those shameless hussies, or soldiers' wives, throw their babies into ponds or wells, and they of course must be put in prison, but we do it all at the proper time and in a clean way.

"We lived like that for another two years. The means employed by those scoundrel-doctors evidently began to bear fruit; she became physically stouter and handsomer, like the late beauty of summer's end. She felt this and paid attention to her appearance. She developed a provocative kind of beauty which made people restless. She was in the full vigour of a well-fed and excited woman of thirty who is not bearing children. Her appearance disturbed people. When she passed men she attracted their notice. She was like a fresh, well-fed, harnessed horse, whose bridle has been removed. There was no bridle, as is the case with ninety-nine hundredths of our women. And I felt this—and was frightened."

XIX

He suddenly rose and sat down close to the window. "Pardon me," he muttered and, with his eyes fixed on the window, he remained silent for about three minutes. Then he sighed deeply and moved back to the seat opposite mine. His face was quite changed, his eyes looked pathetic, and his lips puckered strangely, almost as if he were smiling. "I am rather tired but I will go on with it. We have still plenty of time, it is not dawn yet. Ah, yes," he began after lighting a cigarette, "she grew plumper after she stopped having babies, and here malady—that everlasting worry about the children—began to pass . . . at least not actually to pass, but she as it were woke up from an intoxication, came to herself, and saw that there was a whole divine world with its joys which she had forgotten, but a divine world she did not know how to live in and did not at all understand. 'I must not miss it! Time is passing and won't come back!' So, I imagine, she thought, or rather felt, nor could she have thought or felt differently: she had been brought up in the belief that there was only one thing in the world worthy of attention—love. She had married and received something of that love, but not nearly what had been promised and was expected. Even that had been accompanied by many disappointments and sufferings, and then this un-expected torment: so many children! The torments ex-hausted her. And then, thanks to the obliging doctors, she learnt that it is possible to avoid having children. She was very glad, tried it, and became alive again for the one thing she knew—for love. But love with a husband, be-fouled by jealousy and all kinds of anger, was no longer the thing she wanted. She had visions of some other, clean, new love; at least I thought she had. And she began to look about her as if expecting something. I saw this and could not help feeling anxious. It happened again and again that while talking to me, as usual through other people—that is, telling a third person what she meant for me—she boldly, wihout remembering that she had ex-pressed the opposite opinion an hour before, declared, though half-jokingly, that a mother's cares are a fraud and that it is not worth while to devote one's life to children when one is young and can enjoy life. She gave less attention to the children, and less frenziedly than before, but gave more and more attention to herself, to her appearance (though she tried to conceal this), and to her pleasures, even to her accomplishments. She again enthusiastically took to the piano which she had quite abandoned, and it all began from that."

He turned his weary eyes to the window again but, evidently making an effort, immediately continued once more.

"Yes, that man made his appearance . . ." he became confused and once or twice made that peculiar sound with his nose.

I could see that it was painful for him to name that man, to recall him, or speak about him. But he made an effort and, as if he had broken the obstacle that hindered him, continued resolutely.

"He was a worthless man in my opinion and according to my estimate. And not because of the significance he acquired in my life but because he really was so. How-ever, the fact that he was a poor sort of fellow only served to show how irresponsible she was. If it had not been he then it would have been another. It had to be!"

Again he paused. "Yes, he was a musician, a violinist;

not a professional, but a semi-professional semi-society man.

"His father, a landowner, was a neighbour of my father's. He had been ruined, and his children—there were three boys—had obtained settled positions; only this one, the youngest, had been handed over to his god-mother in Paris. There he was sent to the *Conservatoire* because he had a talent for music, and he came out as a violinist and played at concerts. He was a man . . ." Having evidently intended to say something bad about him, Pózdnyshev restrained himself and rapidly said: "Well, I don't really know how he lived, I only know that he returned to Russia that year and appeared in my house.

"With moist almond-shaped eyes, red smiling lips, a small waxed moustache, hair done in the latest fashion, and an insipidly pretty face, he was what women call 'not bad looking.'" His figure was weak though not misshapen, and he had a specially developed posterior, like a woman's, or such as Hottentots are said to have. They too are reported to be musical. Pushing himself as far as possible into familiarity, but sensitive and always ready to yield at the slightest resistance, he maintained his dignity in externals, wore buttoned boots of a special Parisian fashion, bright-coloured ties, and other things foreigners acquire in Paris, which by their noticeable novelty always attract women. There was an affected external gaiety in his manner. That manner, you know, of speaking about everything in allusions and unfinished sentences, as if you knew it all, remembered it, and could complete it yourself.

"It was he with his music who was the cause of it all. You know at the trial the case was put as if it was all caused by jealousy. No such thing—that is, I don't mean—no such thing—it was and yet it was not. At the trial it was decided that I was a wronged husband and that I had killed her while defending my outraged honour (that is the phrase they employ, you know). That is why I was acquitted. I tried to explain matters at the trial but they took it that I was trying to rehabilitate my wife's honour.

"What my wife's relations with that musician may have been has no meaning for me, or for her either. What has a meaning is what I have told you about—my swinishness. The whole thing was an outcome of the terrible abyss between us of which I have told you—that dreadful tension of mutual hatred which made the first excuse sufficient to produce a crisis. The quarrels between us had for some time past become frightful and were all the more startling because they alternated with similarly intense animal passion.

"If he had not appeared there would have been some-one else. If the occasion had not been jealousy it would have been something else. I maintain that all husbands who live as I did must either live dissolutely, separate, or kill themselves or their wives as I have done. If there is anybody who has not done so, he is a rare exception. Before I ended as I did, I had several times been on the verge of suicide, and she too had repeatedly tried to poison herself."

XX

"Well, that is how things were going not long before it happened. We seemed to be living in a state of truce and had no reason to infringe it. Then we chanced to speak about a dog which I said had been awarded a medal at an exhibition. She remarked, 'Not a medal, but an honourable mention.' A dispute ensues. We jump from one subject to another, reproach one another, 'Oh, that's nothing new, it's always been like that.' 'You said . . .' 'No, I didn't say so.' 'Then I am telling lies! . . .' You feel that at any moment that dreadful quarrelling which makes you wish to kill yourself or her will begin. You know it will begin immediately and fear it like fire and therefore wish to restrain yourself, but your whole being is seized with fury. She being in the same or even a worse condition purposely misinterprets every word you say, giving it a wrong meaning. Her every word is venomous; where she alone knows that I am most sensi-tive, she stabs. It gets worse and worse. I shout: 'Be quiet!' or something of that kind.

"She rushes out of the room and into the nursery. I try to hold her back in order to finish what I was saying, to prove my point, and I seize her by the arm. She pretends that I have hurt her and screams: 'Children, your father is striking me!' I shout: 'Don't lie!' 'But it's not the first time!' she screams, or something like that. The children rush to her. She calms them down. I say, 'Don't sham!' She says, 'Everything is sham in your eyes, you would kill any one and say they were shamming. Now I have understood you. That's just what you want!' 'Oh, I wish you were dead as a dog!' I shout. I remember how those dreadful words horrified me. I never thought I could utter such dreadful, coarse words and am surprised that they escaped me. I shout them and rush away into my study and sit down and smoke. I hear her go out into the hall preparing to go away. I ask, 'Where are you going to?' She does not reply. 'Well, devil take her,' I say to myself and go back to my study and lie down and smoke. A thousand different plans of how to revenge myself on her and get rid of her, and how to improve matters and go on as if nothing had happened, come into my head. I think all that and go on smoking and smoking. I think of running away from her, hiding myself, going to America. I get as far as dreaming of how I shall get rid of her, how splendid that will be, and how I shall unite with another, an admirable woman—quite different. I shall get rid of her either by her dying or by a divorce, and I plan how it is to be done. I notice that I am getting confused and not thinking of what is necessary and to prevent myself from perceiving that my thoughts are not to the point I go on smoking.

"Life in the house goes on. The governess comes in and asks: 'Where is madame? When will she be back?' The footman asks whether he is to serve tea. I go to the dining-room. The children, especially Lisa who already understands, gaze inquiringly and disapprovingly at me. We drink tea in silence. She has still not come back. The evening passes, she has not returned, and two different feelings alternate within me. Anger because she torments me and all the children by her absence which will end by her returning; and fear that she will not return but will do something to herself. I would go to fetch her, but where am I to look for her? At her sister's? But it would be so stupid to go and ask. And it's all the better: if she is bent on tormenting someone, let her torment herself.

Besides, that is what she is waiting for, and next time it would be worse still. But suppose she is not with her sister but is doing something to herself or has already done it! It's past ten, past eleven! I don't go to the bedroom—it would be stupid to lie there alone waiting—but I'll not lie down here either. I wish to occupy my mind, to write a letter or to read, but I can't do anything. I sit alone in my study, tortured, angry, and listening. It's three o'clock, four o'clock, and she is not back. Towards morning I fall asleep. I wake up, she has still not come!

"Everything in the house goes on in the usual way, but all are perplexed and look at me inquiringly and reproachfully, considering me to be the cause of it all. And in me the same struggle still continues: anger that she is torturing me, and anxiety for her.

"At about eleven in the morning her sister arrives as her envoy. And the usual talk begins. 'She is in a terrible state. What does it all mean?' 'After all, nothing has happened.' I speak of her impossible character and say that I have not done anything.

"'But, you know, it can't go on like this,' says her sister.

"'It's all her doing and not mine,' I say. 'I won't take the first step. If it means separation, let it be separation.'

"My sister-in-law goes away having achieved nothing. I had boldly said that I would not take the first step; but after her departure, when I came out of my study and saw the children piteous and frightened, I was prepared to take the first step. I should be glad to do it, but I don't know how. Again I pace up and down and smoke; at lunch I drink vodka and wine and attain what I unconsciously desire—I no longer see the stupidity and humiliation of my position.

"At about three she comes. When she meets me she does not speak. I imagine that she has submitted, and begin to say that I had been provoked by her reproaches. She, with the same stern expression on her terribly harassed face, says that she has not come for explanations but to fetch the children, because we cannot live together. I begin telling her that the fault is not mine and that she provoked me beyond endurance. She looks severely and solemnly at me and says: 'Do not say any more, you will repent it.' I tell her that I cannot stand comedies. Then she cries out something I don't catch and rushes into her room. The key clicks behind her,— she has locked herself in. I try the door but, getting no answer, go away angrily. Half an hour later Lisa runs in crying. 'What is it? Has anything happened?' 'We can't hear mama.' We go. I pull at the double doors with all my might. The bolt had not been firmly secured, and the two halves both open. I approach the bed, on which she is lying awkwardly in her petticoats and with a pair of high boots on. An empty opium bottle is on the table. She is brought to herself. Tears follow, and a reconciliation. No, not a reconciliation: in the heart of each there is still the old animosity, with the additional irritation produced by the pain of this quarrel which each attributes to the other. But one must of course finish it all somehow, and life goes on in the old way. And so the same kind of quarrel, and even worse ones, occurred continually: once a week, once a month, or at times every day. It was always the same. Once I had already procured a passport to go abroad—the quarrel had continued for two days. But there was again a partial explanation, a partial reconciliation, and I did not go."

XXI

"So those were our relations when that man appeared. He arrived in Moscow—his name is Trukhachévski—and came to my house. It was in the morning. I received him. We had once been on familiar terms and he tried to maintain a familiar tone by using non-committal expressions, but I definitely adopted a conventional tone and he at once submitted to it. I disliked him from the first glance. But curiously enough a strange and fatal force led me not to repulse him, not to keep him away, but on the contrary to invite him to the house. After all, what could have been simpler than to converse with him coldly and say good-bye without introducing him to my wife? But no, as if purposely, I began talking about his playing and said I had been told he had given up the violin. He replied that, on the contrary, he now played more than ever. He referred to the fact that there had been a time when I myself played. I said I had given it up but that my wife played well. It is an astonishing thing that from the first day, from the first hour of my meeting him, my relations with him were such as they might have been only after all that subsequently happened. There was something strained in them: I noticed every word, every expression he or I used, and attributed importance to them.

"I introduced him to my wife. The conversation immediately turned to music, and he offered to be of use to her by playing with her. My wife was, as usual of late, very elegant, attractive, and disquietingly beautiful. He evidently pleased her at first sight. Besides she was glad that she would have someone to accompany her on a violin, which she was so fond of that she used to engage a violinist from the theatre for the purpose, and her face reflected her pleasure. But catching sight of me she at once understood my feeling and changed her expression, and a game of mutual deception began. I smiled pleasantly to appear as if I liked it. He, looking at my wife as all immoral men look at pretty women, pretended that he was only interested in the subject of the conversation— which no longer interested him at all; while she tried to seem indifferent, though my false smile of jealousy with which she was familiar, and his lustful gaze, evidently excited her. I saw that from their first encounter her eyes were particularly bright and, probably as a result of my jealousy, it seemed as if an electric current had been established between them, evoking as it were an identity of expressions, looks, and smiles. She blushed and he blushed. She smiled and he smiled. We spoke about music, Paris, and all sorts of trifles. Then he rose to go and stood smilingly, holding his hat against his twitching thigh and looking now at her and now at me, as if in expectation of what we would do. I remember that instant just because at that moment I might not have invited him, and then nothing would have happened. But I glanced at him and at her and said silently to myself, 'Don't suppose that I am jealous,' 'or that I am afraid of you," I added mentally addressing him, and I invited him to come some evening and bring his violin to play with my wife. She glanced at me with surprise, flushed, and as if frightened began to decline, saying that she did not play well enough. This refusal irritated me still more, and I insisted the more on his coming. I remember the curious feeling with which I looked at the back of his head, with the black hair parted in the middle contrasting with the white nape of his neck, as he went out with his peculiar springing gait suggestive of some kind of a bird. I could not conceal from myself that that man's presence tormented me. 'It depends on me,' I reflected, 'to act so as to see nothing more of him. But that would be to admit that I am afraid of him. No, I am not afraid of him; it would be too humiliating,' I said to myself. And there in the ante-room, knowing that my wife heard me, I insisted that he should come that evening with his violin. He promised to do so, and left.

"In the evening he brought his violin and they played. But it took a long time to arrange matters—they had not the music they wanted, and my wife could not without preparation play what they had. I was very fond of music and sympathized with their playing, arranging a music-stand for him and turning over the pages. They played a few things, some songs without words, and a little sonata by Mozart. They played splendidly, and he had an exceptionally fine tone. Besides that, he had a refined and elevated taste not at all in correspondence with his character.

"He was of course a much better player than my wife, and he helped her, while at the same time politely praising her playing. He behaved himself very well. My wife seemed interested only in music and was very simple and natural. But though I pretended to be interested in the music I was tormented by jealousy all the evening.

"From the first moment his eyes met my wife's I saw that the animal in each of them, regardless of all conditions of their position and of society, asked, 'May I?' and answered, 'Oh, yes, certainly.' I saw that he had not at all expected to find my wife, a Moscow lady, so attractive, and that he was very pleased. For he had no doubt whatever that she was *willing*. The only crux was whether that unendurable husband could hinder them. Had I been pure I should not have understood this, but, like the majority of men, I had myself regarded women in that way before I

married and therefore could read his mind like a manuscript. I was particularly tormented because I saw without
doubt that she had no other feeling towards me than a
continual irritation only occasionally interrupted by the
habitual sensuality; but that this man—by his external
refinement and novelty and still more by his undoubtedly
great talent for music, by the nearness that comes of playing
together, and by the influence music, especially the violin,
exercises on impressionable natures—was sure not only to
please but certainly and without the least hesitation to
conquer, crush, bind her, twist her round his little finger
and do whatever he liked with her. I could not help seeing
this and I suffered terribly. But for all that, or perhaps on
account of it, some force obliged me against my will to be
not merely polite but amiable to him. Whether I did it
for my wife or for him, to show that I was not afraid of
him, or whether I did it to deceive myself I don't know,
but I know that from the first I could not behave naturally
with him. In order not to yield to my wish to kill him
there and then, I had to make much of him. I gave him
expensive wines at supper, went into raptures over his
playing, spoke to him with a particularly amiable smile,
and invited him to dine and play with my wife again the
next Sunday. I told him I would ask a few friends who
were fond of music to hear him. And so it ended."

Greatly agitated, Pózdnyshev changed his position and
emitted his peculiar sound.

"It is strange how the presence of that man acted on
me," he began again, with an evident effort to keep calm.
"I come home from the Exhibition a day or two later, enter
the ante-room, and suddenly feel something heavy, as if a
stone had fallen on my heart, and I cannot understand
what it is. It was that passing through the ante-room I
noticed something which reminded me of him. I realized
what it was only in my study and went back to the ante-
room to make sure. Yes, I was not mistaken, there was his
overcoat. A fashionable coat, you know. (Though I did
not realize it, I observed everything connected with him
with extraordinary attention.) I inquire: sure enough he is
there. I pass on to the dancing-room, not through the
drawing-room but through the schoolroom. My daughter,
Lisa, sits reading a book and the nurse sits with the young-

est boy at the table, making a lid of some kind spin round. The door to the dancing-room is shut but I hear the sound of a rhythmic arpeggio and his and her voices. I listen but cannot make out anything.

"Evidently the sound of the piano is purposely made to drown the sound of their voices, their kisses . . . perhaps. My God! What was aroused in me! Even to think of the beast that then lived in me fills me with horror! My heart suddenly contracted, stopped, and then began to beat like a hammer. My chief feeling, as usual whenever I was enraged, was one of self-pity. 'In the presence of the children! of their nurse!' thought I. Probably I looked awful, for Lisa gazed at me with strange eyes. 'What am I to do?' I asked myself. 'Go in? I can't: heaven only knows what I should do. But neither can I go away.' The nurse looked at me as if she understood my position. 'But it is impossible not to go in,' I said to myself, and I quickly opened the door. He was sitting at the piano playing those arpeggios with his large white upturned fingers. She was standing in the curve of the piano, bending over some open music. She was the first to see or hear and glanced at me. Whether she was frightened and pretended not to be, or whether she was really not frightened, anyway she did not start or move but only blushed, and that not at once.

" 'How glad I am that you have come: we have not decided what to play on Sunday,' she said in a tone she would not have used to me had we been alone. This, and her using the word 'we' of herself and him, filled me with indignation. I greeted him silently.

"He pressed my hand, and at once, with a smile which I thought distinctly ironic, began to explain that he had brought some music to practise for Sunday, but that they disagreed about what to play: a classical but more difficult piece, namely Beethoven's sonata for the violin, or a few little pieces. It was all so simple and natural that there was nothing one could cavil at, yet I felt certain that it was all untrue and that they had agreed how to deceive me.

"One of the most distressing conditions of life for a jealous man (and everyone is jealous in our world) is certain society conventions which allow a man and woman the greatest and most dangerous proximity. You would become a laughing-stock to others if you tried to prevent such nearness at balls, or the nearness of doctors to their women-patients, or of people occupied with art, sculpture, and especially music. A couple are occupied with the noblest of arts, music; this demands a certain nearness, and there is nothing reprehensible in that and only a stupid jealous husband can see anything undesirable in it. Yet everybody knows that it is by means of those very pursuits, especially of music, that the greater part of the adulteries in our society occur. I evidently confused them by the confusion I betrayed: for a long time I could not speak. I was like a bottle held upside down from which the water does not flow because it is too full. I wanted to abuse him and to turn him out, but again felt that I must treat him courteously and amiably. And I did so. I acted as though I approved of it all, and again because of the strange feeling which made me behave to him the more amiably the more his presence distressed me. I told him that I trusted his taste and advised her to do the same. He stayed as long as was necessary to efface the unpleasant impression caused by my sudden entrance—looking frightened and remaining silent—and then left, pretending that it was now decided what to play next day. I was however fully convinced that compared to what interested them the question of what to play was quite indifferent.

"I saw him out to the ante-room with special politeness. (How could one do less than accompany a man who had come to disturb the peace and destroy the happiness of a whole family?) And I pressed his soft white hand with particular warmth.

XXII

"I did not speak to her all that day—I could not. Nearness to her aroused in me such hatred of her that I was afraid of myself. At dinner in the presence of the children she asked me when I was going away. I had to go next week to the District Meetings of the Zémstvo. I told her the date. She asked whether I did not want anything for the journey. I did not answer but sat silent at table and then went in silence to my study. Latterly she used never to come to my room, especially not at that time of day. I lay in my study filled with anger. Suddenly I heard her familiar step, and

the terrible, monstrous idea entered my head that she, like
Uriah's wife, wished to conceal the sin she had already
committed and that that was why she was coming to me at
such an unusual time. 'Can she be coming to me?' thought
I, listening to her approaching steps. 'If she is coming here,
then I am right,' and an inexpressible hatred of her took
possession of me. Nearer and nearer came the steps. Is it
possible that she won't pass on to the dancing-room? No,
the door creaks and in the doorway appears her tall handsome figure, on her face and in her eyes a timid ingratiating
look which she tries to hide, but which I see and the meaning of which I know. I almost choked, so long did I hold
my breath, and still looking at her I grasped my cigarette-
case and began to smoke.

" 'Now how can you? One comes to sit with you for a
bit, and you begin smoking'—and she sat down close to
me on the sofa, leaning against me. I moved away so as
not to touch her.

" 'I see you are dissatisfied at my wanting to play on
Sunday,' she said.

" 'I am not at all dissatisfied,' I said.

" 'As if I don't see!'

" 'Well, I congratulate you on seeing. But I only see
that you behave like a coquette. . . . You always find
pleasure in all kinds of vileness, but to me it is terrible!'

" 'Oh, well, if you are going to scold like a cabman I'll
go away.'

" 'Do, but remember that if you don't value the family
honour, I value not you (devil take you) but the honour
of the family!'

" 'But what is the matter? What?'

" 'Go away, for God's sake be off!'

"Whether she pretended not to understand what it was
about or really did not understand, at any rate she took
offence, grew angry, and did not go away but stood in the
middle of the room.

" 'You have really become impossible,' she began. 'You
have a character that even an angel could not put up with.'
And as usual trying to sting me as painfully as possible,
she reminded me of my conduct to my sister (an incident
when, being exasperated, I said rude things to my sister);
she knew I was distressed about it and she stung me just

on that spot. 'After that, nothing from you will surprise me,' she said.

" 'Yes! Insult me, humiliate me, disgrace me, and then put the blame on me,' I said to myself, and suddenly I was seized by such terrible rage as I had never before experienced.

"For the first time I wished to give physical expression to that rage. I jumped up and went towards her; but just as I jumped up I remember becoming conscious of my rage and asking myself: 'It is right to give way to this feeling?' and at once I answered that it was right, that it would frighten her, and instead of restraining my fury I immediately began inflaming it still further and was glad it burnt yet more fiercely within me.

" 'Be off, or I'll kill you!' I shouted, going up to her and seizing her by the arm. I consciously intensified the anger in my voice as I said this. And I suppose I was terrible, for she was so frightened that she had not even the strength to go away, but only said: 'Vásya, what is it? What is the matter with you?'

" 'Go!' I roared louder still. 'No one but you can drive me to fury. I do not answer for myself!'

"Having given reins to my rage, I revelled in it and wished to do something still more unusual to show the extreme degree of my anger. I felt a terrible desire to beat her, to kill her, but knew that this would not do, and so to give vent to my fury I seized a paper-weight from my table, again shouting 'Go!' and hurled it to the floor near her. I aimed it very exactly past her. Then she left the room but stopped at the doorway, and immediately, while she still saw it (I did it so that she might see), I began snatching things from the table—candlesticks and inkstand—and hurling them on the floor, still shouting 'Go! Get out! I don't answer for myself!' She went away—and I immediately stopped.

"An hour later the nurse came to tell me that my wife was in hysterics. I went to her; she sobbed, laughed, could not speak, and her whole body was convulsed. She was not pretending, but was really ill.

"Towards morning she grew quiet, and we made peace under the influence of the feeling we called love.

"In the morning when, after our reconciliation, I confessed to her that I was jealous of Trukhachévski, she was not at all confused, but laughed most naturally; so strange did the very possibility of an infatuation for such a man seem to her, she said.

" 'Could a decent woman have any other feeling for such a man than the pleasure of his music? Why, if you like I am ready never to see him again . . . not even on Sunday, though everybody has been invited. Write and tell him that I am ill, and there's an end of it! Only it is unpleasant that anyone, especially he himself, should imagine that he is dangerous. I am too proud to allow anyone to think that of me!'

"And you know, she was not lying, she believed what she was saying; she hoped by those words to evoke in herself contempt for him and so to defend herself from him, but she did not succeed in doing so. Everything was against her, especially that accursed music. So it all ended, and on the Sunday the guests assembled and they again played together.

XXIII

"I suppose it is hardly necessary to say that I was very vain: if one is not vain there is nothing to live for in our usual way of life. So on that Sunday I arranged the dinner and the musical evening with much care. I bought the provisions myself and invited the guests.

"Towards six the visitors assembled. He came in evening dress with diamond studs that showed bad taste. He behaved in a free and easy manner, answered everything hurriedly with a smile of agreement and understanding, you know, with that peculiar expression which seems to say that all you may do or say is just what he expected. Everything that was not in good taste about him I noticed with particular pleasure, because it ought all to have had the effect of tranquillizing me and showing that he was so far beneath my wife that, as she had said, she could not lower herself to his level. I did not now allow myself to be jealous. In the first place I had worried through that torment and needed rest, and secondly I wanted to believe my wife's assurances and did believe them. But though I was not jealous I was nevertheless not natural with either of them, and at dinner and during the first half of the evening before the music began I still followed their movements and looks.

"The dinner was, as dinners are, dull and pretentious. The music began pretty early. Oh, how I remember every detail of that evening! I remember how he brought in his violin, unlocked the case, took off the cover a lady had embroidered for him, drew out the violin, and began tuning it. I remember how my wife sat down at the piano with pretended unconcern, under which I saw that she was trying to conceal great timidity—chiefly as to her own ability—and then the usual A on the piano began, the pizzicato of the violin, and the arrangement of the music. Then I remember how they glanced at one another, turned to look at the audience who were seating themselves, said something to one another, and began. He took the first chords. His face grew serious, stern, and sympathetic, and listening to the sounds he produced, he touched the strings with careful fingers. The piano answered him. The music began. . . ."

Pózdnyshev paused and produced his strange sound several times in succession. He tried to speak, but sniffed, and stopped.

"They played Beethoven's Kreutzer Sonata," he continued. "Do you know the first presto? You do?" he cried. "Ugh! Ugh! It is a terrible thing, that sonata. And especially that part. And in general music is a dreadful thing! What is it? I don't understand it. What is music? What does it do? And why does it do what it does? They say music exalts the soul. Nonsense, it is not true! It has an effect, an awful effect—I am speaking of myself—but not of an exalting kind. It has neither an exalting nor a debasing effect but it produces agitation. How can I put it? Music makes me forget myself, my real position; it transports me to some other position not my own. Under the influence of music it seems to me that I feel what I do not really feel, that I understand what I do not understand, that I can do what I cannot do. I explain it by the fact that music acts like yawning, like laughter: I am not sleepy, but I yawn when I see someone yawning; there is nothing for me to laugh at, but I laugh when I hear people laughing.

"Music carries me immediately and directly into the

mental condition in which the man was who composed it.
My soul merges with his and together with him I pass from
one condition into another, but why this happens I don't
know. You see, he who wrote, let us say, the Kreutzer
Sonata—Beethoven—knew of course why he was in that
condition; that condition caused him to do certain actions
and therefore that condition had a meaning for him, but
for me—none at all. That is why music only agitates and
doesn't lead to a conclusion. Well, when a military march
is played the soldiers march to the music and the music
has achieved its object. A dance is played, I dance and the
music has achieved its object. Mass has been sung, I receive Communion, and that music too has reached a conclusion. Otherwise it is only agitating, and what ought to
be done in that agitation is lacking. That is why music
sometimes acts so dreadfully, so terribly. In China, music
is a State affair. And that is as it should be. How can one
allow anyone who pleases to hypnotize another, or many
others, and do what he likes with them? And especially that
this hypnotist should be the first immoral man who
turns up?

"It is a terrible instrument in the hands of any chance
user! Take that Kreutzer Sonata, for instance, how can
that first presto be played in a drawing-room among
ladies in low-necked dresses? To hear that played, to clap
a little, and then to eat ices and talk of the latest scandal?
Such things should only be played on certain important
significant occasions, and then only when certain actions
answering to such music are wanted; play it then and do
what the music has moved you to. Otherwise an awakening
of energy and feeling unsuited both to the time and the
place, to which no outlet is given, cannot but act harm-
fully. At any rate that piece had a terrible effect on me; it
was as if quite new feelings, new possibilities, of which
I had till then been unaware, had been revealed to me.
'That's how it is: not at all as I used to think and live, but
that way,' something seemed to say within me. What this
new thing was that had been revealed to me I could not
explain to myself, but the consciousness of this new condition was very joyous. All those same people, including my
wife and him, appeared in a new light.

"After that allegro they played the beautiful, but

common and unoriginal, andante with trite variations, and the very weak finale. Then, at the request of the visitors, they played Ernst's Elegy and a few small pieces. They were all good, but they did not produce on me a one-hundredth part of the impression the first piece had. The effect of the first piece formed the background for them all.

"I felt light-hearted and cheerful the whole evening. I had never seen my wife as she was that evening. Those shining eyes, that severe, significant expression while she played, and her melting languor and feeble, pathetic, and blissful smile after they had finished. I saw all that but did not attribute any meaning to it except that she was feeling what I felt, and that to her as to me new feelings, never before experienced, were revealed or, as it were, recalled. The evening ended satisfactorily and the visitors departed.

"Knowing that I had to go away to attend the Zémstvo Meetings two days later, Trukhachévski on leaving said he hoped to repeat the pleasure of that evening when he next came to Moscow. From this I concluded that he did not consider it possible to come to my house during my absence, and this pleased me.

"It turned out that as I should not be back before he left town, we should not see one another again.

"For the first time I pressed his hand with real pleasure and thanked him for the enjoyment he had given us. In the same way he bade a final farewell to my wife. Their leave-taking seemed to be most natural and proper. Everything was splendid. My wife and I were both very well satisfied with our evening party."

XXIV

"Two days later I left for the Meetings, parting from my wife in the best and most tranquil of moods.

"In the district there was always an enormous amount to do and a quite special life, a special little world of its own. I spent two ten-hour days at the Council. A letter from my wife was brought me on the second day and I read it there and then.

"She wrote about the children, about uncle, about the nurse, about shopping, and among other things she mentioned, as a most natural occurrence, that Trukhachévski had called, brought some music he had promised, and had offered to play again, but that she had refused.

"I did not remember his having promised any music but thought he had taken leave for good, and I was therefore unpleasantly struck by this. I was however so busy that I had no time to think of it, and it was only in the evening when I had returned to my lodgings that I re-read her letter.

"Besides the fact the Trukhachévski had called at my house during my absence, the whole tone of the letter seemed to me unnatural. The mad beast of jealousy began to growl in its kennel and wanted to leap out, but I was afraid of that beast and quickly fastened him in. 'What an abominable feeling this jealousy is!' I said to myself. 'What could be more natural than what she writes?'

"I went to bed and began thinking about the affairs awaiting me next day. During those Meetings, sleeping in a new place, I usually slept badly, but now I fell asleep very quickly. And as sometimes happens, you know, you feel a kind of electric shock and wake up. So I woke thinking of her, of my physical love for her, and of Trukhachévski, and of everything being accomplished between them. Horror and rage compressed my heart. But I began to reason with myself. 'What nonsense!' said I to myself. 'There are no grounds to go on, there is nothing and there has been nothing. How can I so degrade her and myself as to imagine such horrors? He is a sort of hired violinist, known as a worthless fellow, and suddenly an honourable woman, the respected mother of a family, *my* wife. . . . What absurdity!' So it seemed to me on the one hand. 'How could it help being so?' it seemed on the other. 'How could that simplest and most intelligible thing help happening—that for the sake of which I married her, for the sake of which I have been living with her, what alone I wanted of her, and which others including this musician must therefore also want? He is an unmarried man, healthy (I remember how he crunched the gristle of a cutlet and how greedily his red lips clung to the glass of wine), well-fed, plump, and not merely unprincipled but evidently making it a principle to accept the pleasures that present themselves. And they have music, that most exquisite voluptuousness of the senses, as a link between them. What then could make him refrain? She? But who is she? She was, and still is, a mystery. I don't know her. I only know her as an animal. And nothing can or should restrain an animal.'

"Only then did I remember their faces that evening when, after the Kreutzer Sonata, they played some impassioned little piece, I don't remember by whom, impassioned to the point of obscenity. 'How dared I go away?' I asked myself, remembering their faces. Was it not clear that everything had happened between them that evening? Was it not evident already then that there was not only no barrier between them, but that they both, and she chiefly, felt a certain measure of shame after what had happened? I remember her weak, piteous, and beatific smile as she wiped the perspiration from her flushed face when I came up to the piano. Already then they avoided looking at one another, and only at supper when he was pouring out some water for her, they glanced at each other with the vestige of a smile. I now recalled with horror the glance and scarcely perceptible smile I had then caught. 'Yes, it is all over,' said one voice, and immediately the other voice said something entirely different. 'Something has come over you, it can't be that it is so,' said that other voice. It felt uncanny lying in the dark and I struck a light and felt a kind of terror in that little room with its yellow wall-paper. I lit a cigarette and, as always happens when one's thoughts go round and round in a circle of insoluble contradictions, I smoked, taking one cigarette after another in order to befog myself so as not to see those contradictions.

"I did not sleep all night, and at five in the morning, having decided that I could not continue in such a state of tension, I rose, woke the caretaker who attended me, and sent him to get horses. I sent a note to the Council saying that I had been recalled to Moscow on urgent business and asking that one of the members should take my place. At eight o'clock I got into my trap and started."

XXV

The conductor entered and, seeing that our candle had burnt down, put it out, without supplying a fresh one. The day was dawning. Pózdnyshev was silent but sighed deeply all the time the conductor was in the carriage. He continued his story only after the conductor had gone out, and in the semi-darkness of the carriage only the rattle of the windows of the moving carriage and the rhythmic snoring of the clerk could be heard. In the half-light of dawn I could not see Pózdnyshev's face at all but only heard his voice becoming ever more and more excited and full of suffering.

"I had to travel twenty-four miles by road and eight hours by rail. It was splendid driving. It was frosty autumn weather, bright and sunny. The roads were in that condition when the tyres leave their dark imprint on them, you know. They were smooth, the light brilliant, and the air invigorating. It was pleasant driving in the tarantas. When it grew lighter and I had started I felt easier. Looking at the houses, the fields, and the passers-by, I forgot where I was going. Sometimes I felt that I was simply taking a drive, and that nothing of what was calling me back had taken place. This oblivion was peculiarly enjoyable. When I remembered where I was going, I said to myself, 'We shall see when the time comes; I must not think about it.' When we were half-way an incident occurred which detained me and still further distracted my thoughts. The tarantas broke down and had to be repaired. That break-down had a very important effect, for it caused me to arrive in Moscow at midnight, instead of at seven o'clock as I had expected, and to reach home between twelve and one, as I missed the express and had to travel by an ordinary train. Going to fetch a cart, having the tarantas mended, settling up, tea at the inn, a talk with the innkeeper—all this still further diverted my attention. It was twilight before all was ready and I started again. By night it was even pleasanter driving than during the day. There was a new moon, a slight frost, still good roads, good horses, and a jolly driver, and as I went on I enjoyed it, hardly thinking at all of what lay before me; or perhaps I enjoyed it because I knew what awaited me and was saying good-bye to the joys of life. But that tranquil mood, that ability to suppress my feelings, ended with my drive. As soon as I entered the train something entirely different began. That eight-hour journey in a railway carriage was something dreadful, which I shall never forget all my life. Whether it was that having taken my seat in the carriage

I vividly imagined myself as having already arrived, or that railway travelling has such an exciting effect on people, at any rate from the moment I sat down in the train I could no longer control my imagination, and with extraordinary vividness which inflamed my jealousy it painted incessantly, one after another, pictures of what had gone on in my absence, of how she had been false to me. I burnt with indignation, anger, and a peculiar feeling of intoxication with my own humiliation, as I gazed at those pictures, and I could not tear myself from them; I could not help looking at them, could not efface them, and could not help evoking them.

"That was not all. The more I gazed at those imaginary pictures the stronger grew my belief in their reality. The vividness with which they presented themselves to me seemed to serve as proof that what I imagined was real. It was as if some devil against my will invented and suggested to me the most terrible reflections. An old conversation I had had with Trukhachévski's brother came to my mind, and in a kind of ecstasy I rent my heart with that conversation, making it refer to Trukhachévski and my wife.

"That had occurred long before, but I recalled it. Trukhachévski's brother, I remember, in reply to a question whether he frequented houses of ill-fame, had said that a decent man would not go to places where there was danger of infection and it was dirty and nasty, since he could always find a decent woman. And now his brother had found my wife! 'True, she is not in her first youth, has lost a side-tooth, and there is a slight puffiness about her; but it can't be helped, one has to take advantage of what one can get,' I imagined him to be thinking. 'Yes, it is condescending of him to take her for his mistress!' I said to myself. 'And she is safe. . . .' 'No, it is impossible!' I thought, horror-struck. 'There is nothing of the kind, nothing!' There are not even any grounds for suspecting such things. Didn't she tell me that the very thought that I could be jealous of him was degrading to her? 'Yes, but she is lying, she is always lying!' I exclaimed, and everything began anew. . . . There were only two other people in the carriage; an old woman and her husband, both very taciturn, and even they got out at one of the stations and I was quite alone. I was like a caged animal: now I jumped up and went to the window, now I began to walk up and down trying to speed the carriage up; but the carriage with all its seats and windows went jolting on in the same way, just as ours does. . . ."

Pózdnyshev jumped up, took a few steps, and sat down again.

"Oh, I am afraid, afraid of railway carriages, I am seized with horror. Yes, it is awful!" he continued. "I said to myself, 'I will think of something else. Suppose I think of the innkeeper where I had tea,' and there in my mind's eye appears the innkeeper with his long beard and his grandson, a boy of the age of my Vásya. 'My Vásya! He will see how the musician kisses his mother. What will happen in his poor soul? But what does she care? She loves' . . . and again the same thing rose up in me. 'No, no . . . I will think about the inspection of the District Hospital. Oh, yes, about the patient who complained of the doctor yesterday. The doctor has a moustache like Trukhachévski's. And how impudent he is . . . they both deceived me when he said he was leaving Moscow,' and it began afresh. Everything I thought of had some connexion with them. I suffered dreadfully. The chief cause of the suffering was my ignorance, my doubt, and the contradictions within me: my not knowing whether I ought to love or hate her. My suffering was of a strange kind. I felt a hateful consciousness of my humiliation and of his victory, but a terrible hatred for her. 'It will not do to put an end to myself and leave her; she must at least suffer to some extent, and at least understand that I have suffered,' I said to myself. I got out at every station to divert my mind. At one station I saw some people drinking, and I immediately drank some vodka. Beside me stood a Jew who was also drinking. He began to talk and to avoid being alone in my carriage I went with him into his dirty third-class carriage reeking with smoke and bespattered with shells of sunflower seeds. There I sat down beside him and he chattered a great deal and told anecdotes. I listened to him but could not take in what he was saying because I continued to think about my own affairs. He noticed this and demanded my attention. Then I rose and went back to my carriage. 'I must think it over,' I said to myself. 'Is what I suspect true, and is there any reason for me to suffer?' I sat down, wishing to think it over calmly, but immediately, instead of calm reflection, the same thing began again: instead of reflection, pictures and fancies. 'How often I have suffered like this,' I said to myself (recalling former similar attacks of jealousy), 'and afterwards it all ended in nothing. So it will be now perhaps, yes certainly it will. I shall find her calmly asleep, she will wake up, be pleased to see me, and by her words and looks I shall know that there has been nothing and that this is all nonsense. Oh, how good that would be! But no, that has happened too often and won't happen again now,' some voice seemed to say; and it began again. Yes, that was where the punishment lay! I wouldn't take a young man to a lock-hospital to knock the hankering after women out of him, but into my soul, to see the devils that were rending it! What was terrible, you know, was that I considered myself to have a complete right to her body as if it were my own, and yet at the same time I felt I could not control that body, that it was not mine and she could dispose of it as she pleased, and that she wanted to dispose of it not as I wished her to. And I could do nothing either to her or to him. He, like Vánka the Steward,[1] could sing a song before the gallows of how he kissed the sugared lips and so forth. And he would triumph. If she has not yet done it but wishes to—and I know that she does wish to—it is still worse; it would be better if she had done it and I knew it, so that there would be an end to this uncertainty. I could not have said what it was I wanted. I wanted her not to desire that which she was bound to desire. It was utter insanity."

XXVI

"At the last station but one, when the conductor had been to collect the tickets, I gathered my things together and went out onto the brake-platform, and the consciousness that the crisis was at hand still further increased my agita-

[1] *Vánka the Steward* is the subject and name of some old Russian poems. Vánka seduces his master's wife, boasts of having done so, and is hanged.

tion. I felt cold, and my jaw trembled so that my teeth chattered. I automatically left the terminus with the crowd, took a cab, got in, and drove off. I rode looking at the few passers-by, the night-watchmen, and the shadows of my trap thrown by the street lamps, now in front and now behind me, and did not think of anything. When we had gone about half a mile my feet felt cold, and I remembered that I had taken off my woollen stockings in the train and put them in my satchel. 'Where is the satchel? Is it here? Yes.' And my wicker trunk? I remembered that I had entirely forgotten about my luggage, but finding that I had the luggage-ticket I decided that it was not worth while going back for it, and so continued my way.

"Try now as I will, I cannot recall my state of mind at the time. What did I think? What did I want? I don't know at all. All I remember is a consciousness that something dreadful and very important in my life was imminent. Whether that important event occurred because I thought it would, or whether I had a presentiment of what was to happen, I don't know. It may even be that after what has happened all the foregoing moments have acquired a certain gloom in my mind. I drove up to the front porch. It was past midnight. Some cabmen were waiting in front of the porch expecting, from the fact that there were lights in the windows, to get fares. (The lights were in our flat, in the dancing-room and drawing-room.) Without considering why it was still light in our windows so late, I went up-stairs in the same state of expectation of something dreadful, and rang. Egór, a kind, willing, but very stupid footman, opened the door. The first thing my eyes fell on in the hall was a man's cloak hanging on the stand with other outdoor coats. I ought to have been surprised but was not, for I had expected it. 'That's it!' I said to myself. When I asked Egór who the visitor was and he named Trukha-chévski, I inquired whether there was anyone else. He replied, 'Nobody, sir.' I remember that he replied in a tone as if he wanted to cheer me and dissipate my doubts of there being anybody else there. 'So it is, so it is,' I seemed to be saying to myself. 'And the children.' 'All well, heaven be praised. In bed, long ago.'

"I could not breathe and could not check the trembling of my jaw. 'Yes, so it is not as I thought: I used to expect a misfortune but things used to turn out all right and in the usual way. Now it is not as usual but is all as I pictured to myself. I thought it was only fancy, but here it is, all real. Here it all is . . .!'

"I almost began to sob, but the devil immediately suggested to me: 'Cry, be sentimental, and they will get away quietly. You will have no proof and will continue to suffer and doubt all your life.' And my self-pity immediately vanished, and a strange sense of joy arose in me, that my torture would now be over, that now I could punish her, could get rid of her, and could vent my anger. And I gave vent to it—I became a beast, a cruel and cunning beast.

" 'Don't!' I said to Egór, who was about to go to the drawing-room. 'Here is my luggage-ticket, take a cab as quick as you can and go and get my luggage. Go!' He went down the passage to fetch his overcoat. Afraid that he might alarm them, I went as far as his little room and waited while he put on his overcoat. From the drawing-room, beyond another room, one could hear voices and the clatter of knives and plates. They were eating and had not heard the bell. 'If only they don't come out now,' thought I. Egór put on his overcoat, which had an astrakhan collar, and went out. I locked the door after him and felt creepy when I knew I was alone and must act at once. How, I did not yet know. I only knew that all was now over, that there could be no doubt as to her guilt, and that I should punish her immediately and end my relations with her.

"Previously I had doubted and had thought: 'Perhaps after all it's not true, perhaps I am mistaken.' But now it was so no longer. It was all irrevocably decided. 'Without my knowledge she is alone with him at night! That is a complete disregard of everything! Or worse still: it is intentional boldness and impudence in crime, that the boldness may serve as a sign of innocence. All is clear. There is no doubt.' I only feared one thing—their parting hastily, inventing some fresh lie, and thus depriving me of clear evidence and of the possibility of proving the fact. So as to catch them more quickly I went on tiptoe to the dancing-room where they were, not through the drawing-room but through the passage and nurseries.

"In the first nursery slept the boys. In the second nursery the nurse moved and was about to wake, and I imagined to myself what she would think when she knew all; and such pity for myself seized me at that thought that I could not restrain my tears, and not to wake the children I ran on tiptoe into the passage and on into my study, where I fell sobbing on the sofa.

" 'I, an honest man, I, the son of my parents, I, who have all my life dreamt of the happiness of married life; I, a man who was never unfaithful to her. . . . And now! Five children, and she is embracing a musician because he has red lips!

" 'No, she is not a human being. She is a bitch, an abominable bitch! In the next room to her children whom she has all her life pretended to love. And writing to me as she did! Throwing herself so barefacedly on his neck! But what do I know? Perhaps she long ago carried on with the footmen and so got the children who are considered mine!

" 'To-morrow I should have come back and she would have met me with her fine coiffure, with her elegant waist, and her indolent, graceful movements' (I saw all her attractive, hateful face), 'and that beast of jealousy would for ever have sat in my heart lacerating it. What will the nurse think? . . . And Egór? And poor little Lisa! She already understands something. Ah, that impudence, those lies! And that animal sensuality which I know so well,' I said to myself.

"I tried to get up but could not. My heart was beating so that I could not stand on my feet. 'Yes, I shall die of a stroke. She will kill me. That is just what she wants. What is killing to her? But no, that would be too advantageous for her and I will not give her that pleasure. Yes, here I sit while they eat and lunch and . . . Yes, though she was no longer in her first freshness he did not disdain her. For in spite of that she is not bad-looking, and above all she is at any rate not dangerous to his precious health. And why did I not throttle her then?' I said to myself, recalling the moment when, the week before, I drove her out of my study and hurled things about. I vividly recalled the state I had then been in; I not only recalled it but again felt the need to strike and destroy that I had felt then. I remember how I wished to act, and how all considerations except those necessary for action went out of my head. I entered into that condition when an animal or a man, under the influence of physical excitement at a time of danger, acts with precision and deliberation but without losing a moment and always with a single definite aim in view.

"The first thing I did was to take off my boots and, in my socks, approach the sofa, on the wall above which guns and daggers were hung. I took down a curved Damascus dagger that had never been used and was very sharp. I drew it out of its scabbard. I remember the scabbard fell behind the sofa, and I remember thinking 'I must find it afterwards or it will get lost.' Then I took off my overcoat which I was still wearing, and stepping softly in my socks I went there."

XXVII

"Having crept up stealthily to the door, I suddenly opened it. I remember the expression of their faces. I remember that expression because it gave me a painful pleasure—it was an expression of terror. That was just what I wanted. I shall never forget the look of desperate terror that appeared on both their faces the first instant they saw me. He I think was sitting at the table, but on seeing or hearing me he jumped to his feet and stood with his back to the cupboard. His face expressed nothing but quite unmistakable terror. Her face too expressed terror but there was something else besides. If it had expressed only terror, perhaps what happened might not have happened; but on her face there was, or at any rate so it seemed to me at the first moment, also an expression of regret and annoyance that love's raptures and her happiness with him had been disturbed. It was as if she wanted nothing but that her present happiness should not be interfered with. These expressions remained on their faces but an instant. The look of terror on his changed immediately to one of inquiry: might he, or might he not, begin lying? If he might, he must begin at once; if not, something else would happen. But what? . . . He looked inquiringly at her face. On her face the look of vexation and regret changed as she looked at him (so it seemed to me) to one of solicitude for him.

"At that moment he smiled and in a ridiculously indifferent tone remarked: 'And we have been having some music.'

" 'What a surprise!' she began, falling into his tone. But neither of them finished; the same fury I had experienced the week before overcame me. Again I felt that need of destruction, violence, and a transport of rage and yielded to it. Neither finished what they were saying. That something else began which he had feared and which immediately destroyed all they were saying. I rushed towards her, still hiding the dagger that he might not prevent my striking her in the side under her breast. I selected that spot from the first. Just as I rushed at her he saw it, and—a thing I never expected of him—seized me by the arm and shouted: 'Think what you are doing! . . . Help, someone! . . .'

"I snatched my arm away and rushed at him in silence. His eyes met mine and he suddenly grew as pale as a sheet to his very lips. His eyes flashed in a peculiar way, and—what again I had not expected—he darted under the piano and out at the door. I was going to rush after him, but a weight hung on my left arm. It was she. I tried to free myself, but she hung on yet more heavily and would not let me go. This unexpected hindrance, the weight, and her touch, which was loathsome to me, inflamed me still more. I felt that I was quite mad and that I must look frightful, and this delighted me. I swung my left arm with all my might, and my elbow hit her straight in the face. She cried out and let go my arm. I wanted to run after him but remembered that it is ridiculous to run after one's wife's lover in one's socks; and I did not wish to be ridiculous but terrible. In spite of the fearful frenzy I was in, I was all the time aware of the impression I might produce on others and was even partly guided by that impression. I turned towards her. She fell on the couch and holding her hand to her bruised eyes, looked at me. Her face showed fear and hatred of me, the enemy, as a rat's does when one lifts the trap in which it has been caught. At any rate I saw nothing in her expression but this fear and hatred of me. It was just the fear and hatred of me which would be evoked by love for another. But still I might perhaps have restrained myself and not done what I did had she remained silent. But she suddenly began to speak and to catch hold of the hand in which I held the dagger.

" 'Come to yourself! What are you doing? What is the matter? There has been nothing, nothing, nothing—I swear it!'

"I might still have hesitated, but those last words of hers, from which I concluded just the opposite—that everything had happened—called forth a reply. And the reply had to correspond to the temper to which I had brought myself, which continued to increase and had to go on increasing. Fury, too, has its laws.

" 'Don't lie, you wretch!' I howled, and seized her arm with my left hand, but she wrenched herself away. Then, still without letting go of the dagger, I seized her by the throat with my left hand, threw her backwards, and began throttling her. What a firm neck it was . . .! She seized my hand with both hers, trying to pull it away from her throat, and as if I had only waited for that, I struck her with all my might with the dagger in the side below the ribs.

"When people say they don't remember what they do in a fit of fury, it is rubbish, falsehood. I remembered everything and did not for a moment lose consciousness of what I was doing. The more frenzied I became the more brightly the light of consciousness burnt in me, so that I could not help knowing everything I did. I knew what I was doing every second. I cannot say that I knew beforehand what I was going to do; but I knew what I was doing when I did it, and even I think a little before, as if to make repentance possible and to be able to tell myself that I could stop. I knew I was hitting below the ribs and that the dagger would enter. At the moment I did it I knew I was doing an awful thing such as I had never done before, which would have terrible consequences. But that consciousness passed like a flash of lightning and the deed immediately followed the consciousness. I realized the action with extraordinary clearness. I felt, and remember, the momentary resistance of her corset and of something else, and then the plunging of the dagger into something soft. She seized the dagger with her hands, and cut them, but could not hold it back.

"For a long time afterwards, in prison when the moral change had taken place in me, I thought of that moment, recalled what I could of it, and considered it. I remembered that for an instant, only an instant, before the action I had a terrible consciousness that I was killing, had killed, a defenceless woman, my wife! I remember the horror of that consciousness and conclude from that, and even dimly remember, that having plunged the dagger in I pulled it out immediately, trying to remedy what had been done and to stop it. I stood for a second motionless waiting to see what would happen, and whether it could be remedied.

"She jumped to her feet and screamed: 'Nurse! He has killed me.'

"Having heard the noise the nurse was standing by the door. I continued to stand waiting and not believing the truth. But the blood rushed from under her corset. Only then did I understand that it could not be remedied, and I immediately decided that it was not necessary it should be, that I had done what I wanted and had to do. I waited till she fell down, and the nurse, crying, 'Good God!' ran to her, and only then did I throw away the dagger and leave the room.

" 'I must not be excited; I must know what I am doing,' I said to myself without looking at her and at the nurse. The nurse was screaming—calling for the maid. I went down the passage, sent the maid, and went into my study. 'What am I to do now?' I asked myself, and immediately realized what it must be. On entering the study I went straight to the wall, took down a revolver and examined it; it was loaded—I put it on the table. Then I picked up the scabbard from behind the sofa and sat down there.

"I sat thus for a long time. I did not think of anything or call anything to mind. I heard the sounds of bustling outside. I heard someone drive up, then someone else. Then I heard and saw Egór bring into the room my wicker trunk he had fetched. As if anyone wanted that!

" 'Have you heard what has happened?' I asked. 'Tell the yard-porter to inform the police.' He did not reply and went away. I rose, locked the door, got out my

cigarettes and matches, and began to smoke. I had not
finished the cigarette before sleep overpowered me. I must
have slept for a couple of hours. I remember dreaming
that she and I were friendly together, that we had quarrelled but were making it up, there was something rather
in the way, but we were friends. I was awakened by
someone knocking at the door. 'That is the police!' I
thought, waking up. 'I have committed murder, I think.
But perhaps it is *she*, and nothing has happened.' There
was again a knock at the door. I did not answer but was
trying to solve the question whether it had happened or
not. Yes, it had! I remembered the resistance of the corset
and the plunging in of the dagger, and a cold shiver ran
down my back. 'Yes, it has. Yes, and now I must do
away with myself too,' I thought. But I thought this
knowing that I should *not* kill myself. Still I got up and
took the revolver in my hand. But it is strange: I remember
how I had many times been near suicide, how even that
day on the railway it had seemed easy, easy just because
I thought how it would stagger her—now I was not only
unable to kill myself but even to think of it. 'Why should
I do it?' I asked myself, and there was no reply. There
was more knocking at the door. 'First I must find out
who is knocking. There will still be time for this.'
I put down the revolver and covered it with a newspaper.
I went to the door and unlatched it. It was my wife's sister,
a kindly, stupid widow. 'Vásya, what is this?' and her
ever-ready tears began to flow.

   " 'What do you want?' I asked rudely. I knew I ought
not to be rude to her and had no reason to be, but I
could think of no other tone to adopt.

   " 'Vásya, she is dying! Iván Zakhárych says so.' Iván
Zakhárych was her doctor and adviser.

   " 'Is he here?' I asked, and all my animosity against
her surged up again. 'Well, what of it?'

   " 'Vásya, go to her. Oh, how terrible it is!' said she.

   " 'Shall I go to her?' I asked myself and immediately
decided that I must go to her. Probably it is always
done, when a husband has killed his wife, as I had—
he must certainly go to her. 'If that is what is done,
then I must go,' I said to myself. 'If necessary I shall
always have time,' I reflected, referring to the shooting

of myself, and I went to her. 'Now we shall have phrases, grimaces, but I will not yield to them,' I thought. 'Wait,' I said to her sister, 'it is silly without boots, let me at least put on slippers.' "

XXVIII

"Wonderful to say, when I left my study and went through the familiar rooms, the hope that nothing had happened again awoke in me; but the smell of that doctor's nastiness —iodoform and carbolic—took me aback. 'No, it had happened.' Going down the passage past the nursery I saw little Lisa. She looked at me with frightened eyes. It even seemed to me that all the five children were there and all looked at me. I approached the door, and the maid opened it from inside for me and passed out. The first thing that caught my eye was her light-grey dress thrown on a chair and all stained black with blood. She was lying on one of the twin beds (on mine because it was easier to get at), with her knees raised. She lay in a very sloping position supported by pillows, with her dressing jacket unfastened. Something had been put on the wound. There was a heavy smell of iodoform in the room. What struck me first and most of all was her swollen and bruised face, blue on part of the nose and under the eyes. This was the result of the blow with my elbow when she had tried to hold me back. There was nothing beautiful about her, but something repulsive as it seemed to me. I stopped on the threshold. 'Go up to her, do,' said her sister. 'Yes, no doubt she wants to confess,' I thought. 'Shall I forgive her? Yes, she is dying and may be forgiven,' I thought, trying to be magnanimous. I went up close to her. She raised her eyes to me with difficulty, one of them was black, and with an effort said falteringly: " 'You've got your way, killed . . .' and through the look of suffering and even the nearness of death her face had the old expression of cold animal hatred that I knew so well. 'I shan't . . . let you have . . . the children, all the same. . . . She '(her sister)' will take . . .'

"Of what to me was the most important matter, her guilt, her faithlessness, she seemed to consider it beneath her to speak.

" 'Yes, look and admire what you have done,' she said looking towards the door, and she sobbed. In the doorway stood her sister with the children. 'Yes, see what you have done.'

"I looked at the children and at her bruised disfigured face, and for the first time I forgot myself, my rights, my pride, and for the first time saw a human being in her. And so insignificant did all that had offended me, all my jealousy, appear, and so important what I had done, that I wished to fall with my face to her hand, and say, 'Forgive me,' but dared not do so.

"She lay silent with her eyes closed, evidently too weak to say more. Then her disfigured face trembled and puckered. She pushed me feebly away.

" 'Why did it all happen? Why?'

" 'Forgive me,' I said.

" 'Forgive! That's all rubbish! . . . Only not to die! . . .' she cried, raising herself, and her glittering eyes were bent on me. Yes, you have had your way! . . . I hate you! Ah! Ah!' she cried, evidently already in delirium and frightened at something. 'Shoot! I'm not afraid! . . . Only kill everyone . . .! He has gone . . .! Gone . . .!'

"After that the delirium continued all the time. She did not recognize anyone. She died towards noon that same day. Before that they had taken me to the police-station and from there to prison. There, during the eleven months I remained awaiting trial, I examined myself and my past, and understood it. I began to understand it on the third day: on the third day they took me *there* . . ."

He was going on but, unable to repress his sobs, he stopped. When he recovered himself he continued: "I only began to understand when I saw her in her coffin . . ."

He gave a sob but immediately continued hurriedly: "Only when I saw her dead face did I understand all that I had done. I realized that I, I, had killed her; that it was my doing that she, living, moving, warm, had now become motionless, waxen, and cold, and that this could never, anywhere, or by any means, be remedied. He who has not lived through it cannot understand. . . . Ugh! Ugh! Ugh! . . ." he cried several times and then was silent.

We sat in silence a long while. He kept sobbing and

trembling as he sat opposite me without speaking. His face had grown narrow and elongated and his mouth seemed to stretch right across it.

"Yes," he suddenly said. "Had I then known what I know now, everything would have been different. Nothing would have induced me to marry her. . . . I should not have married at all."

Again we remained silent for a long time.

"Well, forgive me. . . ."[1] He turned away from me and lay down on the seat, covering himself up with his plaid. At the station where I had to get out (it was at eight o'clock in the morning) I went up to him to say good-bye. Whether he was asleep or only pretended to be, at any rate he did not move. I touched him with my hand. He uncovered his face, and I could see he had not been asleep.

"Good-bye," I said, holding out my hand. He gave me his and smiled slightly, but so piteously that I felt ready to weep.

"Yes, forgive me . . ." he said, repeating the same words with which he had concluded his story.

NOTE

We have chosen to omit an Appendix which the translators conscientiously prepared to follow the text of The Kreutzer Sonata. *It contains brief incidental material that the Maudes had omitted from their translation. While this would be necessary for a literal translation, they did not feel that it was needed in the English reading version, and the editor of this Portable agreed.*

THE PUBLISHERS

---

[1] In Russian the word for "forgive me" is very similar to that for "good-bye" and is sometimes used in place of the latter.

MASTER AND MAN

I

It happened in the 'seventies in winter, on the day after St. Nicholas's Day. There was a fête in the parish and the innkeeper, Vasíli Andréevich Brekhunóv, a Second Guild merchant, being a church elder had to go to church and had also to entertain his relatives and friends at home.

But when the last of them had gone he at once began to prepare to drive over to see a neighbouring proprietor about a grove which he had been bargaining over for a long time. He was now in a hurry to start, lest buyers from the town might forestall him in making a profitable purchase.

The youthful landowner was asking ten thousand rubles for the grove simply because Vasíli Andréevich was offering seven thousand. Seven thousand was, however, only a third of its real value. Vasíli Andréevich might perhaps have got it down to his own price, for the woods were in his district and he had a long-standing agreement with the other village dealers that no one should run up the price in another's district, but he had now learnt that some timber-dealers from town meant to bid for the Goryáchkin grove, and he resolved to go at once and get the matter settled. So as soon as the feast was over, he took seven hundred rubles from his strong box, added to them two thousand three hundred rubles of church money he had in his keeping, so as to make up the sum to three thousand, carefully counted the notes, and having put them into his pocket-book made haste to start.

Nikíta, the only one of Vasíli Andréevich's labourers who was not drunk that day, ran to harness the horse.

Nikíta, though an habitual drunkard, was not drunk that
day because since the last day before the fast, when he had
drunk his coat and leather boots, he had sworn off drink
and had kept his vow for two months, and was still keeping it despite the temptation of the vodka that had been
drunk everywhere during the first two days of the feast.

Nikíta was a peasant of about fifty from a neighbouring village; "not a manager" as the peasants said of
him, meaning that he was not the thrifty head of a household but lived most of his time away from home as a
labourer. He was valued everywhere for his industry,
dexterity, and strength at work, and still more for his
kindly and pleasant temper. But he never settled down
anywhere for long because about twice a year, or even
oftener, he had a drinking bout, and then besides spending
all his clothes on drink he became turbulent and quarrel-
some. Vasíli Andréevich himself had turned him away
several times but had afterwards taken him back again—
valuing his honesty, his kindness to animals, and especially
his cheapness. Vasíli Andréevich did not pay Nikíta the
eighty rubles a year such a man was worth, but only about
forty, which he gave him haphazard, in small sums, and
even that mostly not in cash but in goods from his own
shop and at high prices.

Nikíta's wife Martha, who had once been a handsome
vigorous woman, managed the homestead with the help
of her son and two daughters and did not urge Nikíta to
live at home: first because she had been living for some
twenty years already with a cooper, a peasant from another
village who lodged in their house; and secondly because
though she managed her husband as she pleased when he
was sober, she feared him like fire when he was drunk.
Once when he had got drunk at home, Nikíta, probably to
make up for his submissiveness when sober, broke open her
box, took out her best clothes, snatched up an axe, and
chopped all her under-garments and dresses to bits. All
the wages Nikíta earned went to his wife, and he raised
no objection to that: so now, two days before the holiday,
Martha had been twice to see Vasíli Andréevich and had
got from him wheat flour, tea, sugar, and a quart of
vodka, the lot costing three rubles, and also five rubles

in cash, for which she thanked him as for a special favour though he owed Nikíta at least twenty rubles.

"What agreement did we ever draw up with you?" said Vasíli Andréevich to Nikíta. "If you need anything, take it; you will work it off. I'm not like others to keep you waiting, and making up accounts and reckoning fines. We deal straightforwardly. You serve me and I don't neglect you."

And when saying this Vasíli Andréevich was honestly convinced that he was Nikíta's benefactor, and he knew how to put it so plausibly that all those who depended on him for their money, beginning with Nikíta, confirmed him in the conviction that he was their benefactor and did not overreach them.

"Yes, I understand, Vasíli Andréevich. You know that I serve you and take as much pains as I would for my own father. I understand very well!" Nikíta would reply. He was quite aware that Vasíli Andréevich was cheating him, but at the same time he felt that it was useless to try to clear up his accounts with him or explain his side of the matter and that as long as he had nowhere else to go he must accept what he could get.

Now, having heard his master's order to harness, he went as usual cheerfully and willingly to the shed, stepping briskly and easily on his rather turned-in feet, took down from a nail the heavy tasselled leather bridle, and jingling the rings of the bit went to the closed stable where the horse he was to harness was standing by himself.

"What, feeling lonely, feeling lonely, little silly?" said Nikíta in answer to the low whinny with which he was greeted by the good-tempered, medium-sized bay stallion, with a rather slanting crupper, who stood alone in the shed. "Now then, now then, there's time enough. Let me water you first," he went on, speaking to the horse just as to someone who understood the words he was using, and having whisked the dusty grooved back of the well-fed young stallion with the skirt of his coat, he put a bridle on his handsome head, straightened his ears and forelock, and having taken off his halter led him out to water.

Picking his way out of the dung-strewn stable, Mukhórty frisked and, making play with his hind leg pretended that

he meant to kick Nikíta, who was running at a trot beside
him to the pump.

"Now then, now then, you rascal!" Nikíta called out,
well knowing how carefully Mukhórty threw out his hind
leg just to touch his greasy sheepskin coat but not to
strike him—a trick Nikíta much appreciated.

After a drink of the cold water the horse sighed,
moving his strong wet lips, from the hairs of which
transparent drops fell into the trough; then standing still
as if in thought, he suddenly gave a loud snort.

"If you don't want any more, you needn't. But don't
go asking for any later," said Nikíta quite seriously and
fully explaining his conduct to Mukhórty. Then he ran
back to the shed pulling the playful young horse, who
wanted to gambol all over the yard, by the rein.

There was no one else in the yard except a stranger,
the cook's husband, who had come for the holiday.

"Go and ask which sledge is to be harnessed—the wide
one or the small one—there's a good fellow!"

The cook's husband went into the house, which stood
on an iron foundation and was iron-roofed, and soon returned saying that the little one was to be harnessed. By
that time Nikíta had put the collar and brass-studded belly-
band on Mukhórty and, carrying a light, painted shaft-bow
in one hand, was leading the horse with the other up to
two sledges that stood in the shed.

"All right, let it be the little one!" he said, backing the
intelligent horse, which all the time kept pretending to bite
him, into the shafts, and with the aid of the cook's husband
he proceeded to harness. When everything was nearly ready
and only the reins had to be adjusted, Nikíta sent the other
man to the shed for some straw and to the barn for a
drugget.

"There, that's all right! Now, now, don't bristle up!"
said Nikíta, pressing down into the sledge the freshly
threshed oat straw the cook's husband had brought. "And
now let's spread the sacking like this, and the drugget over
it. There, like that it will be comfortable sitting," he went
on, suiting the action to the words and tucking the drugget
all round over the straw to make a seat.

"Thank you, dear man. Things always go quicker with

two working at it!" he added. And gathering up the leather reins fastened together by a brass ring, Nikíta took the driver's seat and started the impatient horse over the frozen manure which lay in the yard, towards the gate.

"Uncle Nikíta! I say, Uncle, Uncle!" a high-pitched voice shouted, and a seven-year-old boy in a black sheepskin coat, new white felt boots, and a warm cap ran hurriedly out of the house into the yard. "Take me with you!" he cried, fastening up his coat as he ran.

"All right, come along, darling!" said Nikíta, and stopping the sledge he picked up the master's pale thin little son, radiant with joy, and drove out into the road.

It was past two o'clock and the day was windy, dull, and cold, with more than twenty degrees Fahrenheit of frost. Half the sky was hidden by a lowering dark cloud. In the yard it was quiet, but in the street the wind was felt more keenly. The snow swept down from a neighbouring shed and whirled about in the corner near the bathhouse.

Hardly had Nikíta driven out of the yard and turned the horse's head to the house before Vasíli Andréevich emerged from the high porch in front of the house, with a cigarette in his mouth and wearing a cloth-covered sheepskin coat tightly girdled low at his waist, and stepped onto the hard-trodden snow which squeaked under the leather soles of his felt boots, and stopped. Taking a last whiff of his cigarette he threw it down, stepped on it, and letting the smoke escape through his moustache and looking askance at the horse that was coming up, began to tuck in his sheepskin collar on both sides of his ruddy face, clean-shaven except for the moustache, so that his breath should not moisten the collar.

"See now! The young scamp is there already!" he exclaimed when he saw his little son in the sledge. Vasíli Andréevich was excited by the vodka he had drunk with his visitors, and so he was even more pleased than usual with everything that was his and all that he did. The sight of his son, whom he always thought of as his heir, now gave him great satisfaction. He looked at him, screwing up his eyes and showing his long teeth.

His wife—pregnant, thin and pale, with her head and shoulders wrapped in a shawl so that nothing of her face could be seen but her eyes—stood behind him in the vestibule to see him off.

"Now really, you ought to take Nikíta with you," she said timidly, stepping out from the doorway.

Vasíli Andréevich did not answer. Her words evidently annoyed him and he frowned angrily and spat.

"You have money on you," she continued in the same plaintive voice. "What if the weather gets worse! Do take him, for goodness' sake!"

"Why? Don't I know the road that I must needs take a guide?" exclaimed Vasíli Andréevich, uttering every word very distinctly and compressing his lips unnaturally, as he usually did when speaking to buyers and sellers.

"Really you ought to take him. I beg you in God's name!" his wife repeated, wrapping her shawl more closely round her head.

"There, she sticks to it like a leech! . . . Where am I to take him?"

"I'm quite ready to go with you, Vasíli Andréevich," said Nikíta cheerfully. "But they must feed the horses while I am away," he added, turning to his master's wife.

"I'll look after them, Nikíta dear. I'll tell Simon," replied the mistress.

"Well, Vasíli Andréevich, am I to come with you?" said Nikíta, awaiting a decision.

"It seems I must humour my old woman. But if you're coming you'd better put on a warmer cloak," said Vasíli Andréevich, smiling again as he winked at Nikíta's short sheepskin coat, which was torn under the arms and at the back, was greasy and out of shape, frayed to a fringe round the skirt, and had endured many things in its lifetime.

"Hey, dear man, come and hold the horse!" shouted Nikíta to the cook's husband, who was still in the yard.

"No, I will myself, I will myself!" shrieked the little boy, pulling his hands, red with cold, out of his pockets, and seizing the cold leather reins.

"Only don't be too long dressing yourself up. Look alive!" shouted Vasíli Andréevich, grinning at Nikíta.

"Only a moment, father, Vasíli Andréevich!" replied Nikíta, and running quickly with his inturned toes in his felt boots with their soles patched with felt, he hurried across the yard and into the workmen's hut.

"Arínushka! Get my coat down from the stove. I'm going with the master," he said, as he ran into the hut and took down his girdle from the nail on which it hung.

The workmen's cook, who had had a sleep after dinner and was now getting the samovar ready for her husband, turned cheerfully to Nikíta and infected by his hurry began to move as quickly as he did, got down his miserable worn-out cloth coat from the stove where it was drying, and began hurriedly shaking it out and smoothing it down.

"There now, you'll have a chance of a holiday with your goodman," said Nikíta, who from kindhearted politeness always said something to anyone he was alone with.

Then, drawing his worn narrow girdle round him, he drew in his breath, pulling in his lean stomach still more, and girdled himself as tightly as he could over his sheepskin.

"There now," he said, addressing himself no longer to the cook but the girdle, as he tucked the ends in at the waist, "now you won't come undone!" And working his shoulders up and down to free his arms, he put the coat over his sheepskin, arched his back more strongly to ease his arms, poked himself under the armpits, and took down his leather-covered mittens from the shelf. "Now we're all right!"

"You ought to wrap your feet up, Nikíta. Your boots are very bad."

Nikíta stopped as if he had suddenly realized this.

"Yes, I ought to. . . . But they'll do like this. It isn't far!" and he ran out into the yard.

"Won't you be cold, Nikíta?" said the mistress as he came up to the sledge.

"Cold? No, I'm quite warm," answered Nikíta as he pushed some straw up to the forepart of the sledge so that it should cover his feet and stowed away the whip, which the good horse would not need, at the bottom of the sledge.

Vasíli Andréevich, who was wearing two fur-lined coats one over the other, was already in the sledge, his broad back filling nearly its whole rounded width, and taking the reins he immediately touched the horse. Nikíta jumped in just as the sledge started, and seated himself in front of the left side, with one leg hanging over the edge.

II

The good stallion took the sledge along at a brisk pace over the smooth-frozen road through the village, the runners squeaking slightly as they went.

"Look at him hanging on there! Hand me the whip, Nikíta!" shouted Vasíli Andréevich, evidently enjoying the sight of his "heir," who standing on the runners was hanging on at the back of the sledge. "I'll give it you! Be off to mamma, you dog!"

The boy jumped down. The horse increased his amble and, suddenly changing foot, broke into a fast trot.

The Crosses, the village where Vasíli Andréevich lived, consisted of six houses. As soon as they had passed the blacksmith's hut, the last in the village, they realized that the wind was much stronger than they had thought. The road could hardly be seen. The tracks left by the sledge-runners were immediately covered by snow and the road was only distinguished by the fact that it was higher than the rest of the ground. There was a whirl of snow over the fields and the line where sky and earth met could not be seen. The Telyátin forest, usually clearly visible, now only loomed up occasionally and dimly through the driving snowy dust. The wind came from the left, insistently blowing over to one side the mane on Mukhórty's sleek neck and carrying aside even his fluffy tail, which was tied in a simple knot. Nikíta's wide coat-collar, as he sat on the windy side, pressed close to his cheek and nose.

"This road doesn't give him a chance—it's too snowy," said Vasíli Andréevich, who prided himself on his good horse. "I once drove to Pashútino with him in half an hour."

"What?" asked Nikíta, who could not hear on account of his collar.

"I say I once went to Pashútino in half an hour," shouted Vasíli Andréevich.

"It goes without saying that he's a good horse," replied Nikíta.

They were silent for awhile. But Vasíli Andréevich wished to talk.

"Well, did you tell your wife not to give the cooper any

vodka?" he began in the same loud tone, quite convinced that Nikíta must feel flattered to be talking with so clever and important a person as himself, and he was so pleased with his jest that it did not enter his head that the remark might be unpleasant to Nikíta.

The wind again prevented Nikíta's hearing his master's words.

Vasíli Andréevich repeated the jest about the cooper in his loud, clear voice.

"That's their business, Vasíli Andréevich. I don't pry into those affairs. As long as she doesn't ill-treat our boy—God be with them."

"That's so," said Vasíli Andréevich. "Well, and will you be buying a horse in spring?" he went on, changing the subject.

"Yes, I can't avoid it," answered Nikíta, turning down his collar and leaning back towards his master.

The conversation now became interesting to him and he did not wish to lose a word.

"The lad's growing up. He must begin to plough for himself, but till now we've always had to hire someone," he said.

"Well, why not have the lean-cruppered one. I won't charge much for it," shouted Vasíli Andréevich, feeling animated and consequently starting on his favourite occupation—that of horse-dealing—which absorbed all his mental powers.

"Or you might let me have fifteen rubles and I'll buy one at the horse-market," said Nikíta, who knew that the horse Vasíli Andréevich wanted to sell him would be dear at seven rubles but that if he took it from him it would be charged at twenty-five, and then he would be unable to draw any money for half a year.

"It's a good horse. I think of your interest as of my own—according to conscience. Brekhunóv isn't a man to wrong anyone. Let the loss be mine. I'm not like others. Honestly!" he shouted in the voice in which he hypnotized his customers and dealers, "it's a real good horse."

"Quite so!" said Nikíta with a sigh, and convinced that there was nothing more to listen to, he again released his collar, which immediately covered his ear and face.

They drove on in silence for about half an hour. The

wind blew sharply onto Nikíta's side and arm where his sheepskin was torn.

He huddled up and breathed into the collar which covered his mouth, and was not wholly cold.

"What do you think—shall we go through Karamýshevo or by the straight road?" asked Vasíli Andréevich.

The road through Karamýshevo was more frequented and was well marked with a double row of high stakes. The straight road was nearer but little used and had no stakes, or only poor ones covered with snow.

Nikíta thought awhile.

"Though Karamýshevo is farther, it is better going," he said.

"But by the straight road, when once we get through the hollow by the forest, it's good going—sheltered," said Vasíli Andréevich, who wished to go the nearest way.

"Just as you please," said Nikíta and again let go of his collar.

Vasíli Andréevich did as he had said, and having gone about half a verst came to a tall oak stake which had a few dry leaves still dangling on it, and there he turned to the left.

On turning they faced directly against the wind, and snow was beginning to fall. Vasíli Andréevich, who was driving, inflated his cheeks, blowing the breath out through his moustache. Nikíta dosed.

So they went on in silence for about ten minutes. Suddenly Vasíli Andréevich began saying something.

"Eh, what?" asked Nikíta, opening his eyes.

Vasíli Andréevich did not answer but bent over, looking behind them and then ahead of the horse. The sweat had curled Mukhórty's coat between his legs and on his neck. He went at a walk.

"What is it?" Nikíta asked again.

"What is it? What is it?" Vasíli Andréevich mimicked him angrily. "There are no stakes to be seen! We must have got off the road!"

"Well, pull up then, and I'll look for it," said Nikíta, and jumping down lightly from the sledge and taking the whip from under the straw, he went off to the left from his own side of the sledge.

The snow was not deep that year, so that it was

possible to walk anywhere, but still in places it was knee-deep and got into Nikíta's boots. He went about feeling the ground with his feet and the whip, but could not find the road anywhere.

"Well, how it is?" asked Vasíli Andréevich when Nikíta came back to the sledge.

"There is no road this side. I must go to the other side and try there," said Nikíta.

"There's something there in front. Go and have a look."

Nikíta went to what had appeared dark but found that it was earth which the wind had blown from the bare fields of winter oats and had strewn over the snow, colouring it. Having searched to the right also, he returned to the sledge, brushed the snow from his coat, shook it out of his boots, and seated himself once more.

"We must go to the right," he said decidedly. "The wind was blowing on our left before, but now it is straight in my face. Drive to the right," he repeated with decision.

Vasíli Andréevich took his advice and turned to the right, but still there was no road. They went on in that direction for some time. The wind was as fierce as ever and it was snowing lightly.

"It seems, Vasíli Andréevich, that we have gone quite astray," Nikíta suddenly remarked, as if it were a pleasant thing. "What is that?" he added, pointing to some potato bines that showed up from under the snow.

Vasíli Andréevich stopped the perspiring horse, whose deep sides were heaving heavily.

"What is it?"

"Why, we are on the Zakhárov lands. See where we've got to!"

"Nonsense!" retorted Vasíli Andréevich.

"It's not nonsense, Vasíli Andréevich. It's the truth," replied Nikíta. "You can feel that the sledge is going over a potato-field, and there are the heaps of bines which have been carted here. It's the Zakhárov factory land."

"Dear me, how we have gone astray!" said Vasíli Andréevich. "What are we to do now?"

"We must go straight on, that's all. We shall come out somewhere—if not at Zakhárova then at the proprietor's farm," said Nikíta.

Vasíli Andréevich agreed and drove as Nikíta had indicated. So they went on for a considerable time. At times they came onto bare fields and the sledge-runners rattled over frozen lumps of earth. Sometimes they got onto a winter-rye field, or a fallow field on which they could see stalks of wormwood, and straws sticking up through the snow and swaying in the wind; sometimes they came onto deep and even white snow, above which nothing was to be seen.

The snow was falling from above and sometimes rose from below. The horse was evidently exhausted, his hair had all curled up from sweat and was covered with hoar-frost, and he went at a walk. Suddenly he stumbled and sat down in a ditch or water-course. Vasíli Andréevich wanted to stop, but Nikíta cried to him: "Why stop? We've got in and must get out. Hey, pet! Hey, darling! Gee up, old fellow!" he shouted in a cheerful tone to the horse, jumping out of the sledge and himself getting stuck in the ditch.

The horse gave a start and quickly climbed out onto the frozen bank. It was evidently a ditch that had been dug there.

"Where are we now?" asked Vasíli Andréevich.

"We'll soon find out!" Nikíta replied. "Go on, we'll get somewhere."

"Why, this must be the Goryáchkin forest!" said Vasíli Andréevich, pointing to something dark that appeared amid the snow in front of them.

"We'll see what forest it is when we get there," said Nikíta.

He saw that beside the black thing they had noticed, dry, oblong willow-leaves were fluttering, and so he knew it was not a forest but a settlement, but he did not wish to say so. And in fact they had not gone twenty-five yards beyond the ditch before something in front of them, evidently trees, showed up black, and they heard a new and melancholy sound. Nikíta had guessed right: it was not a wood, but a row of tall willows with a few leaves still fluttering on them here and there. They had evidently been planted along the ditch round a threshing-floor. Coming up to the willows, which moaned sadly in the wind, the horse suddenly planted his forelegs above the height of the sledge, drew up his hind legs also, pulling the sledge onto higher ground, and turned to the left, no longer sinking up to his knees in snow. They were back on a road.

"Well, here we are, but heaven only knows where!" said Nikíta.

The horse kept straight along the road through the drifted snow, and before they had gone another hundred yards the straight line of the dark wattle wall of a barn showed up black before them, its roof heavily covered with snow which poured down from it. After passing the barn the road turned to the wind and they drove into a snow-drift. But ahead of them was a lane with houses on either side, so evidently the snow had been blown across the road and they had to drive through the drift. And so in fact it was. Having driven through the snow they came out into a street. At the end house of the village some frozen clothes hanging on a line—shirts, one red and one white, trousers, leg-bands, and a petticoat—fluttered wildly in the wind. The white shirt in particular struggled desperately, waving its sleeves about.

"There now, either a lazy woman or a dead one has not taken her clothes down before the holiday," remarked Nikíta, looking at the fluttering shirts.

III

At the entrance to the street the wind still raged and the road was thickly covered with snow, but well within the village it was calm, warm, and cheerful. At one house a dog was barking; at another a woman, covering her head with her coat, came running from somewhere and entered the door of a hut, stopping on the threshold to have a look at the passing sledge. In the middle of the village, girls could be heard singing.

Here in the village there seemed to be less wind and snow, and the frost was less keen.

"Why, this is Gríshkino," said Vasíli Andréevich.

"So it is," responded Nikíta.

It really was Gríshkino, which meant that they had

gone too far to the left and had travelled some six miles, not quite in the direction they aimed at but towards their destination for all that.

From Gríshkino to Goryáchkin was about another four miles.

In the middle of the village they almost ran into a tall man walking down the middle of the street.

"Who are you?" shouted the man, stopping the horse, and recognizing Vasíli Andréevich he immediately took hold of the shaft, went along it hand over hand till he reached the sledge, and placed himself on the driver's seat.

He was Isáy, a peasant of Vasíli Andréevich's acquaintance and well known as the principal horse-thief in the district.

"Ah, Vasíli Andréevich! Where are you off to?" said Isáy, enveloping Nikíta in the odour of the vodka he had drunk.

"We were going to Goryáchkin."

"And look where you've got to! You should have gone through Molchánovka."

"Should have, but didn't manage it," said Vasíli Andréevich, holding in the horse.

"That's a good horse," said Isáy, with a shrewd glance at Mukhórty, and with a practised hand he tightened the loosened knot high in the horse's bushy tail.

"Are you going to stay the night?"

"No, friend. I must get on."

"Your business must be pressing. And who is this? Ah, Nikíta Stepánych!"

"Who else?" replied Nikíta. "But I say, good friend, how are we to avoid going astray again?"

"Where can you go astray here? Turn back straight down the street and then when you come out keep straight on. Don't take to the left. You will come out onto the high road, and then turn to the right."

"And where do we turn off the high road? As in summer, or the winter way?" asked Nikíta.

"The winter way. As soon as you turn off you'll see some bushes, and opposite them there is a way-mark—a large oak one with branches—and that's the way."

Vasíli Andréevich turned the horse back and drove through the outskirts of the village.

"Why not stay the night?" Isáy shouted after them.

But Vasíli Andréevich did not answer and touched up the horse. Four miles of good road, two of which lay through the forest, seemed easy to manage, especially as the wind was apparently quieter and the snow had stopped.

Having driven along the trodden village street, darkened here and there by fresh manure, past the yard where the clothes hung out and where the white shirt had broken loose and was now attached only by one frozen sleeve, they again came within sound of the weird moan of the willows, and again emerged on the open fields. The storm, far from ceasing, seemed to have grown yet stronger. The road was completely covered with drifting snow, and only the stakes showed that they had not lost their way. But even the stakes ahead of them were not easy to see, since the wind blew in their faces.

Vasíli Andréevich screwed up his eyes, bent down his head, and looked out for the way-marks but trusted mainly to the horse's sagacity, letting it take its own way. And the horse really did not lose the road but followed its windings, turning now to the right and now to the left and sensing it under his feet, so that though the snow fell thicker and the wind strengthened they still continued to see way-marks now to the left and now to the right of them.

So they travelled on for about ten minutes, when suddenly, through the slanting screen of wind-driven snow, something black showed up which moved in front of the horse.

This was another sledge with fellow-travellers. Mukhórty overtook them and struck his hoofs against the back of the sledge in front of him.

"Pass on . . . hey there . . . get in front!" cried voices from the sledge.

Vasíli Andréevich swerved aside to pass the other sledge. In it sat three men and a woman, evidently visitors returning from a feast. One peasant was whacking the snow-covered croup of their little horse with a long switch, and the other two sitting in front waved their arms and shouted something. The woman, completely wrapped up and covered with snow, sat drowsing and bumping at the back.

"Who are you?" shouted Vasíli Andréevich.

"From A-a-a . . ." was all that could be heard.

"I say, where are you from?"

"From A-a-a-a!" one of the peasants shouted with all his might, but still it was impossible to make out who they were.

"Get along! Keep up!" shouted another, ceaselessly beating his horse with the switch.

"So you're from a feast, it seems?"

"Go on, go on! Faster, Simon! Get in front! Faster!"

The wings of the sledges bumped against one another, almost got jammed but managed to separate, and the peasants' sledge began to fall behind.

Their shaggy, big-bellied horse, all covered with snow, breathed heavily under the low shaft-bow and, evidently using the last of its strength, vainly endeavoured to escape from the switch, hobbling with its short legs through the deep snow which it threw up under itself.

Its muzzle, young-looking, with the nether lip drawn up like that of a fish, nostrils distended and ears pressed back from fear, kept up for a few seconds near Nikíta's shoulder and then began to fall behind.

"Just see what liquor does!" said Nikíta. "They've tired that little horse to death. What pagans!"

For a few minutes they heard the panting of the tired little horse and the drunken shouting of the peasants. Then the panting and the shouts died away, and around them nothing could be heard but the whistling of the wind in their ears and now and then the squeak of their sledge-runners over a wind-swept part of the road.

This encounter cheered and enlivened Vasíli Andréevich, and he drove on more boldly without examining the way-marks, urging on the horse and trusting to him.

Nikíta had nothing to do, and as usual in such circumstances he drowsed, making up for much sleepless time. Suddenly the horse stopped and Nikíta nearly fell forward onto his nose.

"You know we're off the track again!" said Vasíli Andréevich.

"How's that?"

"Why, there are no way-marks to be seen. We must have got off the road again."

"Well, if we've lost the road we must find it," said Nikíta curtly, and getting out and stepping lightly on his pigeon-toed feet he started once more going about on the snow.

He walked about for a long time, now disappearing and now reappearing, and finally he came back.

"There is no road here. There may be farther on," he said, getting into the sledge.

It was already growing dark. The snow-storm had not increased but had also not subsided.

"If we could only hear those peasants!" said Vasíli Andréevich.

"Well they haven't caught us up. We must have gone far astray. Or maybe they have lost their way too."

"Where are we to go then?" asked Vasíli Andréevich.

"Why, we must let the horse take its own way," said Nikíta. "He will take us right. Let me have the reins."

Vasíli Andréevich gave him the reins, the more willingly because his hands were beginning to feel frozen in his thick gloves.

Nikíta took the reins but only held them, trying not to shake them and rejoicing at his favourite's sagacity. And indeed the clever horse, turning first one ear and then the other now to one side and then to the other, began to wheel round.

"The one thing he can't do is to talk," Nikíta kept saying. "See what he is doing! Go on, go on! You know best. That's it, that's it!"

The wind was now blowing from behind and it felt warmer.

"Yes, he's clever," Nikíta continued, admiring the horse. "A Kirgiz horse is strong but stupid. But this one—just see what he's doing with his ears! He doesn't need any telegraph. He can scent a mile off."

Before another half-hour had passed they saw something dark ahead of them—a wood or a village—and stakes again appeared to the right. They had evidently come out onto the road.

"Why, that's Gríshkino again!" Nikíta suddenly exclaimed.

And indeed, there on their left was that same barn with the snow flying from it, and farther on the same line with the frozen washing, shirts and trousers, which still fluttered desperately in the wind.

Again they drove into the street and again it grew quiet, warm, and cheerful, and again they could see the manure-stained street and hear voices and songs and the barking of a dog. It was already so dark that there were lights in some of the windows.

Half-way through the village Vasíli Andréevich turned the horse towards a large double-fronted brick house and stopped at the porch.

Nikíta went to the lighted snow-covered window, in the rays of which flying snow-flakes glittered, and knocked at it with his whip.

"Who is there?" a voice replied to his knock.

"From Krestý, the Brekhunóvs, dear fellow," answered Nikíta. "Just come out for a minute."

Someone moved from the window, and a minute or two later there was the sound of the passage door as it came unstuck, then the latch of the outside door clicked and a tall white-bearded peasant, with a sheepskin coat thrown over his white holiday shirt, pushed his way out holding the door firmly against the wind, followed by a lad in a red shirt and high leather boots.

"Is that you, Andréevich?" asked the old man.

"Yes, friend, we've gone astray," said Vasíli Andréevich. "We wanted to get to Goryáchkin but found ourselves here. We went a second time but lost our way again."

"Just see how you have gone astray!" said the old man. "Petrúshka, go and open the gate!" he added, turning to the lad in the red shirt.

"All right," said the lad in a cheerful voice and ran back into the passage.

"But we're not staying the night," said Vasíli Andréevich.

"Where will you go in the night? You'd better stay!"

"I'd be glad to, but I must go on. It's business and it can't be helped."

"Well, warm yourself at least. The samovar is just ready."

"Warm myself? Yes, I'll do that," said Vasíli Andréevich. "It won't get darker. The moon will rise and it will be lighter. Let's go in and warm ourselves, Nikíta."

"Well, why not? Let us warm ourselves," replied Nikíta,

who was stiff with cold and anxious to warm his frozen limbs.

Vasíli Andréevich went into the room with the old man, and Nikíta drove through the gate opened for him by Petrúshka, by whose advice he backed the horse under the penthouse. The ground was covered with manure and the tall bow over the horse's head caught against the beam. The hens and the cock had already settled to roost there and clucked peevishly, clinging to the beam with their claws. The disturbed sheep shied and rushed aside, trampling the frozen manure with their hooves. The dog yelped desperately with fright and anger and then burst out barking like a puppy at the stranger.

Nikíta talked to them all, excused himself to the fowls and assured them that he would not disturb them again, rebuked the sheep for being frightened without knowing why, and kept soothing the dog, while he tied up the horse.

"Now that will be all right," he said, knocking the snow off his clothes. "Just hear how he barks!" he added, turning to the dog. "Be quiet, stupid! Be quiet. You are only troubling yourself for nothing. We're not thieves, we're friends. . . ."

"And these are, it's said, the three domestic counsellors," remarked the lad, and with his strong arms he pushed under the pent-roof the sledge that had remained outside.

"Why counsellors?" asked Nikíta.

"That's what is printed in Paulson. A thief creeps to a house—the dog barks, that means, 'Be on your guard!' The cock crows, that means, 'Get up!' The cat licks herself—that means, 'A welcome guest is coming. Get ready to receive him!'" said the lad with a smile.

Petrúshka could read and write and knew Paulson's primer, his only book, almost by heart, and he was fond of quoting sayings from it that he thought suited the occasion, especially when he had had something to drink, as to-day.

"That's so," said Nikíta.

"You must be chilled through and through," said Petrúshka.

"Yes, I am rather," said Nikíta, and they went across the yard and the passage into the house.

IV

The household to which Vasíli Andréevich had come was one of the richest in the village. The family had five allotments, besides renting other land. They had six horses, three cows, two calves, and some twenty sheep. There were twenty-two members belonging to the homestead: four married sons, six grandchildren (one of whom, Petrúshka, was married), two great-grandchildren, three orphans, and four daughters-in-law with their babies. It was one of the few homesteads that remained still undivided, but even here the dull internal work of disintegration which would inevitably lead to separation had already begun, starting as usual among the women. Two sons were living in Moscow as water-carriers, and one was in the army. At home now were the old man and his wife, their second son who managed the homestead, the eldest who had come from Moscow for the holiday, and all the women and children. Besides these members of the family there was a visitor, a neighbour who was godfather to one of the children.

Over the table in the room hung a lamp with a shade, which brightly lit up the tea-things, a bottle of vodka, and some refreshments, besides illuminating the brick walls, which in the far corner were hung with icons on both sides of which were pictures. At the head of the table sat Vasíli Andréevich in a black sheepskin coat, sucking his frozen moustache and observing the room and the people around him with his prominent hawk-like eyes. With him sat the old, bald, white-bearded master of the house in a white homespun shirt, and next him the son home from Moscow for the holiday—a man with a sturdy back and powerful shoulders and clad in a thin print shirt—then the second son, also broad-shouldered, who acted as head of the house, and then a lean red-haired peasant—the neighbour.

Having had a drink of vodka and something to eat, they were about to take tea, and the samovar standing on the floor beside the brick oven was already humming. The children could be seen in the top bunks and on the top of the oven. A woman sat on a lower bunk with a cradle beside her. The old housewife, her face covered with wrinkles which wrinkled even her lips, was waiting on Vasíli Andréevich.

As Nikíta entered the house she was offering her guest a small tumbler of thick glass which she had just filled with vodka.

"Don't refuse, Vasíli Andréevich, you mustn't! Wish us a merry feast. Drink it, dear!" she said.

The sight and smell of vodka, especially now when he was chilled through and tired out, much disturbed Nikíta's mind. He frowned, and having shaken the snow off his cap and coat, stopped in front of the icons as if not seeing anyone, crossed himself three times, and bowed to the icons. Then, turning to the old master of the house and bowing first to him, then to all those at table, then to the women who stood by the oven, and muttering, "A merry holiday!" he began taking off his outer things without looking at the table.

"Why, you're all covered with hoar-frost, old fellow!" said the eldest brother, looking at Nikíta's snow-covered face, eyes, and beard.

Nikíta took off his coat, shook it again, hung it up beside the oven, and came up to the table. He too was offered vodka. He went through a moment of painful hesitation and nearly took up the glass and emptied the clear fragrant liquid down his throat, but he glanced at Vasíli Andréevich, remembered his oath and the boots that he had sold for drink, recalled the cooper, remembered his son for whom he had promised to buy a horse by spring, sighed, and declined it.

"I don't drink, thank you kindly," he said frowning, and sat down on a bench near the second window.

"How's that?" asked the eldest brother.

"I just don't drink," replied Nikíta without lifting his eyes but looking askance at his scanty beard and moustache and getting the icicles out of them.

"It's not good for him," said Vasíli Andréevich, munching a cracknel after emptying his glass.

"Well, then, have some tea," said the kindly old hostess. 'You must be chilled through, good soul. Why are you women dawdling so with the samovar?"

"It is ready," said one of the young women, and after flicking with her apron the top of the samovar which was now boiling over, she carried it with an effort to the table, raised it, and set it down with a thud.

Meanwhile Vasíli Andréevich was telling how he had lost his way, how they had come back twice to this same village, and how they had gone astray and had met some drunken peasants. Their hosts were surprised, explained where and why they had missed their way, said who the tipsy people they had met were, and told them how they ought to go.

"A little child could find the way to Molchánovka from here. All you have to do is to take the right turning from the high road. There's a bush you can see just there. But you didn't even get that far!" said the neighbour.

"You'd better stay the night. The women will make up beds for you," said the old woman persuasively.

"You could go on in the morning and it would be pleasanter," said the old man, confirming what his wife had said.

"I can't, friend. Business!" said Vasíli Andréevich. "Lose an hour and you can't catch it up in a year," he added, remembering the grove and the dealers who might snatch that deal from him. "We shall get there, shan't we?" he said, turning to Nikíta.

Nikíta did not answer for some time, apparently still intent on thawing out his beard and moustache.

"If only we don't go astray again," he replied gloomily.

He was gloomy because he passionately longed for some vodka, and the only thing that could assuage that longing was tea and he had not yet been offered any.

"But we have only to reach the turning and then we shan't go wrong. The road will be through the forest the whole way," said Vasíli Andréevich.

"It's just as you please, Vasíli Andréevich. If we're to go, let us go," said Nikíta, taking the glass of tea he was offered.

"We'll drink our tea and be off."

Nikíta said nothing but only shook his head, and carefully pouring some tea into his saucer began warming his hands, the fingers of which were always swollen with hard work, over the steam. Then, biting off a tiny bit of sugar, he bowed to his hosts, said, "Your health!" and drew in the steaming liquid.

"If somebody would see us as far as the turning," said Vasíli Andréevich.

"Well, we can do that," said the eldest son. "Petrúshka will harness and go that far with you."

"Well, then, put in the horse, lad, and I shall be thankful to you for it."

"Oh, what for, dear man?" said the kindly old woman. "We are heartily glad to do it."

"Petrúshka, go and put in the mare," said the eldest brother.

"All right," replied Petrúshka with a smile, and promptly snatching his cap down from a nail he ran away to harness.

While the horse was being harnessed the talk returned to the point at which it had stopped when Vasíli Andréevich drove up to the window. The old man had been complaining to his neighbour, the village elder, about his third son who had not sent him anything for the holiday though he had sent a French shawl to his wife.

"The young people are getting out of hand," said the old man.

"And how they do!" said the neighbour. "There's no managing them! They know too much. There's Demóchkin now, who broke his father's arm. It's all from being too clever, it seems."

Nikíta listened, watched their faces and evidently would have liked to share in the conversation, but he was too busy drinking his tea and only nodded his head approvingly. He emptied one tumbler after another and grew warmer and warmer and more and more comfortable. The talk continued on the same subject for a long time—the harmfulness of a household dividing up—and it was clearly not an abstract discussion but concerned the question of a separation in that house; a separation demanded by the second son who sat there morosely silent.

It was evidently a sore subject and absorbed them all, but out of propriety they did not discuss their private affairs before strangers. At last, however, the old man could not restrain himself and with tears in his eyes declared that he would not consent to a break-up of the family during his lifetime, that his house was prospering, thank God, but that if they separated they would all have to go begging.

"Just like the Matvéevs," said the neighbour. "They used to have a proper house, but now they've split up none of them has anything."

"And that is what you want to happen to us," said the old man, turning to his son.

The son made no reply and there was an awkward pause. The silence was broken by Petrúshka, who having harnessed the horse had returned to the hut a few minutes before this and had been listening all the time with a smile.

"There's a fable about that in Paulson," he said. "A father gave his sons a broom to break. At first they could not break it, but when they took it twig by twig they broke it easily. And it's the same here," and he gave a broad smile. "I'm ready!" he added.

"If you're ready, let's go," said Vasíli Andréevich. "And as to separating, don't you allow it, grandfather. You got everything together and you're the master. Go to the Justice of the Peace. He'll say how things should be done."

"He carries on so, carries on so," the old man continued in a whining tone. "There's no doing anything with him. It's as if the devil possessed him."

Nikíta having meanwhile finished his fifth tumbler of tea laid it on its side instead of turning it upside down, hoping to be offered a sixth glass. But there was no more water in the samovar, so the hostess did not fill it up for him. Besides, Vasíli Andréevich was putting his things on, so there was nothing for it but for Nikíta to get up too, put back into the sugar-basin the lump of sugar he had nibbled all round, wipe his perspiring face with the skirt of his sheepskin, and go to put on his overcoat.

Having put it on he sighed deeply, thanked his hosts, said good-bye, and went out of the warm bright room into the cold dark passage, through which the wind was howling and where snow was blowing through the cracks of the shaking door, and from there into the yard.

Petrúshka stood in his sheepskin in the middle of the yard by his horse, repeating some lines from Paulson's primer. He said with a smile:

> "Storms with mist the sky conceal,
>   Snowy circles wheeling wild.
> Now like savage beast 'twill howl,
>   And now 'tis wailing like a child."

Nikíta nodded approvingly as he arranged the reins. The old man, seeing Vasíli Andréevich off, brought a lantern into the passage to show him a light, but it was blown out at once. And even in the yard it was evident that the snow-storm had become more violent.

"Well, this is weather!" thought Vasíli Andréevich. "Perhaps we may not get there after all. But there is nothing to be done. Business! Besides, we have got ready, our host's horse has been harnessed, and we'll get there with God's help!"

Their aged host also thought they ought not to go, but he had already tried to persuade them to stay and had not been listened to.

"It's no use asking them again. Maybe my age makes me timid. They'll get there all right, and at least we shall get to bed in good time and without any fuss," he thought.

Petrúshka did not think of danger. He knew the road and the whole district so well, and the lines about "snowy circles wheeling wild" described what was happening outside so aptly that it cheered him up. Nikíta did not wish to go at all, but he had been accustomed not to have his own way and to serve others for so long that there was no one to hinder the departing travellers.

V

Vasíli Andréevich went over to his sledge, found it with difficulty in the darkness, climbed in, and took the reins.

"Go on in front!" he cried.

Petrúshka, kneeling in his low sledge, started his horse. Mukhórty, who had been neighing for some time past, now scenting a mare ahead of him started after her, and they drove out into the street. They drove again through the outskirts of the village and along the same road, past the yard where the frozen linen had hung (which, however, was no longer to be seen), past the same barn, which was now snowed up almost to the roof and from which the snow was still endlessly pouring, past the same dismally moaning, whistling, and swaying willows, and again entered into the sea of blustering snow raging from above and below. The wind was so strong that when it blew from the side and the travellers steered against it, it tilted the sledges and turned the horses to one side. Petrúshka drove his good

mare in front at a brisk trot and kept shouting lustily.
Mukhórty pressed after her.

After travelling so for about ten minutes, Petrúshka
turned round and shouted something. Neither Vasíli Andréevich nor Nikíta could hear anything because of the wind,
but they guessed that they had arrived at the turning. In
fact Petrúshka had turned to the right, and now the wind
that had blown from the side blew straight in their faces,
and through the snow they saw something dark on their
right. It was the bush at the turning.

"Well, now, God speed you!"

"Thank you, Petrúshka!"

"Storms with mist the sky conceal!" shouted Petrúshka
as he disappeared.

"There's a poet for you!" muttered Vasíli Andréevich,
pulling at the reins.

"Yes, a fine lad—a true peasant," said Nikíta.

They drove on.

Nikíta, wrapping his coat closely about him and pressing
his head down so close to his shoulders that his short beard
covered his throat, sat silently trying not to lose the warmth
he had obtained while drinking tea in the house. Before
him he saw the straight lines of the shafts which constantly
deceived him into thinking they were a well-travelled road
and the horse's swaying crupper with his knotted tail blown
to one side, and farther ahead the high shaft-bow and the
swaying head and neck of the horse with its waving mane.
Now and then he caught sight of a way-sign, so that he
knew they were still on a road and that there was nothing
for him to be concerned about.

Vasíli Andréevich drove on, leaving it to the horse to
keep to the road. But Mukhórty, though he had had a
breathing-space in the village, ran reluctantly, and seemed
now and then to get off the road, so that Vasíli Andréevich
had repeatedly to correct him.

"Here's a stake to the right, and another, and here's
a third," Vasíli Andréevich counted, "and here in front is
the forest," thought he, as he looked at something dark
in front of him. But what had seemed to him a forest was
only a bush. They passed the bush and drove on for another
hundred yards but there was no fourth way-mark nor
any forest.

"We must reach the forest soon," thought Vasíli André-evich, and animated by the vodka and the tea he did not stop but shook the reins, and the good obedient horse responded, now ambling, now slowly trotting in the direction in which he was sent, though he knew that he was not going the right way. Ten minutes went by, but there was still no forest.

"There now, we must be astray again," said Vasíli André-evich, pulling up.

Nikíta silently got out of the sledge and holding his coat, which the wind now wrapped closely about him and now almost tore off, started to feel about in the snow, going first to one side and then to the other. Three or four times he was completely lost to sight. At last he returned and took the reins from Vasíli Andréevich's hand.

"We must go to the right," he said sternly and peremptorily, as he turned the horse.

"Well, if it's to the right, go to the right," said Vasíli Andréevich, yielding up the reins to Nikíta and thrusting his freezing hands into his sleeves.

Nikíta did not reply.

"Now then, friend, stir yourself!" he shouted to the horse, but in spite of the shake of the reins Mukhórty moved only at a walk.

The snow in places was up to his knees, and the sledge moved by fits and starts with his every movement.

Nikíta took the whip that hung over the front of the sledge and struck him once. The good horse, unused to the whip, sprang forward and moved at a trot, but immediately fell back into an amble and then to a walk. So they went on for five minutes. It was dark and the snow swirled from above and rose from below, so that sometimes the shaft-bow could not be seen. At times the sledge seemed to stand still and the field to run backwards. Suddenly the horse stopped abruptly, evidently aware of something close in front of him. Nikíta sprang again lightly out, throwing down the reins, and went ahead to see what had brought him to a standstill, but hardly had he made a step in front of the horse before his feet slipped and he went rolling down an incline.

"Whoa, whoa, whoa!" he said to himself as he fell, and he tried to stop his fall but could not and only stopped when his feet plunged into a thick layer of snow that had drifted to the bottom of the hollow.

The fringe of a drift of snow that hung on the edge of the hollow, disturbed by Nikíta's fall, showered down on him and got inside his collar.

"What a thing to do!" said Nikíta reproachfully, addressing the drift and the hollow and shaking the snow from under his collar.

"Nikíta! Hey, Nikíta!" shouted Vasíli Andréevich from above.

But Nikíta did not reply. He was too occupied in shaking out the snow and searching for the whip he had dropped when rolling down the incline. Having found the whip he tried to climb straight up the bank where he had rolled down, but it was impossible to do so: he kept rolling down again, and so he had to go along at the foot of the hollow to find a way up. About seven yards farther on he managed with difficulty to crawl up the incline on all fours, then he followed the edge of the hollow back to the place where the horse should have been. He could not see either horse or sledge, but as he walked against the wind he heard Vasíli Andréevich's shouts and Mukhórty's neighing, calling him.

"I'm coming! I'm coming! What are you cackling for?" he muttered.

Only when he had come up to the sledge could he make out the horse and Vasíli Andréevich standing beside it and looking gigantic.

"Where the devil did you vanish to? We must go back, if only to Gríshkino," he began reproaching Nikíta.

"I'd be glad to get back, Vasíli Andréevich, but which way are we to go? There is such a ravine here that if we once get in it we shan't get out again. I got stuck so fast there myself that I could hardly get out."

"What shall we do, then? We can't stay here! We must go somewhere!" said Vasíli Andréevich.

Nikíta said nothing. He seated himself in the sledge with his back to the wind, took off his boots, shook out the snow that had got into them, and taking some straw from the bottom of the sledge, carefully plugged with it a hole in his left boot.

Vasíli Andréevich remained silent, as though now leaving

everything to Nikíta. Having put his boots on again, Nikíta drew his feet into the sledge, put on his mittens and took up the reins, and directed the horse along the side of the ravine. But they had not gone a hundred yards before the horse again stopped short. The ravine was in front of him again.

Nikíta again climbed out and again trudged about in the snow. He did this for a considerable time and at last appeared from the opposite side to that from which he had started.

"Vasíli Andréevich, are you alive?" he called out.

"Here!" replied Vasíli Andréevich. "Well, what now?"

"I can't make anything out. It's too dark. There's nothing but ravines. We must drive against the wind again."

They set off once more. Again Nikíta went stumbling through the snow, again he fell in, again climbed out and trudged about, and at last quite out of breath he sat down beside the sledge.

"Well, how now?" asked Vasíli Andréevich.

"Why, I am quite worn out and the horse won't go."

"Then what's to be done?"

"Why, wait a minute."

Nikíta went away again but soon returned.

"Follow me!" he said, going in front of the horse.

Vasíli Andréevich no longer gave orders but implicitly did what Nikíta told him.

"Here, follow me!" Nikíta shouted, stepping quickly to the right, and seizing the rein he led Mukhórty down towards a snow-drift.

At first the horse held back, then he jerked forward, hoping to leap the drift, but he had not the strength and sank into it up to his collar.

"Get out!" Nikíta called to Vasíli Andréevich who still sat in the sledge, and taking hold of one shaft he moved the sledge closer to the horse. "It's hard, brother!" he said to Mukhórty, "but it can't be helped. Make an effort! Now, now, just a little one!" he shouted.

The horse gave a tug, then another, but failed to clear himself and settled down again as if considering something.

"Now, brother, this won't do!" Nikíta admonished him. "Now once more!"

Again Nikíta tugged at the shaft on his side, and Vasíli Andréevich did the same on the other.

Mukhórty lifted his head and then gave a sudden jerk.

"That's it! That's it!" cried Nikíta. "Don't be afraid—you won't sink!"

One plunge, another, and a third, and at last Mukhórty was out of the snow-drift, and stood still, breathing heavily and shaking the snow off himself. Nikíta wished to lead him farther, but Vasíli Andréevich, in his two fur coats, was so out of breath that he could not walk farther and dropped into the sledge.

"Let me get my breath!" he said, unfastening the kerchief with which he had tied the collar of his fur coat at the village.

"It's all right here. You lie there," said Nikíta. "I will lead him along." And with Vasíli Andréevich in the sledge he led the horse by the bridle about ten paces down and then up a slight rise, and stopped.

The place where Nikíta had stopped was not completely in the hollow where the snow sweeping down from the hillocks might have buried them altogether, but still it was partly sheltered from the wind by the side of the ravine. There were moments when the wind seemed to abate a little, but that did not last long and as if to make up for that respite the storm swept down with ten-fold vigour and tore and whirled the more fiercely. Such a gust struck them at the moment when Vasíli Andréevich, having recovered his breath, got out of the sledge and went up to Nikíta to consult him as to what they should do. They both bent down involuntarily and waited till the violence of the squall should have passed. Mukhórty too laid back his ears and shook his head discontentedly. As soon as the violence of the blast had abated a little, Nikíta took off his mittens, stuck them into his belt, breathed on to his hands, and began to undo the straps of the shaft-bow.

"What's that you are doing there?" asked Vasíli Andréevich.

"Unharnessing. What else is there to do? I have no strength left," said Nikíta as though excusing himself.

"Can't we drive somewhere?"

"No, we can't. We shall only kill the horse. Why, the

poor beast is not himself now," said Nikíta, pointing to the horse, which was standing submissively waiting for what might come, with his steep wet sides heaving heavily. "We shall have to stay the night here," he said, as if preparing to spend the night at an inn, and he proceeded to unfasten the collar-straps. The buckles came undone.

"But shan't we be frozen?" remarked Vasíli Andréevich.

"Well, if we are we can't help it," said Nikíta.

VI

Although Vasíli Andréevich felt quite warm in his two fur coats, especially after struggling in the snow-drift, a cold shiver ran down his back on realizing that he must really spend the night where they were. To calm himself he sat down in the sledge and got out his cigarettes and matches.

Nikíta meanwhile unharnessed Mukhórty. He unstrapped the belly-band and the back-band, took away the reins, loosened the collar-strap, and removed the shaft-bow, talking to him all the time to encourage him.

"Now come out! Come out!" he said, leading him clear of the shafts. "Now we'll tie you up here and I'll put down some straw and take off your bridle. When you've had a bite you'll feel more cheerful."

But Mukhórty was restless and evidently not comforted by Nikíta's remarks. He stepped now on one foot and now on another, and pressed close against the sledge, turning his back to the wind and rubbing his head on Nikíta's sleeve. Then, as if not to pain Nikíta by refusing his offer of the straw he put before him, he hurriedly snatched a wisp out of the sledge but immediately decided that it was now no time to think of straw and threw it down, and the wind instantly scattered it, carried it away, and covered it with snow.

"Now we will set up a signal," said Nikíta, and turning the front of the sledge to the wind he tied the shafts together with a strap and set them up on end in front of the sledge. "There now, when the snow covers us up, good folk will see the shafts and dig us out," he said, slapping his mittens together and putting them on. "That's what the old folk taught us!"

Vasíli Andréevich meanwhile had unfastened his coat and, holding its skirt up for shelter, struck one sulphur match after another on the steel box. But his hands trembled, and one match after another either did not kindle or was blown out by the wind just as he was lifting it to the cigarette. At last a match did burn up, and its flame lit up for a moment the fur of his coat, his hand with the gold ring on the bent forefinger, and the snow-sprinkled oat-straw that stuck out from under the drugget. The cigarette lighted, he eagerly took a whiff or two, inhaled the smoke, let it out through his moustache, and would have inhaled again, but the wind tore off the burning tobacco and whirled it away as it had done the straw.

But even these few puffs had cheered him.

"If we must spend the night here, we must!" he said with decision. "Wait a bit, I'll arrange a flag as well," he added, picking up the kerchief which he had thrown down in the sledge after taking it from round his collar, and drawing off his gloves and standing up on the front of the sledge and stretching himself to reach the strap, he tied the handkerchief to it with a tight knot.

The kerchief immediately began to flutter wildly, now clinging round the shaft, now suddenly streaming out, stretching and flapping.

"Just see what a fine flag!" said Vasíli Andréevich, admiring his handiwork and letting himself down into the sledge. "We should be warmer together, but there's not room enough for two," he added.

"I'll find a place," said Nikíta. "But I must cover up the horse first—he sweated so, poor thing. Let go!" he added, drawing the drugget from under Vasíli Andréevich.

Having got the drugget he folded it in two, and after taking off the breechband and pad, covered Mukhórty with it.

"Anyhow it will be warmer, silly!" he said, putting back the breechband and the pad on the horse over the drugget. Then having finished that business he returned to the sledge and, addressing Vasíli Andréevich, said: "You won't need the sackcloth, will you? And let me have some straw."

And having taken these things from under Vasíli Andréevich, Nikíta went behind the sledge, dug out a hole for himself in the snow, put straw into it, wrapped his coat well round him, covered himself with the sackcloth, and pulling his cap well down seated himself on the straw he had spread, and leant against the wooden back of the sledge to shelter himself from the wind and the snow.

Vasíli Andréevich shook his head disapprovingly at what Nikíta was doing, as in general he disapproved of the peasants' stupidity and lack of education, and he began to settle himself down for the night.

He smoothed the remaining straw over the bottom of the sledge, putting more of it under his side, then he thrust his hands into his sleeves and settled down, sheltering his head in the corner of the sledge from the wind in front.

He did not wish to sleep. He lay and thought: thought ever of the one thing that constituted the sole aim, meaning, pleasure, and pride of his life— of how much money he had made and might still make, of how much other people he knew had made and possessed, and of how those others had made and were making it, and how he, like them, might still make much more. The purchase of the Goryách-kin grove was a matter of immense importance to him. By that one deal he hoped to make perhaps ten thousand rubles. He began mentally to reckon the value of the wood he had inspected in autumn, and on five acres of which he had counted all the trees.

"The oaks will go for sledge-runners. The undergrowth will take care of itself, and there'll still be some thirty sázheens of fire-wood left on each desyatín," said he to himself. "That means there will be at least two hundred and twenty-five rubles' worth left on each desyatín. Fifty-six desyatíns means fifty-six hundreds, and fifty-six hundreds, and fifty-six tens, and another fifty-six tens, and then fifty-six fives . . ." He saw that it came out to more than twelve thousand rubles, but could not reckon it up exactly without a counting-frame. "But I won't give ten thousand, anyhow. I'll give about eight thousand with a deduction on account of the glades. I'll grease the sur-veyor's palm—give him a hundred rubles, or a hundred and fifty, and he'll reckon that there are some five desyatíns of glade to be deducted. And he'll let it go for eight thousand. Three thousand cash down. That'll move him, no fear!" he thought, and he pressed his pocket-book with his forearm.

"God only knows how we missed the turning. The forest

ought to be there, and a watchman's hut, and dogs barking. But the damned things don't bark when they're wanted." He turned his collar down from his ear and listened, but as before only the whistling of the wind could be heard, the flapping and fluttering of the kerchief tied to the shafts, and the pelting of the snow against the woodwork of the sledge. He again covered up his ear.

"If I had known I would have stayed the night. Well, no matter, we'll get there to-morrow. It's only one day lost. And the others won't travel in such weather." Then he remembered that on the 9th he had to receive payment from the butcher for his oxen. "He meant to come himself, but he won't find me, and my wife won't know how to receive the money. She doesn't know the right way of doing things," he thought, recalling how at their party the day before she had not known how to treat the police-officer who was their guest. "Of course she's only a woman! Where could she have seen anything? In my father's time what was our house like? Just a rich peasant's house: just an oat-mill and an inn—that was the whole property. But what have I done in these fifteen years? A shop, two taverns, a flour mill, a grain-store, two farms leased out, and a house with an iron-roofed barn," he thought proudly. "Not as it was in father's time! Who is talked of in the whole district now? Brekhunóv! And why? Because I stick to business. I take trouble, not like others who lie abed or waste their time on foolishness while I don't sleep of nights. Blizzard or no blizzard I start out. So business gets done. They think money-making is a joke. No, take pains and rack your brains! You get overtaken out of doors at night, like this, or keep awake night after night till the thoughts whirling in your head make the pillow turn," he meditated with pride. "They think people get on through luck. After all, the Mirónovs are now millionaires. And why? Take pains and God gives. If only He grants me health!"

The thought that he might himself be a millionaire like Mironóv, who began with nothing, so excited Vasíli Andréevich that he felt the need of talking to somebody. But there was no one to talk to. . . . If only he could have reached Goryáchkin he would have talked to the landlord and shown him a thing or two.

"Just see how it blows! It will snow us up so deep that

we shan't be able to get out in the morning!" he thought, listening to a gust of wind that blew against the front of the sledge, bending it and lashing the snow against it. He raised himself and looked around. All he could see through the whirling darkness was Mukhórty's dark head, his back covered by the fluttering drugget, and his thick knotted tail; while all round, in front and behind, was the same fluctuating whity darkness, sometimes seeming to get a little lighter and sometimes growing denser still.

"A pity I listened to Nikíta," he thought. "We ought to have driven on. We should have come out somewhere, if only back to Gríshkino and stayed the night at Tarás's. As it is we must sit here all night. But what was I thinking about? Yes, that God gives to those who take trouble, but not to loafers, lie-abeds, or fools. I must have a smoke!"

He sat down again, got out his cigarette-case, and stretched himself flat on his stomach, screening the matches with the skirt of his coat. But the wind found its way in and put out match after match. At last he got one to burn and lit a cigarette. He was very glad that he had managed to do what he wanted, and though the wind smoked more of the cigarette than he did, he still got two or three puffs and felt more cheerful. He again leant back, wrapped himself up, started reflecting and remembering, and suddenly and quite unexpectedly lost consciousness and fell asleep.

Suddenly something seemed to give him a push and awoke him. Whether it was Mukhórty who had pulled some straw from under him, or whether something within him had startled him, at all events it woke him, and his heart began to beat faster and faster so that the sledge seemed to tremble under him. He opened his eyes. Everything around him was just as before. "It looks lighter," he thought. "I expect it won't be long before dawn." But he at once remembered that it was lighter because the moon had risen. He sat up and looked first at the horse. Mukhórty still stood with his back to the wind, shivering all over. One side of the drugget, which was completely covered with snow, had been blown back, the breeching had slipped down and the snow-covered head with its waving forelock and mane were now more visible. Vasíli Andréevich leant over the back of the sledge and looked behind. Nikíta still sat in the same position in which he had settled himself. The sacking with which he was covered, and his legs, were thickly covered with snow.

"If only that peasant doesn't freeze to death! His clothes are so wretched. I may be held responsible for him. What shiftless people they are—such a want of education," thought Vasíli Andréevich, and he felt like taking the drugget off the horse and putting it over Nikíta, but it would be very cold to get out and move about and, more-over, the horse might freeze to death. "Why did I bring him with me? It was all her stupidity!" he thought, recalling his unloved wife, and he rolled over into his old place at the front part of the sledge. "My uncle once spent a whole night like this," he reflected, "and was all right." But another case came at once to his mind. "But when they dug Sebastian out he was dead—stiff like a frozen carcass. If I'd only stopped the night in Gríshkino all this would not have happened!"

And wrapping his coat carefully round him so that none of the warmth of the fur should be wasted but should warm him all over, neck, knees, and feet, he shut his eyes and tried to sleep again. But try as he would he could not get drowsy, on the contrary he felt wide awake and animated. Again he began counting his gains and the debts due to him, again he began bragging to himself and feeling pleased with himself and his position, but all this was continually disturbed by a stealthily approaching fear and by the unpleasant regret that he had not remained in Gríshkino.

"How different it would be to be lying warm on a bench!" He turned over several times in his attempts to get into a more comfortable position more sheltered from the wind, he wrapped up his legs closer, shut his eyes, and lay still. But either his legs in their strong felt boots began to ache from being bent in one position or the wind blew in somewhere, and after lying still for a short time he again began to recall the disturbing fact that he might now have been lying quietly in the warm hut at Gríshkino. He again sat up, turned about, muffled himself up, and settled down once more.

Once he fancied that he heard a distant cock-crow. He felt glad, turned down his coat-collar and listened with strained attention, but in spite of all his efforts nothing could be heard but the wind whistling between the shafts, the flapping of the kerchief, and the snow pelting against the frame of the sledge.

Nikíta sat just as he had done all the time, not moving and not even answering Vasíli Andréevich who had addressed him a couple of times. "He doesn't care a bit—he's probably asleep!" thought Vasíli Andréevich with vexation, looking behind the sledge at Nikíta who was covered with a thick layer of snow.

Vasíli Andréevich got up and lay down again some twenty times. It seemed to him that the night would never end. "It must be getting near morning," he thought, getting up and looking around. Let's have a look at my watch. It will be cold to unbutton, but if I only know that it's getting near morning I shall at any rate feel more cheerful. We could begin harnessing."

In the depth of his heart Vasíli Andréevich knew that it could not yet be near morning, but he was growing more and more afraid and wished both to get to know and yet to deceive himself. He carefully undid the fastening of his sheepskin, pushed in his hand, and felt about for a long time before he got to his waistcoat. With great difficulty he managed to draw out his silver watch with its enamelled flower design and tried to make out the time. He could not see anything without a light. Again he went down on his knees and elbows as he had done when he lighted a cigarette, got out his matches, and proceeded to strike one. This time he went to work more carefully, and feeling with his fingers for a match with the largest head and the greatest amount of phosphorus, lit it at the first try. Bringing the face of the watch under the light he could hardly believe his eyes. . . . It was only ten minutes past twelve. Almost the whole night was still before him.

"Oh, how long the night is!" he thought, feeling a cold shudder run down his back, and having fastened his fur coats again and wrapped himself up, he snuggled into a corner of the sledge intending to wait patiently. Suddenly, above the monotonous roar of the wind, he clearly distinguished another new and living sound. It steadily strengthened and having become quite clear diminished just as gradually. Beyond all doubt it was a wolf, and he was so near that the movement of his jaws as he changed his cry was brought down the wind. Vasíli Andréevich turned back the collar of his coat and listened attentively. Mukhórty too strained to listen, moving his ears, and when the wolf had ceased its howling he shifted from foot to foot and gave a warning snort. After this Vasíli Andréevich could not fall asleep again or even calm himself. The more he tried to think of his accounts, his business, his reputation, his worth, and his wealth, the more and more was he mastered by fear; and regrets that he had not stayed the night at Gríshkino dominated and mingled in all his thoughts.

"Devil take the forest! Things were all right without it, thank God. Ah, if we had only put up for the night!" he said to himself. "They say it's drunkards that freeze," he thought, "and I have had some drink." And observing his sensations he noticed that he was beginning to shiver, without knowing whether it was from cold or from fear. He tried to wrap himself up and lie down as before but could no longer do so. He could not stay in one position. He wanted to get up, to do something to master the gathering fear that was rising in him and against which he felt himself powerless. He again got out his cigarettes and matches, but only three matches were left and they were bad ones. The phosphorus rubbed off them all without lighting.

"The devil take you! Damned thing! Curse you!" he muttered, not knowing whom or what he was cursing, and he flung away the crushed cigarette. He was about to throw away the matchbox too, but checked the movement of his hand and put the box in his pocket instead. He was seized with such unrest that he could no longer remain in one spot. He climbed out of the sledge and standing with his back to the wind began to shift his belt again, fastening it lower down in the waist and tightening it.

"What's the use of lying and waiting for death? Better mount the horse and get away!" The thought suddenly occurred to him. "The horse will move when he has someone on his back. As for him"—he thought of Nikíta—

"it's all the same to him whether he lives or dies. What is his life worth? He won't grudge his life, but I have something to live for, thank God."

He untied the horse, threw the reins over his neck and tried to mount, but his coats and boots were so heavy that he failed. Then he clambered up in the sledge and tried to mount from there, but the sledge tilted under his weight, and he failed again. At last he drew Mukhórty nearer to the sledge, cautiously balanced on one side of it, and managed to lie on his stomach across the horse's back. After lying like that for a while he shifted forward once and again, threw a leg over, and finally seated himself, supporting his feet on the loose breeching-straps. The shaking of the sledge awoke Nikíta. He raised himself, and it seemed to Vasíli Andréevich that he said something.

"Listen to such fools as you! Am I to die like this for nothing?" exclaimed Vasíli Andréevich. And tucking the loose skirts of his fur coat in under his knees, he turned the horse and rode away from the sledge in the direction in which he thought the forest and the forester's hut must be.

VII

From the time he had covered himself with the sackcloth and seated himself behind the sledge, Nikíta had not stirred. Like all those who live in touch with nature and have known want, he was patient and could wait for hours, even days, without growing restless or irritable. He heard his master call him but did not answer because he did not want to move or talk. Though he still felt some warmth from the tea he had drunk and from his energetic struggle when clambering about in the snowdrift, he knew that this warmth would not last long and that he had no strength left to warm himself again by moving about, for he felt as tired as a horse when it stops and refuses to go further in spite of the whip, and its master sees that it must be fed before it can work again. The foot in the boot with a hole in it had already grown numb, and he could no longer feel his big toe. Besides that, his whole body began to feel colder and colder.

The thought that he might, and very probably, would, die that night occurred to him but did not seem particularly unpleasant or dreadful. It did not seem particularly unpleasant, because his whole life had been not a continual holiday, but on the contrary an unceasing round of toil of which he was beginning to feel weary. And it did not seem particularly dreadful, because besides the masters he had served here, like Vasíli Andréevich, he always felt himself dependent on the Chief Master, who had sent him into this life, and he knew that when dying he would still be in that Master's power and would not be ill-used by Him. "It seems a pity to give up what one is used to and accustomed to. But there's nothing to be done; I shall get used to the new things."

"Sins?" he thought and remembered his drunkenness, the money that had gone on drink, how he had offended his wife, his cursing, his neglect of church and of the fasts, and all the things the priest blamed him for at confession. "Of course they are sins. But then, did I take them on of myself? That's evidently how God made me. Well, and the sins? Where am I to escape to?"

So at first he thought of what might happen to him that night and then did not return to such thoughts but gave himself up to whatever recollections came into his head of themselves. Now he thought of Martha's arrival, of the drunkenness among the workers and his own renunciation of drink, then of their present journey and of Tará's house and the talk about the breaking-up of the family, then of his own lad, and of Mukhórty now sheltered under the drugget, and then of his master who made the sledge creak as he tossed about in it. "I expect you're sorry yourself that you started out, dear man," he thought. "It would seem hard to leave a life such as his! It's not like the likes of us."

Then all these recollections began to grow confused and got mixed in his head, and he fell asleep.

But when Vasíli Andréevich, getting on the horse, jerked the sledge against the back of which Nikíta was leaning, and it shifted away and hit him in the back with one of its runners, he awoke and had to change his position whether he liked it or not. Straightening his legs with difficulty and shaking the snow off them he got up, and an agonizing cold immediately penetrated his whole body. On making out what was happening he called to Vasíli Andréevich to leave him the drugget which the horse no longer needed, so that he might wrap himself in it.

But Vasíli Andréevich did not stop, but disappeared amid the powdery snow.

Left alone, Nikíta considered for a moment what he should do. He felt that he had not the strength to go off in search of a house. It was no longer possible to sit down in his old place—it was by now all filled with snow. He felt that he could not get warmer in the sledge either, for there was nothing to cover himself with, and his coat and sheepskin no longer warmed him at all. He felt as cold as though he had nothing on but a shirt. He became frightened. "Lord, heavenly Father!" he muttered and was comforted by the consciousness that he was not alone but that there was One who heard him and would not abandon him. He gave a deep sigh, and keeping the sackcloth over his head he got inside the sledge and lay down in the place where his master had been.

But he could not get warm in the sledge either. At first he shivered all over, then the shivering ceased and little by little he began to lose consciousness. He did not know whether he was dying or falling asleep but felt equally prepared for the one as for the other.

VIII

Meanwhile Vasíli Andréevich, with his feet and the ends of the reins, urged the horse on in the direction in which for some reason he expected the forest and the forester's hut to be. The snow covered his eyes and the wind seemed intent on stopping him, but bending forward and constantly lapping his coat over and pushing it between himself and the cold harness pad which prevented him from sitting properly, he kept urging the horse on. Mukhórty ambled on obediently though with difficulty, in the direction in which he was driven.

Vasíli Andréevich rode for about five minutes straight

ahead, as he thought, seeing nothing but the horse's head and the white waste, and hearing only the whistle of the wind about the horse's ears and his coat collar.

Suddenly a dark patch showed up in front of him. His heart beat with joy, and he rode towards the object, already seeing in imagination the walls of village houses. But the dark patch was not stationary, it kept moving; and it was not a village but some tall stalks of wormwood sticking up through the snow on the boundary between two fields, and desperately tossing about under the pressure of the wind which beat it all to one side and whistled through it. The sight of that wormwood tormented by the pitiless wind made Vasíli Andréevich shudder, he knew not why, and he hurriedly began urging the horse on, not noticing that when riding up to the wormwood he had quite changed his direction and was now heading the opposite way, though still imagining that he was riding towards where the hut should be. But the horse kept making towards the right, and Vasíli Andréevich kept guiding it to the left.

Again something dark appeared in front of him. Again he rejoiced, convinced that now it was certainly a village. But once more it was the same boundary line overgrown with wormwood, once more the same wormwood desperately tossed by the wind and carrying unreasoning terror to his heart. But its being the same wormwood was not all, for beside it there was a horse's track partly snowed over. Vasíli Andréevich stopped, stooped down and looked carefully. It was a horse-track only partially covered with snow and could be none but his own horse's hoofprints. He had evidently gone round in a small circle. "I shall perish like that!" he thought, and not to give way to his terror he urged on the horse still more, peering into the snowy darkness in which he saw only flitting and fitful points of light. Once he thought he heard the barking of dogs or the howling of wolves, but the sounds were so faint and indistinct that he did not know whether he heard them or merely imagined them, and he stopped and began to listen intently.

Suddenly some terrible, deafening cry resounded near his ears, and everything shivered and shook under him.

He seized Mukhórty's neck, but that too was shaking all over and the terrible cry grew still more frightful. For some seconds Vasíli Andréevich could not collect himself or understand what was happening. It was only that Mukhórty, whether to encourage himself or to call for help, had neighed loudly and resonantly. "Ugh, you wretch! How you frightened me, damn you!" thought Vasíli Andréevich. But even when he understood the cause of his terror he could not shake it off.

"I must calm myself and think things over," he said to himself, but yet he could not stop and continued to urge the horse on, without noticing that he was now going with the wind instead of against it. His body, especially between his legs where it touched the pad of the harness and was not covered by his overcoats, was getting painfully cold, especially when the horse walked slowly. His legs and arms trembled and his breathing came fast. He saw himself perishing amid this dreadful snowy waste and could see no means of escape.

Suddenly the horse under him tumbled into something and, sinking into a snow-drift, began to plunge and fell on his side. Vasíli Andréevich jumped off, and in so doing dragged to one side the breechband on which his foot was resting, and twisted round the pad to which he held as he dismounted. As soon as he had jumped off, the horse struggled to his feet, plunged forward, gave one leap and another, neighed again, and dragging the drugget and the breechband after him, disappeared, leaving Vasíli Andréevich alone in the snowdrift.

The latter pressed on after the horse, but the snow lay so deep and his coats were so heavy that, sinking above his knees at each step, he stopped breathless after taking not more than twenty steps. "The copse, the oxen, the leasehold, the shop, the tavern, the house with the iron-roofed barn, and my heir," thought he. "How can I leave all that? What does this mean? It cannot be!" These thoughts flashed through his mind. Then he thought of the wormwood tossed by the wind, which he had twice ridden past, and he was seized with such terror that he did not believe in the reality of what was happening to him. "Can this be a dream?" he thought and tried to wake up but could not. It was real snow that lashed his face and covered him and chilled his right hand from which he had lost the glove, and this was a real desert in which he was now left alone like that wormwood, awaiting an inevitable, speedy, and meaningless death.

"Queen of Heaven! Holy Father Nicholas, teacher of temperance!" he thought, recalling the service of the day before and the holy icon with its black face and gilt frame, and the tapers which he sold to be set before that icon and which were almost immediately brought back to him scarcely burnt at all, and which he put away in the store-chest.[1] He began to pray to that same Nicholas the Wonder-Worker to save him, promising him a thanksgiving service and some candles. But he clearly and indubitably realized that the icon, its frame, the candles, the priest, and the thanksgiving service, though very important and necessary in church, could do nothing for him here and that there was and could be no connexion between those candles and services and his present disastrous plight. "I must not despair," he thought. "I must follow the horse's track before it is snowed under. He will lead me out, or I may even catch him. Only I must not hurry, or I shall stick fast and be more lost than ever."

But in spite of his resolution to go quietly, he rushed forward and even ran, continually falling, getting up and falling again. The horse's track was already hardly visible in places where the snow did not lie deep. "I am lost!" thought Vasíli Andréevich. "I shall lose the track and not catch the horse." But at that moment he saw something black. It was Mukhórty, and not only Mukhórty, but the sledge with the shafts and the kerchief. Mukhórty, with the sacking and the breechband twisted round to one side, was standing not in his former place but nearer to the shafts, shaking his head which the reins he was stepping on drew downwards. It turned out that Vasíli Andréevich had sunk in the same ravine Nikíta had previously fallen into, and that Mukhórty had been bringing

---

[1] As churchwarden Vasíli Andréevich sold the tapers the worshippers bought to set before the icons. These were collected at the end of the service and could afterwards be resold to the advantage of the church revenue.

him back to the sledge and he had got off his back no more than fifty paces from where the sledge was.

IX

Having stumbled back to the sledge Vasíli Andréevich caught hold of it and for a long time stood motionless, trying to calm himself and recover his breath. Nikíta was not in his former place, but something, already covered with snow, was lying in the sledge and Vasíli Andréevich concluded that this was Nikíta. His terror had now quite left him, and if he felt any fear it was lest the dreadful terror should return that he had experienced when on the horse and especially when he was left alone in the snow-drift. At any cost he had to avoid that terror, and to keep it away he must do something—occupy himself with something. And the first thing he did was to turn his back to the wind and open his fur coat. Then, as soon as he recovered his breath a little, he shook the snow out of his boots and out of his left-hand glove (the right-hand glove was hopelessly lost and by this time probably lying somewhere under a dozen inches of snow), then, as was his custom when going out of his shop to buy grain from the peasants, he pulled his girdle low down and tightened it and prepared for action. The first thing that occurred to him was to free Mukhórty's leg from the rein. Having done that, and tethered him to the iron cramp at the front of the sledge where he had been before, he was going round the horse's quarters to put the breechband and pad straight and cover him with the cloth, but at that moment he noticed that something was moving in the sledge and Nikíta's head rose up out of the snow that covered it. Nikíta, who was half frozen, rose with great difficulty and sat up, moving his hand before his nose in a strange manner just as if he were driving away flies. He waved his hand and said something and seemed to Vasíli Andréevich to be calling him. Vasíli Andréevich left the cloth unadjusted and went up to the sledge.

"What is it?" he asked. "What are you saying?"

"I'm dying, that's what," said Nikíta brokenly and with difficulty. "Give what is owing to me to my lad, or to my wife, no matter."

"Why, are you really frozen?" asked Vasíli Andréevich.

"I feel it's my death. Forgive me for Christ's sake . . ." said Nikíta in a tearful voice, continuing to wave his hand before his face as if driving away flies.

Vasíli Andréevich stood silent and motionless for half a minute. Then suddenly, with the same resolution with which he used to strike hands when making a good purchase, he took a step back and turning up his sleeves began raking the snow off Nikíta and out of the sledge. Having done this he hurriedly undid his girdle, opened out his fur coat, and having pushed Nikíta down, lay down on top of him, covering him not only with his fur coat but with the whole of his body, which glowed with warmth. After pushing the skirts of his coat between Nikíta and the sides of the sledge, and holding down its hem with his knees, Vasíli Andréevich lay like that face down, with his head pressed against the front of the sledge. Here he no longer heard the horse's movements or the whistling of the wind, but only Nikíta's breathing. At first and for a long time Nikíta lay motionless, then he sighed deeply and moved.

"There, and you say you are dying! Lie still and get warm, that's our way . . ." began Vasíli Andréevich.

But to his great surprise he could say no more, for tears came to his eyes and his lower jaw began to quiver rapidly. He stopped speaking and only gulped down the risings in his throat. "Seems I was badly frightened and have gone quite weak," he thought. But this weakness was not only not unpleasant but gave him a peculiar joy such as he had never felt before.

"That's our way!" he said to himself, experiencing a strange and solemn tenderness. He lay like that for a long time, wiping his eyes on the fur of his coat and tucking under his knee the right skirt, which the wind kept turning up.

But he longed so passionately to tell somebody of his joyful condition that he said: "Nikíta!"

"It's comfortable, warm!" came a voice from beneath.

"There, you see, friend, I was going to perish. And you would have been frozen, and I should have . . ."

But again his jaws began to quiver and his eyes to fill with tears, and he could say no more.

"Well, never mind," he thought. "I know about myself what I know."

He remained silent and lay like that for a long time. Nikíta kept him warm from below and his fur coats from above. Only his hands, with which he kept his coat-skirts down round Nikíta's sides, and his legs which the wind kept uncovering, began to freeze, especially his right hand which had no glove. But he did not think of his legs or of his hands but only of how to warm the peasant who was lying under him. He looked out several times at Mukhórty and could see that his back was uncovered and the drugget and breeching lying on the snow, and that he ought to get up and cover him, but he could not bring himself to leave Nikíta and disturb even for a moment the joyous condition he was in. He no longer felt any kind of terror.

"No fear, we shan't lose him this time!" he said to himself, referring to his getting the peasant warm with the same boastfulness with which he spoke of his buying and selling.

Vasíli Andréevich lay in that way for one hour, another, and a third, but he was unconscious of the passage of time. At first, impressions of the snow-storm, the sledge-shafts, and the horse with the shaft-bow shaking before his eyes kept passing through his mind, then he remembered Nikíta lying under him, then recollections of the festival, his wife, the police officer, and the box of candles began to mingle with these; then again Nikíta, this time lying under that box, then the peasants, customers and traders, and the white walls of his house with its iron roof with Nikíta lying underneath, presented themselves to his imagination. Afterwards all these impressions blended into one nothingness. As the colours of the rainbow unite into one white light, so all these different impressions mingled into one, and he fall asleep.

For a long time he slept without dreaming, but just before dawn the visions recommenced. It seemed to him that he was standing by the box of tapers and that Tíkhon's wife was asking for a five-kopek taper for the Church fête. He wished to take one out and give it to her, but his hands would not lift, being held tight in his pockets. He wanted to walk round the box but his feet would not move and his new clean goloshes had grown to the stone floor, and he could neither lift them nor get his feet out of the goloshes. Then the taper-box was no longer a box but a bed, and suddenly Vasíli Andréevich saw himself lying in his bed at home. He was lying in his bed and could not get up. Yet it was necessary for him to get up because Iván Matvéich, the police officer, would soon call for him and he had to go with him—either to bargain for the forest or to put Mukhórty's breeching straight.

He asked his wife: "Nikoláevna,[1] hasn't he come yet?" "No, he hasn't," she replied. He heard someone drive up to the front steps. "It must be him." "No, he's gone past." "Nikoláevna! I say, Nikoláevna, isn't he here yet?" "No." He was still lying on his bed and could not get up but was always waiting. And this waiting was uncanny and yet joyful. Then suddenly his joy was completed. He whom he was expecting came; not Iván Matvéich the police officer, but someone else—yet it was he whom he had been waiting for. He came and called him; and it was he who had called him and told him to lie down on Nikíta. And Vasíli Andréevich was glad that that one had come for him.

"I'm coming!" he cried joyfully, and that cry awoke him but woke him up not at all the same person he had been when he fell asleep. He tried to get up but could not, tried to move his arm and could not, to move his leg and also could not, to turn his head and could not. He was surprised but not at all disturbed by this. He understood that this was death, and was not at all disturbed by that either. He remembered that Nikíta was lying under him and that he had got warm and was alive, and it seemed to him that he was Nikíta and Nikíta was he, and that his life was not in himself but in Nikíta. He strained his ears and heard Nikíta breathing and even slightly snoring. "Nikíta is alive, so I too am alive!" he said to himself triumphantly.

And he remembered his money, his shop, his house, the buying and selling, and Mirónov's millions, and it was hard for him to understand why that man called

---

[1] A familiar peasant use of the patronymic in place of the Christian name.

Vasíli Brekhunóv had troubled himself with all those things with which he had been troubled.

"Well, it was because he did not know what the real thing was," he thought, concerning that Vasíli Brekhunóv. "He did not know, but now I know and know for sure. Now I know!" And again he heard the voice of the one who had called him before. "I'm coming! Coming!" he responded gladly, and his whole being was filled with joyful emotion. He felt himself free and that nothing could hold him back any longer.

After that Vasíli Andréevich neither saw, heard, nor felt anything more in this world.

All around the snow still eddied. The same whirlwinds of snow circled about, covering the dead Vasíli Andréevich's fur coat, the shivering Mukhórty, the sledge, now scarcely to be seen, and Nikíta lying at the bottom of it, kept warm beneath his dead master.

X

Nikíta awoke before daybreak. He was aroused by the cold that had begun to creep down his back. He had dreamt that he was coming from the mill with a load of his master's flour and when crossing the stream had missed the bridge and let the cart get stuck. And he saw that he had crawled under the cart and was trying to lift it by arching his back. But strange to say the cart did not move, it stuck to his back and he could neither lift it nor get out from under it. It was crushing the whole of his loins. And how cold it felt! Evidently he must crawl out. "Have done!" he exclaimed to whoever was pressing the cart down on him. "Take out the sacks!" But the cart pressed down colder and colder, and then he heard a strange knocking, awoke completely, and remembered everything. The cold cart was his dead and frozen master lying upon him. And the knock was produced by Mukhórty, who had twice struck the sledge with his hoof.

"Andréeich! Eh, Andréeich!"[1] Nikíta called cautiously,

---

[1] Again the characteristic peasant use of the patronymic without the Christian name preceding it.

beginning to realize the truth, and straightening his back. But Vasíli Andréevich did not answer and his stomach and legs were stiff and cold and heavy like iron weights.

"He must have died! May the Kingdom of Heaven be his!" thought Nikíta.

He turned his head, dug with his hand through the snow about him, and opened his eyes. It was daylight; the wind was whistling as before between the shafts, and the snow was falling in the same way, except that it was no longer driving against the frame of the sledge but silently covered both sledge and horse deeper and deeper, and neither the horse's movements nor his breathing were any longer to be heard.

"He must have frozen too," thought Nikíta of Mukhórty, and indeed those hoof knocks against the sledge, which had awakened Nikíta, were the last efforts the already numbed Mukhórty had made to keep on his feet before dying.

"O Lord God, it seems Thou art calling me too!" said Nikíta. "Thy Holy Will be done. But it's uncanny. . . . Still, a man can't die twice and must die once. If only it would come soon!"

And he again drew in his head, closed his eyes, and became unconscious, fully convinced that now he was certainly and finally dying.

It was not till noon that day that peasants dug Vasíli Andréevich and Nikíta out of the snow with their shovels, not more than seventy yards from the road and less than half a mile from the village.

The snow had hidden the sledge, but the shafts and the kerchief tied to them were still visible. Mukhórty, buried up to his belly in snow, with the breeching and drugget hanging down, stood all white, his dead head pressed against his frozen throat: icicles hung from his nostrils, his eyes were covered with hoar-frost as though filled with tears, and he had grown so thin in that one night that he was nothing but skin and bone.

Vasíli Andréevich was stiff as a frozen carcase, and when they rolled him off Nikíta his legs remained apart and his arms stretched out as they had been. His bulging hawk eyes were frozen, and his open mouth under his clipped moustache was full of snow. But Nikíta though chilled through was still alive. When he had been brought to, he felt sure that he was already dead and that what was taking place with him was no longer happening in this world but in the next. When he heard the peasants shouting as they dug him out and rolled the frozen body of Vasíli Andréevich from off him, he was at first surprised that in the other world peasants should be shouting in the same old way and had the same kind of body, and then when he realized that he was still in this world he was sorry rather than glad, especially when he found that the toes on both his feet were frozen.

Nikíta lay in hospital for two months. They cut off three of his toes, but the others recovered so that he was still able to work and went on living for another twenty years, first as a farm-labourer, then in his old age as a watchman. He died at home as he had wished, only this year, under the icons with a lighted taper in his hands. Before he died he asked his wife's forgiveness and forgave her for the cooper. He also took leave of his son and grandchildren and died sincerely glad that he was relieving his son and daughter-in-law of the burden of having to feed him and that he was now really passing from this life of which he was weary into that other life which every year and every hour grew clearer and more desirable to him. Whether he is better or worse off there where he awoke after his death, whether he was disappointed or found there what he expected, we shall all soon learn.

1895

PART FOUR
The Older Self

$\infty\infty\infty\infty\infty\infty\infty\infty\infty\infty\infty\infty\infty\infty\infty$

THE MEMOIRS
OF
A MADMAN

20th October 1883.

To-day I was taken to the Provincial Government Board to be certified. Opinions differed. They disputed and finally decided that I was not insane—but they arrived at this decision only because during the examination I did my utmost to restrain myself and not give myself away. I did not speak out, because I am afraid of the madhouse, where they would prevent me from doing my mad work. So they came to the conclusion that I am subject to hallucinations and something else but am of sound mind.

They came to that conclusion, but I myself know that I am mad. A doctor prescribed a treatment for me and assured me that if I would follow his instructions exactly all would be right—all that troubled me would pass. Ah, what would I not give that it might pass! The torment is too great. I will tell in due order how and from what this medical certification came about—how I went mad and how I betrayed myself.

Up to the age of thirty-five I lived just as everybody else does and nothing strange was noticed about me. Perhaps in early childhood, before the age of ten, there was at times something resembling my present condition, but only by fits, and not continually as now. Moreover, in childhood it used to affect me rather differently. For instance I remember that once when going to bed, at the age of five or six, my nurse Eupraxia, a tall thin woman who wore a brown dress and a cap and had flabby skin under her chin, was undressing me and lifting me up to put me into my cot. "I will get into bed by myself —myself!" I said, and stepped over the side of the cot.

"Well, lie down then. Lie down, Fédya! Look at Mítya. He's a good boy and is lying down already," she said, indicating my brother with a jerk of her head.

I jumped into the bed still holding her hand and then let it go, kicked about under my bedclothes, and wrapped myself up. And I had such a pleasant feeling. I grew quiet and thought: "I love Nurse; Nurse loves me and Mítya; and I love Mítya, and Mítya loves me and Nurse. Nurse loves Tarás, and I love Tarás, and Mítya loves him. And Tarás loves me and Nurse. And Mamma loves me and Nurse, and Nurse loves Mamma and me and Papa—and everybody loves everybody and everybody is happy!"

Then suddenly I heard the housekeeper run in and angrily shout something about a sugar-basin and Nurse answering indignantly that she had not taken it. And I felt pained, frightened, and bewildered, and horror, cold horror, seized me, and I hid my head under the bedclothes but felt no better in the dark.

I also remembered how a serf-boy was once beaten in my presence, how he screamed, and how dreadful Fóka's face looked when he was beating the boy. "Then you won't do it any more, you won't?" he kept repeating as he went on beating. The boy cried, "I won't!" but Fóka still repeated, "You won't!" and went on beating him.

And then it came upon me! I began to sob, and went on so that they could not quiet me for a long time. That sobbing and despair were the first attacks of my present madness.

I remember another attack when my aunt told us about Christ. She told the story and was about to go away, but we said: "Tell us some more about Jesus Christ!"

"No, I have no time now," she said.

"Yes, do tell us!"

Mítya also asked her to, and my aunt began to repeat what she had told us. She told us how they crucified, beat, and tortured him, and how he went on praying and did not reproach them.

"Why did they torment him, Auntie?"

"They were cruel people."

"But why, when he was good?"

"There, that's enough. It's past eight! Do you hear?"

"Why did they beat him? He forgave them, then why did they hit him? Did it hurt him, Auntie? Did it hurt?"

"That will do! I'm going to tea now."

"But perhaps it isn't true and they didn't beat him?"

"Now, now, that will do!"

"No, no! Don't go away!"

And again I was overcome by it. I sobbed and sobbed and began knocking my head against the wall.

That was how it befell me in my childhood. But by the time I was fourteen, and from the time the instincts of sex were aroused and I yielded to vice, all that passed away and I became a boy like other boys, like all the rest of us reared on rich, over-abundant food, effeminate, doing no physical work, surrounded by all possible temptations that inflamed sensuality, and among other equally spoilt children. Boys of my own age taught me vice, and I indulged in it. Later on that vice was replaced by another, and I began to know women. And so, seeking enjoyments and finding them, I lived till the age of thirty-five. I was perfectly well and there were no signs of my madness.

Those twenty years of my healthy life passed for me so that I can hardly remember anything of them and now recall them with difficulty and disgust. Like all mentally healthy boys of our circle I entered the high school and afterwards the university, where I completed the course of law-studies. Then I was in the Civil Service for a short time, and then I met my present wife, married, had a post in the country, and, as it is called, "brought up" our children, managed the estates, and was Justice of the Peace.

In the tenth year of my married life I again had an attack—the first since my childhood.

My wife and I had saved money—some inherited by her and some from the bonds I, like other landowners, received from the Government at the time of the emancipation of the serfs—and we decided to buy an estate. I was much interested, as was proper, in the growth of our property and in increasing it in the shrewdest way—better than other people. At that time I inquired everywhere where there were estates for sale, and read all the advertisements in the papers. I wanted to buy an estate so that the income from it, or the timber on it, should cover the whole purchase price and I should get it for nothing. I looked out for some fool who did not understand business and thought I had found such a man.

An estate with large forests was being sold in Pénza province. From all I could learn about it, it seemed that its owner was just such a fool as I wanted and the timber would cover the whole cost of the estate. So I got ready and set out.

We (my servant and I) travelled at first by rail and then by road in a post-chaise. The journey was a very pleasant one for me. My servant, a young good-natured fellow, was in just as good spirits as I. We saw new places and met new people and enjoyed ourselves. To reach our destination we had to go about a hundred and forty miles, and decided to go without stopping except to change horses. Night came and we still went on. We grew drowsy. I fell asleep but suddenly awoke feeling that there was something terrifying. As often happens, I woke up thoroughly alert and feeling as if sleep had gone for ever. "Why am I going? Where am I going to?" I suddenly asked myself. It was not that I did not like the idea of buying an estate cheaply, but it suddenly occurred to me that there was no need for me to travel all that distance, that I should die here in this strange place, and I was filled with dread. Sergéy, my servant, woke up, and I availed myself of the opportunity to talk to him. I spoke about that part of the country, he replied and joked, but I felt depressed. I spoke about our folks at home, and of the business before us, and I was surprised that his answers were so cheerful. Everything seemed pleasant and amusing to him while it nauseated me. But for all that while we were talking I felt easier. But besides everything seeming wearisome and uncanny, I began to feel tired and wished to stop. It seemed to me that I should feel better if I could enter a house, see people, drink tea, and above all have some sleep.

We were nearing the town of Arzamás.

"Shall we put up here and rest a bit?"

"Why not? Splendid!"

"Are we still far from the town?"

"About five miles from the last mile-post."

The driver was a respectable man, careful and taciturn, and he drove rather slowly and wearily.

We drove on. I remained silent and felt better because I was looking forward to a rest and hoped that the discomfort would pass. We went on and on in the darkness for a terribly long time as it seemed to me. We reached the town. Everybody was already in bed. Mean little houses showed up through the darkness, and the sound of our jingling bells and the clatter of the horses' feet re-echoed, especially near the houses, and all this was far from cheerful. We passed large white houses here and there. I was impatient to get to the post-station and a samovar, and to lie down and rest.

At last we came up to a small house with a post beside it. The house was white but appeared terribly melancholy to me, so much so that it seemed uncanny and I got out of the carriage slowly.

Sergéy briskly took out all that would be wanted, running clattering up the porch, and the sound of his steps depressed me. I entered a little corridor. A sleepy man with a spot on his cheek (which seemed to me terrifying) showed us into a room. It was gloomy. I entered, and the uncanny feeling grew worse.

"Haven't you got a bed-room? I should like to rest."

"Yes, we have. This is it."

It was a small square room, with whitewashed walls. I remember that it tormented me that it should be square. It had one window with a red curtain, a birchwood table, and a sofa with bent-wood arms. We went in Sergéy prepared the samovar and made tea, while I took a pillow and lay down on the sofa. I was not asleep and heard how Sergéy was busy with the tea and called me to have some. But I was afraid of getting up and arousing myself completely, and I thought how frightful it would be to sit up in that room. I did not get up but began to doze. I must have fallen asleep, for when I awoke I found myself alone in the room and it was dark. I was again as wide awake as I had been in the chaise. I felt that to sleep would be quite impossible. "Why have I come here? Where am I betaking myself? Why and whither am I escaping? I am running away from something dreadful and cannot escape it. I am always with myself, and it is I who am my tormentor. Here I am, the whole of me. Neither the Pénza nor any other property will add anything to or take anything from me. And it is myself I am weary of and find intolerable and a torment. I want to fall asleep and forget myself and cannot. I cannot get away from myself!"

I went out into the passage. Sergéy was sleeping on a narrow bench with one arm hanging down, but he was sleeping peacefully and the man with the spot was also asleep. I had gone out into the corridor thinking to escape from what tormented me. But *it* had come out with me and cast a gloom over everything. I felt just as filled with horror or even more so.

"But what folly this is!" I said to myself. "Why am I depressed? What am I afraid of?"

"Me!" answered the voice of Death, inaudibly. "I am here!"

A cold shudder ran down my back. Yes! Death! It will come—here it is—and it ought not to be. Had I been actually facing death I could not have suffered as much as I did then. Then I should have been frightened. But now I was not frightened. I saw and felt the approach of death, and at the same time I felt that such a thing ought not to exist.

My whole being was conscious of the necessity and the right to live, and yet I felt that Death was being accomplished. And this inward conflict was terrible. I tried to throw off the horror. I found a brass candlestick, the candle in which had a long wick, and lighted it. The red glow of the candle and its size—little less than the candlestick itself—told me the same thing. Everything told me the same: "There is nothing in life. Death is the only real thing, and death ought not to exist."

I tried to turn my thoughts to things that had interested me—to the estate I was to buy and to my wife—but found nothing to cheer me. It had all become nothing. Everything was hidden by the terrible consciousness that my life was ebbing away. I needed sleep. I lay down, but the next instant I jumped up again in terror. A fit of

the spleen seized me—spleen such as the feeling before
one is sick, but spiritual spleen. It was uncanny and
dreadful. It seems that death is terrible, but when
remembering and thinking of life it is one's dying life
that is terrible. Life and death somehow merged into
one another. Something was tearing my soul apart and
could not complete the severance. Again I went to look
at the sleepers, and again I tried to go to sleep. Always
the same horror: red, white, and square. Something tearing within that yet could not be torn apart. A painful,
painfully dry and spiteful feeling, no atom of kindliness,
but just a dull and steady spitefulness towards myself and
towards that which had made me.

What created me? God, they say. God . . . what about
prayer? I remembered. For some twenty years I had
not prayed, and I did not believe in anything, though as
a matter of propriety I fasted and went to communion
every year. Now I began to pray. "Lord have mercy!" "Our
Father." "Holy Virgin." I began to compose new prayers,
crossing myself, bowing down to the ground and glancing
around me for fear that I might be seen. This seemed to
divert me—the fear of being seen distracted my terror—
and I lay down. But I had only to lie down and close
my eyes for the same feeling of terror to knock and
rouse me. I could bear it no longer. I woke the hotel
servant and Sergéy, gave orders to harness, and we drove
off again.

The fresh air and the drive made me feel better. But
I realized that something new had come into my soul
and poisoned my former life.

By nightfall we reached our destination. The whole
day I had been fighting my depression and had mastered
it, but it had left its terrible dregs in my soul as if
some misfortune had befallen me, and I could forget it
only for a time. There it remained at the bottom of my
soul and had me in its power.

The old steward of the estate received me well,
though without any pleasure. He was sorry the estate
was to be sold.

The furniture in the little rooms was upholstered.
There was a new, brightly polished samovar, a large-sized

tea-service, and honey for tea. Everything was good. But I questioned him about the estate unwillingly, as if it were some old forgotten lesson. However, I fell asleep without any depression, and this I attributed to my having prayed again before going to bed.

After that I went on living as before, but the fear of that spleen always hung over me. I had to live without stopping to think, and above all to live in my accustomed surroundings. As a schoolboy repeats a lesson learnt by heart without thinking, so I had to live to avoid falling a prey to that awful depression I had first experienced at Arzamás.

I returned home safely. I did not buy the estate—I had not enough money—and I continued to live as before, only with this difference, that I began to pray and went to church. As before—it seemed to me, but I now remember that it was not as before—I lived on what had been previously begun. I continued to go along the rails already laid by my former strength, but I did not undertake anything new. And I took less part in those things I had previously begun. Everything seemed dull to me and I became pious. My wife noticed this and scolded and nagged me on account of it. But my spleen did not recur at home.

But once I had unexpectedly to go to Moscow. I got ready in the afternoon and left in the evening. It was in connexion with a lawsuit. I arrived in Moscow cheerful. On the way I had talked with a landowner from Khárkov about estate-management and banks, and about where to put up, and about the theatre. We both decided to stop at the Moscow Hotel on the Myasnítsky Street and to go to see *Faust* that same evening.

When we arrived I was shown into a small room. The oppressive air of the corridor filled my nostrils. A porter brought in my portmanteau and a chambermaid lighted a candle. The wick was lighted and then as usual the flame went down. In the next room someone coughed, probably an old man. The maid went out, but the porter remained and asked if he should uncord my luggage. The flame of the candle burnt up, revealing the blue wallpaper with yellow stripes on the partition, a shabby table, a small sofa, a looking-glass, a window, and the narrow dimensions of the room. And suddenly I was seized with an attack of the same horror as in Arzamás. "My God! How can I stay here all night?" I thought.

"Yes, uncord, my good fellow," I told the porter to keep him longer in the room. "I'll dress quickly and go to the theatre." When the porter had uncorded, I said: "Please go to Number Eight and tell the gentleman who came here with me that I shall be ready immediately and will come to him."

The porter went out and I dressed hurriedly, afraid to look at the walls. "What nonsense!" I thought. "What am I afraid of? Just like a child! I am not afraid of ghosts. Ghosts! Ghosts would be better than what I am afraid of. Why, what is it? Nothing. Myself. . . . Oh, nonsense!"

However, I put on a hard, cold, starched shirt, inserted the studs, donned my evening coat and new boots, and went to find the Khárkov landowner, who was ready. We started for the opera. He stopped on the way at a hairdresser's to have his hair curled, and I had mine cut by a French assistant and had a chat with him, and bought a pair of gloves. All was well, and I quite forgot my oblong room with its partition. In the theatre, too, it was pleasant. After the opera the Khárkov landowner suggested that we should have supper. That was contrary to my habit, but just then I again remembered the partition in my room and accepted his suggestion.

We got back after one. I had had two glasses of wine, to which I was unaccustomed, but in spite of that I felt cheerful. But no sooner had we entered the corridor in which the lamp was turned low, and I was surrounded by the hotel smell, than a shiver of horror ran down my spine. There was nothing to be done however, and I pressed my companion's hand and went into my room.

I spent a terrible night—worse than at Arzamás. Not till dawn, when the old man at the other side of the door was coughing again, did I fall asleep, and then not in the bed, in which I had lain down several times during the night, but on the sofa. I had suffered all night unbearably. Again my soul and body were being painfully torn asunder. "I am living, have lived, and ought to live, and suddenly—here is death to destroy everything. Then what is life for? To die? To kill myself at once? No, I am afraid. To wait for death till it comes? I fear that even more. Then I must live. But what for? In order to die?" And I could not escape from that circle. I took up a book, read, and forgot myself for a moment, but then again the same question and the same horror. I lay down in bed and closed my eyes. It was worse still!

God has so arranged it. Why? They say: "Don't ask, but pray!" Very well. I prayed, and prayed as I had done at Arzamás. Then and afterwards I prayed simply, like a child. But now my prayers had a meaning. "If Thou dost exist, reveal to me why and what I am!" I bowed down, repeated all the prayers I knew, composed my own, and added: "Then reveal it!" and became silent, awaiting an answer. But no answer came. It was just as if there were no one who could give an answer. And I remained alone with myself. And in place of Him who would not reply I answered my own questions. "Why? In order to live in a future life," I said to myself. "Then why this obscurity, this torment? I cannot believe in a future life. I believed when I did not ask with my whole soul, but now I cannot, I cannot. If Thou didst exist Thou wouldst speak to me and to all men. And if Thou dost not exist there is nothing but despair. And I do not want that. I do not want that!"

I became indignant. I asked Him to reveal the truth to me, to reveal Himself to me. I did all that everybody does, but He did not reveal Himself. "Ask and it shall be given you," I remembered, and I had asked and in that asking had found not consolation but relaxation. Perhaps I did not pray to Him but repudiated Him. "You recede a span and He recedes a mile," as the proverb has it. I did not believe in Him but I asked, and He did not reveal anything to me. I was balancing accounts with Him and blaming Him. I simply did not believe.

The next day I did all in my power to get through my ordinary affairs so as to avoid another night in the hotel. Although I did not finish everything, I left for home that evening. I did not feel any spleen. That night in Moscow still further changed my life which had begun to change from the time I was at Arzamás. I now attended still less to my affairs and became apathetic. I also grew weaker in health. My wife insisted that I should undergo a treatment. She said that my talks about faith and God arose from ill health. But I knew that my weakness and ill health were the effect of the unsolved question within me. I tried not to let that question dominate me, and tried to fill my life amid my customary surroundings. I went to church on Sundays and feast days, prepared to receive Communion, and even fasted, as I had begun to do since my visit to Pénza, and I prayed, though more as a custom. I did not expect any result from this but as it were kept the demand-note and presented it at the due date, though I knew it was impossible to secure payment. I only did it on the chance. I did not fill my life by estate-management—it repelled me by the struggle it involved (I had no energy)—but by reading magazines, newspapers, and novels, and playing cards for small stakes. I only showed energy by hunting, which I did from habit. I had been fond of hunting all my life.

One winter day a neighbouring huntsman came with his wolf-hounds. I rode out with him. When we reached the place we put on snow-shoes and went to the spot where the wolf might be found. The hunt was unsuccessful, the wolves broke through the ring of beaters. I became aware of this from a distance and went through the forest following the fresh tracks of a hare. These led me far into a glade, where I spied the hare, but it jumped out so that I lost it. I went back through the thick forest. The snow was deep, my snowshoes sank in, and branches of the trees entangled me. The trees grew ever more and more dense. I began to ask myself: "Where am I?" The snow had altered the look of everything.

Suddenly I realized that I had lost my way. I was far from the house, and from the hunters too, and could hear nothing. I was tired and bathed in perspiration. If I stopped I should freeze. If I went on my strength would fail me. I shouted. All was still. No one answered. I turned back, but it was the same again. I looked around—nothing but trees, impossible to tell which was east or west. Again I turned back. My legs were tired. I grew frightened, stopped, and was seized with the same horror as in Arzamás and Moscow, but a hundred times worse.

My heart palpitated; my arms and legs trembled. "Is this death? I won't have it! Why death? What is death?" Once again I wanted to question and reproach God, but here I suddenly felt that I dare not and must not do so, that it is impossible to present one's account to God, that He had said what is needful and I alone was to blame. I began to implore His forgiveness, and felt disgusted with myself.

The horror did not last long. I stood there for a while, came to myself, went on in one direction and soon emerged from the forest. I had not been far from its edge, and came out on to the road. My arms and legs still trembled and my heart was beating, but I felt happy. I found the hunting party and we returned home. I was cheerful, but I knew there was something joyful which I would make out when alone. And so it was. I remained by myself in my study and began to pray, asking forgiveness and remembering my sins. There seemed to me to be but few, but when I recalled them they became hateful to me.

After that I began to read the scriptures. The Old Testament I found unintelligible though enchanting, but the Gospels moved me profoundly. But most of all I read the Lives of the Saints, and that reading consoled me, presenting examples that it seemed more and more possible to follow. From that time forth farming and family matters occupied me less and less. They even repelled me. They all seemed to me wrong. What it was that was "right" I did not know, but what had formerly constituted my life had now ceased to do so. This became plain to me when I was going to buy another estate.

Not far from us an estate was for sale on very advantageous terms. I went to see it. Everything was excellent and advantageous; especially so was the fact that the peasants there had no land of their own except their kitchen-gardens. I saw that they would have to work on the landlord's land merely for permission to use his pastures. And so it was. I grasped all this and by old habit felt pleased about it. But on my way home I met an old woman who asked her way. I had a talk with her, during which she told me about her poverty. I got home, and when telling my wife of the advantages that estate

offered, I suddenly felt ashamed and disgusted. I told ₊
I could not buy it because the advantages we should ge₊
would be based on the peasants' destitution and sorrow. As
I said this I suddenly realized the truth of what I was
saying—the chief truth, that the peasants, like ourselves,
want to live, that they are human beings, our brothers, and
sons of the Father as the Gospels say. Suddenly something
that had long troubled me seemed to have broken away,
as though it had come to birth. My wife was vexed and
scolded me, but I felt glad.

That was the beginning of my madness. But my utter
madness began later—about a month after that.

It began by my going to church. I stood there through
the liturgy and prayed well, and listened and was touched.
Then suddenly they brought me some consecrated bread:
after that we went up to the Cross, and people began
pushing one another. Then at the exit there were beggars.
And it suddenly became clear to me that this ought not
to be, and not only ought not to be but in reality was
not. And if this was not, then neither was there either
death or fear, and there was no longer the former tearing
asunder within me and I no longer feared anything.

Then the light fully illumined me and I became what
I now am. If there is nothing of all that—then it certainly
does not exist within me. And there at the church door
I gave away to the beggars all I had with me—some
thirty-five rubles—and went home on foot talking with
the peasants.

1884

A CONFESSION

1

I was baptized and brought up in the Orthodox Christian faith. I was taught it in childhood and throughout my boyhood and youth. But when I abandoned the second course of the university at the age of eighteen I no longer believed any of the things I had been taught.

Judging by certain memories, I never seriously believed them but had merely relied on what I was taught and on what was professed by the grown-up people around me, and that reliance was very unstable.

I remember that before I was eleven a grammar school pupil, Vladímir Milyútin (long since dead), visited us one Sunday and announced as the latest novelty a discovery made at his school. This discovery was that there is no God and that all we are taught about Him is a mere invention (this was in 1838). I remember how interested my elder brothers were in this information. They called me to their council, and we all, I remember, became very animated, and accepted it as something very interesting and quite possible.

I remember also that when my elder brother, Dmítri, who was then at the university, suddenly, in the passionate way natural to him, devoted himself to religion and began to attend all the church services, to fast, and to lead a pure and moral life, we all—even our elders—unceasingly held him up to ridicule and for some unknown reason called him "Noah." I remember that Músin-Púshkin, the then Curator of Kazán University, when inviting us to a dance at his house, ironically persuaded my brother (who was declining the invitation) by the argument that even David danced before the Ark. I sympathized with these jokes made by my elders and drew from them the conclusion that, though it is necessary to learn the catechism and go to church, one must not take such things too seriously. I remember also that I read Voltaire when I was very young, and that his raillery, far from shocking me, amused me very much.

My lapse from faith occurred as is usual among people on our level of education. In most cases, I think, it happens thus: a man lives like everybody else, on the basis of principles not merely having nothing in common with religious doctrine but generally opposed to it; religious doctrine does not play a part in life, in intercourse with others it is never encountered, and in a man's own life he never has to reckon with it. Religious doctrine is professed far away from life, and independently of it. If it is encountered, it is only as an external phenomenon disconnected from life.

Then as now, it was and is quite impossible to judge by a man's life and conduct whether he is a believer or not. If there be a difference between a man who publicly professes Orthodoxy and one who denies it, the difference is not in favour of the former. Then as now, the public profession and confession of Orthodoxy was chiefly met with among people who were dull and cruel and who considered themselves very important. Ability, honesty, reliability, good-nature, and moral conduct were more often met with among unbelievers.

The schools teach the catechism and send the pupils to church, and government officials must produce certificates of having received communion. But a man of our circle who has finished his education and is not in the government service may even now (and formerly it was still easier for him to do so) live for ten or twenty years without once remembering that he is living among Christians and is himself reckoned a member of the Orthodox Christian Church.

So that, now as formerly, religious doctrine, accepted on trust and supported by external pressure, thaws away gradually under the influence of knowledge and experience of life which conflict with it, and a man very often lives on, imagining that he still holds intact the religious doctrine imparted to him in childhood whereas in fact not a trace of it remains.

S., a clever and truthful man, once told me the story of how he ceased to believe. On a hunting expedition, when he was already twenty-six, he once, at the place where they put up for the night, knelt down in the evening to pray—a habit retained from childhood. His elder brother, who was at the hunt with him, was lying on some hay and watching him. When S. had finished and was settling down for the night, his brother said to him: "So you still do that?"

They said nothing more to one another. But from that day S. ceased to say his prayers or go to church. And now he has not prayed, received communion, or gone to church for thirty years. And this not because he knows his brother's convictions and has joined him in them, nor because he has decided anything in his own soul, but simply because the word spoken by his brother was like the push of a finger on a wall that was ready to fall by its own weight. The word only showed that where he thought there was faith, in reality there had long been an empty space, and that therefore the utterance of words and the making of signs of the cross and genuflections while praying were quite senseless actions. Becoming conscious of their senselessness he could not continue them.

So it has been and is, I think, with the great majority of people. I am speaking of people of our educational level who are sincere with themselves, and not of those who make the profession of faith a means of attaining worldly aims. (Such people are the most fundamental infidels, for if faith is for them a means of attaining any worldly aims, then certainly it is not faith.) These people of our education are so placed that the light of knowledge and life has caused an artificial erection to melt away, and they have either already noticed this and swept its place clear, or they have not yet noticed it.

The religious doctrine taught me from childhood disappeared in me as in others, but with this difference, that as from the age of fifteen I began to read philosophical works, my rejection of the doctrine became a conscious one at a very early age. From the time I was sixteen I ceased to say my prayers and ceased to go to church or to fast of my own volition. I did not believe what had been taught me in childhood but I believed in something. What it was I believed in I could not at all have said. I believed in a God, or rather I did not deny God—but I could not have said what sort of God. Neither did I deny Christ and his teaching, but what his teaching consisted in I again could not have said.

Looking back on that time, I now see clearly that my faith—my own real faith, that which apart from my animal instincts gave impulse to my life—was a belief in perfecting myself. But in what this perfecting consisted and what its object was, I could not have said. I tried to perfect myself mentally—I studied everything I could, anything life threw in my way; I tried to perfect my will, I drew up rules I tried to follow; I perfected myself physically, cultivating my strength and agility by all sorts of exercises, and accustoming myself to endurance and patience by all kinds of privations. And all this I considered to be the pursuit of perfection. The beginning of it all was of course moral perfection, but that was soon replaced by perfection in general: by the desire to be better not in my own eyes or those of God but in the eyes of other people. And very soon this effort again changed into a desire to be stronger than others: to be more famous, more important, and richer than others.

II

Some day I will narrate the touching and instructive history of my life during those ten years of my youth. I think very many people have had a like experience. With all my soul I wished to be good, but I was young, passionate, and alone, completely alone when I sought goodness. Every time I tried to express my most sincere desire, which was to be morally good, I met with contempt and ridicule, but as soon as I yielded to low passions I was praised and encouraged.

Ambition, love of power, covetousness, lasciviousness, pride, anger, and revenge were all respected.

Yielding to those passions I became like the grown-up

folk and felt that they approved of me. The kind aunt with whom I lived, herself the purest of beings, always told me that there was nothing she so desired for me as that I should have relations with a married woman: *"Rien ne forme un jeune homme comme une liaison avec une femme comme il faut."*[1] Another happiness she desired for me was that I should become an aide-de-camp, and if possible aide-de-camp to the Emperor. But the greatest happiness of all would be that I should marry a very rich girl and so become possessed of as many serfs as possible.

I cannot think of those years without horror, loathing, and heartache. I killed men in war and challenged men to duels in order to kill them. I lost at cards, consumed the labour of the peasants, sentenced them to punishments, lived loosely, and deceived people. Lying, robbery, adultery of all kinds, drunkenness, violence, murder—there was no crime I did not commit, and in spite of that people praised my conduct and my contemporaries considered and consider me to be a comparatively moral man.

So I lived for ten years.

During that time I began to write from vanity, covetousness, and pride. In my writings I did the same as in my life. To get fame and money, for the sake of which I wrote, it was necessary to hide the good and to display the evil. And I did so. How often in my writings I contrived to hide under the guise of indifference, or even of banter, those strivings of mine towards goodness which gave meaning to my life! And I succeeded in this and was praised.

At twenty-six years of age[2] I returned to Petersburg after the war and met the writers. They received me as one of themselves and flattered me. And before I had time to look round I had adopted the views on life of the set of authors I had come among, and these views completely obliterated all my former strivings to improve —they furnished a theory which justified the dissoluteness of my life.

[1] "Nothing so forms a young man as an intimacy with a woman of good breeding."

[2] Tolstóy makes a slip here: he was twenty-seven.

The view of life of these people, my comrades in authorship, consisted in this: that life in general goes on developing, and in this development we—men of thought —have the chief part; and among men of thought it is we—artists and poets—who have the greatest influence. Our vocation is to teach mankind. And lest the simple question should suggest itself: What do I know, and what can I teach? it was explained in this theory that this need not be known, and that the artist and poet teach unconsciously. I was considered an admirable artist and poet, and therefore it was very natural for me to adopt this theory. I, artist and poet, wrote and taught without myself knowing what. For this I was paid money; I had excellent food, lodging, women, and society; and I had fame, which showed that what I taught was very good.

This faith in the meaning of poetry and in the development of life was a religion, and I was one of its priests. To be its priest was very pleasant and profitable. And I lived a considerable time in this faith without doubting its validity. But in the second and still more in the third year of this life I began to doubt the infallibility of this religion and to examine it. My first cause of doubt was that I began to notice that the priests of this religion were not all in accord among themselves. Some said: We are the best and most useful teachers, we teach what is needed, but the others teach wrongly. Others said: No! we are the real teachers, and you teach wrongly. And they disputed, quarrelled, abused, cheated, and tricked one another. There were also many among us who did not care who was right and who was wrong but were simply bent on attaining their covetous aims by means of this activity of ours. All this obliged me to doubt the validity of our creed.

Moreover, having begun to doubt the truth of the authors' creed itself, I also began to observe its priests more attentively, and I became convinced that almost all the priests of that religion, the writers, were immoral, and for the most part men of bad, worthless character, much inferior to those whom I had met in my former dissipated and military life; but they were self-confident and self-satisfied as only those can be who are quite holy or who do not know what holiness is. These people revolted me, I became revolting to myself, and I realized that that faith was a fraud.

But strange to say, though I understood this fraud and renounced it, yet I did not renounce the rank these people gave me: the rank of artist, poet, and teacher. I naïvely imagined that I was a poet and artist and could teach everybody without myself knowing what I was teaching, and I acted accordingly.

From my intimacy with these men I acquired a new vice: abnormally developed pride and an insane assurance that it was my vocation to teach men, without knowing what.

To remember that time, and my own state of mind and that of those men (though there are thousands like them to-day), is sad and terrible and ludicrous and arouses exactly the feeling one experiences in a lunatic asylum.

We were all then convinced that it was necessary for us to speak, write, and print as quickly as possible and as much as possible, and that it was all wanted for the good of humanity. And thousands of us, contradicting and abusing one another, all printed and wrote—teaching others. And without noticing that we knew nothing, and that to the simplest of life's questions: What is good and what is evil? we did not know how to reply, we all talked at the same time, not listening to one another, sometimes seconding and praising one another in order to be seconded and praised in turn, sometimes getting angry with one another—just as in a lunatic asylum.

Thousands of workmen laboured to the extreme limit of their strength day and night, setting the type and printing millions of words which the post carried all over Russia, and we still went on teaching and could in no way find time to teach enough and were always angry that sufficient attention was not paid us.

It was terribly strange, but is now quite comprehensible. Our real innermost concern was to get as much money and praise as possible. To gain that end we could do nothing except write books and papers. So we did that. But in order to do such useless work and to feel assured that we were very important people we required a theory justifying our activity. And so among us this theory was devised: "All that exists is reasonable. All that exists develops. And it all develops by means of Culture. And Culture is measured by the circulation of books and newspapers. And we are paid money and are respected because we write books and newspapers, and therefore we are the most useful and the best of men." This theory would have been all very well if we had been unanimous, but as every thought expressed by one of us was always met by a diametrically opposite thought expressed by another, we ought to have been driven to reflection. But we ignored this; people paid us money and those on our side praised us, so each of us considered himself justified.

It is now clear to me that this was just as in a lunatic asylum, but then I only dimly suspected this and, like all lunatics, simply called all men lunatics except myself.

III

So I lived, abandoning myself to this insanity for another six years, till my marriage. During that time I went abroad. Life in Europe and my acquaintance with leading and learned Europeans[1] confirmed me yet more in the faith of striving after perfection in which I believed, for I found the same faith among them. That faith took with me the common form it assumes with the majority of educated people of our day. It was expressed by the word "progress." It then appeared to me that this word meant something. I did not as yet understand that, being tormented (like every vital man) by the question how it is best for me to live, in my answer, "Live in conformity with progress," I was like a man in a boat who when carried along by wind and waves should reply to what for him is the chief and only question, "whither to steer," by saying, "We are being carried somewhere."

I did not then notice this. Only occasionally—not by reason but by instinct—I revolted against this superstition so common in our day, by which people hide from themselves their lack of understanding of life. . . . So, for instance, during my stay in Paris, the sight of an execution revealed to me the instability of my superstitious

[1] Russians generally make a distinction between Europeans and Russians.

belief in progress. When I saw the head part from the body and how they thumped separately into the box, I understood, not with my mind but with my whole being, that no theory of the reasonableness of our present progress could justify this deed; and that though everybody from the creation of the world had held it to be necessary, on whatever theory, I knew it to be unnecessary and bad; and therefore the arbiter of what is good and evil is not what people say and do, nor is it progress, but it is my heart and I. Another instance of a realization that the superstitious belief in progress is insufficient as a guide to life, was my brother's death. Wise, good, serious, he fell ill while still a young man, suffered for more than a year, and died painfully, not understanding why he had lived and still less why he had to die. No theories could give me, or him, any reply to these questions during his slow and painful dying. But these were only rare instances of doubt, and I actually continued to live professing a faith only in progress. "Everything evolves and I evolve with it: and why it is that I evolve with all things will be known some day." So I ought to have formulated my faith at that time.

On returning from abroad I settled in the country and chanced to occupy myself with peasant schools. This work was particularly to my taste because in it I had not to face the falsity which had become obvious to me and stared me in the face when I tried to teach people by literary means. Here also I acted in the name of progress, but I already regarded progress itself critically. I said to myself: "In some of its developments progress has pro- ceeded wrongly, and with primitive peasant children one must deal in a spirit of perfect freedom, letting them choose what path of progress they please." In reality I was ever revolving round one and the same insoluble problem, which was how to teach without knowing what to teach. In the higher spheres of literary activity I had realized that one could not teach without knowing what, for I saw that people all taught differently, and by quarrelling among themselves only succeeded in hiding their ignorance from one another. But here, with peasant children, I thought to evade this difficulty by letting them learn what they liked. It amuses me now when I remember how I shuffled in trying to satisfy my desire to teach, while in the depth of my soul I knew very well that I could not teach anything needful for I did not know what was needful. After spending a year at school work I went abroad a second time to discover how to teach others while myself knowing nothing.

And it seemed to me that I had learnt this abroad, and in the year of the peasants' emancipation (1861) I returned to Russia armed with all this wisdom, and having become an Arbiter[2] I began to teach, both the uneducated peasants in schools and the educated classes through a magazine I published. Things appeared to be going well, but I felt I was not quite sound mentally and that matters could not long continue in that way. And I should perhaps then have come to the state of despair I reached fifteen years later had there not been one side of life still unexplored by me which promised me happiness: that was marriage.

For a year I busied myself with arbitration work, the schools, and the magazine; and I became so worn out— as a result especially of my mental confusion—and so hard was my struggle as Arbiter, so obscure the results of my activity in the schools, so repulsive my shuffling in the magazine (which always amounted to one and the same thing: a desire to teach everybody and to hide the fact that I did not know what to teach) that I fell ill, mentally rather than physically, threw up everything, and went away to the Bashkírs in the steppes, to breathe fresh air, drink kumiss,[3] and live a merely animal life.

Returning from there I married. The new conditions of happy family life completely diverted me from all search for the general meaning of life. My whole life was centred at that time in my family, wife and children, and therefore in care to increase our means of livelihood. My striving after self-perfection, for which I had already substituted a striving for perfection in general—that is, progress—was now again replaced by the effort simply to secure the best possible conditions for myself and my family.

[2] To keep peace between peasants and owners.
[3] A fermented drink prepared from mare's milk

So another fifteen years passed.

In spite of the fact that I now regarded authorship as of no importance, I still continued to write during those fifteen years. I had already tasted the temptation of authorship—the temptation of immense monetary rewards and applause for my insignificant work—and I devoted myself to it as a means of improving my material position and of stifling in my soul all questions as to the meaning of my own life or life in general.

I wrote: teaching what was for me the only truth—namely, that one should live so as to have the best for oneself and one's family.

So I lived; but five years ago something very strange began to happen to me. At first I experienced moments of perplexity and arrest of life, as though I did not know what to do or how to live; and I felt lost and became dejected. But this passed, and I went on living as before. Then these moments of perplexity began to recur oftener and oftener, and always in the same form. They were always expressed by the questions: What is it for? What does it lead to?

At first it seemed to me that these were aimless and irrelevant questions. I thought that it was all well known, and that if I should ever wish to deal with the solution it would not cost me much effort: just at present I had no time for it, but when I wanted to I should be able to find the answer. The questions however began to repeat themselves frequently, and to demand replies more and more insistently; and like drops of ink always falling on one place they ran together into one black blot.

Then occurred what happens to everyone sickening with a mortal internal disease. At first trivial signs of indisposition appear to which the sick man pays no attention; then these signs reappear more and more often and merge into one uninterrupted period of suffering. The suffering increases and, before the sick man can look round, what he took for a mere indisposition has already become more important to him than anything else in the world—it is death!

That was what happened to me. I understood that it was no casual indisposition but something very important, and that if these questions constantly repeated themselves they would have to be answered. And I tried to answer them. The questions seemed such stupid, simple, childish ones; but as soon as I touched them and tried to solve them I at once became convinced, first, that they are not childish and stupid but the most important and profound of life's questions; and secondly that, try as I would, I could not solve them. Before occupying myself with my Samára estate, the education of my son, or the writing of a book, I had to know *why* I was doing it. As long as I did not know why, I could do nothing and could not live. Amid the thoughts of estate management which greatly occupied me at that time, the question would suddenly occur: "Well, you will have 6,000 *desyatínas*[4] of land in Samára Government and 300 horses, and what then?" . . . And I was quite disconcerted and did not know what to think. Or when considering plans for the education of my children, I would say to myself: "What for?" Or when considering how the peasants might become prosperous, I would suddenly say to myself: "But what does it matter to me?" Or when thinking of the fame my works would bring me, I would say to myself, "Very well; you will be more famous than Gógol or Púshkin or Shakespeare or Molière, or than all the writers in the world—and what of it?" And I could find no reply at all. The questions would not wait, they had to be answered at once, and if I did not answer them it was impossible to live. But there was no answer.

I felt that what I had been standing on had collapsed and that I had nothing left under my feet. What I had lived on no longer existed, and there was nothing left.

IV

My life came to a standstill. I could breathe, eat, drink, and sleep, and I could not help doing these things; but there was no life, for there were no wishes the fulfilment of which I could consider reasonable. If I desired anything, I knew in advance that whether I satisfied my desire or not, nothing would come of it. Had a fairy come and offered to fulfil my desires I should not have known what

---

[4] The *desyatína* is about 2¾ acres.

to ask. If in moments of intoxication I felt something which, though not a wish, was a habit left by former wishes, in sober moments I knew this to be a delusion and that there was really nothing to wish for. I could not even wish to know the truth, for I guessed of what it consisted. The truth was that life is meaningless. I had as it were lived, lived, and walked, walked, till I had come to a precipice and saw clearly that there was nothing ahead of me but destruction. It was impossible to stop, impossible to go back, and impossible to close my eyes or avoid seeing that there was nothing ahead but suffering and real death—complete annihilation.

It had come to this, that I, a healthy, fortunate man, felt I could no longer live: some irresistible power impelled me to rid myself one way or other of life. I cannot say I *wished* to kill myself. The power which drew me away from life was stronger, fuller, and more widespread than any mere wish. It was a force similar to the former striving to live, only in a contrary direction. All my strength drew me away from life. The thought of self-destruction now came to me as naturally as thoughts of how to improve my life had come formerly. And it was so seductive that I had to be cunning with myself lest I should carry it out too hastily. I did not wish to hurry, because I wanted to use all efforts to disentangle the matter. "If I cannot unravel matters, there will always be time." And it was then that I, a man favoured by fortune, hid a cord from myself lest I should hang myself from the crosspiece of the partition in my room where I undressed alone every evening, and I ceased to go out shooting with a gun lest I should be tempted by so easy a way of ending my life. I did not myself know what I wanted: I feared life, desired to escape from it, yet still hoped something of it.

And all this befell me at a time when all around me I had what is considered complete good fortune. I was not yet fifty; I had a good wife who loved me and whom I loved, good children, and a large estate which without much effort on my part improved and increased. I was respected by my relations and acquaintances more than at any previous time. I was praised by others and without much self-deception could consider that my name was famous. And far from being insane or mentally diseased, I enjoyed on the contrary a strength of mind and body such as I have seldom met with among men of my kind; physically I could keep up with the peasants at mowing, and mentally I could work for eight and ten hours at a stretch without experiencing any ill results from such exertion. And in this situation I came to this—that I could not live, and, fearing death, had to employ cunning with myself to avoid taking my own life.

My mental condition presented itself to me in this way: my life is a stupid and spiteful joke someone has played on me. Though I did not acknowledge a "someone" who created me, yet such a presentation—that someone had played an evil and stupid joke on me by placing me in the world—was the form of expression that suggested itself most naturally to me.

Involuntarily it appeared to me that there, somewhere, was someone who amused himself by watching how I lived for thirty or forty years: learning, developing, maturing in body and mind; and how, having with matured mental powers reached the summit of life from which it all lay before me, I stood on that summit—like an arch-fool—seeing clearly that there is nothing in life, and that there has been and will be nothing. And *he* was amused. . . .

But whether that "someone" laughing at me existed or not, I was none the better off. I could give no reasonable meaning to any single action or to my whole life. I was only surprised that I could have avoided understanding this from the very beginning—it has been so long known to all. To-day or to-morrow sickness and death will come (they had come already) to those I love or to me; nothing will remain but stench and worms. Sooner or later my affairs, whatever they may be, will be forgotten, and I shall not exist. Then why go on making any effort? . . . How can man fail to see this? And how go on living? That is what is surprising! One can only live while one is intoxicated with life; as soon as one is sober it is impossible not to see that it is all a mere fraud and a stupid fraud! That is precisely what it is: there is nothing either amusing or witty about it, it is simply cruel and stupid.

There is an Eastern fable, told long ago, of a traveller overtaken on a plain by an enraged beast. Escaping from the beast he gets into a dry well and sees at the bottom of the well a dragon that has opened its jaws to swallow him. And the unfortunate man, not daring to climb out lest he should be destroyed by the enraged beast, and not daring to leap to the bottom of the well lest he should be eaten by the dragon, seizes a twig growing in a crack in the well and clings to it. His hands are growing weaker and he feels he will soon have to resign himself to the destruction that awaits him above or below, but still he clings on. Then he sees that two mice, a black and a white one, go regularly round and round the stem of the twig to which he is clinging and gnaw at it. And soon the twig itself will snap and he will fall into the dragon's jaws. The traveller sees this and knows that he will inevitably perish; but while still hanging he looks around, sees some drops of honey on the leaves of the twig, reaches them with his tongue, and licks them. So I too clung to the twig of life, knowing that the dragon of death was inevitably awaiting me, ready to tear me to pieces, and I could not understand why I had fallen into such torment. I tried to lick the honey which formerly consoled me, but the honey no longer gave me pleasure, and the white and black mice of day and night gnawed at the branch by which I hung. I saw the dragon clearly and the honey no longer tasted sweet. I only saw the unescapable dragon and the mice, and I could not tear my gaze from them. And this is not a fable but the real unanswerable truth intelligible to all.

The deception of the joys of life which formerly allayed my terror of the dragon now no longer deceived me. No matter how often I may be told, "You cannot understand the meaning of life, so do not think about it, but live," I can no longer do it: I have already done it too long. I cannot now help seeing day and night going round and bringing me to death. That is all I see, for that alone is true. All else is false.

The two drops of honey which diverted my eyes from the cruel truth longer than the rest, my love of family and of writing—art as I called it—were no longer sweet to me.

"Family" . . . said I to myself. But my family—
wife and children—are also human. They are placed just
as I am: they must either live in a lie or see the terrible
truth. Why should they live? Why should I love them,
guard them, bring them up, or watch them? That they
may come to the despair that I feel, or else be stupid?
Loving them, I cannot hide the truth from them: each
step in knowledge leads them to the truth. And the truth
is death.

"Art, poetry?" . . . Under the influence of success
and the praise of men, I had long assured myself that
this was a thing one could do though death was drawing
near—death which destroys all things, including my work
and its remembrance; but soon I saw that that too was a
fraud. It was plain to me that art is an adornment of
life, an allurement to life. But life had lost its attraction
for me, so how could I attract others? As long as I was
not living my own life but was borne on the waves of
some other life—as long as I believed that life had a
meaning, though one I could not express—the reflection
of life in poetry and art of all kinds afforded me pleasure:
it was pleasant to look at life in the mirror of art. But
when I began to seek the meaning of life and felt the
necessity of living my own life, that mirror became for
me unnecessary, superfluous, ridiculous, or painful. I could
no longer soothe myself with what I now saw in the
mirror—namely, that my position was stupid and desperate.
It was all very well to enjoy the sight when in the depth
of my soul I believed that my life had a meaning. Then
the play of lights—comic, tragic, touching, beautiful, and
terrible—in life amused me. But when I knew life to
be meaningless and terrible, the play in the mirror could
no longer amuse me. No sweetness of honey could be
sweet to me when I saw the dragon and saw the mice
gnawing away my support.

Nor was that all. Had I simply understood that life
had no meaning I could have borne it quietly, knowing
that that was my lot. But I could not satisfy myself with
that. Had I been like a man living in a wood from
which he knows there is no exit, I could have lived; but
I was like one lost in a wood who, horrified at having
lost his way, rushes about wishing to find the road. He

knows that each step he takes confuses him more and more, but still he cannot help rushing about.

It was indeed terrible. And to rid myself of the terror I wished to kill myself. I experienced terror at what awaited me—knew that that terror was even worse than the position I was in, but still I could not patiently await the end. However convincing the argument might be that in any case some vessel in my heart would give way, or something would burst, and all would be over, I could not patiently await that end. The horror of darkness was too great, and I wished to free myself from it as quickly as possible by noose or bullet. That was the feeling which drew me most strongly towards suicide.

V

"But perhaps I have overlooked something, or misunderstood something?" said I to myself several times. "It cannot be that this condition of despair is natural to man!" And I sought for an explanation of these problems in all the branches of knowledge acquired by men. I sought painfully and long, not from idle curiosity or listlessly, but painfully and persistently day and night—sought as a perishing man seeks for safety—and I found nothing.

I sought in all the sciences but, far from finding what I wanted, became convinced that all who like myself had sought in knowledge for the meaning of life had found nothing. And not only had they found nothing, but they had plainly acknowledged that the very thing which made me despair—namely the senselessness of life —is the one indubitable thing man can know.

I sought everywhere; and thanks to a life spent in learning, and thanks also to my relations with the scholarly world, I had access to scientists and scholars in all branches of knowledge, and they readily showed me all their knowledge, not only in books but also in conversation, so that I had at my disposal all that science has to say on this question of life.

I was long unable to believe that it gives no other reply to life's questions than that which it actually does give. It long seemed to me, when I saw the important and serious air with which science announces its conclusions which have nothing in common with the real questions of human life, that there was something I had not understood. I long was timid before science, and it seemed to me that the lack of conformity between the answers and my questions arose not by the fault of science but from my ignorance, but the matter was for me not a game or an amusement but one of life and death, and I was involuntarily brought to the conviction that my questions were the only legitimate ones, forming the basis of all knowledge, and that I with my questions was not to blame, but science, if it pretends to reply to those questions.

My question—that which at the age of fifty brought me to the verge of suicide—was the simplest of questions, lying in the soul of every man from the foolish child to the wisest elder: it was a question without an answer to which one cannot live, as I had found by experience. It was: "What will come of what I am doing to-day or shall do to-morrow? What will come of my whole life?"

Differently expressed, the question is: "Why should I live, why wish for anything, or do anything?" It can also be expressed thus: "Is there any meaning in my life that the inevitable death awaiting me does not destroy?"

To this one question, variously expressed, I sought an answer in science. And I found that in relation to that question all human knowledge is divided as it were into two opposite hemispheres at the ends of which are two poles: the one a negative and the other a positive; but that neither at the one nor the other pole is there an answer to life's questions.

The one series of sciences seems not to recognize the question but replies clearly and exactly to its own independent questions: that is the series of experimental sciences, and at the extreme end of it stands mathematics. The other series of sciences recognizes the question but does not answer it: that is the series of abstract sciences, and at the extreme end of it stands metaphysics.

From early youth I had been interested in the abstract sciences, but later the mathematical and natural sciences attracted me, and until I put my question definitely to myself, until that question had itself grown up within me urgently demanding a decision, I contented myself with those counterfeit answers which science gives.

Now in the experimental sphere I said to myself: "Everything develops and differentiates itself, moving towards complexity and perfection, and there are laws directing this movement. You are a part of the whole. Having learnt as far as possible the whole, and having learnt the law of evolution, you will understand also your place in the whole and will know yourself." Ashamed as I am to confess it, there was a time when I seemed satisfied with that. It was just the time when I was myself becoming more complex and was developing. My muscles were growing and strengthening, my memory was being enriched, my capacity to think and understand was increasing, I was growing and developing; and feeling this growth in myself it was natural for me to think that such was the universal law in which I should find the solution of the question of my life. But a time came when the growth within me ceased. I felt that I was not developing, but fading, my muscles were weakening, my teeth falling out, and I saw that the law not only did not explain anything to me, but that there never had been or could be such a law, and that I had taken for a law what I had found in myself at a certain period of my life. I regarded the definition of that law more strictly, and it became clear to me that there could be no law of endless development; it became clear that to say, "in infinite space and time everything develops, becomes more perfect and more complex, is differentiated," is to say nothing at all. These are all words with no meaning, for in the infinite there is neither complex nor simple, neither forward nor backward, nor better or worse.

Above all, my personal question, "What am I with my desires?" remained quite unanswered. And I understood that those sciences are very interesting and attractive, but that they are exact and clear in inverse proportion to their applicability to the question of life: the less their applicability to the question of life, the more exact and clear they are, while the more they try to reply to the question of life, the more obscure and unattractive they become. If one turns to the division of sciences which attempt to reply to the questions of life—to physiology, psychology, biology, sociology—one encounters an appalling poverty of thought, the greatest obscurity, a quite unjustifiable pretension to solve irrelevant questions, and a continual contradiction of each authority by others and even by himself. If one turns to the branches of science which are not concerned with the solution of the questions of life, but which reply to their own special scientific questions, one is enraptured by the power of man's mind, but one knows in advance that they give no reply to life's questions. Those sciences simply ignore life's questions. They say: "To the question of what you are and why you live we have no reply, and are not occupied with that; but if you want to know the laws of light, of chemical combinations, the laws of development of organisms, if you want to know the laws of bodies and their form, and the relation of numbers and quantities, if you want to know the laws of your mind, to all that we have clear, exact, and unquestionable replies."

In general, the relation of the experimental sciences to life's question may be expressed thus: *Question*: "Why do I live?" *Answer*: "In infinite space, in infinite time, infinitely small particles change their forms in infinite complexity, and when you have understood the laws of those mutations of form you will understand why you live on the earth."

Then in the sphere of abstract science I said to myself: "All humanity lives and develops on the basis of spiritual principles and ideals which guide it. Those ideals are expressed in religions, in sciences, in arts, in forms of government. Those ideals become more and more elevated, and humanity advances to its highest welfare. I am part of humanity, and therefore my vocation is to forward the recognition and the realization of the ideals of humanity." And at the time of my weak-mindedness I was satisfied with that; but as soon as the question of life presented itself clearly to me, those theories immediately crumbled away. Not to speak of the unscrupulous obscurity with which those sciences announce conclusions formed on the study of a small part of mankind as general conclusions, not to speak of the mutual contradictions of different adherents of this view as to what are the ideals of humanity, the strangeness, not to say stupidity, of the theory consists in the fact that in order to reply to the question facing each man: "What am I?" or "Why do I live?" or "What must I do?" one has first to decide the question: "What is the life of the whole?" (which is to him unknown and of which he is acquainted with one tiny part in one minute period of time). To understand what he is, man must first understand all this mysterious humanity, consisting of people such as himself who do not understand one another.

I have to confess that there was a time when I believed this. It was the time when I had my own favourite ideals justifying my own caprices, and I was trying to devise a theory which would allow one to consider my caprices as the law of humanity. But as soon as the question of life arose in my soul in full clearness that reply at once flew to dust. And I understood that as in the experimental sciences there are real sciences, and semi-sciences which try to give answers to questions beyond their competence, so in this sphere there is a whole series of most diffused sciences which try to reply to irrelevant questions. Semi-sciences of that kind, the juridical and the social-historical, endeavour to solve the questions of a man's life by pretending to decide, each in its own way, the question of the life of all humanity.

But as in the sphere of man's experimental knowledge one who sincerely inquires how he is to live cannot be satisfied with the reply: "Study in endless space the mutations, infinite in time and in complexity, of innumerable atoms, and then you will understand your life," so also a sincere man cannot be satisfied with the reply: "Study the whole life of humanity of which we cannot know either the beginning or the end, of which we do not even know a small part, and then you will understand your own life." And like the experimental semi-sciences, so these other semi-sciences are the more filled with obscurities, inexactitudes, stupidities, and contradictions, the further they diverge from the real problems. The problem of experimental science is the sequence of cause and

effect in material phenomena. It is only necessary for experimental science to introduce the question of a final
cause for it to become nonsensical. The problem of abstract
science is the recognition of the primordial essence of
life. It is only necessary to introduce the investigation of
consequential phenomena (such as social and historical
phenomena) and it also becomes nonsensical.

Experimental science only then gives positive knowledge and displays the greatness of the human mind when
it does not introduce into its investigations the question
of an ultimate cause. And, on the contrary, abstract science
is only then science and displays the greatness of the
human mind when it puts quite aside questions relating to
the consequential causes of phenomena and regards man
solely in relation to an ultimate cause. Such in this realm
of science—forming the pole of the sphere—is metaphysics
or philosophy. That science states the question clearly:
"What am I, and what is the universe? And why do
I exist, and why does the universe exist?" And since
it has existed, it has always replied in the same way.
Whether the philosopher calls the essence of life existing
within me, and in all that exists, by the name of "ideal,"
or "substance," or "spirit," or "will," he says one and
the same thing: that this essence exists and that I am of
that same essence; but why it is he does not know, and
does not say, if he is an exact thinker. I ask: "Why
should this essence exist? What results from the fact
that it is and will be?" . . . And philosophy not merely
does not reply but is itself only asking that question. And
if it is real philosophy all its labour lies merely in trying
to put that question clearly. And if it keeps firmly to
its task it cannot reply to the question otherwise than
thus: "What am I, and what is the universe?" "All and
nothing"; and to the question "Why?" by "I do not know."

So that however I may turn these replies of philosophy
I can never obtain anything like an answer—and not
because, as in the clear experimental sphere, the reply
does not relate to my question, but because here, though
all the mental work is directed just to my question,
there is no answer, but instead of an answer one gets
the same question, only in a complex form.

VI

In my search for answers to life's questions I experienced just what is felt by a man lost in a forest.

He reaches a glade, climbs a tree, and clearly sees the limitless distance, but sees that his home is not and cannot be there; then he goes into the dark wood and sees the darkness, but there also his home is not.

So I wandered in that wood of human knowledge, amid the gleams of mathematical and experimental science which showed me clear horizons but in a direction where there could be no home, and also amid the darkness of the abstract sciences where I was immersed in deeper gloom the further I went, and where I finally convinced myself that there was, and could be, no exit.

Yielding myself to the bright side of knowledge, I understood that I was only diverting my gaze from the question. However alluringly clear those horizons which opened out before me might be, however alluring it might be to immerse oneself in the limitless expanse of those sciences, I already understood that the clearer they were the less they met my need and the less they replied to my question.

"I know," said I to myself, "what science so persistently tries to discover, and along that road there is no reply to the question as to the meaning of my life." In the abstract sphere I understood that notwithstanding the fact, or just because of the fact, that the direct aim of science is to reply to my question, there is no reply but that which I have myself already given: "What is the meaning of my life?" "There is none." Or: "What will come of my life?" "Nothing." Or: "Why does everything exist that exists, and why do I exist?" "Because it exists."

Inquiring for one region of human knowledge, I received an innumerable quantity of exact replies concerning matters about which I had not asked: about the chemical constituents of the stars, about the movement of the sun towards the constellation Hercules, about the origin of species and of man, about the forms of infinitely minute imponderable particles of ether; but in this sphere of knowledge the only answer to my question, "What is the meaning of my life?" was: "You are what you call your 'life'; you are a transitory, casual cohesion of particles. The mutual interactions and changes of these particles produce in you what you call your 'life.' That cohesion will last some time; afterwards the interaction of these particles will cease and what you call 'life' will cease, and so will all your questions. You are an accidentally united little lump of something. That little lump ferments. The little lump calls that fermenting its 'life.' The lump will disintegrate and there will be an end of the fermenting and of all the questions." So answers the clear side of science and cannot answer otherwise if it strictly follows its principles.

From such a reply one sees that the reply does not answer the question. I want to know the meaning of my life, but that it is a fragment of the infinite, far from giving it a meaning, destroys its every possible meaning. The obscure compromises which that side of experimental exact science makes with abstract science when it says that the meaning of life consists in development and in co-operation with development, owing to their inexactness and obscurity, cannot be considered as replies.

The other side of science—the abstract side—when it holds strictly to its principles, replying directly to the question, always replies, and in all ages has replied, in one and the same way: "The world is something infinite and incomprehensible. Human life is an incomprehensible part of that incomprehensible 'all.'" Again I exclude all those compromises between abstract and experimental sciences which supply the whole ballast of the semi-sciences called juridical, political, and historical. In those semi-sciences the conception of development and progress is again wrongly introduced, only with this difference, that there it was the development of everything while here it is the development of the life of mankind. The error is there as before: development and progress in infinity can have no aim or direction, and, as far as my question is concerned, no answer is given.

In truly abstract science, namely in genuine philosophy —not in that which Schopenhauer calls "professorial philosophy" which serves only to classify all existing phenomena in new philosophic categories and to call them by new names—where the philosopher does not lose sight of the essential question, the reply is always one and the same—the reply given by Socrates, Schopenhauer, Solomon, and Buddha.

"We approach truth only inasmuch as we depart from life," said Socrates when preparing for death. "For what do we, who love truth, strive after in life? To free ourselves from the body, and from all the evil that is caused by the life of the body! If so, then how can we fail to be glad when death comes to us?

"The wise man seeks death all his life and therefore death is not terrible to him."

And Schopenhauer says:

"Having recognized the inmost essence of the world as *will*, and all its phenomena—from the unconscious working of the obscure forces of Nature up to the completely conscious action of man—as only the objectivity of that will, we shall in no way avoid the conclusion that together with the voluntary renunciation and self-destruction of the will all those phenomena also disappear, that constant striving and effort without aim or rest on all the stages of objectivity in which and through which the world exists; the diversity of successive forms will disappear, and together with the form all the manifestations of will, with its most universal forms, space and time, and finally **its** most fundamental form—subject and object. Without will there is no concept and no world. Before us, certainly, nothing remains. But what resists this transition into annihilation, our nature, is only that same wish to live—*Wille zum Leben*—which forms ourselves as well as our world. That we are so afraid of annihilation or, what is the same thing, that we so wish to live merely means that we are ourselves nothing else but this desire to live, and know nothing but it. And so what remains after the complete annihilation of the will, for us who are so full of the will, is, of course, nothing; but on the other hand, for those in whom the will has turned and renounced itself, this so real world of ours with all its suns and Milky Way is nothing."

"Vanity of vanities," says Solomon—"vanity of vanities—all is vanity. What profit hath a man of all his labour which he taketh under the sun? One generation passeth away, and another generation cometh: but the earth abideth for ever. . . . The thing that hath been, is that which shall be; and that which is done is that which shall be done: and there is no new thing under the sun. Is there anything whereof it may be said, See, this is new? It hath been already of old time, which was before us. There is no remembrance of former things; neither shall there be any remembrance of things that are to come with those that shall come after. I the Preacher was King over Israel in Jerusalem. And I gave my heart to seek and search out by wisdom concerning all that is done under heaven: this sore travail hath God given to the sons of man to be exercised therewith. I have seen all the works that are done under the sun; and behold, all is vanity and vexation of spirit. . . . I communed with my own heart, saying, Lo, I am come to great estate, and have gotten more wisdom than all they that have been before me over Jerusalem: yea, my heart hath great experience of wisdom and knowledge. And I gave my heart to know wisdom, and to know madness and folly: I perceived that this also is vexation of spirit. For in much wisdom is much grief: and he that increaseth knowledge increaseth sorrow.

"I said in my heart, Go to now, I will prove thee with mirth, therefore enjoy pleasure: and behold this also is vanity. I said of laughter, It is mad: and of mirth, What doeth it? I sought in my heart how to cheer my flesh with wine, and while my heart was guided by wisdom, to lay hold on folly, till I might see what it was good for the sons of men that they should do under heaven the number of the days of their life. I made me great works; I builded me houses; I planted me vineyards: I made me gardens and orchards, and I planted trees in them of all kinds of fruits: I made me pools of water, to water therefrom the forest where trees were reared: I got me servants and maidens, and had servants born in my house; also I had great possessions of herds and flocks above all that were before me in Jerusalem: I gathered me also silver and gold and the peculiar treasure from kings and from the provinces: I got me men singers and women singers; and the delights of the sons of men, as musical instruments and that of all sorts. So I was great, and increased more than all that were before me in Jerusalem: also my wisdom remained with me. And whatever mine eyes desired I kept not from them. I withheld not my heart from any joy. . . . Then I looked on all the works that my hands had wrought, and on the labour that I had laboured to do: and, behold, all was vanity and vexation of spirit, and there was no profit from them under the sun. And I turned myself to behold wisdom, and madness, and folly. . . . But I perceived that one event happeneth to them all. Then said I in my heart, As it happeneth to the fool, so it happeneth even to me, and why was I then more wise? Then I said in my heart, that this also is vanity. For there is no remembrance of the wise more than of the fool for ever; seeing that which now is in the days to come shall all be forgotten. And how dieth the wise man? as the fool. Therefore I hated life; because the work that is wrought under the sun is grievous unto me: for all is vanity and vexation of spirit. Yea, I hated all my labour which I had taken under the sun: seeing that I must leave it unto the man that shall be after me. . . . For what hath man of all his labour, and of the vexation of his heart, wherein he hath laboured under the sun? For all his days are sorrows, and his travail grief; yea, even in the night his heart taketh no rest. This is also vanity. Man is not blessed with security that he should eat and drink and cheer his soul from his own labour. . . . All things come alike to all: there is one event to the righteous and to the wicked; to the good and to the evil; to the clean and to the unclean; to him that sacrificeth and to him that sacrificeth not; as is the good, so is the sinner; and he that sweareth, as he that feareth an oath. This is an evil in all that is done under the sun, that there is one event unto all; yea, also the heart of the sons of men is full of evil, and madness is in their heart while they live, and after that they go to the dead. For him that is among the living there is hope: for a living dog is better than a dead lion. For the living know that they shall die: but the dead know not any thing, neither have they any more a reward; for the memory of them is forgotten. Also their love, and their hatred, and their envy, is now perished; neither have they any more a portion for ever in any thing that is done under the sun."

So said Solomon, or whoever wrote those words.[1]

And this is what the Indian wisdom tells:

Sakya Muni, a young, happy prince, from whom the existence of sickness, old age, and death had been hidden, went out to drive and saw a terrible old man, toothless and slobbering. The prince, from whom till then old age had been concealed, was amazed and asked his driver what it was, and how that man had come to such a wretched and disgusting condition, and when he learnt that this was the common fate of all men, that the same thing inevitably awaited him—the young prince—he could not continue his drive but gave orders to go home, that he might consider this fact. So he shut himself up alone and considered it. And he probably devised some consolation for himself, for he subsequently again went out to drive, feeling merry and happy. But this time he saw a sick man. He saw an emaciated, livid, trembling man with dim eyes. The prince, from whom sickness had been concealed, stopped and asked what this was. And when he learnt that this was sickness, to which all men are liable, and that he himself—a healthy and happy prince— might himself fall ill to-morrow, he again was in no mood to enjoy himself but gave orders to drive home, and again sought some solace, and probably found it, for he drove out a third time for pleasure. But this third time he saw another new sight: he saw men carrying something. "What is that?" "A dead man." "What does *dead* mean?" asked the prince. He was told that to become dead means to become like that man. The prince approached the corpse, uncovered it, and looked at it. "What will happen to him now?" asked the prince. He was told that the corpse would be buried in the ground. "Why?" "Because he will certainly not return to life and will only produce a stench and worms." "And is that the fate of all men? Will the same thing happen to me?

---

[1] Tolstóy's version differs slightly in a few places from our own Authorized or Revised version. I have followed his text, for in a letter to Fet, quoted on p. 18, vol. ii, of my *Life of Tolstoy*, he says that "The Authorized English version [of Ecclesiastes] is bad."

Will they bury me, and shall I cause a stench and be eaten by worms?" "Yes." "Home! I shall not drive out for pleasure and never will so drive out again!"

And Sakya Muni could find no consolation in life and decided that life is the greatest of evils; and he devoted all the strength of his soul to free himself from it, and to free others; and to do this so that, even after death, life shall not be renewed any more but be completely destroyed at its very roots. So speaks all the wisdom of India.

These then are the direct replies that human wisdom gives when it replies to life's question.

"The life of the body is an evil and a lie. Therefore the destruction of the life of the body is a blessing, and we should desire it," says Socrates.

"Life is that which should not be—an evil; and the passage into Nothingness is the only good in life," says Schopenhauer.

"All that is in the world—folly and wisdom and riches and poverty and mirth and grief—is vanity and emptiness. Man dies and nothing is left of him. And that is stupid," says Solomon.

"To live in the consciousness of the inevitability of suffering, of becoming enfeebled, of old age and of death, is impossible—we must free ourselves from life, from all possible life," says Buddha.

And what these strong minds said has been said and thought and felt by millions upon millions of people like them. And I have thought it and felt it.

So my wandering among the sciences, far from freeing me from my despair, only strengthened it. One kind of knowledge did not reply to life's question; the other kind replied directly confirming my despair, indicating not that the result at which I had arrived was the fruit of error or of a diseased state of my mind, but on the contrary that I had thought correctly, and that my thoughts coincided with the conclusions of the most powerful of human minds.

It is no good deceiving oneself. It is all—vanity! Happy is he who has not been born: death is better than life, and one must free oneself from life.

VII

Not finding an explanation in science I began to seek for it in life, hoping to find it among the people around me. And I began to observe how the people around me—people like myself—lived, and what their attitude was to this question which had brought me to despair.

And this is what I found among people who were in the same position as myself as regards education and manner of life.

I found that for people of my circle there were four ways out of the terrible position in which we are all placed.

The first was that of ignorance. It consists in not knowing, not understanding, that life is an evil and an absurdity. People of this sort—chiefly women, or very young or very dull people—have not yet understood that question of life which presented itself to Schopenhauer, Solomon, and Buddha. They see neither the dragon that awaits them nor the mice gnawing the shrub by which they are hanging, and they lick the drops of honey. But they lick those drops of honey only for a while: something will turn their attention to the dragon and the mice, and there will be an end to their licking. From them I had nothing to learn—one cannot cease to know what one does know.

The second way out is epicureanism. It consists, while knowing the hopelessness of life, in making use meanwhile of the advantages one has, disregarding the dragon and the mice, and licking the honey in the best way, especially if there is much of it within reach. Solomon expresses this way out thus: "Then I commended mirth, because a man hath no better thing under the sun, than to eat, and to drink, and to be merry: and that this should accompany him in his labour the days of his life, which God giveth him under the sun.

"Therefore eat thy bread with joy and drink thy wine with a merry heart. . . . Live joyfully with the wife whom thou lovest all the days of the life of thy vanity . . . for this is thy portion in life and in thy labours which thou takest under the sun. . . . Whatsoever thy hand findeth to do, do it with thy might, for there is no work, nor device, nor knowledge, nor wisdom, in the grave, whither thou goest."

That is the way in which the majority of people of our circle make life possible for themselves. Their circumstances furnish them with more of welfare than of hardship, and their moral dullness makes it possible for them to forget that the advantage of their position is accidental, and that not everyone can have a thousand wives and palaces like Solomon, that for everyone who has a thousand wives there are a thousand without a wife, and that for each palace there are a thousand people who have to build it in the sweat of their brows; and that the accident that has to-day made me a Solomon may to-morrow make me a Solomon's slave. The dullness of these people's imagination enables them to forget the things that gave Buddha no peace—the inevitability of sickness, old age, and death, which to-day or to-morrow will destroy all these pleasures.

So think and feel the majority of people of our day and our manner of life. The fact that some of these people declare the dullness of their thoughts and imaginations to be a philosophy, which they call Positive, does not remove them, in my opinion, from the ranks of those who, to avoid seeing the question, lick the honey. I could not imitate these people; not having their dullness of imagination I could not artificially produce it in myself. I could not tear my eyes from the mice and the dragon, as no vital man can after he has once seen them.

The third escape is that of strength and energy. It consists in destroying life, when one has understood that it is an evil and an absurdity. A few exceptionally strong and consistent people act so. Having understood the stupidity of the joke that has been played on them, and having understood that it is better to be dead than to be alive, and that it is best of all not to exist, they act accordingly and promptly end this stupid joke, since there are means: a rope round one's neck, water, a knife to stick into one's heart, or the trains on the railways; and the number of those of our circle who act in this way becomes greater and greater, and for the most part they act so at the best time of their life, when the strength of their mind is in full bloom and few habits degrading to the mind have as yet been acquired.

I saw that this was the worthiest way of escape and I wished to adopt it.

The fourth way out is that of weakness. It consists in seeing the truth of the situation and yet clinging to life, knowing in advance that nothing can come of it. People of this kind know that death is better than life but not having the strength to act rationally—to end the deception quickly and kill themselves—they seem to wait for something. This is the escape of weakness, for if I know what is best and it is within my power, why not yield to what is best? . . . I found myself in that category.

So people of my class evade the terrible contradiction in four ways. Strain my attention as I would, I saw no way except those four. One way was not to understand that life is senseless, vanity, and an evil, and that it is better not to live. I could not help knowing this, and when I once knew it could not shut my eyes to it. The second way was to use life such as it is without thinking of the future. And I could not do that. I, like Sakya Muni, could not ride out hunting when I knew that old age, suffering, and death exist. My imagination was too vivid. Nor could I rejoice in the momentary accidents that for an instant threw pleasure to my lot. The third way, having understood that life is evil and stupid, was to end it by killing oneself. I understood that but somehow still did not kill myself. The fourth way was to live like Solomon and Schopenhauer—knowing that life is a stupid joke played upon us, and still to go on living, washing oneself, dressing, dining, talking, and even writing books. This was to me repulsive and tormenting, but I remained in that position.

I see now that if I did not kill myself it was due to some dim consciousness of the invalidity of my thoughts. However convincing and indubitable appeared to me the sequence of my thoughts and of those of the wise that have brought us to the admission of the senselessness of life, there remained in me a vague doubt of the justice of my conclusion.

It was like this: I, my reason, have acknowledged that

life is senseless. If there is nothing higher than reason (and there is not: nothing can prove that there is), then reason is the creator of life for me. If reason did not exist there would be for me no life. How can reason deny life when it is the creator of life? Or to put it the other way: were there no life, my reason would not exist; therefore reason is life's son. Life is all. Reason is its fruit, yet reason rejects life itself! I felt that there was something wrong here.

Life is a senseless evil, that is certain, said I to myself. Yet I have lived and am still living, and all mankind lived and lives. How is that? Why does it live, when it is possible not to live? Is it that only I and Schopenhauer are wise enough to understand the senselessness and evil of life?

The reasoning showing the vanity of life is not so difficult and has long been familiar to the very simplest folk; yet they have lived and still live. How is it they all live and never think of doubting the reasonableness of life?

My knowledge, confirmed by the wisdom of the sages, has shown me that everything on earth—organic and inorganic—is all most cleverly arranged; only my own position is stupid. And those fools—the enormous masses of people—know nothing about how everything organic and inorganic in the world is arranged; but they live, and it seems to them that their life is very wisely arranged! . . .

And it struck me: "But what if there is something I do not yet know? Ignorance behaves just in that way. Ignorance always says just what I am saying. When it does not know something, it says that what it does not know is stupid. Indeed, it appears that there is a whole humanity that lived and lives as if it understood the meaning of its life, for without understanding it it could not live; but I say that all this life is senseless and that I cannot live.

"Nothing prevents our denying life by suicide. Well then, kill yourself, and you won't discuss. If life displeases you, kill yourself! You live, and cannot understand the meaning of life—then finish it, and do not fool about in life, saying and writing that you do not understand it.

You have come into good company where people are contented and know what they are doing; if you find it dull and repulsive—go away!"

Indeed, what are we who are convinced of the necessity of suicide yet do not decide to commit it, but the weakest, most inconsistent, and to put it plainly, the stupidest of men, fussing about with our own stupidity as a fool fusses about with a painted hussy? For our wisdom, however indubitable it may be, has not given us the knowledge of the meaning of our life. But all mankind who sustain life—millions of them—do not doubt the meaning of life.

Indeed, from the most distant times of which I know anything, when life began, people have lived knowing the argument about the vanity of life which has shown me its senselessness, and yet they lived attributing some meaning to it.

From the time when any life began among men they had that meaning of life, and they led that life which has descended to me. All that is in me and around me, all, corporeal and incorporeal, is the fruit of their knowledge of life. Those very instruments of thought with which I consider this life and condemn it were all devised not by me but by them. I myself was born, taught, and brought up thanks to them. They dug out the iron, taught us to cut down the forests, tamed the cows and horses, taught us to sow corn and to live together, organized our life, and taught me to think and speak. And I, their product, fed, supplied with drink, taught by them, thinking with their thoughts and words, have argued that they are an absurdity! "There is something wrong," said I to myself. "I have blundered somewhere." But it was a long time before I could find out where the mistake was.

VIII

All these doubts, which I am now able to express more or less systematically, I could not then have expressed. I then only felt that however logically inevitable were my conclusions concerning the vanity of life, confirmed as they were by the greatest thinkers, there was something not right about them. Whether it was in the reasoning itself or in the statement of the question I did not know—I only felt that the conclusion was rationally convincing, but that that was insufficient. All these conclusions could not so convince me as to make me do what followed from my reasoning—that is to say, kill myself. And I should have told an untruth had I, without killing myself, said that reason had brought me to the point I had reached. Reason worked, but something else was also working which I can only call a consciousness of life. A force was working which compelled me to turn my attention to this and not to that; and it was this force which extricated me from my desperate situation and turned my mind in quite another direction. This force compelled me to turn my attention to the fact that I and a few hundred similar people are not the whole of mankind, and that I did not yet know the life of mankind.

Looking at the narrow circle of my equals, I saw only people who had not understood the question, or who had understood it and drowned it in life's intoxication, or had understood it and ended their lives, or had understood it and yet from weakness were living out their desperate life. And I saw no others. It seemed to me that that narrow circle of rich, learned, and leisured people to which I belonged formed the whole of humanity, and that those milliards of others who have lived and are living were cattle of some sort—not real people.

Strange, incredibly incomprehensible as it now seems to me that I could, while reasoning about life, overlook the whole life of mankind that surrounded me on all sides; that I could to such a degree blunder so absurdly as to think that my life, and Solomon's and Schopenhauer's, is the real, normal life, and that the life of the milliards is a circumstance undeserving of attention—strange as this now is to me, I see that so it was. In the delusion of my pride of intellect it seemed to me so indubitable that I and Solomon and Schopenhauer had stated the question so truly and exactly that nothing else was possible—so indubitable did it seem that all those milliards consisted of men who had not yet arrived at an apprehension of all the profundity of the question—that I sought for the meaning of my life without it once occurring to me to ask: "But what meaning is and has been given to their lives by all the milliards of common folk who live and have lived in the world?"

I long lived in this state of lunacy, which, in fact if not in words, is particularly characteristic of us very liberal and learned people. But thanks either to the strange physical affection I have for the real labouring people, which compelled me to understand them and to see that they are not so stupid as we suppose, or thanks to the sincerity of my conviction that I could know nothing beyond the fact that the best I could do was to hang myself, at any rate I instinctively felt that if I wished to live and understand the meaning of life, I must seek this meaning not among those who have lost it and wish to kill themselves, but among those milliards of the past and the present who make life and who support the burden of their own lives and of ours also. And I considered the enormous masses of those simple, un-learned, and poor people who have lived and are living and I saw something quite different. I saw that, with rare exceptions, all those milliards who have lived and are living do not fit into my divisions and that I could not class them as not understanding the question, for they themselves state it and reply to it with extraordinary clear-ness. Nor could I consider them epicureans, for their life consists more of privations and sufferings than of enjoy-ments. Still less could I consider them as irrationally dragging on a meaningless existence, for every act of their life, as well as death itself, is explained by them. To kill themselves they consider the greatest evil. It ap-peared that all mankind had a knowledge, unacknowledged and despised by me, of the meaning of life. It appeared that reasonable knowledge does not give the meaning of life but excludes life: while the meaning attributed to life by milliards of people, by all humanity, rests on some despised pseudo-knowledge.

Rational knowledge, presented by the learned and wise, denies the meaning of life, but the enormous masses of men, the whole of mankind, receive that meaning in irra-tional knowledge. And that irrational knowledge is faith, that very thing which I could not but reject. It is God, One in Three; the creation in six days; the devils and angels, and all the rest that I cannot accept as long as I retain my reason.

My position was terrible. I knew I could find nothing along the path of reasonable knowledge except a denial of life; and there—in faith—was nothing but a denial of reason, which was yet more impossible for me than a denial of life. From rational knowledge it appeared that life is an evil, people know this and it is in their power to end life; yet they lived and still live, and I myself live, though I have long known that life is senseless and an evil. By faith it appears that in order to understand the meaning of life I must renounce my reason, the very thing for which alone a meaning is required.

IX

A contradiction arose from which there were two exits. Either that which I called reason was not so rational as I supposed, or that which seemed to me irrational was not so irrational as I supposed. And I began to verify the line of argument of my rational knowledge.

Verifying the line of argument of rational knowledge I found it quite correct. The conclusion that life is nothing was inevitable; but I noticed a mistake. The mistake lay in this, that my reasoning was not in accord with the question I had put. The question was: "Why should I live—that is to say, what real, permanent result will come out of my illusory transitory life; what meaning has my finite existence in this infinite world?" And to reply to that question I had studied life.

The solution of all the possible questions of life could evidently not satisfy me, for my question, simple as it at first appeared, included a demand for an explanation of the finite in terms of the infinite, and vice versa.

I asked: "What is the meaning of my life, beyond time, cause, and space?" And I replied to quite another question: "What is the meaning of my life within time, cause, and space?" With the result that, after long efforts of thought, the answer I reached was: "None."

In my reasonings I constantly compared (nor could I do otherwise) the finite with the finite, and the infinite with the infinite, but for that reason I reached the inevitable result: force is force, matter is matter, will is will, the infinite is the infinite, nothing is nothing—and that was all that could result.

It was something like what happens in mathematics, when thinking to solve an equation, we find we are working on an identity. The line of reasoning is correct but results in the answer that a equals a, or x equals x, or o equals o. The same thing happened with my reasoning in relation to the question of the meaning of my life. The replies given by all science to that question only result in—identity.

And really, strictly scientific knowledge—that knowledge which begins, as Descartes's did, with complete doubt about everything—rejects all knowledge admitted on faith and builds everything afresh on the laws of reason and experience, and cannot give any other reply to the question of life than that which I obtained: an indefinite reply. Only at first had it seemed to me that knowledge had given a positive reply—the reply of Schopenhauer: that life has no meaning and is an evil. But on examining the matter I understood that the reply is not positive, it was only my feeling that so expressed it. Strictly expressed, as it is by the Brahmins and by Solomon and Schopenhauer, the reply is merely indefinite, or an identity: o equals o; life is nothing. So that philosophic knowledge denies nothing but only replies that the question cannot be solved by it—that for it the solution remains indefinite.

Having understood this, I understood that it was not possible to seek in rational knowledge for a reply to my question and that the reply given by rational knowledge is a mere indication that a reply can only be obtained by a different statement of the question and only when the relation of the finite to the infinite is included in the question. And I understood that, however irrational and distorted might be the replies given by faith, they have this advantage, that they introduce into every answer a relation between the finite and the infinite, without which there can be no solution.

In whatever way I stated the question, that relation appeared in the answer. How am I to live?—According to the law of God. What real result will come of my life?—Eternal torment or eternal bliss. What meaning has life that death does not destroy?—Union with the eternal God: heaven.

So that besides rational knowledge, which had seemed to me the only knowledge, I was inevitably brought to acknowledge that all live humanity has another irrational knowledge—faith which makes it possible to live. Faith still remained to me as irrational as it was before, but I could not but admit that it alone gives mankind a reply to the questions of life, and that consequently it makes life possible. Reasonable knowledge had brought me to acknowledge that life is senseless—my life had come to a halt and I wished to destroy myself. Looking around on the whole of mankind I saw that people live and declare that they know the meaning of life. I looked at myself— I had lived as long as I knew a meaning of life. As to others so also to me faith had given a meaning to life and had made life possible.

Looking again at people of other lands, at my contemporaries and at their predecessors, I saw the same thing. Where there is life, there since man began faith has made life possible for him, and the chief outline of that faith is everywhere and always identical.

Whatever the faith may be, and whatever answers it may give, and to whomsoever it gives them, every such answer gives to the finite existence of man an infinite meaning, a meaning not destroyed by sufferings, deprivations, or death. This means that only in faith can we find for life a meaning and a possibility. What, then, is this faith? And I understood that faith is not merely "the evidence of things not seen," etc., and is not a revelation (that defines only one of the indications of faith), is not the relation of man to God (one has first to define faith and then God, and not define faith through God); it is not only agreement with what has been told one (as faith is most usually supposed to be), but faith is a knowledge of the meaning of human life in consequence of which man does not destroy himself but lives. Faith is the strength of life. If a man lives he believes in something. If he did not believe that one must live for something, he would not live. If he does not see and recognize the illusory nature of the finite, he believes in the finite; if he understands the illusory nature of the finite, he must believe in the infinite. Without faith he cannot live.

And I recalled the whole course of my mental labour and was horrified. It was now clear to me that for man to be able to live he must either not see the infinite or have such an explanation of the meaning of life as will connect the finite with the infinite. Such an explanation I had had; but as long as I believed in the finite I did not need the explanation, and I began to verify it by reason. And in the light of reason the whole of my former explanation flew to atoms. But a time came when I ceased to believe in the finite. And then I began to build up on rational foundations, out of what I knew, an explanation which would give a meaning to life; but nothing could I build. Together with the best human intellects I reached the result that o equals o and was much astonished at that conclusion, though nothing else could have resulted.

What was I doing when I sought an answer in the experimental sciences? I wished to know why I live and for this purpose studied all that is outside me. Evidently I might learn much, but nothing of what I needed.

What was I doing when I sought an answer in philosophical knowledge? I was studying the thoughts of those who had found themselves in the same position as I, lacking a reply to the question, "Why do I live?" Evidently I could learn nothing but what I knew myself, namely that nothing can be known.

What am I?—A part of the infinite. In those few words lies the whole problem.

Is it possible that humanity has only put that question to itself since yesterday? And can no one before me have set himself that question—a question so simple, and one that springs to the tongue of every wise child?

Surely that question has been asked since man began; and naturally for the solution of that question since man began it has been equally insufficient to compare the finite with the finite and the infinite with the infinite, and since man began the relation of the finite to the infinite has been sought out and expressed.

All these conceptions in which the finite has been adjusted to the infinite and a meaning found for life—

the conception of God, of will, of goodness—we submit to logical examination. And all those conceptions fail to stand reason's criticism.

Were it not so terrible it would be ludicrous with what pride and self-satisfaction we, like children, pull the watch to pieces, take out the spring, make a toy of it, and are then surprised that the watch does not go.

A solution of the contradiction between the finite and the infinite, and such a reply to the question of life as will make it possible to live, is necessary and precious. And that is the only solution which we find everywhere, always, and among all peoples: a solution descending from times in which we lose sight of the life of man, a solution so difficult that we can compose nothing like it—and this solution we light-heartedly destroy in order again to set the same question, which is natural to everyone and to which we have no answer.

The conception of an infinite God, the divinity of the soul, the connexion of human affairs with God, the unity and existence of the soul, man's conception of moral goodness and evil are conceptions formulated in the hidden infinity of human thought; they are those conceptions without which neither life nor I should exist; yet rejecting all that labour of the whole of humanity, I wished to remake it afresh myself and in my own manner.

I did not then think like that, but the germs of these thoughts were already in me. I understood, in the first place, that my position with Schopenhauer and Solomon, notwithstanding our wisdom, was stupid: we see that life is an evil and yet continue to live. That is evidently stupid, for if life is senseless and I am so fond of what is reasonable, it should be destroyed, and then there would be no one to challenge it. Secondly, I understood that all one's reasonings turned in a vicious circle like a wheel out of gear with its pinion. However much and however well we may reason we cannot obtain a reply to the question, and o will always equal o, and therefore our path is probably erroneous. Thirdly, I began to understand that in the replies given by faith is stored up the deepest human wisdom and that I had no right to deny them on the ground of reason, and that those answers are the only ones which reply to life's question.

X

I understood this, but it made matters no better for me. I was now ready to accept any faith if only it did not demand of me a direct denial of reason—which would be a falsehood. And I studied Buddhism and Mohammedanism from books, and most of all I studied Christianity both from books and from the people around me.

Naturally I first of all turned to the Orthodox of my circle, to people who were learned: to Church theologians, monks, to theologians of the newest shade, and even to Evangelicals who profess salvation by belief in the Redemption. And I seized on these believers and questioned them as to their beliefs and their understanding of the meaning of life.

But though I made all possible concessions, and avoided all disputes, I could not accept the faith of these people. I saw that what they gave out as their faith did not explain the meaning of life but obscured it, and that they themselves affirm their belief, not to answer that question of life which brought me to faith, but for some other aims alien to me.

I remember the painful feeling of fear of being thrown back into my former state of despair, after the hope I often and often experienced in my intercourse with these people.

The more fully they explained to me their doctrines, the more clearly did I perceive their error and realized that my hope of finding in their belief an explanation of the meaning of life was vain.

It was not that in their doctrines they mixed many unnecessary and unreasonable things with the Christian truths that had always been near to me: that was not what repelled me. I was repelled by the fact that these people's lives were like my own, with only this difference—that such a life did not correspond to the principles they expounded in their teachings. I clearly felt that they deceived themselves and that they, like myself, found no other meaning in life than to live while life lasts, taking all one's hands can seize. I saw this because if they had had a meaning which destroyed the fear of loss, suffering, and death, they would not have feared these things. But they, these believers of our circle, just like myself, living in sufficiency and superfluity, tried to increase or preserve them, feared privations, suffering, and death, and just like myself and all of us unbelievers, lived to satisfy their desires, and lived just as badly, if not worse, than the unbelievers.

No arguments could convince me of the truth of their faith. Only deeds which showed that they saw a meaning in life making what was so dreadful to me—poverty, sickness, and death—not dreadful to them, could convince me. And such deeds I did not see among the various believers in our circle. On the contrary, I saw such deeds done[1] by people of our circle who were the most unbelieving, but never by our so-called believers.

And I understood that the belief of these people was not the faith I sought, and that their faith is not a real faith but an epicurean consolation in life.

I understood that that faith may perhaps serve, if not for a consolation at least for some distraction for a repentant Solomon on his death-bed, but it cannot serve for the great majority of mankind, who are called on not to amuse themselves while consuming the labour of others but to create life.

For all humanity to be able to live, and continue to live attributing a meaning to life, they, those milliards, must have a different, a real, knowledge of faith. Indeed, it was not the fact that we, with Solomon and Schopenhauer, did not kill ourselves that convinced me of the existence of faith but the fact that those milliards of people have lived and are living, and have borne Solomon and us on the current of their lives.

And I began to draw near to the believers among the poor, simple, unlettered folk: pilgrims, monks, sectarians, and peasants. The faith of these common people was the same Christian faith as was professed by the pseudo-believers of our circle. Among them, too, I found a

[1] This passage is noteworthy as being one of the few references made by Tolstóy at this period to the revolutionary or "Back-to-the-People" movement, in which many young men and women were risking and sacrificing home, property, and life itself from motives which had much in common with his own perception that the upper layers of Society are parasitic and prey on the vitals of the people who support them.

great deal of superstition mixed with the Christian truths; but the difference was that the superstitions of the believers of our circle were quite unnecessary to them and were not in conformity with their lives, being merely a kind of epicurean diversion; but the superstitions of the believers among the labouring masses conformed so with their lives that it was impossible to imagine them to oneself without those superstitions, which were a necessary condition of their life. The whole life of believers in our circle was a contradiction of their faith, but the whole life of the working-folk believers was a confirmation of the meaning of life which their faith gave them. And I began to look well into the life and faith of these people, and the more I considered it the more I became convinced that they have a real faith which is a necessity to them and alone gives their life a meaning and makes it possible for them to live. In contrast with what I had seen in our circle—where life without faith is possible and where hardly one in a thousand acknowledges himself to be a believer—among them there is hardly one unbeliever in a thousand. In contrast with what I had seen in our circle, where the whole of life is passed in idleness, amusement, and dissatisfaction, I saw that the whole life of these people was passed in heavy labour, and that they were content with life. In contradistinction to the way in which people of our circle oppose fate and complain of it on account of deprivations and sufferings, these people accepted illness and sorrow without any perplexity or opposition, and with a quiet and firm conviction that all is good. In contradistinction to us, who the wiser we are the less we understand the meaning of life and see some evil irony in the fact that we suffer and die, these folk live and suffer, and they approach death and suffering with tranquillity and in most cases gladly. In contrast to the fact that a tranquil death, a death without horror and despair, is a very rare exception in our circle, a troubled, rebellious, and unhappy death is the rarest exception among the people. And such people, lacking all that for us and for Solomon is the only good of life and yet experiencing the greatest happiness, are a great multitude. I looked more widely around me. I considered the life of the enormous mass of the people in the past and the present. And of such people, understanding the meaning of life and able to live and to die, I saw not two or three, or tens, but hundreds, thousands, and millions. And they all—endlessly different in their manners, minds, education, and position as they were—all alike, in complete contrast to my ignorance, knew the meaning of life and death, laboured quietly, endured deprivations and sufferings, and lived and died seeing therein not vanity but good.

And I learnt to love these people. The more I came to know their life, the life of those who are living and of others who are dead of whom I read and heard, the more I loved them and the easier it became for me to live. So I went on for about two years, and a change took place in me which had long been preparing and the promise of which had always been in me. It came about that the life of our circle, the rich and learned, not merely became distasteful to me, but lost all meaning in my eyes. All our actions, discussions, science, and art presented itself to me in a new light. I understood that it is all merely self-indulgence and that to find a meaning in it is impossible; while the life of the whole labouring people, the whole of mankind who produce life, appeared to me in its true significance. I understood that *that* is life itself, and that the meaning given to that life is true: and I accepted it.

XI

And remembering how those very beliefs had repelled me and had seemed meaningless when professed by people whose lives conflicted with them, and how these same beliefs attracted me and seemed reasonable when I saw that people lived in accord with them, I understood why I had then rejected those beliefs and found them meaningless, yet now accepted them and found them full of meaning. I understood that I had erred, and why I erred. I had erred not so much because I thought incorrectly as because I lived badly. I understood that it was not an error in my thought that had hid truth from me so much as my life itself in the exceptional conditions of epicurean gratification of desires in which I passed it. I understood that my question as to what my life is, and the answer—

an evil—was quite correct. The only mistake was that the answer referred only to my life, while I had referred it to life in general. I asked myself what my life is, and got the reply: An evil and an absurdity. And really my life—a life of indulgence of desires—was senseless and evil, and therefore the reply, "Life is evil and an absurdity," referred only to my life, but not to human life in general. I understood the truth which I afterwards found in the Gospels, "that men loved darkness rather than the light, for their works were evil. For everyone that doeth ill hateth the light, and cometh not to the light, lest his works should be reproved." I perceived that to understand the meaning of life it is necessary first that life should not be meaningless and evil, then we can apply reason to explain it. I understood why I had so long wandered round so evident a truth, and that if one is to think and speak of the life of mankind, one must think and speak of that life and not of the life of some of life's parasites. That truth was always as true as that two and two are four, but I had not acknowledged it, because on admitting two and two to be four I had also to admit that I was bad; and to feel myself to be good was for me more important and necessary than for two and two to be four. I came to love good people, hated myself, and confessed the truth. Now all became clear to me.

What if an executioner passing his whole life in torturing people and cutting off their heads, or a hopeless drunkard, or a madman settled for life in a dark room which he has fouled and imagines that he would perish if he left—what if he asked himself: "What is life?" Evidently he could get no other reply to that question than that life is the greatest evil, and the madman's answer would be perfectly correct, but only as applied to himself. What if I am such a madman? What if all we rich and leisured people are such madmen? and I understood that we really are such madmen. I at any rate was certainly such.

And indeed a bird is so made that it must fly, collect food, and build a nest, and when I see that a bird does this I have pleasure in its joy. A goat, a hare, and a wolf are so made that they must feed themselves and must breed and feed their family, and when they do so I feel firmly assured that they are happy and that their life is a reasonable one. Then what should a man do? He too should produce his living as the animals do, but with this difference, that he will perish if he does it alone; he must obtain it not for himself but for all. And when he does that, I have a firm assurance that he is happy and that his life is reasonable. But what had I done during the whole thirty years of my responsible life? Far from producing sustenance for all, I did not even produce it for myself. I lived as a parasite, and on asking myself, what is the use of my life? I got the reply: "No use." If the meaning of human life lies in supporting it, how could I—who for thirty years had been engaged not on supporting life but on destroying it in myself and in others—how could I obtain any other answer than that my life was senseless and an evil? . . . It was both senseless and evil.

The life of the world endures by someone's will—by the life of the whole world and by our lives someone fulfils his purpose. To hope to understand the meaning of that will one must first perform it by doing what is wanted of us. But if I will not do what is wanted of me, I shall never understand what is wanted of me, and still less what is wanted of us all and of the whole world.

If a naked, hungry beggar has been taken from the cross-roads, brought into a building belonging to a beautiful establishment, fed, supplied with drink, and obliged to move a handle up and down, evidently, before discussing why he was taken, why he should move the handle, and whether the whole establishment is reasonably arranged—the beggar should first of all move the handle. If he moves the handle he will understand that it works a pump, that the pump draws water, and that the water irrigates the garden beds; then he will be taken from the pumping station to another place where he will gather fruits and will enter into the joy of his master, and, passing from lower to higher work, will understand more and more of the arrangements of the establishment, and taking part in it will never think of asking why he is there, and will certainly not reproach the master.

So those who do his will, the simple, unlearned working folk, whom we regard as cattle, do not reproach the master;

but we, the wise, eat the master's food but do not do what the master wishes, and instead of doing it sit in a circle and discuss: "Why should that handle be moved? Isn't it stupid?" So we have decided. We have decided that the master is stupid or does not exist and that we are wise, only we feel that we are quite useless and that we must somehow do away with ourselves.

XII

The consciousness of the error in reasonable knowledge helped me to free myself from the temptation of idle ratiocination. The conviction that knowledge of truth can only be found by living led me to doubt the rightness of my life; but I was saved only by the fact that I was able to tear myself from my exclusiveness and to see the real life of the plain working people, and to understand that it alone is real life. I understood that if I wish to understand life and its meaning, I must not live the life of a parasite but must live a real life and—taking the meaning given to life by real humanity and merging myself in that life—verify it.

During that time this is what happened to me. During that whole year, when I was asking myself almost every moment whether I should not end matters with a noose or a bullet—all that time, together with the course of thought and observation about which I have spoken, my heart was oppressed with a painful feeling, which I can only describe as a search for God.

I say that that search for God was not reasoning, but a feeling, because that search proceeded not from the course of my thoughts—it was even directly contrary to them—but proceeded from the heart. It was a feeling of fear, orphanage, isolation in a strange land, and a hope of help from someone.

Though I was quite convinced of the impossibility of proving the existence of a Deity (Kant had shown, and I quite understood him, that it could not be proved), I yet sought for God, hoped that I should find Him, and from old habit addressed prayers to that which I sought but had not found. I went over in my mind the arguments of Kant and Schopenhauer showing the impossibility of proving the existence of a God, and I began to verify those arguments and to refute them. Cause, said I to myself, is not a category of thought such as are Time and Space. If I exist, there must be some cause for it, and a cause of causes. And that first cause of all is what men have called "God." And I paused on that thought and tried with all my being to recognize the presence of that cause. And as soon as I acknowledged that there is a force in whose power I am, I at once felt that I could live. But I asked myself: "What is that cause, that force? How am I to think of it? What are my relations to that which I call 'God'?" And only the familiar replies occurred to me: "He is the Creator and Preserver." This reply did not satisfy me, and I felt I was losing within me what I needed for my life. I became terrified and began to pray to Him whom I sought, that He should help me. But the more I prayed the more apparent it became to me that He did not hear me and that there was no one to whom to address myself. And with despair in my heart that there is no God at all, I said: "Lord, have mercy, save me! Lord, teach me!" But no one had mercy on me, and I felt that my life was coming to a standstill.

But again and again, from various sides, I returned to the same conclusion that I could not have come into the world without any cause or reason or meaning; I could not be such a fledgling fallen from its nest as I felt myself to be. Or, granting that I be such, lying on my back crying in the high grass, even then I cry because I know that a mother has borne me within her, has hatched me, warmed me, fed me, and loved me. Where is she—that mother? If I have been deserted, who has deserted me? I cannot hide from myself that someone bore me, loving me. Who was that someone? Again "God"? He knows and sees my searching, my desire, and my struggle.

"He exists," said I to myself. And I had only for an instant to admit that, and at once life rose within me, and I felt the possibility and joy of being. But again, from the admission of the existence of a God I went on to seek my relation with Him; and again I imagined *that* God—our Creator in Three Persons who sent His Son, the Saviour—and again *that* God, detached from the world and from me, melted like a block of ice, melted before my eyes, and again nothing remained, and again the spring of life dried up within me, and I despaired and felt that I had nothing to do but to kill myself. And the worst of all was that I felt I could not do it.

Not twice or three times, but tens and hundreds of times, I reached those conditions, first of joy and animation, and then of despair and consciousness of the impossibility of living.

I remember that it was in early spring: I was alone in the wood listening to its sounds. I listened and thought ever of the same thing, as I had constantly done during those last three years. I was again seeking God.

"Very well, there is no God," said I to myself; "there is no one who is not my imagination but a reality like my whole life. He does not exist, and no miracles can prove His existence, because the miracles would be my imagination, besides being irrational.

"But my *perception* of God, of Him whom I seek," I asked myself, "where has that perception come from?" And again at this thought the glad waves of life rose within me. All that was around me came to life and received a meaning. But my joy did not last long. My mind continued its work.

"The conception of God is not God," said I to myself. "The conception is what takes place within me. The conception of God is something I can evoke or can refrain from evoking in myself. That is not what I seek. I seek that without which there can be no life." And again all around me and within me began to die, and again I wished to kill myself.

But then I turned my gaze upon myself, on what went on within me, and I remembered all those cessations of life and reanimations that recurred within me hundreds of times. I remembered that I only lived at those times when I believed in God. As it was before, so it was now; I need only be aware of God to live; I need only forget Him, or disbelieve Him, and I died.

What is this animation and dying? I do not live when I lose belief in the existence of God. I should long ago have killed myself had I not had a dim hope of finding Him. I live, really live, only when I feel Him and seek

Him. "What more do you seek?" exclaimed a voice within me. "This is He. He is that without which one cannot live. To know God and to live is one and the same thing. God is life."

"Live seeking God, and then you will not live without God." And more than ever before, all within me and around me lit up, and the light did not again abandon me.

And I was saved from suicide. When and how this change occurred I could not say. As imperceptibly and gradually the force of life in me had been destroyed and I had reached the impossibility of living, a cessation of life and the necessity of suicide, so imperceptibly and gradually did that force of life return to me. And strange to say the strength of life which returned to me was not new, but quite old—the same that had borne me along in my earliest days.

I quite returned to what belonged to my earliest childhood and youth. I returned to the belief in that Will which produced me and desires something of me. I returned to the belief that the chief and only aim of my life is to be better—that is, to live in accord with that Will. And I returned to the belief that I can find the expression of that Will in what humanity, in the distant past hidden from me, has produced for its guidance: that is to say, I returned to a belief in God, in moral perfection, and in a tradition transmitting the meaning of life. There was only this difference, that then all this was accepted unconsciously, while now I knew that without it I could not live.

What happened to me was something like this: I was put into a boat (I do not remember when) and pushed off from an unknown shore, shown the direction to the opposite shore, had oars put into my unpractised hands, and was left alone. I rowed as best I could and moved forward, but the further I advanced towards the middle of the stream the more rapid grew the current bearing me away from my goal and the more frequently did I encounter others, like myself, borne away by the stream. There were a few rowers who continued to row; there were others who had abandoned their oars; there were large boats and immense vessels full of people. Some struggled against the current; others yielded to it. And the further I went the more, seeing the progress down the current of all those who were adrift, I forgot the direction given me. In the very centre of the stream, amid the crowd of boats and vessels which were being borne downstream, I quite lost my direction and abandoned my oars. Around me on all sides, with mirth and rejoicing, people with sails and oars were borne down the stream, assuring me and each other that no other direction was possible. And I believed them and floated with them. And I was carried far; so far that I heard the roar of the rapids in which I must be shattered, and I saw boats shattered in them. And I recollected myself. I was long unable to understand what had happened to me. I saw before me nothing but destruction, towards which I was rushing and which I feared. I saw no safety anywhere and did not know what to do; but, looking back, I perceived innumerable boats which unceasingly and strenuously pushed across the stream and I remembered about the shore, the oars, and the direction and began to pull back upward against the stream and towards the shore.

That shore was God; that direction was tradition; the oars were the freedom given me to pull for the shore and unite with God. And so the force of life was renewed in me and I again began to live.

XIII

I turned from the life of our circle, acknowledging that ours is not life but a simulation of life—that the conditions of superfluity in which we live deprive us of the possibility of understanding life, and that in order to understand life I must understand not an exceptional life such as ours who are parasites on life, but the life of the simple labouring folk—those who make life—and the meaning which they attribute to it. The simplest labouring people around me were the Russian people, and I turned to them and to the meaning of life which they give. That meaning, if one can put it into words, was as follows: Every man has come into this world by the will of God. And God has so made man that every man can destroy his soul or save it. The aim of man in life is to save his soul, and to save his soul he must live "godly" and to live "godly" he must renounce all the pleasures of life, must labour, humble himself, suffer, and be merciful. That meaning the people obtain from the whole teaching of faith transmitted to them by their pastors and by the traditions that live among the people. This meaning was clear to me and near to my heart. But together with this meaning of the popular faith of our non-sectarian folk, among whom I live, much was inseparably bound up that revolted me and seemed to me inexplicable: Sacraments, Church services, fasts, and the adoration of relics and icons. The people cannot separate the one from the other, nor could I. And strange as much of what entered into the faith of these people was to me, I accepted everything and attended the services, knelt morning and evening in prayer, fasted, and prepared to receive the Eucharist: and at first my reason did not resist anything. The very things that had formerly seemed to me impossible did not now evoke in me any opposition.

My relations to faith before and after were quite different. Formerly life itself seemed to me full of meaning and faith presented itself as the arbitrary assertion of propositions to me quite unnecessary, unreasonable, and disconnected from life. I then asked myself what meaning those propositions had and, convinced that they had none, I rejected them. Now on the contrary I knew firmly that my life otherwise has, and can have, no meaning, and the articles of faith were far from presenting themselves to me as unnecessary—on the contrary I had been led by indubitable experience to the conviction that only these propositions presented by faith give life a meaning. Formerly I looked on them as on some quite unnecessary gibberish, but now, if I did not understand them, I yet knew that they had a meaning, and I said to myself that I must learn to understand them.

I argued as follows, telling myself that the knowledge of faith flows, like all humanity with its reason, from a mysterious source. That source is God, the origin both of the human body and the human reason. As my body has descended to me from God, so also has my reason and my understanding of life, and consequently the various stages of the development of that understanding of life cannot be false. All that people sincerely believe in must be true; it may be differently expressed but it cannot be a lie, and therefore if it presents itself to me as a lie, that only means that I have not understood it. Furthermore I said to myself, the essence of every faith consists in its giving life a meaning which death does not destroy. Naturally for a faith to be able to reply to the questions of a king dying in luxury, of an old slave tormented by overwork, of an unreasoning child, of a wise old man, of a half-witted old woman, of a young and happy wife, of a youth tormented by passions, of all people in the most varied conditions of life and education—if there is one reply to the one eternal question of life: "Why do I live and what will result from my life?"—the reply, though one in its essence, must be endlessly varied in its presentation; and the more it is one, the more true and profound it is, the more strange and deformed must it naturally appear in its attempted expression, conformably to the education and position of each person. But this argument, justifying in my eyes the queerness of much on the ritual side of religion, did not suffice to allow me in the one great affair of life—religion—to do things which seemed to me questionable. With all my soul I wished to be in a position to mingle with the people, fulfilling the ritual side of their religion; but I could not do it. I felt that I should lie to myself and mock at what was sacred to me, were I to do so. At this point, however, our new Russian theological writers came to my rescue.

According to the explanation these theologians gave, the fundamental dogma of our faith is the infallibility of the Church. From the admission of that dogma follows inevitably the truth of all that is professed by the Church. The Church as an assembly of true believers united by love and therefore possessed of true knowledge became the basis of my belief. I told myself that divine truth cannot be accessible to a separate individual; it is revealed only to the whole assembly of people united by love. To attain truth one must not separate, and in order not to separate one must love and must endure things one may not agree with.

Truth reveals itself to love, and if you do not submit to the rites of the Church you transgress against love; and by transgressing against love you deprive yourself of the possibility of recognizing the truth. I did not then see the sophistry contained in this argument. I did not see that union in love may give the greatest love but certainly cannot give us divine truth expressed in the definite words of the Nicene Creed. I also did not perceive that love cannot make a certain expression of truth an obligatory condition of union. I did not then see these mistakes in the argument and thanks to it was able to accept and perform all the rites of the Orthodox Church without understanding most of them. I then tried with all the strength of my soul to avoid all arguments and contradictions and tried to explain as reasonably as possible the Church statements I encountered.

When fulfilling the rites of the Church I humbled my reason and submitted to the tradition possessed by all humanity. I united myself with my forefathers: the father, mother, and grandparents I loved. They and all my predecessors believed and lived, and they produced me. I united myself also with the millions of the common people whom I respected. Moreover, those actions had nothing bad in themselves ("bad" I considered the indulgence of one's desires). When rising early for Church services I knew I was doing well, if only because I was sacrificing my bodily ease to humble my mental pride, for the sake of union with my ancestors and contemporaries, and for the sake of finding the meaning of life. It was the same with my preparations to receive Communion, and with the daily reading of prayers, with genuflections, and also with the observance of all the fasts. However insignificant these sacrifices might be I made them for the sake of something good. I fasted, prepared for Communion, and observed the fixed hours of prayer at home and in church. During Church service I attended to every word and gave them a meaning whenever I could. In the Mass the most important words for me were: "Let us love one another in conformity!" The further words, "In unity we believe in the Father, the Son, and Holy Ghost," I passed by, because I could not understand them.

XIV

It was then so necessary for me to believe in order to live that I unconsciously concealed from myself the contradictions and obscurities of theology. But this reading of meanings into the rites had its limits. If the chief words in the prayer for the Emperor became more and more clear to me, if I found some explanation for the words "and remembering our Sovereign Most-Holy Mother of God and all the Saints, ourselves and one another, we give our whole life to Christ our God," if I explained to myself the frequent repetition of prayers for the Tsar and his relations by the fact that they are more exposed to temptations than other people and therefore are more in need of being prayed for—the prayers about subduing our enemies and evil under our feet (even if one tried to say that *sin* was the enemy prayed against), these and other prayers, such as the "cherubic song" and the whole sacrament of the oblation, or "the chosen warriors," etc.— quite two-thirds of all the services—either remained completely incomprehensible or, when I forced an explanation into them, made me feel that I was lying, thereby quite destroying my relation to God and depriving me of all possibility of belief.

I felt the same about the celebration of the chief holidays. To remember the Sabbath—that is, to devote one day to God—was something I could understand. But the chief holiday was in commemoration of the Resurrection, the reality of which I could not picture to myself or understand. And that name of "Resurrection" was also given to the weekly holiday.[1] And on those days the Sacrament of the Eucharist was administered, which was quite unintelligible to me. The rest of the twelve great holidays, except Christmas, commemorated miracles—the things I tried not to think about in order not to deny: the Ascension, Pentecost, Epiphany, the Feast of the Intercession of the Holy Virgin, etc. At the celebration of these holidays, feeling that importance was being attributed to the very things that to me presented a negative impor-

[1] In Russia, Sunday was called Resurrection-day.

tance, I either devised tranquillizing explanations or shut my eyes in order not to see what tempted me.

Most of all this happened to me when taking part in the most usual Sacraments, which are considered the most important: Baptism and Communion. There I encountered not incomprehensible but fully comprehensible doings: doings which seemed to me to lead into temptation, and I was in a dilemma—whether to lie or to reject them.

Never shall I forget the painful feeling I experienced the day I received the Eucharist for the first time after many years. The service, confession, and prayers were quite intelligible and produced in me a glad consciousness that the meaning of life was being revealed to me. The Communion itself I explained as an act performed in remembrance of Christ and indicating a purification from sin and the full acceptance of Christ's teaching. If that explanation was artificial I did not notice its artificiality: so happy was I at humbling and abasing myself before the priest—a simple, timid country clergyman—turning all the dirt out of my soul and confessing my vices, so glad was I to merge in thought with the humility of the fathers who wrote the prayers of the office, so glad was I of union with all who have believed and now believe, that I did not notice the artificiality of my explanation. But when I approached the altar gates, and the priest made me say that I believed that what I was about to swallow was truly flesh and blood, I felt a pain in my heart: it was not merely a false note, it was a cruel demand made by someone or other who evidently had never known what faith is.

I now permit myself to say that it was a cruel demand, but I did not then think so: only it was indescribably painful to me. I was no longer in the position in which I had been in youth when I thought all in life was clear; I had indeed come to faith because, apart from faith, I had found nothing, certainly nothing, except destruction; therefore to throw away that faith was impossible and I submitted. And I found in my soul a feeling which helped me to endure it. This was the feeling of self-abasement and humility. I humbled myself, swallowed that flesh and blood without any blasphemous feelings and with a wish to believe. But the blow had been struck and, knowing what awaited me, I could not go a second time.

I continued to fulfill the rites of the Church and still believed that the doctrine I was following contained the truth, when something happened to me which I now understand but which then seemed strange.

I was listening to the conversation of an illiterate peasant, a pilgrim, about God, faith, life, and salvation, when a knowledge of faith revealed itself to me. I drew near to the people, listening to their opinions on life and faith, and I understood the truth more and more. So also was it when I read the lives of holy men, which became my favourite books. Putting aside the miracles and regarding them as fables illustrating thoughts, this reading revealed to me life's meaning. There were the lives of Makarius the Great; the story of Buddha; there were the words of St. John Chrysostom; and there were the stories of the traveller in the well, the monk who found some gold, and of Peter the publican. There were stories of the martyrs, all announcing that death does not exclude life, and there were the stories of ignorant, stupid men, who knew nothing of the teaching of the Church but who yet were saved.

But as soon as I met learned believers or took up their books, doubt of myself, dissatisfaction, and exasperated disputation were roused within me, and I felt that the more I entered into the meaning of these men's speech, the more I went astray from truth and approached an abyss.

XV

How often I envied the peasants their illiteracy and lack of learning! Those statements in the creeds which to me were evident absurdities for them contained nothing false; they could accept them and could believe in the truth— the truth I believed in. Only to me, unhappy man, was it clear that with truth falsehood was interwoven by finest threads, and that I could not accept it in that form.

So I lived for about three years. At first, when I was only slightly associated with truth as a catechumen and was only scenting out what seemed to me clearest, these encounters struck me less. When I did not understand anything, I said, "It is my fault, I am sinful"; but the more I became imbued with the truths I was learning, the more they became the basis of my life, the more oppressive and the more painful became these encounters and the sharper became the line between what I do not understand because I am not able to understand it and what cannot be understood except by lying to oneself.

In spite of my doubts and sufferings I still clung to the Orthodox Church. But questions of life arose which had to be decided; and the decision of these questions by the Church—contrary to the very bases of the belief by which I lived—obliged me at last to renounce communion with Orthodoxy as impossible. These questions were: first, the relation of the Orthodox Eastern Church to other Churches—to the Catholics and to the so-called sectarians. At that time, in consequence of my interest in religion, I came into touch with believers of various faiths: Catholics, Protestants, Old Believers, Molokáns,[1] and others. And I met among them many men of lofty morals who were truly religious. I wished to be a brother to them. And what happened? That teaching which promised to unite all in one faith and love—that very teaching, in the person of its best representatives, told me that these men were all living a lie; that what gave them their power of life was a temptation of the devil; and that we alone possess the only possible truth. And I saw that all who do not profess an identical faith with themselves are considered by the Orthodox to be heretics, just as the Catholics and others consider the Orthodox to be heretics. And I saw that the Orthodox (though they try to hide this) regard with hostility all who do not express their faith by the same external symbols and words as themselves; and this is naturally so: first because the assertion that you are in falsehood and I am in truth is the most cruel thing one man can say to another; and secondly, because a man loving his children and brothers cannot help being hostile to those who wish to pervert his children and brothers to a false belief. And

---

[1] A sect that rejects sacraments and ritual.

that hostility is increased in proportion to one's greater knowledge of theology. And to me who considered that truth lay in union by love, it became self-evident that theology was itself destroying what it ought to produce.

This offence is so obvious to us educated people who have lived in countries where various religions are professed and have seen the contempt, self-assurance, and invincible contradiction with which Catholics behave to the Orthodox Greeks and to the Protestants, and the Orthodox to Catholics and Protestants, and the Protestants to the two others, and the similar attitude of Old Believers, Páshkovites (Russian Evangelicals), Shakers, and all religions— that the very obviousness of the temptation at first perplexes us. One says to oneself: it is impossible that it is so simple and that people do not see that if two assertions are mutually contradictory, then neither of them has the sole truth which faith should possess. There is something else here; there must be some explanation. I thought there was and sought that explanation and read all I could on the subject and consulted all whom I could. And no one gave me any explanation, except the one which causes the Súmsky Hussars to consider the Súmsky Hussars the best regiment in the world, and the Yellow Uhlans to consider that the best regiment in the world is the Yellow Uhlans. The ecclesiastics of all the different creeds, through their best representatives, told me nothing but that they believed themselves to have the truth and the others to be in error and that all they could do was to pray for them. I went to archimandrites, bishops, elders, monks of the strictest orders and asked them; but none of them made any attempt to explain the matter to me except one man, who explained it all and explained it so that I never asked any one any more about it. I said that for every unbeliever turning to belief (and all our young generation are in a position to do so) the question that presents itself first is, why is truth not in Lutheranism nor in Catholicism, but in Orthodoxy? Educated in the high school he cannot help knowing—what the peasants do not know—that the Protestants and Catholics equally affirm that their faith is the only true one. Historical evidence, twisted by each religion in its own favour, is insufficient. Is it not possible, said I, to understand the teaching in a loftier way, so that from its height the differences should disappear, as they do for one who believes truly? Can we not go further along a path like the one we are following with the Old Believers? They emphasize the fact that they have a differently shaped cross and different alleluias and a different procession round the altar. We reply: You believe in the Nicene Creed, in the seven Sacraments, and so do we. Let us hold to that, and in other matters do as you please. We have united with them by placing the essentials of faith above the unessentials. Now with the Catholics can we not say: You believe in so and so and in so and so, which are the chief things, and as for the Filioque clause and the Pope—do as you please. Can we not say the same to the Protestants, uniting with them in what is most important?

My interlocutor agreed with my thoughts but told me that such concessions would bring reproach on the spiritual authorities for deserting the faith of our forefathers and this would produce a schism; and the vocation of the spiritual authorities is to safeguard in all its purity the Greco-Russian Orthodox faith inherited from our forefathers.

And I understood it all. I am seeking a faith, the power of life; and they are seeking the best way to fulfil in the eyes of men certain human obligations. And fulfilling these human affairs they fulfil them in a human way. However much they may talk of their pity for their erring brethren, and of addressing prayers for them to the throne of the Almighty—to carry out human purposes violence is necessary, and it has always been applied and is and will be applied. If of two religions each considers itself true and the other false, then men desiring to attract others to the truth will preach their own doctrine. And if a false teaching is preached to the inexperienced sons of their Church—which has the truth—then that Church cannot but burn the books and remove the man who is misleading its sons. What is to be done with a sectarian—burning, in the opinion of the Orthodox, with the fire of false doctrine—who in the most important affair of life, in faith, misleads the sons of the Church? What can be done with him except to cut off his head or to incarcerate him? Under the Tsar Aléxis Mikháylovich people were burned at the stake—that is to say, the severest method of punishment of the time was applied— and in our day also the severest method of punishment is applied—detention in solitary confinement.[2]

And I turned my attention to what is done in the name of religion and was horrified, and I almost entirely abjured Orthodoxy.

The second relation of the Church to a question of life was with regard to war and executions.

At that time Russia was at war. And Russians, in the name of Christian love, began to kill their fellow men. It was impossible not to think about this and not to see that killing is an evil repugnant to the first principles of any faith. Yet prayers were said in the churches for the success of our arms, and the teachers of the Faith acknowledged killing to be an act resulting from the Faith. And besides the murders during the war, I saw, during the disturbances which followed the war, Church dignitaries and teachers and monks of the lesser and stricter orders who approved the killing of helpless, erring youths. And I took note of all that is done by men who profess Christianity, and I was horrified.

XVI

And I ceased to doubt, and became fully convinced that not all was true in the religion I had joined. Formerly I should have said that it was all false, but I could not say so now. The whole of the people possessed a knowledge of the truth, for otherwise they could not have lived. Moreover, that knowledge was accessible to me, for I had felt it and had lived by it. But I no longer doubted that there was also falsehood in it. And all that had previously repelled me now presented itself vividly before me. And though I saw that among the peasants there was a smaller admixture of the lies that repelled me than among the representatives of the Church, I still saw that in the people's belief also falsehood was mingled with the truth.

[2] At the time this was written capital punishment was considered to be abolished in Russia.

But where did the truth and where did the falsehood come from? Both the falsehood and the truth were contained in the so-called holy tradition and in the Scriptures. Both the falsehood and the truth had been handed down by what is called the Church.

And whether I liked or not, I was brought to the study and investigation of these writings and traditions —which till now I had been so afraid to investigate.

And I turned to the examination of that same theology which I had once rejected with such contempt as unnecessary. Formerly it seemed to me a series of unnecessary absurdities, when on all sides I was surrounded by manifestations of life which seemed to me clear and full of sense; now I should have been glad to throw away what would not enter a healthy head, but I had nowhere to turn to. On this teaching religious doctrine rests or at least with it the only knowledge of the meaning of life that I have found is inseparably connected. However wild it may seem to my firm old mind, it was the only hope of salvation. It had to be carefully, attentively examined in order to understand it, and not even to understand it as I understand the propositions of science: I do not seek that, nor can I seek it, knowing the special character of religious knowledge. I shall not seek the explanation of everything. I know that the explanation of everything, like the commencement of everything, must be concealed in infinity. But I wish to understand in a way which will bring me to what is inevitably inexplicable. I wish to recognize anything that is inexplicable as being so not because the demands of my reason are wrong (they are right, and apart from them I can understand nothing), but because I recognize the limits of my intellect. I wish to understand in such a way that everything that is inexplicable shall present itself to me as being necessarily inexplicable, and not as being something I am under an arbitrary obligation to believe.

That there is truth in the teaching is to me indubitable, but it is also certain that there is falsehood in it, and I must find what is true and what is false, and must disentangle the one from the other. I am setting to work upon this task. What of falsehood I have found in the teaching and what I have found of truth, and to what conclusions I came, will form the following parts of this work, which if it be worth it and if anyone wants it, will probably some day be printed somewhere.

1879

The foregoing was written by me some three years ago and will be printed.

Now, a few days ago, when revising it and returning to the line of thought and to the feelings I had when I was living through it all, I had a dream. This dream expressed in condensed form all that I had experienced and described, and I think therefore that, for those who have understood me, a description of this dream will refresh and elucidate and unify what has been set forth at such length in the foregoing pages. The dream was this:

I saw that I was lying on a bed. I was neither comfortable nor uncomfortable: I was lying on my back. But I began to consider how, and on what, I was lying—a question which had not till then occurred to me. And observing my bed, I saw I was lying on plaited string supports attached to its sides: my feet were resting on one such support, my calves on another, and my legs felt uncomfortable. I seemed to know that those supports were movable, and with a movement of my foot I pushed away the furthest of them at my feet—it seemed to me that it would be more comfortable so. But I pushed it away too far and wished to reach it again with my foot, and that movement caused the next support under my calves to slip away also, so that my legs hung in the air. I made a movement with my whole body to adjust myself, fully convinced that I could do so at once; but the movement caused the other supports under me to slip and to become entangled, and I saw that matters were going quite wrong: the whole of the lower part of my body slipped and hung down, though my feet did not reach the ground. I was holding on only by the upper part of my back, and not only did it become uncomfortable but I was even frightened. And then only did I ask myself about something that had not before occurred to me. I asked myself: "Where am I and what am I lying on?" and I began to look around, and first of all to look down in the direction in which my body was hanging and whither I felt I must soon fall. I looked down and did not believe my eyes. I was not only at a height comparable to the height of the highest towers or mountains, but at a height such as I could never have imagined.

I could not even make out whether I saw anything there below, in that bottomless abyss over which I was hanging and whither I was being drawn. My heart contracted, and I experienced horror. To look thither was terrible. If I looked thither I felt that I should at once slip from the last support and perish. And I did not look. But not to look was still worse, for I thought of what would happen to me directly I fell from the last support. And I felt that from fear I was losing my last supports, and that my back was slowly slipping lower and lower. Another moment and I should drop off. And then it occurred to me that this cannot be real. It is a dream. Wake up! I try to arouse myself but cannot do so. "What am I to do? What am I to do?" I ask myself, and look upwards. Above, there is also an infinite space. I look into the immensity of sky and try to forget about the immensity below, and I really do forget it. The immensity below repels and frightens me; the immensity above attracts and strengthens me. I am still supported above the abyss by the last supports that have not yet slipped from under me; I know that I am hanging, but I look only upwards and my fear passes. As happens in dreams, a voice says: "Notice this, this is it!" And I look more and more into the infinite above me and feel that I am becoming calm. I remember all that has happened, and remember how it all happened; how I moved my legs, how I hung down, how frightened I was, and how I was saved from fear by looking upwards. And I ask myself: "Well, and now am I not hanging just the same?" And I do not so much look round as experience with my whole body the point of support on which I am held. I see that I no longer hang as if about to fall but am firmly held. I ask myself how I am held: I feel about, look round, and see that under me, under the middle of my body, there is one support, and that when

I look upwards I lie on it in the position of securest balance, and that it alone gave me support before. And then, as happens in dreams, I imagined the mechanism by means of which I was held; a very natural, intelligible, and sure means, though to one awake that mechanism has no sense. I was even surprised in my dream that I had not understood it sooner. It appeared that at my head there was a pillar, and the security of that slender pillar was undoubted though there was nothing to support it. From the pillar a loop hung very ingeniously and yet simply, and if one lay with the middle of one's body in that loop and looked up, there could be no question of falling. This was all clear to me, and I was glad and tranquil. And it seemed as if someone said to me: "See that you remember."

And I awoke.

1882

I CANNOT BE SILENT

"Seven death sentences: two in Petersburg, one in Moscow, two in Pénza, and two in Riga. Four executions: two in Khersón, one in Vílna, one in Odessa."

This, repeated daily in every newspaper and continued not for weeks, not for months, not for a year, but for years. And this in Russia, that Russia where the people regard every criminal as a man to be pitied and where till quite recently capital punishment was not recognized by law! I remember how proud I used to be of that when talking to Western Europeans. But now for a second and even a third year we have executions, executions, executions, unceasingly!

I take up to-day's paper.

To-day, May 9th, the paper contains these few words: "To-day in Khersón on the Strelbítsky Field, twenty peasants[1] were hung for an attack, made with intent to rob, on a landed proprietor's estate in the Elisabetgrad district."

Twelve of those by whose labour we live, the very men whom we have depraved and are still depraving by every means in our power—from the poison of vodka to the terrible falsehood of a creed we impose on them with all our might but do not ourselves believe in—twelve of these men strangled with cords by those whom they feed and clothe and house, and who have depraved and

[1] The papers have since contradicted the statement that twenty peasants were hung. I can only be glad of the mistake, glad not only that eight less have been strangled than was stated at first, but glad also that the awful figure moved me to express in these pages a feeling that has long tormented me. I leave the rest unchanged, therefore, merely substituting the word twelve for the word twenty, since what I said refers not only to the twelve who were hung but to all the thousands who have lately been crushed and killed—L. T.

still continue to deprave them. Twelve husbands, fathers, and sons, from among those upon whose kindness, industry, and simplicity alone rests the whole of Russian life, are seized, imprisoned, and shackled. Then their hands are tied behind their backs lest they should seize the ropes by which they are to be hung, and they are led to the gallows. Several peasants similar to those about to be hung, but armed, dressed in clean soldiers' uniforms with good boots on their feet and with guns in their hands, accompany the condemned men. Beside them walks a long-haired man, wearing a stole and vestments of gold or silver cloth and bearing a cross. The procession stops. The man in command of the whole business says something, the secretary reads a paper; and when the paper has been read the long-haired man, addressing those whom other people are about to strangle with cords, says something about God and Christ. Immediately after these words the hangmen (there are several, for one man could not manage so complicated a business) dissolve some soap, and, having soaped the loops in the cords that they may tighten better, seize the shackled men, put shrouds on them, lead them to a scaffold, and place the well-soaped nooses round their necks.

And then, one after another, living men are pushed off the benches which are drawn from under their feet, and by their own weight suddenly tighten the nooses round their necks and are painfully strangled. Men, alive a minute before, become corpses dangling from a rope, at first swinging slowly and then resting motionless.

All this is carefully arranged and planned by learned and enlightened people of the upper class. They arrange to do these things secretly at daybreak so that no one shall see them done, and they arrange that the responsibility for these iniquities shall be so subdivided among those who commit them that each may think and say that it is not he who is responsible for them. They arrange to seek out the most depraved and unfortunate of men and, while obliging them to do this business planned and approved by themselves, still keep up an appearance of abhorring those who do it. They even plan such a subtle device as this: sentences are pronounced by a military tribunal, yet it is not military people but civilians who have to be present at the execution. And the business is performed by unhappy, deluded, perverted, and despised men who have nothing left them but to soap the cords well that they may grip the necks without fail and then to get well drunk on poison sold them by these same enlightened upper-class people in order the more quickly and fully to forget their souls and their quality as men. A doctor makes his round of the bodies, feels them, and reports to those in authority that the business has been done properly—all twelve are certainly dead. And those in authority depart to their ordinary occupations with the consciousness of a necessary though painful task performed. The bodies, now grown cold, are taken down and buried.

The thing is awful!

And this is done not once, and not only to these twelve unhappy, misguided men from among the best class of the Russian people; it is done unceasingly for years, to hundreds and thousands of similar misguided men, misguided by the very people who do these terrible things to them.

And it is not this dreadful thing alone that is being done. All sorts of other tortures and violence are being perpetrated in prisons, fortresses, and convict settlements, on the same plea and with the same cold-blooded cruelty.

This is dreadful, but most dreadful of all is the fact that it is not done impulsively under the sway of feelings that silence reason, as occurs in fights, war, or even burglary, but on the contrary it is done at the demand of reason and calculation that silence feeling. That is what makes these deeds so particularly dreadful. Dreadful because these acts—committed by men who, from the judge to the hangman, do not wish to do them—prove more vividly than anything else how pernicious to human souls is despotism; the power of man over man.

It is revolting that one man can take from another his labour, his money, his cow, his horse, nay, even his son or his daughter—but how much more revolting it is that one man can take another's soul by forcing him to do what destroys his spiritual ego and deprives him of spiritual welfare. And that is just what is done by these men who arrange executions, and who by bribes, threats, and deceptions calmly force men—from the judge to the hangman—to commit deeds that certainly deprive them of their true welfare though they are committed in the name of the welfare of mankind.

And while this goes on for years all over Russia, the chief culprits—those by whose order these things are done, those who could put a stop to them—fully convinced that such deeds are useful and even absolutely necessary, either compose speeches and devise methods to prevent the Finns from living as they want to live, and to compel them to live as certain Russian personages wish them to live or else publish orders to the effect that: "In Hussar regiments the cuffs and collars of the men's jackets are to be of the same colour as the latter, while those entitled to wear pelisses are not to have braid round the cuffs over the fur."

What is most dreadful in the whole matter is that all this inhuman violence and killing, besides the direct evil done to the victims and their families, brings a yet more enormous evil on the whole people by spreading depravity—as fire spreads amid dry straw—among every class of Russians. This depravity grows with special rapidity among the simple working folk because all these iniquities — exceeding as they do a hundredfold all that is or has been done by thieves, robbers, and all the revolutionaries put together—are done as though they were something necessary, good, and unavoidable and are not merely excused but supported by different institutions inseparably connected in the people's minds with justice, and even with sanctity—namely, the Senate, the Synod, the Duma, the Church, and the Tsar.

And this depravity spreads with remarkable rapidity.

A short time ago there were not two executioners to be found in all Russia. In the eighties there was only one. I remember how joyfully Vladímir Solovëv then told me that no second executioner could be found in all Russia and so the one was taken from place to place. Not so now.

A small shopkeeper in Moscow whose affairs were in a bad way offered his services to perform the murders arranged by the government and, receiving a hundred rubles (£10) for each person hung, soon mended his affairs so well that he no longer required this additional business and has now reverted to his former trade.

In Orël last month, as elsewhere, an executioner was wanted, and a man was immediately found who agreed with the organizers of governmental murders to do the business for fifty rubles per head. But this volunteer hangman, after making the agreement, heard that more was paid in other towns, and at the time of the execution, having put the shroud sack on the victim, instead of leading him to the scaffold, stopped and, approaching the superintendent, said: "You must add another twenty-five rubles, your Excellency, or I won't do it!" And he got the increase and did the job.

A little later five people were to be hanged, and the day before the execution a stranger came to see the organizer of governmental murders on a private matter. The organizer went out to him, and the stranger said: "The other day so-and-so charged you seventy-five rubles a man. I hear five are to be done to-morrow. Let me have the whole job and I'll do it at fifteen rubles a head, and you can rely on its being done properly!"

I do not know whether the offer was accepted or not, but I know it was made.

That is how the crimes committed by the government act on the worst, the least moral, of the people, and these terrible deeds must also have an influence on the majority of men of average morality. Continually hearing and reading about the most terrible inhuman brutality committed by the authorities—that is, by persons whom the people are accustomed to honour as the best of men— the majority of average people, especially the young, pre-occupied with their own affairs, instead of realizing that those who do such horrible deeds are unworthy of honour, involuntarily come to the opposite conclusion and argue that if men generally honoured do things that seem to us horrible, these things cannot be as horrible as we suppose.

Of executions, hangings, murders, and bombs, people now write and speak as they used to speak about the weather. Children play at hangings. Lads from the high schools who are almost children go out on expropriating expeditions, ready to kill, just as they used to go out hunting. To kill off the large landed proprietors in order to seize their estates appears now to many people to be the very best solution of the land question.

In general, thanks to the activity of the government which has allowed killing as a means of obtaining its ends, all crimes, robbery, theft, lies, tortures, and murders are now considered by miserable people who have been perverted by that example to be most natural deeds, proper to a man.

Yes! Terrible as are the deeds themselves, the moral, spiritual, unseen evil they produce is incomparably more terrible.

You say you commit all these horrors to restore peace and order.

You restore peace and order!

By what means do you restore them? By destroying the last vestige of faith and morality in men—you, representatives of a Christian authority, leaders and teachers approved and encouraged by the servants of the Church! By committing the greatest crimes: lies, perfidy, torture of all sorts, and this last and most terrible of crimes, the one most abhorrent to every human heart that is not utterly depraved— not just a single murder but murders innumerable, which you think to justify by stupid references to such and such statutes written by yourselves in those stupid and lying books of yours which you blasphemously call "the laws."

You say that this is the only means of pacifying the people and quelling the revolution; but that is evidently false! It is plain that you cannot pacify the people unless you satisfy the demand of most elementary justice advanced by Russia's whole agricultural population (that is, the demand for the abolition of private property in land) and refrain from confirming it and in various ways irritating the peasants, as well as those unbalanced and envenomed people who have begun a violent struggle with you. You cannot pacify people by tormenting them and worrying, exiling, imprisoning, and hanging women and children! However hard you may try to stifle in yourselves the reason and love natural to human beings, you still have them within you and need only come to your senses and think, in order to see that by acting as you do—that is, by taking part in such terrible crimes—you not only fail to cure the disease, but by driving it inwards make it worse.

That is only too evident.

The cause of what is happening does not lie in physical events but depends entirely on the spiritual mood of the people, which has changed and which no efforts can bring back to its former condition, just as no efforts can turn a grown-up man into a child again. Social irritation or tranquillity cannot depend on whether Peter is hanged or allowed to live, or on whether John lives in Tambóv or in penal servitude at Nerchínsk. Social irritation or tranquillity must depend not on Peter or John alone but on how the great majority of the nation regard their position, and on the attitude of this majority to the government, to landed property, to the religion taught them, and on what this majority consider to be good or bad. The power of events does not lie in the material conditions of life at all, but in the spiritual condition of the people. Even if you were to kill and torture a tenth of the Russian nation, the spiritual condition of the rest would not become what you desire.

So that all you are now doing, with all your searchings, spying, exiling, prisons, penal settlements, and gallows, does not bring the people to the state you desire but on the contrary increases the irritation and destroys all possibility of peace and order.

"But what is to be done?" you say. "What is to be done? How are the iniquities that are now perpetrated to be stopped?"

The answer is very simple: "Cease to do what you are doing."

Even if no one knew what ought to be done to pacify "the people"—the whole people (many people know very well that what is most wanted to pacify the Russian people is the freeing of the land from private ownership, just as fifty years ago what was wanted was to free the peasants from serfdom)—if no one knew this, it would still be evident that to pacify the people one ought not to do what only increases its irritation. Yet that is just what you are doing!

What you are doing, you do, not for the people but for yourselves, to retain the position you occupy, a position you consider advantageous but which is really a most pitiful and abominable one. So do not say that you do it for the people; that is not true! All the abominations you do are done for yourselves, for your own covetous, ambitious, vain, vindictive, personal ends, in order to continue for a little longer in the depravity in which you live and which seems to you desirable.

However much you may declare that all you do is done for the good of the people, men are beginning to understand you and despise you more and more, and to regard your measures of restraint and suppression not as you wish them to be regarded—as the action of some kind of higher collective Being, the government—but as the personal evil deeds of individual and evil self-seekers.

Then again you say: "The revolutionaries began all this, not we, and their terrible crimes can only be suppressed by firm measures" (so you call your crimes) "on the part of the government."

You say the atrocities committed by the revolutionaries are terrible.

I do not dispute it. I will add that besides being terrible they are stupid, and—like your own actions—fall beside the mark. Yet however terrible and stupid may be their actions—all those bombs and tunnellings, those revolting murders and thefts of money—still all these deeds do not come anywhere near the criminality and stupidity of the deeds you commit.

They are doing just the same as you and for the same motives. They are in the same (I would say "comic" were its consequences not so terrible) delusion that men, having formed for themselves a plan of what in their opinion is the desirable and proper arrangement of society, have the right and possibility of arranging other people's lives according to that plan. The delusion is the same. These methods are violence of all kinds—including taking life. And the excuse is that an evil deed committed for the benefit of many ceases to be immoral, and that therefore without offending against the moral law, one may lie, rob, and kill whenever this tends to the realization of that supposed good condition for the many which we imagine that we know and can foresee, and which we wish to establish.

You government people call the acts of the revolutionaries "atrocities" and "great crimes"; but the revolutionaries have done and are doing nothing that you have not done, and done to an incomparably greater extent. They only do what you do; you keep spies, practise deception, and spread printed lies, and so do they. You take people's property by all sorts of violent means and use it as you consider best, and they do the same. You execute those whom you think dangerous, and so do they.

So you certainly cannot blame the revolutionaries while you employ the same immoral means as they do for the attainment of your aim. All that you can adduce for your own justification, they can equally adduce for theirs; not to mention that you do much evil that they do not commit, such as squandering the wealth of the nation, preparing for war, making war, subduing and oppressing foreign nationalities, and much else.

You say you have the traditions of the past to guard and the actions of the great men of the past as examples. They, too, have their traditions, also arising from the past—even before the French Revolution. And as to great men, models to copy, martyrs that perished for truth and freedom—they have no fewer of these than you.

So that if there is any difference between you it is only that you wish everything to remain as it has been and is, while they wish for a change. And in thinking that everything cannot always remain as it has been they would be more right than you, had they not adopted from you that curious, destructive delusion that one set of men can know the form of life suitable for all men in the future, and that this form can be established by force. For the rest, they only do what you do, using the same means. They are altogether your disciples. They have, as the saying is, picked up all your little dodges. They are not only your disciples, they are your products, your children. If you did not exist neither would they, so that when you try to suppress them by force you behave like a man who presses with his whole weight against a door that opens towards him.

If there be any difference between you and them it is certainly not in your favour but in theirs. The mitigating circumstances on their side are, firstly, that their crimes are committed under conditions of greater personal danger than you are exposed to, and risks and danger excuse much in the eyes of impressionable youth. Secondly, the immense majority of them are quite young people to whom it is natural to go astray, while you for the most part are men of mature age—old men to whom reasoned calm and leniency towards the deluded should be natural. A third mitigating circumstance in their favour is that however odious their murders may be, they are still not so coldly, systematically cruel as are your Schlüsselburgs, transportations, gallows, and shootings. And a fourth mitigating circumstance for the revolutionaries is that they all quite categorically repudiate all religious teaching and consider that the end justifies the means. Therefore when they kill one or more men for the sake of the imaginary welfare of the majority, they act quite consistently; whereas you government men—from the lowest hangman to the highest official—all support religion and Christianity, which is altogether incompatible with the deeds you commit.

And it is you elderly men, leaders of other men, professing Christianity, it is you who say, like children who have been fighting, "We didn't begin—they did!" That is the best you can say—you who have taken on yourselves the role of rulers of the people. And what sort of men are you? Men who acknowledge as God one who most definitely forbade not only judgement and punishment, but even condemnation of others; one who in clearest terms repudiated all punishment and affirmed the necessity of continual forgiveness however often a crime may be repeated; one who commanded us to turn the other cheek to the smiter and not return evil for evil; one who, in the case of the woman sentenced to be stoned, showed so simply and clearly the impossibility of judgement and punishment between man and man. And you, acknowledging that teacher to be God, can find nothing better to say in your defence than: "They began it! They kill people, so let us kill them!"

An artist of my acquaintance thought of painting a picture of an execution, and he wanted a model for the executioner. He heard that the duty of executioner in Moscow was at that time performed by a watchman, so he went to the watchman's house. It was Easter-time. The family were sitting in their best clothes at the tea-table, but the master of the house was not there. It turned out afterwards that on catching sight of a stranger he had hidden himself. His wife also seemed abashed and said that her husband was not at home; but his little girl betrayed him by saying: "Daddy's in the garret." She did not know that her father was aware that what he did was evil and therefore could not help being afraid of everybody. The artist explained to the wife that he wanted her husband as a model because his face suited the picture he had planned (of course he did not say what the picture was). Having got into conversation with the wife, the artist, in order to conciliate her, offered to take her little son as a pupil, an offer which evidently tempted her. She went out and after a time the husband entered, morose, restless, frightened, and looking askance. For a long time he tried to get the artist to say why he required just him. When the artist told him he had met him in the street and his face seemed suitable to the projected picture, the watchman asked where had he met him? At what time? In what clothes? And he would not come to terms, evidently fearing and suspecting something bad.

Yes, this executioner at first-hand knows that he is an executioner, he knows that he does wrong and is therefore hated, and he is afraid of men: and I think that this consciousness and this fear before men atone for at least a part of his guilt. But none of you—from the Secretary of the Court to the Premier and the Tsar—who are indirect participators in the iniquities perpetrated every day seem to feel your guilt or the shame that your participation in these horrors ought to evoke. It is true that like the executioner you fear men, and the greater your responsibility for the crimes the more your fear: the Public Prosecutor feels more fear than the Secretary; the President of the Court more than the Public Prosecutor; the General Governor more than the President; the

President of the Council of Ministers more still, and the Tsar most of all. You are all afraid, but unlike the executioner you are afraid not because you know you are doing evil, but because you think other people do evil.

Therefore I think that, low as that unfortunate watchman has fallen, he is morally immeasurably higher than you participators and part authors of these awful crimes: you who condemn others instead of yourselves and carry your heads so high.

I know that men are but human, that we are all weak, that we all err, and that one cannot judge another. I have long struggled against the feeling that was and is aroused in me by those responsible for these awful crimes, and aroused the more the higher they stand on the social ladder. But I cannot and will not struggle against that feeling any longer.

I cannot and will not. First, because an exposure of these people who do not see the full criminality of their actions is necessary for them as well as for the multitude which, influenced by the external honour and laudation accorded to these people, approves their terrible deeds and even tries to imitate them. And secondly because (I frankly confess it) I hope my exposure of those men will in one way or other evoke the expulsion I desire from the set in which I am now living, and in which I cannot but feel myself a participant in the crimes committed around me.

Everything now being done in Russia is done in the name of the general welfare, in the name of the protection and tranquillity of the people of Russia. And if this be so, then it is also done for me who live in Russia. For me, therefore, exists the destitution of the people deprived of the first and most natural right of man—the right to use the land on which he is born; for me those half-million men torn away from wholesome peasant life and dressed in uniforms and taught to kill; for me that false so-called priesthood whose chief duty it is to pervert and conceal true Christianity; for me all these transportations of men from place to place; for me these hundreds of thousands of hungry migratory workmen; for me these hundreds of thousands of unfortunates dying of typhus and scurvy in the fortresses and prisons which are insufficient for such a multitude; for me the mothers, wives, and fathers of the exiles, the prisoners, and those who are hanged are suffering; for me are these spies and this bribery; for me the interment of these dozens and hundreds of men who have been shot; for me the horrible work of these hangmen goes on—who were at first enlisted with difficulty but now no longer so loathe their work; for me exist these gallows with well-soaped cords from which hang women, children, and peasants; and for me exists this terrible embitterment of man against his fellow man.

Strange as it seems to say that all this is done for me, and that I am a participator in these terrible deeds, I cannot but feel that there is an indubitable interdependence between my spacious room, my dinner, my clothing, my leisure, and the terrible crimes committed to get rid of those who would like to take from me what I have. And though I know that these homeless, embittered, depraved people—who but for the government's threats would deprive me of all I am using—are products of that same government's actions, still I cannot help feeling that at present my peace really is dependent on all the horrors that are now being perpetrated by the government.

And being conscious of this I can no longer endure it, but must free myself from this intolerable position!

It is impossible to live so! I, at any rate, cannot and will not live so.

That is why I write this and will circulate it by all means in my power both in Russia and abroad—that one of two things may happen: either that these inhuman deeds may be stopped, or that my connexion with them may be snapped and I put in prison, where I may be clearly conscious that these horrors are not committed on my behalf; or still better (so good that I dare not even dream of such happiness) that they may put on me, as on those twelve or twenty peasants, a shroud and a cap and may push me also off a bench, so that by my own weight I may tighten the well-soaped noose round my old throat.

To attain one of these two aims I address myself to all participators in these terrible deeds, beginning with those who put on their brother men and women and children those caps and nooses—from the prison warders up to you, chief organizers and authorizers of these terrible crimes.

Brother men! Come to your senses, stop and think, consider what you are doing! Remember who you are!

Before being hangmen, generals, public prosecutors, judges, premier or Tsar, are you not men—to-day allowed a peep into God's world, to-morrow ceasing to be? (You hangmen of all grades in particular, who have evoked and are evoking special hatred, should remember this.) Is it possible that you who have had this brief glimpse of God's world (for even if you be not murdered, death is always close behind us all), is it possible that in your lucid moments you do not see that your vocation in life cannot be to torment and kill men, yourselves trembling with fear of being killed, lying to yourselves, to others, and to God, assuring yourselves and others that by participating in these things you are doing an important and grand work for the welfare of millions? Is it possible that—when not intoxicated by your surroundings, by flattery, and by the customary sophistries—you do not each one of you know that this is all mere talk, only invented that, while doing most evil deeds, you may still consider yourself a good man? You cannot but know that you, like each of us, have but one real duty which includes all others—the duty of living the short space granted us in accord with the Will that sent you into this world and of leaving it in accord with that Will. And that Will desires only one thing: love from man to man.

But what are you doing? To what are you devoting your spiritual strength? Whom do you love? Who loves you? Your wife? Your child? But that is not love. The love of wife and children is not human love. Animals love in that way even more strongly. Human love is the love of man for man—for every man as a son of God and there-fore a brother. Whom do you love in that way? No one. Who loves you in that way? No one.

You are feared as a hangman or a wild animal is feared. People flatter you because at heart they despise and hate you—and how they hate you! And you know it and are afraid of men.

Yes, consider it—all you accomplices in murder from

the highest to the lowest, consider who you are and cease to do what you are doing. Cease, not for your own sakes, not for the sake of your own personality, not for the sake of men, not that you may cease to be blamed, but for your soul's sake and for the God who lives within you!

1908

~~~~~~

THE POWER OF DARKNESS
or, If a Claw Is Caught the Bird Is Lost
A Drama in Five Acts

(1886)
CHARACTERS

PETER IGNATICH, a well-to-do peasant, 42 years old, married for the second time, and sickly.

ANISYA, his wife, 32 years old, fond of dress.

AKULINA, Peter's daughter by his first marriage, 16 years old, hard of hearing, mentally undeveloped.

NAN (ANNA PETROVNA OR ANYUTA), his daughter by his second marriage, 10 years old.

NIKITA, their labourer, 25 years old, fond of dress.

AKIM, Nikita's father, 50 years old, a plain-looking, God-fearing peasant.

MATRENA (the *e* is pronounced like a broad *yo*), his wife and Nikita's mother, 50 years old.

MARINA, an orphan girl, 22 years old.

MARTHA, Peter's sister.

MITRICH, an old labourer, ex-soldier.

SIMON, Marina's husband.

BRIDEGROOM, engaged to Akulina.

IVAN, his father.

FIRST NEIGHBOUR.

SECOND NEIGHBOUR.

FIRST GIRL.

SECOND GIRL.

POLICE OFFICER.

DRIVER.

BEST MAN.

MATCHMAKER.

VILLAGE ELDER.

Visitors, women, girls, and folk who have come to see the wedding

ACT
I

*The act takes place in autumn in a large village. The scene
represents Peter's roomy hut. Peter is sitting on a wooden
bench, mending a horse-collar. Anisya and Akulina are
spinning and singing a part-song.*

PETER, *looking out of the window*: The horses have got
loose again. If we don't look out they'll be killing the colt.
Nikita! Hey, Nikita! Is the fellow deaf? *Listens. To the
women*: Shut up, one can't hear anything.

NIKITA, *from outside*: What?

PETER: Drive the horses in.

NIKITA: We'll drive 'em in. All in good time.

PETER, *shaking his head*: Ah, these labourers! If I were
well, I'd not keep one on no account. There's nothing
but bother with 'em. *Rises and sits down again.* Nikita!
. . . It's no good shouting. One of you'd better go. Go,
Akul, drive 'em in.

AKULINA: What? The horses?

PETER: What else?

AKULINA: All right. *Exit.*

PETER: Ah, but he's a loafer, that lad . . . no good
at all. Won't stir a finger if he can help it.

ANISYA: You're so mighty brisk yourself. When you're
not sprawling on the top of the oven[1] you're squatting on
the bench. To goad others to work is all you're fit for.

PETER: If one weren't to goad you on a bit, one'd have
no roof left over one's head before the year's out. Oh,
what people!

ANISYA: You go shoving a dozen jobs on to one's
shoulders, and then do nothing but scold. It's easy to lie
on the oven and give orders.

PETER, *sighing*: Oh, if 'twere not for this sickness that's
got hold of me, I'd not keep him on another day.

AKULINA, *off the scene*: Gee up, gee, whoa.

*A colt neighs, the stamping of horses' feet and the creak-
ing of the gate are heard.*

---

[1] The usual large brick Russian baking-oven. The top of it outside is
flat, so that more than one person can lie on it.

PETER: Bragging, that's what he's good at. I'd like to sack him, I would indeed.

ANISYA, *mimicking him*: "Like to sack him." You buckle to yourself, and then talk.

AKULINA (*enters*): It's all I could do to drive 'em in. That piebald always will. . . .

PETER: And where's Nikita?

AKULINA: Where's Nikita? Why, standing out there in the street.

PETER: What's he standing there for?

AKULINA: What's he standing there for? He stands there jabbering.

PETER: One can't get any sense out of her! Who's he jabbering with?

AKULINA (*does not hear*): Eh, what?

Peter waves her off. She sits down to her spinning.

NAN, *running in to her mother*: Nikita's father and mother have come. They're going to take him away. It's true!

ANISYA: Nonsense!

NAN: Yes. Blest if they're not! *Laughing.* I was just going by, and Nikita, he says, "Good-bye, Anna Petrovna," "you must come and dance at my wedding. I'm leaving you," he says, and laughs.

ANISYA, *to her husband*: There now. Much he cares. You see, he wants to leave of himself. "Sack him," indeed!

PETER: Well, let him go. Just as if I couldn't find somebody else.

ANISYA: And what about the money he's had in advance?

Nan stands listening at the door for a while, and then exit.

PETER, *frowning*: The money? Well, he can work it off in summer, anyhow.

ANISYA: Well, of course you'll be glad if he goes and you've not got to feed him. It's only me as'll have to work like a horse all the winter. That lass of yours isn't over-fond of work either. And you'll be lying up on the oven. I know you.

PETER: What's the good of wearing out one's tongue before one has the hang of the matter?

ANISYA: The yard's full of cattle. You've not sold the cow and have kept all the sheep for the winter:

feeding and watering 'em alone takes all one's time, and you want to sack the labourer. But I tell you straight, I'm not going to do a man's work! I'll go and lie on the top of the oven same as you, and let everything go to pot! You may do what you like.

PETER, *to Akulina*: Go and see about the feeding, will you? It's time.

AKULINA: The feeding? All right. *Puts on a coat and takes a rope.*

ANISYA: I'm not going to work for you. You go and work yourself. I've had enough of it, so there!

PETER: That'll do. What are you raving about? Like a sheep with the staggers!

ANISYA: You're a crazy cur, you see! One gets neither work nor pleasure from you. Eating your fill, that's all you do, you palsied cur, you!

PETER (*spits and puts on coat*): Faugh! The Lord have mercy! I'd better go myself and see what's up. *Exit.*

ANISYA, *after him*: Scurvy long-nosed devil!

AKULINA: What are you swearing at dad for?

ANISYA: Hold your noise, you idiot!

AKULINA, *going to the door*: I know why you're swearing at him. You're an idiot yourself, you bitch. I'm not afraid of you.

ANISYA: What do you mean? *Jumps up and looks round for something to hit her with.* You look out, or I'll give you one with the poker.

AKULINA, *opening the door*: Bitch! devil! that's what you are! Devil! bitch! bitch! devil! *Runs off.*

ANISYA (*ponders*): "Come and dance at my wedding!" What new plan is this? Marry? Mind, Nikita, if that's what you mean, I'll go and . . . No, I can't live without him. I won't let him go.

NIKITA (*enters, looks round, and seeing Anisya alone approaches quickly; in a low tone*): Here's a go; I'm in a regular fix! That governor of mine wants to take me away—tells me I'm to come home. Says quite straight I'm to marry and live at home.

ANISYA: Well, go and marry! What's that to me?

NIKITA: Is that it? Why, here am I reckoning how best to arrange matters, and just hear her! She tells me to go and marry. Why's that? *Winking.* Has she forgotten?

ANISYA: Yes, go and marry! What do I care?

NIKITA: What are you spitting for? Just see, she won't even let me stroke her. . . . What's the matter?

ANISYA: This! That you want to play me false. . . . If you do—why, I don't want you either. So now you know!

NIKITA: That'll do, Anisya. Do you think I'll forget you? Never while I live! I'll not play you false, that's flat. I've been thinking that supposing they do go and make me marry, I'd still come back to you. If only he don't make me live at home!

ANISYA: Much need I'll have of you, once you're married.

NIKITA: There's a go now. How can one go against a father's will?

ANISYA: Yes, I dare say, shove it all on your father. You know it's your own doing. You've long been plotting with that slut of yours, Marina. It's she has put you up to it. She didn't come here for nothing t'other day.

NIKITA: Marina? What's she to me? Much I care about her! . . . Plenty of them buzzing around.

ANISYA: Then what has made your father come here? It's you have told him to. You've gone and deceived me. *Cries.*

NIKITA: Anisya, do you believe in a God or not? I never so much as dreamt of it. I know nothing at all about it. I never even dreamt of it—that's flat! My old dad has got it all out of his own pate.

ANISYA: If you don't wish it yourself who can force you? He can't drive you like an ass.

NIKITA: Well, I reckon it's not possible to go against one's parents. But it's not by my wish.

ANISYA: Don't you budge, that's all about it!

NIKITA: There was a fellow wouldn't budge, and the village elder gave him such a hiding. . . . That's what it might come to! I've no great wish for that sort of thing. They say it touches one up. . . .

ANISYA: Shut up with your nonsense. Nikita, listen to me: if you marry that Marina I don't know what I won't do to myself. . . . I shall lay hands on myself! I have sinned, I have gone against the law, but I can't go back now. If you go away I'll . . .

NIKITA: Why should I go? Had I wanted to go—I

should have gone long ago. There was Ivan Seménich t'other day—offered me a place as his coachman. . . . Only fancy what a life that would have been! But I did not go. Because, I reckon, I am good enough for any one. Now if you did not love me it would be a different matter.

ANISYA: Yes, and that's what you should remember. My old man will die one of these fine days, I'm thinking; then we could cover our sin, make it all right and lawful, and then you'll be master here.

NIKITA: Where's the good of making plans? What do I care? I work as hard as if I were doing it for myself. My master loves me, and his missus loves me. And if the wenches run after me, it's not my fault, that's flat.

ANISYA: And you'll love me?

NIKITA, *embracing her*: There, as you have ever been in my heart . . .

MATRENA *enters and crosses herself a long time before the icon. Nikita and Anisya step apart.*

MATRENA: What I saw I didn't perceive; what I heard I didn't hearken to. Playing with the lass, eh? Well— even a calf will play. Why shouldn't one have some fun when one's young? But your master is out in the yard a-calling you, sonnie.

NIKITA: I only came to get the axe.

MATRENA: I know, sonnie, I know; them sort of axes are mostly to be found where the women are.

NIKITA, *stooping to pick up axe*: I say, mother, is it true you want me to marry? By my reckoning, that's quite unnecessary. Besides, I've got no wish that way.

MATRENA: Eh, honey! why should you marry? Go on as you are. It's all the old man. You'd better go, sonnie, we can talk these matters over without you.

NIKITA: It's a queer go! One moment I'm to be married, the next, not. I can't make head or tail of it. *Exit.*

ANISYA: What's it all about then? Do you really want him to get married?

MATRENA: Eh, why should he marry, my jewel? It's all nonsense, all my old man's drivel. "Marry, marry." But he's reckoning without his host. You know the saying, "From oats and hay, why should horses stray?" When you've enough and to spare, why look elsewhere? And so in this case. *Winks.* Don't I see which way the wind blows?

ANISYA: Where's the good of my pretending to you, Mother Matrena? You know all about it. I have sinned. I love your son.

MATRENA: Dear me, here's news! D'you think Mother Matrena didn't know? Eh, lassie—Mother Matrena's been ground, and ground again, ground fine! This much I can tell you, my jewel: Mother Matrena can see through a brick wall three feet thick. I know it all, my jewel! I know what young wives need sleeping draughts for, so I've brought some along. *Unties a knot in her handkerchief and brings out paper-packets.* As much as is wanted I see, and what's not wanted I neither see nor perceive! There! Mother Matrena has also been young. I had to know a thing or two to live with my old fool. I know seventy and seven dodges. But I see your old man's quite seedy, quite seedy! How's one to live with such as him? Why, if you pricked him with a hay-fork it wouldn't fetch blood. See if you don't bury him before the spring. Then you'll need some one in the house. Well, what's wrong with my son? He'll do as well as another. Then where's the advantage of my taking him away from a good place? Am I my child's enemy?

ANISYA: Oh, if only he does not go away.

MATRENA: He won't go away, birdie. It's all nonsense. You know my old man. His wits are always wool-gathering; yet sometimes he takes a thing into his pate, and it's as if it were wedged in, you can't knock it out with a hammer.

ANISYA: And what started this business?

MATRENA: Well, you see, my jewel, you yourself know what a fellow with women the lad is—and he's handsome too, though I say it as shouldn't. Well, you know, he was living at the railway, and they had an orphan wench there to cook for them. Well, that same wench took to running after him.

ANISYA: Marina?

MATRENA: Yes, the plague seize her! Whether anything happened or not, anyhow something got to my old man's ears. Maybe he heard from the neighbours, maybe she's been and blabbed . . .

ANISYA: Well, she is a bold hussy!

MATRENA: So my old man—the old blockhead—off he goes: "Marry, marry," he says, "he must marry her and cover the sin," he says. "We must take the lad home," he says, "and he shall marry," he says. Well, I did my best to make him change his mind, but, dear me, no. So, all right, thinks I, I'll try another dodge. One always has to entice them fools in this way, just pretend to be of their mind, and when it comes to the point one goes and turns it all one's own way. You know, a woman has time to think seventy and seven thoughts while falling off the oven, so how's such as he to see through it? "Well, yes," says I, "it would be a good job—only we must consider well beforehand. Why not go and see our son, and talk it over with Peter Ignatich and hear what he has to say?" So here we are.

ANISYA: Oh dear, oh dear, how will it all end? Supposing his father just orders him to marry her?

MATRENA: Orders, indeed! Chuck his orders to the dogs! Don't you worry; that'll never come off. I'll go to your old man myself and sift and strain this matter clear—there will be nothing of it left. I have come here only for the look of the thing. A very likely thing! Here's my son living in happiness and expecting happiness, and I'll go and match him with a slut! No fear, I'm not a fool!

ANISYA: And she—this Marina—came dangling after him here! Mother, would you believe, when they said he was going to marry, it was as if a knife had gone right through my heart. I knew he cared for her.

MATRENA: Oh, my jewel! Why, you don't think him such a fool, that he should go and care for a homeless baggage like that? Nikita is a sensible fellow, you see. He knows whom to love. So don't you go and fret, my jewel. We'll not take him away, and we won't marry him. No, we'll let him stay on, if you'll only oblige us with a little money.

ANISYA: All I know is, that I could not live if Nikita went away.

MATRENA: Naturally, when one's young it's no easy matter! You, a wench in full bloom, to be living with the dregs of a man like that husband of yours.

ANISYA: Mother Matrena, would you believe it? I'm

that sick of him, that sick of this long-nosed cur of mine,
I can hardly bear to look at him.

MATRENA: Yes, I see, it's one of them cases. Just look
here (*looks round and whispers*), I've been to see that
old man, you know—he's given me simples of two kinds.
This, you see, is a sleeping draught. "Just give him one
of these powders," he says, "and he'll sleep so sound you
might jump on him!" And this here, "This is that kind
of simple," he says, "that if you give one some of it
to drink it has no smell whatever, but its strength is very
great. There are seven doses here, a pinch at a time. Give
him seven pinches," he says, "and she won't have far to
look for freedom," he says.

ANISYA: O-o-oh! What's that?

MATRENA: "No sign whatever," he says. He's taken a
ruble for it. "Can't sell it for less," he says. Because it's
no easy matter to get 'em, you know. I paid him, dearie,
out of my own money. If she takes them, thinks I, it's
all right; if she don't, I can let old Michael's daughter
have them.

ANISYA: O-o-oh! But mayn't some evil come of them?
I'm frightened!

MATRENA: What evil, my jewel? If your old man was
hale and hearty, 'twould be a different matter, but he's
neither alive nor dead as it is. He's not for this world.
Such things often happen.

ANISYA: O-o-oh, my poor head! I'm afeared, Mother
Matrena, lest some evil come of them. No. It can't be done.

MATRENA: Just as you like. I might even return them
to him.

ANISYA: And are they to be used in the same way
as the others? Mixed in water?

MATRENA: Better in tea, he says. "You can't notice anything," he says, "no smell nor nothing." He's a cute old
fellow too.

ANISYA, *taking the powder*: O-oh, my head aches so!
Could I have ever thought of such a thing if my life
were not a very hell?

MATRENA: You'll not forget that ruble? I promised
to take it to the old man. He's had some trouble, too.

ANISYA: Of course. *Goes to her box and hides the
powders.*

MATRENA: And now, my jewel, keep it as close as you can, so that no one should find it out. Heaven defend that it should happen, but *if* any one notices it, tell 'em it's for the black-beetles. *Takes the ruble.* It's also used for beetles. *Stops short.*

Enter Akim, who crosses himself in front of the icon, and then Peter, who sits down.

PETER: Well then, how's it to be, Daddy Akim?

AKIM: As it's best, Peter Ignatich, as it's best . . . I mean—as it's best. 'Cos why? I'm afeared of what d'you call 'em, some tomfoolery, you know. I'd like to, what d'you call it . . . to start, you know, start the lad honest, I mean. But supposing you'd rather, what d'you call it, we might, I mean, what's its name? As it's best . . .

PETER: All right. All right. Sit down and let's talk it over. *Akim sits down.* Well then, what's it all about? You want him to marry?

MATRENA: As to marrying, he might bide a while, Peter Ignatich. You know our poverty, Peter Ignatich. What's he to marry on? We've hardly enough to eat ourselves. How can he marry, then?

PETER: You must consider what will be best.

MATRENA: Where's the hurry for him to get married? Marriage is not that sort of thing, it's not like ripe raspberries that drop off if not picked in time.

PETER: If he were to get married, 'twould be a good thing in a way.

AKIM: We'd like to . . . what d'you call it? 'Cos why, you see? I've what d'you call it . . . a job. I mean, I've found a paying job in town, you know.

MATRENA: And a fine job too—cleaning out cesspools. The other day when he came home, I could do nothing but spew and spew. Faugh!

AKIM: It's true, at first it does seem what d'you call it . . . knocks one clean over, you know—the smell, I mean. But one gets used to it, and then it's nothing, no worse than malt grain, and then it's what d'you call it . . . pays, pays, I mean. And as to the smell being, what d'you call it, it's not for the like of us to complain. And one changes one's clothes. So we'd like to take what's his name . . . Nikita, I mean, home. Let him manage things at home while I, what d'you call it—earn something in town.

PETER: You want to keep your son at home? Yes, that would be all right: but how about the money he has had in advance?

AKIM: That's it, that's it! It's just as you say, Peter Ignatich, it's just what d'you call it. 'Cos why? If you go into service, it's as good as if you had sold yourself, they say. That will be all right. I mean he may stay and serve his time, only he must, what d'you call it, get married. I mean—so: you let him off for a little while, that he may, what d'you call it?

PETER: Yes, we could manage that.

MATRENA: Ah, but it's not yet settled between our-selves, Peter Ignatich. I'll speak to you as I would before God, and you may judge between my old man and me. He goes on harping on that marriage. But just ask—who it is he wants him to marry. If it were a girl of the right sort now—I am not my child's enemy, but the wench is not honest.

AKIM: No, that's wrong! Wrong, I say. 'Cos why? She, that same girl—it's my son as has offended, offended the girl I mean.

PETER: How offended?

AKIM: That's how. She's what d'you call it, with him, with my son, Nikita. With Nikita, what d'you call it, I mean.

MATRENA: You wait a bit, my tongue runs smoother—let me tell it. You know, this lad of ours lived at the railway before he came to you. There was a girl there as kept dangling after him. A girl of no account, you know, her name's Marina. She used to cook for the men. So now this same girl accuses our son, Nikita, that he, so to say, deceived her.

PETER: Well, there's nothing good in that.

MATRENA: But she's no honest girl herself; she runs after the fellows like a common slut.

AKIM: There you are again, old woman, and it's not at all . . . what d'you call it, it's all not . . . what d'you call it, I mean . . .

MATRENA: There now, that's all the sense one gets

from my old owl—"what d'you call it, what d'you call it," and he doesn't know himself what he means. Peter Ignatich, don't listen to me, but go yourself and ask any one you like about the girl, everybody will say the same. She's just a homeless good-for-nothing.

PETER: You know, Daddy Akim, if that's how things are, there's no reason for him to marry her. A daughter-in-law's not like a shoe, you can't kick her off.

AKIM, *excitedly*: It's false, old woman, it's . . . what d'you call it, false; I mean, about the girl; false! 'Cos why? The lass is a good lass, a very good lass, you know. I'm sorry, sorry for the lassie, I mean.

MATRENA: It's an old saying: "For the wide world old Miriam grieves, and at home without bread her children she leaves." He's sorry for the girl, but not sorry for his own son! Sling her round your neck and carry her about with you! That's enough of such empty cackle!

AKIM: No, it's not empty.

MATRENA: There, don't interrupt, let me have my say.

AKIM (*interrupts*): No, not empty! I mean, you twist things your own way, about the lass or about yourself. Twist them, I mean, to make it better for yourself; but God, what d'you call it, turns them His way. That's how it is.

MATRENA: Eh! One only wears out one's tongue with you.

AKIM: The lass is hard-working and spruce, and keeps everything round herself . . . what d'you call it. And in our poverty, you know, it's a pair of hands, I mean; and the wedding needn't cost much. But the chief thing's the offence, the offence to the lass, and she's a what d'you call it, an orphan, you know; that's what she is, and there's the offence.

MATRENA: Eh! they'll all tell you a tale of that sort . . .

ANISYA: Daddy Akim, you'd better listen to us women; we can tell you a thing or two.

AKIM: And God, how about God? Isn't she a human being, the lass? A what d'you call it—also a human being I mean, before God. And how do you look at it?

MATRENA: Eh! . . . started off again?

PETER: Wait a bit, Daddy Akim. One can't believe all these girls say, either. The lad's alive, and not far away;

send for him, and find out straight from him if it's true. He won't wish to lose his soul. Go and call the fellow (*Anisya rises*) and tell him his father wants him. *Exit Anisya.*

MATRENA: That's right, dear friend; you've cleared the way clean, as with water. Yes, let the lad speak for himself. Nowadays, you know, they'll not let you force a son to marry; one must first of all ask the lad. He'll never consent to marry her and disgrace himself, not for all the world. To my thinking, it's best he should go on living with you and serving you as his master. And we need not take him home for the summer either; we can hire a help. If you would only give us ten rubles now, we'll let him stay on.

PETER: All in good time. First let us settle one thing before we start another.

AKIM: You see, Peter Ignatich, I speak, 'cos why? you know how it happens. We try to fix things up as seems best for ourselves, you know; and as to God, we what d'you call it, we forget Him. We think it's best so, turn it our own way, and lo! we've got into a fix, you know. We think it will be best, I mean; and lo! it turns out much worse—without God, I mean.

PETER: Of course one must not forget God.

AKIM: It turns out worse! But when it's the right way —God's way—it . . . what d'you call it, it gives one joy; seems pleasant, I mean. So I reckon, you see, get him, the lad, I mean, get him to marry her, to keep him from sin, I mean, and let him . . . what d'you call it at home, as it's lawful, I mean, while I go and get the job in town. The work is of the right sort—it's payin', I mean. And in God's sight it's what d'you call it—it's best, I mean. Ain't she an orphan? Here, for example, a year ago some fellows went and took timber from the steward— thought they'd do the steward, you know. Yes, they did the steward, but they couldn't . . . what d'you call it . . . do God, I mean. Well, and so . . .

Enter Nikita and Nan.

NIKITA: You called me? *Sits down and takes out his tobacco-pouch.*

PETER, *in a low reproachful voice*: What are you thinking about—have you no manners? Your father is

going to speak to you, and you sit down and fool about
with tobacco. Come, get up!

*Nikita rises, leans carelessly with his elbow on the
table, and smiles.*

AKIM: It seems there's a complaint, you know, about
you, Nikita—a complaint, I mean, a complaint.

NIKITA: Who's been complaining?

AKIM: Complaining? It's a maid, an orphan maid, complaining, I mean. It's her, you know—a complaint against
you, from Marina, I mean.

NIKITA (*laughs*): Well, that's a good one. What's the
complaint? And who's told you—she herself?

AKIM: It's I am asking you, and you must now, what
d'you call it, give me an answer. Have you got mixed up
with the lass, I mean—mixed up, you know?

NIKITA: I don't know what you mean. What's up?

AKIM: Foolin', I mean, what d'you call it, foolin'.
Have you been foolin' with her, I mean?

NIKITA: Never mind what's been! Of course one does
have some fun with a cook now and then to while away
the time. One plays the concertina and gets her to dance.
What of that?

PETER: Don't shuffle, Nikita, but answer your father
straight out.

AKIM, *solemnly*: You can hide it from men but not
from God, Nikita. You . . . what d'you call it . . . think,
I mean, and don't tell lies. She's an orphan; so, you see,
any one is free to insult her. An orphan, you see. So
you should say what's rightest.

NIKITA: But what if I have nothing to say? I have
told you everything—because there isn't anything to tell,
that's flat! *Getting excited.* She can go and say anything
about me, same as if she was speaking of one as is dead.
Why don't she say anything about Fedka Mikishin? Besides,
how's this, that one mayn't even have a bit of fun
nowadays? And as for her, well, she's free to say anything she likes.

AKIM: Ah, Nikita, mind! A lie will out. Did anything
happen?

NIKITA, *aside*: How he sticks to it; it's too bad. *To Akim*:
I tell you, I know nothing more. There's been nothing
between us. *Angrily*. By God! and may I never leave this

spot (*crosses himself*) if I know anything about it. *Silence. Then still more excitedly*: Why! have you been thinking of getting me to marry her? What do you mean by it?—it's a confounded shame. Besides, nowadays you've got no such rights as to force a fellow to marry. That's plain enough. Besides, haven't I sworn I know nothing about it?

MATRENA, *to her husband*: There now, that's just like your silly pate, to believe all they tell you. He's gone and put the lad to shame all for nothing. The best thing is to let him live as he is living, with his master. His master will help us in our present need, and give us ten rubles, and when the time comes . . .

PETER: Well, Daddy Akim, how's it to be?

AKIM (*looks at his son, clicking his tongue disapprovingly*): Mind, Nikita, the tears of one that's been wronged never . . . what d'you call it—never fall beside the mark but always on, what's name—the head of the man as did the wrong. So mind, don't . . . what d'you call it.

NIKITA (*sits down*): What's there to mind? mind yourself.

NAN, *aside*: I must run and tell mother. *Exit.*

MATRENA, *to Peter*: That's always the way with this old mumbler of mine, Peter Ignatich. Once he's got anything wedged in his pate there's no knocking it out. We've gone and troubled you all for nothing. The lad can go on living as he has been. Keep him; he's your servant.

PETER: Well, Daddy Akim, what do you say?

AKIM: Why, the lad's his own master, if only he . . . what d'you call it. . . . I only wish that . . . what d'you call it . . . I mean.

MATRENA: You don't know yourself what you're jawing about. The lad himself has no wish to leave. Besides, what do we want with him at home? We can manage without him.

PETER: Only one thing, Daddy Akim—if you are thinking of taking him back in summer, I don't want him here for the winter. If he is to stay at all, it must be for the whole year.

MATRENA: And it's for a year he'll bind himself. If we want help when the press of work comes, we can hire help, and the lad shall remain with you. Only give us ten rubles now. . . .

PETER: Well then, is it to be for another year?

AKIM, *sighing*: Yes, it seems, it . . . what d'you call it . . . if it's so, I mean, it seems that it must be . . . what d'you call it.

MATRENA: For a year, counting from St. Dimitri's day. We know you'll pay him fair wages. But give us ten rubles now. Help us out of our difficulties. *Gets up and bows to Peter.*

Enter Nan and Anisya. The latter sits down at one side.

PETER: Well, if that's settled we might step across to the inn and have a drink. Come, Daddy Akim, what do you say to a glass of vodka?

AKIM: No, I never drink that sort of thing.

PETER: Well, you'll have some tea?

AKIM: Ah, tea! yes, I do sin that way. Yes, tea's the thing.

PETER: And the women will also have some tea. Come. And you, Nikita, go and drive the sheep in and clear away the straw.

NIKITA: All right.

Exeunt all but Nikita. Nikita lights a cigarette. It grows darker. Just see how they bother one. Want a fellow to tell 'em how he larks about with the wenches! It would take long to tell 'em all those stories—"Marry her," he says. Marry them all! One would have a good lot of wives! And what need have I to marry? Am as good as married now! There's many a chap as envies me. Yet how strange it felt when I crossed myself before the icon. It was just as if some one shoved me. The whole web fell to pieces at once. They say it's frightening to swear what's not true. That's all humbug. It's all talk, that is. It's simple enough.

Akulina enters with a rope, which she puts down. She takes off her outdoor things and goes into closet.

AKULINA: You might at least have got a light.

NIKITA: What, to look at you? I can see you well enough without.

AKULINA: Oh, bother you!

Nan enters and whispers to Nikita.

NAN: Nikita, there's a person wants you. There is!

NIKITA: What person?

NAN: Marina from the railway; she's out there, round the corner.

NIKITA: Nonsense!

NAN: Blest if she isn't.

NIKITA: What does she want?

NAN: She wants you to come out. She says, "I only want to say a word to Nikita." I began asking, but she won't tell, but only says, "Is it true he's leaving you?" And I say, "No, only his father wanted to take him away and get him to marry, but he won't, and is going to stay with us another year." And she says, "For goodness' sake send him out to me. I must see him," she says, "I must say a word to him somehow." She's been waiting a long time. Why don't you go?

NIKITA: Bother her! What should I go for?

NAN: She says, "If he don't come, I'll go into the hut to him." Blest if she didn't say she'd come in!

NIKITA: Not likely. She'll wait a bit and then go away.

NAN: "Or is it," she says, "that they want him to marry Akulina?"

Re-enter Akulina, passing near Nikita to take her distaff.

AKULINA: Marry whom to Akulina?

NAN: Why, Nikita.

AKULINA: A likely thing! Who says it?

NIKITA (*looks at her and laughs*): It seems people do say it. Would you marry me, Akulina?

AKULINA: Who, you? Perhaps I might have afore, but I won't now!

NIKITA: And why not now?

AKULINA: 'Cos you wouldn't love me.

NIKITA: Why not?

AKULINA: 'Cos you'd be forbidden to. *Laughs.*

NIKITA: Who'd forbid it?

AKULINA: Who? My step-mother. She does nothing but grumble and is always staring at you.

NIKITA, *laughing*: Just hear her! Ain't she cute?

AKULINA: Who? Me? What's there to be cute about? Am I blind? She's been rowing and rowing at dad all day. The fat-muzzled witch! *Goes into closet.*

NAN, *looking out of the window*: Look, Nikita, she's coming! I'm blest if she isn't! I'll go away. *Exit.*

MARINA (*enters*): What are you doing with me?

NIKITA: Doing? I'm not doing anything.

MARINA: You mean to desert me.

NIKITA (*gets up angrily*): What does this look like, your coming here?

MARINA: Oh, Nikita!

NIKITA: Well, you are strange! What have you come for?

MARINA: Nikita!

NIKITA: That's my name. What do you want with Nikita? Well, what next? Go away, I tell you!

MARINA: I see, you do want to throw me over.

NIKITA: Well, and what's there between us? You yourself don't know. When you stood out there round the corner and sent Nan for me, and I didn't come, wasn't it plain enough that you're not wanted? It seems pretty simple. So there—go!

MARINA: Not wanted! So now I'm not wanted! I believed you when you said you'd love me. And now that you've ruined me, I'm not wanted.

NIKITA: Where's the good of talking? This is quite improper. You've been telling tales to father. Now, do go away, will you?

MARINA: You know yourself I never loved any one but you. Whether you married me or not, I'd not have been angry. I've done you no wrong, then why have you left off caring for me? Why?

NIKITA: Where's the use of baying at the moon? You go away. Goodness me! What a stupid!

MARINA: It's not that you deceived me when you promised to marry me that hurts, but that you've left off loving. No, it's not that you've stopped loving me either, but that you've left me for another, that's what hurts. I know who it is!

NIKITA (*comes up to her viciously*): Eh! what's the good of talking to the likes of you, that won't listen to reason? Be off, or you'll drive me to do something you'll be sorry for.

MARINA: What, will you strike me, then? Well then, strike me! What are you turning away for? Ah, Nikita!

NIKITA: Supposing some one came in. Of course it's quite improper. And what's the good of talking?

MARINA: So this is the end of it! What has been has flown. You want me to forget it? Well then, Nikita, listen.

I kept my maiden honour as the apple of my eye. You have ruined me for nothing, you have deceived me. You have no pity on a fatherless and motherless girl! *Weeping.* You have deserted, you have killed me, but I bear you no malice. God forgive you! If you find a better one you'll forget me; if a worse one you'll remember me. Yes, you will remember, Nikita! Good-bye, then, if it is to be. Oh, how I loved you! Good-bye for the last time. *Takes his head in her hands and tries to kiss him.*

NIKITA, *tossing his head back*: I'm not going to talk with the likes of you. If you won't go away I will, and you may stay here by yourself.

MARINA (*screams*): You are a brute. *In the doorway*: God will give you no joy. *Exit, crying.*

AKULINA (*comes out of closet*): You're a dog, Nikita!

NIKITA: What's up?

AKULINA: What a cry she gave! *Cries.*

NIKITA: What's up with you?

AKULINA: What's up? You've hurt her so. That's the way you'll hurt me too. You're a dog. *Exit into closet. Silence.*

NIKITA: Here's a fine muddle. I'm as sweet as honey on the lasses, but when a fellow's sinned with 'em it's a bad look-out!

ACT
II

The scene represents the village street. To the left the outside of Peter's hut, built of logs, with a porch in the middle; to the right of the hut the gates and a corner of the yard buildings. Anisya is beating hemp in the street near the corner of the yard. Six months have elapsed since the first act.

ANISYA (*stops and listens*): Mumbling something again. He's probably got off the stove.

Akulina enters, carrying two pails on a yoke.

ANISYA: He's calling. You go and see what he wants, kicking up such a row.

AKULINA: Why don't you go?

ANISYA: Go, I tell you! *Exit Akulina into hut.* He's

bothering me to death. Won't let out where the money is, and that's all about it. He was out in the passage the other day. He must have been hiding it there. Now I don't know myself where it is. Thank goodness he's afraid of parting with it, so that at least it will stay in the house. If only I could manage to find it. He hadn't it on him yesterday. Now I don't know where it can be. He has quite worn the life out of me.

Enter Akulina, tying her kerchief over her head.

ANISYA: Where are you off to?

AKULINA: Where? Why, he's told me to go for Aunt Martha. "Fetch my sister," he says. "I am going to die," he says. "I have a word to say to her."

ANISYA, *aside*: Asking for his sister? Oh my poor head! Sure he wants to give it her. What shall I do? Oh! *To Akulina*: Don't go! Where are you off to?

AKULINA: To call Aunt.

ANISYA: Don't go, I tell you, I'll go myself. You go and take the clothes to the river to rinse. Else you'll not have finished by the evening.

AKULINA: But he told me to go.

ANISYA: You go and do as you're bid. I tell you I'll fetch Martha myself. Take the shirts off the fence.

AKULINA: The shirts? But maybe you'll not go. He's given the order.

ANISYA: Didn't I say I'd go? Where's Nan?

AKULINA: Nan? Minding the calves.

ANISYA: Send her here. I dare say they'll not run away. *Akulina collects the clothes, and exit.*

ANISYA: If some one doesn't go he'll scold. If any one goes he'll give the money to his sister. All my trouble will be wasted. I don't myself know what I'm to do. My poor head's splitting. *Continues to work.*

Enter Matrena, with a stick and a bundle, in outdoor clothes.

MATRENA: May the Lord help you, honey.

ANISYA (*looks round, stops working, and claps her hands with joy*): Well, I never expected this! Mother Matrena, God has sent the right guest at the right time.

MATRENA: Well, how are things?

ANISYA: Ah, I'm driven well-nigh crazy. It's awful!

MATRENA: Well, still alive, I hear?

ANISYA: Oh, don't talk about it. He doesn't live and doesn't die!

MATRENA: But the money—has he given it to anybody?

ANISYA: He's just sending for his sister Martha— probably about the money.

MATRENA: Well, naturally! But hasn't he given it to any one else?

ANISYA: To no one. I watch like a hawk.

MATRENA: And where is it?

ANISYA: He doesn't let out. And I can't find out in any way. He hides it now here, now there, and I can't do anything because of Akulina. Idiot though she is, she keeps watch and is always about. Oh my head! I'm bothered to death.

MATRENA: Oh, my jewel, if he gives the money to any one but you, you'll never cease regretting it as long as you live! They'll turn you out of house and home without anything. You've been worriting, and worriting all your life with one you don't love, and will have to go a-begging when you are a widow.

ANISYA: No need to tell me that, mother. My heart's that weary, and I don't know what to do. No one to get a bit of advice from. I told Nikita, but he's frightened of the job. The only thing he did was to tell me yesterday it was hidden under the floor.

MATRENA: Well, and did you look there?

ANISYA: I couldn't. The old man himself was in the room. I notice that sometimes he carries it about on him, and sometimes he hides it.

MATRENA: But, my lass, you must remember that if once he gives you the slip there's no getting it right again! *Whispering*: Well, and did you give him the strong tea?

ANISYA: Oh! oh! . . . *About to answer, but sees neighbour and stops.*

The neighbour (a woman) passes the hut and listens to a call from within.

NEIGHBOUR, *to Anisya*: I say, Anisya! Eh, Anisya! There's your old man calling, I think.

ANISYA: That's the way he always coughs—just as if he were screaming. He's getting very bad.

NEIGHBOUR (*approaches Matrena*): How do you do, granny? Have you come far?

MATRENA: Straight from home, dear. Come to see my son. Brought him some shirts—can't help thinking of these things, you see, when it's one's own child.

NEIGHBOUR: Yes, that's always so. *To Anisya*: And I was thinking of beginning to bleach the linen, but it is a bit early, no one has begun yet.

ANISYA: Where's the hurry?

MATRENA: Well, and has he had communion?

ANISYA: Oh dear yes, the priest was here yesterday.

NEIGHBOUR: I had a look at him yesterday. Dearie me! one wonders his body and soul keep together. And, O Lord, the other day he seemed just at his last gasp, so that they laid him under the holy icons.[1] They started lamenting and got ready to lay him out.

ANISYA: He came to, and creeps about again.

MATRENA: Well, and is he to have extreme unction?

ANISYA: The neighbours advise it. If he lives till to-morrow we'll send for the priest.

NEIGHBOUR: Oh, Anisya dear, I should think your heart must be heavy. As the saying goes, "Not he is sick that's ill in bed, but he that sits and waits in dread."

ANISYA: Yes, if it were only over, one way or other!

NEIGHBOUR: Yes, that's true, dying for a year, it's no joke. You're bound hand and foot like that.

MATRENA: Ah, but a widow's lot is also bitter. It's all right as long as one's young, but who'll care for you when you're old? Oh yes, old age is not pleasure. Just look at me. I've not walked very far and yet am so footsore I don't know how to stand. Where's my son?

ANISYA: Ploughing. But you come in and we'll get the samovar ready; the tea'll set you up again.

MATRENA, *sitting down*: Yes, it's true, I'm quite done up, my dears. As to extreme unction, that's absolutely necessary. Besides, they say it's good for the soul.

ANISYA: Yes, we'll send to-morrow.

MATRENA: Yes, you had better. And we've had a wedding down in our parts.

---

[1] It is customary to place a dying person under the icon. One or more icons hung in the hut of each Orthodox peasant.

NEIGHBOUR: What, in spring?[2]

MATRENA: Ah, now if it were a poor man, then, as the saying is, it's always unseasonable for a poor man to marry. But it's Simon Matveich, he's married that Marina.

ANISYA: What luck for her!

NEIGHBOUR: He's a widower. I suppose there are children?

MATRENA: Four of 'em. What decent girl would have him? Well, so he's taken her, and she's glad. You see, the vessel was not sound, so the wine trickled out.

NEIGHBOUR: Oh my! And what do people say to it? And he a rich peasant!

MATRENA: They are living well enough so far.

NEIGHBOUR: Yes, it's true enough. Who wants to marry where there are children? There now, there's our Michael. He's such a fellow, dear me. . .

PEASANT'S VOICE: Hullo, Mavra. Where the devil are you? Go and drive the cow in. *Exit Neighbour.*

MATRENA (*while the Neighbour is within hearing speaks in her ordinary voice*): Yes, lass, thank goodness, she's married. At any rate my old fool won't go bothering about Nikita. Now (*suddenly changing her tone*), she's gone! *Whispers*: I say, did you give him the tea?

ANISYA: Don't speak about it. He'd better die of himself. It's no use—he doesn't die, and I have only taken a sin on my soul. O-oh, my head, my head! Oh, why did you give me those powders?

MATRENA: What of the powders? The sleeping powders, lass—why not give them? No evil can come of them.

ANISYA: I am not talking of the sleeping ones, but the others, the white ones.

MATRENA: Well, honey, those powders are medicinal.

ANISYA (*sighs*): I know, yet it's frightening. Though he's worried me to death.

MATRENA: Well, and did you use many?

ANISYA: I gave two doses.

MATRENA: Was anything noticeable?

ANISYA: I had a taste of the tea myself—just a little

---

2 Peasant weddings are usually in autumn. They are forbidden in Lent, and soon after Easter the peasants become too busy to marry till harvest is over.

bitter. And he drank them with the tea and says, "Even tea disgusts me," and I say, "Everything tastes bitter when one's sick." But I felt that scared, mother.

MATRENA: Don't go thinking about it. The more one thinks the worse it is.

ANISYA: I wish you'd never given them to me and led me into sin. When I think of it something seems to tear my heart. Oh dear, why did you give them to me?

MATRENA: What do you mean, honey? Lord help you! Why are you turning it on to me? Mind, lass, don't go twisting matters from the sick on to the healthy. If anything were to happen, I stand aside! I know nothing! I'm aware of nothing! I'll kiss the cross on it; I never gave you any kind of powders, never saw any, never heard of any, and never knew there were such powders. You think about yourself, lass. Why, we were talking about you the other day. "Poor thing, what torture she endures! The step-daughter an idiot; the old man rotten, sucking her life-blood. What wouldn't one be ready to do in such a case!"

ANISYA: I'm not going to deny it. A life such as mine could make one do worse than that. It could make you hang yourself or throttle him. Is this a life?

MATRENA: That's just it. There's no time to stand gaping; the money must be found one way or other, and then he must have his tea.

ANISYA: O-oh, my head, my head! I can't think what to do. I am so frightened; he'd better die of himself. I don't want to have it on my soul.

MATRENA, *viciously*: And why doesn't he show the money? Does he mean to take it along with him? Is no one to have it? Is that right? God forbid such a sum should be lost all for nothing. Isn't that a sin? What's he doing? Is he worth considering?

ANISYA: I don't know anything. He's worried me to death.

MATRENA: What is it you don't know? The business is clear. If you make a slip now, you'll repent it all your life. He'll give the money to his sister and you'll be left without.

ANISYA: O-oh dear! Yes, and he did send for her—I must go.

MATRENA: You wait a bit and light the samovar first. We'll give him some tea and search him together—we'll find it, no fear.

ANISYA: Oh dear, oh dear; supposing something were to happen.

MATRENA: What now? What's the good of waiting? Do you want the money to slip from your hand when it's just in sight? You go and do as I say.

ANISYA: Well, I'll go and light the samovar.

MATRENA: Go, honey, do the business so as not to regret it afterwards. That's right! *Anisya turns to go. Matrena calls her back.* Just a word. Don't tell Nikita about the business. He's silly. God forbid he should find out about the powders. The Lord only knows what he would do. He's so tender-hearted. D'you know, he usen't to be able to kill a chicken. Don't tell him. 'Twould be a fine go, he wouldn't understand things. *Stops horror-struck as Peter appears in the doorway.*

PETER (*holding on to the wall, creeps out into the porch and calls with a faint voice*): How's it one can't make you hear? Oh, oh, Anisya! Who's there? *Drops on the bench.*

ANISYA (*steps from behind the corner*): Why have you come out? You should have stayed where you were lying.

PETER: Has the girl gone for Martha? It's very hard. . . . Oh, if only death would come quicker!

ANISYA: She had no time. I sent her to the river. Wait a bit, I'll go myself when I'm ready.

PETER: Send Nan. Where's she? Oh, I'm that bad! Oh, death's at hand!

ANISYA: I've sent for her already.

PETER: Oh dear! Then where is she?

ANISYA: Where's she got to, the plague seize her!

PETER: Oh, dear! I can't bear it. All my inside's on fire. It's as if a gimlet were boring me. Why have you left me as if I were a dog? . . . no one to give me a drink. . . . Oh . . . send Nan to me.

ANISYA: Here she is. Nan, go to father.

Nan runs in. Anisya goes behind the corner of the house.

PETER: Go you, . . . oh . . . to Aunt Martha, tell her father wants her; say she's to come, I want her.

NAN: All right.

PETER: Wait a bit. Tell her she's to come quick. Tell her I'm dying. O-oh!

NAN: I'll just get my shawl and be off. *Runs off.*

MATRENA, *winking*: Now then, mind and look sharp, lass. Go into the hut, hunt about everywhere, like a dog that's hunting for fleas: look under everything, and I'll search him.

ANISYA, *to Matrena*: I feel a bit bolder, somehow, now you're here. *Goes up to porch. To Peter*: Hadn't I better light the samovar? Here's Mother Matrena come to see her son; you'll have a cup of tea with her?

PETER: Well then, light it.

Anisya goes into the house. Matrena comes up to the porch.

PETER: How do you do?

MATRENA, *bowing*: How d'you do, my benefactor; how d'you do, my precious . . . still ill, I see. And my old man, he's that sorry! "Go," says he, "see how he's getting on." He sends his respects to you. *Bows again.*

PETER: I'm dying.

MATRENA: Ah yes, Peter Ignatich, now I look at you I see, as the saying has it, "Sickness lives where men live." You've shrivelled, shrivelled, all to nothing, poor dear, now I come to look at you. Seems illness does not add to good looks.

PETER: My last hour has come.

MATRENA: Oh well, Peter Ignatich, it's God's will you know, you've had communion, and you'll have unction, God willing. Your missus is a wise woman, the Lord be thanked; she'll give you a good burial, and have prayers said for your soul, all most respectable! And my son, he'll look after things meanwhile.

PETER: There'll be no one to manage things! She's not steady. Has her head full of folly—why, I know all about it, I know. And my girl is silly and young. I've got the homestead together and there's no one to attend to things. One can't help feeling it. *Whimpers.*

MATRENA: Why, if it's money, or something, you can leave orders.

PETER, *to Anisya inside the house*: Has Nan gone?

MATRENA, *aside*: There now, he's remembered!

ANISYA, *from inside*: She went then and there. Come inside, won't you? I'll help you in.

PETER: Let me sit here a bit for the last time. The air's so stuffy inside. Oh, how bad I feel! Oh, my heart's burning. . . . Oh, if death would only come.

MATRENA: If God don't take a soul, the soul can't go out. Death and life are in God's will, Peter Ignatich. You can't be sure of death either. Maybe you'll recover yet. There was a man in our village just like that, at the very point of death . . .

PETER: No, I feel I shall die to-day, I feel it. *Leans back and shuts his eyes.*

ANISYA (*enters*): Well now, are you coming in or not? You do keep one waiting. Peter! eh, Peter!

MATRENA (*steps aside and beckons to Anisya with her finger*): Well?

ANISYA (*comes down the porch steps*): Not there.

MATRENA: But have you searched everywhere? Under the floor?

ANISYA: No, it's not there either. In the shed perhaps; he was rummaging there yesterday.

MATRENA: Go, search, search for all you're worth. Go all over everywhere, as if you licked with your tongue! But I see he'll die this very day; his nails are turning blue and his face looks earthy. Is the samovar ready?

ANISYA: Just on the boil.

NIKITA (*comes from the other side, if possible on horseback, up to the gate, and does not see Peter*) to Matrena: How d'you do, mother, is all well at home?

MATRENA: The Lord be thanked, we're all alive and have a crust to bite.

NIKITA: Well, and how's master?

MATRENA: Hush, there he sits. *Points to porch.*

NIKITA: Well, let him sit. What's it to me?

PETER (*opens his eyes*): Nikita, I say, Nikita, come here! *Nikita approaches. Anisya and Matrena whisper together.*

PETER: Why have you come back so early?

NIKITA: I've finished ploughing.

PETER: Have you done the strip beyond the bridge?

NIKITA: It's too far to go there.

PETER: Too far? From here it's still farther. You'll have to go just for that now. You might have made one job of it.

Anisya, without showing herself, stands and listens.

MATRENA (*approaches*): Oh, sonnie, why don't you take more pains for your master? Your master is ill and depends on you; you should serve him as you would your own father, straining every muscle just as I always tell you to.

PETER: Well then—o-oh! . . . Get out the seed potatoes, and the women will go and sort them.

ANISYA, *aside*: No fear, I'm not going. He's sending every one away again; he must have the money on him now, and wants to hide it somewhere.

PETER: Else . . . o-oh! when the time comes for planting, they'll all be rotten. Oh, I can't stand it! *Rises.*

MATRENA (*runs up into the porch and holds Peter up*): Shall I help you into the hut?

PETER: Help me in. *Stops.* Nikita!

NIKITA, *angrily*: What now?

PETER: I shan't see you again . . . I'll die to-day. . . . Forgive me,[3] for Christ's sake, forgive me if I have ever sinned against you. . . . If I have sinned in word or deed. . . . There's been all sorts of things. Forgive me!

NIKITA: What's there to forgive? I'm a sinner myself.

MATRENA: Ah, sonnie, have some feeling.

PETER: Forgive me, for Christ's sake. *Weeps.*

NIKITA (*snivels*): God will forgive you, Daddy Peter. I have no cause to complain of you. You've never done me any wrong. You forgive me; maybe I've sinned worse against you. *Weeps.*

Peter goes in whimpering, Matrena supporting him.

ANISYA: Oh, my poor head! It's not without some purpose that he's sending for her. *Approaches Nikita.* Why did you say the money was under the floor? It's not there.

NIKITA (*does not answer, but cries*): I have never had anything bad from him, nothing but good, and what have I gone and done!

---

[3] A formal request for forgiveness is customary among Russians, but it is often no mere formality. Nikita's first reply is evasive; his second reply, "God will forgive you," is the correct one sanctioned by custom.

ANISYA: Enough now! Where's the money?

NIKITA, *angrily*: How should I know? Go and look for it yourself!

ANISYA: What's made you so tender-hearted?

NIKITA: I am sorry for him—that sorry. How he cried! Oh dear!

ANISYA: Look at him—seized with pity! He has found some one to pity too! He's been treating you like a dog and even just now was giving orders to have you turned out of the house. You'd better show me some pity!

NIKITA: What are you to be pitied for?

ANISYA: If he dies, and the money's been hidden away . . .

NIKITA: No fear, he'll not hide it . . .

ANISYA: Oh, Nikita darling! he's sent for his sister, and wants to give it to her. It will be a bad lookout for us. How are we going to live, if he gives her the money? They'll turn me out of the house! You try and manage somehow! You said he went to the shed last night.

NIKITA: I saw him coming from there, but where he's shoved it to who can tell?

ANISYA: Oh, my poor head! I'll go and have a look there. *Nikita steps aside.*

MATRENA (*comes out of the hut and down the steps of the porch to Anisya and Nikita*): Don't go anywhere. He's got the money on him. I felt it on a string round his neck.

ANISYA: Oh my head, my head!

MATRENA: If you don't keep wide awake now, then you may whistle for it. If his sister comes—then good-bye to it!

ANISYA: That's true. She'll come and he'll give it her. What's to be done? Oh my poor head!

MATRENA: What is to be done? Why, look here: the samovar is boiling, go and make the tea and pour him out a cup, and then (*whispers*) put in all that's left in the paper. When he's drunk the cup, then just take it. He'll not tell, no fear.

ANISYA: Oh! I'm afeared!

MATRENA: Don't be talking now, but look alive, and I'll keep his sister off if need be. Mind, don't make a blunder! Get hold of the money and bring it here, and Nikita will hide it.

ANISYA: Oh my head, my head! I don't know how I'm going to . . .

MATRENA: Don't talk about it, I tell you, do as I bid you. Nikita!

NIKITA: What is it?

MATRENA: You stay here—sit down—in case something is wanted.

NIKITA (*waves his hand*): Oh these women, what won't they be up to? Muddle one up completely. Bother them! I'll really go and fetch out the potatoes.

MATRENA (*catches him by the arm*): Stay here, I tell you.

Nan enters.

ANISYA: Well?

NAN: She was down in her daughter's vegetable plot —she's coming.

ANISYA: Coming! What shall we do?

MATRENA: There's plenty of time if you do as I tell you.

ANISYA: I don't know what to do; I know nothing, my brain's all in a whirl. Nan! Go, daughter, and see to the calves, they'll have run away, I'm afraid. . . . Oh dear, I haven't the courage.

MATRENA: Go on! I should think the samovar's boiling over.

ANISYA: Oh my head, my poor head. *Exit.*

MATRENA (*approaches Nikita*): Now then, sonnie. *Sits down beside him.* Your affairs must be thought about too, and not left anyhow.

NIKITA: What affairs?

MATRENA: Why, this affair—how you're to live your life.

NIKITA: How I'm to live my life? Others manage to live, and I shall live!

MATRENA: The old man will probably die to-day.

NIKITA: Well, if he dies, God give him rest! What's that to me?

MATRENA (*keeps looking towards the porch while she speaks*): Eh, sonnie! Those that are alive have to think about living. One needs plenty of sense in these matters, honey. What do you think? I've tramped all over the place on your business, I've got quite footsore bothering about matters. And you must not forget me when the time comes.

NIKITA: And what is it you've been bothering about?

MATRENA: About your affairs, about your future. If you don't take trouble in good time you'll get nothing. You know Ivan Moseich? Well, I've been to him too. I went there the other day. I had something else to settle, you know. Well, so I sat and chatted awhile and then came to the point. "Tell me, Ivan Moseich," says I, "how's one to manage an affair of this kind? Supposing," says I, "a peasant as is a widower married a second wife, and supposing all the children he has is a daughter by the first wife and a daughter by the second. Then," says I, "when that peasant dies, could an outsider get hold of the homestead by marrying the widow? Could he," says I, "give both the daughters in marriage and remain master of the house himself?" "Yes, he could," says he, "but," says he, "it would mean a deal of trouble; still the thing could be managed by means of money, but if there's no money it's no good trying."

NIKITA (*laughs*): That goes without saying, only fork out the money. Who does not want money?

MATRENA: Well then, honey, so I spoke out plainly about the affair. And he says, "First and foremost, your son will have to get himself on the register of that village —that will cost something. The elders will have to be treated. And they, you see, they'll sign. Everything," says he, "must be done sensibly." Look (*unwraps her kerchief and takes out a paper*), he's written out this paper; just read it, you're a scholar, you know. *Nikita reads.*

NIKITA: This paper's only a decision for the elders to sign. There's no great wisdom needed for that.

MATRENA: But you just hear what Ivan Moscich bids us do. "Above all," he says, "mind and don't let the money slip away, dame. If she don't get hold of the money," he says, "they'll not let her do it. Money's the great thing!" So look out, sonnie; things are coming to a head.

NIKITA: What's that to me? The money's hers—so let her look out.

MATRENA: Ah, sonnie, how foolishly you look at it! How can a woman manage such affairs? Even if she does get the money, is she capable of arranging it all? One knows what a woman is! You're a man anyhow. You can hide it, and all that. You see, you've after all got more sense, in case of anything happening.

NIKITA: Oh, your woman's notions are all so inexpedient!

MATRENA: Why inexpedient? You just collar the money, and the woman's in your hands. And then should she ever turn snappish you'd be able to tighten the reins!

NIKITA: Bother you all—I'm going.

ANISYA (*quite pale, runs out of the hut and round the corner to Matrena*): So it was, it was on him! Here it is! *Shows that she has something under her apron.*

MATRENA: Give it to Nikita; he'll hide it. Nikita, take it and hide it somewhere.

NIKITA: All right, give here!

ANISYA: O-oh, my poor head! No, I'd better do it myself. *Goes towards the gate.*

MATRENA (*seizing her by the arm*): Where are you going to? You'll be missed. There's the sister coming; give it him; he knows what to do. Eh, you blockhead!

ANISYA (*stops irresolutely*): Oh, my head, my head!

NIKITA: Well, give it here. I'll shove it away somewhere.

ANISYA: Where will you shove it to?

NIKITA, *laughing*: Why, are you afraid?

Akulina is seen approaching.

ANISYA: O-oh, my poor head! *Gives the money.* Mind, Nikita.

NIKITA: What are you afraid of? I'll hide it so that I'll not be able to find it myself. *Exit.*

ANISYA (*stands in terror*): Oh dear, and supposing he . . .

MATRENA: Well, is he dead?

ANISYA: Yes, he seems dead. He did not move when I took it.

MATRENA: Go in, there's Akulina.

ANISYA: Well there, I've done the sin and he has the money. . . .

MATRENA: Have done and go in! There's Martha coming!

ANISYA: There now, I've trusted him. What's going to happen now? *Exit.*

Martha having entered from the other side meets Akulina.

MARTHA, *to Akulina*: I should have come before, but I was at my daughter's. Well, how's the old man? Is he dying?

AKULINA (*puts down the clothes*): Don't know, I've been to the river.

MARTHA (*pointing to Matrena*): Who's that?

MATRENA: I'm from Zuevo. I'm Nikita's mother from Zuevo, my dearie. Good afternoon to you. He's withering, withering away, poor dear—your brother, I mean. He came out himself. "Send for my sister," he said, "because," said he . . . Dear me, why, I do believe he's dead!

ANISYA (*runs out screaming, clings to a post, and begins wailing*⁴): Oh, oh, ah! who-o-o-m have you left me to, why-y-y have you dese-e-e-rted me—a miserable widow . . . to live my life alone . . . Why have you closed your bright eyes . . .

Enter Neighbour. Matrena and Neighbour catch hold of Anisya under the arms to support her. Akulina and Martha go into the hut. A crowd assembles.

A VOICE IN THE CROWD: Send for the old women to lay out the body.

MATRENA (*rolls up her sleeves*): Is there any water in the copper? But I daresay the samovar is still hot. I'll go too and help a bit.

ACT
III

The same scene as in Act I. Winter. Nine months have passed since Act II. Anisya, plainly dressed, sits before a loom weaving. Nan is on the oven.

MITRICH (*enters and slowly takes off his outdoor things*): Oh Lord, have mercy! Well, hasn't the master come home yet?

---

⁴ Loud public wailing of this kind is customary, and considered indispensable, among the peasants.

ANISYA: What?

MITRICH: Nikita isn't back from town, is he?

ANISYA: No.

MITRICH: Must have been on the spree. Oh Lord!

ANISYA: Have you finished in the stackyard?

MITRICH: What d'you think? Got it all as it should be, and covered everything with straw! I don't like doing things by halves! Oh Lord! holy Nicholas! *Picks at the corns on his hands.* But it's time he was back.

ANISYA: What need has he to hurry? He's got money. Merry-making with that girl, I daresay . . .

MITRICH: Why shouldn't one make merry if one has the money? And why did Akulina go to town?

ANISYA: You'd better ask her. How do I know what the devil took her there!

MITRICH: What! to town? There's all sorts of things to be got in town if one's got the means. Oh Lord!

NAN: Mother, I heard myself. "I'll get you a little shawl," he says, blest if he didn't; "you shall choose it yourself," he says. And she got herself up so fine; she put on her velveteen coat and the French shawl.

ANISYA: Really, a girl's modesty reaches only to the door. Step over the threshold and it's forgotten. She is a shameless creature.

MITRICH: Oh my! What's the use of being ashamed? While there's plenty of money make merry. Oh Lord! It is too soon to have supper, eh? *Anisya does not answer.* I'll go and get warm meanwhile. *Climbs on the stove.* Oh Lord! Blessed Virgin Mother! holy Nicholas!

NEIGHBOUR (*enters*): Seems your goodman's not back yet?

ANISYA: No.

NEIGHBOUR: It's time he was. Hasn't he perhaps stopped at our inn? My sister, Thekla, says there's heaps of sledges standing there as have come from the town.

ANISYA: Nan! Nan, I say!

NAN: Yes?

ANISYA: You run to the inn and see! Mayhap, being drunk, he's gone there.

NAN (*jumps down from the oven and dresses*): All right.

NEIGHBOUR: And he's taken Akulina with him?

ANISYA: Else he'd not have had any need of going. It's because of her he's unearthed all the business there. "Must go to the bank," he says; "it's time to receive the payments," he says. But it's all her fooling.

NEIGHBOUR (*shakes her head*): It's a bad look-out. *Silence.*

NAN, *at the door*: And if he's there, what am I to say?

ANISYA: You only see if he's there.

NAN: All right. I'll be back in a winking. *Long silence.*

MITRICH (*roars*): Oh Lord, merciful Nicholas!

NEIGHBOUR, *starting*: Oh, how he scared me? Who is it?

ANISYA: Why, Mitrich, our labourer.

NEIGHBOUR: Oh dear, oh dear, what a fright he did give me! I had quite forgotten. But tell me, dear, I've heard some one's been wooing Akulina?

ANISYA (*gets up from the loom and sits down by the table*): There was some one from Dedlovo; but it seems the affair's got wind there too. They made a start, and then stopped; so the thing fell through. Of course, who'd care to?

NEIGHBOUR: And the Lizunovs from Zuevo?

ANISYA: They made some steps too, but it didn't come off either. They won't even see us.

NEIGHBOUR: Yet it's time she was married.

ANISYA: Time and more than time! Ah, my dear, I'm that impatient to get her out of the house; but the thing does not get done. He does not wish it, nor she either. He's not yet had enough of his beauty, you see.

NEIGHBOUR: Eh, eh, eh, what doings! Only think of it. Why, he's her step-father!

ANISYA: Ah, friend, they've taken me in completely. They've done me so fine it's beyond saying. I, fool that I was, noticed nothing, suspected nothing, and so I married him. I guessed nothing, but they already understood one another.

NEIGHBOUR: Oh dear, what goings on!

ANISYA: So it went on from bad to worse, and I see they begin hiding from me. Ah, friend, I was that sick —that sick of my life! It's not as if I didn't love him.

NEIGHBOUR: That goes without saying.

ANISYA: Ah, how hard it is to bear such treatment from him! Oh, how it hurts!

NEIGHBOUR: Yes, and I've heard say he's becoming too free with his fists?

ANISYA: And that too! There was a time when he was gentle when he'd had a drop. He used to hit out before, but of me he was always fond! But now when he's in a temper he goes for me and is ready to trample me under his feet. The other day he got both hands entangled in my hair so that I could hardly get away. And the girl's worse than a serpent; it's a wonder the earth bears such furies.

NEIGHBOUR: Ah, ah, my dear, now I look at you, you are a sufferer! To suffer like that is no joke. To have given shelter to a beggar, and he to lead you such a dance! Why don't you pull in the reins?

ANISYA: Ah but, my dear, if it weren't for my heart! Him as is gone was stern enough, still I could twist him about any way I liked; but with this one I can do nothing. As soon as I see him all my anger goes. I haven't a grain of courage before him; I go about like a drowned hen.

NEIGHBOUR: Ah, neighbour, you must be under a spell. I've heard that Matrena goes in for that sort of thing. It must be her.

ANISYA: Yes, dear; I think so myself sometimes. Gracious me, how hurt I feel at times! I'd like to tear him to pieces. But when I set eyes on him, my heart won't go against him.

NEIGHBOUR: It's plain you're bewitched. It don't take long to blight a body. There now, when I look at you, what you have dwindled to!

ANISYA: Growing a regular spindle-shanks. And just look at that fool Akulina. Wasn't the girl a regular untidy slattern, and just look at her now! Where has it all come from? Yes, he has fitted her out. She's grown so smart, so puffed up, just like a bubble that's ready to burst. And, though she's a fool, she's got it into her head; "I'm the mistress," she says; "the house is mine; it's me father wanted him to marry." And she's that vicious! Lord help us, when she gets into a rage she's ready to tear the thatch off the house.

NEIGHBOUR: Oh dear, what a life yours is, now I come to look at you. And yet there's people envying you: "They're rich," they say; but it seems that gold don't keep tears from falling.

ANISYA: Much reason for envy indeed! And the riches too will soon be made ducks and drakes of. Dear me, how he squanders money!

NEIGHBOUR: But how is it, dear, you've been so simple to give up the money? It's yours.

ANISYA: Ah, if you knew all! The thing is that I've made one little mistake.

NEIGHBOUR: Well, if I were you, I'd go straight and have the law on him. The money's yours; how dare he squander it? There's no such rights.

ANISYA: They don't pay heed to that nowadays.

NEIGHBOUR: Ah, my dear, now I come to look at you, you've got that weak.

ANISYA: Yes, quite weak, dear, quite weak. He's got me into a regular fix. I don't myself know anything. Oh, my poor head!

NEIGHBOUR, *listening:* There's some one coming, I think. *The door opens and Akim enters.*

AKIM (*crosses himself, knocks the snow off his feet, and takes off his coat*): Peace be to this house! How do you do? Are you well, daughter?

ANISYA: How d'you do, father? Have you come straight from home?

AKIM: I've been a thinking, I'll go and see what's name, go to see my son, I mean—my son. I didn't start early —had my dinner, I mean; I went, and it's so what d'you call it—so snowy, hard walking, and so there I'm . . . what d'you call it—late, I mean. And my son—is he at home? At home? My son, I mean.

ANISYA: No; he's gone to the town.

AKIM (*sits down on a bench*): I've some business with him, d'you see, some business, I mean. I told him t'other day, told him I was in need—told him, I mean, that our horse was done for, our horse, you see. So we must, what d'ye call it, get a horse, I mean, some kind of a horse, I mean. So there, I've come, you see.

ANISYA: Nikita told me. When he comes back you'll have a talk. *Goes to the oven.* Have some supper now, and he'll soon come. Mitrich, eh Mitrich, come and have your supper.

MITRICH: Oh Lord! merciful Nicholas!

ANISYA: Come to supper.

NEIGHBOUR: I shall go now. Good-night. *Exit.*

MITRICH (*gets down from the oven*): I never noticed how I fell asleep. Oh Lord! gracious Nicholas! How d'you do, Daddy Akim?

AKIM: Ah, Mitrich! What are you, what d'ye call it, I mean? . . .

MITRICH: Why, I'm working for your son, Nikita.

AKIM: Dear me! What d'ye call . . . working for my son, I mean. Dear me!

MITRICH: I was living with a tradesman in town, but drank all I had there. Now I've come back to the village. I've no home, so I've gone into service. *Gapes.* Oh Lord!

AKIM: But how's that, what d'you call it, or what's name, Nikita, what does he do? Has he some business I mean besides, that he should hire a labourer, a labourer I mean, hire a labourer?

ANISYA: What business should he have? He used to manage, but now he's other things on his mind, so he's hired a labourer.

MITRICH: Why shouldn't he, seeing he has money?

AKIM: Now that's what d'you call it, that's wrong, I mean, quite wrong, I mean. That's spoiling oneself.

ANISYA: Oh, he has got spoilt, that spoilt, it's just awful.

AKIM: There now, what d'you call it, one thinks how to make things better, and it gets worse I mean. Riches spoil a man, spoil, I mean.

MITRICH: Fatness makes even a dog go mad; how's one not to get spoilt by fat living? Myself now; how I went on with fat living. I drank for three weeks without being sober. I drank my last breeches. When I had nothing left, I gave it up. Now I've determined not to. Bother it!

AKIM: And where's what d'you call, your old woman?

MITRICH: My old woman has found her right place, old fellow. She's hanging about the gin-shops in town. She's a swell too: one eye knocked out, and the other black, and her muzzle twisted to one side. And she's never sober; drat her!

AKIM: Oh, oh, oh, how's that?

MITRICH: And where's a soldier's wife to go? She has found her right place. *Silence.*

AKIM, *to Anisya*: And Nikita—has he what d'you call it, taken anything up to town? I mean, anything to sell?

ANISYA, *laying the table and serving up*: No, he's taken nothing. He's gone to get money from the bank.

AKIM, *sitting down to supper*: Why? D'you wish to put it to another use, the money I mean?

ANISYA: No, we don't touch it. Only some twenty or thirty rubles as have come due; they must be taken.

AKIM: Must be taken? Why take it, the money I mean? You'll take some to-day I mean, and some to-morrow; and so you'll what d'you call it, take it all, I mean.

ANISYA: We get this extra. The money is all safe.

AKIM: All safe? How's that, safe? You take it, and it's what d'you call it, it's all safe. How's that? You put a heap of meal into a bin, or a barn, I mean, and go on taking meal, will it remain there what d'you call it, all safe I mean? That's, what d'you call it, it's cheating. You'd better find out, or else they'll cheat you. Safe indeed! I mean, you, what d'ye call . . . you take it and it remains all safe there?

ANISYA: I know nothing about it. Ivan Moseich advised us at the time. "Put the money in the bank," he said, "the money will be safe, and you'll get interest," he said.

MITRICH, *having finished his supper*: That's so. I've lived with a tradesman. They all do like that. Put the money in the bank, then lie down on the oven and it will keep coming in.

AKIM: That's queer talk. How's that—what d'ye call, coming in, how's that coming in, and they, who do they get it from I mean, the money I mean?

ANISYA: They take the money out of the bank.

MITRICH: Get along! 'Tain't a thing a woman can understand! You look here, I'll make it all plain to you. Mind and remember. You see, suppose you've got some money, and I, for instance, have spring coming on, my land's idle, I've got no seeds, or I have to pay taxes. So, you see, I go to you. "Akim," I say, "give us a ten-ruble note, and when I've harvested in autumn I'll return it, and till two acres for you besides, for having obliged me!" And you, seeing I've something to fall back on—a horse say, or a cow—you say, "No, give two or three rubles for the obligation," and there's an end of it. I'm stuck in the mud and can't do without. So I say, "All right!" and take a tenner. In the autumn, when I've made my turnover, I bring it back, and you squeeze the extra three rubles out of me.

AKIM: Yes, but that's what peasants do when they, what d'ye call it, when they forget God. It's not honest, I mean, it's no good, I mean.

MITRICH: You wait. You'll see it comes just to the same thing. Now don't forget how you've skinned me. And Anisya, say, has got some money lying idle. She does not know what to do with it, besides, she's a woman and does not know how to use it. She comes to you. "Couldn't you make some profit with my money too?" she says. "Why not?" say you, and you wait. Before the summer I come again and say, "Give me another tenner, and I'll be obliged." Then you find out if my hide isn't all gone, and if I can be skinned again you give me Anisya's money. But supposing I'm clean shorn—have nothing to eat— then you see I can't be fleeced any more, and you say, "Go your way, friend," and you look out for another, and lend him your own and Anisya's money and skin him. That's what the bank is. So it goes round and round. It's a cute thing, old fellow!

AKIM, *excitedly*: Gracious me, whatever is that like? It's what d'ye call it, it's filthy! The peasants—what d'ye call it, the peasants do so I mean, and know it's, what d'ye call it, a sin! It's what d'you call, not right, not right, I mean. It's filthy! How can people as have learnt . . . what d'ye call it . . .

MITRICH: That, old fellow, is just what they're fond of! And remember, them that are stupid, or the women folk, as can't put their money into use themselves, they take it to the bank, and they there, deuce take 'em, clutch hold of it, and with this money they fleece the people. It's a cute thing!

AKIM, *sighing*: Oh dear, I see, what d'ye call it, without money it's bad, and with money it's worse! How's that? God told us to work, but you, what d'ye call . . . I mean you put money into the bank and go to sleep, and the money will what d'ye call it, will feed you while you sleep. It's filthy, that's what I call it; it's not right.

MITRICH: Not right? Eh, old fellow, who cares about that nowadays? And how clean they pluck you, too! That's the fact of the matter.

AKIM (*sighs*): Ah yes, seems the time's what d'ye call it, the time's growing ripe. There, I've had a look at the closets in town. What they've come to! It's all polished and polished I mean, it's fine, it's what d'ye call it, it's like inside an inn. And what's it all for? What's the good of it? Oh, they've forgotten God. Forgotten, I mean. We've forgotten, forgotten God, God I mean! Thank you, my dear, I've had enough. I'm quite satisfied. *Rises. Mitrich climbs on to the oven.*

ANISYA (*collects the dishes while she eats*): If his father would only take him to task! But I'm ashamed to tell him.

AKIM: What d'you say?

ANISYA: Oh! it's nothing.

Enter Nan.

AKIM: Here's a good girl, always busy! You're cold, I should think?

NAN: Yes, I am, terribly. How d'you do, grandfather?

ANISYA: Well? Is he there?

NAN: No. But Andriyan is there. He's been to town, and he says he saw them at an inn in town. He says Dad's as drunk as drunk can be!

ANISYA: Do you want anything to eat? Here you are.

NAN (*goes to the oven*): Well, it is cold. My hands are quite numb.

Akim takes off his leg-bands and bast-shoes. Anisya washes up.

ANISYA: Father!

AKIM: Well, what is it?

ANISYA: Is Marina living well?

AKIM: Yes, she's living all right. The little woman is what d'ye call it, clever and steady; she's living, and what d'ye call it, doing her best. She's all right; the little woman's of the right sort I mean; painstaking and what d'ye call it, submissive; the little woman's all right I mean, all right, you know.

ANISYA: And is there no talk in your village that a relative of Marina's husband thinks of marrying our Akulina? Have you heard nothing of it?

AKIM: Ah; that's Mironov. Yes, the women did chatter something. But I didn't pay heed, you know. It don't interest me, I mean, I don't know anything. Yes, the old women did say something, but I've a bad memory, bad memory, I mean. But the Mironovs are what d'ye call it, they're all right, I mean they're all right.

ANISYA: I'm that impatient to get her settled.

AKIM: And why?

NAN (*listens*): They've come!

ANISYA: Well, don't you go bothering them. *Goes on washing the spoons without turning her head.*

NIKITA (*enters*): Anisya! Wife! who has come? *Anisya looks up and turns away in silence.*

NIKITA, *severely*: Who has come? Have you forgotten?

ANISYA: Now don't humbug. Come in!

NIKITA, *still more severely*: Who's come?

ANISYA (*goes up and takes him by the arm*): Well then, husband has come. Now then, come in!

NIKITA (*holds back*): Ah, that's it! Husband! And what's husband called? Speak properly.

ANISYA: Oh bother you! Nikita!

NIKITA: Where have you learnt manners? The full name.

ANISYA: Nikita Akimich! Now then!

NIKITA, *still in the doorway*: Ah, that's it! But now— the surname?

ANISYA (*laughs and pulls him by the arm*): Chilikin. Dear me, what airs!

NIKITA: Ah, that's it. *Holds on to the door-post.* No, now say with which foot Chilikin steps into this house!

ANISYA: That's enough! You're letting the cold in!

NIKITA: Say with which foot he steps. You've got to say it—that's flat.

ANISYA, *aside*: He'll go on worrying. *To Nikita*: Well then, with the left. Come in!

NIKITA: Ah, that's it.

ANISYA: You look who's in the hut!

NIKITA: Ah, my parent! Well, what of that? I'm not ashamed of my parent. I can pay my respects to my parent. How d'you do, father? *Bows and puts out his hand.* My respects to you.

AKIM (*does not answer*): Drink, I mean drink, what it does! It's filthy!

NIKITA: Drink, what's that? I've been drinking? I'm to blame, that's flat! I've had a glass with a friend, drank his health.

ANISYA: Go and lie down, I say.

NIKITA: Wife, say where am I standing?

ANISYA: Now then, it's all right, lie down!

NIKITA: No, I'll first drink a samovar with my parent.
Go and heat the samovar. Akulina, I say, come here!

Enter Akulina, smartly dressed and carrying their
purchases.

AKULINA: Why have you thrown everything about?
Where's the yarn?

NIKITA: The yarn? The yarn's there. Hullo, Mitrich,
where are you? Asleep? Asleep? Go and put the horse up.

AKIM, *not seeing Akulina but looking at his son*: Dear
me, what is he doing? The old man's what d'ye call it,
quite done up, I mean—been thrashing—and look at him,
what d'ye call it, putting on airs! Put up the horse!
Faugh, what filth!

MITRICH (*climbs down from the oven, and puts on felt*
boots): Oh, merciful Lord! Is the horse in the yard? Done
it to death, I dare say. Just see how he's been swilling,
the deuce take him. Up to his very throat. Oh Lord, holy
Nicholas! *Puts on sheepskin, and exit.*

NIKITA (*sits down*): You must forgive me, father. It's
true I've had a drop; well, what of that? Even a hen will
drink. Ain't it true? So you must forgive me. Never mind
Mitrich, he doesn't mind, he'll put it up.

ANISYA: Shall I really heat the samovar?

NIKITA: Heat it! My parent has come. I wish to talk
to him, and shall drink tea with him. *To Akulina*: Have
you brought all the parcels?

AKULINA: The parcels? I've brought mine, the rest's in
the sledge. Hi, take this, this isn't mine!

Throws a parcel on the table and puts the others into
her box. Nan watches her while she puts them away. Akim
does not look at his son, but puts his leg-bands and bast-
shoes on the oven.

ANISYA, *going out with the samovar*: Her box is full
as it is, and still he's brought more!

NIKITA, *pretending to be sober*: You must not be
cross with me, father. You think I'm drunk? I am all
there, that's flat! As they say, "Drink, but keep your wits
about you." I can talk with you at once, father. I can
attend to any business. You told me about the money;
your horse is worn out—I remember! That can all be

managed. That's all in our hands. If it was an enormous sum that's wanted, then we might wait; but as it is I can do everything. That's how it is.

AKIM (*goes on fidgeting with the leg-bands*): Eh, lad, "It's ill sledging when the thaw has set in."

NIKITA: What d'you mean by that? "And it's ill talking with one who is drunk?" But don't you worry, let's have some tea. And I can do anything; that's flat! I can put everything to rights.

AKIM (*shakes his head*): Eh, eh, eh!

NIKITA: The money, here it is. *Puts his hand in his pocket, pulls out pocket-book, handles the notes in it, and takes out a ten-ruble note.* Take this to get a horse; I can't forget my parent. I shan't forsake him, that's flat. Because he's my parent! Here you are, take it! Really now, I don't grudge it. *Comes up and pushes the note towards Akim, who won't take it. Nikita catches hold of his father's hand.* Take it, I tell you. I don't grudge it.

AKIM: I can't, what d'you call it, I mean, can't take it! And can't what d'ye call it, talk to you because you're not yourself, I mean.

NIKITA: I'll not let you go! Take it! *Puts the money into Akim's hand.*

ANISYA (*enters, and stops*): You'd better take it, he'll give you no peace!

AKIM (*takes it, and shakes his head*): Oh! that liquor. Not like a man, I mean!

NIKITA: That's better! If you repay it you'll repay it, if not I'll make no bother. That's what I am! *Sees Akulina.* Akulina, show your presents.

AKULINA: What?

NIKITA: Show your presents.

AKULINA: The presents, what's the use of showing 'em? I've put 'em away.

NIKITA: Get them, I tell you. Nan will like to see 'em. Undo the shawl. Give it here.

AKIM: Oh, oh! It's sickening! *Climbs on the oven.*

AKULINA (*gets out the parcels and puts them on the table*): Well, there you are—what's the good of looking at 'em?

NAN: Oh how lovely! It's as good as Stepanida's.

AKULINA: Stepanida's? What's Stepanida's compared to

this? *Brightening up and undoing the parcels.* Just look here—see the quality! It's a French one.

NAN: The print *is* fine! Mary has a dress like it, only lighter on a blue ground. This *is* pretty.

NIKITA: Ah, that's it!

Anisya passes angrily into the closet, returns with a tablecloth and the chimney of the samovar, and goes up to the table.

ANISYA: Drat you, littering the table!

NIKITA: You look here!

ANISYA: What am I to look at? Have I never seen anything? Put it away! *Sweeps the shawl on to the floor with her arm.*

AKULINA: What are you pitching things down for? You pitch your own things about! *Picks up the shawl.*

NIKITA: Anisya! Look here!

ANISYA: Why should I look?

NIKITA: You think I have forgotten you? Look here! *Shows her a parcel and sits down on it.* It's a present for you. Only you must earn it! Wife, where am I sitting?

ANISYA: Enough of your humbug. I'm not afraid of you. Whose money are you going on the spree with and buying your fat wench presents with? Mine!

AKULINA: Yours indeed! No fear! You wished to steal it, but it did not come off! Get out of the way! *Pushes her while trying to pass.*

ANISYA: What are you shoving for? I'll teach you to shove!

AKULINA: Shove me? You try! *Presses against Anisya.*

NIKITA: Now then, now then, you women. Have done now! *Steps between them.*

AKULINA: Comes shoving herself in! You ought to keep quiet and remember your own goings on! You think no one knows!

ANISYA: Knows what? Out with it, out with it! What do they know?

AKULINA: I know something about you!

ANISYA: You're a slut who goes with another's husband!

AKULINA: And you did yours to death!

ANISYA, *throwing herself on Akulina:* You're raving!

NIKITA, *holding her back:* Anisya, you seem to have forgotten!

ANISYA: Want to frighten me! I'm not afraid of you!

NIKITA (*turns Anisya round and pushes her out*): Be off!

ANISYA: Where am I to go? I'll not go out of my own house!

NIKITA: Be off, I tell you, and don't dare to come in here!

ANISYA: I won't go! *Nikita pushes her; Anisya cries and screams and clings to the door.* What! am I to be turned out of my own house by the scruff of the neck? What are you doing, you scoundrel? Do you think there's no law for you? You wait a bit!

NIKITA: Now then!

ANISYA: I'll go to the Elder! To the policeman!

NIKITA: Off, I tell you! *Pushes her out.*

ANISYA, *behind the door*: I'll hang myself!

NIKITA: No fear!

NAN: Oh, oh, oh! Mother, dear, darling! *Cries.*

NIKITA: Me frightened of her! A likely thing! What are you crying for? She'll come back, no fear. Go and see to the samovar. *Exit Nan.*

AKULINA (*collects and folds her presents*): The mean wretch, how she's messed it up. But wait a bit, I'll cut up her jacket for her! Sure I will!

NIKITA: I've turned her out, what more do you want?

AKULINA: She's dirtied my new shawl. If that bitch hadn't gone away, I'd have torn her eyes out!

NIKITA: That's enough. Why should you be angry? Now if I loved her . . .

AKULINA: Loved her? She's worth loving, with her fat mug! If you'd have given her up, then nothing would have happened. You should have sent her to the devil. And the house was mine all the same, and the money was mine! Says she is the mistress, but what sort of mistress is she to her husband? She's a murderess, that's what she is! She'll serve you the same way!

NIKITA: Oh dear, how's one to stop a woman's jaw? You don't yourself know what you're jabbering about!

AKULINA: Yes, I do. I'll not live with her! I'll turn her out of the house! She can't live here with me. The mistress indeed! She's not the mistress—that jailbird!

NIKITA: That's enough! What have you to do with

her? Don't mind her. You look at me! I am the master.
I do as I like. I've ceased to love her, and now I love you.
I love who I like! The power is mine, she's under me. That's
where I keep her. *Points to his feet.* A pity we've no concertina. *Sings:*

> We have loaves on the stoves,
> We have porridge on the shelf.
> So we'll live and be gay,
> Making merry every day,
> And when death comes,
> Then we'll die!
> We have loaves on the stoves,
> We have porridge on the shelf . . .

*Enter Mitrich. He takes off his outdoor things and
climbs on the oven.*

MITRICH: Seems the women have been fighting again!
Tearing each other's hair. Oh Lord, gracious Nicholas!

AKIM (*sitting on the edge of the oven, takes his leg-
bands and shoes and begins putting them on*): Get in, get
into the corner.

MITRICH: Seems they can't settle matters between them.
Oh Lord!

NIKITA: Get out the liquor, we'll have some with our
tea.

NAN, *to Akulina:* Sister, the samovar is just boiling over.

NIKITA. And where's your mother?

NAN: She's standing and crying out there in the
passage.

NIKITA: Oh, that's it! Call her, and tell her to bring
the samovar. And you, Akulina, get the tea things.

AKULINA: The tea things? All right. *Brings the things.*

NIKITA (*unpacks spirits, rusks, and salt herrings*): That's
for myself. This is yarn for the wife. The paraffin is
out there in the passage, and here's the money. Wait a
bit (*takes a counting-frame*), I'll add it up. *Adds.* Wheat-
flour, 80 kopeks, oil . . . Father, 10 rubles. . . . Father,
come let's have some tea!

*Silence. Akim sits on the oven and winds the bands
round his legs. Enter Anisya with samovar.*

ANISYA: Where shall I put it?

NIKITA: Here on the table. Well! have you been to the Elder? Ah, that's it! Have your say and then eat your words. Now then, that's enough. Don't be cross, sit down and drink this. *Fills a wine-glass for her.* And here's your present. *Gives her the parcel he had been sitting on. Anisya takes it silently and sways her head disapprovingly.*

AKIM (*gets down and puts on his sheepskin, then comes up to the table and puts down the money*): Here, take your money back! Put it away.

NIKITA (*does not see the money*): Why have you put on your things?

AKIM: I'm going, going I mean; forgive me for the Lord's sake. *Takes up his cap and belt.*

NIKITA: My gracious! Where are you going to at this time of night!

AKIM: I can't, I mean, what d'ye call 'em, in your house, what d'ye call 'em, can't stay I mean, stay, can't stay, forgive me.

NIKITA: But are you going without having any tea?

AKIM (*fastens his belt*): Going, because, I mean, it's not right in your house, I mean, what d'you call it, not right, Nikita, in the house, what d'ye call it, not right! I mean, you are living a bad life, Nikita, bad—I'll go.

NIKITA: Eh now! Have done talking! Sit down and drink your tea!

ANISYA: Why, father, you'll shame us before the neighbours. What has offended you?

AKIM: Nothing, what d'ye call it, nothing has offended me, nothing at all! I mean only, I see, what d'you call it, I mean, I see my son, to ruin I mean, to ruin, I mean my son's on the road to ruin, I mean.

NIKITA: What ruin? Just prove it!

AKIM: Ruin, ruin; you're in the midst of it! What did I tell you that time?

NIKITA: You said all sorts of things!

AKIM: I told you, what d'ye call it, I told you about the orphan lass. That you had wronged an orphan— Marina, I mean, wronged her!

NIKITA: Eh! he's at it again. Let bygones be bygones. . . . All that's past!

AKIM, *excited*: Past! No, lad, it's not past. Sin, I mean, fastens on to sin—drags sin after it, and you've stuck fast, Nikita, fast in sin! Stuck fast in sin! I see you're fast in sin. Stuck fast, sunk in sin, I mean!

NIKITA: Sit down and drink your tea, and have done with it!

AKIM: I can't, I mean can't what d'ye call it, can't drink tea. Because of your filth, I mean; I feel what d'ye call it, I feel sick, very sick! I can't what d'ye call it, I can't drink tea with you.

NIKITA: Eh! There he goes rambling! Come to the table.

AKIM: You're in your riches same as in a net—you're in a net, I mean. Ah, Nikita, it's the soul that God needs!

NIKITA: Now really, what right have you to scold me in my own house? Why do you keep on at me? Am I a child that you can pull by the hair? Nowadays those things have been dropped!

AKIM: That's true. I have heard that nowadays, what d'ye call it, that nowadays children pull their fathers' beards, I mean! But that's ruin, that's ruin, I mean!

NIKITA, *angrily*: We are living without help from you, and it's you who came to us with your wants!

AKIM: The money? There's your money! I'll go begging, begging I mean, before I'll take it, I mean.

NIKITA: That's enough! Why be angry and upset the whole company! *Holds him by the arm.*

AKIM (*shrieks*): Let go! I'll not stay. I'd rather sleep under some fence than in the midst of your filth! Faugh! God forgive me! *Exit.*

NIKITA: Here's a go!

AKIM (*reopens the door*): Come to your senses, Nikita! It's the soul that God wants! *Exit.*

AKULINA (*takes cups*): Well, shall I pour out the tea? Takes a cup. All are silent.

MITRICH (*roars*): Oh Lord, be merciful to me a sinner! *All start.*

NIKITA (*lies down on the bench*): Oh, it's dull, it's dull! *To Akulina*: Where's the concertina?

AKULINA: The concertina? He's remembered it! Why, you took it to be mended. I've poured out your tea. Drink it!

NIKITA: I don't want it! Put out the light. . . . Oh, how dull I feel, how dull! *Sobs.*

ACT
IV

Autumn. Evening. The moon is shining. The stage repre-
sents the interior of the court-yard. The scenery at the
back shows, in the middle, the back porch of the hut. To
the right the winter half of the hut and the gate; to the
left the summer half and the cellar. To the right of
the stage is a shed. The sounds of tipsy voices and shouts
are heard from the hut.[1] *Second Neighbour Woman*
comes out of the hut and beckons to First Neighbour
Woman.

SECOND NEIGHBOUR: How's it Akulina has not shown
herself?

FIRST NEIGHBOUR: Why hasn't she shown herself?
She'd have been glad to; but she's too ill, you know. The
suitor's relatives have come, and want to see the girl;
and she, my dear, she's lying in the cold hut and can't
come out, poor thing!

SECOND NEIGHBOUR: But how's that?

FIRST NEIGHBOUR: They say she's been bewitched by
an evil eye! She's got pains in the stomach!

SECOND NEIGHBOUR: You don't say so?

FIRST NEIGHBOUR: What else could it be? *Whispers.*

SECOND NEIGHBOUR: Dear me! There's a go! But his
relatives will surely find it out?

FIRST NEIGHBOUR: They find it out! They're all drunk!
Besides, they are chiefly after her dowry. Just think what
they give with the girl! Two furs, my dear, six dresses, a
French shawl, and I don't know how many pieces of linen,
and money as well—two hundred rubles it's said!

SECOND NEIGHBOUR: That's all very well, but even
money can't give much pleasure in the face of such a disgrace.

FIRST NEIGHBOUR: Hush! . . . There's his father, I
think. *They cease talking, and go into the hut.*

The Bridegroom's Father comes out of the hut hiccough-
ing.

---

[1] Where not otherwise mentioned in the stage directions, it is always
the winter half of the hut that is referred to as "the hut." The
summer half is not heated, and not used in winter in ordinary
circumstances.

THE FATHER: Oh, I'm all in a sweat. It's awfully hot! Will just cool myself a bit. *Stands puffing.* The Lord only knows what—something is not right. I can't feel happy. Well, it's the old woman's affair.

Enter Matrena from hut.

MATRENA: And I was just thinking, where's the father? Where's the father? And here you are, dear friend. . . . Well, dear friend, the Lord be thanked! Everything is as honourable as can be! When one's arranging a match one should not boast. And I have never learnt to boast. But as you've come about the right business, so with the Lord's help, you'll be grateful to me all your life! She's a wonderful girl! There's no other like her in all the district!

THE FATHER: That's true enough, but how about the money?

MATRENA: Don't you trouble about the money! All she had from her father goes with her. And it's more than one gets easily, as things are nowadays. Three times fifty rubles!

THE FATHER: We don't complain, but it's for our own child. Naturally we want to get the best we can.

MATRENA: I'll tell you straight, friend: if it hadn't been for me, you'd never have found anything like her! They've had an offer from the Karmilins, but I stood out against it. And as for the money, I'll tell you truly: when her father, God be merciful to his soul, was dying, he gave orders that the widow should take Nikita into the homestead—of course I know all about it from my son, and the money was to go to Akulina. Why, another one might have thought of his own interests, but Nikita gives everything clean! It's no trifle. Fancy what a sum it is!

THE FATHER: People are saying that more money was left her? The lad's sharp too!

MATRENA: Oh, dear soul alive! A slice in another's hand always looks big; all she had will be handed over. I tell you, throw doubts to the wind and make all sure! What a girl she is! as fresh as a daisy!

THE FATHER: That's so. But my old woman and I were only wondering about the girl; why has she not come out? We've been thinking, suppose she's sickly?

MATRENA: Oh, ah. . . . Who? She? Sickly? Why, there's

none to compare with her in the district. The girl's as sound as a bell; you can't pinch her. But you saw her the other day! And as for work, she's wonderful! She's a bit deaf, that's true, but there are spots on the sun, you know. And her not coming out, you see, it's from an evil eye! A spell's been cast on her! And I know the bitch who's done the business! They know of the betrothal and they bewitched her. But I know a counter-spell. The girl will get up to-morrow. Don't you worry about the girl!

THE FATHER: Well, of course, the thing's settled.

MATRENA: Yes, of course! Don't you turn back. And don't forget me, I've had a lot of trouble. Don't forget . . .

A woman's voice from the hut.

VOICE: If we are to go, let's go. Come along, Ivan!

THE FATHER: I'm coming.

Exeunt. Guests crowd together in the passage and prepare to go away.

NAN (*runs out of the hut and calls to Anisya*): Mother!

ANISYA, *from inside*: What d'you want?

NAN: Mother, come here, or they'll hear.

Anisya enters and they go together to the shed.

ANISYA: Well? What is it? Where's Akulina?

NAN: She's gone into the barn. It's awful what's she's doing there! I'm blest! "I can't bear it," she says. "I'll scream," she says, "I'll scream out loud." Blest if she didn't.

ANISYA: She'll have to wait. We'll see our visitors off first.

NAN: Oh mother! She's so bad! And she's angry too. "What's the good of their drinking my health?" she says. "I shan't marry," she says. "I shall die," she says. Mother, supposing she does die! It's awful. I'm so frightened!

ANISYA: No fear, she'll not die. But don't you go near her. Come along. *Exeunt Anisya and Nan.*

MITRICH (*comes in at the gate and begins collecting the scattered hay*): Oh Lord! Merciful Nicholas! What a lot of liquor they've been and swilled, and the smell they've made! It smells even out here! But no, I don't want any, drat it! See how they've scattered the hay about. They don't eat it, but only trample it under foot. A truss gone before you know it. Oh, that smell, it seems to be just under my nose! Drat it! *Yawns.* It's time to go to sleep! But I don't care to go into the hut. It seems to float just round my nose! It has a strong scent, the damned stuff! *The guests are heard driving off.* They're off at last. Oh Lord! Merciful Nicholas! There they go, binding themselves and gulling one another. And it's all gammon!

Enter Nikita.

NIKITA: Mitrich, you get off to sleep and I'll put this straight.

MITRICH: All right, you throw it to the sheep. Well, have you seen 'em all off?

NIKITA: Yes, they're off! But things are not right! I don't know what to do!

MITRICH: It's a fine mess. But there's the Foundlings'[2] for that sort of thing. Whoever likes may drop one there; they'll take 'em all. Give 'em as many as you like, they ask no questions, and even pay—if the mother goes in as a wet-nurse. It's easy enough nowadays.

NIKITA: But mind, Mitrich, don't go blabbing.

MITRICH: It's no concern of mine. Cover the tracks as you think best. Dear me, how you smell of liquor! I'll go in. Oh Lord! *Exit, yawning.*

Nikita is silent a long time. Sits down on a sledge.

NIKITA: Here's a go!

Enter Anisya.

ANISYA: Where are you?

NIKITA: Here.

ANISYA: What are you doing there? There's no time to be lost! We must take it out directly!

NIKITA: What are we to do?

ANISYA: I'll tell you what you are to do. And you'll have to do it!

NIKITA: You'd better take it to the Foundlings'—if anything.

ANISYA: Then you'd better take it there yourself if you like! You've a hankering for smut, but you're weak when it comes to settling up, I see!

---

[2] The Foundlings' Hospital in Moscow, where 80 to 90 per cent of the children used to die.

NIKITA: What's to be done?

ANISYA: Go down into the cellar, I tell you, and dig a hole!

NIKITA: Couldn't you manage, somehow, some other way?

ANISYA, *imitating him*: "Some other way?" Seems we can't "some other way!" You should have thought about it a year ago. Do what you're told to!

NIKITA: Oh dear, what a go!

Enter Nan.

NAN: Mother! Grandmother's calling! I think sister's got a baby! I'm blest if it didn't scream!

ANISYA: What are you babbling about? Plague take you! It's kittens whining there. Go into the hut and sleep, or I'll give it you!

NAN: Mammy dear, truly, I swear . . .

ANISYA, *raising her arm as if to strike*: I'll give it you! You be off and don't let me catch sight of you! *Nan runs into hut. To Nikita*: Do as you're told, or else mind! *Exit.*

NIKITA, *alone; after a long silence*: Here's a go! Oh these women! What a fix! Says you should have thought of it a year ago. When's one to think beforehand? When's one to think? Why, last year this Anisya dangled after me. What was I to do? Am I a monk? The master died; and I covered my sin as was proper, so I was not to blame there. Aren't there lots of such cases? And then those powders. Did I put her up to that? Why, had I known what the bitch was up to, I'd have killed her! I'm sure I should have killed her! She's made me her partner in these horrors—that jade! And she became loathsome to me from that day! She became loathsome, loathsome, to me as soon as mother told me about it. I can't bear the sight of her! Well then, how could I live with her! And then it began. . . . That wench began hanging round. Well, what was I to do! If I had not done it, some one else would. And this is what comes of it! Still I'm not to blame in this either. Oh, what a go! *Sits thinking.* They are bold, these women! What a plan to think of! But I won't have a hand in it!

Enter Matrena with a lantern and spade, panting.

MATRENA: Why are you sitting there like a hen on a

perch? What did your wife tell you to do? You just get things ready!

NIKITA: What do you mean to do?

MATRENA: We know what to do. You do your share!

NIKITA: You'll be getting me into a mess!

MATRENA: What? You're not thinking of backing out, are you? Now it's come to this, and you back out!

NIKITA: Think what a thing it would be! It's a living soul.

MATRENA: A living soul indeed! Why, it's more dead than alive. And what's one to do with it? Go and take it to the Foundlings'—it will die just the same, and the rumour will get about, and people will talk, and the girl be left on our hands.

NIKITA: And supposing it's found out?

MATRENA: Not manage to do it in one's own house? We'll manage it so that no one will have an inkling. Only do as I tell you. We women can't do it without a man. There, take the spade and get it done there—I'll hold the light.

NIKITA: What am I to get done?

MATRENA, *in a low voice*: Dig a hole; then we'll bring it out and get it out of the way in a trice! There, she's calling again. Now then, get in, and I'll go.

NIKITA: Is it dead then?

MATRENA: Of course it is. Only you must be quick, or else people will notice! They'll see or they'll hear! The rascals must needs know everything. And the policeman went by this evening. Well then, you see (*gives him the spade*), you get down into the cellar and dig a hole right in the corner; the earth is soft there, and you'll smooth it over. Mother earth will not blab to any one; she'll keep it close. Go then; go, dear.

NIKITA: You'll get me into a mess, confound you! I'll go away! You do it alone as best you can!

ANISYA, *through the doorway*: Well? Has he dug it?

MATRENA: Why have you come away? What have you done with it?

ANISYA: I've covered it with rags. No one can hear it. Well, has he dug it?

MATRENA: He doesn't want to!

ANISYA (*springs out enraged*): Doesn't want to! How will he like feeding vermin in prison! I'll go straight away and tell everything to the police! It's all the same if one must perish. I'll go straight and tell!

NIKITA, *taken aback*: What will you tell?

ANISYA: What? Everything! Who took the money? You! *Nikita is silent.* And who gave the poison? I did! But you knew! You knew! You knew! We were in agreement!

MATRENA: That's enough now. Nikita dear, why are you obstinate? What's to be done now? One must take some trouble. Go, honey.

ANISYA: See the fine gentleman! He doesn't like it! You've put upon me long enough! You've trampled me under foot! Now it's my turn! Go, I tell you, or else I'll do what I said. . . . There, take the spade; there, now go!

NIKITA: Drat you! Can't you leave a fellow alone! *Takes the spade, but shrinks.* If I don't choose to, I'll not go!

ANISYA: Not go? *Begins to shout*: Neighbours! Heh! heh!

MATRENA (*closes her mouth*): What are you about? You're mad! He'll go. . . . Go, sonnie; go, my own.

ANISYA: I'll cry murder!

NIKITA: Now stop! Oh what people! You'd better be quick. . . . As well be hung for a sheep as a lamb! *Goes towards the cellar.*

MATRENA: Yes, that's just it, honey. If you know how to amuse yourself, you must know how to hide the consequences.

ANISYA, *still excited*: He's trampled on me . . . he and his slut! But it's enough! I'm not going to be the only one! Let him also be a murderer! Then he'll know how it feels!

MATRENA: There, there! How she flares up! Don't you be cross, lass, but do things quietly little by little, as it's best. You go to the girl, and he'll do the work. *Follows Nikita to the cellar with a lantern. He descends into the cellar.*

ANISYA: And I'll make him strangle his dirty brat! *Still excited*: I've worried myself to death all alone, with

Peter's bones weighing on my mind! Let him feel it too!
I'll not spare myself; I've said I'll not spare myself!

NIKITA, *from the cellar*: Show a light!

MATRENA (*holds up the lantern to him*) *to Anisya*:
He's digging. Go and bring it.

ANISYA: You stay with him, or he'll go away, the
wretch! And I'll go and bring it.

MATRENA: Mind, don't forget to baptize it, or I will
if you like. Have you a cross?

ANISYA: I'll find one. I know how to do it. *Exit.*[3]

MATRENA: How the woman bristled up! But one must
allow she's been put upon. Well, but with the Lord's help,
when we've covered this business, there'll be an end of
it. We'll shove the girl off without any trouble. My son
will live in comfort. The house, thank God, is as full as
an egg. They'll not forget me either. Where would they
have been without Matrena? They'd not have known
how to contrive things. *Peering into the cellar.* Is it ready,
sonnie?

NIKITA (*puts out his head*): What are you about there?
Bring it quick! What are you dawdling for? If it is to
be done, let it be done.

*Matrena goes towards door of the hut and meets Anisya.
Anisya comes out with a baby wrapped in rags.*

MATRENA: Well, have you baptized it?

ANISYA: Why, of course! It was all I could do to take
it away—she wouldn't give it up! *Comes forward and
hands it to Nikita.*

NIKITA (*does not take it*): You bring it yourself!

ANISYA: Take it, I tell you! *Throws the baby to him.*

NIKITA (*catches it*): It's alive! Gracious me, it's moving!
It's alive! What am I to . . .

ANISYA (*snatches the baby from him and throws it
into the cellar*): Be quick and smother it, and then it
won't be alive! *Pushes Nikita down.* It's your doing, and
you must finish it.

MATRENA (*sits on the doorstep of the hut*): He's
tender-hearted. It's hard on him, poor dear. Well, what
of that? Isn't it also his sin?

---

[3] See at end of Act IV, Variation, which may be used instead of
what follows.

Anisya stands by the cellar.

MATRENA (*sits looking at her and discourses*): Oh, oh, oh! How frightened he was: well, but what of that? If it *is* hard, it's the only thing to be done. Where was one to put it? And just think how often it happens that people pray to God to have children! But no, God gives them none; or they are still-born. Look at our priest's wife now. . . . And here, where it's not wanted, here it lives. *Looks towards the cellar.* I suppose he's finished. *To Anisya:* Well?

ANISYA, *looking into the cellar:* He's put a board on it and is sitting on it. It must be finished!

MATRENA: Oh, oh! One would be glad not to sin, but what's one to do?

Re-enter Nikita from cellar, trembling all over.

NIKITA: It's still alive! I can't! It's alive!

ANISYA: If it's alive, where are you off to? *Tries to stop him.*

NIKITA (*rushes at her*): Go away! I'll kill you! *Catches hold of her arms; she escapes, he runs after her with the spade. Matrena runs towards him and stops him. Anisya runs into the porch. Matrena tries to wrench the spade from him. To his mother:* I'll kill you! I'll kill you! Go away! *Matrena runs to Anisya in the porch. Nikita stops.* I'll kill you! I'll kill you all!

MATRENA: That's because he's so frightened! Never mind, it will pass!

NIKITA: What have they made me do? What have they made me do? How it whimpered. . . . How it crunched under me! What have they done with me? . . . And it's really alive, still alive! *Listens in silence.* It's whimpering. . . . There, it's whimpering. *Runs to the cellar.*

MATRENA, *to Anisya:* He's going; it seems he means to bury it. Nikita, you'd better take the lantern!

NIKITA (*does not heed her, but listens by the cellar door*): I can hear nothing! I suppose it was fancy! *Moves away, then stops.* How the little bones crunched under me! Krr . . . krr . . . What have they made me do? *Listens again.* Again whimpering! It's really whimpering! What can it be? Mother! Mother! I say! *Goes up to her.*

MATRENA: What is it, sonnie?

NIKITA: Mother, my own mother, I can't do any

more! Can't do any more! My own mother, have some pity on me!

MATRENA: Oh dear, how frightened you are, my darling! Come, come, drink a drop to give you courage!

NIKITA: Mother, mother! It seems my time has come! What have you done with me? How the little bones crunched, and how it whimpered! My own mother! What have you done with me? *Steps aside and sits down on the sledge.*

MATRENA: Come, my own, have a drink! It certainly does seem uncanny at night-time. But wait a bit. When the day breaks, you know, and one day and another passes, you'll forget even to think of it. Wait a bit; when the girl's married we'll even forget to think of it. But you go and have a drink; have a drink! I'll go and put things straight in the cellar myself.

NIKITA (*rouses himself*): Is there any drink left? Perhaps I can drink it off! *Exit.*

Anisya, who has stood all the time by the door, silently makes way for him.

MATRENA: Go, go, honey, and I'll set to work! I'll go down myself and dig! Where has he thrown the spade to? *Finds the spade, and goes down into cellar.* Anisya, come here! Hold the light, will you?

ANISYA: And what of him?

MATRENA: He's so frightened! You've been too hard on him. Leave him alone, he'll come to his senses. God help him! I'll set to work myself. Put the lantern down here. I can see.

Matrena disappears into the cellar.

ANISYA, *looking towards the door by which Nikita entered the hut*: Well, have you had enough spree? You've been puffing yourself up, but now you'll know how it feels! You'll lose some of your bluster!

NIKITA (*rushes out of the hut towards the cellar*): Mother! mother, I say!

MATRENA (*puts out her head*): What is it, sonnie?

NIKITA, *listening*: Don't bury it, it's alive! Don't you hear? Alive! There—it's whimpering! There . . . quite plain!

MATRENA: How can it whimper? Why, you've flattened it into a pancake! The whole head is smashed to bits!

NIKITA: What is it then? *Stops his ears.* It's still whimpering! I am lost! Lost! What have they done with me? . . . Where shall I go? *Sits down on the step.*

VARIATION

Instead of the end of Act IV (from the words: "ANISYA: I'll find one. I know how to do it. *Exit"), the following variation may be read, and is the one usually acted.*

Scene 2

The interior of the hut as in Act I. Nan lies on the bench and is covered with a coat. Mitrich is sitting on the oven smoking.

MITRICH: Dear me! How they've made the place smell! Drat 'em! They've been spilling the fine stuff. Even tobacco don't get rid of the smell! It keeps tickling one's nose so. Oh Lord! But it's bed-time, I guess. *Approaches the lamp to put it out.*

NAN (*jumps up, and remains sitting up*): Daddy dear,[1] don't put it out!

MITRICH: Not put it out? Why?

NAN: Didn't you hear them making a row in the yard? *Listens.* D'you hear, there in the barn again now?

MITRICH: What's that to you? I guess no one's asked you to mind! Lie down and sleep! And I'll turn down the light. *Turns down lamp.*

NAN: Daddy darling! Don't put it right out; leave a little bit if only as big as a mouse's eye, else it's so frightening!

MITRICH (*laughs*): All right, all right. *Sits down by her.* What's there to be afraid of?

NAN: How can one help being frightened, daddy! Sister did go on so! She was beating her head against the box! *Whispers.* You know, I know . . . a little baby is going to be born. . . . It's already born, I think. . . .

MITRICH: Eh, what a little busybody it is! May the frogs kick her! Must needs know everything. Lie down

[1] Nan calls Mitrich "daddy" merely as a term of endearment.

and sleep! *Nan lies down.* That's right! *Tucks her up.* That's right! There now, if you know too much you'll grow old too soon.

NAN: And you are going to lie on the oven?

MITRICH: Well, of course! What a little silly you are, now I come to look at you! Must needs know everything. *Tucks her up again, then stands up to go.* There now, lie still and sleep! *Goes up to the oven.*

NAN: It gave just one cry, and now there's nothing to be heard.

MITRICH: Oh Lord! Gracious Nicholas! What is it you can't hear?

NAN: The baby.

MITRICH: There is none, that's why you can't hear it!

NAN: But I heard it! Blest if I didn't hear it! Such a thin voice!

MITRICH: Heard indeed! Much you heard! Well, if you know—why then it was just such a little girl as you that the bogey popped into his bag and made off with.

NAN: What bogey?

MITRICH: Why, just his very self! *Climbs up on to the oven.* The oven is beautifully warm to-night. Quite a treat! Oh Lord! Gracious Nicholas!

NAN: Daddy! are you going to sleep?

MITRICH: What else? Do you think I'm going to sing songs? *Silence.*

NAN: Daddy! Daddy, I say! They are digging! they're digging—don't you hear? Blest if they're not, they're digging!

MITRICH: What are you dreaming about? Digging! Digging in the night! Who's digging? The cow's rubbing herself, that's all. Digging indeed! Go to sleep, I tell you, else I'll just put out the light!

NAN: Daddy darling, don't put it out! I won't . . . truly, truly, I won't. It's so frightful!

MITRICH: Frightful? Don't be afraid and then it won't be frightful. Look at her, she's afraid and then says it's frightful. How can it help being frightful if you are afraid? Eh, what a stupid little girl! *Silence. The cricket chirps.*

NAN (*whispers*): Daddy! I say, daddy! Are you asleep?

MITRICH: Now then, what d'you want?

NAN: What's the bogey like?

MITRICH: Why, like this! When he finds such a one as you, who won't sleep, he comes with a sack and pops the girl into it, then in he gets himself, head and all, lifts her dress, and gives her a fine whipping!

NAN: What with?

MITRICH: He takes a birch-broom with him.

NAN: But he can't see there—inside the sack!

MITRICH: He'll see, no fear!

NAN: But I'll bite him.

MITRICH: No, friend, him you can't bite!

NAN: Daddy, there's some one coming! Who is it? Oh gracious goodness! Who can it be?

MITRICH: Well, if some one's coming, let them come! What's the matter with you? I suppose it's your mother!

Enter Anisya.

ANISYA: Nan! *Nan pretends to be asleep.* Mitrich!

MITRICH: What?

ANISYA: What's the lamp burning for? We are going to sleep in the summer-hut.

MITRICH: Why, you see I've only just got straight. I'll put the light out all right.

ANISYA (*rummages in her box and grumbles*): When a thing's wanted one never can find it!

MITRICH: Why, what is it you are looking for?

ANISYA: I'm looking for a cross. Suppose it were to die unbaptized. It would be a sin, you know!

MITRICH: Of course it would! Everything in due order. . . . Have you found it?

ANISYA: Yes, I've found it. *Exit.*

MITRICH: That's right, else I'd have lent her mine. Oh Lord!

NAN (*jumps up trembling*): Oh, oh, daddy! Don't go to sleep; for goodness' sake, don't! It's so frightful!

MITRICH: What's frightful?

NAN: It will die—the little baby will! At Aunt Irene's the old woman baptized the baby, and it died!

MITRICH: If it dies, they'll bury it!

NAN: But maybe it wouldn't have died, only old Granny Matrena's there! Didn't I hear what granny was saying? I heard her! Blest if I didn't.

MITRICH: What did you hear? Go to sleep, I tell you.

Cover yourself up, head and all, and let's have an end of it!

NAN: If it lived, I'd nurse it!

MITRICH (*roars*): Oh Lord!

NAN: Where will they put it?

MITRICH: In the right place! It's no business of yours! Go to sleep, I tell you, else mother will come; she'll give it you! *Silence.*

NAN: Daddy! Eh, daddy! That girl, you know, you were telling about—they didn't kill her?

MITRICH: That girl? Oh yes. That girl turned out all right!

NAN: How was it? You were saying you found her?

MITRICH: Well, we just found her!

NAN: But where did you find her? Do tell!

MITRICH: Why, in their own house; that's where! We came to a village, the soldiers began hunting about in the house, when suddenly there's that same little girl lying on the floor, flat on her stomach. We were going to give her a knock on the head, but all at once I felt that sorry, that I took her up in my arms; but no, she wouldn't let me! Made herself so heavy, quite a hundred-weight, and caught hold where she could with her hands, so that one couldn't get them off! Well, so I began stroking her head. It was so bristly—just like a hedgehog! So I stroked and stroked, and she quieted down at last. I soaked a bit of rusk and gave it her. She understood that, and began nibbling. What were we to do with her? We took her; took her, and began feeding and feeding her, and she got so used to us that we took her with us on the march, and so she went about with us. Ah, she was a fine girl!

NAN: Yes, and not baptized?

MITRICH: Who can tell! They used to say, not altogether. 'Cos why, those people weren't our own.

NAN: Germans?

MITRICH: What an idea! Germans! Not Germans, but Asiatics. They are just the same as Jews, but still not Jews. Polish, yet Asiatics. Curls . . . or, Curdlys is their name. . . . I've forgotten what it is![2] We called the girl

2 Probably Kurds.

Sashka. She was a fine girl, Sashka was! There now, I've forgotten everything I used to know! But that girl—the deuce take her—seems to be before my eyes now! Out of all my time of service, I remember how they flogged me, and I remember that girl. That's all I remember! She'd hang around one's neck, and one 'ud carry her so. That was a girl—if you wanted a better you'd not find one! We gave her away afterwards. The captain's wife took her to bring up as her daughter. So—she was all right! How sorry the soldiers were to let her go!

NAN: There now, daddy, and I remember when father was dying—you were not living with us then. Well, he called Nikita and says, "Forgive me, Nikita!" he says, and begins to cry. *Sighs.* That was very sad too!

MITRICH: Yes; there now, so it is . . .

NAN: Daddy! Daddy, I say! There they are again, making a noise in the cellar! Oh gracious heavens! Oh dear! Oh dear! Oh, daddy! They'll do something to it! They'll make away with it, and it's so little! Oh, oh! *Covers up her head and cries.*

MITRICH, *listening*: Really they're up to some villainy, blow 'em to shivers! Oh, these women are vile creatures! One can't say much for men either; but women! . . . They are like wild beasts, and stick at nothing!

NAN, *rising*: Daddy! I say, daddy!

MITRICH: Well, what now?

NAN: The other day a traveller stayed the night; he said that when an infant died its soul goes up straight to heaven. Is that true?

MITRICH: Who can tell? I suppose so. Well?

NAN: Oh, it would be best if I died too. *Whimpers.*

MITRICH: Then you'd be off the list!

NAN: Up to ten one's an infant, and maybe one's soul would go to God. Else one's sure to go to the bad!

MITRICH: Sure enough, to the bad? How should the likes of you not go to the bad? Who teaches you? What do you see? What do you hear? Only vileness! I, though I've not been taught much, still know a thing or two. I'm not quite like a peasant woman. A peasant woman, what is she? Just mud! There are many millions of the likes of you in Russia, and all as blind as moles

—knowing nothing! All sorts of spells: how to stop the cattle-plague with a plough, and how to cure children by putting them under the perches in the hen-house! That's what they know!

NAN: Yes, mother did that too.

MITRICH: Yes—there it is—just so! So many millions of girls and women, and all like beasts in a forest! As she grows up, so she dies! Never sees anything; never hears anything. A peasant—he may learn something at the inn, or maybe in prison, or in the army—as I did. But a woman? Let alone about God, she doesn't even know rightly what Friday it is! Friday! Friday! But ask her what's Friday? She don't know! They're like blind puppies, creeping about and poking their noses into the dung-heap. . . . All they know are their silly songs. Ho, ho, ho, ho! But what they mean by ho-ho, they don't know themselves!

NAN: But I, daddy, I do know half the Lord's Prayer!

MITRICH: A lot you know! But what can one expect of you? Who teaches you? Only a tipsy peasant—with the strap perhaps! That's all the teaching you get! I don't know who'll have to answer for you. For a recruit, the drill sergeant or the corporal has to answer; but for the likes of you there's no one responsible! Just as the cattle that have no herdsman are the most mischievous, so with you women—you are the stupidest class! The most foolish class is yours!

NAN: Then what's one to do?

MITRICH: That's what one has to do. . . . You just cover up your head and sleep! Oh Lord!

Silence. The cricket chirps.

NAN (*jumps up*): Daddy! Some one's screaming awfully! Blest if some one isn't screaming! Daddy darling, it's coming here!

MITRICH: Cover up your head, I tell you!

Enter Nikita, followed by Matrena.

NIKITA: What have they done with me? What have they done with me?

MATRENA: Have a drop, honey; have a drop of drink! What's the matter? *Fetches the spirits and sets the bottle before him.*

NIKITA: Give it here! Perhaps the drink will help me!

MATRENA: Mind! They're not asleep! Here you are, have a drop!

NIKITA: What does it all mean? Why did you plan it? You might have taken it somewhere!

MATRENA (*whispers*): Sit still a bit and drink a little more, or have a smoke. It will ease your thoughts!

NIKITA: My own mother! My turn seems to have come! How it began to whimper, and how the little bones crunched . . . krr . . . I'm not a man now!

MATRENA: Eh, now, what's the use of talking so silly! Of course it does seem fearsome at night, but wait till the daylight comes, and a day or two passes, and you'll forget to think of it! *Goes up to Nikita and puts her hand on his shoulder.*

NIKITA: Go away from me! What have you done with me?

MATRENA: Come, come, sonnie! Now really, what's the matter with you? *Takes his hand.*

NIKITA: Go away from me! I'll kill you! It's all one to me now! I'll kill you!

MATRENA: Oh, oh, how frightened he's got! You should go and have a sleep now!

NIKITA: I have nowhere to go; I'm lost!

MATRENA, *shaking her head*: Oh, oh, I'd better go and tidy things up. He'll sit and rest a bit, and it will pass! *Exit.*

Nikita sits with his face in his hands. Mitrich and Nan seem stunned.

NIKITA: It's whining! It's whining! It is really—there, there, quite plain! She'll bury it, really she will! *Runs to the door.* Mother, don't bury it, it's alive. . . .

Enter Matrena.

Matrena (*whispers*): Now then, what is it! Heaven help you! Why won't you get to rest? How can it be alive? All its bones are crushed!

NIKITA: Give me more drink! *Drinks.*

MATRENA: Now go, sonnie. You'll fall asleep now all right.

NIKITA (*stands listening*): Still alive . . . there . . . it's whining! Don't you hear? . . . There!

MATRENA (*whispers*): No! I tell you!

NIKITA: Mother! My own mother! I've ruined my life!
What have you done with me? Where am I to go? *Runs
out of the hut; Matrena follows him.*

NAN: Daddy dear, darling, they've smothered it!

MITRICH (*angrily*): Go to sleep, I tell you! Oh dear,
may the frogs kick you! I'll give it to you with the broom!
Go to sleep, I tell you!

NAN: Daddy, my treasure! Something is catching hold
of my shoulders, something is catching hold with its paws!
Daddy dear . . . really, really . . . I must go! Daddy,
darling! let me get up on the oven with you! Let me,
for Heaven's sake! Catching hold . . . catching hold!
Oh! *Runs to the stove.*

MITRICH: See how they've frightened the girl. . . .
What vile creatures they are! May the frogs kick them!
Well then, climb up.

NAN (*climbs on oven*): But don't you go away!

MITRICH: Where should I go to? Climb up, climb up!
Oh Lord! Gracious Nicholas! Holy Mother! . . . How
they have frightened the girl. *Covers her up.* There's a little
fool—really a little fool! How they've frightened her;
really, they are vile creatures! The deuce take 'em!

ACT
V

Scene I

*In front of scene a stack-stand, to the left a thrashing
ground, to the right a barn. The barn doors are open.
Straw is strewn about in the doorway. The hut with yard
and out-buildings is seen in the background, whence
proceed sounds of singing and of a tambourine. Two girls
are walking past the barn towards the hut.*

FIRST GIRL: There, you see we've got round without
so much as getting our boots dirty! But to come by the
street is terribly muddy! *They stop and wipe their boots
on the straw. First Girl looks at the straw and sees something.* What's that?

SECOND GIRL (*looks where the straw lies and sees some one*): It's Mitrich, their labourer. Just look how drunk he is!

FIRST GIRL: Why, I thought he didn't drink.

SECOND GIRL: It seems he didn't until it was going around.

FIRST GIRL: Just see! He must have come to fetch some straw. Look! he's got a rope in his hand, and he's fallen asleep.

SECOND GIRL, *listening*: They're still singing the praises.[1] So I s'pose the bride and bridegroom have not yet been blessed! They say Akulina didn't even lament![2]

FIRST GIRL: Mammie says she is marrying against her will. Her step-father threatened her, or else she'd not have done it for the world! Why, you know what they've been saying about. her?

MARINA, *catching up the girls*: How d'you do, lassies?

GIRLS: How d'you do?

MARINA: Going to the wedding, my dears?

FIRST GIRL: It's nearly over! We've come just to have a look.

MARINA: Would you call my old man for me? Simon, from Zuevo; you surely know him?

FIRST GIRL: To be sure we do; he's a relative of the bridegroom's, I think?

MARINA: Of course; he's my old man's nephew, the bridegroom is.

SECOND GIRL: Why don't you go yourself? Fancy not going to a wedding!

MARINA: I have no mind for it, and no time either. It's time for us to be going home. We didn't mean to come to the wedding. We were taking oats to town. We only stopped to feed the horse, and they made my old man go in.

FIRST GIRL: Where did you put up then? At Fedorich's?

MARINA: Yes. Well then, I'll stay here and you go and call him, my dear—my old man. Call him, my pet, and

---

[1] This refers to the songs customary at the wedding of Russian peasants, praising the bride and bridegroom.

[2] It is etiquette for a bride to bewail the approaching loss of her maidenhood.

say "Your missis Marina says you must go now!" His mates are harnessing.

FIRST GIRL: Well, all right—if you won't go in yourself. *The girls go away towards the house along a footpath. Sounds of songs and tambourine.*

MARINA (*alone, stands thinking*): I might go in, but I don't like to, because I have not met him since that day he threw me over. It's more than a year now. But I'd have liked to have a peep and see how he lives with his Anisya. People say they don't get on. She's a coarse woman, and with a character of her own. I should think he's remembered me more than once. He's been caught by the idea of a comfortable life and has changed me for it. But, God help him, I don't cherish ill-will! Then it hurt! Oh dear, it was pain! But now it's worn away and been forgotten. But I'd like to have seen him. *Looks towards hut and sees Nikita.* Look there! Why, he is coming here! Have the girls told him? How is it he has left his guests? I'll go away! *Nikita approaches, hanging his head down, swinging his arms, and muttering.* And how sullen he looks!

NIKITA (*sees and recognizes Marina*): Marina, dearest friend, little Marina, what do you want?

MARINA: I have come for my old man.

NIKITA: Why didn't you come to the wedding? You might have had a look round, and a laugh at my expense!

MARINA: What have I to laugh at? I've come for my husband.

NIKITA: Ah, Marina dear! *Tries to embrace her.*

MARINA (*steps angrily aside*): You'd better drop that sort of thing, Nikita! What has been, is past! I've come for my husband. Is he in your house?

NIKITA: So I must not remember the past? You won't let me?

MARINA: It's no use recalling the past! What used to be is over now!

NIKITA: And can never come back, you mean?

MARINA: And will never come back! But why have you gone away? You, the master—and to go away from the feast!

NIKITA (*sits down on the straw*): Why have I gone away? Eh, if you knew, if you had any idea . . . I'm wretched, Marina, so wretched that I wish my eyes would not see! I rose from the table and left them, to get away from the people. If I could only avoid seeing any one!

MARINA, *coming nearer to him*: How's that?

NIKITA: This is how it is: when I eat, it's there! When I drink, it's there! When I sleep, it's there! I'm so sick of it —so sick! But it's chiefly because I'm all alone that I'm so sick, little Marina. I have no one to share my trouble.

MARINA: You can't live your life without trouble, Nikita. However, I've wept over mine and wept it away.

NIKITA: The former, the old trouble! Ah, dear friend, you've wept yours away, and I've got mine up to there! *Puts his hand to his throat.*

MARINA: But why?

NIKITA: Why, I'm sick of my whole life! I am sick of myself! Ah, Marina, why did you not know how to keep me? You've ruined me, and yourself too! Is this life?

MARINA (*stands by the barn crying, but restrains herself*): I do not complain of my life, Nikita! God grant every one a life like mine. I do not complain. I confessed to my old man at the time, and he forgave me. And he does not reproach me. I'm not discontented with my life. The old man is quiet, and is fond of me, and I keep his children clothed and washed! He is really kind to me. Why should I complain? It seems God willed it so. And what's the matter with your life? You are rich . . .

NIKITA: My life! . . . It's only that I don't wish to disturb the wedding feast, or I'd take this rope here (*takes hold of the rope on the straw*) and throw it across that rafter there. Then I'd make a noose and stretch it out, and I'd climb on to that rafter and jump down with my head in the noose! That's what my life is!

MARINA: That's enough! Lord help you!

NIKITA: You think I'm joking? You think I'm drunk? I'm not drunk! To-day even drink takes no hold on me! I'm devoured by misery! Misery is eating me up completely, so that I care for nothing! Oh, little Marina, it's only with you I ever lived! Do you remember how we used to while away the nights together at the railway?

MARINA: Don't you rub the sores, Nikita! I'm bound legally now, and you too. My sin has been forgiven, don't disturb . . .

NIKITA: What shall I do with my heart? Where am I to turn to?

MARINA: What is there to be done? You've got a wife. Don't go looking at others, but keep to your own! You loved Anisya, then go on loving her!

NIKITA: Oh, that Anisya, she's gall and wormwood to me, but she's round my feet like rank weeds!

MARINA: Whatever she is, still she's your wife. . . . But what's the use of talking; you'd better go to your visitors, and send my husband to me.

NIKITA: Oh dear, if you knew the whole business . . . but there's no good talking!

Enter Marina's Husband, red and tipsy, and Nan.

MARINA'S HUSBAND: Marina! Missis! My old woman! are you here?

NIKITA: There's your husband calling you. Go!

MARINA: And you?

NIKITA: I? I'll lie down here for a bit! *Lies down on the straw.*

HUSBAND: Where is she then?

NAN: There she is, near the barn.

HUSBAND: What are you standing there for? Come to the feast! The hosts want you to come and do them honour! The wedding party is just going to start, and then we can go too.

MARINA, *going towards her husband*: I didn't want to go in.

HUSBAND: Come on, I tell you! You'll drink a glass to our nephew Peter's health, the rascal! Else the hosts might take offence! There's plenty of time for our business.

Marina's Husband puts his arm around her, and goes reeling out with her.

NIKITA (*rises and sits down on the straw*): Ah, now that I've seen her, life seems more sickening than ever! It was only with her that I ever really lived! I've ruined my life for nothing! I've done for myself! *Lies down.* Where can I go? If mother earth would but open and swallow me!

NAN (*sees Nikita, and runs towards him*): Daddy, I

say, daddy! They're looking for you! Her godfather and all of them have already blessed her. Truly they have, they're getting cross!

NIKITA, *aside*: Where can I go to?

NAN: What? What are you saying?

NIKITA: I'm not saying anything! Don't bother!

NAN: Daddy! Come, I say! *Nikita is silent; Nan pulls him by the hand.* Dad, go and bless them! My word, they're angry, they're grumbling!

NIKITA (*drags away his hand*): Leave me alone!

NAN: Now then!

NIKITA (*threatens her with the rope*): Go, I say! I'll give it you!

NAN: Then I'll send mother! *Runs away.*

NIKITA (*rises*): How can I go? How can I take the holy icon in my hands? How am I to look her in the face! *Lies down again.* Oh, if there were a hole in the ground, I'd jump in! No one should see me, and I should see no one! *Rises again.* No, I shan't go. . . . May they all go to the devil, I shan't go. *Takes the rope and makes a noose and tries it on his neck.* That's the way!

Enter Matrena. Nikita sees his mother, takes the rope off his neck, and again lies down in the straw.

MATRENA (*comes in hurriedly*): Nikita! Nikita, I say! He don't even answer! Nikita, what's the matter? Have you had a drop too much? Come, Nikita dear; come, honey! The people are tired of waiting.

NIKITA: Oh dear, what have you done with me? I'm a lost man!

MATRENA: But what is the matter then? Come, my own; come, give them your blessing, as is proper and honourable, and then it'll all be over! Why, the people are waiting!

NIKITA: How can I give blessings?

MATRENA: Why, in the usual way! Don't you know?

NIKITA: I know, I know! But who is it I am to bless? What have I done to her?

MATRENA: What have you done? Eh, now he's going to remember it? Why, who knows anything about it? Not a soul! And the girl is going of her own accord.

NIKITA: Yes, but how?

MATRENA: Because she's afraid, of course. But still

she's going. Besides, what's to be done now? She should have thought sooner! Now she can't refuse. And his kinsfolk can't take offence either. They saw the girl twice, and get money with her too! It's all safe and sound!

NIKITA: Yes, but what's in the cellar?

MATRENA (*laughs*): In the cellar? Why, cabbages, mushrooms, potatoes, I suppose! Why remember the past?

NIKITA: I'd be only too glad to forget it; but I can't! When I let my mind go, it's just as if I heard . . . Oh, what have you done with me?

MATRENA: Now, what are you humbugging for?

NIKITA (*turns face downward*): Mother! Don't torment me! I've got it up to here! *Puts his hand to his throat.*

MATRENA: Still it has to be done! As it is, people are talking. "The master's gone away and won't come; he can't make up his mind to give his blessing." They'll be putting two and two together. As soon as they see you're frightened they'll begin guessing. "The thief none suspect who walks bold and erect!" But you'll be getting out of the frying-pan into the fire! Above all, lad, don't show it, don't lose courage, else they'll find out all the more!

NIKITA: Oh dear! You have snared me into a trap!

MATRENA: That'll do, I tell you; come along! Come in and give your blessing, as is right and honourable; and there's an end of the matter!

NIKITA (*lies face down*): I can't!

MATRENA, *aside*: What has come over him? He seemed all right, and suddenly this comes over him! It seems he's bewitched! Get up, Nikita! See! There's Anisya coming; she's left her guests!

Anisya enters, dressed up, red, and tipsy.

ANISYA: Oh, how fine it is, mother! So fine, so respectable! And how pleased the people are. . . . But where is he?

MATRENA: Here, honey, he's here; he's laid down on the straw and there he lies! He won't come!

NIKITA, *looking at his wife*: Just see, she's tipsy too! When I look at her my heart seems to turn! How can one live with her? *Turns on his face.* I'll kill her some day! It'll be worse then!

ANISYA: Only look, how he's got all among the straw! Is it the drink? *Laughs.* I'd not mind lying down there with you, but I've no time! Come, I'll lead you! It is so fine in the house! It's a treat to look on! A concertina! And the women singing so well! All tipsy! Everything so respectable, so fine!

NIKITA: What's fine?

ANISYA: The wedding—such a jolly wedding! They all say it's quite an uncommon fine wedding! All so respectable, so fine! Come along! We'll go together! I have had a drop, but I can give you a hand yet! *Takes his hand.*

NIKITA (*pulls it back with disgust*): Go on alone! I'll come!

ANISYA: What are you humbugging for? We've got rid of all the bother, we've got rid of her as came between us; now we have nothing to do but to live and be merry! And all so respectable, and quite legal! I'm so pleased! I have no words for it! It's just as if I were going to marry you over again! And oh, the people, they *are* pleased! They're all thanking us! And the guests are all of the best: Ivan Moseich is there, and the Police Officer; they too have been singing songs of praise!

NIKITA: Then you should have stayed with them! What have you come for?

ANISYA: True enough, I must go back! Else what does it look like! The hosts both go and leave the visitors! And the guests are all of the best!

NIKITA (*gets up and brushes the straw off himself*): Go, and I'll come at once!

MATRENA: Just see! He listens to the young bird, but wouldn't listen to the old one! He would not hear me, but he follows his wife at once! *Matrena and Anisya turn to go.* Well, are you coming?

NIKITA: I'll come directly! You go and I'll follow! I'll come and give my blessing! *The women stop.* Go on! I'll follow! Now then, go! *Exit women. Sits down and takes his boots off.* Yes, I'm going! A likely thing! No, you'd better look at the rafter for me! I'll fix the noose and jump with it from the rafter, then you can look for me! And the rope is here just handy. *Ponders.* I'd have got over it, over any sorrow—I'd have got over that. But this now—here it is, deep in my heart, and I can't get over it! *Looks towards the yard.* Surely she's not coming back? *Imitates Anisya:* "So fine, so fine. I'd lie down here with you." Oh, the baggage! Well then, here I am! Come and cuddle when they've taken me down from the rafter! There's only one way! *Takes the rope and pulls it.*

Mitrich, who is tipsy, sits up and won't let go of the rope.

MITRICH: Shan't give it up! Shan't give it to no one! I'll bring it myself! I said I'd bring the straw—and so I will! Nikita, is that you? *Laughs.* Oh, the devil! Have you come to get the straw?

NIKITA: Give me the rope!

MITRICH: No, you wait a bit! The peasants sent me! I'll bring it. . . . *Rises to his feet and begins getting the straw together, but reels for a time, then falls.* It has beaten me. It's stronger . . .

NIKITA: Give me the rope!

MITRICH: Didn't I say I won't! Oh, Nikita, you're as stupid as a hog! *Laughs.* I love you, but you're a fool! You see that I'm drunk . . . devil take you! You think I need you? . . . You just look at me; I'm a Non . . . fool, can't say it—Non-commissioned Officer of Her Majesty's very First Regiment of Grenadier Guards! I've served Tsar and country, loyal and true! But who am I? You think I'm a warrior? No, I'm not a warrior; I'm the very least of men, a poor lost orphan! I swore not to drink, and now I had a smoke, and . . . Well then, do you think I'm afraid of you? No fear; I'm afraid of no man! I've taken to drink, and I'll drink! Now I'll go it for a fortnight; I'll go it hard! I'll drink my last shirt; I'll drink my cap; I'll pawn my passport; and I'm afraid of no one! They flogged me in the army to stop me drinking! They switched and switched! "Well," they say, "will you leave off?" "No," says I! Why should I be afraid of them? Here I am! Such as I am, God made me! I swore off drinking, and didn't drink. Now I've took to drink, and I'll drink! And I fear no man! 'Cos I don't lie; but just as . . . Why should one mind them— such muck as they are! "Here you are," I say; that's me. A priest told me the devil's the biggest bragger! "As soon," says he, "as you begin to brag, you get frightened; and as soon as you fear men, then the hoofed one just collars you and pushes you where he likes!" But as I don't fear men, I'm easy! I can spit in the devil's beard, and at the sow his mother! He can't do me no harm! There, put that in your pipe!

NIKITA, *crossing himself*: True enough! What was I about? *Throws down the rope.*

MITRICH: What?

NIKITA (*rises*): You tell me not to fear men?

MITRICH: Why fear such muck as they are? You look at 'em in the bath-house! All made of one paste! One has a bigger belly, another a smaller; that's all the difference there is! Fancy being afraid of 'em! Deuce take 'em!

MATRENA, *from the yard*: Well, are you coming?

NIKITA: Ah! Better so! I'm coming! *Goes towards yard.*

Scene 2

Interior of hut, full of people, some sitting round tables and others standing. In the front corner Akulina and the Bridegroom. On one of the tables an icon and a loaf of rye-bread. Among the visitors are Marina, her Husband, a Police Officer, a Hired Driver, the Matchmaker, and the Best Man. The women are singing. Anisya carries round the drink. The singing stops.

THE DRIVER: If we are to go, let's go! The church ain't so near.

THE BEST MAN: All right; you wait a bit till the step-father has given his blessing. But where is he?

ANISYA: He is coming—coming at once, dear friends! Have another glass all of you; don't refuse!

THE MATCHMAKER: Why is he so long? We've been waiting such a time!

ANISYA: He's coming; coming directly, coming in no time! He'll be here before one could plait a girl's hair who's had it cropped! Drink, friends! *Offers drink.* Coming at once! Sing again, my pets, meanwhile!

THE DRIVER: They've sung all their songs, waiting here!

The women sing. Nikita and Akim enter during the singing.

NIKITA (*holds his father's arm and pushes him in before him*): Go, father; I can't do without you!

AKIM: I don't like—I mean what d'ye call it . . .

NIKITA, *to the women*: Enough! Be quiet! *Looks round the hut.* Marina, are you there?

THE MATCHMAKER: Go, take the icon, and give them your blessing!

NIKITA: Wait a while! *Looks round.* Akulina, are you there?

MATCHMAKER: What are you calling everybody for? Where should she be? How queer he seems!

ANISYA: Gracious goodness! Why, he's barefoot!

NIKITA: Father, you are here! Look at me! Christian Commune, you are all here, and I am here! I am . . . *Falls on his knees.*

ANISYA: Nikita darling, what's the matter with you? Oh my head, my head!

MATCHMAKER: Here's a go!

MATRENA: I did say he was taking too much of that French wine! Come to your senses; what are you about? *They try to lift him; he takes no heed of them, but looks in front of him.*

NIKITA: Christian Commune! I have sinned, and I wish to confess!

MATRENA (*shakes him by the shoulder*): Are you mad? Dear friends, he's gone crazy! He must be taken away!

NIKITA (*shakes her off*): Leave me alone! And you, father, hear me! And first, Marina, look here! *Bows to the ground to her and lifts himself.* I have sinned towards you! I promised to marry you, I tempted you, and forsook you! Forgive me, in Christ's name! *Again bows to the ground before her.*

ANISYA: And what are you drivelling about? It's not becoming! No one wants to know! Get up! It's like your impudence!

MATRENA: Oh, oh, he's bewitched! And however did it happen? It's a spell! Get up! What nonsense are you jabbering? *Pulls him.*

NIKITA (*shakes his head*): Don't touch me! Forgive me my sin towards you, Marina! Forgive me, for Christ's sake!

Marina covers her face with her hands in silence.

ANISYA: Get up, I tell you! Don't be so impudent! What are you thinking about—to recall it? Enough humbug! It's shameful! Oh my poor head! He's quite crazy!

NIKITA (*pushes his wife away and turns to Akulina*): Akulina, now I'll speak to you! Listen, Christian Commune! I'm a fiend, Akulina! I have sinned against you! Your father died no natural death! He was poisoned!

ANISYA (*screams*): Oh my head! What's he about?

MATRENA: The man's beside himself! Lead him away! *The folk come up and try to seize him.*

AKIM (*motions them back with his arms*): Wait! You lads, what d'ye call it, wait, I mean!

NIKITA: Akulina, I poisoned him! Forgive me, in Christ's name!

AKULINA (*jumps up*): He's telling lies! I know who did it!

MATCHMAKER: What are you about? You sit still!

AKIM: Oh Lord, what sins, what sins!

POLICE OFFICER: Seize him, and send for the Elder! We must draw up an indictment and have witnesses to it! Get up and come here!

AKIM, *to Police Officer*: Now you—with the bright buttons—I mean, you wait! Let him, what d'ye call it, speak out, I mean!

POLICE OFFICER: Mind, old man, and don't interfere! I have to draw up an indictment!

AKIM: Eh, what a fellow you are; wait, I say! Don't talk, I mean, about, what d'ye call it, 'ditements! Here God's work is being done. . . . A man is confessing, I mean! And you, what d'ye call it . . . 'ditements!

POLICE OFFICER: The Elder!

AKIM: Let God's work be done, I mean, and then you, I mean, you do your business!

NIKITA: And, Akulina, my sin is great towards you; I seduced you; forgive me in Christ's name! *Bows to the ground before her.*

AKULINA (*leaves the table*): Let me go! I shan't be married! He told me to, but I shan't now!

POLICE OFFICER: Repeat what you have said.

NIKITA: Wait, sir, let me finish!

AKIM, *with rapture*: Speak, my son! Tell everything—

you'll feel better! Confess to God, don't fear men! God —God! It is He!

NIKITA: I poisoned the father, dog that I am, and I ruined the daughter! She was in my power and I ruined her, and her baby!

AKULINA: True, that's true!

NIKITA: I smothered the baby in the cellar with a board! I sat on it and smothered it—and its bones crunched! *Weeps.* And I buried it! I did it, all alone!

AKULINA: He raves! I told him to!

NIKITA: Don't shield me! I fear no one now! Forgive me, Christian Commune! *Bows to the ground. Silence.*

POLICE OFFICER: Bind him! The marriage is evidently off!

Men come up with their belts.

NIKITA: Wait, there's plenty of time! *Bows to the ground before his father.* Father, dear father, forgive me too— fiend that I am! You told me from the first, when I took to bad ways, you said then, "If a claw is caught, the bird is lost!" I would not listen to your words, dog that I was, and it has turned out as you said! Forgive me, for Christ's sake!

AKIM, *rapturously*: God will forgive you, my own son! *Embraces him.* You have had no mercy on yourself, He will show mercy on you! God—God! It is He!

Enter Elder.

ELDER: There are witnesses enough here.

POLICE OFFICER: We will have the examination at once. *Nikita is bound.*

AKULINA (*goes and stands by his side*): I shall tell the truth! Ask me!

NIKITA, *bound*: No need to ask! I did it all myself. The design was mine, and the deed was mine. Take me where you like. I will say no more!

1886

PART SIX

Arts
and Letters

From WHAT IS ART?

IV

*Definitions of art founded on beauty. Taste not definable. A
clear definition needed to enable us to recognize works of art.*

To what do these definitions of beauty amount? Not
reckoning the thoroughly inaccurate definitions of beauty
which fail to cover the conception of art and suppose
beauty to consist either in utility, or in adjustment to a
purpose, or in symmetry, or in order, or in proportion,
or in smoothness, or in harmony of the parts, or in unity
amid variety, or in various combinations of these—not
reckoning these unsatisfactory attempts at objective definition, all the aesthetic definitions of beauty lead to two
fundamental conceptions. The first is that beauty is something having an independent existence (existing in itself),
that it is one of the manifestations of the absolutely Perfect,
of the Idea, of the Spirit, of Will, or of God; the other
is that beauty is a kind of pleasure received by us not
having personal advantage for its object.

The first of these definitions was accepted by Fichte,
Schelling, Hegel, Schopenhauer, and the philosophizing
Frenchmen: Cousin, Jouffroy, Ravaisson, and others, not
to enumerate the second-rate aesthetic philosophers. And
this same objective-mystical definition of beauty is held

by a majority of educated people of our day. It is a conception very widely spread especially among the elder generation.

The second view, that beauty is a certain kind of pleasure received by us not having personal advantage for its aim, finds favour chiefly among the English aesthetic writers and is shared by the other part of our society, principally by the younger generation.

So there are (and it could not be otherwise) only two definitions of beauty: the one objective, mystical, merging this conception into that of the highest perfection, God—a fantastic definition, founded on nothing; the other on the contrary a very simple, and intelligible, subjective one, which considers beauty to be that which pleases (I do not add to the word "pleases" the words "without the aim of advantage," because "pleases" naturally presupposes the absence of the idea of profit).

On the one hand beauty is viewed as something mystical and very elevated, but unfortunately at the same time very indefinite, and consequently embracing philosophy, religion, and life itself (as in the theories of Schelling and Hegel and their German and French followers); or on the other hand (as necessarily follows from the definition of Kant and his adherents) beauty is simply a certain kind of disinterested pleasure received by us. And this conception of beauty, although it seems very clear, is unfortunately again inexact; for it widens out on the other side—that is, it includes the pleasure derived from drink, from food, from touching a delicate skin, and so forth, as is acknowledged by Guyau, Kralik, and others.

It is true that, following the development of the aesthetic doctrines of beauty, we may notice that though at first (in the times when the foundations of the science of aesthetics were being laid) the metaphysical definition of beauty prevailed, yet the nearer we get to our own times the more does an experimental definition (recently assuming a physiological form) come to the front, so that at last we even meet with aestheticians such as Véron and Sully, who try to escape entirely from the conception of beauty. But such aestheticians have very little success, and with the majority of the public as well as of artists and the learned, a conception of beauty is firmly held which agrees with the definitions contained in most of the aesthetic treatises—that is, which regards beauty either as something mystical or metaphysical, or as a special kind of enjoyment.

What then is this conception of beauty, so stubbornly held to by people of our circle and day as furnishing a definition of art?

In its subjective aspect, we call beauty that which supplies us with a particular kind of pleasure.

In its objective aspect, we call beauty something absolutely perfect, and we acknowledge it to be so only because we receive from the manifestation of this absolute perfection a certain kind of pleasure: so that this objective definition is nothing but the subjective conception differently expressed. In reality both conceptions of beauty amount to one and the same thing, namely, the reception by us of a certain kind of pleasure; that is to say, we call "beauty" that which pleases us without evoking in us desire.

Such being the position of affairs it would seem only natural that the science of art should decline to content itself with a definition of art based on beauty (that is, on that which pleases) and should seek a general definition applicable to all artistic productions, by reference to which we might decide whether a certain article belonged to the realm of art or not. But no such definition is supplied, as the reader may see from those summaries of aesthetic theories which I have given, and as he may discover even more clearly from the original aesthetic works if he will be at the pains to read them. All attempts to define absolute beauty in itself—whether as an imitation of nature, or as suitability to its object, or as a correspondence of parts, or as symmetry, or as harmony, or as unity in variety, and so forth—either define nothing at all or define only some traits of some artistic productions and are far from including all that everybody has always held and still holds to be art.

There is no objective definition of beauty. The existing definitions (both the metaphysical and the experimental) amount only to one and the same subjective definition, which is (strange as it seems to say so), that art is that which makes beauty manifest, and beauty is that which pleases (without exciting desire). Many aestheticians have felt the insufficiency and instability of such a definition and in order to give it a firm basis have asked themselves why a thing pleases. And they have converted the discussion on beauty into a question of taste, as did Hutcheson, Voltaire, Diderot, and others. But all attempts to define what taste is must lead to nothing, as the reader may see both from the history of aesthetics and experimentally. There is and can be no explanation of why one thing pleases one man and displeases another, or vice versa; so that the whole existing science of aesthetics fails to do what we might expect from it as a mental activity calling itself a science: namely, it does not define the qualities and laws of art, or of the beautiful (if that be the content of art), or the nature of taste (if taste decides the question of art and its merit), and then on the basis of such definitions acknowledge as art those productions which correspond to these laws and reject those which do not come under them. But this science of aesthetics consists in first acknowledging a certain set of productions to be art (because they please us) and then framing such a theory of art as all these productions which please a certain circle of people can be fitted into. There exists an art-canon according to which certain productions favoured by our circle are acknowledged as being art— the works of Phidias, Sophocles, Homer, Titian, Raphael, Bach, Beethoven, Dante, Shakespeare, Goethe, and others —and the aesthetic laws must be such as to embrace all these productions. In aesthetic literature you will constantly meet with opinions on the merit and importance of art, founded not on any certain laws by which this or that is held to be good or bad, but merely on consideration as to whether this art tallies with the art-canon we have drawn up.

The other day I was reading a far from ill-written book by Folgeldt. Discussing the demand for morality in works of art, the author plainly says that we must not demand morality in art. And in proof of this he advances the fact that, if we admit such a demand, Shakespeare's *Romeo and Juliet* and Goethe's *Wilhelm Meister* would not come within the definition of good art; but since both these books are included in our canon of art, he concludes that the demand is unjust. And therefore it is necessary to find a definition of art which shall fit the works, and instead of a demand for morality Folgeldt postulates as the basis of art a demand for the important (*Bedeutungsvolles*).

All the existing aesthetic standards are built on this plan. Instead of giving a definition of true art and then deciding what is and what is not good art by judging whether a work conforms or does not conform to this definition, a certain class of works which for some reason pleases a certain circle of people is accepted as being art, and a definition of art is then devised to cover all these productions. I recently came upon a remarkable instance of this method in a very good German work, *The History of Art in the Nineteenth Century*, by Muther. Describing the pre-Raphaelites, the Decadents, and the Symbolists (who are already included in the canon of art), he not only does not venture to blame their tendency but earnestly endeavours to widen his standard so that it may include them all, since they appear to him to represent a legitimate reaction from the excesses of realism. No matter what insanities appear in art, when once they find acceptance among the upper classes of our society a theory is quickly invented to explain and sanction them; just as if there had never been periods in history when certain special circles of people recognized and approved false, deformed, and insensate art which subsequently left no trace and has been utterly forgotten. And to what lengths the insanity and deformity of art may go, especially when as in our days it knows that it is considered infallible, may be seen by what is being done in the art of our circle to-day.

So that the theory of art founded on beauty, expounded by aesthetics and in dim outline professed by the public, is nothing but the setting up as good of that which has pleased and pleases us—that is, pleases a certain class of people.

In order to define any human activity, it is necessary to understand its sense and importance; and in order to do this it is primarily necessary to examine that activity in itself, in its dependence on its causes and in connexion with its effects, and not merely in relation to the pleasure we can get from it.

If we say that the aim of any activity is merely our pleasure and define it solely by that pleasure, our definition will evidently be a false one. But this is precisely what has occurred in the efforts to define art. Now if we consider the food question it will not occur to any one to affirm that the importance of food consists in the pleasure we receive when eating it. Everybody understands that the satisfaction of our taste cannot serve as a basis for our definition of the merits of food, and that we have therefore no right to presuppose that dinners with cayenne pepper, Limburg cheese, alcohol, and so on, to which we are accustomed and which please us, form the very best human food.

In the same way beauty, or that which pleases us, can in no sense serve as a basis for the definition of art; nor can a series of objects which afford us pleasure serve as the model of what art should be.

To see the aim and purpose of art in the pleasure we get from it is like assuming (as is done by people of the lowest moral development, for instance by savages) that the purpose and aim of food is the pleasure derived when consuming it.

Just as people who conceive the aim and purpose of food to be pleasure cannot recognize the real meaning of eating, so people who consider the aim of art to be pleasure cannot realize its true meaning and purpose, because they attribute to an activity the meaning of which lies in its connexion with the other phenomena of life the false and exceptional aim of pleasure. People come to understand that the meaning of eating lies in the nourishment of the body only when they cease to consider that the object of that activity is pleasure. And it is the same with regard to art. People will come to understand the meaning of art only when they cease to consider that the aim of that activity is beauty—that is to say, pleasure. The acknowledgement of beauty (that is, of a certain kind of pleasure received from art) as being the aim of art not only fails to assist us in finding a definition of what art is, but, on the contrary, by transferring the question into a region quite foreign to art (into metaphysical, psychological, physiological, and even historical discussions as to why such a production pleases one person and such another displeases or pleases some one else), it renders such definition impossible. And since discussions as to why one man likes pears and another prefers meat do not help towards finding a definition of what is essential in nourishment, so the solution of questions of taste in art (to which the discussions on art involuntarily come) not only does not help to make clear in what this particular human activity which we call art really consists but renders such elucidation quite impossible until we rid ourselves of a conception which justifies every kind of art at the cost of confusing the whole matter.

To the question, what is this art to which is offered up the labour of millions, the very lives of men, and even morality itself? we have extracted replics from the existing aesthetics which all amount to this: that the aim of art is beauty, that beauty is recognized by the enjoyment it gives, and that artistic enjoyment is a good and important thing, because it *is* enjoyment. In a word, that enjoyment is good because it is enjoyment. Thus what is considered the definition of art is no definition at all but only a shuffle to justify existing art. Therefore, however strange it may seem to say so, in spite of the mountains of books written about art, no exact definition of art has been constructed. And the reason of this is that the conception of art has been based on the conception of beauty.

V

Definitions of art not founded on beauty. Tolstóy's definition. The extent and necessity of art. How people in the past distinguished good from bad in art.

What is art if we put aside the conception of beauty, which confuses the whole matter? The latest and most comprehensible definitions of art, apart from the conception of beauty, are the following: (1) *a*, Art is an activity arising even in the animal kingdom, and springing from sexual desire and the propensity to play (Schiller, Darwin, Spencer), and *b*, accompanied by a pleasurable excitement of the nervous system (Grant Allen). This is the physiolog-

ical-evolutionary definition. (2) Art is the external manifestation, by means of lines, colours, movements, sounds,
or words, of emotions felt by man (Véron). This is the
experimental definition. According to the very latest definition (Sully), (3) Art is "the production of some permanent
object or passing action which is fitted not only to supply
an active enjoyment to the producer, but to convey a
pleasurable impression to a number of spectators or listen-
ers, quite apart from any personal advantage to be derived
from it."

Notwithstanding the superiority of these definitions to
the metaphysical definitions which depended on the conception of beauty, they are yet far from exact. The first,
the physiological-evolutionary definition (1) *a*, is inexact,
because instead of speaking about the artistic activity
itself, which is the real matter in hand, it treats of the
derivation of art. The modification of it, *b*, based on the
physiological effects on the human organism, is inexact
because within the limits of such definition many other
human activities can be included, as has occurred in the
neo-aesthetic theories which reckon as art the preparation
of handsome clothes, pleasant scents, and even of victuals.

The experimental definition, (2), which makes art
consist in the expression of emotions, is inexact because
a man may express his emotions by means of lines,
colours, sounds, or words and yet may not act on others
by such expression—and then the manifestation of his
emotions is not art.

The third definition (that of Sully) is inexact because
in the production of objects or actions affording pleasure
to the producer and a pleasant emotion to the spectators
or hearers apart from personal advantage may be included
the showing of conjuring tricks or gymnastic exercises, and
other activities which are not art. And further, many things
the production of which does not afford pleasure to the
producer and the sensation received from which is unpleasant, such as gloomy, heart-rending scenes in a poetic
description or a play, may nevertheless be undoubted works
of art.

The inaccuracy of all these definitions arises from the
fact that in them all (as also in the metaphysical definitions) the object considered is the pleasure art may give,

and not the purpose it may serve in the life of man and of humanity.

In order to define art correctly it is necessary first of all to cease to consider it as a means to pleasure, and to consider it as one of the conditions of human life. Viewing it in this way we cannot fail to observe that art is one of the means of intercourse between man and man.

Every work of art causes the receiver to enter into a certain kind of relationship both with him who produced or is producing the art and with all those who, simultaneously, previously, or subsequently, receive the same artistic impression.

Speech transmitting the thoughts and experiences of men serves as a means of union among them, and art serves a similar purpose. The peculiarity of this latter means of intercourse, distinguishing it from intercourse by means of words, consists in this, that whereas by words a man transmits his thoughts to another, by art he transmits his feelings.

The activity of art is based on the fact that a man receiving through his sense of hearing or sight another man's expression of feeling is capable of experiencing the emotion which moved the man who expressed it. To take the simplest example: one man laughs and another who hears becomes merry, or a man weeps and another who hears feels sorrow. A man is excited or irritated, and another man seeing him is brought to a similar state of mind. By his movements or by the sounds of his voice a man expresses courage and determination or sadness and calmness, and this state of mind passes on to others. A man suffers, manifesting his sufferings by groans and spasms, and this suffering transmits itself to other people; a man expresses his feelings of admiration, devotion, fear, respect, or love to certain objects, persons, or phenomena, and others are infected by the same feelings of admiration, devotion, fear, respect, or love to the same objects, persons, or phenomena.

And it is on this capacity of man to receive another man's expression of feeling and to experience those feelings himself, that the activity of art is based.

If a man infects another or others directly, immediately, by his appearance or by the sounds he gives vent to at the very time he experiences the feeling; if he causes another man to yawn when he himself cannot help yawning, or to laugh or cry when he himself is obliged to laugh or cry, or to suffer when he himself is suffering—that does not amount to art.

Art begins when one person, with the object of joining another or others to himself in one and the same feeling, expresses that feeling by certain external indications. To take the simplest example: a boy having experienced, let us say, fear on encountering a wolf relates that encounter, and in order to evoke in others the feeling he has experienced describes himself, his condition before the encounter, the surroundings, the wood, his own light-heartedness, and then the wolf's appearance, its movements, the distance between himself and the wolf, and so forth. All this, if only the boy when telling the story again experiences the feelings he had lived through, and infects the hearers and compels them to feel what he had experienced, is art. Even if the boy had not seen a wolf but had frequently been afraid of one, and if, wishing to evoke in others the fear he had felt, he invented an encounter with a wolf and recounted it so as to make his hearers share the feelings he experienced when he feared the wolf, that also would be art. And just in the same way it is art if a man, having experienced either the fear of suffering or the attraction of enjoyment (whether in reality or in imagination), expresses these feelings on canvas or in marble so that others are infected by them. And it is also art if a man feels, or imagines to himself, feelings of delight, gladness, sorrow, despair, courage, or despondency, and the transition from one to another of these feelings, and expresses them by sounds so that the hearers are infected by them and experience them as they were experienced by the composer.

The feelings with which the artist infects others may be most various—very strong or very weak, very important or very insignificant, very bad or very good: feelings of love of one's country, self-devotion and submission to fate or to God expressed in a drama, raptures of lovers described in a novel, feelings of voluptuousness expressed in a picture, courage expressed in a triumphal march, merriment evoked by a dance, humour evoked by a funny story, the feeling of quietness transmitted by an evening landscape or by a lullaby, or the feeling of admiration evoked by a beautiful arabesque—it is all art.

If only the spectators or auditors are infected by the feelings which the author has felt, it is art.

To evoke in oneself a feeling one has once experienced and having evoked it in oneself then by means of movements, lines, colours, sounds, or forms expressed in words so to transmit that feeling that others experience the same feeling—this is the activity of art.

Art is a human activity consisting in this, that one man consciously, by means of certain external signs, hands on to others feelings he has lived through, and that others are infected by these feelings and also experience them.

Art is not, as the metaphysicians say, the manifestation of some mysterious Idea of beauty or God; it is not, as the aesthetic physiologists say, a game in which man lets off his excess of stored-up energy; it is not the expression of man's emotions by external signs; it is not the production of pleasing objects; and, above all, it is not pleasure; but it is a means of union among men, joining them together in the same feelings, and indispensable for the life and progress towards well-being of individuals and of humanity.

As every man, thanks to man's capacity to express thoughts by words, may know all that has been done for him in the realms of thought by all humanity before his day and can in the present, thanks to this capacity to understand the thoughts of others, become a sharer in their activity and also himself hand on to his contemporaries and descendants the thoughts he has assimilated from others as well as those that have arisen in himself; so, thanks to man's capacity to be infected with the feelings of others by means of art, all that is being lived through by his contemporaries is accessible to him, as well as the feelings experienced by men thousands of years ago, and he has also the possibility of transmitting his own feelings to others.

If people lacked the capacity to receive the thoughts conceived by men who preceded them and to pass on to others their own thoughts, men would be like wild beasts, or like Kaspar Hauser.[1]

And if men lacked this other capacity of being infected by art, people might be almost more savage still, and above all more separated from, and more hostile to, one another.

And therefore the activity of art is a most important one, as important as the activity of speech itself and as generally diffused.

As speech does not act on us only in sermons, orations, or books, but in all those remarks by which we interchange thoughts and experiences with one another, so also art in the wide sense of the word permeates our whole life, but it is only to some of its manifestations that we apply the term in the limited sense of the word.

We are accustomed to understand art to be only what we hear and see in theatres, concerts, and exhibitions; together with buildings, statues, poems, and novels. . . . But all this is but the smallest part of the art by which we communicate with one another in life. All human life is filled with works of art of every kind—from cradle-song, jest, mimicry, the ornamentation of houses, dress, and utensils, to church services, buildings, monuments, and triumphal processions. It is all artistic activity. So that by art, in the limited sense of the word, we do not mean all human activity transmitting feelings but only that part which we for some reason select from it and to which we attach special importance.

This special importance has always been given by men to that part of this activity which transmits feelings flowing from their religious perception, and this small part they have specifically called art, attaching to it the full meaning of the word.

That was how men of old—Socrates, Plato, and Aristotle—looked on art. Thus did the Hebrew prophets and the ancient Christians regard art. Thus it was, and still is, understood by the Mohammedans, and thus it still is understood by religious folk among our own peasantry.

[1] "The foundling of Nuremberg," found in the market-place of that town on 23rd May 1828, apparently some sixteen years old. He spoke little and was almost totally ignorant even of common objects. He subsequently explained that he had been brought up in confinement underground and visited by only one man, whom he saw but seldom.

Some teachers of mankind—such as Plato in his *Republic*, and people like the primitive Christians, the strict Mohammedans, and the Buddhists—have gone so far as to repudiate all art.

People viewing art in this way (in contradiction to the prevalent view of to-day which regards any art as good if only it affords pleasure) held and hold that art (as contrasted with speech, which need not be listened to) is so highly dangerous in its power to infect people against their wills that mankind will lose far less by banishing all art than by tolerating each and every art.

Evidently such people were wrong in repudiating all art, for they denied what cannot be denied—one of the indispensable means of communication without which mankind could not exist. But not less wrong are the people of civilized European society of our class and day in favouring any art if it but serves beauty—that is, gives people pleasure.

Formerly people feared lest among works of art there might chance to be some causing corruption, and they prohibited art altogether. Now they only fear lest they should be deprived of any enjoyment art can afford, and they patronize any art. And I think the last error is much grosser than the first and that its consequences are far more harmful.

∞∞∞

XIV

Truths fatal to preconceived views not readily recognized. Proportion of works of art to counterfeits. Perversion of taste, and incapacity to recognize art. Examples.

I know that most men—not only those considered clever, but even those who are very clever and capable of understanding most difficult scientific, mathematical, or philosophic problems—can seldom discern even the simplest and most obvious truth if it be such as obliges them to admit the falsity of conclusions they have formed, perhaps with much difficulty—conclusions of which they are proud, which they have taught to others, and on which they have built their lives. And therefore I have little hope that what I adduce as to the perversion of art and taste in our society will be accepted or even seriously considered. Nevertheless I must state fully the inevitable conclusion to which my investigation into the question of art has brought me. This investigation has brought me to the conviction that almost all that our society considers to be art, good art, and the whole of art, far from being real and good art and the whole of art, is not even art at all but only a counterfeit of it. This position I know will seem very strange and paradoxical, but if we once acknowledge art to be a human activity by means of which some people transmit their feelings to others (and not a service of Beauty, or a manifestation of the Idea, and so forth), we shall inevitably have to admit this further conclusion also. If it is true that art is an activity by means of which one man having experienced a feeling intentionally transmits it to others, then we have inevitably to admit further that of all that among us is termed art (the art of the upper classes), of all those novels, stories, dramas, comedies, pictures, sculptures, symphonies, operas, operettas, ballets, etc., which profess to be works of art, scarcely one in a hundred thousand proceeds from an emotion felt by its author, all the rest being but manufactured counterfeits of art in which borrowing, imitation, effects, and interest replace the contagion of feeling. That the proportion of real productions of art is to the counterfeits as one to some hundreds of thousands or even more may be seen by the following calculation: I have read somewhere that the artist painters in Paris alone number 30,000; there will probably be as many in England, as many in Germany, and as many in Russia, Italy, and the smaller states combined. So that in all there will be in Europe, say, 120,000 painters, and there are probably as many musicians and as many literary artists. If these 360,000 individuals produce three works a year each (and many of them produce ten or more), then each year yields over a million so-called works of art. How many then must have been produced in the last ten years, and how many in the whole time since upper-class art broke off from the art of the whole people? Evidently millions. Yet who of all the connoisseurs of art has received impressions from all these pseudo works of art? Not to mention the labouring classes who have no conception of these productions, even people of the upper classes cannot know one in a thousand of them all and cannot remember those they have known. These works all appear under the guise of art, produce no impression on any one (except when they serve as pastimes for an idle crowd of rich people), and vanish utterly.

In reply to this it is usually said that without this enormous number of unsuccessful attempts we should not have the real works of art. But such reasoning is as though a baker, in reply to a reproach that his bread was bad, were to say that if it were not for the hundreds of spoiled loaves there would not be any well-baked ones. It is true that where there is gold there is also much sand, but that cannot serve as a reason for talking a lot of nonsense in order to say something wise.

We are surrounded by productions considered artistic. Thousands of verses, thousands of poems, thousands of novels, thousands of dramas, thousands of pictures, thousands of musical pieces follow one after another. All the verses describe love, or nature, or the author's state of mind, and in all of them rhyme and rhythm are observed. The dramas and comedies are all splendidly staged and are performed by admirably trained actors. All the novels are divided into chapters; all of them describe love, contain effective situations, and correctly describe the details of life. All the symphonies contain *allegro, andante, scherzo,* and *finale;* all consist of modulations and chords and are played by highly trained musicians. All the pictures, in gold frames, saliently depict faces and sundry accessories. But among these productions in the various branches of art there is in each branch one among hundreds of thousands not only somewhat better than the rest, but differing from them as a diamond differs from paste. The one is priceless; the others not only have no value but are worse than valueless for they deceive and pervert taste. And yet externally they are, to a man of perverted or atrophied artistic perception, precisely alike.

In our society the difficulty of recognizing real works of art is further increased by the fact that the external quality of the work in false productions is not only no worse, but often better, than in real ones; the counterfeit is often more effective than the real, and its subject more interesting. How is one to discriminate? How is one to find a production in no way distinguished in externals from hundreds of thousands of others intentionally made precisely to imitate it?

For a country peasant of unperverted taste this is as easy as it is for an animal of unspoilt scent to follow the trace he needs among a thousand others in wood or forest. The animal unerringly finds what he needs. So also the man, if only his natural qualities have not been perverted, will without fail select from among thousands of objects the real work of art he requires—that which infects him with the feeling experienced by the artist. But it is not so with those whose taste has been perverted by their education and life. The receptive feeling of these people is atrophied, and in valuing artistic productions they must be guided by discussion and study, which discussion and study completely confuse them. So that most people in our society are quite unable to distinguish a work of art from the grossest counterfeits. People sit for whole hours in concert-rooms and theatres listening to the new composers, consider it a duty to read the novels of the famous modern novelists and to look at pictures representing either something incomprehensible or just the very things they see much better in real life; and above all they consider it incumbent on them to be enraptured by all this, imagining it all to be art, while at the same time they will pass real works of art by, not only without attention but even with contempt, merely because in their circle these works are not included in the list of works of art.

A few days ago I was returning home from a walk feeling depressed, as sometimes happens. On nearing the house I heard the loud singing of a large choir of peasant women. They were welcoming my daughter, celebrating her return home after her marriage. In this singing, with its cries and cianging of scythes, such a definite feeling of joy, cheerfulness, and energy was expressed that without noticing how it infected me I continued my way towards the house in a better mood and reached home smiling and quite in good spirits. That same evening a visitor, an admirable musician, famed for his execution of classical music and particularly of Beethoven, played us Beethoven's sonata, Opus 101. For the benefit of those who might otherwise attribute my judgment of that sonata of Beethoven to non-comprehension of it, I should mention that whatever other people understand of that sonata and of other productions of Beethoven's later period, I, being very susceptible to music, understand equally. For a long time I used to attune myself to delight in those shapeless improvisations which form the subject-matter of the works of Beethoven's later period, but I had only to consider the question of art seriously, and to compare the impression I received from Beethoven's later works with those pleasant, clear, and strong musical impressions which are transmitted, for instance, by the melodies of Bach (his arias), Haydn, Mozart, Chopin (when his melodies are not overloaded with complications and ornamentation), of Beethoven himself in his earlier period, and above all, with the impressions produced by folk-songs—Italian, Norwegian, or Russian—by the Hungarian *csárdás*, and other such simple, clear, and powerful music, for the obscure, almost unhealthy excitement from Beethoven's later pieces, which I had artificially evoked in myself, to be immediately destroyed.

On the completion of the performance (though it was noticeable that every one had become dull) those present warmly praised Beethoven's profound production in the accepted manner and did not forget to add that formerly they had not been able to understand that last period of his, but that they now saw he was really then at his very best. And when I ventured to compare the impression made on me by the singing of the peasant women—an impression which had been shared by all who heard it—with the effect of this sonata, the admirers of Beethoven only smiled contemptuously, not considering it necessary to reply to such strange remarks.

But for all that, the song of the peasant women was real art transmitting a definite and strong feeling, while the 101st sonata of Beethoven was only an unsuccessful attempt at art containing no definite feeling and therefore not infectious.

For my work on art I have this winter read diligently, though with great effort, the celebrated novels and stories

praised by all Europe, written by Zola, Bourget, Huysmans, and Kipling. At the same time I chanced on a
story in a child's magazine, by a quite unknown writer,
which told of the Easter preparations in a poor widow's
family. The story tells how the mother managed with
difficulty to obtain some wheat-flour, which she poured
on the table ready to knead. She then went out to procure
some yeast, telling the children not to leave the hut
and to take care of the flour. When the mother had gone,
some other children ran shouting near the window calling
those in the hut to come to play. The children forgot their
mother's warning, ran into the street, and were soon engrossed in the game. The mother on her return with the
yeast finds a hen on the table throwing the last of the
flour to her chickens, who were busily picking it out of
the dust of the earthen floor. The mother, in despair,
scolds the children, who cry bitterly. And the mother
begins to feel pity for them—but the white flour has all
gone. So to mend matters she decides to make the Easter
cake with sifted rye-flour, brushing it over with white
of egg and surrounding it with eggs. "Rye-bread we
bake is as good as a cake," says the mother, using a rhyming
proverb to console the children for not having an Easter
cake of white flour, and the children, quickly passing from
despair to rapture, repeat the proverb and await the Easter
cake more merrily even than before.

Well! the reading of the novels and stories by Zola,
Bourget, Huysmans, Kipling, and others, handling the most
harrowing subjects, did not touch me for one moment,
and I was provoked with the authors all the while
as one is provoked with a man who considers you so
naïve that he does not even conceal the trick by which
he intends to take you in. From the first lines one sees
the intention with which the book is written, the details
all become superfluous, and one feels dull. Above all,
one knows that the author had no other feeling all the
time than a desire to write a story or a novel, and so
one receives no artistic impression. On the other hand I
could not tear myself away from the unknown author's
tale of the children and the chickens, because I was at
once infected by the feeling the author had evidently experienced, re-evoked in himself, and transmitted.

Vasnetsóv is one of our Russian painters. He has painted ecclesiastical pictures in Kíev Cathedral and every one praises him as the founder of some new, elevated kind of Christian art. He worked at those pictures for ten years, was paid tens of thousands of rubles for them, and they are all simply bad imitations of imitations of imitations, destitute of any spark of feeling. And this same Vasnetsóv once drew a picture for Turgénev's story "The Quail" (in which it is told how a son pitied a quail he had seen his father kill) showing the boy asleep with pouting upper lip, and above him, as a dream, the quail. And this picture is a true work of art.

In the English Academy of 1897 two pictures were exhibited together; one of these, by J. C. Dollman, was the Temptation of St. Anthony. The saint is on his knees praying. Behind him stands a naked woman and animals of some kind. It is apparent that the naked woman pleased the artist very much, but that Anthony did not concern him at all, and that so far from the temptation being terrible to him (the artist) it is highly agreeable. Therefore if there be any art in this picture, it is very nasty and false. Next in the same book of academy pictures comes a picture by Langley, showing a stray beggar boy, who has evidently been called in by a woman who has taken pity on him. The boy, pitifully drawing his bare feet under the bench, is eating; the woman is looking on, probably considering whether he will not want some more; and a girl of about seven, leaning on her arm, is carefully and seriously looking on, not taking her eyes from the hungry boy and evidently understanding for the first time what poverty is and what inequality among people is, and asking herself why she has everything provided for her while this boy goes barefoot and hungry? She feels sorry and yet pleased, and she loves both the boy and goodness. . . . One feels that the artist loved this girl and that she too loves. And this picture, by an artist who, I think, is not very widely known, is an admirable and true work of art.

I remember seeing a performance of *Hamlet* by Rossi. Both the tragedy itself and the performer who took the chief part are considered by our critics to represent the climax of supreme dramatic art. And yet, both from the subject-matter of the drama and from the performance,

I experienced all the time that peculiar suffering which is caused by false imitations of works of art. But I lately read of a theatrical performance among a savage tribe—the Voguls. A spectator describes the play. A big Vogul and a little one, both dressed in reindeer skins, represent a reindeer-doe and its young. A third Vogul with a bow represents a huntsman on snow-shoes, and a fourth imitates with his voice a bird that warns the reindeer of their danger. The play is that the huntsman follows the track the doe with its young one has travelled. The deer run off the scene and again reappear. (Such performances take place in a small tent-house.) The huntsman gains more and more on the pursued. The little deer is tired and presses against its mother; the doe stops to draw breath. The hunter comes up with them and draws his bow. But just then the bird sounds its note warning the deer of their danger. They escape. Again there is a chase and again the hunter gains on them, catches them, and lets fly his arrow. The arrow strikes the young deer. Unable to run, the little one presses against its mother. The mother licks its wound. The hunter draws another arrow. The audience, as the eye-witness describes them, are paralysed with suspense; deep groans and even weeping are heard among them. And from the mere description I felt that this was a true work of art.

What I am saying will be considered irrational paradox at which one can only be amazed, but for all that I must say what I think: namely, that people of our circle, of whom some compose verses, stories, novels, operas, symphonies, and sonatas, paint all kinds of pictures, and make statues, while others hear and look at these things, and others again appraise and criticise them all: discuss, condemn, triumph, and generation after generation raise monuments to one another—that all these people with very few exceptions, artists, and public, and critics, have never (except in childhood and earliest youth before hearing any discussions on art) experienced that simple feeling familiar to the plainest man and even to a child, that sense of infection with another's feeling—compelling us to rejoice in another's gladness, to sorrow at another's grief, and to mingle souls with another—which is the very essence of art. And therefore these people not only cannot distinguish true works of art from counterfeits but continually mistake for real art the worst and most artificial, while they do not even perceive works of real art, because the counterfeits are always more ornate, while true art is modest.

XV

The quality of art (which depends on its form) considered apart from its subject-matter. The sign of art: infectiousness. Art is incomprehensible to those whose taste is perverted. Conditions of infection: Individuality, Clearness, and Sincerity of the feeling conveyed.

Art in our society has become so perverted that not only has bad art come to be considered good, but even the very perception of what art really is has been lost. In order to be able to speak about the art of our society it is, therefore, first of all necessary to distinguish art from counterfeit art.

There is one indubitable sign distinguishing real art from its counterfeit—namely, the infectiousness of art. If a man, without exercising effort and without altering his standpoint, on reading, hearing, or seeing another man's work experiences a mental condition which unites him with that man and with others who are also affected by that work, then the object evoking that condition is a work of art. And however poetic, realistic, striking, or interesting a work may be, it is not a work of art if it does not evoke that feeling (quite distinct from all other feelings) of joy and of spiritual union with another (the author) and with others (those who are also infected by it).

It is true that this indication is an *internal* one and that there are people who, having forgotten what the action of real art is, expect something else from art (in our society the great majority are in this state), and that therefore such people may mistake for this aesthetic feeling the feeling of diversion and a certain excitement which they receive from counterfeits of art. But though it is impossible to undeceive these people, just as it may be impossible to convince a man suffering from colour-blindness that green is not red, yet for all that, this indication remains perfectly definite to those whose feeling for art is neither perverted nor atrophied, and it clearly distinguishes the feeling produced by art from all other feelings.

The chief peculiarity of this feeling is that the recipient of a truly artistic impression is so united to the artist that he feels as if the work were his own and not some one else's—as if what it expresses were just what he had long been wishing to express. A real work of art destroys in the consciousness of the recipient the separation between himself and the artist, and not that alone, but also between himself and all whose minds receive this work of art. In this freeing of our personality from its separation and isolation, in this uniting of it with others, lies the chief characteristic and the great attractive force of art.

If a man is infected by the author's condition of soul, if he feels this emotion and this union with others, then the object which has effected this is art; but if there be no such infection, if there be not this union with the author and with others who are moved by the same work, then it is not art. And not only is infection a sure sign of art, but the degree of infectiousness is also the sole measure of excellence in art.

The stronger the infection the better is the art, as art, speaking of it now apart from its subject-matter—that is, not considering the value of the feelings its transmits.

And the degree of the infectiousness of art depends on three conditions: (1) on the greater or lesser individuality of the feeling transmitted; (2) on the greater or lesser clearness with which the feeling is transmitted; (3) on the sincerity of the artist—that is, on the greater or lesser force with which the artist himself feels the emotion he transmits.

The more individual the feeling transmitted the more strongly does it act on the recipient; the more individual the state of soul into which he is transferred the more pleasure does the recipient obtain and therefore the more readily and strongly does he join in it.

Clearness of expression assists infection because the recipient who mingles in consciousness with the author is the better satisfied the more clearly that feeling is transmitted which, as it seems to him, he has long known and felt and for which he has only now found expression.

But most of all is the degree of infectiousness of art increased by the degree of sincerity in the artist. As soon as the spectator, hearer, or reader feels that the artist is infected by his own production and writes, sings, or plays for himself, and not merely to act on others, this mental condition of the artist infects the recipient; and, on the contrary, as soon as the spectator, reader, or hearer feels that the author is not writing, singing, or playing for his own satisfaction—does not himself feel what he wishes to express, but is doing it for him, the recipient—resistance immediately springs up, and the most individual and the newest feelings and the cleverest technique not only fail to produce any infection but actually repel.

I have mentioned three conditions of contagion in art, but they may all be summed up into one, the last, sincerity; that is, that the artist should be impelled by an inner need to express his feeling. That condition includes the first; for if the artist is sincere he will express the feeling as he experienced it. And as each man is different from every one else, his feeling will be individual for every one else; and the more individual it is—the more the artist has drawn it from the depths of his nature—the more sympathetic and sincere will it be. And this same sincerity will impel the artist to find clear expression for the feeling which he wishes to transmit.

Therefore this third condition—sincerity—is the most important of the three. It is always complied with in peasant art, and this explains why such art always acts so powerfully; but it is a condition almost entirely absent from our upper-class art, which is continually produced by artists actuated by personal aims of covetousness or vanity.

Such are the three conditions which divide art from its counterfeits, and which also decide the quality of every work of art considered apart from its subject-matter.

The absence of any one of these conditions excludes a work from the category of art and relegates it to that of art's counterfeits. If the work does not transmit the artist's peculiarity of feeling and is therefore not individual, if it is unintelligibly expressed, or if it has not proceeded from the author's inner need for expression—it is not a work of art.

The presence in various degrees of these three conditions—individuality, clearness, and sincerity—decides the merit of a work of art as art, apart from subject-matter. All works of art take order of merit according to the degree in which they fulfil the first, the second, and the third of these conditions. In one the individuality of the feeling transmitted may predominate; in another, clearness of expression; in a third, sincerity; while a fourth may have sincerity and individuality but be deficient in clearness; a fifth, individuality and clearness, but less sincerity; and so forth, in all possible degrees and combinations.

Thus is art divided from what is not art, and thus is the quality of art, as art, decided, independently of its subject-matter—that is to say, apart from whether the feelings it transmits are good or bad.

But how are we to define good and bad art with reference to its content or subject-matter?

∽∽∽

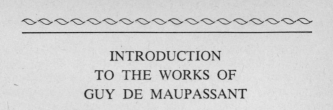

INTRODUCTION
TO THE WORKS OF
GUY DE MAUPASSANT

This article was written by Tolstoy to serve as preface to a Russian edition of a selection of Guy de Maupassant's stories.

It was, I think, in 1881 that Turgénev while visiting me took out of his portmanteau a small French book entitled *La Maison Tellier* and gave it to me.

"Read it some time," said he in an off-hand way, just as, a year before, he had given me a number of *Russian Wealth* that contained an article by Gárshin, who was then only beginning to write. Evidently on this occasion, as in Gárshin's case, he was afraid of influencing me one way or the other and wished to know my own unbiassed opinion.

"It is by a young French writer," said he. "Have a look at it. It isn't bad. He knows you and esteems you highly," he added, as if wishing to propitiate me. "As a man he reminds me of Druzhínin. He is, like Druzhínin, an excellent son, an admirable friend, *un homme d'un commerce sûr,*[1] and besides that he associates with the working people, guides them, and helps them. Even in his relations with women he reminds me of Druzhínin." And Turgénev told me something astonishing, incredible, of Maupassant's conduct in that respect.

That time (1881) was for me a period of most ardent inner reconstruction of my whole outlook on life, and in this reconstruction the activity called the fine arts, to which I had formerly devoted all my powers, had not only lost the importance I formerly attributed to it but had become simply obnoxious to me on account of the unnatural position it had hitherto occupied in my life,

---

[1] A reliable man.

as it generally does in the estimation of the people of the well-to-do classes.

And therefore such works as the one Turgénev was recommending to me did not then interest me in the least. But to please him I read the book he had handed me.

From the first story, *La Maison Tellier*, despite the indecency and insignificance of the subject, I could not help recognizing that the author had what is called talent.

He possessed that particular gift called talent, which consists in the capacity to direct intense concentrated attention, according to the author's tastes, on this or that subject, in consequence of which the man endowed with this capacity sees in the things to which he directs his attention some new aspect which others have overlooked; and this gift of seeing what others have not seen Maupassant evidently possessed. But judging by the little volume I read, he unfortunately lacked the chief of the three conditions, besides talent, essential to a true work of art. These are: (1) a correct, that is, a moral, relation of the author to his subject; (2) clearness of expression, or beauty of form—the two are identical; and (3) sincerity—that is, a sincere feeling of love or hatred of what the artist depicts. Of these three, Maupassant possessed only the two last and was quite lacking in the first. He had not a correct, that is a moral, relation to the subjects depicted.

Judging by what I read I was convinced that Maupassant possessed talent—that is to say, the gift of attention revealing in the objects and facts of life with which he deals qualities others have not perceived. He was also master of a beautiful style, expressing what he wanted to say clearly, simply, and with charm. He was also master of that condition of true artistic production without which a work of art does not produce its effect, namely, sincerity; that is, he did not pretend that he loved or hated but really loved or hated what he described. But unfortunately, lacking the first and perhaps the chief condition of good artistic production, a correct moral relation to what he described —that is to say, a knowledge of the difference between good and evil—he loved and described things that should not have been loved and described. Thus in this little volume, the author described with great detail and fondness how women seduce men, and men women; and in

La Femme de Paul he even describes certain obscenities difficult to understand. And he presents the country labouring folk not merely with indifference but even with contempt, as though they were animals.

This unconsciousness of the difference between good and evil is particularly striking in the story *Une Partie de campagne*, in which is given, as a very pleasant and amusing joke, a detailed description of how two men rowing with bare arms in a boat tempt and afterwards seduce, at the same time, one of them an elderly mother and the other a young girl, her daughter.

The sympathy of the author is evidently all the time so much on the side of these two wretches that he not merely ignores, but simply does not see, what must have been felt by the seduced mother and the maid (her daughter), by the father, and by a young man who is evidently engaged to the daughter; and therefore not merely is an objectionable description of a revolting crime presented in the form of an amusing jest, but the occurrence itself is described falsely, for what is given is only one side, and that the most insignificant—namely, the pleasure received by the rascals.

In that same little volume there is a story, *Histoire d'une fille de ferme*, which Turgénev particularly recommended to me and which particularly displeased me, again by this incorrect relation of the author to his subject. He evidently sees in all the working folk he describes mere animals, who rise to nothing more than sexual and maternal love, so that his descriptions give one an incomplete and artificial impression.

Lack of understanding of the life and interests of working people, and the presentation of them as semi-brutes moved only by sensuality, spite, and greed, is one of the chief and most important defects of most recent French writers, including Maupassant, who not only in this but in all his other stories where he refers to the people, always describes them as coarse, dull animals at whom one can only laugh. Of course the French writers should know the nature of their own people better than I do; but despite the fact that I am a Russian and have not lived among the French peasants, I nevertheless affirm that in so representing their people the French authors are wrong, and that the French labourers cannot be such as they represent them to be. If France—such as we know her, with her truly great men and the great contributions those great men have made to science, art, citizenship, and the moral development of mankind—if this France exists, then that working class which has maintained and maintains on its shoulders this France with its great men, must consist not of brutes but of people with great spiritual qualities; and I therefore do not believe what I read in novels such as *La Terre*[2] and in Maupassant's stories; just as I should not believe it if I were told of the existence of a beautiful house standing without foundations. It may very well be that these high qualities of the people are not such as are described to us in *La Petite Fadette* and *La Mare aux diables*,[3] but I am firmly convinced that these qualities exist, and a writer who portrays the people only as Maupassant does, describing with sympathy only the *hanches* and *gorges*[4] of the Breton servant-girls, and describing with detestation and ridicule the life of the labouring men, commits a great artistic mistake, because he describes his subject only from one, and that the least interesting, physical, side and leaves quite out of sight another, and the most important, spiritual, side wherein the essence of the matter lies.

On the whole, the perusal of the little book handed me by Turgénev left me quite indifferent to the young writer.

So repugnant to me were the stories *Une Partie de campagne, La Femme de Paul, L'Histoire d'une fille de ferme* that I did not then notice the beautiful story, *Le Papa de Simon*, and the story, excellent in its description of the night, *Sur l'eau*.

"Are there not in our time, when so many people want to write, plenty of men of talent who do not know to what to apply this gift or who boldly apply it to what should not, and need not, be described?" thought I. And so I said to Turgénev and thereupon forgot about Maupassant.

The first thing of his that fell into my hands after that

---

[2] By Zola.
[3] Stories by George Sand.
[4] Hips and throats.

was *Une Vie,* which some one advised me to read. That book at once compelled me to change my opinion of Maupassant, and since then I have read with interest everything signed by him. *Une Vie* is excellent, not only incomparably the best of his novels, but perhaps the best French novel since Hugo's *Les Misérables,* Here, besides remarkable talent—that special strenuous attention applied to the subject, by which the author perceives quite new features in the life he describes—are united in almost equal degree all three qualities of a true work of art: first, a correct, that is a moral, relation of the author to his subject; secondly, beauty of form; and thirdly, sincerity—that is, love of what the author describes. Here the meaning of life no longer presents itself to the author as consisting in the adventures of various male and female libertines; here the subject, as the title indicates, is life—the life of a ruined, innocent, amiable woman, predisposed to all that is good but ruined by precisely the same coarse animal sensuality which in his former stories the author presented as if it were the central feature of life, dominant over all else. And in this book the author's whole sympathy is on the side of what is good.

The form, which was beautiful in the first stories, is here brought to such a pitch of perfection as, in my opinion, has been attained by no other French writer of prose. And above all, the author here really loves, and deeply loves, the good family he describes; and he really hates that coarse debauchee who destroys the happiness and peace of this charming family and, in particular, ruins the life of the heroine.

That is why all the events and characters of this novel are so life-like and memorable. The weak, kindly, debilitated mother; the upright, weak, attractive father; the daughter, still more attractive in her simplicity, artlessness, and sympathy with all that is good; their mutual relations, their first journey, their servants and neighbours; the calculating, grossly sensual, mean, petty, insolent suitor, who as usual deceives the innocent girl by the customary empty idealization of the foulest instincts; the marriage, Corsica with the beautiful descriptions of nature, and then village life, the husband's coarse faithlessness, his seizure of power over the property, his qua-

with his father-in-law, the yielding of the good people and the victory of insolence; the relations with the neighbours—all this is life itself in its complexity and variety. And not only is all this vividly and finely described, but the sincere pathetic tone of it all involuntarily infects the reader. One feels that the author loves this woman, and loves her not for her external form but for her soul, for the goodness there is in her; that he pities her and suffers on her account, and this feeling is involuntarily communicated to the reader. And the questions: Why, for what end, is this fine creature ruined? Ought it indeed to be so? arise of themselves in the reader's soul and compel him to reflect on the meaning of human life.

Despite the false notes which occur in the novel, such as the minute description of the young girl's skin, or the impossible and unnecessary details of how, by the advice of an abbé, the forsaken wife again became a mother—details which destroy all the charm of the heroine's purity—and despite the melodramatic and unnatural story of the injured husband's revenge; notwithstanding these blemishes, the novel not only seemed to me excellent, but I saw behind it no longer a talented chatterer and jester who neither knew nor wished to know right from wrong—as from his first little book Maupassant had appeared to me to be—but a serious man penetrating deeply into life and already beginning to see his way in it.

The next novel of Maupassant's that I read was *Bel-Ami*.

Bel-Ami is a very dirty book. The author evidently gives himself a free hand in describing what attracts him and at times seems to lose his main negative attitude towards his hero and to pass over to his side: but on the whole *Bel-Ami*, like *Une Vie*, has at its base a serious idea and sentiment. In *Une Vie*, the fundamental idea is perplexity in face of the cruel senselessness of the suffering life of an excellent woman ruined by a man's coarse sensuality; whereas here it is not only perplexity, but indignation, at the prosperity and success of a coarse, sensual brute who by that very sensuality makes his career and attains a high position in society, and indignation also at the depravity of the whole sphere in which the hero attains his success. In the former novel the author seems to ask: "For what, and why, was a fine creature ruined?

Why did it happen?" Here in the latter novel he seems to answer: all that is pure and good has perished and is perishing in our society, because that society is depraved, senseless, and horrible.

The last scene in the novel—the marriage in a fashionable church of the triumphant scoundrel, decorated with the Legion of Honour, to the pure girl, the daughter of an elderly and formerly irreproachable mother whom he had seduced; a wedding blessed by a bishop and regarded as something good and proper by everybody—expresses this idea with extraordinary force. In this novel, despite the fact that it is encumbered with dirty details (in which it is to be regretted that the author seems to find pleasure) the same serious questions are presented to life.

Read the conversation of the old poet with Duroy when after dinner, if I remember rightly, they are leaving the Walters. The old poet bares life to his young companion and shows it as it is, with its eternal and inevitable concomitant and end—death.

"She has hold of me already, *la gueuse*,"[5] says he of death. "She has already shaken out my teeth, torn out my hair, crippled my limbs, and is now ready to swallow me. I am already in her power. She is only playing with me as a cat does with a mouse, knowing that I cannot escape. Fame? Riches? What is the use of them since they cannot buy a woman's love? For it is only a woman's love that makes life worth living, and that too death takes away. It takes that away, and then one's health, strength, and life itself. It is the same for every one, and there is nothing else."

Such is the meaning of what the old poet says. But Duroy, the successful lover of all the women who please him, is so full of sensual energy and strength that he hears and does not hear, understands and does not understand, the old poet's words. He hears and understands, but the source of sensual life throbs in him so strongly that this unquestionable truth, foretelling the same end for him, does not disturb him.

This inner contradiction, besides its satirical value, gives

[5] The old hag.

the novel its chief significance. The same idea gleams in the fine scenes of the death of the consumptive journalist. The author sets himself the question: What is this life? How solve the contradiction between the love of life and the knowledge of inevitable death? He seems to seek, pauses, and decides neither one way nor the other. And therefore the moral relation to life in this novel continues to be correct.

But in the novels that follow, this moral relation to life grows confused. The appraisement of the phenomena of life begins to waver, to grow obscure, and in the last novels it is quite perverted.

In *Mont-Oriol* Maupassant seems to unite the motives of his two previous novels and repeats himself to order. Despite the fine descriptions of the fashionable watering-place and of the medical activity in it, which is executed with delicate taste, we have here the same bull-like Paul, just as empty and despicable as the husband in *Une Vie*, and the same deceived, frank, meek, weak, lonely—always lonely—good woman, and the same impassive triumph of pettiness and triviality as in *Bel-Ami*.

The thought is the same, but the author's moral relation to what he describes is already much lower, lower especially than in *Une Vie*. The author's inner estimate of right and wrong begins to get confused. Notwithstanding his abstract wish to be impartially objective, the scoundrel Paul evidently has all his sympathy, and therefore the love story of this Paul and his attempts at, and success in, seduction produce a discordant impression. The reader does not know what the author intends: is it to show the whole emptiness and vileness of Paul (who turns indifferently away from and insults a woman merely because her waist has been spoilt by her pregnancy with his child); or, on the contrary, is it to show how pleasant and easy it is to live as this Paul lives?

In the next novels, *Pierre et Jean, Fort comme la mort*, and *Notre coeur*, the author's moral attitude towards his characters becomes still more confused, and in the last-named is quite lost. All these novels bear the stamp of indifference, haste, unreality, and, above all, again that same absence of a correct moral relation to life which was present in his first writings. This began from the time when Maupassant's reputation as a fashionable author had become established and he became liable to the temptation, so terrible in our day, to which every celebrated writer is subject, especially one so attractive as Maupassant. In the first place the success of his first novels, the praise of the press, and the flattery of society, especially of women; in the second the ever increasing amount of remuneration (never however keeping up with his continually increasing wants); in the third the pertinacity of editors outbidding one another, flattering, begging, and no longer judging the merits of the works the author offers, but enthusiastically accepting everything signed by a name now established with the public—all these temptations are so great that they evidently turn his head, and he succumbs to them; and though he continues to elaborate the form of his work as well as or sometimes even better than before, and even though he is fond of what he describes, yet he no longer loves it because it is good or moral and lovable to all, or hates it because it is evil and hateful to all, but only because one thing pleases and another thing happens to displease him.

On all Maupassant's novels, beginning with *Bel-Ami*, there lies this stamp of haste and still more of artificiality. From that time Maupassant no longer did what he had done in his first two novels. He did not take as his basis certain moral demands and on that ground describe the actions of his characters, but wrote as all hack novelists do—that is, he devised the most interesting and pathetic, or most up-to-date, persons and situations and made a novel out of them, adorning it with whatever observations he had opportunity to make which fitted into the framework of the story, quite indifferent as to how the incidents described were related to the demands of morality. Such are *Pierre et Jean, Fort comme la mort*, and *Notre coeur*.

Accustomed as we are to read in French novels of how families live in threes, always with a lover known to every one except the husband, it still remains quite unintelligible to us how it happens that all husbands are always fools, *cocus et ridicules*,[6] but all lovers (who themselves in the end marry and become husbands) are

---

[6] Deceived and ridiculous.

not only not *cocus et ridicules*, but are heroic. And still less comprehensible is it how all women can be depraved, and yet all mothers saintly.

And on these unnatural and unlikely, and above all profoundly immoral, propositions *Pierre et Jean* and *Fort comme la mort* are built, and therefore the sufferings of the characters so situated affect us but little. The mother of Pierre and Jean, who can live her whole life deceiving her husband, evokes little sympathy when she is obliged to confess her sin to her son, and still less when she justifies herself by asserting that she could not but avail herself of the chance of happiness which presented itself. Still less can we sympathize with the gentleman who, in *Fort comme la mort*, having all his life deceived his friend and debauched his friend's wife, now only regrets that having grown old he cannot seduce his mistress's daughter. The last novel, *Notre coeur*, has even no kernel at all beyond the description of various kinds of sex-love. The satiated emotions of an idle debauchee are described, who does not know what he wants, and who first lives with a woman yet more depraved than himself—a mentally depraved woman, who lacks even the excuse of sensuality—then leaves her and lives with a servant-girl, and then again rejoins the former, and, it seems, lives with them both. If in *Pierre et Jean* and *Fort comme la mort* there are still some touching scenes, this last novel excites only disgust.

The question in Maupassant's first novel, *Une Vie*, consists in this: here is a human being, good, wise, pleasing, predisposed to all that is good, and this creature is for some reason offered up as a sacrifice first to a coarse, small-minded, stupid animal of a husband without having given anything to the world. Why is this? The author puts that question and as it were gives no answer, but his whole novel, all his feeling of pity for her and abhorrence of what has ruined her, serves as answer. If there is a man who has understood her suffering and expressed it, then it is redeemed, as Job put it to his friends when they said that no one would know of his sufferings. When suffering is recognized and understood, it is redeemed; and here the author has recognized and understood and shown men this suffering, and the suffering is redeemed, for once it is understood by men it will sooner or later be done away with.

In the next novel, *Bel-Ami*, the question no longer is Why do good persons suffer? but Why do wealth and fame go to the unworthy? What are wealth and fame? How are they obtained? And as before, these questions carry with them their own answers, which consist in the repudiation of all that the crowd of men so highly prize. The subject of this second novel is still serious, but the moral relation of the author to the subject he describes already weakens considerably, and whereas in the first novel blots and sensuality which spoil it only appear here and there, in *Bel-Ami* these blots have increased, and many chapters are filled with dirt alone, which seems to please the author.

In the next book, *Mont-Oriol*, the questions: Why, and to what end, does the amiable woman suffer and the savage male secure success and happiness? are no longer put; but it seems tacitly admitted that it should be so, and hardly any moral demands are felt. But without the least necessity, uncalled for by any artistic consideration, dirty, sensual descriptions are presented. As an example of this violation of artistic taste, resulting from the author's incorrect relation to his subject, the detailed description in this novel of the heroine in her bath is specially striking. This description is quite unnecessary and is in no way connected either with the external or the inner purpose of the novel: "Bubbles appear on her pink skin."

"Well, what of that?" asks the reader.

"Nothing more," replies the author. "I describe it because I like such descriptions."

In the next novels, *Pierre et Jean* and *Fort comme la mort*, no moral demand at all is perceptible. Both novels are built on debauchery, deceit, and falsehood, which bring the actors to tragic situations.

In the last novel, *Notre coeur*, the position of the actors is most monstrous, wild, and immoral; they no longer struggle with anything but only seek satisfaction for their vanity, sensuality, and sexual desires, and the author appears quite to sympathize with their aims. The only deduction one can draw from this last novel is that the greatest pleasure in life consists in sexual intercourse, and that therefore one must secure that happiness in the pleasantest way.

Yet more striking is this immoral relation to life in the half-novel, *Yvette*. The subject, which is horrible in its immorality, is as follows: A charming girl, innocent in soul and depraved only in the manners she has learned in her mother's dissolute circle, leads a libertine into error. He falls in love with her, but imagining that this girl knowingly chatters the obscene nonsense she has picked up in her mother's society and repeats parrot-like without understanding—imagining that she is already depraved— he coarsely offers her an immoral union. This proposal horrifies and offends her (for she loves him); it opens her eyes to her own position and to that of her mother, and she suffers profoundly. This deeply touching scene is admirably described: the collision between a beautiful innocent soul and the depravity of the world. And with that it might end; but the author, without either external or inner necessity, continues to write and makes this man penetrate by night to the girl and seduce her. Evidently in the first part of the story the author was on the girl's side, but in the later part he has suddenly gone over to the debauchee, and the one impression destroys the other— the whole novel crumbles and falls to pieces like ill-kneaded bread.

In all his novels after *Bel-Ami* (I am not now speaking of the short stories, which constitute his chief merit and glory—of them later), Maupassant evidently submitted to the theory which ruled not only in his circle in Paris but which now rules everywhere among artists: that for a work of art it is not only unnecessary to have any clear conception of what is right and wrong, but that on the contrary an artist should completely ignore all moral questions, there being even a certain artistic merit in so doing. According to this theory the artist may or should depict what is true to life, what really is, what is beautiful and therefore pleases him, or even what may be useful as material for "science"; but that to care about what is moral or immoral, right or wrong, is not an artist's business.

I remember a celebrated painter showing me one of his pictures representing a religious procession. It was all excellently painted, but no relation of the artist to his subject was perceptible.

"And do you regard these ceremonies as good and consider that they should be performed, or not?" I asked him.

With some condescension to my naïveté, he told me that he did not know about that and did not want to know it; his business was to represent *life*.

"But at any rate you sympathize with this?"

"I cannot say I do."

"Well then do you dislike these ceremonies?"

"Neither the one thing nor the other," with a smile of compassion at my silliness replied this modern, highly cultured artist who depicted life without understanding its purpose and neither loving nor hating its phenomena.

And so unfortunately thought Maupassant.

In his preface to *Pierre et Jean* he says that people say to a writer, *"Consolez-moi, amusez-moi, attristez-moi, attendrissez-moi, faites-moi rêver, faites-moi rire, faites-moi frémir, faites-moi pleurer, faites-moi penser. Seuls quelques esprits d'élite demandent à l'artiste: faites-moi quelque chose de beau dans la forme qui vous conviendra le mieux d'après votre tempérament."*[7]

Responding to this demand of the *élite* Maupassant wrote his novels, naïvely imagining that what was considered beautiful in his circle was that beauty which art should serve.

And in the circle in which Maupassant moved, the beauty which should be served by art was, and is, chiefly woman—young, pretty, and for the most part naked—and sexual connexion with her. It was so considered not only by all Maupassant's comrades in art—painters, sculptors, novelists, and poets—but also by philosophers, the teachers of the rising generation. Thus the famous Renan, in his work *Marc-Aurèle*, p. 555, when blaming Christianity for not understanding feminine beauty, plainly says:

"Le défaut du christianisme apparaît bien ici. Il est trop uniquement moral; la beauté, chez lui, est tout-à-fait sacrifiée. Or, aux yeux d'une philosophie complète,

---

[7] "Console me, amuse me, sadden me, touch my heart, make me dream, make me laugh, make me tremble, make me weep, make me think. Only a few chosen spirits bid the artist compose something beautiful, in the form that best suits his temperament."

*la beauté, loin d'être un avantage superficiel, un danger,
un inconvénient, est un don de Dieu, comme la vertu. Elle
vaut la vertu; la femme belle exprime aussi bien une face
du but divin, une des fins de Dieu, que l'homme de génie
ou la femme vertueuse. Elle le sent et de là sa fierté. Elle
sent instinctivement le trésor infini qu'elle porte en son
corps; elle sait bien que, sans esprit, sans talent, sans
grande vertu, elle compte entre les premières manifestations de Dieu. Et pourquoi lui interdire de mettre en
valeur le don qui lui a été fait, de sertir le diamant qui
lui est échu? La femme, en se parant, accomplit un devoir;
elle pratique un art, art exquis, en un sens le plus charmant
des arts. Ne nous laissons pas égarer par le sourire que
certains mots provoquent chez* LES GENS FRIVOLES. *On
décerne le palme du génie à l'artiste grec qui a su résoudre
le plus délicat des problèmes, orner le corps humain, c'est
à dire orner la perfection même, et l'on ne veut voir qu'une
affaire de chiffons dans l'essai de collaborer à la plus belle
oeuvre de Dieu, à la beauté de la femme! La toilette de la
femme, avec tous ses raffinements, est du grand art à sa
manière. Les siècles et les pays qui savent y réussir sont
les grands siècles, les grands pays, et le christianisme
montra, par l'exclusion dont il frappa ce genre de re-
cherches, que l'idéal social qu'il concevait ne deviendrait
le cadre d'une société complète que bien plus tard, quand
la révolte des gens du monde aurait brisé le joug étroit
imposé primitivement à la secte par un piétisme exalté."*[8]

---

[8] "The defect of Christianity is clearly seen in this. It is too exclusively moral; it quite sacrifices beauty. But in the eyes of a complete
philosophy beauty, far from being a superficial advantage, a danger,
an inconvenience, is a gift of God, like virtue. It is worth as much
as virtue; the beautiful woman expresses an aspect of the divine
purpose, one of God's aims, as well as a man of genius does, or a
virtuous woman. She feels this, and hence her pride. She is instinctively conscious of the infinite treasure she possesses in her body;
she is well aware that without intellect, without talent, without great
virtue, she counts among the chief manifestations of God. And why
forbid her to make the most of the gift bestowed upon her, or
to give the diamond allotted to her its due setting? By adorning
herself woman accomplishes a duty; she practises an art, an exquisite art, in a sense the most charming of arts. Do not let us be
misled by the smile which certain words provoke in the *frivolous.*
We award the palm of genius to the Greek artist who succeeded in
solving the most delicate of problems, that of adorning the human
body, that is to say, adorning perfection itself, and yet some people

(So that, in the opinion of this leader of the young generation, only now have Paris milliners and coiffeurs corrected the mistake committed by Christianity, and re-established beauty in the true and lofty position due to it.)

In order that there should be no doubt as to how one is to understand beauty, the same celebrated writer, historian, and savant wrote the drama *L'Abbesse de Jouarre*, in which he showed that to have sexual intercourse with a woman is a service of this beauty—that is to say, is an elevated and good action. In that drama, which is striking by its lack of talent and especially by the coarseness of the conversations between d'Arcy and the abbesse, in which the first words make it evident what sort of love that gentleman is discussing with the supposedly innocent and highly moral maiden, who is not in the least offended thereby—in that drama it is shown that the most highly moral people, at the approach of death to which they are condemned, a few hours before it arrives, can do nothing more beautiful than yield to their animal passions.

So that in the circle in which Maupassant grew up and was educated, the representation of feminine beauty and sex-love was and is regarded quite seriously, as a matter long ago determined and recognized by the wisest and most learned men, as the true object of the highest art— *Le grand art.*

And it is this theory, dreadful in its folly, to which Maupassant submitted when he became a fashionable writer; and, as was to be expected, this false ideal led him in his novels into a series of mistakes and to ever weaker and weaker production.

In this the fundamental difference between the demands of the novel and of the short story is seen. A novel has for its aim, even for external aim, the description of a whole human life or of many human lives, and therefore

---

wish to see nothing more than an affair of *chiffons* in the attempt to collaborate with the finest work of God—woman's beauty! Woman's toilette with all its refinements is a great art in its own way. The epochs and countries which can succeed in this are the great epochs and great countries, and Christianity, by the embargo it laid on this kind of research, showed that the social ideal it had conceived would only become the framework of a complete society at a much later period, when the revolt of men of the world had broken the narrow yoke originally imposed on the sect by a fanatical pietism."

its writer should have a clear and firm conception of what is good and bad in life, and this Maupassant lacked; indeed, according to the theory he held, that is just what should be avoided. Had he been a novelist like some talentless writers of sensual novels, he would, being without talent, have quietly described what was evil as good, and his novels would have had unity and would have been interesting to people who shared his view. But Maupassant had talent, that is to say, he saw things in their essentials and therefore involuntarily discerned the truth. He involuntarily saw the evil in what he wished to consider good. That is why, in all his novels except the first, his sympathies continually waver, now presenting the evil as good and now admitting that the evil is evil and the good good, but continually shifting from the one standpoint to the other. And this destroys the very basis of any artistic impression—the framework on which it is built. People of little artistic sensibility often think that a work of art possesses unity when the same people act in it throughout, or when it is all constructed on one plot, or describes the life of one man. That is a mistake. It only appears so to a superficial observer. The cement which binds any artistic production into one whole, and therefore produces the illusion of being a reflection of life, is not the unity of persons or situations, but the unity of the author's independent moral relation to his subject. In reality, when we read or look at the artistic production of a new author, the fundamental question that arises in our soul is always of this kind: "Well, what sort of a man are you? Wherein are you different from all the people I know, and what can you tell me that is new about how we must look at this life of ours?" Whatever the artist depicts—saints, robbers, kings, or lackeys—we seek and see only the artist's own soul. If he is an established writer with whom we are already familiar, the question no longer is, "What sort of a man are you?" but, "Well, what more can you tell me that is new?" or, "From what new side will you now illumine life for me?" And therefore a writer who has not a clear, definite, and just view of the universe, and especially a man who considers that this is not even wanted, cannot produce a work of art. He may write much and admirably, but a work of art will not result.

So it was with Maupassant in his novels. In his first two novels, and particularly in the first, *Une Vie*, there was a clear, definite, and new relation to life, and it was an artistic production; but as soon as, submitting to the fashionable theory, he decided that this relation of the author to life was quite unnecessary and began to write merely in order to *faire quelque chose de beau* (to produce something beautiful), his novels ceased to be works of art. In *Une Vie* and *Bel-Ami* the author knows whom he should love and whom he should hate, and the reader agrees with him and believes in him—believes in the people and events he describes. But in *Notre coeur* and *Yvette* the author does not know whom he should love and whom he should hate, and the reader does not know either. And not knowing this the reader does not believe in the events described and is not interested in them. And therefore, except the two first, or, strictly speaking, only the first one, all Maupassant's novels, as such, are weak; and if he had left us only his novels he would have been merely a striking instance of the way in which brilliant talents may perish as a result of the false environment in which the author has developed, and of those false theories of art that have been devised by people who neither love nor understand it. But fortunately Maupassant wrote short stories in which he did not subject himself to the false theory he had accepted and wrote not *quelque chose de beau*, but what touched or revolted his moral feeling. And in these short stories—not in all, but in the best of them—we see how that moral feeling grew in the author.

And it is in this that the wonderful quality of every true artist lies, if only he does not do violence to himself under the influence of a false theory. His talent teaches its possessor and leads him forward along the path of moral development, compelling him to love what deserves love and to hate what deserves hate. An artist is an artist because he sees things not as he wishes to see them but as they really are. The man, the possessor of a talent, may make mistakes, but if only his talent is allowed free play, as Maupassant gave it free play in his short stories, it discloses, undrapes the object, and compels love of it if it deserves love, and hatred of it if it deserves hatred. With every true artist, when under the influence of hi·

circle he begins to represent what should not be represented, there happens what happened to Balaam, who, wishing to bless, cursed what should be cursed, and wishing to curse, blessed what should be blessed: involuntarily he does not what he wishes to do but what he should do. And this happened to Maupassant.

There has hardly been another writer who so sincerely thought that all the good, all the meaning of life, lies in woman, in love, and who with such strength of passion described woman and her love from all sides; and there has hardly ever been a writer who reached such clearness and exactitude in showing all the awful phases of that very thing which had seemed to him the highest and the greatest of life's blessings. The more he penetrated into the question the more it revealed itself, and the more did the coverings fall from it and only its horrible results and yet more horrible essence remain.

Read of the idiot son, of the night with a daughter (*L'Ermite*), of the sailor with his sister (*Le Port*), *Le Champ d'oliviers, La Petite Roque,* of the English girl (*Miss Harriet*), *Monsieur Parent, L'Armoire* (the girl who fell asleep in the cupboard), the wedding in *Sur l'eau*, and last expression of all, *Un Cas de divorce.* Just what was said by Marcus Aurelius when devising means to destroy the attractiveness of this sin in his imagination is what Maupassant does in most vivid artistic forms, turning one's soul inside out. He wished to extol sex-love, but the better he came to know it the more he cursed it. He cursed sex-love for the misfortunes and sufferings it bears within it, and for the disillusionments, and above all the falsification of real love, the fraud which is in it—from which the more trustingly he has yielded to the deception the more acutely man suffers.

The powerful moral development of the author in the course of his literary activity is recorded in indelible traits in these charming short stories and in his best book, *Sur l'eau.*

And not alone in this involuntary and therefore all the more powerful dethronement of sex-love is the moral growth of the author seen, but also in the more and more exalted moral demands he makes upon life.

Not alone in sex-love does he see the innate contradiction between the demands of animal and rational man; he sees it in the whole organization of the world.

He sees that the world as it is, the material world, is not only not the best of worlds but might on the contrary be quite different—this thought is strikingly expressed in *Horla*—and that it does not satisfy the demands of reason and life. He sees that there is some other world, or at least the demand for such another world, in the soul of man.

He is tormented not only by the irrationality of the material world and its ugliness, but by its unlovingness, its discord. I do not know a more heart-rending cry of horror from one who has lost his way and is conscious of his loneliness than the expression of this idea in that most charming story, *Solitude*.

The thing that most tormented Maupassant and to which he returns many times is the painful condition of isolation —spiritual isolation—of man; the barrier standing between him and his fellows; a barrier, he says, the more painfully felt the nearer one's bodily connexion.

What is it torments him, and what would he have? What can destroy this barrier? What end this isolation? Love—not woman's love, which has become disgusting to him, but pure, spiritual, divine love. And that is what Maupassant seeks. Towards it, towards this saviour of life long since plainly disclosed to all men, he painfully strains from those fetters in which he feels himself bound.

He does not yet know how to name what he seeks. He does not wish to name it with his lips alone lest he should profane his holy-of-holies. But his unexpressed striving, shown in his dread of loneliness, is so sincere that it infects and attracts one more strongly than many and many a sermon about love, uttered only by the lips.

The tragedy of Maupassant's life is that in a most monstrous and immoral circle he was escaping by the strength of his talent, by that extraordinary light which was in him, from the outlook on life held by that circle and was already near to deliverance, was already breathing the air of freedom, but—having exhausted his last strength in the struggle and not being able to make a final effort —perished without having attained freedom.

The tragedy of that ruin lies in what still afflicts the majority of the so called cultured men of our time.

Men in general have never lived without an expression of the meaning of their life. Always and everywhere, highly gifted men going in advance of others have appeared—the prophets, as they are called—who have explained to men the meaning and purport of their life; and always the ordinary, average men, who had not the strength to explain that meaning for themselves, have followed the explanation of life their prophets have disclosed to them.

That meaning was explained eighteen hundred years ago by Christianity, simply, clearly, indubitably, and joyfully, as is proved by the lives of all who acknowledge it and follow the guidance of life which results from that conception.

But then people appeared who misinterpreted that meaning so that it became meaningless, and men are placed in the dilemma either of acknowledging Christianity as interpreted by Orthodoxy, Lourdes, the Pope, the dogma of the Immaculate Conception, and so forth, or of going on with life according to the teachings of Renan and his kind—that is, living without any guidance or understanding of life, following only their lusts as long as they are strong, and their habits when their lusts become feeble.

And people, ordinary people, choose the one or the other —sometimes both: first dissoluteness and then Orthodoxy; and thus whole generations live, shielding themselves with various theories invented not to disclose the truth but to hide it. And ordinary and, more especially, dull people are content.

But there are others—not many, they are rare—such as Maupassant, who with their own eyes see things as they are, see their significance, see the contradictions in life concealed from others, and vividly realize to what these contradictions must inevitably lead them—and seek to solve them in advance. They seek these solutions everywhere except where they are to be found, namely in Christianity, because Christianity appears to them outlived and discarded, repelling them by its absurdity. And vainly trying to find these solutions for themselves, they come to the conviction that there are no solutions, and that it is inherent in life that one should always bear in oneself these unsolved contradictions. And having come to such a conclusion, if these people are feeble unenergetic natures, they put up with such meaningless life' and are even proud of their position, accounting their ignorance a quality and a sign of culture. But if they are energetic, truthful, and gifted natures, such as Maupassant was, they do not endure it but one way or other try to get out of this senseless life.

It is as if men thirsting in a desert sought water everywhere except near those people who standing round a spring pollute it and offer stinking mire instead of the water that unceasingly flows beneath the mire. Maupassant was in this position; he could not believe—evidently it never even entered his head—that the truth he sought had long ago been found and was so near him; but neither could he believe that man can live in such contradiction as that in which he felt himself to be living.

Life—according to the theories in which he had been brought up, which surrounded him and were corroborated by all the lusts of his young and mentally and physically strong being—life consists in pleasure, of which the chief is to be found in woman with her love and in the reproduction of this pleasure in its reflection, in the presentation of this love, and in exciting it in others. All this might be well; but on examining these pleasures other quite different things emerge, alien and hostile to this love and this beauty: woman for some reason is disfigured, becomes unpleasantly pregnant and repulsive, gives birth to children, unwanted children; then come deceptions, cruelties, moral suffering, then mere old age, and ultimately death.

Then is this beauty indeed beauty? And why is all this so? It would be all very well if one could arrest life, but life goes on. And what does that mean? "Life goes on" means that the hair falls out, turns grey, the teeth decay, and there are wrinkles and offensive breath. Even before all is finished, everything becomes dreadful, disgusting: the rouge, the powder, the sweat, the smell, and the repulsiveness are evident. Where then is that which I serve? Where is beauty? But she is all! And if she is not, there is nothing left. There is no life!

But not merely is there no life in what seemed to be

life: one begins to forsake it oneself, one becomes weaker, more stupid; one decays; others before one's eyes seize those delights in which all the good of life lay. Nor is that all. Some other possibility of life begins to glimmer in one's mind; something else, some other kind of union with men, with the whole world, one which does not admit of all these deceptions, something which cannot by any means be infringed, which is true and forever beautiful. But this cannot be. It is only the tantalizing vision of an oasis when we know that it does not exist and that there is nothing but sand everywhere.

Maupassant reached that tragic moment in life when the struggle begins between the falseness of the life about him and the truth of life of which he began to be conscious. Pangs of spiritual birth had already begun in him.

And it is the pangs of this birth that are expressed in his best work, especially in the short stories printed in this edition.

Had he been fated not to die while still suffering but to fulfil all his possibilities, he would have left us great and illuminating works; but even what he gave us in the midst of his pain is much. Let us then be thankful to this strong and truthful man for what he has given us.

1894

PREFACE TO
WILHELM VON POLENZ'S NOVEL
DER BÜTTNERBAUER [1]

For you will find, if you think deeply of it, that the chief of all the curses of this unhappy age is the universal gabble of its fools, and of the flocks that follow them, rendering the quiet voices of the wise men of all past time inaudible. This is, first, the result of the invention of printing, and of the easy power and extreme pleasure to vain persons of seeing themselves in print. When it took a twelvemonth's hard work to make a single volume legible, men considered a little the difference between one book and another; but now, when not only anybody can get themselves made legible through any quantity of volumes, in a week, but the doing so becomes a means of living to them, and they can fill their stomachs with the foolish foam of their lips, the universal pestilence of falsehood fills the mind of the world as cicadas do olive-leaves, and the first necessity for our mental government is to extricate from among the insectile noise, the few books and words that are Divine.

—JOHN RUSKIN, *Fors Clavigera*, Letter 81

Last year a friend of mine in whose taste I have confidence gave me a German novel, *Der Büttnerbauer*, by von Polenz, to read. I read it and was astonished that such a work, which appeared a couple of years ago, was hardly known by any one.

This novel is not one of those works of imitation-art that are produced in such enormous quantities in our time but is a really artistic production. It is not one of those descriptions of events and of people, destitute of all interest, which are artificially put together merely because the author, having learned the technique of artistic descriptions, wants to write a new novel; nor is it one of those disserta-

---

[1] Wilhelm von Polenz was born in 1861 and died in 1903. His novels *Der Pfarrer von Breitendorf* (1893) and *Der Büttnerbauer* (1895), are descriptions of village life. His *Grabenhäger*, *Thekla Lüdekind*, and *Liebe ist ewig* (1900) describe the life of the landowning and town classes. *Wurzellocker* (1902) treats of a literary society.

tions on a given theme set in the form of a drama or novel, which also in our day pass as artistic productions; nor does it belong to the class of works called "decadent," which particularly please the modern public just because, resembling the ravings of a madman, they present something of the nature of rebuses the guessing of which forms a pleasant occupation besides being considered a sign of refinement.

This novel belongs neither to the first, nor to the second, nor to the third, of these categories, but is a real work of art, in which the author says what he feels he must say because he loves what he is speaking about and says it not by reflections or hazy allegories but in the one manner by which artistic content can be conveyed, by poetic images, not fantastic, extraordinary, unintelligible images with no essential inner connexion one with another, but by the presentation of the most ordinary, simple persons and events, united one with another by an inner artistic necessity.

But not only is this novel a genuine work of art, it is also an admirable work of art, uniting in a high degree the three chief conditions of really good artistic production.

In the first place its content is important, relating as it does to the life of the peasantry—that is, to the majority of mankind who stand at the basis of every social structure and in our day, not only in Germany but in all European countries, are enduring trying alterations of their ancient, age-long condition. (It is remarkable that almost simultaneously with *Der Büttnerbauer* there has appeared a French novel, René Bazin's *La Terre qui meurt*, which is not at all bad, though far less artistic.)

In the second place, this novel is written with great mastery in admirable German, particularly forcible when the author makes his characters speak the coarse peasant-labourer's *Plattdeutsch*.

In the third place this novel is thoroughly indued with love of the people whom the author sets before us.

In one of the chapters, for instance, there is a description of how after a night passed in drunkenness with his comrades, the husband when it is already morning returns home and knocks at the door. The wife looks out of the window and recognizes him; she loads him with abuse and is purposely slow about letting him in. When at last she opens the door for him, the husband tumbles in and wants to go into the large living-room, but the wife does not let him, lest the children should see their father drunk, and she pushes him back. But he catches hold of the lintel of the door and struggles with her. Usually a mild man, he suddenly becomes terribly exasperated (the cause of his exasperation is that the day before she had taken out of his pocket some money his master had given him, and had hidden it) and in his rage he flings himself upon her, seizes her by the hair, and demands his money.

"I won't give it up, I won't give it up for anything!" says she in reply to his demands, trying to free herself from him.

Then he, forgetting himself in his anger, strikes her where and as he can.

"I'll die before I'll give it up!" says she.

"You won't give it up!" he answers, knocking her off her feet and falling on her himself, while continuing to demand his money. Not receiving a reply, in his mad drunken anger he tries to throttle her. But the sight of blood which trickles from under her hair and flows over her forehead and nose, causes him to stop. He becomes frightened at what he has done and, letting go of her, staggers and falls down on his bed.

The scene is truthful and terrible. But the author loves his protagonists and adds one small detail which suddenly illumines everything with such a vivid ray as compels the reader not only to pity but also to love these people, despite their coarseness and cruelty. The wife who has been beaten comes to herself, rises from the floor, wipes her bleeding head with the hem of her skirt, feels her limbs, and opening the door leading to the crying children quiets them, and then seeks her husband with her eyes. He is lying on the bed as he had fallen, but his head has slipped from the pillow. The wife walks over to him, carefully raises his head on the pillow, and after that adjusts her dress and picks off some of her hair that had been pulled out.

Dozens of pages of dialogue would not have said all that is said by this detail. Here at once the reader is shown the consciousness of conjugal duty educated by tradition, and the triumph of a decision maintained—not to give up the money, needed not for herself but for the family—here also is the offence, forgiveness of the beating, and pity, and if not love, at least the memory of love for her husband, the father of her children. Nor is that all. Such a detail, illuminating the inner life of this woman and this man, lights up for the reader the inner life of millions of such husbands and wives, who have lived or are now living, and not only teaches respect and love for these people who are crushed by toil but compels us to consider why and wherefore they, strong in soul and body, with such possibilities in them of good, loving life, are so neglected, crushed, and ignorant.

And such truly artistic traits, which are revealed to an author only by love of what he is describing, are met with in every chapter of this novel.

It is undoubtedly a beautiful work of art, as all who read it will agree. And yet it appeared three years ago and though translated into Russian in the *Messenger of Europe* has passed unnoticed both in Russia and in Germany. I have asked several literary Germans whom I have met recently about this novel—they had heard von Polenz's name but had not read his book, though they had all read the last novels of Zola, the last stories by Kipling, and the plays of Ibsen, d'Annunzio, and even of Maeterlinck.

Some twenty years ago Matthew Arnold wrote an admirable article on the purpose of criticism.[2] In his opinion the purpose of criticism is to find among all that has been written, whenever and wherever it may be, that which is most important and good and to direct the attention of readers to this that is important and good.

In our time, when readers are deluged with newspapers, periodicals, books, and by the profusion of advertisements, not only does such criticism seem to me essential, but the whole future culture of the educated class of our European world depends on whether such criticism appears and acquires authority.

The over-production of any kind of article is harmful;

[2] "The Function of Criticism at the Present Time," in *Essays in Criticism*.

but the over-production of articles which are not an aim but a means is particularly harmful when people consider this means to be an aim.

Horses and carriages as means of conveyance, clothing and houses as means of protection against changes of weather, good food to maintain the strength of one's organism are very useful. But as soon as men begin to regard the possession of means as an end in itself, considering it good to have as many horses, clothes, and houses and as much food as possible, such articles become not only useless but simply harmful. And this has come about with book-production among the well-to-do circle of people of our European society. Printing, which is undoubtedly useful for the great masses of uneducated people, among well-to-do people has long ago become the chief organ for the dissemination of ignorance, and not of enlightenment.

It is easy to convince oneself of this. Books, periodicals, and especially newspapers have become in our time great financial undertakings for the success of which the largest possible number of purchasers is required. But the interests and tastes of the largest number of purchasers are always low and vulgar, and so for the success of the productions of the press it is necessary that these productions should correspond to the demands of this great mass of purchasers—that is, that they should treat of mean interests and correspond to vulgar tastes. And the press fully satisfies these demands, having ample opportunity to do so, since among those who work for the press there are many more with the same mean interests and coarse tastes as the public than there are men with lofty interests and refined taste. And since with the diffusion of printing and the commercial methods applied to newspapers, periodicals, and books, these people receive good pay for matter they supply corresponding to the demands of the masses, there appears that terrible, ever and ever increasing deluge of printed paper, which by its quantity alone, not to speak of the harmfulness of its contents, forms a vast obstacle to enlightenment.

If in our day a clever young man of the people, wishing to educate himself, is given access to all books, periodicals, and newspapers, and the choice of his reading is left to himself, he will, if he reads for ten years assiduously every day, in all probability read nothing but stupid and immoral books. It is as improbable that he will strike on a good book as it would be that he should find a marked pea in a bushel of peas. What is worst of all is that, continually reading bad books, he will more and more pervert his understanding and his taste, so that when he does come on a good work he will either be quite unable to understand it or will understand it perversely.

Besides this, thanks to accident or to masterly advertisement, some bad works, such, for instance, as *The Christian* by Hall Caine, a novel false in its content and inartistic, which has been sold to the extent of a million copies, obtain, without the proper merit, as great a notoriety as Odol or Pears' Soap. And this great publicity causes an ever-growing number of people to read such books, and the fame of an insignificant or often harmful book grows and grows like a snowball, and in the heads of the great majority of men an ever and ever greater confusion of ideas is formed, also like a snowball, involving complete incapacity to understand the qualities of literary productions. Therefore in proportion to the greater and greater diffusion of newspapers, periodicals, books, and printing in general, the level of the quality of what is printed falls lower and lower, and the great mass of the so-called educated public is ever more and more immersed in the most hopeless, self-satisfied, and therefore incurable ignorance.

Within my own memory, during the last fifty years, this striking debasement of the taste and common sense of the reading public has occurred. One may trace this debasement in all branches of literature, but I will indicate only a few notable instances best known to me. In Russian poetry, for instance, after Púshkin and Lérmontov (Tyúchev is generally forgotten) poetic fame passes first to the very doubtful poets, Máykov, Polónski, and Fet, then to Nekrásov, who was quite destitute of the poetic gift, then to the artificial and prosaic versifier Alexéy Tolstóy, then to the monotonous and weak Nádson, then to the quite ungifted Apúkhtin, and after that everything becomes confused, and versifiers appear whose name is legion—who do not even know what poetry is, or the meaning of what they write, or why they write.

Another astonishing example is that of the English prose writers. From the great Dickens we descend, first to George Eliot, then to Thackeray, from Thackeray to Trollope, and then there already begin the indifferent fabrications of Kipling, Hall Caine, Rider Haggard, and so forth. The same thing is yet more striking in American literature. After the great galaxy of Emerson, Thoreau, Lowell, Whittier, and others, suddenly everything crumbles, and there appear beautiful publications with beautiful illustrations, but with stories and novels it is impossible to read because of their lack of any content.

In our time the ignorance of the educated crowd has reached such a pass that all the really great thinkers, poets, and prose writers, both of ancient times and of the nineteenth century, are considered obsolete and no longer satisfy the lofty and refined demands of the new men; it is all regarded with contempt or with a smile of condescension. The immoral, coarse, inflated disconnected babble of Nietzsche is recognized as the last word of the philosophy of our day, and the senseless artificial arrangements of words in various decadent poems united by measure and rhythm is regarded as poetry of the highest order. In all the theatres plays are produced the meaning of which is unknown to any one, even to the authors, and novels that have no content and no artistic merit are printed and circulated by millions under the guise of artistic productions.

"What shall I read to supplement my education?" asks a young man or girl who has finished his or her studies at the high-school.

The same question is put by a man of the people who has learned to read, and to understand what he reads, and is seeking true enlightenment.

To answer such questions the naïve attempts made to interrogate prominent men as to which they consider to be the best hundred books is of course insufficient.

Nor is the matter helped by the classification existing in our European society and tacitly accepted by all, which divides writers into first, second, and third class, and so on—into those of genius, those who are very talented, and those simply good. Such a division, far from helping a true understanding of the excellences of literature and the search of what is good amid the sea of what is bad, still more confuses this aim. To say nothing of the fact that this division into classes is often incorrect and is maintained only because it was made long ago and is accepted by everybody, such a division is harmful because writers acknowledged to be first class have written some very bad things, and writers of the lowest class have produced some excellent things. So that a man who believes in the division of writers into classes and thinks everything by first-class writers to be admirable and everything by writers of the lower class, or those quite unknown, to be weak will only become confused and deprive himself of much that is useful and truly enlightening.

Only real criticism can reply to that most important question of our day, put by the youth of the educated class who seeks education and by the man of the people who seeks enlightenment—not such criticism as now exists, which sets itself the task of praising such works as have obtained notoriety and devising foggy philosophic aesthetic theories to justify them; and not criticism that makes it its task more or less wittily to ridicule bad works, or works proceeding from a different camp; still less such criticism as has functioned and still functions in Russia and sets itself the task of deducing the direction of the movement of our whole society from some types depicted by certain writers, or in general of finding opportunities to express particular economic and political opinions under guise of discussing literary productions.

To that enormously important question, "What, of all that has been written, is one to read?" only real criticism can furnish a reply: criticism which, as Matthew Arnold says, sets itself the task of bringing to the front and pointing out to people all that is best, both in former and in contemporary writers.

On whether such disinterested criticism, which understands and loves art and is independent of any party, makes its appearance or not, and on whether its authority becomes sufficiently established for it to be stronger than mercenary advertisement, depends, in my opinion, the decision of the question whether the last rays of enlightenment are to perish in our so-called educated European society without having reached the masses of the people, or whether they will revive, as they did in the Middle Ages, and reach the great mass of the people who are now without any enlightenment.

The fact that the mass of the public do not know of this admirable novel of von Polenz's, any more than they do of many other admirable works which are drowned in the sea of printed rubbish, while senseless, insignificant, and even simply nasty literary productions are discussed from every aspect, invariably praised, and sold by millions of copies, has evoked in me these thoughts, and I avail myself of the opportunity, which will hardly present itself to me again, of expressing them, though it be but briefly.

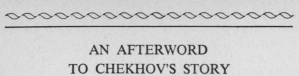

AN AFTERWORD
TO CHEKHOV'S STORY
"THE DARLING"

There is profound meaning in the story in the Book of Numbers which tells how Balak, king of the Moabites, sent for Balaam to curse the people of Israel who had come to his borders. Balak promised Balaam many gifts for his service; and Balaam being tempted went to Balak but was stopped on the way by an angel, who was seen by his ass but whom Balaam did not see. In spite of this, Balaam went on to Balak and went with him up a mountain, where an altar had been prepared with calves and lambs slaughtered in readiness for the imprecation. Balak waited for the curse to be pronounced, but instead of cursing them Balaam blessed the people of Israel.

And Balak said unto Balaam, What hast thou done unto me? I took thee to curse mine enemies, and, behold, thou hast blessed them altogether.

And he answered and said, Must I not take heed to speak that which the Lord hath put in my mouth?

And Balak said unto nim, Come with me unto another place . . . and curse me them from thence.

And he took him to another place, where also altars had been prepared.

But again Balaam, instead of cursing, blessed them.

And so it was a third time. . . .

And Balak's anger was kindled against Balaam, and he smote his hands together; and Balak said unto Balaam, I called thee to curse mine enemies, and thou hast altogether blessed them these three times.

Therefore now flee thou to thy place: I thought to promote thee unto great honour; but, lo, the Lord hath kept thee back from honour. [And so Balaam departed without receiving the gifts, because instead of cursing Balak's enemies he had blessed them.] (Numbers 23:11–15; 24:10–11)

What happened to Balaam very often happens to true poets and artists. Tempted by Balak's promises of popularity, or by false views suggested to them, the poet does not even see the angel that bars his way, whom the ass sees, and he wishes to curse but yet he blesses.

This is just what happened with the true poet and artist Chékhov when he wrote his charming story "The Darling."

The author evidently wanted to laugh at this pitiful creature—as he judged her with his intellect, not with his heart—this "darling," who, after sharing Kúkin's troubles about his theatre and then immersing herself in the interests of the timber business, under the influence of the veterinary surgeon considers the struggle against bovine tuberculosis to be the most important matter in the world, and is finally absorbed in questions of grammar and the interests of the little school-boy in the big cap. Kúkin's name is ridiculous, and so even is his illness and the telegram announcing his death. The timber-dealer with his sedateness is ridiculous, and the veterinary surgeon and the boy are ridiculous; but the soul of "darling," with her capacity for devoting herself with her whole being to the one she loves, is not ridiculous but wonderful and holy.

I think that in the mind, though not in the heart, of the author when he wrote "The Darling," there was a dim idea of the new woman, of her equality of rights with man; of woman, developed, learned, working independently, and as well as man if not better, for the benefit of society; of the woman who has raised, and insists upon, the woman question; and in beginning to write "The Darling," he wanted to show what woman ought not to be. The Balak of public opinion invited Chékhov to curse the weak, submissive, undeveloped woman devoted to man, and Chékhov ascended the mountain and the calves and sheep were laid upon the altar, but when he began to speak, the author blessed what he had meant to curse. Despite the wonderful gay humour of the whole work, I, at any rate, cannot read without tears some passages of this beautiful story. I am touched by the description of the complete devotion with which she loved Kúkin and all that he cared for, and also the timber-dealer, and also the veterinary surgeon, and yet more by her sufferings when she was left alone and had no one to love, and by the account of how finally, with all the strength of her womanly and motherly feeling (which she had never had the opportunity to expend on children of her own), she devoted her unbounded love to the future man, the school-boy in the big cap.

The author makes her love the ridiculous Kúkin, the insignificant timber-dealer, and the unpleasant veterinary surgeon; but love is not less sacred whether its object be a Kúkin or a Spinoza, a Pascal or a Schiller, whether its object changes as rapidly as in the case of "darling," or remains the same for a whole lifetime.

I happened not long ago to read in the *Nóvoe Vrémya* an excellent feuilleton by M. Ata about women. In this feuilleton the author expressed a remarkably wise and profound thought. "Women," he says, "try to prove to us that they can do everything we men can do. I not only do not dispute this, but am ready to agree that women can do all that men do and perhaps even do it better, but the trouble is that men cannot do anything even approximately approaching what women can accomplish."

Yes, that is certainly so, and it is true not only of the bearing, nursing, and early education of children, but men cannot do what is loftiest, best, and brings man nearest to God—the work of loving, of complete devotion to the beloved, which has been so well and naturally done, and is done and will be done, by good women. What would become of the world, what would become of us men, if women had not that faculty and did not exercise it? Without women doctors, women telegraphists, women lawyers and scientists and authors, we might get on, but without mothers, helpers, friends, comforters, who love in man all that is best in him—without such women it would be hard to live in the world. Christ would be without Mary or Magdalene, Francis of Assisi would have lacked Claire, there would have been no wives of the Decembrists in their exile, nor would the Dukhobors have had their wives, who did not restrain their husbands but supported them in their martyrdom for truth. There would not have been those thousands and thousands of unknown women—the very best (as the unknown generally are)—comforters of the drunken, the weak, and the dissolute, who more than any one else need the consolation of love. In that love, whether directed to Kúkin or to Christ, is the chief, grand strength of women, irreplaceable by anything else.

What a wonderful misconception is the whole so-called woman's question, which has obsessed (as is natural with every empty idea) the majority of women and even of men!

"Woman wants to improve herself!" What can be more legitimate or more just than that?

But the business of a woman, by her very vocation, is different from that of a man. And therefore the ideal of perfection for a woman cannot be the same as the ideal for a man. Let us grant that we do not know in what that ideal consists, but in any case it is certainly not the ideal of perfection for a man. And yet to the attainment of that masculine ideal all the absurd and unwholesome activity of the fashionable woman's movement, which now so confuses women, is directed.

I am afraid that Chékhov when writing "The Darling" was under the influence of this misunderstanding.

He, like Balaam, intended to curse, but the God of poetry forbade him to do so and commanded him to bless, and he blessed, and involuntarily clothed that sweet creature in such a wonderful radiance that she will always remain a type of what woman can be in order to be happy herself and to cause the happiness of those with whom her fate is united.

This story is so excellent because its effect was unintentional.

I learned to ride a bicycle in the great Moscow riding-school in which army-divisions are reviewed. At the other end of the riding-school a lady was learning to ride. I thought of how to avoid incommoding that lady and began looking at her. And, looking at her, I began involuntarily to draw nearer and nearer to her, and although she, noticing the danger, hastened to get out of the way, I rode against her and upset her—that is to say, I did exactly the opposite of what I wished to do, simply because I had concentrated my attention upon her.

The same thing has happened with Chékhov but in an inverse sense: he wanted to knock down "darling," and directing the close attention of a poet upon her he has exalted her.

A TOLSTOY
BIBLIOGRAPHY

BIOGRAPHY

Leon, Derrick. *Tolstoy, His Life and Work*. London: Routledge, 1944; reprinted, 1946.

Maude, Aylmer. *The Life of Tolstoy*. London: Oxford, 1930; reprinted in World's Classics, Oxford University Press, 1938.

Redpath, Theodore. *Tolstoy*. London: Bowes & Bowes, 1960; New York: Hillary House, 1961.

Simmons, Ernest J. *Leo Tolstoy*. 2 vols. Boston: Little, Brown, 1945, 1956; paperback, New York: Vintage Books, 1960.

CRITICAL STUDIES

Bayley, John. *Tolstoy and the Novel*. London: Chatto & Windus, 1966; New York: Viking, 1967.

Berlin, Isaiah. *The Hedgehog and the Fox: An Essay on Tolstoy's View of History*. London: Curwell Press, 1953; New York: Simon & Schuster, 1953; New York: New American Library, 1957.

Christian, Reginald F. *Tolstoy's* War and Peace: *A Study*. London: Oxford, 1962.

————. *Tolstoy: A Critical Introduction*. Cambridge: The University Press, 1969.

Knight, G. Wilson. *Shakespeare and Tolstoy*. London: H. Milford, Oxford University Press, 1934; New York: Haskell, 1970.

Lavrin, Janko. *Tolstoy: An Approach*. London: W. Collins, 1924; New York: Macmillan, 1946; New York: Russell & Russell, 1968.

Mann, Thomas. "Goethe and Tolstoy" in *Three Essays*.

Translated from German by H. T. Lowe-Porter. New York: A. A. Knopf, 1929.

COLLECTIONS

Dane, R., ed. *Russian Literature and Modern English Fiction*. Chicago: University of Chicago Press, 1965.

Matlaw, Ralph E., ed. *Tolstoy: A Collection of Critical Essays*. Englewood Cliffs, N.J.: Prentice-Hall, 1967.

A selection of books published by Penguin is listed on the following pages.

For a complete list of books available from Penguin in the United States, write to Dept. DG, Penguin Books, 299 Murray Hill Parkway, East Rutherford, New Jersey 07073.

PENGUIN CLASSICS

The Penguin Classics, the earliest and most varied series of world masterpieces to be published in paperback, began in 1946 with E. V. Rieu's now famous translation of *The Odyssey*. Since then the series has commanded the unqualified respect of scholars and teachers throughout the English-speaking world. It now includes more than three hundred volumes, and the number increases yearly. In them, the great writings of all ages and civilizations are rendered into vivid, living English that captures both the spirit and the content of the original. Each volume begins with an introductory essay, and most contain notes, maps, glossaries, or other material to assist the reader in appreciating the work fully. Some volumes available include:

Aeschylus, THE ORESTEIAN TRILOGY
Honoré de Balzac, COUSIN BETTE
Geoffrey Chaucer, THE CANTERBURY TALES
THE EPIC OF GILGAMESH
Gustave Flaubert, MADAME BOVARY
Nikolai Gogol, DEAD SOULS
Henrik Ibsen, HEDDA GABLER AND OTHER PLAYS
Friedrich Nietzsche, THUS SPOKE ZARATHUSTRA
Plato, THE LAST DAYS OF SOCRATES
Sophocles, THE THEBAN PLAYS
Stendhal, SCARLET AND BLACK
Émile Zola, GERMINAL

SOME RUSSIAN
PENGUIN CLASSICS

Leo Tolstoy
ANNA KARENIN
Translated and with an Introduction by Rosemary Edmonds

Leo Tolstoy
CHILDHOOD, BOYHOOD, YOUTH
Translated and with an Introduction by Rosemary Edmonds

Leo Tolstoy
THE COSSACKS AND OTHER STORIES
Translated and with an Introduction by Rosemary Edmonds

Leo Tolstoy
RESURRECTION
Translated and with an Introduction by Rosemary Edmonds

Leo Tolstoy
WAR AND PEACE
(two volumes)
Translated and with an Introduction by Rosemary Edmonds

Ivan Turgenev
FATHERS AND SONS
Translated and with an Introduction by Rosemary Edmonds

Ivan Turgenev
HOME OF THE GENTRY
Translated and with an Introduction by Richard Freeborn

Ivan Turgenev
ON THE EVE
Translated and with an Introduction by Gilbert Gardiner

Ivan Turgenev
RUDIN
Translated and with an Introduction by Richard Freeborn

Ivan Turgenev
SKETCHES FROM A HUNTER'S ALBUM
Translated and with an Introduction by Richard Freeborn

SOME FRENCH
PENGUIN CLASSICS

Honoré de Balzac
OLD GORIOT
Translated and with an Introduction by Marion Ayton Crawford

René Descartes
DISCOURSE ON METHOD AND THE MEDITATIONS
Translated and with an Introduction by F. E. Sutcliffe

Gustave Flaubert
THREE TALES
(A SIMPLE HEART, THE LEGEND OF ST. JULIAN HOSPITATOR,
HERODIAS)
Translated and with an Introduction by Robert Baldick

Guy de Maupassant
SELECTED SHORT STORIES
Translated and with an Introduction by Roger Colet

Molière
THE MISANTHROPE AND OTHER PLAYS
(TARTUFFE, THE IMAGINARY INVALID, THE SICILIAN,
A DOCTOR IN SPITE OF HIMSELF)
THE MISER AND OTHER PLAYS
(THE WOULD-BE GENTLEMAN, DON JUAN, THAT SCOUNDREL SCAPIN,
LOVE'S THE BEST DOCTOR)
Translated and with an Introduction by John Wood

Michel de Montaigne
ESSAYS
Translated and with an Introduction by J. M. Cohen

Jean-Jacques Rousseau
THE SOCIAL CONTRACT
Translated and with an Introduction by Maurice Cranston

Voltaire
CANDIDE
Translated and with an Introduction by John Butt

Émile Zola
NANA
Translated and with an Introduction by George Holden

PENGUIN ENGLISH LIBRARY

The Penguin English Library Series reproduces, in convenient but authoritative editions, many of the greatest classics in English literature from Elizabethan times through the nineteenth century. Each volume is introduced by a critical essay, enhancing the understanding and enjoyment of the work for the student and general reader alike. A few selections from the list of more than one hundred titles follow:

BEN JONSON: THREE COMEDIES
Edited by Michael Jamieson
VOLPONE, THE ALCHEMIST, BARTHOLOMEW FAIR

JOHN WEBSTER: THREE PLAYS
Edited by D. C. Gunby
THE WHITE DEVIL, THE DUCHESS OF MALFI,
THE DEVIL'S LAW-CASE

THREE JACOBEAN TRAGEDIES
Edited by Gāmini Salgādo
THE REVENGER'S TRAGEDY, *Cyril Tourneur*
THE WHITE DEVIL, *John Webster*
THE CHANGELING, *Thomas Middleton and William Rowley*

FOUR JACOBEAN CITY COMEDIES
Edited by Gāmini Salgādo
THE DUTCH COURTESAN, *John Marston*
A MAD WORLD, MY MASTERS, *Thomas Middleton*
THE DEVIL IS AN ASS, *Ben Jonson*
A NEW WAY TO PAY OLD DEBTS, *Philip Massinger*

THREE RESTORATION COMEDIES
Edited by Gāmini Salgādo
THE MAN OF MODE, *George Etherege*
THE COUNTRY WIFE, *William Wycherley*
LOVE FOR LOVE, *William Congreve*

Also works by Jane Austen, Charlotte Brontë, Emily Brontë, John Bunyan, Samuel Butler, Wilkie Collins, Daniel Defoe, Charles Dickens, George Eliot, Henry Fielding, Elizabeth Gaskell, Thomas Malory, Herman Melville, Edgar Allan Poe, Tobias Smollett, Laurence Sterne, Jonathan Swift, William Makepeace Thackeray, Anthony Trollope, Mark Twain, and others

THE VIKING PORTABLE LIBRARY

In single volumes, The Viking Portable Library has gathered the very best work of individual authors or works of a period of literary history, writings that otherwise are scattered in a number of separate books. These are not condensed versions, but rather selected masterworks assembled and introduced with critical essays by distinguished authorities. Over fifty volumes of The Viking Portable Library are now in print in paperback, making the cream of ancient and modern Western writing available to bring pleasure and instruction to the student and the general reader. An assortment of subjects follows:

891.733 Tolstoi, Lev
TOL   Nikolaevich,
          graf, 1828-1910.

          The portable
          Tolstoy

DATE